THE
GUARDIAN
INTERVIEWS

MICHAEL CLARY

A PERMUTED PRESS BOOK
ISBN: 978-1-61868-512-4

THE GUARDIAN INTERVIEWS
©2015 by Michael Clary
All Rights Reserved

Cover Art by Dean Samed, Conzpiracy Digital Arts

Permuted Press
109 International Drive, Suite 300
Franklin, TN 37067
http://permutedpress.com

CONTENTS

THE GUARDIAN

THE REGULATORS

BROKEN

THE
GUARDIAN

BOOK 1 OF THE GUARDIAN INTERVIEWS

BY MICHAEL CLARY

Chapter 1

JAXON

I became nervous the moment he walked into the room. This was going to be the biggest interview of my career. Every reporter in the country would kill to be in my position, but for the life of me, I couldn't seem to stop my hands from shaking. He had wider shoulders than I thought he would, but he didn't look like some sort of superman. More like a regular guy. Handsome...certainly, but he didn't seem like the kind of person that would be interested in saving lives. He looked more like the guy your mother always warned you to stay away from. Still, there was an aura of power surrounding him...or maybe not...maybe it was just me. Maybe I was star struck at being in the same room as a real, honest to God, hero?

Right now, this man was currently much more famous than any movie star or musician. He also earned his fame the hard way. I couldn't stop thinking about that famous fifteen minutes of footage as I looked at him. I couldn't stop thinking about the things he was able to do. For a moment, I was speechless, and then he offered me his hand, and gave me a lopsided smile.

My name's Jaxon, where would you like to start?

"Um...can I ask what finally made you agree to meet with me?"

I guess it's about time people know what really happened in the beginning of my...career. All they ever seem to hear about is me getting into some kind of trouble. Thought it might explain some things if I agreed to let you tell my story. I've also been thinking about archiving our...situations. It might be helpful in the future. This is probably the easiest way to do it. So, by all means, fire away.

"How about the day it began?"

All right, the day it began. I can do that. It was a Sunday, I think; the beginning of summer. It was early morning and the sun was shining brightly. I remember this quite clearly because I'd stopped on top of Trans Mountain to check out the view.

I was coming back from Ruidoso, New Mexico, where my parents live. I had taken the bike out over the weekend, because it had been raining pretty hard in El Paso during that time, and I wasn't able to ride as much as I'd liked.

I own a Harley Davidson Super Glide. I love it. Black, chrome, drag bars, loud pipes, it's the bike I've always wanted. I can't explain in words, the freedom that comes from riding a motorcycle; it's something that every person needs to experience for themselves.

I remember cruising over the mountain with music that wasn't really playing pounding in my head. I was in heaven. Life was perfect. At least, that's the kind of feeling I get when I ride. Maybe it's different for everybody, but that's the feeling that belongs to me. The sound of the engine, and the almost violent response of the throttle, there's nothing like it in the world. As soon as I'm off the bike, well that's a different story, at least around this time of year.

The morning air was getting humid. I could tell it was going to be bad today. My home was cooled by evaporative air, like most homes in the Southwest. This kind of air conditioning works like crap when it is humid, and let me tell ya, El Paso summers are always humid. So, during that time of year, when you needed your air-conditioning the most…it won't work worth a damn. Whatever, there are certainly worse things in the world than faulty air conditioning, trust me…I'm an expert on that.

Still, El Paso is one of the best places to live in my opinion. I love the Southwest. Don't get me wrong, I'm very much the outdoors type and I love my trips into the woods, but there's something about living in the desert. Something about that city always brings me back. Maybe it the culture, maybe it's just because I grew up there. El Paso has everything that I could possibly want. It's too small to be a big busy city, and way too large to have anything near a small town atmosphere. The population is also pretty damn big, five hundred thousand, or somewhere around there, I believe. Lots of people, maybe that's why everything spread so fast…at least, that's my guess.

"'Why everything spread so fast.'" I know exactly what he's referring to. He doesn't have to spell it out for me.

Anyway, yeah…I love the place. I grew up there. It's just that this time of year always kind of created a sort of melancholy ache inside of me. It wasn't the rain. Living in the desert, rain is pretty scarce most times of the year except for about three months in the summer. During those three months I actually enjoyed the wetness.

I tend to think that my melancholy was caused more by my lack of direction, but why it only hit me in the summer was far beyond me.

I guess I always expected something great from myself. I always wanted something more than what I had. I tried my hand at many different things, but so far nothing had panned out for me. I was in my mid-thirties, and I just didn't know where to turn.

I was nowhere near lazy, but the idea of doing some sort of office job bothered me. I simply wasn't cut out for one of those nine to five lifestyles. I had friends that went that route, and they were always miserable. Besides, the last boss I had almost drove me to the point of throwing his condescending ass out of a window.

Yeah…I was looking for something. I just didn't know what it was.

At the time, I was teaching cage fighting on the Northeast side of town. I enjoyed it. It kept me in shape, and it seemed kinda right but it just wasn't enough. The money wasn't great and I just knew it wouldn't be long before I started searching for something new and different. That's how life was back in those days. I continually searched for, and wished for a way to leave my mark upon the world. I just never knew that I was wishing on a monkey's paw.

He laughed at this. It wasn't a nice laugh. It was very cynical, as if he himself caused all the trouble that would soon be crashing its way into his life. Some people would bask in fame, but Jaxon seemed to wish that he could go back to his unsatisfying former life. I was anticipating the return of my familiar melancholy ache as I rumbled to a stop at the top of the mountain, and took in the view. I'd seen it a million times before, but this time—and don't ask me why—it was different. There was something in the air. It took a few moments to be sure, but something was definitely different. I wasn't the only one that had pulled over; fifteen other people were also taking in the view. The sun was shining, and the Westside of El Paso was opened up, and stretched out before me. The city was the same as always, but my heavy heart, and melancholy feelings, had vanished. Change was coming. That's all I knew. I didn't question it. I just enjoyed the feeling.

It felt like I might be able to make something out of myself very soon. It felt positive, like I would soon find my place in the world, but I had no idea what had caused this change inside of me.

I sat there for about twenty minutes just taking it all in.

The loud yawn that exploded from my mouth told me I was tired before I even felt the need for sleep. Once I noticed the yawn however, I realized just how exhausted I was. It wasn't a big deal; I was about ten minutes away from my house, which was in the Upper Valley. This is about as far west as you can go in El Paso any farther than the Upper Valley, and you're crossing into New Mexico.

I hit the ignition, rumbled the engine, and put my half helmet back on as the other people watched me. I always enjoy being the center of attention when I'm on my bike, and the loud growl of the engine makes me feel like Fonzie. I rode the rest of the way home slowly just to enjoy the ride.

At home, I pulled the bike into the garage; I was too tired to wash it. I called out for my wife, but there was no answer. I assumed she had taken her kids over to her parent's house, which was over on the Eastside of town, (pretty far away), so she probably wouldn't be back until much later in the evening.

Actually, I should explain this. It's real simple. El Paso is divided into four parts, Eastside, Westside, Northeast and Downtown. Downtown is the city area, it's between the Westside and the Eastside. The Eastside is on the other side of town from the Westside. The Northeast is easiest to get to, by going over Trans Mountain road, and it's just a little ways north of the Eastside.

I looked around the house to see if my nephew Dudley was awake, he stays with us over the summers but he hadn't managed to crawl out of his bed just yet. This wasn't a surprise; he normally wakes up well into the afternoon, and then hogs the computer for the rest of the day. The kid looked young, and though he was only about one hundred and fifty pounds, he was in excellent shape from all the weight lifting he did when he wasn't acting like a computer nerd.

With nothing else to do, I figured it was time for a hot shower, and a long nap. I guess it might be interesting that I remember all of these little details, but then again, it was the last time in my life that I was able to experience any kind of normality.

I woke up around 2:00 in the afternoon with my pit bull, Merrick, lying on top of me. She's a great dog and I consider her a member of the family. She's black with a white splotch on her chest, and is great with people. Kind of like a child to me, and don't ever let people tell you that pit bulls are dangerous; they are great dogs.

I'd have to take his word for it. The dog looked somewhat intimidating to me. I'd forgotten to mention her earlier, but she came into the room right behind Jaxon. Every now and then, she would paw at his leg for attention, and glare over towards me when she received it.

I crawled out of bed still feeling good when I heard what sounded like screaming in the distance. I guess in every neighborhood you hear the odd noise now and again, so the scream itself didn't really set off any alarm bells, or hold my attention. I figured that it was probably just some neighborhood kids playing a game.

Then I realized that the scream wasn't stopping.

I went through the front door with Merrick at my side, and walked outside to the front patio. From where I was standing in the courtyard, I couldn't tell where the screaming was coming from but it sort of sounded like it might be coming from inside one of the houses on my block.

I heard the sound of traffic in the distance; screeching tires, blaring horns, and crunching bumpers. Yet, the chaos was far away, and disconnected. Still, I knew something was wrong. I just didn't know how wrong. I couldn't focus past those violent screams. It was a woman's voice, shrill, and in terror.

And then the screaming stopped.

I didn't like the way it just shut off like that. It was like someone just clicked a light switch, that sudden. Dudley was suddenly behind me rubbing his eyes.

"What the hell was that?"

"No idea," I replied, and immediately changed the subject. "Do you happen to know where my wife is?"

"Just woke up," Dudley said with a yawn. "I have no idea."

The neighborhood had gone quiet. Even the traffic noises in the distance had begun to quiet down. Somewhere above us, I heard the sound of a helicopter. I didn't see the helicopter; I just heard the sound of one as it moved farther, and farther, away. Something was definitely off. There should be some sort of noise out there. Where were the loud, hyperactive, kids? Where were the teenagers with their motorcycles that constantly ran up, and down, the road?

I couldn't hear a single sound.

Not even a breeze.

The neighbor from across the street suddenly stumbled out of his front door.

He walked, tripped over his own feet and then fell. He was wearing a light colored shirt, and the front of this shirt was stained in red. In a moment, I realized that it was blood, and there was a lot of it. Like someone took a ketchup bottle, and emptied it all over him. His mouth was also stained red.

Dudley and I were frozen solid. All we could do was watch him flounder about on the ground with horrified expressions plastered upon our faces.

The man obviously needed help, but the situation was just wrong, and that made me hesitate. The man suddenly stopped moving.

"Maybe we should call 911," Dudley said.

It took me awhile to answer but I finally snapped just a little bit out of my daze, and tried to respond.

"I think…"

That was all that came out. My neighbor was climbing to his feet, and staring straight at us.

He screamed, or maybe he roared. I don't know. If you've ever heard the sound, all you can really say is that it's inhuman.

I know exactly what he's talking about. I hate the sound of those all too familiar screams. I'm sure everyone does. Even now, if I have the misfortune of hearing it on the radio or on a news broadcast during the day, I'm not able to sleep in the evening.

The neighbor charged us, and when I say charged, that's exactly what I mean. Just like a bull, head down, and full speed ahead. He ran across the street, past our drive way, and head first into the metal front gate of our patio.

Both Dudley and I fell backwards in shock. We'd been standing right behind the gate, and looking through the bars, when my neighbor charged. The gate bent, and warped, but it held. My neighbor went down with a grunt, paused, and stood right back up.

He blared out another bone chilling scream, and rammed the gate once again. His head, and face, collided with the metal bars. His nose shattered on impact and, miraculously, he had no reaction to what should have been some intense pain. Instead, he began banging away with his fists on the metal barrier that stood between us.

He periodically stopped pounding the bars in an attempt to reach us through the open spaces with his clawing hands. He was also blaring out that guttural filth of a scream while he was banging, and reaching, for us. It chilled me to the bone.

Dudley and I were frozen again. Our faces were petrified in a terrible expression of horror as this lunatic went crazy on our gate.

Then, there was a woman with him. We never even saw her approach. It was like she had appeared out of thin air. She made the same noises, with the same actions. Now there were two of them trying to get at us through the bars.

Though bent from the initial charge, the metal gate was still holding up rather well. Unfortunately, the walls on either side of it were made of stucco, and I could see that the bolts holding the gates hinges were beginning to rip free from the flimsy material. In no time at all, they would be through the barrier, and on top of us.

"Look at her face," Dudley said over the maniacal screaming.

I looked and I saw what I really truly wished I hadn't ever seen. Most of her cheek had been ripped off. All that remained was a large jagged gash with hanging pieces of skin. We could see her bloody teeth through the wound, and every time she screamed at us, flecks of blood would spray out into the air.

I couldn't stop watching the little pieces of skin around the gash flop around as she reached between the bars to grab and claw in our direction.

"What the fuck?" Dudley asked.

"Let's call the cops," I replied.

I didn't notice the rampant barking that was coming from Merrick until she launched herself at my neighbors.

If I wasn't convinced that things were seriously fucked up before, I was certainly convinced after Merrick got involved. At first, she bit at the flailing arms. Each bite left vicious, dripping wounds but my neighbors didn't bother to pull their arms away from her attack. They just kept on screaming, and reaching for us.

Then, Merrick latched herself onto the man's forearm. Biting deeply, she shook her head from side to side creating a terrible gash, and crunching the bone with her efforts. Even with that kind of damage, there was still no response from the man. Nothing! Not even a wail.

"Yeah," Dudley said. "Let's call the cops."

We backed up rapidly towards the front door. Merrick followed us immediately after I gave her a whistle. I thought this odd in a distant sort of way. Normally, if something caught her attention she was quite difficult to get back into the house. I ran to our home phone and tried to dial 911. The line was dead.

"Use your cell phone," I said. "This one's not working."Dudley dialed, and the 911 operator picked up her end of the line after what seemed to me a ridiculously long pause. I didn't hear what she said, because at that moment, the neighbors finally broke through my front gate. The cracking of stucco, and the twisting of metal, was so loud, I heard the noise through the walls of the house.

Seconds later, they were banging on my front door. I ran forward, jumped over Merrick, and slid the deadbolt home. It was a heavy wooden door. It would hold, for a while at least. Dudley was off the phone and not looking happy.

"The operator said that it's happening all over town. She said that we should lock ourselves inside the house, and barricade all the windows."

"What about the cops?" I asked. "Are they coming?"

"Not anytime soon," Dudley answered.

I looked around the house. From where I was standing in the living room, I could see the entire layout. We were in a very bad position. The place was filled with windows and sliding glass doors, and we lacked the materials to barricade them all.

Dudley must have realized the same thing. He was staring at me with the same worried expression that I must have been wearing.

"They're gonna get in here aren't they?" Dudley asked.

I didn't answer him. I was just now realizing that my wife was out there somewhere, and I didn't know if she was safe or not.

I took the stairs to my bedroom two at a time. Merrick was right next to me. I grabbed my cell phone from the nightstand, and called her number. She didn't answer. I slapped the phone shut and called again. She still didn't answer.

I repeated the process over and over until Dudley walked into the room.

"We can't stay here," Dudley said. "They are going to get inside the house soon. We gotta leave."

"And go where?" I asked.

"I dunno, let's go to Georgie's," Dudley answered.

It was a good idea, but first I had to see how bad the neighborhood was. How many of those things were out there.

"I'm going to check the view from upstairs," I said. "I wanna know how bad it is."

"I'll go with you," Dudley muttered.

My bedroom has yet another sliding glass door. This one led to the backyard balcony, which stood over the kitchen.

From here, we could see over our back wall, and across the open field behind it. The field wasn't empty. Four of them were down there, wandering around in different directions. They were pretty easy to identify, since their clothes were torn and bloody. They also walked in a sluggish sort of shamble.

"Oh fuck," Dudley said.

"Relax," I replied. "None of them are headed our way."

I climbed up from the balcony to the roof. From there I could see the entire street. I didn't like the view.

"Oh hell," I grumbled.

Dudley cursed and climbed up to join me. The previously empty street was now in a state of utter chaos. I saw neighbors packing up cars. I saw neighbors running from other bloody neighbors. I saw neighbors fighting neighbors, and last but by far, not the least, I had neighbors eating neighbors.

The screams, both human, and inhuman were loud, and for a brief moment I thought I could actually smell the metallic scent of blood in the air.

"They're dead aren't they?" Dudley asked.

"I don't know," I answered honestly.

"That woman out front, with her throat all torn up, there's no way she could have been alive. Did you see how cloudy her eyes were?"

"Yeah, I saw."

"We need to go. We need to get out of here."

I agreed with him. I didn't voice it, but I most certainly agreed. I climbed back down to the balcony and glanced over to the field behind my house. Their numbers had grown.

One of them saw me watching and let out one of those gut-twisting screams. The others in the field looked over from the screamer to me, almost in unison, and began to scream as well.

Lovely.

Dudley was next to me. Merrick had both her front paws on the top of the balcony wall, and was watching as well.

"The back of the house is all windows," Dudley said. "We gotta move."

"Go to your room and grab your backpack," I ordered in a voice that was much too shrill for my tastes. "Fill it with as much water and food as you can."

"Georgie, here we come," I thought. I hope you're home.

I had a little military backpack that fit quite comfortably in the small of my back. It contained various survival items from the different camping trips I'd taken over the years. I tossed it on the bed and began filling it up with anything I thought I might need.One thing about me that is not very well known is that I have always had a fondness for weapons. Ever since I was a little boy, I collected various types of knives, swords, and axes. I was far from being defenseless. In fact, I was pretty much locked and loaded for anything that came my way. The only thing I never spent a lot of time on was guns. In my immediate possession, I had two shotguns and no shells for either of them.

I had everything else in abundance. I grabbed my favorite knife at the time, which was a Seal Pup, made by a company called SOG. Probably one the best fixed blades I have ever owned and it was definitely coming with me. The nylon sheath had an extra pocket, and inside I kept a Victorinox Swiss Army Ranger knife (my preferred Swiss Army knife). I threw the ensemble on the bed next to the backpack.

I ignored the swords. I didn't think any of them were for more than show. Instead, I grabbed a neat looking tomahawk, and a machete, from the closet, and threw them on the bed as well.

I was only wearing a white t-shirt and boxers. I threw on some socks and a pair of jeans. I yanked on my boots, my watch, my belt, and for whatever reason, a pair of nylon gloves that I used for riding.

I threw my day to day pocket knife which was a Special Forces folding tanto made by BokerPlus into my right front pocket, strapped my Seal Pup to my belt on the right hand side, slung the backpack over my shoulder, and grabbed the machete in one hand, and the tomahawk in the other.

"I notice that you give a lot of description to the tools and weapons that you took with you."

Hell yeah, these things were a part of my survival, and the survival of many others. I guess I kind of have a bit of fondness, and pride about them.

"I get you. It makes perfect sense. What happened next?"

I ran down the stairs as quick as I could. Dudley met me at the bottom. I handed him the machete, and he looked, if only slightly, somewhat relieved to have a weapon.

The first slam on the glass doors on the side of the house rang out loudly, even over the pounding noises still coming from the front door. The sound was unmistakable. I looked over Dudley's shoulder, and stared through the glass into a cloudy-eyed face filled with rage.It screamed at me, and was soon joined by another, and another. All three of them rammed, and slammed, against the glass. To my immense relief and great surprise, the glass door actually held, but it also began to crack in the middle.

Dudley, Merrick, and I, immediately ran to the garage. A flimsy wooden door was all that separated the garage from the house. On the way there I heard the unmistakable sound of the sliding glass door bursting inward in an explosion of glass shards, as another one of our unwanted visitors slammed into it.

Those things, whatever they were, ran right for us the minute they were inside the house. We barely had enough time to slam the weak, wooden door, shut behind us. It was close. It was way, way too close.

I love my Harley, but sometimes you just need a four-wheeled vehicle. I have nothing against sports cars, but they just aren't my thing. I never wanted a truck, because anytime someone has to move, they call you. I preferred one kind of vehicle above all others.

Jeep.

They're probably the most functional vehicle ever made. The one I had in the garage was a gift from my father. It was a black, four-cylinder, Jeep Wrangler. It currently had the full canvas top on due to the rain, but the three back windows were off because of the heat.

Dudley and I tossed our backpacks and weapons in the backseat. Merrick hopped inside with Dudley. I jumped into the driver's seat, and hit the button to open the garage door while I turned the ignition.

The flimsy wooden door burst apart, just as I was peeling out of the garage. Those things that were once human ran straight for us, but as soon as they grabbed hold of the vehicle, Merrick began to ravage their hands, and fingers. They let go quickly but it wasn't from the pain, it was from the damage Merrick inflicted upon their grasping hands.

Before I came to the stop sign at the end of my road, we had ten of them chasing after us.

"Run the stop sign!" Dudley shouted in a voice even more shrill than mine was earlier. "Run the fucking stop sign!"

I slowed down enough just to make sure we wouldn't be hit by another car, and then took off again when I was sure the way was clear only to end up smack dab in the middle of a fucking traffic jam the second I came to a major street.

We had to stop. We had no choice. There were too many abandoned cars littering the street, and the cars that were still occupied were now moving at a snail's pace as they tried to weave their way around the empty ones. Horns were blaring, and curses were being shouted from windows.

I looked into the rearview mirror. The ten pursuing us had gained in number, and they weren't very far behind. Oh hell.

I began to honk my horn furiously. Dudley had his head out the window, and was shouting for people to get out of the way.

Our pursuers were getting closer, and closer. Dudley panicked, and grabbed for his machete. He was pulling it out of its nylon sheath when I slapped the Jeep into reverse, and peeled out.

I had no idea what I was going to do. I only knew that we couldn't stay where we were. I guess I was going to ram through them in reverse, until I noticed the canal on my left hand side.

There are a lot of farms in the Upper Valley irrigated by canals branching off from the Rio Grande. These canals litter the entire area, and all of them have trails running on top of them that people use for walking, motorcycles, ATV's, and now…Jeeps.

I was still moving backwards when I hit the brakes. The bloody man, or thing, that was leading our pursuers was only four feet away from the back of the Jeep. He let out a scream just as I jammed the stick into first gear, hit the gas, and aimed for the trail on top of the canal.

Thank God for off road vehicles. Thank God for my Jeep. The way ahead was clear.

I stopped when we were a safe distance away, and I noticed that the shouting and blaring horns had gone quiet.

Dudley and I watched the group that had been chasing us swarm around the vehicles that were caught in the traffic jam. We saw some of the drivers make a run for it with their wives and children in tow. A few of them may have even made it. Many of them didn't.

We didn't watch for long. We just wanted to know.

I drove along the trail as fast as I could, which wasn't very fast at all. It was littered with weeds, bumps, and potholes. On one side of the trail was a drop off, and on the other was the actual water in the canal.

It took us about ten or fifteen minutes before we reached the Rio Grande. The river was full due to the recent rains, and the water was moving fast. I reversed until the back of the Jeep was about two feet from the river. That way I could see if anything was coming our way.

I would have preferred not to stop at all, but we needed to figure out which direction we wanted to take as we made our way to Georgie's.

The rains had also made the weeds and grasses grow and they climbed high on either side of the Jeep. It didn't seem like we were in El Paso anymore. It felt more like Africa. It was hot like Africa, and I realized for the first time that I was drenched in sweat.

Dudley handed me a large water bottle that he had, intelligently enough, brought with him. I drank greedily and just sat quietly while my heart settled itself down. I even tried to relax a bit by listening to the soft insect noises coming from all around us.

In the far off distance we could hear the occasional scream coming from both humans, and… well, whatever those things were.

"All those people," Dudley said in a soft voice. "We led them to all those people."

I was feeling just as guilty as he was, but I couldn't let him know.

"We couldn't have known that there would be a traffic jam there," I said. "We couldn't have known."

He was quiet for a while. Probably trying to see if his mind could accept what I just told him. Personally, mine couldn't. I felt very much responsible. Those things were chasing us, we escaped, and most of those people stuck in that traffic jam weren't so lucky. Words couldn't begin to describe how terrible I felt, but it sure as hell wasn't Dudley's fault. He wasn't the one driving the damn Jeep.

"I was right earlier, when I said what I said."

I didn't know what he was talking about. This of course wasn't anything unusual. He often said the oddest and most random things that made no sense whatsoever.

Jaxon tends to pick on just about everybody. I've been told that it's something he's always done, especially with his very close friends.

"Those things," he continued. "They aren't alive. They can't be. Not with those wounds, and all that blood, and those screams. They're dead. They can't be alive."

I agreed with him; I didn't need to say anything, I just nodded my head.

"It's like a horror movie," Dudley continued. "The dead are attacking us. They're eating us, just like a fucking movie."

He didn't say what kind of movie. We both knew, of course, but it just seemed easier to refrain from using the one word that summed up exactly what those things were.

And that was fine by me.

The humidity was horrendous. I looked up at the sky and saw some seriously dark rain clouds gathering in the distance. We were in for a storm. It would probably begin sometime after sunset, that's how El Paso weather usually works.

I reached into the console and removed a couple of dark blue bandanas. I gave one to Dudley, and we both tied them around our necks, cowboy style, hoping it would help with the sweat.

Twenty minutes later, I was getting drowsy. We should have already been on the move but after narrowly escaping what we had just been through, neither one of us was in a big hurry to jump back into the maelstrom again.

"We won't be safe here forever," I said. "We still need to get to Georgie's."

"I agree," Dudley replied.

"Well, if Redd Road is blocked," I said, referring to the road where the traffic jam was. "We can go the longer way around through the access road. They opened it up a few months ago. It's really wide, about four lanes, and there aren't a lot of stores around the area yet, so there hopefully won't be a lot of traffic. We should be able to get through."

"All right," Dudley said. "Just give me a few more…"

The scream interrupted him. One of the dead had found us. It was a young man, whose left arm was mangled. He wasn't a danger to Dudley and me at the moment; he was on the opposite side of the river.

"Never mind," Dudley continued. "Let's get the hell out of here."

"Hold on a second," I said. "I wanna see what he's gonna do."

We watched as the dead man made a bee-line right for us despite the fast moving water. He didn't hesitate for even a second at the water's edge, he just ran right in.

With both of his arms reaching out for us, we watched as he stumbled against the strong current of the river. His screams meanwhile, had attracted more company on the opposite shore. It was a woman in a white sundress. She also made that beeline right for us.

"We should leave," Dudley warned.

"Wait up," I replied. "There's no way they can cross, the waters moving too fast."

I was right, fortunately. Less than halfway across, the man lost his footing, and was unable to get back up. We watched him splash in the water for a brief moment before the current carried him far away from us.

The woman came next. It was the same thing. She lost her footing, fell, and floated away downstream.

After that, there were others. They weren't far behind the first two, just a few minutes if I remember correctly.

I don't know why I stayed there and kept watching. It was like being unable to turn your head when you pass by the scene of a traffic accident. I was mesmerized.

I began to shake. I guess it was my nerves finally reacting to what we had been through.

What I didn't realize is that I was learning about my enemy.

My mind was taking in the things that would come in handy later.

I learned that their screams attracted others. I don't know if this was a purposeful call or not, but the end result was the same. When one of the dead screams out, more of them appear to investigate.

I learned that they were stupid. It was evident that they couldn't cross the river. The ones in the back saw the ones in front wash away. Yet, they still waded in right behind their friends. They weren't only stupid about wading into the water to get at us; they also didn't seem to care if they drowned. Which they couldn't drown being that they were already dead, and I had no doubt that they were indeed dead. Still, all that water rushing into their lungs couldn't feel good and it made me remember back to when Merrick was savaging the arms of my neighbors at the front gate of my patio. They didn't react to the bites, didn't care if they were injured; and didn't seem to even notice that they were being injured.

They didn't feel pain.

I was measuring my enemy without even realizing that I was doing so.

We sat there for a long time, watching at least thirty of them wash away down the river. It was getting late in the day, and I began to worry that Georgie might not even be home. There was every chance in the world that he could have tried his luck, and attempted to get out of town. Then I began to wonder if this was happening anywhere else.

It must be. What could possibly be containing everything inside of El Paso? We could hold up at Georgie's for a while but eventually we had to go somewhere. Was there any place in the country that was still safe? Had the government come in to help us yet? Would the government come in to help us?

I started the Jeep, and slowly drove away from the river. I took the trail to an exit ramp that came off the freeway to Doniphan, which is a pretty major road in my neck of the woods. At the moment, it was deserted, nothing but empty cars, lifeless bodies, and bloodstains, on the street. We crossed the road slowly and carefully, on the lookout for the living dead.

We only saw one of them. She looked to be half eaten, but she reached out for us anyway. She couldn't pursue us; there wasn't enough left of her body. All she could do was reach out and growl. I was thankful she didn't scream.

I'd heard about roads like this from other survivors, empty except for the dead. It seems to leave a mark on people, more so than a lot of other terrifying situations. I always wondered if it had something to do with the emptiness.

We were fortunate that Doniphan was so empty. There were enough deserted cars to cause serious problems if anything began to chase after us. The weaving in and out slowed us down too almost a standstill.

When we hit the access road, we were able to speed up a bit. Still, I didn't go crazy. I didn't want to be hauling ass, and run into something that would damage the Jeep. It was our only safe way of travel. The four lanes were spread out nice and wide, so it was easy to go around any deserted cars we came across. I saw some wet bloodstains, but never any bodies, either dead, or undead.

That was a relief.

I was beginning to relax. Either that or I was getting used to things. I can't really say which.

When we came to Redd Road again, it was at the opposite side of where we encountered the traffic jam. We made our way slowly, on the lookout for any signs of danger.

We were all alone.

It was as if the earlier horror hadn't known this area existed. There weren't even any of those deserted cars. It just looked empty…like a ghost town.

We drove up a street called Dakota Ridge. This was Georgie's street. His house was a red brick number at the corner of the first left turn.

We sat in the Jeep with the engine running for a bit while we watched the house, and checked up and down the road.

"What if everyone around here is dead?" Dudley asked.

"There's no sign of anything going on over here," I answered. "Maybe everyone was able to get indoors, and safe, before…"

Georgie's windows were all boarded up. It was right in front of my face, and I only just now noticed it.

"Look at Georgie's windows," I said. "He's already sealed himself in. He's safe."

"Look at the other houses," Dudley said. "Same thing, it looks like everyone managed to board up their windows before they got hit."

"Hopefully, those things already passed through here," I said. "Everyone was safely boarded up, and they just went on by."

I reversed the Jeep into Georgie's driveway. We hopped out with all our belongings, and went to his front door.

"Georgie, it's us," I called out as I banged on his front door.

There was no answer but I could hear movement from inside.

"Georgie let us in."

There was still no answer, but I thought I could hear some shushing sounds from somewhere inside the house.

"Georgie," I shouted. "Are you guys okay in there?"

No answer, just more shushing noises from inside.

"Just break down the door," Dudley said. "I can hear him in there."

"I'll tell him that," I said.

"Georgie, we're getting worried. I'm going to kick down the door and come in."

No answer.

I gave the door a sharp kick. Nothing that would come close to causing any damage, I just wanted to see if it would cause Georgie to get off his ass and open up.

"Go away," Georgie said in a muffled voice from behind the wood.

"What do you mean go away?" I shouted. "Open the damn door. We need to get inside."

"I can only take care of my wife," Georgie's muffled voice answered.

"Are you for real, asshole?" Dudley shouted. "Open the fucking door before I rip it off the hinges."

Then I heard another muffled voice from inside.

"Georgie, open the door. They're our friends."

"No Lucy. I'm only taking care of you."

"Are you serious? Let them in, or I'll be leaving with them."

After that, the voices became indistinct, and I couldn't understand what they were saying to one another. I only knew that they were having an argument, and it seemed like Georgie was losing.

I went to the front of the yard by the street to keep watch.

It was as still and silent as a ghost town.

I glanced over at the other houses. We were being watched.

I saw that many of the neighbors were staring from their second story windows, safe inside their boarded up homes. As a matter of fact, all the houses in the vicinity seemed to have lookouts. Excellent! I was right (I normally am). These people boarded up before the danger came through.

That's if the hell of my neighborhood even came through here at all.

Lucy opened the front door.

"Jax," she cried out. "Man, am I glad to see you."

She ran right over, threw her arms around my chest, and ended up nearly crushing my ribs in a bear hug. Just when I began to wonder if I'd ever breathe again, she released me and did the same thing to Dudley.

Inside the house, the air conditioner was pumping. It wasn't the greatest. I hate evaporative coolers so very, very much yet; it was a hell of a lot better than the humid heat from outside.

Georgie was in the next room staring at his feet.

"How ya doin Georgie," I asked.

"It's nothing personal guys," Georgie said. "I just need to keep my wife safe."

"Then she shouldn't be with you, ya pussy," Dudley retorted.

In all honesty, Dudley told it like it was. Georgie wasn't exactly the toughest cat around. In fact, he seemed to kinda go all to pieces whenever a situation became the slightest bit heated.

Another bit of honesty I can share about Georgie is the attachment he has towards his wife. It borders on psychotic. I have no doubts that he would have left us outside to be eaten if she hadn't intervened.

Now Lucy, she adored us. She was the type of person that just really cared about other people, especially her friends.

It made for some interesting weekends.

Lucy would want to hang out with everyone, and Georgie would want to keep Lucy all to himself. Yeah, those were some good times. The arguments that they'd get into over little things like Lucy having friends, those were freaking hilarious. I used to joke that you couldn't buy that kind of entertainment.

His laugh was genuine this time, as was the smile on his face. He allowed himself to enjoy the moment for a few minutes before snapping back to the here and now.

Where was I? Oh yeah. We were finally inside Georgie's house.

"What's going on out there?" Lucy asked.

"I'm not sure," I answered. "It seems like…like…"

"Zombies," Georgie said. "I think those things are zombies."

Stupid Georgie, this was the exact word that Dudley and I had successfully avoided earlier at the river.

"Are you serious?" Lucy asked aloud in response to the silence coming from Dudley and me. "That can't be right."

"It seems right," Dudley said apologetically. "We've seen things."

"Has it come through here yet?" I asked.

"Nothing serious," Georgie said. "There were a few people that ran down the street kinda funny. We were already boarded up when it happened, so none of them stayed."

He mimicked the hard, rage infused face that we saw many times earlier in the day.

"I wonder if it'll come back this way again," I asked.

"The news said to stay put and board up the windows, but now the stations are all off."

"What do you mean off?"

"The signal went down earlier," Georgie said. "No more TV."

That didn't sound good. That didn't sound good at all.

"Should we stay here, Jax?" Lucy asked. "What if more of those…those…things come this way?"

"I think we should stay for a while at least," I answered. "Maybe we can figure something out. Maybe help will come."

"Where's your kid?" Dudley asked. "Georgie and Lucy had a six year old that normally never left her mother's side.

"She's with Georgie's parents," Lucy answered. "They already made it out."

"They're out of El Paso?" I asked.

"How do you know?" Dudley asked.

"They emailed us," Georgie said.

"Wait a minute!" I said. "The Internet is still working?"

"Yeah," Georgie answered.

Georgie's computer was on the second floor. I took about three stairs at a time. In the background, I could hear Lucy asking Dudley about my wife, and Dudley telling her that he had gotten in late the previous evening, and assumed she was asleep. He had no idea where she was at the moment, because he had only woken up when the screaming started.

With trembling fingers I logged on to my account. There were no new messages, just an old email that I never bothered to delete.

Then it came to me.

Nobody I knew ever emailed me there anyway. They always emailed my Facebook account. As a matter of fact, my wife and I bounced emails back and forth all day long whenever she was at work, and by her computer.

I logged into my account. It seemed an eternity before it showed my page. I had new messages. I clicked my inbox. There were two of them, one from my wife and one from my friend Kingsley.

Dudley was suddenly behind me.

I clicked on my wife's email. I read it, breathed a deep sigh of relief, and then reread the damn thing because I had no idea what she was talking about.

"Well?" asked Dudley.

"I'll read it to you," I answered. "Dear Jaxon. I love you very much, and I am safe. We made it out before the trouble started. I understand what you must do, I'm not sure I believe it but please be careful."

"What must you do?"

"Hell if I know. There's a link to a website here though. It's called EPUA.com."

I clicked the website, and it took me to a chat room. Dudley and I began to read the messages. They were from the survivors. Hundreds of messages were being added as we read.

"Help us."

"I am so and so. I made it."

"They killed my brother."

"I am at this or that street. Please send help."

There were also messages from people outside of El Paso.

"Has anyone seen my daughter?"

"Stay safe. Don't go outside."

"The military won't tell us anything."

"El Paso has been closed off."

Georgie walked over to us, took a look at the computer screen and began to read the messages as well.

"Yeah," he said. "That's the best website. EPUA means 'El Paso Under Attack.' I read on there that all the exits out of town are barricaded by the military. Nobody can get in or out."

"Then this thing hasn't spread out of El Paso?" I asked.

"Nope, it's all been contained. The military was on top of things the minute shit began to happen. At first they were letting people out. Then, when the zombies got to the borders, they closed everything down."

"How do you know all this?" Dudley asked.

"I've been on and off this website all day," Georgie answered. "The website address was the last thing the TV was able to broadcast before the signal was lost."

"What about the radio?"

"Nothing in El Paso," Georgie said. "No cell phones either. Those got shut down just a bit ago along with the landlines, and the radio. Some people are thinking that the military did it somehow."

Cell phones...I immediately tried my cell phone once again, just to make sure. Sometimes Georgie was totally full of shit. However, he was right this time; I no longer even got a signal.

"This is fucked," Dudley complained. "Does the outside world not know what's happening to us in here?"

"It's getting out," Georgie answered, "but, the military doesn't want to risk spreading whatever this is outside of the city. That's why all forms of communication are down. They don't want any reporters announcing any exits or weak spots along the borders before everything's sealed up tight, because they don't want people sneaking in or out. What if the entire country was overrun with this shit?"

"How nice for those of us still here," I complained. "The fuckers outside of El Paso get to be safe and sound, while those of us that are trapped get to be eaten by zombies. Why does the Internet still work?"

"My guess is that the military needs at least one way to keep updated with whatever is going on inside the city. Then again, maybe they couldn't shut the Internet down?"

It made sense I guess, even if it was Georgie logic, and it's easy enough to complain about things. Yet, in the end I understood. It's bad enough that it happened in El Paso but things would be a whole lot worse if it began to spread outside the city. Then it hit me, how did they respond so quickly and close off all the borders before there were any leaks?

The outbreak happened quickly and spread fast, yet, they were still able to contain everything. It didn't seem right, but now wasn't the time to ask questions. I had just remembered Kingsley sent me an email.

I read it out loud for everyone.

"Jax, everyone is dead. I can make it to my car. I'm coming to you."

"Shit," I said.

We weren't at my house anymore, and that area wasn't exactly the nicest, or friendliest, place to visit by the time we left. I checked when he sent the email. It had had been over an hour ago. There was no way to stop Kingsley from going to my house.

"There's nothing we can do," Georgie said.

"Maybe he'll come here," Dudley added. "I mean, if he drives up to our house and everything is all gone to shit, he's not going to get out of the car, and next place he'd stop would be here."

"That's true," I said. "If he can even make it to our house, Kingsley lives all the way on the Northeast."

That means Kingsley had a relatively long drive, through all kinds of hell, ahead of him. Nobody spoke for a while. We all just kinda sat around and looked at our own feet.

"Nothing we can do but wait," Georgie said.

And wait is exactly what we did.

For weeks, we simply waited. The rains came at night, and deep puddles littered the streets in the morning. It wasn't an unpleasant wait we had all the luxuries a normal home provides but the anxiety was overwhelming.

Another thing I heard about was how difficult the "waiting" was for the survivors. They were isolated for days upon days, and in some cases, months upon months just hoping that they wouldn't be attacked. It must have been terrible.

EPUA gave us nothing new. It was always one of two messages, trapped people asking for help while being besieged by walking corpses, or people hoping to locate a missing friend or loved one. There were way too many people in need. I sort of stayed away from the computer after a while; it was too depressing. But, we saw nothing in our area. No sign of the zombie hordes that were ravaging the city.

One important fact about Georgie that I should probably mention is his love of guns. Georgie loved a good firearm probably as much as he loved his wife. He collected them, sold them, bought them new, bought them old, and traded out the ones he got bored of. In his house, he probably had around forty pistols and rifles.

So, while we waited, we made bullets.

I chose two firearms for myself: a 9mm Glock, and a Winchester .30-30. Having shot both of these guns in the past, I felt relatively comfortable with them, and I was hopefully still a decent shot. Plus, the bullets weren't gigantic. I didn't want loaded down with ammo if I had to travel. Not that this was a problem just then. We hadn't even tried to leave the house. All my gear was packed up and ready to go by the garage door. Georgie gave me a military style belt that I put the Glock, my knife, and some ammo pouches on. I also rigged a little ring onto the belt so that I could attach my tomahawk. I kept this little ensemble close by at all times.

One morning, after an incredible breakfast of pancakes and bacon, we decided to pull my Jeep into the garage just in case the house was swarmed, and we needed to get out fast.

I went out the front door and walked to the road. Nothing; the coast was perfectly clear. Up the street, down the street, and anywhere else I cared to look, was devoid of any movement, and completely vacant.

The neighbors watched me from their windows as I gave the thumbs up sign to Dudley who then opened the garage door. I hopped into my Jeep, turned the key in the ignition, and began to back it inside the garage.

I was reversing up the driveway when I saw the neighbor across the street pointing frantically down the road. I followed his finger and saw Kingsley's green and battered car veering around like a bat out of hell right towards me.

I was overjoyed to say the least. Kingsley and I have always been very close. I was able to relax a little bit knowing that he was safe.

I parked the Jeep in the garage, and went down to the sidewalk to meet him just as he smacked off his one remaining hubcap against the curb.

He didn't look good; he looked like he'd been through hell. Dried blood covered his clothes, and his face looked like it had aged ten years. We hugged briefly and went inside.

I did not ask Kingsley what happened to him. It wasn't hard to figure that out just by his appearance. Instead, I respected his privacy, and let him shower and change without bombarding him with a hundred questions.

In general, Kingsley is a very quiet, bear of a man, who stands just slightly over six-foot-three. His quietness is often mistaken for menacing, but in all actuality, he's a very sensitive and gentle person.

"How long have you known him?"

About four years at that time, just long enough for him to know that if he needed, or wanted to talk, I would be there for him. I wouldn't push him. I was just happy that he was with us, and safe.

In the end, he was with us for about a week before he said anything.

"Anyone heard anything from Tito?" Kingsley asked.

"No," I answered with a shake of my head.

"Hope he's all right," Kingsley said. "It's bad out there."

Time went by slowly. We were starting to run out of food, and so were the neighbors. They were hanging signs in their windows asking for something to eat. Things weren't horrible yet, at least for us. We still had about three days left of canned food if we rationed everything.

"The supermarket is just down the road," I said. "We may need to grab some things if this doesn't end soon."

"I can't believe nobody is coming for us," Lucy said.

"Well, they may not come for us in a long time," I answered. "So we need to rely on ourselves. Everyone's running out of food, somebody needs to go. If it's bad, we can always turn back."

"I'll go with you," Kingsley said in his quiet voice. "I don't want you wandering off alone. You have a way of getting into trouble even when there aren't zombies running around."

"That's true," Georgie laughed. "I just don't know if it's safe. Last night I heard something making noise outside."

"Did you see anything?" Dudley asked.

"No," Georgie answered.

"Did you bother looking or did you hide under the covers?"

"Bite me."

We had a good laugh at this. Dudley making fun of Georgie was always a good time. The insults started flying back and forth as we sat there in the dining room. Suddenly Lucy, who had been periodically looking out the window between the boards, called our attention.

"The neighbor across the street is coming out," Lucy said.

It was a young girl of about twenty. She looked scared to death as she reached the road, and looked up and down. She started to cross the street, coming towards us, when we heard the scream.

Georgie was right. He did hear something during the night.

The girl froze solid in her tracks as the corpse ran towards her. It came from between two empty houses at a furious run.

I ran to the front door.

"Georgie, let's go," I called out as I passed him by.

He picked up his rifle, the one that looked like an M16. I threw open the door, and Georgie panicked.

"What if it isn't one of them?" He asked.

"Give me a break Georgie," I yelled. "Look at it."

The zombie had already begun to rot in the wet and humid heat. Its graying flesh was peeling off of its fingertips and face. The shock of dark hair on its head was plastered to its skull with what may have been oil. The blood on its clothes looked old, and it was covered in some sort of slimy muck that contrasted only slightly from the substance on its head. Still, as bad as it looked, it was moving in on the frozen girl rapidly.Georgie took aim and fired. The bullet tore a chunk out of the thing's hip. It spun around, landed on its face, got back up, and limped towards the girl at a slower pace.

"In the head you idiot," Dudley screamed. "You gotta shoot them in the head."

Merrick was going nuts. It was all Lucy could do to hold her back, and all the racket and commotion she was making only added to the tension.

Georgie was still aiming for his second shot, when Kingsley shouldered him out of the way, and nailed it with a single blast from his shotgun.

"Hard to miss with one of these," Kingsley said with a smile.

No one said anything for a moment. I think we were all uncomfortable about having just killed something that used to be a man.

"Fuck!" I just about shouted. Then I laughed and turned to Georgie. "All these guns and you can't even shoot them."

Everyone else started laughing, and it broke the tension. It was kill or be killed. There was just no sense in feeling bad for shooting something that wouldn't hesitate to eat you alive. At least, that's how I rationalized things.

The girl began to cry very loudly. She actually fell to her knees with full body wracking sobs that threatened to never stop.

I heard zombie screams come from farther down the street.

I ran towards the driveway. There were three of them running towards her now. I didn't think. There was no time for rational thinking. I ran back inside the house, grabbed my tomahawk, and ran back outside once more.

I was halfway to her when I began to panic. I realized that the zombies were going to reach her at the exact same time I did. I ran faster. I poured all my strength into my legs, and I heard gunshots coming from Georgie, and Kingsley.

I breathed a sigh of relief when I heard those shots. I didn't even look over to see the effect until I reached the girl. I trusted my friends.

Two of the zombies were down for good and the other one was struggling to his feet after being knocked on his ass by what looked to be a shotgun blast.

I didn't hear the pounding footsteps coming from behind me until the surprise zombie was almost on top of me. I spun around, and came just about face to face with the raging corpse. It truly and deeply scared the living hell right out of me. I had no idea there was a fourth zombie. I had no idea where it even came from. I think I maybe even screamed a little bit.

It reached out for my throat as it tackled me to the street. I held its face inches from my own by its neck and somehow, in my panic, still managed to twist my way out from underneath it. I got to my knees and immediately kicked out with my boot. It fell backwards, got quickly back up to its feet, and charged into my swinging tomahawk.

The crunching sound my weapon made as the blade shattered bone and entered the brain, was sickening. I didn't waste any time gagging about it though, I grabbed the girl by the arm, and was already on Georgie's porch before the swaying corpse even hit the pavement.

Lucy closed and locked the door behind us.

"Why the hell didn't you grab the gun?" Georgie asked.

"I dunno, I just grabbed out, and my fingers went for the tomahawk."

"But hell Jaxon," he continued. "If that thing had bitten you…"

He didn't have to finish. Everyone knew the score. We'd all seen the movies. Yet, to be perfectly honest, I felt sort of comfortable with the tomahawk. A blade just feels much more natural in my hands than a gun ever could. I don't know, I guess I've always felt safer and in more control with some sort of edged weapon.

"I'm Lucy," Lucy said to the new girl. "What's your name?"

"Nancy," the girl answered. She wasn't crying anymore; she seemed to be in shock.

"Your front door is wide open. Is the rest of your family still inside the house?" Georgie asked.
"No."

"Where's your family then?" Georgie asked. "I saw other people looking out the windows over the last few days."

"They're dead. My brother killed them all."

"Was that your brother that tackled me?" I asked.

She just nodded her head, and we watched as her silent tears began to trickle down her cheeks. Well, that's great. Nice to meet you, hold on a second, let me just bury a tomahawk into your brother's head. There we go, sorry for the interruption, now where were we?

To put it lightly, I felt pretty bad but at least it explained where the fourth zombie came from. It followed her right out of her front door.

"We're still going to run out of food," Kingsley said in a complete subject change.

"Not like we can do anything about that now," Georgie laughed before continuing on in an uncharacteristically angry and resentful voice. "More of those things are obviously coming this way. We all heard the screams when Jax was running back to the house. They were probably just a few streets over, heard the gunshots, and then followed the noise."

To be fair, Georgie was probably right. What kind of world are we unfortunate enough to live in where something like that happens?

I couldn't seem to tell whether or not he was joking, or whether or not he was actually asking me a question. So after blankly staring at him for a few seconds, I gave him a small courtesy smile. He then continued as if I had never floundered for a response.

"We'd better go soon then," Dudley answered. "It is probably only going to get worse."

"We'll go tonight, after the sun goes down," I said.

"But Jax," Lucy interrupted. "Won't those things be harder to see at night?"

"Let's just hope that we're harder to see as well," I answered.

It was decided then. Dudley, Kingsley, and I would take the Jeep after sunset and look for food. Georgie would stay behind to protect the girls, because he was a pussy. On our way back, after we were loaded up with food, we'd fire two shots in the air at the end of Georgie's street so they'd know to open the garage door for us.

It sounded easy enough. We go out, sneak around, grab some food, fire two shots, they let us back in, and we all have a jolly good time. I hoped it would work!

As the sun was setting I should have been freaking out. I was about to go into the lion's den, and try not to be eaten. Yet, I wasn't freaking out. I don't know why but I was coming back to my usual charming self. In fact, the very second I chopped Nancy's brother in the head with my tomahawk, I began to come to grips with my new environment.

Weird, don't you think?

I just sort of nodded my head. I still had no idea what to say. The things this man went through. I didn't have the words. He wasn't too bothered by my apparent lack of decent feedback however; he just gave me a small grin and once again continued his tale.

It wasn't easy to get into the Jeep without Merrick but eventually we made it. I wish we could have taken her but she's a bit of a barker, and we were trying to be stealthy. Dudley was driving the Jeep, Kingsley was riding shotgun, and I was in the back seat with my rifle. Hopefully, I could blast anything that came running at us.

They opened the garage door manually to keep things quiet. We coasted down the driveway, and into the street. Once there, Dudley keyed the ignition and we crept down the road slowly.

At the end of the road, we turned to the left and continued cautiously.

The first zombie came from the left side of the street. No scream at all. I just heard the pounding footsteps. Dudley gunned the Jeep and I fell back into my seat.

"No," I protested. "Slow down so I can get a decent shot."

He took his foot off the gas. I aimed, squeezed the trigger and blasted the top of the thing's head off before it got within ten feet of us.

"Jax, if you guard the rear," Kingsley said, "I can take care of this side."

"Rock on," I answered.

Of course, I had mistakenly thought that was the plan. I made a mental note to verbally communicate my ideas in the future.

We probably only had to take out another three zombies before we got to the supermarket. It was actually kind of easy; I was expecting a whole lot worse. When we arrived at the supermarket, things got worse.

Apparently, zombies love to shop for groceries, because this place was teeming with them. I'm talking about well over a hundred. We had the Jeep stopped a little ways off to the side of the supermarket's parking lot and we were watching them wander aimlessly in and out of the store and around the lot. It was the weirdest thing. Why in the world would so many zombies gather around a grocery store? I know now that they tend to frequent the places that were familiar to them when they were alive. Still, don't they have any better memories than going to the supermarket?

"Are there any other grocery stores around here?" Kingsley whispered.

"Yes," I answered. "There's one just a little bit farther down the road."

"How are we going to get there?" Kingsley asked. "Is there an alternate route?"

"Fuck if I know," I answered honestly.

"Maybe if we just go real slowly past them, they won't notice," Dudley added.

"Meeerrrrraaaaaahhhh!"

We were pretty much used to what that scream meant. Slowly, the three of us turned our heads to the supermarket to see how bad things were about to get.

I don't think that they could have gotten any worse. Every head in the parking lot was looking our way.

To say the least, it is a very unnerving experience to have a stare down with that many rotted things that used to be human. I don't think mere words can describe what that scene really entailed; slime and mud covered corpses that were well into various stages of decay, sizing you up for dinner.

"Oh fuck me," Dudley moaned, and truer words could not have been spoken. All three of us were frozen solid as we waited for the storm to start. We stared at them and they stared at us. Why they didn't charge us right away, I could not say. Why we didn't run...well...I guess we were just hoping they wouldn't charge.

They charged.

Like a rampaging semi they came forth. It started with only one of them, a grotesque male whose face was peeling off. Before he had even taken five steps, they all decided to follow his example. Over one hundred starving zombies poured through the parking lot, and every one of them was hell bent on taking a bite out of us.

Let me tell ya, they ran fast! We could hear their feet pounding on the cement, even over their screams.

Don't even get me started on the smell. The days spent out in the sun, heat, and humidity, took their toll. We could smell their reek as soon as they came into view. Once they started charging us, the smell became unbearable.

Dudley wasn't moving.

"Hey Duds," I said in a calm voice.

"Yes," he answered in a whisper.

"Hit the fucking gas!" I shouted.

He did, and we took off down the street. The only problem was that we should have taken off in the other direction, because we were headed directly in front of the parking lot, and some of the zombies were already running to cut us off.

Now, I'll go on record saying that zombies are incredibly stupid. There's no doubt about that. All they're really capable of doing is reacting to basic instincts. In other words, if they see a human, they chase it. If they catch a human, they eat it. That's it, nothing more.

But damned if we weren't about to get surrounded.

I readied myself with the tomahawk in my hand.

Kingsley took out a rope from my backpack, and threw it to me.

"I don't want you falling out," he said.

Quickly, I tied it around my waist.

Then, they were upon us.

Dudley did his best to swerve around any that got in front of the Jeep. He did a pretty good job, and the zombies even helped his cause somewhat by dodging the vehicle and trying to grab at us from the sides. Kingsley had a Colt .45, and was blasting everything that rushed in on his side. I was still in the back, swinging and chopping at everything I could reach.

It wasn't easy to hit anything with Dudley's driving jostling me all over the back seat, but as soon as one of those fleshy hands grabbed on, I swung. It was working, even though we couldn't drive too fast without crashing into one of them, we were still pulling away bit by bit. It even looked like we were gonna make it, when Dudley swerved just a little too hard and I fell out of the Jeep.

My tomahawk dropped from my hand as soon as I lost balance. I hit the road in a tumble that probably broke some ribs. To make matters even worse, I felt a hard yank on my stomach before I had even stopped rolling, which meant the rope was still attached to my waist.

I'm not sure what hurt more, the yank of the rope or being dragged behind a Jeep going forty miles per hour. To make matters just a bit more unbearable, the rope decided to slide farther up my torso. It began to dig into what I was positive, at that point, were broken ribs. I was in agony.

Dudley couldn't slow down. If he did, the Jeep would be overtaken.

I reached for the knife on my utility belt. It seemed like an eternity, but I finally managed to find it amidst the dragging and rolling. I hacked at the rope around my waist, and it came away quickly under the sharp blade. I rolled some more, and finally came to a stop, but I didn't have time to take stock of my injuries. The dead were coming.

They reached me just as I stood up. The first one tackled me, and I rolled him off before he could get a firm grip. Damn! They smelled bad, and double damn, they were fast. I was at a dead, albeit limping run in the blink of an eye and I could still feel fingernails scrape against the soft skin of my back.

Obviously, Dudley realized that I fell out. As soon as he was safely out of danger he slowed down as much as he could. I could see his, wide, terrified, eyes in the reflection of the rear view mirror. He wouldn't leave me. Not Dudley.

There was nothing barring my way but behind me was an army of zombies. I ran for all I was worth; it wasn't fast enough. I was just too injured. They were gaining rapidly, and only a few steps from catching me. When I got close enough to the Jeep, I dove for the tailgate.

I hit it hard and my ribs screamed out in a chorus of pain. Kingsley reached over the passenger seat and grabbed my left arm. He pulled me and I crawled up into the backseat of the Jeep. Things were looking up, until I felt the tug on my leg.

One of them, a woman, had managed to run fast enough to latch onto me. One of her hands grabbed my leg, and the other grabbed the tailgate. Her feet were dragging, but she was slowly pulling herself up.

I still had the knife in my right hand. When she pulled herself to within biting range, I shot my arm back as hard as I could, and buried the blade into her temple. She squeezed tighter on my calf for a brief second, and then limply fell away into the road as we drove off.

When she hit the road, she rolled wildly, knocking some of her fellow zombies out of the chase just as Dudley really hit the gas. We careened away, leaving the rotting things to sort it out.

I pulled myself into the back seat, found my tomahawk lying where it had fallen on the floor spared one last look behind us to make sure things were really over and surrendered to the pain.

When I woke up to agony, around fifteen minutes later, Dudley was driving slowly. and cautiously, while Kingsley looked around for any signs of trouble. They were arguing over where to get the food (the grocery store down the street was too close to the danger zone we had just escaped), or if they should stop everything and get me back to Georgie's to see how badly I was hurt.

I was hurt pretty damn bad. By the vast degree of mind numbing pain, my best guess was that my ribs weren't the only things that were broken. I had hurt something on the inside. I didn't know exactly what, but I knew that I had some serious internal problems working against me. Without medical help, I would be in big time trouble.

Dudley drove down a street called Sunland Park Drive, and stopped by the side of a park. I heard them discussing a gas station a little ways down that would probably have some food. They couldn't see any zombies around but they were afraid to leave me in the Jeep alone.

I managed to open my eyes and take in my surroundings.

The park looked wonderful, cool and inviting. The air smelled of the rain that would start falling any moment. I wanted to lie in the cool grass instead of the hard confines of the Jeep.

"Drive into the park," I said.

"There's some trees over that way," Kingsley added. "They'll hide the Jeep while we figure things out."

It was a short and bumpy trip to the trees. I was glad when it was over. I passed out when they pulled me out of the Jeep, but only for a moment.

The damp grass felt like heaven on my body. Dudley and Kingsley looked on in concern. I must have looked pretty bad because I could see the worry in their faces. If I had been able to think coherently, I would have been freaking out. Still, the realization that I was probably dying did not escape me.

The moment sucked, royally.

"I'm not leaving him here," Dudley said.

"I agree," Kingsley said. "We should give him a moment and head back."

"No," I mumbled. "It's safe here. Just go get the food."

In fact, I did feel safe. I was even starting to feel a little bit more comfortable. The cool grass was a soft lullaby welcoming its brother sleep…or death.

In that moment, I didn't care. I just didn't want to move.

"We're not leaving you," Dudley whispered.

"I'm not asking you to. Just let me relax here for a bit while you get the supplies. It'll be fine."

"Let's just give it a try," Kingsley said. "He's got his Glock if he needs it."

I felt Dudley's hot hand on my forehead while he looked me over.

"We'll be back soon."

They were gone when I next opened my eyes, and I had no idea how much time had passed. I heard thunder in the distance, and felt the first slight drops of rain. I closed my eyes again, very much aware that I would be dead before Dudley and Kingsley returned with the supplies.

It turns out I was wrong, but while I was sleeping, I had the strangest dreams I'd ever had in my life.

I woke up to the sound of my name being whispered. At least I thought I was awake. I was pretty sure that I wasn't dreaming their voices, but I couldn't see anything. Great, did I somehow manage to blind myself? I couldn't remember ever hitting my head on anything.

Dudley and Kingsley began calling my name out louder, and I forced myself to answer back. Not because I wanted to, you see. I'd rather have gone back to sleep than deal with the new problem of blindness, but I was afraid of what they might bring down on us with their panicked shouting.

"Over here," Dudley shouted.

I felt him slide to the turf next to me, and then I heard the sound of grass being ripped from the ground.

"It's like the park is trying to swallow him or something," Dudley whispered.

I heard gunshots, three or four of them. Then I heard and felt another hard ripping sound close to my face, and I could see. I could see!

"You okay?" Dudley asked."Yeah, what the hell just happened?"

"You tell me. I have no idea."

I heard two more gunshots, and looked over to see Kingsley bringing down some zombies that had been running towards us. When I looked back at Dudley I noticed my body. It was covered with grass—not grass that someone had thrown over me—grass that had grown over me.

"What the hell is this?" I asked.

"No idea Jax. Let's just get you out of there."

Dudley began ripping at the grass again, but he was having difficulties. It seemed as if the grass didn't want to release me. Dudley was panting from the exertion. I wanted to help him, so I tried sitting up. The grass gave way immediately.

I climbed to my feet, and joined Kingsley, who was now keeping watch. The rain was coming down harder than before. The thunder was impressive in its volume, and the area seemed clear of any hostiles, at least for the moment.

"Did you get the supplies?" I asked.

"Oh yeah, we got lots of stuff," Dudley answered. "Now all we have to do is make our way back. How are you feeling by the way?"

"Huh?" I didn't even notice till he had asked but I felt great. "Um, I feel pretty good."

I lifted my shirt and my body told a different story. Deep, black, bruises ran from my hips to my chest. It looked like I should be in the same agony I was in before the ground tried to swallow me, but somehow, the pain was gone. I was just a little bit stiff.

"Dude, I was sure you broke some ribs or something," Kingsley said.

I did, in fact, agree with him. I also could have sworn that I had some internal damage as well, but that didn't seem to be the case any longer. Things were getting stranger and stranger.

"I thought so too," I answered. "I felt like I was dying, to be honest with you, but right now I'm good to go. I even feel kinda energized."

"The ground healed him," Dudley said in a strange voice. "There was no mistaking how bad he was. We all saw it. He was headed downhill, and now, a few hours later…and…well, now he's all better. The ground healed him. It was even protecting him. I couldn't get him out of the grass, but the minute he wanted to sit up, it let him go."

"That's ridiculous," I laughed. Sometimes, Dudley came up with some really harebrained ideas. He was often funny, sometimes strange, but never boring.

"Oh yeah," he shouted. "That's ridiculous, but the living dead cannibals that keep chasing after us are perfectly normal?"

He had a point. Plus, I'd sat on the ground many times during my life, and it had never before tried to swallow me.

"Wait. What do you mean you left me alone for a few hours?"

"Oh yeah," Dudley sighed. "It sucked. Getting to the gas station was no problem. Getting inside was no problem either. I mean, we saw some zombies and everything, but they were easy enough to sneak by. Once we got in the station however, things went bad. We got spotted somehow. I managed to block the front door, but in about ten minutes we had almost twenty zombies banging on the glass."

"What did you do?" I asked.

"We went out the back, down an alley, and hid inside a restaurant until the coast was clear. Then we were finally able to zig and zag our way back here. There's still a big mess of zombies somewhere in the neighborhood looking for us. And the shooting Kingsley had to do once we got here might have given away our position."

"All right, let's hop back in the Jeep and make our way home. Just avoid the gazillion zombies at the grocery store."

"Wait a minute. What happened at the park?"

How should I know?

"But, it's true then. You are different?"

I guess I'll let you to figure that one out on your own. I don't see the point in trying to prove or disprove any of those rumors about me that are out there swirling around the Internet.

"Fair enough. I'll force myself to be patient."

Good idea.

Where was I then? Oh yeah, Kingsley was trying to figure out another way to Georgie's house, while Dudley and I laughed at him. He's notoriously horrible with directions, the kind of person that has to visit a place five times before they can remember how to get there. Not that I'm any better, but I knew the Westside of town better than he did.

"Don't worry about it," I finally said. "We just need to go around the long way. It's really easy."

It was, in all honesty, a lot more comfortable to watch the rear of the vehicle when I wasn't sitting atop a mound of supplies. I wasn't complaining though. I wasn't about to complain about anything for a good long while. I was just happy that I wasn't feeling horrible and intense agony from my mid-section anymore. I was also still a little freaked out by those weird ass dreams I had while I was being swallowed up by the park. Wow.

They were dreams of violence and destruction, and in them vast numbers of people were screaming out for help. In each dream, the time periods were different. One was in medieval times, another seemed to be in the early 1800s, yet another in the 1920s. The only thing in common was that all of the people I saw were frightened and in pain. That is, until someone fought back.

In every era, a hero answered the call. I could see him rise out of the mounds of fallen bodies and begin to strike back at the monsters and demons that had descended upon the innocent.

"And you had no idea why you were having those dreams?"

Not then I didn't. They got a lot worse before I ever learned why I was having them. That was just a taste of what was yet to come.

So, around we went through the creepily lit streets. The rain had slowed a bit; it was now a soft sprinkling from the sky. El Paso rain is like that, very inconsistent. One minute it's raining hard, and the next it's either a drizzle, or gone entirely. Lightning flashed across the skies, and thunder boomed as we made our way through the deserted neighborhoods.

We heard screams in the distance, some were from the dead, and others seemed like they came from the living. Every now and then, a scream was punctuated with a gunshot. I wanted to help those people. I just didn't think we'd ever be able to find them. And I wondered if we were the only ones stupid enough to be driving around.

The streetlights were out on a few blocks and that, combined with the dark empty houses, created a truly dangerous scene. It was really dark on those streets, and the three of us braced ourselves for an attack that could come from any direction the second we entered one of those neighborhoods. I expected the houses to be dark. Even if there were people still alive in some of them, they wouldn't be turning on lights that could be seen from the outside. That would be a beacon for the zombies. The streetlights however, were a different story. I had no idea why those were out.

Some of the houses really began to make me wonder. They had boarded up windows. Someone worked on them to make them safe. Were the people that boarded them up still inside? Were they waiting for some kind of help to arrive?

A flicker of light caught my attention.

"What was that?"

"What was what?" Dudley asked, in a voice that spelled out, with no uncertainty, he really didn't want to know.

"I saw a light," I said, just as I saw it again from the corner of my eye.

Since I was facing Dudley, I missed where the source of light originated from.

"I saw that," Kingsley said. "Where did it come from?"

"Stop the Jeep," I said to Dudley. "I wanna look."

He stopped, but he wasn't happy about. Can't say I blame him. Who knew what was gonna come charging out of the shadows at us.

We sat there quietly for a few tense moments before the light flickered once again. Kingsley and I found the source. It was three houses down, coming from an upstairs window.

Now what?

"We should check it out," Kingsley said. "It could be another survivor."

"Or it could be a zombie that's playing with a light switch," Dudley answered. "It's too risky. Let's get the hell out of here."

Shit. Shit. And damn it. I really, really, really didn't want to go into that dark house and see what kinda nasty freak was gonna run out and try to eat me. At the same time, I couldn't just walk away and leave a potentially living, breathing human in need of help.

Isn't life wonderful?

"So what did you do?"

I played the hero. That's what I did. I don't always want to, but I just can't bear the thought of not being the hero. Does that make sense? I doubt it. I don't do it for my ego, and I don't do it for fame. I do it because no one else can. I do it because I have to.

So yeah, we backed the Jeep through the yard of the house, right up to the front door, in case we had to get out of there in a hurry.

We left Dudley in the Jeep, and with my Glock un-holstered, I went to the front door with Kingsley. Of course, it was locked. I tried knocking just to see what would happen. Nobody answered, so I gave it a kick, but I must have thrown more power in it than I had planned. The door flew open, and slammed so violently against the nearby wall, that the doorknob buried itself into the plaster. The house appeared to be empty. I shone a flashlight all around the room, and didn't see anything. The smell wasn't so great though. Something had certainly been through this house. The question was whether or not it was still inside.

We entered cautiously.

That's the worst feeling ever, by the way, entering a dark, enclosed area, and having no idea what's going to come running out to rip off your face. I can't tell you how many times I've had to do it but I really, really hate it.

The kitchen was full. We both agreed to grab some food on our way out. The more food we could stockpile, the longer we could last.

Kingsley went to the window, and looked out at the backyard. He motioned me over and pointed.

A dead man was out there, walking around in circles. He hadn't seen us, so he didn't seem to pose that much of a threat. We still watched him for a few moments just to make sure. After we were satisfied that he wasn't going to come charging through the windows at us, we continued our search.

We needed to be quiet.

Slowly, we searched the entire downstairs floor. There were five different rooms, and zero signs of life, or un-life. We found ourselves in front of the stairway that led to the upstairs floor. The beam of our flashlight didn't penetrate very far from our angle. It was dark, it was scary, and we were going up there. Neither one of us was very happy.

Step by step we rose. I had my gun in front of me, at the ready to blow the shit out of anything that needed blasting.

At the top of the stairs, we waited. I put my head on the carpet as Kingsley kept watch. I waited for the light to flicker. I would see it under one of the doors when it did.

It happened just a moment later. In one quick flash of light, I knew where to go.

"I found it," I announced.

"Let's get it done quickly then," Kingsley said.

"We should check the other rooms before we open that door."

"Fuck that. Let's just open the damn door, and get the hell out of here," Kingsley replied.

As it was, I figured we were pushing our luck. If something wasn't currently trying to bite me, that probably meant it was well on its way. So, I took Kinsley's advice.

The door was locked. I tried knocking. Of course there was no answer so I tried again with my ear pressed against the door. I heard a whimper. It was a human whimper.

I was positive.

I pressed my shoulder against the wood of door as gently as possible. It wasn't that quiet, but the door did open.

We went inside, and turned on the light. At first glance it seemed to be empty.

We found ourselves standing in a little girl's room with twin beds. It was all done up in pink with flowers and rainbows drawn onto the walls. There was a desk in the far corner and a closet on the left.

"You sure this is the right room?"

"Yeah," I answered. "I saw the light under the door. Try the closet while I look under the beds."

"Are you fucking kidding me?" Kingsley asked.

To be honest, I laughed, and then I called him a pussy.

I went to the first bed, and keeping as much distance as I could, peered underneath. Toys and dust bunnies. I was about to go to the next bed when Kingsley opened the closet door.

I jumped no less than fifteen feet when he screamed. Something darted out of the closet, ran between his legs, and scrambled under the second bed.

"What the hell," I shouted as I brought my Glock up, and prepared to fire through the bed if I had to.

Kingsley just about tackled my gun arm in response.

"Don't shoot," He screamed. "Don't shoot. She's alive."

"Are you sure?" I asked.

"Yeah, she's just a little girl," he answered.

Well, there ya have it! I kept my distance and peered under the bed. She was a dirty, smudged little girl in a blue dress. A little out of fashion, I imagined, but Kingsley was right; she was alive.

"It must have been difficult for a little girl to stay alive without anyone around to help her."

I agree. She certainly was a survivor. I've seen adults cower and die when things get tense. I can't imagine what it must have been like for her, but nevertheless, she pulled through somehow.

"You okay little girl," I asked.

She nodded just a tiny bit in response. Her eyes were as big as saucers. She was understandably scared to death.

"All right honey," I said in that weird voice adults use for calming children down. "I know you're scared but we need to move you to a much safer place."

"I can't leave," she answered. "My sister's going to come back."

It made sense. There were two beds in the room. The pictures on the desk showed two little girls. By the look of things, our newfound friend was part of a set.

"Part of a set, what do you mean?"

They were twins. The sad thing is the poor kid thought her sister was going to come home and she wanted to wait for her. How the hell was I supposed to burst her bubble and tell her that her twin was probably dead? It looked like a job for Kingsley.

I laughed a little at this. It was by no means funny. In fact, it was terrible. It's just that Jaxon had a way of speaking that both entertained and disarmed. He was with me on the laugh at least. As soon as he heard me chuckle a big smile spread across his face.

You know how it goes. Some people aren't very good at dealing with the emotions of others, and some people aren't very good at dealing with kids. I'm not very good at dealing with either of those. Kingsley, on the hand, has a much gentler soul than I did.

"It's all you buddy," I told him.

"Oh damn it," he replied. Then, he went and sprawled out beside the bed.

"What's your name, sweetie?"

"Tamra," she answered quietly.

"How old are you, Tamra?"

"Nine."

"Nine just happens to be the perfect age, I'd reckon. I remember when I was nine, I used to play with those little green army men."

"I like my dolls."

"Like the ones on top of the bed?"

"Yes."

"Well, what do you say we grab your favorite doll, and drive over to a much safer place to wait for your sister?"

Ah. The chicken shit didn't tell her. I approved. How the hell did we know what to say? We didn't. Better let someone more skilled with kids do that messy job.

"I don't want to," Tamra said.

"You don't want to wait for her in a safe place?" Kingsley asked. "I'm sure she'll be able to find you."

"No, I don't want to leave."

Well, that tore it. I tried, he tried and neither of us felt it was safe to remain in that house longer than we had to.

I shouldered him out of the way, reached under the bed, grabbed Tamra by the arm, and pulled. Damn that little girl could put up a fight.

"I can't believe you did that."

Don't judge me just yet. In the end, I was doing the kid a favor.

She didn't just fight, though. That kid had a set of lungs that made my damn ears ring. I think her scream was probably heard throughout the entire neighborhood.

In other words, we really had to boogie.

"Grab her dolly and let's go," I shouted to Kingsley.

He grabbed it, and we ran for the door.

The growl came from a room farther down the hall. We froze, and I fumbled for the flashlight. Tamra's twin came out of the shadows slowly and into the light. She wore a pink dress. Half her face had been chewed off along with most of her stomach.

Things made sense in a completely new and different sort of way. It wasn't that Tamra was afraid of leaving her sister, she was afraid of being eaten by her sister.

I'm thinking it was the gross out factor that made Kingsley freak a little bit. Whatever it was, when Tamra's dead sister charged, Kingsley jumped back and hit me. I just happened to be standing by the edge of the stairs, so the bump took all of us for a tumble down the stairs.

Tamra's undead twin launched herself right after us.

The next thing I knew, there were three living, breathing, humans and one undead zombie all in a pile at the bottom of the stairs. Kingsley had recovered sufficiently and was holding the zombie girl by the throat away from the rest of us. I was busy trying to untangle myself from the mass of flailing limbs, when one of the windows to the backyard burst inward in an explosion of glass.

It was the zombie we saw earlier, the one that had been wandering around in circles. It was the scream, or maybe even the tumble down the stairs—I don't know, feel free to take your pick—but something gave us away. He screamed into the dark room just as a loud boom of thunder sounded outside. He began to climb furiously through the broken shards around the window, gouging deep marks along his back as he came through. Copious amounts of sticky black blood began to pour from his wounds, hitting the wall and splattering down to the floor. I screamed, Kingsley screamed, Tamra screamed... Hell, even the zombies were screaming.

I finally struggled out of the pileup.

Kingsley would have to handle Tamra's sister. I aimed and pulled off a shot just as the other zombie reached us. Luck was with me; he dropped like a rock. Unfortunately, I pulled the trigger at point blank range; our little group got covered in gore.

"Damn. I would have gone into hysterics a long time ago. It just amazes me that you managed to keep on going after all of those horrible experiences."

Well, what choice did I have? What choice did any one of us have? I couldn't just run and hide, we were running out of food.

"There were people that did exactly that. Hundreds of people actually starved in their own homes right next to their wives, husbands, and children."

Yeah, I'm aware of that.

It bothered him, I could tell, even though he covered up his emotions immediately. Even after all he's done, the loss still affects him. He considers it a personal failure. His reactions were touching. It was bigger than life, and for a brief moment, I was speechless. Fortunately, he didn't seem to notice and continued with his story.

I was a little shocked at the gore that flew out from the zombie. So shocked, that I actually forgot where I was for a second. Then, I heard the crunching sound as Kingsley nailed Tamra's sister in the head with a lamp. I snapped out of my stupor real quick after that, but the gunshots exploding from beyond the front door still managed to take me completely by surprise.

Dudley was in trouble.

We ran to the front yard and into a mess of zombies. I don't know how many there were, but Dudley was already out of the Jeep, loaded down with all the weapons and gear we had left behind. He wasn't trying to shoot anymore; there were too many of them. He was too busy running, shoving, and pushing his way towards the front door. The punk didn't even to slow down as he passed us when he entered the house.

With all those zombies less than a few feet away, Kingsley and I barely paused to look at each other before we turned around, ran after him, and slammed the front door shut behind us.

I grabbed my Winchester out of Dudley's arms, and ran to the back of the house. It was clear. I checked all the windows. All of them were secure, except for the one that had already been broken by the zombie whose gore now covered my clothes.

I ran to the garage next. I ransacked the place as fast as I could, and found the tool chest. Hammer and nails were on the menu. I was on my way back to the broken window when I heard the scream.

A zombie was crawling through the shattered glass and, just like the previous zombie, it was also gouging its back wide open on the shards.

I didn't hesitate for even a second. I simply smacked its head with the hammer and pushed it back out the window.

It wasn't exactly difficult, the whole smacking the head with a hammer thing; therefore, I didn't really understand why everyone was staring at me like I was the monster after I did it.

Whatever. I grabbed a table off the floor and shouted to Dudley for help. While he held the table in place, I nailed the hell out of it to the wall. The window was barricaded.

After that, it was easy enough to board up the rest of the windows around the house. We were safe, and secure, as the outside walls rattled against the pounding fists of many zombies. We were lucky that Tamra's father had plenty of tools and wood to work with.

"Wait a minute, I've heard about this. I don't remember where I heard about it but this is the part where you were trapped inside a house, isn't it?"

Yeah, the story got out almost immediately. We were trapped there for about five days. It wasn't much of a problem though. The house had plenty of food and water.

Tamra got sick that very first morning.

She was pale when the sun came up. She looked bad. I guess it happened before we ever got to her house. It was Dudley who found the small bite mark on her shoulder. We were all saddened by the knowledge but there was simply nothing we could do. That little girl was going to turn; at least, we thought she was.

We had talks about it as we stayed up late into the night, and listened to the dead pound on the walls. What to do? None of us could shoot her. That was a fact. Besides, we didn't even know for sure that she was going to turn. We were basing all of our information on a bunch of zombie movies, and how reliable could information gathered from a bunch of movies actually be?

It was agreed; we'd sit, wait, and watch. If she turned, whoever was closest would handle it. Kingsley was taking care of her. Dudley even tried to make her laugh. They were getting attached. It made me nervous but I guess it was inevitable.

"What were you thinking during all this? What was going on in your mind? You're isolated from the rest of your friends and family. You're taking care of a very sick child, and you're trapped inside an unfamiliar house that's surrounded by zombies."

I guess, at first, I was just able to relax. Maybe I should have been panicking, but we were in a safe place, and it gave me some time to collect my thoughts.

"What kinds of thoughts?"

Well, I was thinking three very different things all at the same time.

The first thing that crossed my mind was how the hell I had managed to heal so quickly from the injuries I received. That shouldn't have been possible. I was in some seriously rough shape. Bad enough shape that I wasn't counting on much of a future, and the next thing I knew, I was covered in grass and feeling a lot better. Still a little bit stiff maybe but a hell of a lot better and the stiffness didn't last very long either. The next evening when I took a shower, all the remaining stiffness and bruises practically melted away when the water made contact with my skin. I couldn't explain any of it. I tried to wrap my brain around it but I had zero answers. So I did the only thing that I could do. I ignored it.

I actually do this quite a bit in life. If I can't explain it or figure it out, I just toss it into the good ol' ignore pile and forget it ever existed.

"What's the second thing that you were thinking about?"

Making contact with Georgie, I wanted him to know that we were still alive, and that we'd get back with the food as soon as possible. This wasn't exactly difficult for us to do. There was a working computer. The only problem was that I couldn't sign into it under my own screen name. I had to use Tamra's fathers screen name.

"What was it?"

The General.

"Is that where the name came from?"

It sure is. At the time, I had absolutely zero experience with the military. Yet, for two days stupid

Georgie wouldn't respond to my messages on EPUA, so I kept leaving messages for him under the General's screen name. I couldn't remember his email address, so a direct email wasn't an option. Finally, I started writing huge paragraphs about what had happened after we had left his house. I skipped the part about the grass growing over me, but I did include Tamra. He eventually got off his ass and answered. After that we spent hours going over all the little details of how we survived.

"And people were reading this?"

Yes.

"They were reading about how some man named 'the General' not only survived numerous life threatening situations but also attempted to help others along the way?"

Yeah.

"And what happened next?"

Well, apparently Georgie kept the party going long after I signed off. I'm not sure what he told everyone, but when I signed back on the next evening, people were still talking about me.

"What were they saying?"

Some of them believed the tales. Some of them didn't. Some of them were telling what had happened accurately, and some of them were embellishing.

"What do you mean embellishing?"

They were talking about me, but they were making me out to be some kind of hero. They were taking the situations we fell into, and exaggerating them into tales where I fought a hundred zombies with just my tomahawk and my knife.

"How did all the attention make you feel?"

To be honest, it was funny. Kingsley and Dudley were getting a kick out of it as well.

"Did you respond to any of these people?"

No. Not until Tito wrote. What could I say to them? I guess I figured that they needed some kind of hope. Maybe this could be it. The stories weren't always true but if they could inspire someone to hang in just a little longer, good for them. I wasn't going to take that away from anybody. Also, don't forget, they were cracking us up.

"Your friend Tito wrote?"

Correct.

"Why do you call him Tito?"

He looks like a Tito.

"I see, and he was able to connect the tales he was reading back to you?"

Yeah, he said later that if the stories were real, only I could be the General. Which is quite a compliment coming from Tito...I think. He's normally a very angry person who becomes rather resentful when someone else achieves any kind of success. You don't usually get compliments from guys like that unless they need something from you. Then again, he did need something from me.

"I should think so. What did he say?"

Help.

He told some stories about the good ol' days as a way of garnering my attention, and proving it was him, but he wanted help. He was trapped in his apartment, and the entire complex was teeming with zombies.

"And what did you tell him?"

I told him to sit tight, and be safe. I was coming.

"What happened next?"

The people who were watching the site reacted. All of them began to send messages at the same time, and the site crashed for the next few hours.

"What messages were the people sending you?"

Help us.

"And what did you think of that?"

I panicked. Kingsley and Dudley were reading over my shoulder. The responses, the crash, it was kinda surreal. We didn't know how to react to that. We just kinda sat there in silence for a while. Then Kingsley began to laugh.

"It figures," Kingsley said. "The whole world is going to shit, and freaking Jax ends up being famous!"

"Yeah, no shit," Dudley said. "Why does all the cool stuff happen to you?"

They were both cracking up. I was trying to laugh along with them, but there was some serious stress involved. I mean, talk about pressure. I'm just one person. I have no training. I was surviving on luck. Never mind the whole healing from my injuries mystery. Never mind that when I was in the thick of things I felt way too comfortable. What the hell could I really do to save anyone?

"I could see how you'd feel under pressure but you seem to have handled it well."

Eventually I handled it. I don't know how well but I eventually dealt with it I guess. At the time I was more concerned with the third thought that was on my mind.

"And that was?"

Getting out of that house.

It took a good long while to figure that one out, and when I finally did, let's just say, my plan bordered somewhere between crazy and stupid. It was mid afternoon on the fourth day, when I looked out a crack in the boarded up window, and saw my new best friend, the sun. That hot, blazing, ball of heat that hangs over the Texas skies, and makes life miserable every single summer…well, I don't think the zombies liked it very much, because the ones that hadn't already entered the nearby houses seeking shelter were all sitting around in whatever shade they could find looking just as miserable as you please.

This is common knowledge now of course. Zombies don't like extremely hot temperatures. They tend to get really sluggish, and seek out whatever shelters they can find, but back then, it was new and welcome news to me.

However, when zombies are stalking humans they tend to be rather relentless. I'd noticed that without much difficulty, as well. So that meant that even though most of them were waiting out the heat in the neighbors' homes, the minute we made a run to the car, they'd snap awake, and attack.

My plan needed a part two since the idea of running to the Jeep and getting surrounded by masses of zombies wasn't very appealing. I wandered around the garage until I saw the ladder, and every bit of my crazy ass plan came together. I also caught sight of some chain link fence. Now that really started to spin my gears. However, I had to keep my mind on the present situation, which included rigging up the ladder and getting back to Georgie's. Just keep chain link fencing in the back of your mind, because I'll get there later.

We spent the entire night stretching out that ladder. It was already pretty long, but we needed it to be even longer for my plan to work, and we also needed to reinforce it so that it would hold our weight.

The zombies snapped out of it as soon as the sun went down. We could hear them outside, as we pounded and hammered on the ladder, they pounded and hammered on the walls. My plan might have been insane, but it was still a halfway decent idea. It was also the best we were gonna come up with. We just needed the sun to make another appearance so we could get a decent head start.

"How was Tamra doing during all of this?"

She wasn't doing very well. She was steadily getting worse. Kingsley refused to leave without her. He's always had a soft spot for kids. He's good with them, and as far as he was concerned, she was alone in this world, and he wasn't about to abandon her.

"How did you feel about her?"

I have no idea. I kept my distance, but Kingsley had made up his mind, and that dude's an Aries. Those people are stubborn as hell. My wife's an Aries as well, so I speak from experience. If Dudley and I left without the girl, we were also going to have to leave without Kingsley, and neither one of us was prepared to do that. So the decision was made without me ever having to think about it.

When we made a break for it, Tamra was coming with us.

"You had no attachment to her?"

I knew what was going to happen, so I kept my distance. If I was wrong, I'd make up for it and buy her an ice cream, but I'm rarely ever wrong. That's one of the many things about me that can really infuriate people, but it's also something that they have to learn to live with if they wanna hang.

I was really hoping that this would be one of those rare occasions and I'd be wrong. I mean, I was still getting my information from a bunch of movies, and most of them weren't even very good movies. There was hope. Not much, but a little.

When the sun rose on the fifth morning, we watched in anticipation. The day grew hotter, and hotter. The majority of the zombies sought shelter once again. The ones that remained sat in the shade or squirmed under bushes. By mid-afternoon, Dudley, Kingsley and, Tamra were on the roof with this incredibly long and awkward homemade bridge that used to be a ladder.

The houses in this neighborhood were rather close together, so the bridge easily spanned the distance to the next home's roof. Kingsley began to make his way across. The zombies hadn't noticed what they were doing yet; they were more concerned about the heat.

The homemade bridge worked, kind of. It wobbled like hell, but Kingsley made it across. Next up was Dudley. He had Tamra secured to his back. Halfway across, a zombie scream broke the silence of the neighborhood into a thousand pieces. In less than five minutes, about two hundred zombies were reaching up for him. He was about five feet over their heads. Safe, but it probably scared the hell out of him when they started jumping up in an effort to grab him.

They approached the next house with our improvised bridge in the same way, and the zombies followed. I watched nervously as they went across the shaky ladder to the next roof. I couldn't believe it was really working.

I waited until they started on the fifth house before I made my move.

I ripped the boards we used to secure the front door off, and after loading up my arms with gear and food I went outside.

It wasn't as clear as I had hoped. There were still some loitering zombies, and a couple of them noticed me and started running my way. I threw the gear and food into the back of the Jeep with the rest of the supplies Dudley didn't grab when he ran for the house. My hands found my tomahawk, and knife, as if they had a mind of their own.

The first one was easy enough to take out. It ran straight for me, so I swung and cleaved the top of its head off. The second zombie, who was right behind the first, ducked under my second swing, and tackled me to the ground. I improvised with a backwards somersault, ending up on top, and stabbed my knife through its ear, into its brain. I was back on my feet in less than a second, and that was a good thing.

More were coming.

Damn.

Shit.

I quickly ran back in the house, and grabbed the rest of the food and gear. On my way back out, the first of the zombies had reached the front door.

It was a female, and I ran straight towards her. She must have been surprised, because she came to a sudden stop. After she got over it, she began the first obscene notes of that famous zombie scream, so I kicked her as hard as I could under the chin.

She went flying.

I kept running, straight to the Jeep, where I threw in the last of the food and the gear.

As soon as I did this, I reached for the tomahawk and knife. About ten zombies were coming for me.

I think I actually smiled as I ran forward to meet them.

We collided in a beautiful cacophony of breaking bones. I was hacking and stabbing and kicking and slicing. When I reached the very last of them, I took out his knee with the axe, and pushed my blade into the top of his head as he fell.

It was over quickly.

I was amazed. I had just taken out ten zombies (yes I counted) in just a few seconds. I turned around, and around looking for more. I was beginning to enjoy this, but unfortunately, the rest of the zombies were in hot pursuit of my buddies.

I ran back to the Jeep, started her up, and began chasing after Dudley, Kingsley, and Tamra.

It didn't take long to find them. They hadn't gotten very far. They were stuck at the seventh house they had reached. The ladder had finally broken, and its two separate pieces had fallen to the ground below. Kingsley was on the edge of the roof trying to climb up with Dudley's help. A couple hundred zombies were crowded below him, reaching up hungrily for his dangling legs.

No big deal.

I pulled up as close as I could, and began to scream for all I was worth. A couple hundred zombies turned, and looked at me. I was now honking the horn, and flipping them off.

For a second, I actually wondered if he was joking around. He's wasn't.

Well, I doubt it was my middle finger that got their attention, but whatever it was, they came a running!

I hit the gas, and tore off down the street with just about all of them running after me. After about two blocks, I slowed my pace, and let them gain some ground on the Jeep. I had to keep them interested, so I waited for them to get about ten feet behind me, and then I kept the Jeep at that pace for the next five blocks.

When I felt that I'd gone far enough with my hungry followers, I really hit the gas. I left them behind, very far behind. A few blocks after that, I headed down some streets that pointed in the right direction, and made my way back to my friends.

I pulled up to the seventh house, and they were already waiting for me in the front yard.

They ran to my Jeep just as Tamra, who was still on Dudley's back, finally turned.

I shot a hole in her head before Dudley even realized what had happened. With all the excitement, neither of them had known she'd even died. I pulled my pistol, and shot purely on reflex just as she was going for Dudley's neck.

He freaked, fell backwards, and rolled with the dead little girl flopping wetly behind him. Kingsley saw the entire thing, yet I shot before he could call out or react. He pulled Tamra off of Dudley's back and helped him back to his feet.

Nobody said a word.

Our escape however, did not go unnoticed. There were survivors behind some of those boarded up windows after all, and they had been watching us from the moment we made our escape. They cheered for us as they emerged from the safety of their homes. I wasn't sure how to react at first. I looked towards Kingsley but he was as shocked as I was. I looked towards Dudley, and he motioned for me to say something.

"Get your cars!" I shouted. "You can follow us."

And that's pretty much how everything started.

The trip back to Georgie's was rather eventful, but not because of the zombies. Hell, the few that rushed us fell under a hail of bullets almost immediately.

It seems that in Texas, everybody owns a gun and if it isn't just one gun its many guns, but that wasn't what made the return trip interesting.

Our group was growing. Some of the people that were joining up with us had laptops, and these people that had laptops had been checking in regularly with EPUA for updates. Therefore, they had read all about my exaggerated little adventures. Since I had also posted Tamra's address when I was talking to Georgie, they were ready when I made my move to escape. I guess they wanted to see what the "General" would do.

"They weren't disappointed."

No, they weren't disappointed. They saw how we made our escape, and then they started writing about it on their laptops. People started coming out in droves to join us as we made our way back to Georgie's. We just kept meeting more and more of them along the way, because our path was being posted all over EPUA.

"How many joined you during the return trip?"

I dunno. It seemed like a couple hundred, but maybe I'm wrong. There were a lot of cars. That made me nervous. If the zombies gathered in huge numbers and gave chase, we'd never be able to stop at Georgie's. I was also worried about where we were gonna put everyone.

In the end, I grabbed some kid with a laptop, and started giving orders.

"Post this message," I told the kid. "I want everybody on Georgie's street to start making their way over to Georgie's house. When they have enough people gathered, I want them to then secure about twenty houses on each side of the street."

Needless to say, Georgie was freaking out. He didn't want those people anywhere near him. I'm sure he would have liked to pretend he never saw the message, but Lucy was there, and she quickly made her way outside to meet the neighbors before Georgie could do anything to stop her.

"If he doesn't move," Dudley said. "I'm kicking his fucking ass."

"If those houses aren't clean, and safe when we get back, I'll join you," I added.

Then I picked the closest hardware store in the vicinity, and told the kid to post where we were going in case more people wanted to join up with us.

It was a Lowe's Hardware, and I wanted my chain link fence.

Fifty or sixty cars and trucks pulled into the parking lot of Lowe's with guns a blazing. I hopped out of the Jeep and told all the rednecks with big trucks to load up on all the chain link fence they could carry in the back of their trucks, along with fence posts and whatever tools we needed to dig up the street.

As they went to work I ordered all the other vehicles to form a defensive line around the trucks, and the building in order to protect the workers.

Amazingly, there were no accidents. More people were joining us, but they weren't shot at like you'd expect. In fact, nobody shot their guns until I gave the order. We probably took out close to a hundred zombies, but only one large group of about forty gave us any real scares.

When most people get excited, they lose hand/eye coordination. The big group of zombies rushed, and with all the excitement, the bullets weren't bringing them down. They were still pretty far up the street—no pressure yet—so I grabbed my rifle and hopped on top of a big truck. That's when I saw what brought such a large group of them together in the same place at the same time.

She screamed for help as soon as she saw me. Not sure how she recognized me from so far away but I recognized her as well. And come hell or high water she was going to live.

Chapter 2

IVANA

People often wonder how this woman fits into such a rowdy crowd. At first appearance, she seems just a little bit too sweet and innocent to fit in with her rambunctious friends. She also tends to shy away from reporters and cameras, yet there's a hidden strength in her that has left many speechless. Has anyone not seen the video where a little girl that just lost both parents reaches out to her? Has anyone not seen her pick up that little girl and hug her tightly? What about the soft tears that gently fell as she whispered into the little girl's ear?

She's not a warrior. It's her kindness that is legendary.

She stands around five-foot-seven. She has short black hair, and the darkest eyes you could possibly imagine. Just about every man I know has a crush on her, but they are unfortunately, out of luck. Ivana is gay. She has no problems admitting or talking about it. It's a part of her character, a part of who she is. She's also very proud of who she is. The horror of what she went through was unable to change that part of her.

When I met with her, she walked into the room with a shy smile on her face. She was wearing baggy cargo pants and a tight t-shirt. Her sunglasses were pushed up on her head, and she had a beer in her hand.

I take it that you've already spoken with Jaxon?

"Yes."

He's pretty intimidating. Are you okay?

"It may take some time to process everything, but I'll manage."

Good for you. I always have to warn my girlfriends before they meet him. Bit of a bad boy that one.

I laughed at this. It's the first time someone close to him actually said it. It's true, it's obvious, but nobody has ever just come right out and admitted it.

"So, you've been friends with him for a long time haven't you?"

I'd say about five or six years before any of the craziness happened. I met him about a year before he met his wife. If you think he's rowdy now, you should have seen him back then.

"That bad?"

I'm not sure I'd refer to it as bad, but it certainly was entertaining. You never knew what he was going to say or do. He kept us all on our toes, that's for sure.

"How did you meet him?"

He hit on me. It was the funniest thing, he knew I was a lesbian but he hit on me anyway. It's just…he did it in such a funny way that I had to get to know him better. He made me laugh, still does. He has no suave moves but, my God, you should see the girls chase after him. He just has that "it factor" I think. Women love him.

"Yeah, I've read the blogs some of these women have posted about him. He does seem to be quite popular."

Even before he got famous he was quite popular. You should have seen how spoiled he was. Now, it's just unbelievable. There have been talks lately of using a security detail to keep him safe from the women after he had a shirt ripped off last week.

"You love him a lot don't you?"

Of course, he's my boy. I mean, I know he's married but I can still love him in that special kind of way that won't interfere with the way things are. Then again, he is the only guy I've ever met that made me consider going straight.

She laughed at her own joke, and I wonder if she's just a little bit serious. It's obvious how devoted she is to him.

My fellow lesbians are going to have a fit because I said that. "Argh! We're losing her to the General. There goes another one."

"You refer to him as the General as well?"

It's kinda hard not to sometimes. Ever since he used that screen name on EPUA, complete strangers that weren't even there, and who have never even fought beside him, refer to him as the General. They even salute him with that crazy fist over the heart thing that they do.

"I've seen that."

It's still a shock to know that my friend has become the man he has become, but I was there. I saw everything. I saw him fall into leadership, and I saw him bear it all on those wide shoulders of his. He's earned his fame. He's earned the recognition.

"And what about you?"

What about me? I was lucky, just like everyone else that found him.

"Can you tell me about it?"

Tell about which part? My personal experience or what happened after I was with Jaxon?

"I'd like to hear both if it's okay with you?"

It might be kind of boring I think. I'm no fighter. My experience is probably very similar to anyone else who happened to be in El Paso when the zombies came.

"That's okay with me."

Well, I had an apartment on the Westside. I had been living there with my girlfriend for about three months or so. The night before the attack, everything was very normal. We went out to the bars, and I ended up drinking quite a bit. That's why I slept through most of the morning. I was hung over.

I had no idea anything was going on until Jill (my girlfriend) woke me up. It was about thirty minutes or so before the TV went dead. The reports were coming in about savage people attacking anyone they could catch.

The madness was spreading. A few images managed to find their way onto the screen. The people didn't look right. No, they didn't look right at all. They looked dead. They looked like they were dead and still moving around.

Then, the reports started coming in about how the savages were eating people. Eventually, they announced some website that we could go to, and after that all the stations went off the air.

Jill was terrified. When we started hearing screams around our apartment complex she stopped speaking altogether. She was just shaking all over. I grabbed her by the shoulders and pulled her close. I tried to talk her down. I even shook her a little bit.

Nothing.

I couldn't reach her. She just went into quiet hysterics. To be honest, I had no idea what to do.

The only thing I could think of was to call my mom. Of course all the phones were dead at that point.

I didn't feel safe in the apartment. I felt that we needed to move. I had no idea what the roads looked like but I had a full size truck, and I was pretty sure that it could get us where we need to go.

"Which was where?"

My mom's, it was still all I could think of.

I was able to move Jill. She didn't put up a fight. We walked to my truck slowly. I was so afraid. I can't even explain to you how terrified I was. The day was so humid, and I was covered in sweat. I could hear the screams of rage and the screams of terror coming from all around me. I saw my neighbor chase his wife down into some bushes and begin biting her. It was like walking through some sort of hell.

I continued to pull Jill down the maze of sidewalks that make up our apartment complex. I would crouch and hide with her whenever I saw movement. Most of the time I tried not to look. I didn't want to see people being killed. It was madness but so far we were safe. We managed to run and hide, run and hide.

And then they saw us.

He came from the side. I don't know who it was; I'd never seen him before. We were moving forward past an apartment with an open door, and he came running out after us.

I saw him immediately.

We ran.

He followed.

Caution was blown to the wind. We had nothing to lose. We ran as fast as we could to the truck.

We never made it. We damn near ran into a group of them. I don't know how many there were. I didn't stop to count. They were all crouched around a red and wet mass of something that used to be human.

Most of the body was already devoured. They looked up at Jill and me and immediately gave chase. We barely even froze for a second before we turned to the left and headed down a walkway as fast as we could.

There was no way we were going to make it to my truck. There were too many of them chasing us, and the path we were on headed in the wrong direction. It was go back to the apartment or die.

Part of me was worried about being stuck in our apartment, but I had still had hopes that the police, or someone, would be able to sort everything soon and come to our rescue. I held onto that hope for as long as I could.

It didn't take us long to reach the apartment. We were inside and locking the door before any of them neared the patio. It was a horrible experience. I shook for hours afterwards but we were very lucky. Another twenty feet or so and they would of had us. Zombies don't seem to tire out like people do. I don't know why.

Another thing we were really lucky about was the lack of a sliding glass door. I remember when we moved into the apartment complex, we were pretty upset about having one of the few apartments without the sliding glass door on the patio. They would have broken through a sliding glass door in seconds. All the apartment had were those tiny little windows. They couldn't fit through them, but they tried anyway. They broke them apart immediately, and reached out for us through the broken glass. I've never been able to get that image out of my mind.

Aside from being trapped, we were safe.

After a half an hour of watching them reach for us, Jill began to scream. I wasn't sure if that was any better than her self induced coma, because the noise she was making was sure to attract even more of them.

I told her to be quiet. She responded by tearing out handfuls of her own hair.

I tried to comfort her. I tried to wrap her in my arms so she couldn't hurt herself, but in the end I think I just ended up getting the wrong end of the stick. By the time she calmed back down into quiet hysterics, I was covered in scratches and bruises.

I managed to move her into the closet with me. I was hoping that if they couldn't see us anymore they'd go away. I grabbed my laptop on the way, and closed the door. It didn't work, they continued to scream, and reach for us through the broken windows, even though we were out of sight.

Eventually, we fell asleep.

I don't know how. I guess we were just so exhausted from everything, and hiding in the dark closet made us feel just a little bit safe. Even the screams were somewhat muffled by the walls.

I don't remember what time it was when I woke up. It was dark out; I know that. I chanced a peek out the closet door.

They were still there. They were still trying to get inside. Yet, their screams had been replaced by moans and low guttural growls.

I guess they had calmed down a little bit. It just took a while but I was positive that if they saw us again they'd go back into a full frenzy.

Jill was still asleep and I didn't want to wake her. I wasn't sure how she'd react, and I didn't want her to start screaming again. I didn't want the frenzy outside to start back up.

I fired up my laptop. I couldn't remember the website that the news stations were talking about, but it wasn't hard to find.

EPUA.

It was there that I learned what was really going on. It was there that I learned that all forms of communication, aside from the Internet, were shut down. It was there that I learned that El Paso was sealed off. It was there that I learned that the dead had risen. It was there that I learned that help was not coming.

I cried for hours. I cried and cried and cried. I was going to die soon. They'd get in somehow. I just knew it.

Eventually, I calmed down enough…no, that's not true. Eventually, through the tears and quiet sobs I started to read the messages that people were posting.

I read the horror stories. I read the fear and sadness in their words.

I didn't feel so alone anymore.

"That website helped a lot of people get through the bad times."

I agree. It helps to know that there are people out there going through the same things you are. Even though we were isolated and stuck in an apartment closet, I was able to connect with others that were also trapped.

I mean, don't get me wrong, I truly wished that I wasn't in El Paso. Paris was sounding especially pretty damn good, but the website made things better.

"Did you talk to any of the other survivors on EPUA?"

I didn't. I just read what they posted. I read and read and read. I barely ate at all. The one time I left the closet to grab food I was spotted and the frenzy began again. The screaming and banging and thrashing; it was horrible. It took hours for them to calm back down again.

Jill wasn't responding to anything anymore; she just lay there. It was like her mind had shut down.

I had headphones and music on my laptop. I put the headphones on Jill, and I played the music loud. Every so often I would try to get her to eat or drink. She refused each time. I was slowly losing her, and there wasn't a thing I could do about it.

I reached a sort of calm as the days, and nights passed. The outrageous fear was gone. It was replaced by an inevitable knowing that I wasn't going to live much longer. I didn't want to starve. I had pills. As soon as Jill was gone, I was going to join her. I didn't think it would be very long.

I don't know how many days, and nights had passed exactly. The time seemed to bleed together. I slept, and read the posts on EPUA. I could do nothing else. I was just waiting for the end.

And then, I heard about the General.

I never noticed it when Jax was trying to reach Georgie. There were thousands of people trying to reach friends and family. I must have been asleep when the two of them actually began to talk, but afterwards when I woke up, I was able to read all the stories people were talking about.

"And you had no idea who the General was?"

None, all I knew was that somewhere out there a man was fighting. Somewhere out there, a man was saving people. In the cold, dark, and lonely night…there was a hero.

My heart began to beat again. My eyes grew wide. It couldn't be true. It was too much to hope for. And yet, despite myself, I began to hope. I wasn't ready to give up. I was excited. Who was this man? Was he sent by the government?

I sat straight up, and read and read and read.

Finally, Tito was there. His apartment was just down the street from mine. He was trapped, just like Jill and I.

"You recognized Tito?"

Yeah, it wasn't hard. I've never met anybody else called Tito, but what really shocked me was that he said he knew the General.

Everybody stopped posting. The page became quiet for the first time. Everyone just watched and waited to see if the General would respond. Tito began to write about the past and the good times that they both had. I felt the tears well up in my eyes as I stared at the laptop screen. I began to pray for the first time in a long time.

It was then that I realized who the General was. It was then that Tito asked for help. It was then that Jaxon responded.

The website crashed right afterwards.

The public solitude was broken with a surge of hope. Everyone reached out at the same time. I squealed with joy. Jax was coming. He said so, and my boy never lies. You may not like what he says, but he's always honest.

"Tell me how you felt at that moment, knowing that the General was a close friend of yours."

It's kind of hard to explain, but I was certainly happy. I felt like I had already been saved. I just had to wait for the site to go back online, and write to him. There was no doubt in my mind that he would come for me. He'd follow me straight into hell if that's where I had been dragged.

That's the kind of guy Jaxon is. He'll be there when you need him.I was beside myself. For the first time in days, my tears were for joy instead of fear. I was going to live. I was going to survive. This wasn't going to be the end. And as much as I had resigned myself to dying, I wanted to live.

That's when things went bad.

I reached out in the darkness of the closet for Jill's leg. I had been doing this periodically, like she was some sort of security blanket. Her leg wasn't there. I turned around, and neither was she. I lost her in my excitement. She had left the closet and I never even noticed.

I panicked.

I was up in a flash. The laptop was still in my hand. The frenzy of the dead had started once again. I could hear the screams, and fists shaking the walls. I opened the closet door all the way, and looked into the apartment. I saw Jill at our front door. The zombies saw her as well.

"I'm leaving now," Jill said. "I hope you take care of yourself."

I screamed for her. I screamed louder than the zombies that were reaching for her through the small windows.

She opened the front door.

They were on her in an instant. A savage, tearing mob of corpses fell upon her so fast. I never even heard her cry out. Hell, I never even saw her being attacked. One moment she was there, and in the blink of an eye, she was underneath…

She didn't finish her thoughts, and I didn't press her. She was tearing up the moment she talked about reaching for Jill in the dark closet. I watched as she brought one hand to her mouth and motioned with the other for me to give her a moment as she quietly mourned her lost love.

After a few minutes she continued.

I'm sorry…It's just…this is the first time I've told anybody the full story.

"Nobody ever asked you what happened to Jill?"

They did. I just told people that she didn't make it. I guess it's a testament to the survivors. After you tell someone that so and so didn't make it, they just say that they're sorry, and drop the subject. Everybody knows what happened. Only the smallest details vary.

She coughed loudly and stretched her arms.

All right, I'm good.

Was she though? Who am I to answer that question, really? I didn't go through what she went through. I felt for her. I truly did. I barely knew her, and yet I shared just a little bit of her pain.

They rushed into the apartment. They filled the room. Yet, none of them had eyes for me. They all went after Jill. I ran straight through them.

In their ferocity, they didn't notice me. I was almost through the door before any of them even reached for me. By the time they did reach for me, it was too late and I was already outside.

Outside wasn't any better. I was in the midst of the dead, and they knew it. I felt fingers clamping hard on my shoulder but I didn't stop. I ran and ran, for all I was worth.

I think that the only reason I survived was because I took them by surprise. I don't think they expected anyone to run right through them. Not that they think at all. I guess they were just used to people running away from them.

So, I ran at them, through them, and in just a few seconds, away from them. Many gave chase. Too many of them gave chase. Only one of them was able to cut me off and I smashed it in the face with my laptop.

The smell had gotten pretty bad. I noticed it when I was still in the closet but it was nowhere near as bad as it was out here in the midst of them. Their flesh was beginning to decay. The rains, the humidity, and then the sun had certainly left their mark.

The sun was a problem for me. After spending so much time in the dark closet, I found the bright sunlight blinding. I ran through shrubs and even slammed into a tree at one point. I never stopped though. I never even slowed down.

I was able to reach my truck.

It was a full sized Chevy. I opened the doors from ten feet away with my keypad. It was then that I noticed that there weren't as many zombies in the apartment complex. When Jill and I first tried to leave, the zombies were everywhere. Now it seemed that the bulk of them were at my apartment.

It was another stroke of luck for me. After the mass, I was able to run from the apartment to my truck with only one zombie getting in my way.

When I made it inside the vehicle, I immediately locked the doors. I barely made it, by the way. The zombies were right behind me. I think I even slammed the door on some fingers. They didn't give up though. I don't think they ever do. They had the truck surrounded in seconds. They were climbing all over it and punching at the windows in an effort to reach me.

I probably don't need to tell you that I was scared to death. I mean, when I started running, it was basically just instinct. Being stuck in a vehicle while a herd of zombies are pummeling their way inside…Wow, that gives terrifying a whole new meaning.

To my credit, I only froze for a moment. One moment of seeing their angry, rotten faces pressed against the windows, and I was off. The zombies that didn't scatter out of my way ended up under the tires. I heard a sickening crunch, a bump, and I was pulling away. I had no idea where I was going mind you, I was just leaving.

Some of the zombies were in the back of the truck. I zigged and zagged out of the parking lot and around the neighborhood. It took about fifteen minutes, and a vast amount of slamming brakes and pedal to the metal accelerating, before I got all of them out of the truck bed.

Then I drove more slowly. I drove until I came to a neighborhood where there were no zombies rushing out from the houses as I passed by. I had a moment to myself. I took stock of what I had. My clothes were disgusting. They were filthy from their dirty fingers and torn from their clenching hands. At this point, I realized how close they actually came to killing me.

As soon as I stopped hyperventilating, I realized I still had my laptop.

I fired it up. The computer found a signal and I went immediately to EPUA.

Unknown to Jaxon, there were other survivors in the neighboring homes. They were reporting everything he was doing to the entire world. And what he was doing was nothing short of incredible.

He was fighting back, and the world was getting a play by play of his success. I waited for his inevitable fall. It was almost too much to bear. The odds against him were too great. Yet, he didn't fall like all the others. He escaped. He, himself, fought the dead, and he won.

People began leaving the safety of their homes to join up with him. I couldn't believe it. I couldn't believe that this trouble-making guy that I love so very much was creating an army. Not by his words but by his deeds.

It was a strange moment. It was a history making moment. I should have known that if anyone could do it, it would be Jaxon. He just isn't very good at following any sort of rules. And the rules now clearly stated that everyone should board up their homes and hide.

Not him. Not the General. I remember laughing out loud. I was so proud.

Then, there came a message from Jaxon himself. He was telling everybody to join together, and meet him at Lowe's.

The first zombie hit the side of my truck at a dead run. It was a woman with grey skin and a ruined face. I don't know why she ran headfirst into the side of my truck. Maybe her eyesight was fucked up. I don't know, but the next zombie hit even harder against the passenger side door. A slam, a punch, it even tried to turn the handle.

I hit the gas and tore off down the street. Lowe's was about ten minutes away, and nothing was going to stop me from getting there.

I took the side streets. I stayed away from the main roads in fear that the dead would be thick on those streets. I had no idea they tended to get lazy in the hot sun.

Some of the streets that I traveled on looked completely normal, as if the dead had never risen. Others were ravaged with beaten cars left out in the middle of the road with open doors, and splatters of blood. This time, I prayed for the victims.

I saw very few bodies. This was probably because most of them rose up after being killed, and joined their fellow zombies in the search for victims. When I did see a body, the remains were either so ravaged that they couldn't rise, or had a head wound that was probably received after they had been turned.

It was a sobering experience.

Once again, I felt very alone.

I started thinking about Jaxon. About how he used to flirt with me back in the day. About how nothing in his personality would lead one to believe that he would ever do what he was doing. I mean, he was always a leader with his friends. He was always very well liked. I began to wonder.

"What were you wondering?"

Umm, just that I never saw him as the hero type. He was always kinda wild. He was fun. He was funny. He'd prefer to sit around and tell jokes, rather than hit the clubs and party it up. He was never much about meeting people or going out. He just didn't seem like the type that would be out there saving all those lives. He's a bad boy, a troublemaker.

She was laughing as she told me this.

"So it was still a shock that Jaxon was the General."

Completely, and as is common with times of stress, I began to wonder if it wasn't just some sort of cruel joke. Or maybe I was wrong, and the General wasn't really Jaxon.

I don't know what I was thinking. I was just worried that my intended destination, my salvation, would turn out to be the place of my death.

Does that make any sense at all? I don't want my interview to turn into a bunch of mindless yammering.

"It makes perfect sense actually. The idea of a hero rising up out of the ashes is almost too good to be true, and by all accounts, there was nothing in Jaxon's personality or the way he lived his life to suggest that he would be that hero. You were worried that there was no light at the end of the tunnel, so to speak."

Exactly.

"Now I have a question."

Lay it on me.

"Some of those personality traits that you mentioned, like him being a troublemaker, or a bad boy, or that he can't follow the rules, or that he's a leader among his friend…aren't they a sort of

vague indication that he would be capable, or that he would at least desire to fight back?"

Hell yeah, they are, but at the time I was running for my life in a zombie infested city. Any doubt that I could possibly have had I was having. But what you said really hit the button. The very traits (so to speak) that made me doubt it was him were also the very same traits that made it possible for him to do those things.

I tell ya, it's the wild ones you gotta look out for. Nothing ever holds them back.

"So, you were driving to Lowe's. You're going there to meet your friend the General. You were understandably worried. What happened next?"

The worst thing imaginable, my truck ran out of gas.

"What?"

Yeah, just like in some cheesy horror movie. Clunk, clunk, clunk, and boom, my truck was dead.

I screamed. I was about two miles from Lowe's. For the first time, I wasn't screaming in terror, I was screaming in rage.

I mean, what the hell kind of cruel joke was happening to me? After everything that I went through, when the ordeal seemed to finally be over, my truck runs out of gas?

So yeah, I screamed with a vengeance. I was finally angry. No more, no more, no more.

It felt good to scream. It was also the stupidest thing that I could have possibly done but for just a few seconds it felt really good.

Then the zombies came.

They came from the houses, they came from under the cars, they came running out of the back-yards, they came from everywhere.

I ducked down in the cab of my truck. I was hoping they wouldn't see me, and for about five minutes they didn't.

They ran out to the street and began wildly looking around. I eventually chanced a glance through the window. Hopefully, they'd go back to hiding if they didn't see anybody. Maybe they would have, but one of them decided to investigate my truck.

Its leg was badly mangled. It limped all the way over to where my truck died. The others were much farther away. Some sort of luck was still with me I guess.

Anyway, it reached my truck, and without any kind of hesitation it looked in the window. We both kinda stared at each other for a while. I could hear its rattling breath through the fogging glass. Its face was a weird, putrid yellow and gray mixture.

Then it slammed its fist through my window. I'm honestly still a little shocked that none of my other encounters ended up breaking the windows on my truck.

In a blind panic, I scurried out the passenger door.

Of course, I tripped and fell. The others were running towards me at this point and there were a lot of them.

I skinned up my elbows pretty badly in the fall. The scent of my blood was in the air. I got up and ran like hell.

I run every day of my life now. I work out with weights as well. Yet, back then, I rarely ever worked out. I should have but I didn't. Jax had even asked me to go to his martial arts class on many occasions. I only went a couple of times.

I was two miles away from Lowe's.

Two miles isn't really that far but when you've spent most of your adult life sitting on your ass, and drinking at the bars, two miles might as well be a thousand.

I don't know how I made it. I almost didn't. My lungs all too quickly began to burn with fire and my legs began to feel as if they were made of jelly.

They started catching up to me and I began pushing myself even harder. Somehow, I managed to stay ahead of them but they were getting closer and closer.

I was dying, literally dying. That's how bad the pain in my lungs and legs had become. I was out of shape and the zombies were only a few feet behind me. I don't think they ever get tired. I fell once more and almost got nabbed but somehow—I don't know if it was an inner strength or just fear—I managed to get back up and take off again.

I started to think about giving up. My body was done. I thought about how much it would hurt when they bit into me. I was hoping that, because there were so many of them, it would be over quickly.

I just couldn't run anymore. I started to slow down. Their grasping hands were inches from my skin. God, I knew it was going to hurt. I knew it was going to be terrible but I just couldn't run anymore.

And then I saw Lowe's in the distance. I began to hear the sounds of gunfire.

I mentally spurred myself on. I was almost there but my legs were shot. They wouldn't cooperate. The zombies were about to catch me.

I refused to look behind me; instead, I looked towards Lowe's and with each step I took, the more details I could make out. There was a great mass of cars and trucks. It was a barricade of some sorts and behind this barricade were men holding rifles.

And then I saw him. I saw Jax. I saw the General.

At first I wasn't sure. I was looking through about a gallon of tears. So, I wiped my eyes, and there he was. I was sure of it. I began to scream his name. At the top of my lungs I screamed. It was a scream even more powerful than the scream I unleashed earlier in my rage and frustration. It was a scream that shouted my fear. I screamed his name over and over.

He heard me.

He was standing there, tall, straight, and proud. He was on top of a truck, and he was looking right at me.

"What were you thinking at that moment?"

Hmmm, well, do you know what a hero is?

"I have my definition but I'd like to hear yours."

A hero is someone who chases away the dark. When you are at the very bottom and the demons are scratching at your door. A hero is the one and only person that chases them away. A hero can wash away all your fears and doubts, because you know that he won't fail. He will save you. No matter how bad things are, he will stand fast against the storm.

That is how I felt at that moment. Jaxon saw me. Jaxon knew I was in trouble. Any doubt born in fear had vanished. It was him; he was the hero

I made it to my boy. I was saved.

"That must have been a huge relief to you?"

For a split second there was a light at the end of my tunnel. I even managed to speed up for a second and gain a little distance. Then my legs gave out. They wobbled and I hit the asphalt hard. The dead were right behind me. They were just about to reach me. I refused to look. Instead, I cast my gaze towards Jaxon. He wasn't on top of the truck anymore.

He was running straight towards me, inhumanly fast. The distance between us was covered almost instantly. The zombies hesitated and slowed when they saw him approaching. The distraction saved my life. Then, he was past me and crashing into the many zombies with the sickening sound of tearing flesh and breaking bone.

I turned to look and what I saw was simply unbelievable.

The dead never stood a chance. It was like he was created to bring them harm. With an axe in one hand, and a big knife in the other, he hacked and slashed and stabbed his way right into their heart.

I couldn't see him anymore. He was hidden from view. They had surrounded him. Then, I saw a corpse fly about eight feet into the air and ten feet away from the main group.

Dudley and Kingsley rushed by a few moments later. They had their guns out and began shooting into the mass of dead. It was probably a wasted effort. I don't think Jax ever truly required their help but I'm sure he appreciated it nonetheless.

I watched as the group of zombies began to diminish. I began to see flashes of the General. He was still cutting and hacking. The dead were falling at an alarming rate. In minutes it was over.

Jaxon walked over to me, flanked by Dudley and Kingsley. I was still lying where I had fallen. I was in shock. Not from what I went through but from what I had just seen. The violence and devastation that seemed so easily made by Jaxon was almost frightening.

He grinned at me.

It was one of those sarcastic, arrogant grins that he so loves to give.

"Picked a bad time for a walk," Jax said.

She laughed at the memory. After a few seconds, I began to laugh as well.

"He actually said that?"

I know. Can you believe it? After all that just happened, those are his first words to me. It's so typical of him.

"What did you say to him?"

I didn't say anything. I began to laugh and then I began to cry.

"What did Jaxon do?"

He picked me up. He did it so easily. One scoop and I was at last safe in his arms. It was a good feeling. Hell, it was a great feeling. I did it. I made it. I was safe.

I had my losses. I had my injuries. Every survivor has those but when you meet him face to face and you're under his protection…it's just…relaxing.

"Relaxing?"

Yeah, I don't know how else to explain it. I was finally able to just relax. I think I was pretty much incoherent for the next ten minutes and that was okay with me. I had my battle. It was over. Reinforcements had arrived. My turn was finished.

"I can imagine, after all you went through, how great it felt."

That's the feeling he brings to people. He makes them feel safe. He makes them feel like fighting back. He inspires them.

"He chases away the dark."

Exactly.

"What happened next?"

He set me down inside his Jeep and went back to barking orders. It took a few moments for everybody to snap out of it; they were just as astonished as I was. Jaxon was able to do what no other man could. He could destroy the zombies. Not just one—that's easy enough when you have a gun—no, he could destroy them in large numbers. The people following him were in awe.

Next thing I knew, everybody was moving around again. It seemed like everybody had a job to do. A man who said he was a doctor came over and started treating my injuries. It hurt like hell but I never cried out. I would have been ashamed to.

Whatever equipment they were gathering, they seemed to have gathered it. The people started getting back into their vehicles. Jaxon came over to me, followed by Dudley and Kingsley.

"How ya feeling?" Jaxon asked with a smile.

"Thanks to you, I'm feeling pretty good."

"Jill?"

"She didn't make it."

"I'm sorry," he said after an awkward pause. "Dudley and Kingsley will be in the Jeep with you. We're headed to Georgie's street. I'm going to go in the back of one of those oversized pickups so I can shoot."

"No way man," Dudley said, angrily. "You don't go anywhere without either Kingsley or me."

"I'll be like two or three cars away."

"Don't care," Dudley said.

"All right," Jax said with a sigh. "Kingsley can come with me. He can't drive worth a shit anyway."

Jaxon strode off rather quickly, leaving Kingsley in a rush to grab his shotgun, and catch up to him.

I was alone in the Jeep with Dudley. Dudley is a very funny young man. He's often very quiet but when he finally deems the rest of us worthy of speaking to, what he says is really quite amusing.

"So little lady, would you like some ice cream?"

"Do you have any ice cream?" I asked.

"No. I just wanted to know if you'd like some," he answered.

"Fucker," I murmured.

He thought this was pretty funny. Or maybe he was just testing me to see if I was still myself. I was ya know?

"You were what?"

I was still myself. The dead couldn't take that away from me. I mourned my losses but I did so privately. There were people who still lived, and these survivors needed my help a lot more than those that were lost.

In other words, I decided right then and there that I wasn't going to fall apart or waste any time feeling sorry for myself.

"You decided to help instead?"

Hah. What could I really do? I'm no fighter. I'll never be a fighter, but yes, I decided to help. Or more to the point, I decided to be beneficial.

I'm only telling you this, because I don't want you to feel that I'm cold. In the end, I lost my entire family but you won't see me crying through the rest of my story. I saved that for when I was alone.

"I understand."

We went to Georgie's. A few of the zombies rushed us on our way but they fell almost as soon as they screamed and charged.

There were one hundred and seventy-two survivors, including Georgie and the rest of the people still hiding on his street.

"A lot of people still wear the 172 patch. Did you know that?"

I did know that. The original 172 survivors that set up the Safe Zone. I have one of those patches on my jacket. It's a badge of honor now.

Men with guns were posted everywhere along the street. Teams were formed to search all the yards. Even more teams were formed to help search the houses. The latter of which had already been started before we got there.

Jax was scouring the dead out of the area.

It was well into the night before Jax was satisfied that we were safe. He still didn't relax though, spotlights went up and they started erecting the fence.

Georgie's street is naturally well guarded. Behind the houses on one side is an eight-foot rock wall. Beyond the wall is a ten-foot drop that ends in a ditch. On the other side of the street, behind the houses, is an even taller rock wall with a sheer cliff rising up immediately behind it.

The chain link fences were built right into each end of the street. They spanned from the outside wall of one house, across the road, and straight through the yard until it reached a neighbor's home.

When the fences were finally finished, dawn was breaking. Jaxon stared at them for a long time and then decided to make them higher. It was late in the afternoon before he was satisfied and both ends of the street were closed off.

We were safe. People cheered. I remember cheering right along with them. Jaxon was smiling.

Georgie, who had previously refused to leave his yard, finally came over to the rest of us at Lucy's request. There were zombies already at the fences but the fences were strong and would not be moved. Georgie had an idea.

Guard towers were built, a total of ten, and each of them could hold about four guards. They were spaced around the fences and behind the houses. When the zombies approached, they were easily spotted and shot down from the high vantage points.

That evening we threw a huge party. Everybody had fun. We were tired but we were safe. I don't remember drinking so much in my entire life and I've had some seriously crazy nights.

I finally passed out in Georgie's house. This is where Georgie, Lucy, Jaxon, Dudley, Kingsley, and I stayed while we were here.

"What happened to Jaxon's dog?"

Oh, ha! Merrick. I love Merrick. Who doesn't love Merrick? As soon as we pulled up, she went so crazy Georgie had to let her out of his house. She never leaves Jaxon's side.

The next night was pretty much the same thing. We even started dancing in the middle of the street. The occasional gunshots coming from the towers didn't even slow us down a bit. I can't tell you how much fun we had. We were living life. We were enjoying. Because…all of us had faced death, and all of us came away loving life.

"Was Jaxon also living it up?"

He was very busy. He seemed to make it his own personal duty to periodically check up on all the guard towers. Finally, someone found some walkie-talkies. It made his job a little easier but he was always talking on the damn thing.

Plus, everybody wanted to meet him. Everybody wanted to talk to him. Everybody wanted to shake his hand. If he accepted half the drinks they had offered him, he would have died from alcohol poisoning during the first party.

Yeah, he was busy.

I remember at one point, maybe it was the third evening, Jaxon was nowhere to be seen for the longest time. So, I went to look for him. He was back at Georgie's house. Georgie was there with him. He was staring at the computer screen, just sitting there in the dark, watching.

It didn't take a genius to figure out which site he was on. I finally looked over his shoulder to see what was so important.

At this point, I guess, the entire world knew what he had done. So, other survivors that weren't able to join him, and even people that were safely outside of El Paso, were asking for some kind of help. Post after post was rolling down the screen. They were crying out to the General; they all needed a hero.

The people outside of El Paso were asking him to save their loved ones that were trapped inside the city. The survivors inside of El Paso were asking to be rescued and still others were asking for revenge.

"The military and the government were not responding to the citizens inside or outside of El Paso, so the citizens were turning to the one person that would do something."

Yeah, there were a lot of family members and fellow human beings left out there in the cold, and many people were getting pretty upset about being ignored. I can't blame them. The government had simply closed off the city, and refused any further action. It's just that Jaxon is only one man. There's only so much that he can do.

"We have to help them," Jaxon whispered in the dark.

"You can't save everybody," Georgie said.

"They need me."

"We need you," Georgie continued. "You're an inspiration. I don't know how the hell you did it but if you leave us to go play hero, these people are gonna fall apart. They feel safe because they are with the General. Their hope rests on your shoulders."

"That's too much pressure," I said rather angrily. I could see how stressed out Jaxon had become.

"I understand that," Georgie answered. "But that doesn't make it any less true. He's needed here. If he leaves, who's going to run this place?"

"Jax," I said. "I don't want you to leave. I think you've done enough. Hell, you've done more than our own government…"

I didn't finish what I was going to say. A scream that came from somewhere outside of Georgie's house interrupted me. It was human, but the scream that followed was from the dead.

Jax moved so fast, he became a blur. The axe or actually, I think he calls it a tomahawk, was off his belt, and in his hand in a flash. It was then that I realized he always carried his weapons.

People were running everywhere. It took a moment for Jaxon to pinpoint where the screams came from. Oddly, Georgie was right behind me as I followed Jaxon between two houses.

A zombie boy of about seventeen was eating his father while the mother watched on in horror. The tomahawk swung twice, once at the boy and once at the dead father. A crowd had formed behind me. Some of the men had brought guns.

The bodies were carried away. The mother was led away. Jaxon reached out as she walked by him.

"Wait," he said. "She can't go."

"Why not?" asked the woman leading the mother.

"She's been bitten," the General answered.

I moved up to him and grabbed his arm. He was so focused. I wasn't sure he even noticed I was there until he suddenly turned to me and whispered.

"Grab the boys. I want a meeting at Georgie's right now."

I was off and moving as fast as my legs could carry me. I was terrified. I don't mind saying that. I just wasn't terrified for my life this time; I was terrified for that woman. They were going to decide whether or not to kill her, to chop or shoot her in the head. That poor woman, she'd just lost her family.

"Wasn't she already dead anyway? I mean now that she was bitten, wasn't she going to turn?"

Yes. She was going to die very soon and turn into a zombie. I knew this—trust me—I knew this. It's just that she wasn't dead yet. My problem wasn't with killing the monsters that were already dead. My problem was with killing the living. It wasn't right and I was going to that meeting to make sure my opinion was heard.

It didn't take me long to find everyone. We gathered in Georgie's dining room and Jaxon told everybody what had happened.

"I'll do it," Kingsley said. "You've done enough Jaxon. I can handle this part."

"No," I answered. "She's not one of them yet. It isn't right to end her life; that would be murder."

"Would you rather wait until she turns into a zombie and attacks you?" Georgie asked.

"Let's just put it to a vote," Dudley said.

"You will be voting on whether or not to end a woman's life," I shouted in anger.

"I agree with the vote," Kingsley said.

"Jaxon," Lucy interrupted. "End this. I don't want someone who will soon become dangerous around here. We've all been through enough. Can't we finally be safe?"

"Let's just vote on it," Dudley said. "That way, Jaxon doesn't have the weight of this on his shoulders."

"My shoulders are fine," Jaxon said. "Has anyone considered that there may be more people out there with bites?"

"Oh hell," Georgie said.

The rest of us sighed. No, it was something none of us had considered, but we were sure as hell thinking about it now.

"What was decided?"

Jaxon picked out the smallest house in our little Safe Zone. Everyone was searched for bite marks. All in all, we found five people that had been bitten. All five of them were sick.

Jaxon brought them into the smallest house and handcuffed each of them to a bed. He made sure that they were comfortable, and then asked for doctors to watch over them.

There were four doctors in our Safe Zone. Two of them volunteered. They took turns watching over them. Over the next couple of weeks, each time one of them turned; they called in Jaxon and Kingsley.

I heard the gunshots. I heard all five of them. I never asked who did it, so I don't know if it was Jaxon or Kingsley who pulled the trigger. and they never once talked about it.

What I do know is that they did the right thing. They made everyone safe by confining the victims and they didn't take a life, they only destroyed monsters.

"So you approve of the way Jaxon handled things?"

Yeah, very much so, he tries very hard to do the right thing.

"What happened afterwards?"

Jaxon didn't sit still. He was on to the next problem. Tito was still out there.

"Just to rehash, Tito is Jaxon's friend right?"

Yeah, Tito is his oldest friend. He was the one on EPUA asking for help.

"Jaxon wanted to leave the Safe Zone and go after him?"

Yeah.

"How did you feel about this?"

I didn't want him to go. I mean, look at all he'd already done. The weight of the city should not rest on his shoulders. He needed a break. It was all too much for one man.

Chapter 3

DUDLEY

Dudley is indeed a quiet person. Once he gets talking though, it's very clear how intelligent he is. There's only one problem; once he gets talking he doesn't seem to stop. It took me about twenty minutes to get him to quiet down about some invisible dimension he's recently read about online. Apparently, he and Jaxon had been arguing about it.

He's in his early twenties by the look of him but he stubbornly refused to discuss his age, and seemed to enjoy my attempts at guessing, even though he never told me whether or not I'm right or wrong.

He's muscular but still somewhat thin. His voice has a very arrogant quality to it, which is somewhat similar to Jaxon's. He's also almost as big a smart ass as Jaxon, as well. He was wearing dark jeans, a skin tight t-shirt, cowboy boots, and Elvis style sunglasses.

Ready when you are, little lady.

"Okay, I've heard about the beginning from Jaxon and Ivana. I'd now like to start after the five infected people were confined to the house."

Kinda obvious isn't it?

"No, I was told all about that. I want to know what happened afterwards."

Ah, you want to know what Jaxon did next.

"Exactly."

No problem. You just have to understand that my uncle is one of the world's greatest trouble-makers. That should probably be somewhat obvious at this point but for the sake of clarification, he follows his own agenda, and he makes his own rules. He's also very difficult to deter once he's made his mind up about something.

"And he's made up his mind about something?"

Yep. The two problems on his mind, at that time were the many, many, survivors not in our Safe Zone, and Tito. He had an answer for Tito.

"So he decided to rescue his friend?"

Yep, and nobody was going to talk him out of it.

I was hanging over his shoulder while he watched the computer screen flash on by with all the 'help us' messages one night. I knew it was time to keep my eye on him. He's a man of action. He isn't one of those people that can sit around and wait. Something was going to happen soon. He just happened to figure out a solution for Tito first.

"I'm going out for Tito tonight," Jax finally announced.

"How are you going to do this?" I asked

"I saw a couple of quads sitting in one of the driveways. I'm going to use a quad to get to the desert, and then I'm going to off road it around all the neighborhoods until I hit Thunderbird.

"What's Thunderbird?"

That's the street Tito's apartment complex is on. If he could make it to the desert, he could easily go around the entire Westside in a sort of half circle close to the Franklin Mountains, and come back down when he got close to Thunderbird.

"Why are you going that way?" I asked.

"I'm hoping that the zombies are staying in the city," he answered. "They don't seem to like the sun and heat. So, maybe I can avoid them a little bit if I go through the desert."

"What happens when you hit Thunderbird?" I asked. "Ivana's apartment is very close to Tito's. She said that whole area is teeming with the undead."

"Easy," Jaxon answered. "I'll leave the quad in the desert. Then, I'll sneak in, grab Tito, and sneak back to the quad."

"You think it'll go that smoothly?" I asked.

"Not really, asshole," Jax snapped. "I'm sure I'll run into a number of problems but it's a decent idea for a rescue mission."

"How many quads did you see?" I asked.

"At least three, and no you're not going."

There was a major tinge of irritation in his voice. I could always manage to irritate my uncle, and he knew exactly what I was getting at. What he didn't know was that I wasn't giving him a choice.

"Well, you can't blame him for trying. He didn't want to endanger you."

Yeah, fuck all that.

"I'm going," I said.

"No," Jax said. "You're staying here."

"How about I kick you in the nuts, and go by myself," I said.

"How about you try it, and I knock your dick in the dirt," He answered.

"How bout I beat you like the bitch you are."

"How bout I make you my bitch." He said.

"Dude, you aren't the boss. I can do what I want," I replied.

He sometimes forgets I'm not a kid anymore.

"Look around, numb nuts," Jax growled. "I am the boss, and you sound like a whining twelve year old."

"What's everyone going to say when you tell them that you're going out to rescue Tito?" I asked.

"I'm not going to tell them," Jaxon said. "They'd freak. I'm gonna sneak out before daybreak, and be back before they start to panic."

"I'll go tell all of them what you're planning, right now, if you don't quit acting like a girl," I sneered.

This one caught his attention. Georgie can throw a tremendous fit when he puts his mind to it. Just ask his wife. It was something that at the very least would cause a delay for Jaxon.

"That's blackmail," Jaxon said.

"Pretty much," I replied.

Then he stood up, knocked over my chair with me in it, before darting off down the stairs. "Get your crap ready, and meet me by the lower gate," Jaxon called over his shoulder.

"So there it was. You were going back into the lion's den so to speak."

Yes I was.

"Were you scared? I mean, you've been through the danger before but after being safe for a while, what were you feeling?"

I was feeling pretty shitty about the whole thing, to be honest with you. This is the real world, no kiddy gloves allowed. People were getting eaten out there. By Georgie's calculations, there were around seventy thousand survivors, not in our Safe Zone—That's only seventy thousand people still alive. That means there were a whole bunch of nasty decaying corpses running around the city that would just love to take a bite out of my happy ass.

Family should stick together.

"Yes, I agree with you."

There was also no way in hell he'd let me go alone if it was me going after a friend of mine. Besides, I kinda like Tito. I grew up around that angry skank.

"I can imagine. Your entire group seems to be very close to one another."

Ain't that the truth?

"So you met at the gates?"

Yeah. We met at the gates. Are you rushing me?

"I'm sorry. I didn't mean to."

He laughed at this, and pointed his finger at me.

Gotcha.

He did indeed, and I laughed along with him even though it was my expense.

Seriously though…be patient. I excel at storytelling.

"I'll do my best."

Lay off the caffeine maybe.

Anyway, we met at the gate, talked to the guards in the tower, and explained that we were going to a little reconnoitering. It's not like anyone was going to argue with the General at this point.

Then he went and talked to the owner of the quads. It wasn't like they were going to argue with him, either. I put a gas tank on the back of the quad I was using, in case we ran low on fuel. Jaxon took the faster quad, which was somewhat irritating considering my superior driving skills. Unfortunately, once he told me Tito would be riding with him, I couldn't really complain.

As the sun began to rise on the horizon, we set off.

It was difficult, or maybe just repulsive, negotiating the quads through the dead bodies that started to accumulate beyond the gates.

"These were the zombies that were shot by the guards?"

Yep. All day, and all night, they came for us. The tower guards shot them on sight. Sometimes they even came in huge groups, and tried to climb the gates. The tower guards nailed all of them. We just didn't know what to do with all the bodies.

I'm not even going to talk about the smell. It was funky as hell.

It took awhile, but soon we were through and hauling ass down the road. A few twists and turns later, and we were in the open desert.

We only had about ten zombies chasing after us. We didn't bother to shoot at them. The noise would have attracted even more, and they weren't likely to catch up anyway.

The desert ride was actually fun. We found a trail, and followed it. Got lost, went off the trail back towards the direction we needed to go, found another trail, and set off down that one.

I guess it took most of the morning. It was getting pretty hot, but it wasn't like we had a map or anything. Jax just had an idea that the top of Thunderbird could be reached from the desert, and away we went.

Finally, Jax slowed to a stop, and pulled out some binoculars from his backpack. Hell, I didn't know he even kept anything else besides ammo in there. He stood on the quad's seat, and looked around.

"You see anything, Skywalker?" I asked.

"Skywalker?"

You must not watch a lot of movies. It's a somewhat comical reference to Star Wars. You know…the scene where Luke is looking through the binoculars for the missing R2D2?

Never mind.

Anyway, he was looking through the binoculars.

"Yeah," he answered. "I see some houses over there. I think we're getting close."

"Any dead guys walking around?" I asked.

"There's some movement in one of the houses. I can't tell if they're alive or dead."

"What do you want to do?" I asked.

"Let's get closer," Jax said, "but we'll take it slow so the quads don't make a lot of noise."

"I'll have my gun ready," I said.

I had brought one of Georgie's favorite pistols. He was gonna be pissed when he found out I took it. It was a Kimber .45 cal if I'm remembering correctly, which I am, because I still have the damn thing.

Dudley then pulled a somewhat battered pistol from the back of his pants, and proudly set it upon the table.

"What happened to it?"

It's seen a lot of abuse. It's seen a lot of action as well. It may not be pretty but it's still wicked accurate.

We started cruising closer to the homes. From our angle, we mainly saw only the backyards at first, but occasionally we saw some movement from inside the houses. Many of the homes in El Paso have large windows or sliding glass doors in the back. We just couldn't tell if the occupants were alive or dead.

"Did you go investigate?"

We couldn't, this little adventure was supposed to be somewhat sneaky. If we went and checked out one of these houses, and it turned out to be filled with zombies, we'd have to fight. If we had to fight, we'd make a lot of noise, and if we made a lot of noise, we'd have a ton of zombies trying to catch and eat us. We'd never make it to Tito.

We finally found where Thunderbird hit the desert. There was one of those metal guard rails with a dead end sign marking the end of the street. We parked the quads right next to it. As soon as Jaxon was off his quad, he began checking his weapons.

"Use your machete as much as possible," Jaxon said. "We want to keep things as quiet as we can."

"Then wouldn't it be preferable to just avoid any trouble?"

"Yes, it would," Jax answered.

"You just don't think it's possible?" I asked.

"It hasn't been possible so far."

He pulled the gas can off of my quad, and filled both of the tanks. Each had made it all the way to our destination without a refill. This was fortunate; it meant we could make it all the way back to the Safe Zone without having to stop. I was more than a little worried we'd end up hoofing it at some point.

The next thing I knew, we were walking down an empty street. It was scary as hell. At any moment hordes of zombie cannibals could have started pouring out of the houses after us.

"It's strange how neither you nor Jaxon has any problems admitting when a situation is frightening."

If anybody told you differently, they'd be lying. That shit is scary. There are no ands, ifs, or buts about it. What's really funny is that we all tend to make light of those fucked up moments after they're over.

"What do you mean?"

We make fun of each other. Talk smack when somebody gets freaked. I guess it's just a way of dealing with all the tension. It's works though. I can't explain it but it works.

One of them came running out of a house at us.

Before I even unsheathed the machete, Jaxon's tomahawk went flying through the air, and landed deep into the zombies head.

"When did you learn how to do that?" I asked as he calmly pulled the weapon out of the corpse's head.

"Do what?"

"Learn how to throw the damn ax," I said.

"I dunno," he answered. "Just kinda feels natural."

Screams began to come from inside the house. There were obviously others in there getting ready to rush us, and if they were still making all that noise when they got out, they were gonna bring the entire street down on us.

"Aw fuck it," Jaxon said as he looked from the front door, and back towards me. "Stay here and keep a look out. I don't want trapped in another fucking house."

He then, calmly walked into the house as I watched the street. I didn't even think about following him. I was still a little shell-shocked. It was the way he was getting so good at dealing out this casual violence. He was getting deadlier with every encounter.

I crouched behind some bushes, and kept my watch. The street remained calm. The inside of the house did not.

"Were you worried?"

Not at all, Jaxon was kicking ass. I'd hear the start of a scream, a nasty crunch, and then another scream would try to start from another room. Jaxon was so efficient, that you'd literally have to be right by the front door to hear anything. But, if you happened to be by that front door, like I was, it sounded like hell erupting. Eventually, I began to hear glass breaking and wood cracking. I never once heard a gun.

"How long did this last?"

Probably about five or ten minutes, it felt like a lot longer. Then, suddenly it was quiet. Dead quiet. That's when I got worried.

The quiet lasted a few minutes. I was just about to go inside, when Jaxon casually strolled out wiping down his knife and tomahawk with what looked like a dishtowel.

"There were more of them than I thought," Jax said casually. "Let's keep going."

I didn't say anything. I never even asked how many. I just followed him back down the street.

"It weird how they normally come in packs," I said in an effort break the silence.

"Is this the only conversation you have prepared for me?" Jaxon replied.

"Yeah, this is my A game," I answered.

"Well, I guess it's better than you coming out of the closet. I've been dreading that eventuality."

"Really, because if I did come out of the closet, I'd think you'd be somewhat proud."

"Why would I be proud?" Jaxon asked.

"You would be proud, because if I were gay, and coming out of the closet, I'd be following in your footsteps."

"Are you for real?"

Not at all, we both have gay friends. We were just fucking around.

"Not about that, I've met Ivana. Are you for real that in the middle of enemy territory so to speak, the two of you were joking around?"

Oh hell yeah. That's what we do. That's just the way things go.

"I would be scared to death. I wouldn't be in any kind of mood to be joking around."

I thought we already covered this. Of course we were scared. We were walking down the middle of the street in broad daylight. We knew some of the houses were occupied with zombie cannibals. As far as I was concerned, it was just a matter of time before we one of them saw us, and a bunch of them rushed us. We were definitely feeling the nerves.

"Then why were you joking around?"

What else could we do?

Ok then. Thinking about it later, I guess his logic actually made sense in a weird sort of way.

Jaxon went inside every house that seemed to get louder as we passed by. Maybe they saw us, maybe they didn't. He wasn't taking any chances; getting rushed out here would probably be fatal. All in all, I guess he cleaned out about five homes. On the last one, he came out with a deep laceration in his head, claw marks all over one of his arms, and zombie blood all over his clothes.

"Fell through a glass table," Jax said.

He was trying to staunch the blood pouring from his head with a dirty rag.

"Maybe we should go inside until you stop bleeding," I suggested.

"Why?"

"These things may be able to smell blood."

"They probably can," Jaxon frowned. That's why I don't want to be inside a house when they do. If we're outside, we can at least make a run for it. Besides, I'm covered in zombie blood as well; maybe it'll mask the scent of my blood."

"But you're injured," I almost shouted. The situation was getting ridiculous. "You're bleeding all over the place."

"We don't have time to stop the bleeding," Jaxon said. "So keep walking."

Are you getting the picture here?

"What do you mean?"

I mean, that Jaxon has always been tough, but this was a deep, gushing head wound, and he was still ready to go. In fact, he was refusing to stop.

"Okay."

Nobody is that tough. I could very clearly remember how badly injured he was in that park when we went looking for supplies. How weird was that? We leave him for a while, and when we get back, I find out that the grass has swallowed him, and he's damn near completely healed. I thought for sure he was a goner but nope. He's right as rain.

My uncle was changing somehow. It was like he was adapting to the environment he was placed in, and he was doing it at a somewhat supernatural rate.

I was just glad he was on our side.

It didn't take us too long to hit a four-way intersection. Down the road somewhat, we could see a group of zombies sitting around a bunch of trees in a parking lot. The dead are always lazy in the hot sun.

"We should shamble zombie style across the street," Jaxon said.

"Are you retarded?" I asked. "Let's just run like hell."

"If we do that, they'll know we're a food source. If we shamble like zombies, and go slow, they might think we're one of them, and ignore us."

"What if they charge?" I asked. "What if they can smell us, and decide to charge?"

"Then we run like hell," Jaxon laughed. "It's not like we're losing our only chance to run. Now let's smear some of the zombie blood on your clothes, and try to cover up your human scent."

Most of the zombie blood on his shirt had dried, but he still managed to fuck up my shirt pretty decently. It was disgusting.

It was also the best idea we were gonna get. I was just worried, because his head was still gushing pretty badly.

We shambled across the road. I knew at least a couple of them were watching us. I could just feel it. If they smelled our human scent or his human blood over the dead blood, they'd be on us in a second.

It turned out, we were far enough away from them, and the masking of Jaxon's blood with the zombie blood ended up working. They still might have been a little suspicious, because I heard one or two of them sort of moan in our direction. They never gave chase though. I guess it was too hot for them to bother without knowing for sure.

"It's working," I said once we were almost across the intersection.

"Of course it's working you fool," Jaxon said. "It was my idea. If it were your idea, we'd be getting eaten right about now."

"How about you go fuck yourself?" I asked.

"Shut up, there are more of them up ahead," Jaxon said.

He was right. There were about twenty or maybe even more sitting by some bushes. They were massed in the same direction we were headed.

Jaxon grabbed my arm, and pulled me towards a little doorway, which was out of their line of sight.

"What are you doing?" I asked rather angrily at being yanked by the arm. His strength was shocking.

"Stay here," Jax said. "I have another idea."

He shambled off towards the group of zombies that we had just passed. In less than five minutes he was back with a severed arm. He began wiping the bloody end of the arm all over my clothes.

"What the fuck?" I asked. "I've already got enough on me."

"Relax," Jaxon laughed. You need more; some of them were watching us in a hungry kind of way. Besides, I think what normally makes them chase a victim isn't only because the victim runs; it's also the human smell coming off them. They probably have an incredible sense of smell, and can easily tell the difference between human and zombie."

"But this is revolting!" I almost shouted.

"That's okay," he answered with another little laugh. "It's dead blood, even the color is different. I'm hoping that the more we use, the more we can hide our human scents, and my bleeding head."

"Oh shit," I complained. "This is fucked up."

"Well," Jaxon said. "Maybe you should have kept your ass back at the Safe Zone if you don't like it."

When we started out again, we kept up the shambling, zombie walk. Just to be safe, we crossed to the other side of the street; away from the new group that was sitting in the direction we were headed.

This time I was positive we were being watched. Many of them even sat up as we shambled in front of them. Twenty zombies were a lot to have to fight, especially if we couldn't use our guns.

"You still couldn't use your guns, even if you were attacked by twenty zombies?"

Twenty zombies would rapidly turn into hundreds if we used a gun. They were definitely attracted to noise. A gunshot is like a diner bell.

"So what did you do?"

We shambled almost all the way to Tito's apartment.

"You mean it worked?"

Yes and no. They didn't rush and attack, but something about us must have seemed wrong, because they began to follow from a distance.

I think we both began to relax just a little bit as we passed them by, and got some distance away. A couple of blocks away from Tito's, however, we heard a moan come from behind our backs. Jaxon and I both turned to look back up the street. More than half the zombies from the large group were following behind us, plus a few extras that probably came from inside one of the buildings we shambled by.

We were in deep, deep, trouble, and we knew it. I was hoping that Jaxon was thinking of something, because I sure couldn't think of shit. I also couldn't ask him. They'd charge for sure if they heard us talking.

"That whole masking our scents thing didn't work as well as I'd hoped," Jaxon whispered. "So get ready."

"Get ready for what?" I asked.

I was seriously freaking out. I could see more corpses creeping out of the nearby buildings. Not like hundreds of them or anything, but more than we could handle in a fight, and it sounded like he was getting ready to make a fight out of it.

"RUN!!!!" Jaxon shouted.

Off we went, like bats out of hell. We ran, and ran. It wasn't more than a minute before we hit Tito's parking lot. I knew what his plan was then. He was hoping to lose them in the maze of buildings, and walkways, that make up an apartment complex.

As soon as we ran, *they knew*. We hauled ass, and so did they. The screams began, and more and more started coming after us. They came from inside the buildings, under bushes, from the alleyways between buildings. They came from everywhere.

Their pounding steps behind us made the ground tremble. There were that many of them. I saw them flooding the street behind me, and the sight was terrible.

After the parking lot, came the maze. We turned left, and right, and left, and right. Then we ran straight ahead past a few more lefts, and rights, and finally lost them.

Jaxon wasn't stopping.

"Keep going!" He shouted at me.

I was admittedly slowing down. I've been working on my cardio ever since, so it wouldn't be a problem now but back then, and at that moment; I was sucking some serious air.

Jaxon ran back to me.

"We're almost there, Dudley," he said. "We need to be inside his apartment, and secure, before they catch up to us."

"Okay."

He was right and I knew it. There were hundreds of them now. Their numbers grew and grew. As soon as we started running, and they started screaming. If they saw us go into Tito's apartment, they'd surely be able to break down the door or, at the very least, trap us inside.

I ran for all I was worth. I cursed my lack of cardio, and pushed harder. I was going to make it. I forced my muscles to obey my commands.

Jaxon was opening the latch on Tito's patio door. Then we were both tumbling through, and slamming it shut, when a group of at least ten zombies rushed by.

Jaxon knocked on Tito's door lightly. There was no answer.

"Tito," I whispered through the wood. "Open the fucking door, dude. It's us."

There was no answer.

"Tito," Jaxon whispered. "I'm Luke Skywalker. I'm here to rescue you."

The door opened.

Tito was standing there with wearing the biggest grin I've ever seen on the man.

"I heard you guys the first time," Tito said. "I just had to move the barricade. How did you get in here with all those things around anyway?"

"With style and finesse," I answered.

I should, at this point, inform you that (most of the time) Tito doesn't enjoy our humor.

"I'm sure he was glad to see you though."

He surely was.

"With style and finesse, huh?" He answered me. "You wouldn't know style or finesse if it jumped out and…oh, fuck me!"

The smile was wiped completely off his face as his eyes went wide in fear.

We must not have closed the patio door properly, and it had swung open behind us. To make matters worse, standing about twenty feet down the walkway leading to his apartment was a huge gang of zombie cannibals.

"Fuck!" Jaxon said. "Get inside."

And inside we went. As soon as the door was closed, Tito rebuilt his barricade of wood, metal, and couches.

The zombies rushed us before we even had the door closed. Once they got to Tito's front door, they began pounding with impressive force. We could hear them screaming through the walls. We were trapped; stuck. We were caught in the very situation we were trying to avoid.

Jaxon was whipping his head around, and around, absorbing his environment. What could he do? What weapon existed that could strike down so many of our enemies? There must have been hundreds of them out there.

I had a lot of faith in my uncle at this point, but when he went into the kitchen and started rummaging around, I was thinking that the man had lost his mind.

"Where's your laptop?" He asked Tito.

"You dumb fucks led them right to me," Tito shouted in return. "I was safe. That door can't keep so many of them out. We're fucked."

"We will be soon," Jaxon said. "Where's the laptop? NOW!"

The next thing I knew, he was talking to Georgie via the laptop. I was looking over his shoulder. He was asking Georgie to look up something dealing with a gas explosion.

"What's going on, Jax?" I asked, with panic in my voice.

"I left Georgie a note, and told him what we were up to. I also told him to stay by his computer in case we needed any help."

I briefly wondered how bad a fit Georgie threw when he read the note, and realized Jaxon wasn't there to protect him. It was smart of my uncle to handle it that way. It was also kind of funny how he avoided the temper tantrum, and still had him waiting to help us. Unfortunately, the humor was escaping me due to our current situation.

"What are you having him look up?" I asked.

"Tito has a gas stove. I'm going to blow it up."

"Well that's wonderful Jaxon," Tito said. "But we're still in here."

"Not for long," Jaxon grumbled.

The directions for blowing up the stove started scrolling across the laptop.

Jaxon started writing back. He was asking Georgie to find another way, one that would take a little longer.

The front door started to crack and splinter.

"Tito," Jaxon barked. "Start putting up more of a barricade. I need more time."

Tito reluctantly went to work, and I began to help him. We were piling everything we could find in front of the door. There were decaying arms reaching out for us through the cracks. I began to hack at them with my machete.

"Tito," Jaxon shouted. "Can you understand these directions?"

Tito left me to the hacking, and went to look at the computer screen. They sat there staring at the screen for a few minutes, while I hacked, and hacked, at the arms that reached out for me.

"I can do it," Tito said at last.

The next thing I knew, he was in the kitchen, and yanking his stove away from the wall. I don't know what he did exactly, and if I did, it probably wouldn't be safe to print it here. The next thing you'd hear about is a bunch of kids somewhere blowing up their kitchen.

However, in just a few seconds, he called out that he was ready.

"That's all great Jaxon," I shouted through the hacking. "But we're still trapped in here, and if your idea is to blow us, and them up, I'm not down for that."

Jaxon wasn't even looking at me. He was cutting off a piece of sofa fabric with his knife, and putting it on a tiny pile of trash. He lit it—a small fire about the size of a fist—and then he turned his attention to one of the nearest walls. After making sure it was the one he wanted, he punched it so hard the whole room shook. His fist went right through the wood, or plaster, or whatever it was. Then he took out his tomahawk and began hacking, and kicking, at the hole until it was big enough for him to fit through.

"Hit it Tito," he shouted.

Tito did indeed "hit it" because, very suddenly, the room was filled with the smell of gas. It almost overpowered the smell of decay that was coming from outside the door.

"Move, Dudley! Move!" Tito shouted as he dived through the hole and into the bedroom of the next apartment.

I was right behind him. Jaxon was next. I must say, the next apartment was very nice. I approved of the decor.

"Same thing," Jaxon shouted to Tito.

The zombies would soon be through the barricade in Tito's apartment, so we started blocking up the hole we had just created while Tito ran to the next kitchen.

In less than three minutes, the zombies were inside Tito's apartment, and working on our new barricade. Jaxon was pounding through another wall. The cut on his head was still bleeding profusely, and he had to periodically wipe the blood away to keep his vision clear.

We were through the next wall, and into the next apartment. There was a dead man in the bathroom. I went to make sure he wasn't going to come at us, while Tito worked on the stove and Jaxon barricaded the new hole.

It was a suicide. The guy stepped into the hot water of the bathtub, and opened his veins. I felt sorry for him. I wanted to just sit and take a minute. The world was going to shit. I don't know why this out of everything I had seen brought it home for me but it did.

Jaxon was grabbing me. He was shoving me through another hole he'd just made. I don't know how far the zombies were behind us. My mind had somehow left the room. Everything became a blur.

I knew I was cracking; I just couldn't get my shit together. It didn't seem to bother Jaxon any; it was almost like he expected it to happen eventually. He had me by the wrist, and was dragging me around. Blood was flying off of him and hitting me in the face. Pieces of drywall and white dust were sticking to the blood.

Suddenly, Jaxon stopped.

"Fucking blood in my eyes," he shouted. Then a slew of obscenities came out of him.

I caught a glimpse of his eyes. The whites had actually been stained pink from all the blood in them. He ran to this new apartment's sink as Tito began to tear the stove from the wall.

Quickly he washed the blood off his face, and out of his eyes.

"Ah," he shouted after dunking his entire head in the water. "It itches."

Tito stepped away from what he was doing, and ran over to Jaxon who was furiously rubbing the area around his wound.

"Holy shit Jaxon," Tito whispered. "That cut is closing up."

Another twenty seconds I'm guessing, I'm still not sure, and Jaxon was back at it. He grabbed my wrist, and dragged me through yet another hole, and into yet another apartment.

I'm guessing we went through about eight of these apartments. I wasn't counting. I was actually trying to get a decent look at Jaxon's head wound. It was tough to see with him moving around so much, but it did seem to have stopped bleeding. I was mesmerized. A couple of minutes ago that wound had been gushing blood, now it wasn't bleeding at all.

"Let me see your head," I asked.

"What?" He asked. He wasn't really paying any attention to me at the moment. He was looking out the window.

"I wanna see your head," I repeated.

This got his attention. He walked over to me and grabbed my shoulders.

"You need to snap out of it," he said, while looking in my eyes.

Boom!

The first apartment had blown. The second apartment followed with a dull whump.

"Move, Tito," Jaxon shouted, as he grabbed my hand, and jerked me out the front door.

The three of us were running back up the street toward the quads. Most of the zombies must have been inside the apartments trying to get at us, because there weren't many of them on the sidewalks. The ones that were there rushed us, of course, but Jaxon shot them down with his pistol. We could see large groups of them running after us from farther down the street in the opposite direction than we were heading. They were only just reaching Tito's apartment building so we weren't that concerned.

It wasn't even a minute before the entire building went up in the loudest explosion I've ever heard in my life. The sheer force of it knocked us all off our feet.

I must have blacked out, because when I came to Tito was screaming. A female zombie was on top of him and trying to bite at his throat. I grabbed my pistol and shot her right in the spine. Jaxon threw her off and helped him to his feet. I think he must have gotten hit with something in the explosion, because the back of his shirt was ripped. The bruise that was forming covered half his back, narrowly missing his Winchester.

"No more need to be quiet," Jaxon said as he pulled his rifle off his back.

I did the same and smiled as Tito held out his hand for a gun.

"You can't shoot, dickhead," Jaxon told him.

"Give me a gun, damn it," Tito growled.

"You still don't have a sense of humor," I added. I felt a lot better at that point. Whatever happened to me had finally passed.

"Look who finally decided to join us," Tito growled.

"I'm not giving the dickhead my gun," I said. "He never went to the range with us. He'll probably end up shooting me in the ass."

Jaxon wasn't paying any attention. I looked over to what he was staring at. Tito's entire apartment building was a huge tower of smoke and flame. The large groups of zombies that had been running after us must have caught some of the blast, because all of them (at least a hundred) that weren't in pieces were slowly rising to their feet.

"We better move," Tito said.

"Wait a minute," I argued. "Look at what's left of the walls."

Tito took another look, and saw what I was pointing at. The walls of Tito's building, or at least what was left of them after that huge explosion, were beginning to buckle. Just as everyone else began to notice this, they collapsed with an ear-shattering screech. The entire building came down as we looked on, then more explosions began to sound off, blowing chunks of metal, wood, and dust, hundreds of feet into the air as the rest of the complex erupted.

The remaining zombies that were littered around the building ended up buried in the rubble. It didn't mean we wiped out all the zombies in the area, but we sure as hell made a huge fucking dent.

"I've seen that explosion on the news. It was a gigantic mushroom cloud that could be seen from the blockades around El Paso. For a while there, the citizens were worried that the government had started bombing the city. It took about five press conferences before people finally began to believe the government had nothing to do with it."

Yeah, it was just my uncle visiting a friend.

"You make it sound all nonchalant."

To be honest, we were just happy to be alive. We knew the military had quarantined the city. After the initial shock wore off, we knew the citizens outside the city were demanding that something be done, but all of it was rather far away and disconnected. We were at ground zero. It was almost like the outside world didn't exist.

"So you never considered that people outside the military blockade would see the explosion?"

I doubt any of us even gave it a second's worth of thought. We still had to get back to the Safe Zone. That's all we cared about. We headed towards the four-way intersection as fast as we could go because, at that point, the neighboring apartment buildings had started to catch fire from all the burning debris. Jaxon was limping; his back was pretty messed up. Every now, and then I would see him wince. Yet, he never complained. I secretly think he used his own body to shield both of us.

There were still zombies afoot, let's not forget that point. At that point, there weren't any large groups, so they were easy enough to shoot down. I finally relented, and gave Tito my pistol, which didn't do him much good since he couldn't shoot worth a damn.

We had crossed the intersection, and were heading back up towards the desert before things got interesting. The houses were now on either side of us, and it was a good thing because Jaxon was reaching his limit of pain tolerance.

"Jaxon," I said. "The sprinklers in that yard are going off."

"So?"

"They're spraying water everywhere," I answered. "Go sit in front of it for a second, and see if that helps any."

He didn't say another word. He just walked over, and dropped in the soggy grass, right in front of a sprinkler. The water began to spray over him. It was cleaning the blood off of his back, and for the first time, I actually saw it happen.

The grass all around him began to writhe and churn. Jaxon didn't seem to notice, it was like he'd found a little slice of heaven. He was just kneeling there as the water hit his back. His eyes even began closing.

It looked painful, but it also looked somewhat relaxing?

"What do you mean?"

Well, there was a definite easing of pain; I could see it in his face. His entire body was relaxing, but he would occasionally twitch an arm or something. So I'm thinking there was a fair amount of pain involved as well.

"What about the grass?"

It was still moving, like it was alive. It grew, and stretched towards him. It wrapped around his fingers, and eased up his arms and back. The weirdest thing was Jaxon didn't seem to mind. Then his eyes opened.

He was looking past our astonished faces and back down the road. After that, his eyes narrowed, and he pointed.

The corpses that hadn't been utterly destroyed in the fire came forth. They were far away, but they were moving as fast as their damaged and burnt bodies could carry them. Personally, I couldn't believe it. I had thought that we'd gotten all of them, but zombies just keep on coming. It's irritating how relentless they are.

We only had moments.

"We need to move," Tito said.

He was right. We needed to get to the quads as soon as possible. The dead were coming fast, and they were many.

Jaxon just stood up. All the grass that was wrapping around his body immediately released him. "That's pretty fucking weird," he said.

We ran as fast as we could. It wasn't easy; I was exhausted and Tito, who constantly bragged about being able to run something like eight miles a day, was really feeling the exhaustion. He later blamed it on being cooped up in his apartment without enough food. I call bullshit.

Jaxon was re-energized. It was like he had all the energy in the world to just burn and throw away. Still, the zombies were gaining on us. We'd been through too much. Jaxon was behind us, pushing at our backs.

I began to smell the charred skin as they got closer, and closer. The zombie screams shattered the once quiet, neighborhood as they rattled forth from the dried out husks that used to be human throats.

Then the fun began. We had cleared some houses when we passed through this area on our way to Tito's, but we only cleared the homes that were getting rambunctious while we passed. Most of the homes, we just ignored.

Well, they weren't empty.

The zombies inside them finally woke up and came outside. It must have been those weird screams coming from our pursuers that got them moving. In seconds, they were pouring into the street ahead of us, blocking us off from the guard rail and the quads behind it.

Jaxon had a tomahawk in his right hand and his pistol in the other. He ran to meet them head on.

The corpses that didn't fall from his bullets met the crunching power of his tomahawk. He was clearing our way.

"Keep moving!" He shouted. "Don't try to fight them, just keep moving forward."

We did what he said and followed the wake of destruction that became our path to survival.

I would have liked to stop and admire his efficient killing abilities, but I was too busy running for my life. I also had to grab a hold of Tito and pull him behind me. The burnt zombies that were chasing after us were too damn close.

Jaxon was over the guard rail and starting the quads. The sound was beautiful. They were so close but still so far away.

With the quads running, he stood on the guard rail and took aim with his rifle. I panicked at that point. If he felt the need to fire off some shots, the zombies must be closer to us than I thought. I should have kept a better eye on them.

I glanced over my shoulder. The dead were less than ten feet away, and gaining.

I poured on the last of my strength.

Crack! Crack! Crack!

The shots rang out. They were deafening; they were salvation. The dead that met the bullets began to fall. The ones behind them began to trip over their fallen brethren. We began to pull away. Not much, but enough.

Enough that when we went over the guard rail, we had time to jump on the quads, and zoom away in a trail of hot sand and small rocks.

The dead could not keep up. We lost them in the desert. No doubt they'd eventually turn up around the fences of our Safe Zone, but they'd be easy enough to deal with there.

"Another daring escape. You survived the un-survivable once again. Mentally, how were you holding up?"

I felt pretty good, to be honest with you. I mean, I was exhausted—worried that we might ride around some large hill and end up in the middle of a large pack of zombies before we made it back to the Safe Zone—but I really felt pretty damn good.

"Did you encounter another large pack of zombies?"

In point of fact, we did not. It was smooth sailing all the way back. We even stopped at one point to have some water and let the quads cool down.

"Well that was fun," Tito said after a few uncomfortable moments of silence.

"You ready to do it again?" asked Jaxon.

"Hell no," Tito shouted back at him. "I never wanna be anywhere near another zombie."

We laughed for a long time. Finally, I couldn't take it anymore.

"What the hell was up with the sprinklers and the water?" I blurted. "I can't believe that actually worked." "Hell if I know," Jax answered. "It was your idea. The water kinda numbed the pain somewhat but it then it started to burn a bit. By the time the grass began to move over me, the damage was just sort of melting away. In fact, I feel a lot better now."

"Yeah," I said. "You look it. Ever since the park, you've been different somehow. Back at the apartment complex, when you ran your head under the water, it healed that deep cut you had."

"Not completely," he answered. "The cut's still there but it's not bleeding anymore."

"I bet the longer you stay under the water, or under the grass, the more it will heal," I said.

"What the hell are the two of you smoking?" Tito asked with a definite annoyance in his tone. "Jaxon is no different from anyone else. He's no champion. He's no hero. He's just a guy that keeps getting lucky."

"Then why do his wounds heal so fast?" I asked.

"They probably weren't as deep or as bad as we thought they were," Tito answered. "It's not like either one of us actually studied the damage before he sat under the sprinklers."

"What about the way the grass moved over him?"

"Maybe the grass was going to eat him or something," Tito said. "Maybe it's infected in the same fucked up way the zombies are."

"All right, Tito," I replied. "Whatever you say."

I wasn't going to waste any more of my time arguing with him. It was the weirdest thing. I, like most people, wanted Jaxon to be special in some way. It very much sounded like Tito was angry at the idea that Jaxon might be special.

"Why did you want Jaxon to be special, and why do you think other people wanted him to be special as well?"

Because we were trapped in hell, and on every side we were staring down evil. It was nice to have hope. These vile, rowdy monsters rose up from their own deaths, and destroyed a city in less than one day. That's a horrible thought. It meant our time was very limited, but what if there was an opposite? What if there was some guy that could right the wrongs, and stamp them out?

"Kind of like an antidote to a poison?"

Exactly, a savior of some sort, that's what everyone wanted. Someone that they could stand behind, someone that could win. Tito just didn't want that someone to be Jaxon.

"Why do you suppose that is?"

Jealousy.

Chapter 4

JAXON

On my second round of questions with Jaxon, he was waiting for me in his backyard. As usual, Merrick was by his side. She gave a quick bark when I entered, and then proceeded to jump all over me.

Jaxon's attitude was still very relaxed, despite all the papers on the table next to him detailing assignments and other emergencies. For a moment I felt what Ivana felt when she first heard that this man was the General; a suspension of belief. Could this seemingly normal looking person who'd rather crack jokes and hang out with his friends, really be the hero I've heard so much about? He wasn't ten feet tall; he didn't wear an "S" on his chest. Where did it all come from?

So how are your interviews coming?

"Pretty good, I've just finished with Dudley telling me about how the two of you rescued Tito."

I heard you talked to Ivana. Is that true?

"Yes. She gave me some interesting insights."

On what?

"What things were like for someone who wasn't really able to fight back."

Ah, you see, I disagree with that. I think, on a basic level, everyone is capable of fighting back. What they don't want is to be put into a position in which they have to fight back.

"Is that what you tell your critics?"

I have critics?

"You didn't know?"

He laughed and so did I. The fact is there have been a number of groups that would like to see the General retired. They believe that, as an average citizen with zero military or government experience, he has been given too much power.

Actually, I don't tell my critics anything.

"Why is that?"

They aren't really important. I mean, at the end of the day, I'm going to be doing exactly what it is that I do. The government sanctions it and, unfortunately, some people really need it. If I stop, people die. That's something I'm not prepared to live with at the moment. Maybe there will come a day when I'm not needed anymore. It's what I'm hoping for at least.

"I think it's entirely fair to say that you're a hero to many."

I've often wondered what would happen if one of those so-called critics were surrounded by an army of the dead. Would they, at that point, stop whining and realize that I'm actually needed?

"That's an interesting thought. Would you help them?"

Of course I would, but I'd be rubbing it in the entire time. I'm no saint.

"So, after rescuing Tito, what happened when you returned to the Safe Zone?"

I took a shower. It was lovely. It was heaven. I can't tell you how glad I was to be able to shower. I guess I'm a bit of a clean freak.

"Did you have trouble getting into the Safe Zone?"

Not really. The guards were keeping everything pretty free of any undead stragglers. This, of course, is a nice way of saying that they shot down every zombie that they saw.

One of the happiest moments was when I realized that our numbers had swelled. More and more people were traveling to our Safe Zone. They were braving the dangers, and joining our ranks. We were barely gone a day, and I think close to a hundred people had already arrived.

Unfortunately, they did bring some bad news with them.

"What was that?"

The zombies were coming.

Our guards killed anywhere from ten to twenty a day. Not a big deal, but some of our new arrivals claimed to have narrowly avoided a mass of thousands.

Maybe it was all the human smells coming from the Safe Zone. I really have no idea. All I knew is that if a mob that large attacked us, there was no way our fence would hold.

Now, the survivors that saw this mass told us that they weren't all traveling together like some great army—zombies don't work that way—but they were more than certain that the zombies were headed right towards us.

"And you think it was the human smell coming from the Safe Zone?"

It's just a guess. The fact is, I have no idea. All I know is that zombies follow humans. I don't know how, but they do. The more humans you have together, the more zombies you'll attract.

They wouldn't all come at once, but once they reached the area, it would only be a few short days before our fences were totally surrounded by the dead. After that, it wouldn't take long before those same fences fell. We simply didn't have enough bullets, or people, for that kind of force.

We needed to act, and we needed to act fast.

Our best guess was that we had two or three days at the most before they'd be on us.

That night, we had a meeting. My usual gang were the only people in attendance. I didn't invite the others in the Safe Zone, because it would have become a free for all, with about a thousand different ideas, and nothing would get done.

The group was small and, after all, whatever we decided to do, we weren't forcing others to do it with us. If they didn't like our ideas, they were free to follow their own path.

I should also mention that Georgie was very glad to have me back safe and sound, but at the same time, he was somewhat pissed at me. I told him to get over it, we had work to do, and to his credit, he did what I asked.

The first thing we realized is that people exaggerate. Someone had to go out into the night, and find out just how large this army of the undead was. That was our first idea. It might end up being something we could handle without a problem. At least, that's what we were hoping for.

As usual for Tito, he was playing devil's advocate.

"I don't think it's right for us to be making these decisions for people," Tito said.

"We aren't making decisions for anyone," I answered. "They don't have to go along with what we decide."

"Yet, they will," he answered. "And sooner or later they'll resent you for it. You weren't elected. They didn't choose you."

"They did choose him," Ivana said. "I chose him. As soon as I found out where he was, I went there. I wanted to be alongside of him."

"Okay, some people may have decided to stand beside this so-called General," Tito said. "But what are his qualifications? Why should they follow Jax? He's just a normal guy that got lucky?"

"Are you seriously saying that the things he accomplished were due to luck?" Dudley asked. "I was there dude. I had a front row seat for everything he did, and I can tell you with the utmost certainty that there was no luck involved. He was born to do this shit."

"I'm sure there was a little luck involved," I laughed, figuring I might as well make light of a tense situation. In truth, I never expect anyone to be on my side. It's always a bit of a shock when they are.

"Why is that?"

I'm just used to fighting my own battles. Plus, most people won't engage themselves in a confrontation. I, however, have never had much of a problem with that.

"Let's make it simple," I said. "If there's anyone here that doesn't think I'm a fit leader, raise your hand."

No hands were raised, including Tito's.

"Tito, are you sure you want involved with this?" I asked with a bit of pleasure. "You were the one so against me leading."

"I'm with you," he answered. "I just think that whatever decisions you make should at least be run by us first."

"I can agree with that," I said. "When I have the time, I'll run my ideas by everyone."

Nobody said a word. All that I meant was that in the middle of a fight or something I didn't want to have to ask permission before I gave out some orders.

"Were you comfortable giving these orders?"

Somebody had to do it. Nobody else was stepping up. I was getting kind of used to it. Still, if the government got off its ass, and threw us a bone, I'd gladly step out of the way. That just wasn't happening. All those people were looking to me. They weren't asking to be led by some group; they were asking to be led by me.

"Now, what do we do if there is indeed an incredibly huge mass of zombies headed this way?" I asked.

"Let's reinforce the fences," Georgie volunteered.

"With the kind of group those people were talking about, the fences will fall, or they'll eventually be able to climb right over them," I answered. "A mass of thousands is just too much. The first time one of them sees our group—and blurts out with one of those fucked up screams—we'll be overrun. We just don't have the forces or ammo."

"Are you serious?" Lucy shouted. "So we're all going to die?"

She seemed to be on the verge of a nervous breakdown, so I pretty much just ignored her. It wasn't something I could deal with anyway. Let her husband handle it.

Nobody else said anything after her outburst.

"Nobody has any ideas?" I asked. "I only have one, and you guys aren't gonna like it."

"What's your idea?" Georgie asked in the same very calm voice that he often used when his wife was freaking out.

"If they are headed this way," I said. "We can't be here when they arrive. We need to move."

"Where the hell are we going to go?" Kingsley asked. He seemed drunk. "Are we just going to bounce around the city? Every time they find us, we run somewhere else? That's not a permanent solution. They said a mass of thousands. That's thousands of zombies?"

"Yes," Tito said. "There are thousands of zombies. What's your point?"

I knew exactly what Kingsley was getting at before he even had a chance to answer. I just didn't like it much.

"That just a small fraction of the zombies running around this city," Kingsley said. "El Paso has a population of about five hundred thousand. Georgie estimated that only around seventy thousand are not infected."

"And?"

"Eventually, we're going to attract a mass of zombies so large that thousands will pale by comparison," I answered for Kingsley. "He's right, if there are only thousands coming this way, we are seriously lucky. Sooner or later, probably when they run out of survivors outside the Safe Zone, every zombie in the city will be heading straight for us."

There was a pause while everyone absorbed what I had just said. My mind, meanwhile, had kicked into overdrive. Eventually, we'd get caught. Eventually, we'd run out of places to hide. The odds were way too stacked against us. We needed to get out of El Paso as soon as possible.

"I'm taking my Jeep," I said. "I'm going to see how far away the mass of zombies really is, or if there actually is a mass. I'll have a plan by the time I get back."

Outside of Georgie's house, the people were waiting for us. The survivors; the lost souls I was trying to help. All of them were looking to me for an answer. If worse came to worse, I could probably survive in this city for years. They couldn't, but I'd never abandon them. Our fates were intertwined.

I needed a plan. I needed a way to open the barriers that blocked our way out of the city.

Their anxious faces watched me as I climbed onto the back of the nearest truck. I hated giving speeches, but this needed to come from me.

"I think everyone knows the score," I said. "The dead are coming. I'm going out to see how far away they are, and how many of them are coming. I want all of you to make yourselves ready."

I let my words sink in. They already knew, but hearing it from someone like me gave it a more menacing tone. They were murmuring amongst themselves. They were afraid. Some of them had just gotten here. They thought this place was safe. It wasn't. In the long run, no place in the entire city was going to be safe.

"Where are we going?" Asked a man whose name I believe was Chewie.

"I don't know yet," I answered honestly. I wasn't going to lie to those people.

"Why can't we stay and fight?" asked another man. I won't even guess his name.

"Maybe we can," I answered. "I haven't seen this horde for myself yet. That's why I'm going out there. I need to see how bad things are."

"But there's a chance that we may be able to stay here and fight them off?" Chewie asked.

"I don't think so," I answered. "There's just too many of them out there. Eventually, this Safe Zone, or any place like it, will become a death trap. It's just a matter of time before we're overrun."

"Then why bother running?" Someone shouted out. The crowd surrounding the truck was quite large, and still growing.

"It ain't over till it's over," I answered. "I also think it is time to leave the city."

The crowd was silenced. It's what everyone wanted, and it was also impossible. The last messages we heard about the barricades blocking the city told of soldiers shooting anybody trying to cross those barricades.

"I don't want everybody getting too excited about this," I added before the questions could begin. "I don't have a way out yet. I'm just not prepared to let that stop me."

They began to laugh. Then someone began to cheer, and someone else joined along. Before I knew it, they were all cheering. Good, they were with me.

As I jumped down from the truck, a cowboy that I'd never met before grabbed my hand and pumped it furiously.

"We're with you," he said. "Wherever the General leads, we're going to follow."

I was dressed in black fatigues and a black t-shirt. I had on my utility belt, and all my weapons. My backpack was slung over my shoulder. Dudley wanted to go, but he just looked too tired. He needed his rest. Tito was the same way, and Kingsley needed to sober up.

"You're the shooter," I told Georgie. "I may need you."

"I can't go," he answered. "My wife needs me."

"You're useless," I said and shouldered by him. "While I'm gone, I want you to find out about the barricades around this city. If I have a question, I'm asking you, and you'd better have an answer."

I didn't wait for his reply.

Dudley and Kingsley were having a fit over my going alone. They were waiting for me by my Jeep.

"Jax," Dudley said. "I can do this. If you think I'm too tired, I can always wait in the Jeep."

"I can go with him," Kingsley added. "It worked the first time we all went out together. He can drive and I can shoot."

They didn't look right. They looked too tired, and Kingsley looked too drunk. Yet, the worry on their faces was difficult to weather. In the end, they were right. They could stay in the Jeep and watch each other's backs. It might be better to have them watching my Jeep anyway.

Shortly after sunset, Dudley drove the three of us out of the Safe Zone and down the road. I brought Merrick with me this time. She'd be a big help making sure no zombies climbed in the Jeep. She was happy to be going with me for once, or maybe she was just glad to get away from that pussy Georgie.

"So, you went back into the fire?"

It certainly felt that way. This time we were just supposed to have a look. There was no need to fight anything. It made things a little bit easier on the nerves but we were still going into hostile territory.

"Did you know where you were going, or were you just going to drive around?"

We knew exactly where we were headed. We were headed Downtown.

"This is the business district of the city right?"

Yeah, it's small, but the buildings are close together, and they rise up kinda tall. Most of El Paso is wide open, and spread out. It's easiest to think of Downtown as a very small version of New York complete with its own offices, restaurants, and clubs. There were lots of places to hide, and hundreds of alleys to jump out of.

"So it's the actual city section of the city of El Paso?"

That sounds kinda funny, but it's accurate. The ride over there was relatively boring in comparison to what we'd been dealing with. We expected hordes of the undead to come chasing after us at any moment.

It never happened. I mean, sure we had some runners come after us but they weren't fast enough to even bother shooting. The street lamps were coming on as we drove by abandoned, and sometimes bloody, vehicles.

"Where the hell are they?" Dudley asked.

"Oh they're out there." Kingsley answered. "We're just lucky enough not to have run into them yet."

"This area was pretty active when we went out for supplies that one time," I added. "So, it does make you wonder where they went."

"I bet they're on the Eastside," Dudley added. He didn't much like the Eastside. "Better eating over there."

Kingsley was looking at him like he was the biggest ass in the world.

"What?" Dudley asked. "I'm talking about the restaurants."

"Well if that's the case," I joined in. "I'm going to have to agree with you."

We were laughing quietly as we drove along. It's a bone of contention between people living on the Eastside and Westside of town. Who has the better restaurants? I'm going to have to go with the Eastside.

"So, while driving through hostile terrain, you are arguing about who has the better restaurants?"

I'm not sure how big of an argument it was; I think we were all in agreement. It was about then that we heard the moans. There was movement down a street to our right. Dudley was slowing down and looking at me. I nodded to him and he nosed the front of the Jeep over towards the commotion.

Zombies had somehow overrun a van. It must have happened recently, the blood was still very fresh. I could smell it in the air over the stench of the undead and decaying bodies.

The dead were feasting on what looked to be the remains of a large family. They must have been trying to make it to the Safe Zone. It was bound to happen as our numbers were swelling. Not everyone was going to make it. I could almost say that death lurked around every corner, but that isn't accurate. Some corners were safe, while others led to a feeding frenzy.

The zombies, and there were many of them, didn't pay us any attention. Their prey was still plentiful, and fresh. More of them were coming from down the street. They wanted the fresh kill; they smelled the blood.

I nodded to Dudley. It was time we left. The area was about to become very dangerous.

"Make sure we take a different route on our way back," I said.

"You got that right," Dudley said.

As we left the neighborhood, we were encountering more and more of the undead. They were swarming in on the fresh kill. I'm not sure where they wander off to, but they sure as hell regroup pretty fast when there's something to eat.

In another ten minutes, we reached the buildings of Downtown. I don't remember the street; I guess it's not that important.

Dudley kept driving inwards; I wasn't stopping him. I was waiting for something, I just didn't know what.

"I've got an idea," Kingsley said. "Let's drive through that above ground parking garage that's by the courthouse."

"Why?" I asked.

"Because it's only a few streets over and it has around six or so levels. We'll be able to see a lot of the city and not have to leave the Jeep."

"Good idea," I answered.

So, we made our way to the parking garage and entered very slowly. Our lights were blazing and our guns were ready. Merrick noticed the tension and started a slow and steady growl.

We took the concrete path at a steady pace and circled our way up.

"The parking garage kind of loops around in circles until you reach the top, correct?"

I see you've been there.

"No, it's just common for parking garages to wind up and down."

Well, I'd been there more than a few times.

"Really?"

Nothing like that; don't get too excited. I used to receive a summons for jury duty every year. It's a real pain in the ass, if you ask me. Working the job I have now, I don't get summoned anymore. One of the perks I guess.

For some reason that made me laugh. Here was a man who risked his life on a constant basis and he was still finding perks in his job.

On about the fourth floor we ran into a traffic jam. Cars were piled up bumper to bumper. There was no way to go around them; it was a one-way kinda direction. About five parking spaces ahead was the left turn that led down to the exit.

The exit route was before the traffic jam and therefore not blocked by any cars.

"Maybe they ran into the garage for shelter, and got cornered," Kingsley said when I mumbled something about the traffic jam.

"Why would they do that?" Dudley asked.

"There are elevators here that lead to entrances in the courthouse. Maybe they thought that they'd find help there?"

"Lots of cops at least," I added. "It sounds feasible. Maybe something happened and they had to leave their cars?"

"Yeah, we've seen that before," Dudley said. "The zombies come from behind while the people are trapped in a traffic jam."

"If that's a possibility, we should get out of here," Kingsley said. "Whatever made them leave their cars may still be up there somewhere."

"To be honest, I think the entire area over here is dangerous. I can feel it in my bones. Something just doesn't feel right."

"I agree," Dudley said. "This place is fucking creepy."

I thought it over for a moment and made my decision.

"All right boys, this is where we part company for the time being. Aim the Jeep towards the exit route. I'm going up to get a view of the city. If anything happens, try not to use your guns. We don't want to attract every zombie in the area."

I was off. I jumped out of the back seat of the Jeep and took off at a quick jog. Merrick was right behind me. She wouldn't let me out of her sight. It wasn't that difficult weaving in and out of the bumper-to-bumper traffic. The dim lights of the parking garage made things overly easy.

I was hoping for more darkness, but I was still pretty sure that I could blend into the shadows if the need arose.Occasionally, I had to hop onto the hoods of the vehicles to make my way. It was a lot like running an obstacle course.

Nearing around the fifth level, I pulled out my small flashlight. It was the smell of blood in the air that made me do it. I was curious. I started to look inside the cars. No problems there, the doors were still open on a lot of them, yet they were all empty.

The flashlight filled in the missing details. What I thought were oil stains on the floor were actually pools of blood. Yep, people had been coming here for help. The zombies followed them, and they had to leave their cars behind because of the traffic jam. Dudley was right.

Now I was wondering, what had caused the traffic jam?

Since I was sure that I was in zombie-infested territory, or at least territory that had been zombie infested, I was extra careful. I took my time. I kept Merrick quiet.

I heard noise coming from the streets below but it wasn't constant.

The silence in the parking garage was near absolute. It gave me time to think as I worked my way to the top floor, and what I realized was actually pretty messed up.

"What was that?"

The survivors back at the Safe Zone were accepting me as their leader, and I was barely there. This was the second time I had left them. When we first arrived at Georgie's house; I also left the folks in his house in a search for food.

I was wondering how good of a leader I actually was.

"Well you united all those people and made them safe. I think that has to count for something."

True, but who wants a leader that's never around?

"People that want to live."

Yeah, and to tell you the truth, I was kind of afraid to turn the leadership mantle over to someone else. What if they fucked up?

Anyway, I guess I was just having some doubts.

"That's completely understandable."

He nodded as if he accepted that doubt was normal. However, I don't truly believe my words mattered very much to him. Maybe Ivana was right? The pressure of his position could indeed be too much for one man.

So yeah, I was telling you about the silence inside of the parking garage. That was probably the only reason I heard the slight noise coming from behind two cars in a dark corner.

It was a strange lapping sound.

I pulled out my knife, and motioned Merrick to stay, while I quietly climbed over the cars to take a peek.

It was repulsive. A zombie that was missing most of his limbs was face down in the bloody mess of what looked like the long ago devoured leftovers of a victim. The zombie could only move in an inchworm style, so he had resorted to lapping up the leftover blood with pieces of guts.

I was on him quickly, and my knife was embedded in his ear before he could scream. I think I was doing him a favor.

Farther up, I saw more evidence of the carnage, bloody remains consisting of mostly bone, and ripped fabric. If the brain was damaged, the victim wouldn't rise and become a zombie. The dead that came through here must have been hungry. They didn't leave enough leftovers to add to their ranks.

The elevator door that led to the courthouse entrance was open and blinking. When I looked inside, I saw large splatters of blood that, literally, covered the walls. I had no interest in taking that elevator.

At the end of the sixth floor I saw what had created the traffic jam. A large truck that must have been hauling ass had hit a concrete support beam and spun around. It blocked the way and two other cars had then slammed into it. Oil and radiator fluid covered the ground.

Merrick's low growl was the only warning I received. The truck wasn't empty. Its occupant came out in a rush. The beginning notes of a scream died in its throat when my tomahawk met its forehead in a sickening crunch.

I carefully shone the light in every dark corner I saw. It seemed clear, and Merrick seemed calm. I moved forward.

Finally, I met open sky. I went immediately to the side of the building facing the courthouse. I looked down at the glass walkway that made a bridge above the street level traffic and connected the courthouse to the parking garage. It was filled with zombies that had been trapped by the metal doors on each side of the buildings. The street below the walkway was empty.

I went to the side of the roof that was directly above our escape route; thankfully it was empty as well.

The next side told an entirely different story. The street below was covered in zombies. It was the weirdest sight imaginable. Without the presence of humans, the zombies seemed quite calm. They just wandered aimlessly around the street.

The smell was putrid. There were hundreds upon hundreds of zombies—maybe even a thousand— just on one street alone. I'm sure you can imagine how badly that many corpses must have reeked.

Some were dressed in suits. Some of the female zombies wore dresses. Others were in their everyday blue jeans. They walked around, and looked in the shop windows; they went in and out of stores. It was almost like they were trying to live the barest possible hints of their past lives.

I even watched one female in a white pant suit walk all the way down to the end of the street, turn around and walk to the other end of the street, then turn around again and enter a clothing store. When she came back out, she was holding an empty shopping bag.

I went to the fourth side of the roof.

It was the same thing. I could see off into some side streets as well and they were also littered with the undead.

Downtown had been overrun by zombies. There were even more of them than what we were told, and we were told it was in the thousands. I wasn't sure they were actually leaving. It seemed like they were quite content to stay here, which was great for us in the Safe Zone, but I had no idea what was so interesting about the area.

I heard the loud crack of a door being broken down before I saw it. I ran back to the side that had the female zombie with the empty shopping bag. I saw a living woman run out of the store and into the street. I reached back for my rifle, but before I could even get my hands on it, she was down. More and more zombies piled on top of her. Despite their numbers, her screams managed to go on for at least a minute as they tore her apart.

There were survivors in these buildings and there was nothing I could do to help them. I hated the zombies. In that moment, I wished I could jump off the roof and land in the middle of all of them. I'd hack and stab and slash until they were all dead. It was just a wish; they'd rip me apart and devour me just as easily as that woman.

BOOM...crack...crack...BOOM.

I heard it loud and clear, and so did just about every zombie in the Downtown area.

I ran over to the side of the building with the glass walkway. The roof and sides of the walkway were now cracked wide open from what was probably a couple shotgun blasts. Inside the walkway, the zombies were rushing forward at the humans who were shooting at them.

It was a brave thing to do, I'm not sure why they left the security of the courthouse, but it was brave. Still, there were just way too many zombies in that walkway for the five living, breathing men and women to handle.

It was a long way down from the roof to the top of the walkway.

I landed with a thud and a roll, all the while cradling Merrick, so she wouldn't get hurt. I was now inside the walkway through the broken glass roof, my back just a little bit stiff from the fall.

"Don't shoot me!" I screamed. "I'm here to help!"

To their credit, they didn't shoot me. Unfortunately, the shock of seeing me drop down through the top of the walkway with a large black pit bull also seemed to stop them from shooting the zombies as well.

"Can you blame them? That's not exactly something you see every day."

I can't blame them at all I guess.

Anyway, my pistol was out, along with my knife. I shot and stabbed my way through the reeking throng of zombies. Let me tell ya, in that enclosed area, it really stank something fierce. Merrick was right by my side. Her teeth and jaws did vast amounts of damage. Finally, and not a moment too soon, the others began shooting again. It wasn't long before the hallway was cleared.

There were three women and two men. The walkway was filled with smoke and the scent of gunpowder. All six of us stood there for a moment eyeing one another and catching our breath.

"My name's Jaxon," I finally said.

"It's the General," one of the women said.

"Yeah," I replied stupidly.

"My name's Beth," she said. "We heard you were headed Downtown. We kept a lookout, and when we saw that Jeep going into the parking garage, we figured it was you."

"How did you hear I was headed Downtown?" I asked.

"EPUA," one of the men answered.

"Ah…well how many people you got down here?" I asked.

"There are twenty of us inside the building. There are hundreds in the neighboring buildings," the other man answered.

I could hear screaming coming from the street below us. I put my head out of the crack in the side of the walkway in order to get a look at the situation.

It was bad.

It was real bad. The street was filled with zombies. All of them were looking at me. Most of them were screaming.

To make matters worse, the side of the street with the glass walkway was also the same side of the street with the entrance to the parking garage.

The zombies were heading into the parking garage. Not all of them some were banging on the doors to the courthouse, but way too many were flooding the entrance. Dudley and Kingsley were in that parking garage waiting for me.

Yeah, it was bad.

"Look," I said. "Go barricade yourselves back inside. Those doors are thick enough to keep them out. I have friends in the parking garage."

"You can't just leave us," Beth shouted in outrage.

"I don't have a choice," I replied. "I can't fit twenty people in the Jeep. I'll be back for you, I promise."

With that I took off running back towards the parking garage. I heard her shouting curses behind me.

"Does that bother you?"

Yes.

"Why?"

They thought my coming there would be their salvation. As I left, they were thinking I abandoned them.

"But you had no choice."

I know that, and as I entered the parking garage through the opposite door, I realized that time was definitely of the essence.

"Why is that?"

I could already hear the zombie screams echoing through the parking garage. I could already hear their feet pounding on the slick cement. It was going to be a race to the Jeep.

"We're never going to make it. What floor is the Jeep on?"

I turned to look behind me. One of the men was following.

"Around the fourth, keep running," I shouted over my shoulder.

We ran and ran and ran. The man wasn't in the greatest of shape. In fact, he was rather large, but I knew if he fell behind he'd never make it.

"MOVE YOUR FAT ASS!" I shouted. He grimaced at me but he kept moving. These business and lawyer types, it's like the minute they put on a suit, they stop taking care of themselves.

Finally, I saw the Jeep, but beyond the Jeep, I also saw the many zombies rushing towards us. Dudley was in the driver's seat. Kingsley was standing up in the back with a rifle. They both looked scared to death.

In a quick swoop I picked up Merrick. I tossed her in the back from about five feet away. It was going to be tough. Kingsley was shooting now. The man running behind me was crying.

I grabbed his arm and pulled him along behind me. His legs were giving out. I don't know if it was from fatigue or fear.

I hopped in the back of the vehicle. I was pulling him in behind me when Dudley started to accelerate. The zombies were right behind us. The man still had the lower half of his body hanging out the back of the Jeep.

Hundreds of zombies chased us down the winding path of the exit. With the constant turning, Dudley just couldn't pick up enough speed to shake them off. With all the jostling, Kingsley and I couldn't pull the man into the Jeep.

The zombies were reaching out for him.

We were almost out of the parking garage when a zombie managed to grab a hold of the man's leg. The speed of the Jeep took the zombie off its feet, and then we were dragging his dead weight behind us. It weighed the man down even more.

When we left the parking garage, we hit a bump, and the man was torn from our grasp. I screamed for Dudley to stop the Jeep but he wouldn't listen. I frantically tried to reach out for Dudley. I had to make him stop, but Kingsley had wrapped me in a bear hug.

"It's too late Jaxon," He said. "They were on him the minute he fell."

I looked back towards the parking garage as we sped off down the street, and left our pursuers behind. I never even heard the man scream, or even learned the man's name.

That's one of the ones that still really bother me. To have your hands on someone and still be unable to save them…it's a bit hard to handle.

"I can see how it would be tough, but you did all you could. If you had stopped the Jeep, they probably would have ended up killing all of you."

He didn't answer me. He just seemed to sort of absorb my words as he pulled himself away from the disturbing memories.

So…yeah…Downtown was certainly a hotspot. If we left well enough alone, it would probably bide us some time. I'm just not very good at leaving well enough alone. Not when hundreds of people are about to be eaten alive.

Eventually, those poor souls would run out of food and water, or the zombies would break down their doors. It was an end for those survivors I wasn't willing to accept.

All of Downtown was in an uproar because of the commotion we caused. We could hear the screams, and moans of the dead echo in and around the city. It took us a while, but we finally found an alleyway that was free of movement. We parked in between two Dumpsters to hide us from the activity on the streets and it gave us a moment to collect our breath. Dudley and Kingsley were talking about the easiest way to get back to the Safe Zone.

"We can't leave just yet," I said.

"What are you talking about?" Kingsley asked. "The zombies aren't about to leave this area. We're home free."

"He's right," Dudley added. "We found out what we wanted to find out. Our job's done, and the Safe Zone isn't in danger of being overrun."

"It's not safe for the survivors that are stuck in those buildings," I replied. "We can't leave them to starve and get eaten. I just can't do it. Already I've seen two people die."

"Two people?" Dudley asked.

"Yeah, these buildings are filled with survivors."

"Oh shit…how many are we talking about?" Kingsley asked.

"Hundreds," I answered.

They took it in for a moment, heads down in thought. Finally, sighing in resignation, they both raised their heads one after another, and looked me in the eye.

"What's your plan?" Kingsley asked.

"I'm not sure yet. We need the zombies to follow us out of the city."

"And then what?" Dudley asked. "We have to be careful not to lead them to the Safe Zone." I thought it over for a moment.

"Why not lead them to the Safe Zone?" I asked. If we can get them all on the freeway, and headed towards the Westside, those survivors will have a chance."

"What about all the survivors currently in the Safe Zone?" Kingsley asked. He either didn't get my plan yet, or he just didn't like it.

"The current occupants of the Safe Zone will be long gone before the zombies get anywhere close," Dudley answered for me.

"There's no way out of the city Jax. I know you told everyone that it's time to leave and all, but I just don't see how you're gonna make that happen."

"Have a little faith," I told him. "As long as we don't give up, we can make something happen."

"I just don't think we'll be able to leave the Safe Zone," Kingsley whined.

"We are leaving the Safe Zone," I said roughly. "Anyone that wants to stay is more than welcome, but my guess is that most everyone will be coming with me."

Kingsley was pissed, but he wasn't going to argue anymore. I knew exactly what he thought. The Safe Zone was the only protection we had. He wanted to stay there, and wait for help. So, he must have believed that help was coming.

"And you?"

I did not believe that help was coming. When the zombies were finished tearing down all the locked doors and eating all the survivors, they would be headed to the next largest concentration of humans…the Safe Zone.

"Here's my idea," I said proudly. "Let's play pied piper but instead of rats, we'll use zombies."

"That makes sense," Dudley said enthusiastically. "We lead them a little ways down the freeway then take off, and leave them in our dust."

"And by the time we take off and leave them on the freeway," I added. "They will have smelled all the humans in the Safe Zone, and continue heading towards the Westside."

"Yeah," Dudley said. "It'll take them another day or two to even reach the Safe Zone. We'll be long gone."

"Are you sure you can get the survivors in the Safe Zone out of the city," Kingsley asked.

"No," I answered truthfully. "But I'm positive that when the zombies are finished here, they will eventually head towards our Safe Zone, and kill all of us regardless."

"All right…fuck it," Kingsley said. "How are we going to get them to follow us to the freeway?"

"You boys aren't going to do shit," a voice said from above. The three of us looked up and saw a man in camouflage staring down at us from a nearby rooftop. Merrick began a low growl.

"So you found another survivor in the city?"

Not really. We stumbled upon some mercenaries who were paid to sneak into El Paso and end the zombie threat.

"Who paid them?"

They wouldn't say. They came out of the building they standing on, and led us (at gunpoint) down the alley and into a two story abandoned leather store. We tried asking questions but none of them would answer anything.

"How many were there?"

There were eight of them in total. Five of them led us into the leather shop and the other three were there waiting for us. In the back of the shop was a large workroom with a metal table in the center. The walls were filled with maps speckled with red circles. We were told to have a seat at the table, and introduced to their leader whose name was Martin.

"Which one of you is the General?" Martin asked.

"I am," I answered.

"Way too young," he said as he sized me up, and down. "What the hell did you think you were doing?"

I was starting to believe that Martin was a dick. I've always had problems kissing people's asses.

"To which incident are you referring?" I asked in a low grumble. Merrick must have noticed my tone. She immediately put her head on my lap and gave a soft growl.

"Is that dog trained?" Martin asked. "I don't want to get bit."

"She's been doing okay," I answered.

"Good, I don't like hurting dogs. I must have something in common with them." Martin's men thought this was pretty funny. I mentally placed my hand on top of my pocket knife, which was in the right leg side pocket of my fatigues. They had removed our backpacks and weapons before leading us inside the building. The idiots just happened to overlook my pocket knife. If they made a move towards any of my party, dog included, I'd try to kill them all.

"Well that's lovely." I said in a calm voice. "It was certainly nice meeting all of you but I suppose it's time we were off."

"Look at this boys," Martin said to his men. "The General thinks he's calling the shots here. Well kid, I guess it's my pleasure to inform you that your time as the king is totally and completely... over."

"So, you wanna be the guy in charge. Is that right?" I asked.

"That's right. There's a new sheriff in town, and that's me."

"Fair enough," I answered. "You're the boss. Have fun with it. Can we leave now?"

Martin's men were still chuckling. I wasn't sure if it was because I was funny or if it was because I was asking to leave.

"Can't let ya leave, Mr. General," Martin said. "I'm gonna need you to lead me to this Safe Zone of yours after I'm finished up here."

"Why do you need that," I asked. This was getting scary.

Before Martin could answer, one of his men whispered something in his ear. They began mumbling back and forth in a heated discussion until Martin finally looked over at me once again and smiled.

"Gerald over there seems to think we're holding a tiger by the tail."

I looked over to the man who had been mumbling with Martin on the assumption that he was Gerald. The man looked worried.

"I've seen one of your types before," Gerald said. "Back in 'Nam."

"My types?" I asked.

"Guardians," he answered.

"Whatever," Martin interrupted. "I don't believe any of it. The General here is just some nobody that got in over his head. Isn't that right, Mr. General?"

"Whatever you say, Martin," I smiled.

"That's right Mr. General. Whatever I say; and I say it's time to annihilate all these zombies."

"You got a plan for that?" I asked.

"First we blow up Downtown...all of Downtown. Then we spend a few hours cleaning up whatever we missed. After that, we take charge of the Safe Zone, imprison all the survivors, and rig that to blow. When the leftover hordes of zombies.that weren't in the Downtown area arrive in enough numbers, we blow the Safe Zone."

"What about all the survivors here in the city and the Safe Zone?" I asked. "What happens to them when you set off the explosions?"

"Unfortunately, they won't be survivors much longer," he answered. "It's not ideal, in fact it's unfortunate, but it is necessary. Humans just happen to make the best zombie bait. We need them to draw in the zombies."

"You're mad," I said. "Do you even have enough explosives for all of this? And even after you blow the Safe Zone, you probably won't get anywhere near all the zombies."

"Yes, we have more than enough explosives. We probably won't get all the zombies but we're only after the large groups you see? If we haven't done enough damage after blowing up the Safe Zone, we'll round up more survivors, and repeat the procedure in different areas until we eliminate the threat. And maybe I am somewhat mad, but my methods will work."

"At what cost?" I asked.

"The cost of many lives, lives that are sooner or later going to end anyway, because the government will never render aid, and they will never let them out of this city. Play your cards right kid, and you might even be remembered as a hero. I doubt it though, not after I've reclaimed the city. Stand in my way or try to escape, and you'll just be dead, simple as that."

It was evident that the man was an asshole. I just didn't exactly know what my next move should be. Dudley and Kingsley weren't saying a word. So, for the time being I had no better option than nodding my head in acceptance of Martin's rule, and that's exactly what I did.

"Didn't you want to argue with him? All those people were about to be killed. Shouldn't you have fought for them?"

You can't argue with people like Martin. I've learned that a long time ago. It's best to just let them believe whatever it is they want to believe. Challenge their authority and you might end up with a bullet in your head for your efforts.

"So you were biding your time?"

Of course. I couldn't exactly do much of anything except get shot in that moment. There were too many guns in the room. I had to wait for a good time. I was just hoping that a good time would present itself before he blew up all of Downtown.

Martin left Gerald in charge of keeping an eye on us, while he went out with the remainder of his men to set the explosives in key buildings around the Downtown area.

Gerald didn't seem very comfortable around me.

"I want you to know something, Mr. General," he said. It only took him about ten minutes after everyone had left to strike up a conversation with me. "I don't much like the plan either but I have to follow my orders."

I just stared at him.

"So…if you're thinking about killing all of us, try and remember that when it comes to me."

"What do you think you know about me?" I asked.

"There was an outbreak back in 'Nam. I was in the Special Forces back then, Green Berets. One of my friends, his name was Max, he began to change…"

"What kind of outbreak?" I asked.

"Same as here," answered Gerald. "The dead began to walk. Max began to fight. All of us were trained soldiers but what Max could do…it was amazing. It was like he was born to kill those things."

"Did he heal fast?" I asked.

"Not on his own. He'd stand out in the rain or jump in a lake whenever he got hurt."

"That sounds a lot like you."

It sure as hell did. I was chomping at the bit.

"I can imagine."

"So what happened to Max?" I asked.

"The outbreak only lasted a month. We were left out in the jungle until it was cleared. Max did most of the work. We just followed his lead. When it was over, men came and took him away. I overheard one of them call him a Guardian."

"A Guardian?"

"That's what I heard. I can remember it even today. I can remember everything about that hell I went through."

"Who were the men that took him?"

"I really couldn't say. It wasn't like I was in the loop, and I never saw him again either, so I couldn't even tell you where they took him."

"So what can you tell me?" I asked.

"Not much at all. It's just that from what I read on EPUA, you seem to be following in his footsteps."

Well, it wasn't much, but at least it was something. He didn't have a lot of the answers but there seemed to have been a guy back in Vietnam that was able to deal with these things just like I was trying to deal with them now.

"And an outbreak of zombies made him change."

Yeah, without knowing a whole lot, Gerald actually knew a whole lot. Still, it was time to move forward. I had to stop these guys.

"Well Gerald, since you seem to know something about me, why don't you put down the gun and let us out of here?"

"If I did that, you would go straight after Martin."

"How do you know that?" I asked. He was right of course. I wasn't about to let Martin kill everyone in the Downtown area, I just wasn't going to admit it to Gerald.

"Because that's what Max would have done back in 'Nam," he answered with a knowing smile. "He felt the need to save everyone, just like you apparently do."

This was going nowhere. The guy was highly trained and armed with an assault rifle. All I had was a freakin' pocket knife. What the hell was I going to do?

The radio against the wall squeaked to life. It was Martin calling in his position.

"Tomcat…Come in Tomcat."

"Tomcat here," Gerald said into the receiver. "What's happening out there?"

"We've divided into three groups…Alpha, Beta, and Gamma."

"I read that Boss. Which group are you?"

"Alpha—"

The sounds of gunfire cut off whatever he was about to say.

"Alpha, do you read me?" Gerald asked. I could tell that he was becoming a little nervous. In fact he seemed on edge before Martin even radioed in.

"Maybe it was you?"

That could be true, but it seemed to go a little deeper than that. I think he maybe didn't like being stuck in an area full of hostile zombies. I can't say I blamed him either.

"So let me get this straight…during our last interview, I believe I heard that radios were not working during a conversation you had with Georgie. Yet these mercenaries were using a radio for communication?"

Right, the household and automobile radios were not getting any signals, but the military radios used for communication between these two parties were working just fine.

"I get it now. Thanks."

No worries.

"Did Martin ever radio back?"

Yeah but it took him about thirty minutes.

"We lost position Tomcat. I repeat…Alpha team has lost position." Martin gasped into the radio.

"What's going on out there?" Gerald asked.

"There's…"

More gunfire interrupted the transmission.

"There's more of the hostiles than we expected," Martin said. "A lot more."

"Were you able to set the explosives?" Gerald asked.

No answer.

"It's bad out there, Gerald. They may not make it back," I taunted.

"Shut the hell up! I'm not getting left out here. There are two other teams!" Gerald screamed as he rounded on me.

"Have you heard from those two other teams?" I asked.

"Shut the hell up," Gerald repeated.

"I'm your only hope, Gerald." I said calmly. "Let me know if you want to live."

After that, I leaned back in my chair and pretended to fall asleep.

"Why?"

Why not?

"Well, that just seems like an odd tactic."

Yeah, I agree. You need to remember, I was trying to deal with an ex Green Beret who was starting to lose it big time. If I made a move before the time was right, he'd blow a big hole in my chest for the effort. I'm not too keen on getting shot. So, I waited it out.

In the next hour Beta team and Gamma team both radioed in. Gerald seemed to calm down just a bit but the calm didn't last long. Both teams were attacked almost immediately. We could hear the two guys in Beta scream as they were eaten.

Gamma survived their initial attack but the two guys on the team were on the run.

"What happened to Alpha team? Isn't that the team with Martin?"

Yeah, that was Martin's team. Initially, they had three teammates, but they lost one during the last transmission. It was a while before they were able to radio back in.

Martin wasn't ready to give up just yet. I could hear him yelling and screaming over the radio. He wanted the Gamma team to regroup with wherever Beta team fell and pick up their explosives.

"How much was this guy getting paid? By my count, he'd lost three of his men and with only four left, he still wanted to continue his mission?"

Yeah. I was hoping he'd get eaten out there. It would make things a lot easier. No such luck. Meanwhile, Gerald was having a shit fit. He was trying to determine exactly where Beta team fell, and his back was finally towards us.

I looked over to Dudley and Kingsley. They looked shocked. I don't blame them; we were in the midst of idiots.

I gave Dudley a smile.

He gave me an *oh shit* look.

I stood up with all the speed and power in my possession. As I did that, I seized the table, and rushed Gerald.

Before the man could even turn around, I had him smashed against the wall with the table. I hit him so hard the table broke in two.

He was unconscious, and Dudley and Kingsley still had that shocked expression on their faces.

"I was wondering when this asshole would give me his back," I laughed.

"His friends are going to come after us," Kingsley said.

"No, they're not," I replied.

"The hell they aren't. We need to get out of the area."

"No they aren't, because we're going after them," I said.

"Fuck, Jax!" He shouted. "Those are trained soldiers. We can't fight them."

"Fine, we won't fight them but we do need to disarm those explosives."

"How are we supposed to do that?" Dudley asked.

"We'll get my buddy Gerald to do it," I answered. "Now let's grab our gear and get the hell out of here."

"So you escaped, and began a new mission, and that was to stop four mercenaries from blowing up the Downtown area. What about everyone back in the Safe Zone? Were they worried at how long you'd been gone?"

To be completely honest…I never even thought about it. We were having a bit of a situation. It would have made things easier if there was a radio in the Safe Zone so that we could communicate, but there wasn't. I also didn't have a laptop on hand to give them an update. They just had to wait it out.

"So what did you do after you grabbed your gear?"

We grabbed some maps, a radio, Gerald, and headed back to where we left the Jeep. Luck was with us, the way was clear, and none of the mercenaries thought to disable the vehicle.

Dudley was driving again. I was in the back with Merrick and Gerald. Luckily, I found some handcuffs that one of the mercenaries left behind back at the leather store, and I was able to handcuff Gerald to the side of the Jeep's roll bar before he woke up. Because, when he woke up, he threw an epic shit fit.

He screamed so damn loud I thought my ears were gonna pop. He also began to thrash around so much that he ended up kicking Merrick right in the face. She retaliated by promptly biting him in the leg and holding on for dear life as he screamed even louder and thrashed even harder.

The little episode caught Dudley by surprise, and he almost ran into a street sign. We were starting to attract attention as well. There were three zombies running after us.

I finally pulled Merrick off of Gerald's leg, and then punched him in the face when he didn't stop struggling.

I pulled my knife.

"Look behind us, asshole," I snarled. "You're attracting attention. Keep it up and I'll cut your Achilles tendon and toss you out the back."

"Would you have really done that?"

I wouldn't have cut him, but I would have tossed him. He was endangering all of us. Not a good thing to do, especially when you were aiming a gun at my face in the not so distant past. Regardless, the threat worked. Gerald shut the hell up. Dudley was able to lose the runners in just a short while. That was a relief. I didn't want to shoot them down and attract even more attention.

"Find us another alley Dudley," I said. "Gerald and I are going to have a little chat."

It took a short amount of time, but soon enough Dudley found a nice quiet alley. As soon as we had safely parked the jeep, a zombie ran for us. It came from behind a Dumpster. This one didn't scream because its throat was missing. It was a young boy of about fifteen. Its clothes were spattered with some sort of grey slime. Its skin was yellow, and slowly peeling away from its face. The sickest thing about it was the fingers. They were rotting away from the bone, and he looked as if he were wearing shredded gloves.

It ran straight for Gerald. Before it could bite down on his arm, I punched my knife straight into its forehead. It dropped dead, and Gerald stared at me with wide eyes.

"You are like Max," he said. "That was too quick, too fluid...too easy."

"Whatever," I answered. "Here's the deal. Four of your buddies are out there dropping some serious explosives. I'm going to stop them. Your job is to lead me to them. If you do that, you live. Fuck with me in any way...you die, any questions?"

Gerald shook his head, no.

"Radio both teams, and find out if they've set up any explosives yet."

It took him only a minute before he raised Martin on the radio. Martin had set three of his six sets of explosives. He was having trouble reaching the rest of the predetermined locations, due to all the zombies.

"He couldn't place them in other locations?"

I guess not. These bombs were huge. They also had a plan to lay waste to the entire Downtown area. I think they needed to be put in the proper locations for the maximum amount of damage. If the explosions didn't cover the entire area, they'd be pretty useless.

Gamma team had only just recovered the explosives from the fallen Beta team, and had just enough time to set one of their twelve charges (an extra six came from Beta). Needless to say, Martin wasn't happy about how far behind schedule Gamma team had fallen, and both teams were pissed at Gerald for his radio silence right when Gamma needed help pinpointing Beta's location. Gerald made his excuses. Radio problems seemed to be acceptable, and everyone went back to work.

"All right Gerald," I said. "Point out on the map where the four charges have been set."

I scratched at the map with the tip of my knife to mark the spots. Kingsley then took a look at the locations. He really came into play here; both Dudley and I suck at reading maps. Kingsley didn't know the area very well due to his shitty sense of direction, but he knew it a lot better than the both of us.

The first charge we went after was naturally the closest one to us. It also happened to be in a McDonald's, which in turn made me kinda hungry. The double cheeseburgers with no onions are to die for.

Anyway, we couldn't park right in front of the restaurant because there was a group of about twenty or so zombies milling around the entrance. They were probably leftovers from when the team planted the explosives, and if we tried to shoot our way through, we'd end up attracting thousands.

"What's that building behind our target area?" Dudley asked, sounding very military.

"I'm guessing it's an old hotel," Kingsley answered.

"Well, the rear of it is right next to the McDonald's. There aren't any zombies around its entrance, which is around the corner."

"I get what you're saying," I said. "Park the Jeep in front of the hotel, go through the building, and out the back exit. From there, I should be able to sneak into the back of the McDonald's."

"Sounds about right," Dudley said.

"What separates the hotel from the McDonald's?" Kingsley asked.

"I can't really tell," I answered, "but it looks like a narrow alleyway."

We quietly backed up the Jeep and went the long way around a couple of blocks until we were able to make our way to the front of the hotel.

"Let's make this simple," I said. "Dudley, you stay in the Jeep and keep a lookout for anything behind you. Kingsley, go to the corner of the street, and make sure the zombies in front of the McDonald's stay in front of the McDonald's. Gerald, Merrick, and I will go disarm the explosives."

"You think that it's a good idea being alone with him?" Kingsley asked.

"Yeah, Jax," Dudley said. "What if he gets away?"

I unlatched the side of the handcuffs attached to the roll bar, and locked it onto my left arm.

"He's not going anywhere," I said. "And you better know how to disarm those charges," I added to Gerald.

"Yeah," he answered. "I know how to disarm them. It's pretty easy, I could show you, and you wouldn't have to take me with you."

"Good luck with that idea," I sneered at him. I wasn't about to let an ex Green Beret out of my sight.

The sky overhead grumbled what sounded like a warning as we left the Jeep. I hadn't even noticed the rising humidity until then. I was surprised to find that I, along with everyone else, was covered in sweat. It hadn't rained since…hell, I couldn't even remember, but it was about to make up for it. I could see the lighting streak across the nighttime sky with the next rumble. I was thankful for the rain; maybe it would mask our scent.

I waited for a loud crack of thunder, and broke down the front door to the hotel. We were inside and moving at a quick trot. Gerald was keeping up with me just fine, but having him handcuffed to my left arm was annoying.

I handed Gerald a flashlight and he shone the beam in the direction that we needed to go. He wasn't armed, so he wasn't about to lead us into any danger. It was in his best interest to keep us both safe. Besides, I had my tomahawk in my right hand, in case he decided to do something stupid.

We were heading down a long, carpeted hallway when the sky above us opened up and let the rain fall. It was a hard, angry rain and once again I was happy about it. If I could hear it pattering off the walls of the hotel, then hopefully all the noise would cover any banging and crashing sounds made by me.

We got a little lost in the maze of hallways. It was really a matter of guesswork to find the alley exit. It took some time—I have no idea how long—but I was getting anxious. Some of the doors we ran past were open. It's never fun running past an open door in a dark hallway. Something could come jumping out at you.

"I take it that you speak from experience?"

Most certainly.

Finally, we found the exit. The rain was still making an obnoxious amount of noise. There was a fire alarm connected to the door. Not good.

"If you open that door, the alarm will go off," Gerald warned, as if I didn't know that was a possibility.

"I don't think there's any power to this building," I answered. "Look at all the dirt and dust. I think this place has been closed for a while. The front door was even boarded up on the inside, when I kicked it down."

"All that could have happened before the first wave of zombies came through."

"If that were true, where are the people that boarded the door?" I asked. "Never mind, I don't want an answer."

I really didn't want to hear Gerald tell me that the place could have been crowded with zombies, with all of them just waiting to pounce on us. It was time to make a move, and as I pushed open the door, I was secretly wishing that I'd paid more attention to the inside of the hotel, so that I could be sure it was truly an abandoned building.

We were lucky. No alarm sounded. The rain outside was pouring. The alleyway was narrow; not enough space to drive a vehicle through. I was trying to blink the rain out of my eyes, and locate a way into the McDonald's when the first zombie tackled me to the ground.

Merrick was attacking immediately, but it paid her no attention. Gerald seemed to have stumbled with my fall, and he was trying to pull away. His efforts were wrenching my arm that was connected to the handcuffs, and keeping me off balance. I could barely keep the zombie from my throat. I could hear the sound of splashing feet from farther down the alley. More of the dead were coming.

Idiot Gerald wasn't even trying to help me. Finally, Merrick grabbed the back of the zombie's head, and began to shake. Her efforts rag-dolled the dead guy and I was free. The zombie was fighting to get its head loose, but Merrick was shaking him so fiercely all over the alley, he couldn't get a firm grip on her jaws.

My tomahawk had come away from my hand when I fell. I couldn't find it in the dark pools of water made by the rain. The zombies I heard earlier were almost upon us; I could count at least five. Gerald was grabbing at the pistol on my belt as I searched the shadow covered, wet ground for my tomahawk.

"No you idiot," I said. "Others will hear the gunshots."

Finally, I felt the wooden handle. It was safe in my hand, and I stood in the pouring rain just as my undead attackers bore down on me.

The first one was easy enough to take out. As it reached for me, I sent the blade of the tomahawk into its forehead, destroying the brain. After that, I slammed the panicking Gerald against the brick wall of the motel, and ducked under the swinging arms of another zombie. I gave it a push kick to get some distance, and chopped it in the neck. It went down with a wet gurgling noise.

The remaining three were trying to surround us.

"Don't get bit," I snarled at Gerald.

They rushed at the same time. Two ran at Gerald and one ran for me.

My attacker ducked under my wild swing and I had to do a weird turn to crack it in the back of the head. It worked, barely, but it worked.

Gerald was on the ground. He was holding one zombie away from his throat, while the other zombie was savaging him at the knee. Suddenly, Merrick was on top of the zombie at his knee. Again, she had the corpse by the back of the head, and began shaking. I was free to dispatch the one at Gerald's throat. I then followed with another swing to the zombie being shaken by Merrick. The fight was over. I slammed the tomahawk into a fallen zombie that was still twitching, just to be on the safe side.

I turned my head over to Gerald who was just now getting to his feet. I raised the tomahawk into the air.

"No, no...wait a minute," Gerald screamed in a panic. "I'm not bit. Look and see, I haven't been bitten."

He was right of course. He had hard plastic kneepads under his green fatigues. The kneepads were now scratched up with teeth marks. I couldn't see any blood, so I lowered my weapon.

"I thought you were Special Forces," I growled at him.

"I was, back in 'Nam."

"Then why the hell are you such a pussy?" I demanded.

"These are dead people that are trying to eat me," he shouted back. "Excuse me if I'm a little freaked out."

"You either defend yourself, or you are going to die out here."

"Then give me a weapon."

I wasn't really sure I liked the idea. He could easily use any weapon I gave him on me the moment my back was turned.

"So, what did you do?"

I took a large Bowie knife from my backpack, and handed it over to him.

"So, you decided to trust him?"

I'm not sure that "trust" is the right word. I just knew that if I left him unarmed he was a liability, and I didn't want him wrenching my arm out of the socket again. I also believed that he had a pretty large desire to live, and that would be greatly diminished without me.

We went over to the McDonald's. The back door was metal. If I broke it down, it would make one hell of a noise. Even with the rain pouring, it would be too loud. We opted to break a window instead.

We did it intelligently. We stood there in the soaking wet, and waited for the next boom of thunder. When it cracked across the sky, and the lightning arced, I swung my tomahawk. The window exploded.

"Off subject...would you say that the tomahawk is your weapon of choice?"

Ya know...I never really even thought about it. I guess it deals the most damage to the enemy, and at the time, the enemy happened to be zombies that need a damaged brain to stay down. However, up until I grabbed a hold of the tomahawk, I'd always been more partial to knives. It's just more difficult to deal massive amounts of damage with them, especially against multiple attackers.

"If you had to choose?"

I'd choose both in a combination slash and hack. It would throw out a lot of damage, especially against more than one zombie...so, both of them.

"I only ask because my nephew wanted to know. He and his friend were arguing about it. I think they each had pictures of you with both weapons."

He laughed at this. I couldn't tell if it was because he's comfortable being a superstar for young boys everywhere, or because he's uncomfortable with his status in general.

Where were we? Oh yeah, we climbed in the window. It wasn't exactly easy; we had to be mindful of the large glass shards around the opening. We certainly didn't want to put the smell of blood in the air, even with the rain.

I also left Merrick in the alley. I didn't want her getting cut, and it wasn't like the zombies had any appetite for dogs.

The McDonald's was dark. I was wondering why Mr. Green Beret didn't have any night vision goggles. It wasn't like we could use the flashlight here. I'm sure everyone has been to a McDonald's. The restaurants are covered with large windows. If we used a flashlight, we'd have every zombie outside those windows licking their chops, and looking for a way in.

Did I mention how eerie it was looking out those windows at the zombies that were milling around? They didn't seem to mind the pouring rain at all, and the street lights outside were casting them in a weird yellow glow that would have been right at home in a horror film. Every now and then, one of them would moan that hungry sound of theirs, and another would answer. The sounds chilled my bones.

The explosives were in the restroom. They were in a large crate that would take at least two men to carry. There was some sort of receiver on the top of the crate. I was guessing that Martin's team put the explosives in the restroom to keep away from the windows. They'd be able to use the flashlights that way, just like we were.

I shone the light, and Gerald went to work on the receiver. He had it disarmed in just a few seconds.

"That's it?" I asked.

"Yeah, I just have to disconnect a couple wires."

"I'm thinking of some way to threaten you," I responded.

"I made it look too easy?" He asked.

"Sounds about right."

"Too bad, it was easy. I helped set these things up."

"Then you're an asshole. You'd solve the problem using the lives of thousands of innocent people. How's that make you feel?"

It really bothered me that they were so willing to blow up all these people.

"I think it sucks but this outbreak is huge, and the government isn't going to let these people out anyway. The borders of this city will remain closed until there isn't a single zombie or living, breathing, human being left standing. The risk of spreading the infection is too high."

A moan came from the street. I cracked the restroom door and took a look outside. It sounded a little loud for my comfort level. Gerald chose this moment to make his move.

He rushed the doo, and slammed my head between it and the wall. It hurt like hell and put stars in my eyes. I'm actually surprised he didn't knock me right out.

He followed this attack up with a neat little kick to my groin with his combat boots. I dropped to my knees. At this point, I was wishing he had knocked me out.

"You just don't wanna go down do you?" He asked.

The man had moves. His training was good. He knew how to hurt, and he knew how to use his environment.

He tried to bring the butt of the knife I'd loaned him down on the back of my head to finish me off, but I caught it with my free hand (we were still handcuffed). I guess I have moves as well.

I shoved his free hand away, and punched him in the gut as hard as I could. I heard the air go out of him, but he wasn't finished. His knee came out, and caught me on the temple. I picked him up off the floor, and slammed his back on the sink.

I was shocked as all hell when he still tried to come after me. I wrapped his handcuffed arm in mine, and broke it at the elbow. He began to scream.

I clamped my right hand over his mouth.

"Shut the hell up," I snarled. He answered by trying to stab me with his knife. I jerked out of the way of the blade, but he began to pull me back with his broken arm. His good arm was swinging the blade in a wild pattern, just trying to cut me. I couldn't escape, so I attacked. I grabbed his good arm and rolled on top of the man. We both struggled and in the end, the Bowie knife landed between his ribs and kissed his heart.

I had killed a man.

I didn't like that at all. It wasn't right. I had no choice, but it wasn't right. I pulled the knife out, cleaned it off, put it back in its sheath, and replaced it in my backpack.

I had killed a man.

I had killed a man.

I had killed a man.

I heard banging on the windows. The zombies had heard us. They wanted in.

Quickly, I shone the flashlight on the explosives. I memorized which wires Gerald had unplugged, unlocked the handcuffs, and then left the restroom. I was zooming down the hallway, and entering the main area of the restaurant when I saw the windows, they were swarmed by zombies.

So many faces pressed against the glass. So many hands cupped around the eyes for a better view, as if they could still think and function as well as they did when they were alive. A spider web of cracks formed on the glass from their pounding hands. I had seconds before they'd get smart enough to surround the building. I ran to my broken window and dove right through it. I was amazed that I cleared it so easily, but there I was, coming out of the dive in a nifty little roll in the rain soaked alley.

Merrick was happy to see me. The pouring rain refreshed me immediately. If I was bleeding at all from having my head smashed between the door and the wall, I wasn't anymore. I felt pretty damn good as a matter of fact.

I was back up and moving just as I heard the crunching of feet on the dirty gravel at the end of the alley. I hurriedly ducked inside the still-open door of the hotel and locked it behind me. Merrick was excited. I think she was having a good time. Things must be easier when the zombies have no interest in eating you.

In less than a second, the walking dead were banging to get in.

Fuck it. I just had to get through the building, make it to the Jeep, and I'd be safe.

That was easier said than done, unfortunately. I got lost almost immediately.

There were too many winding turns and too many dead ends. It sucked royally. I zigged and zagged. Finally, I came to the stairway that led to the upper levels. I was about to turn around and retrace my steps, when I heard a crash and the screams of the undead. They must have broken through the door. No good. They'd be able to sniff me out rapidly, and I was lost in the hotel labyrinth with a horrible sense of direction.

Well, since the dead weren't that far behind me…I took the stairs. If I could lead them up, then maybe I could lose them on the upper floors while I made my way back down. It may have been wishful thinking but I had no time for other options.

"Is your sense of direction really that bad?"

Bad is an understatement. I took a chance and peered over the railing when I was about five floors up. There I was, leaning over the railing and looking down at the ground floor just as one wet and decaying face decided to take a peek upwards at the same time.

It was another one of those *he froze-I froze* moments, and then I ran like hell. I mean, I really poured it on. I used everything I had. When Merrick had problems keeping up, I hoisted her up in my arms, and moved even faster.

The stairwell became a blur. When I reached the twelfth floor, I exited the stairwell and set Merrick back down on her feet. I immediately picked a direction and ran down the hallway. This time, I was hoping to find another stairwell.

What I found was even weirder.

There was a flickering light at the end of the hallway. I was walking cautiously towards the light when I saw debris in the adjoining hall. In the middle of all the debris were cans of gasoline. I ran to the cans of gasoline and checked them. There were four in total, and all were about half full. The debris surrounding them consisted of couches, box springs, and even a few mattresses.

I ran back to the stairwell and gave a listen, the zombies were still coming but they were still some floors down. I guess they had some slower moving corpses in the front of the pack that were holding the faster ones up. Either that, or I really hauled some ass. Not important. I propped open the stairwell door, loaded up a couple of sofas with the surrounding trash, and pushed.

Then, I went back for more flammable trash. I pushed all the new debris down the stairwell as well, and doused all of it with the gasoline.

I was rummaging through my backpack for matches when the zombies arrived. They were trying to shove the debris out of their way, and get to me, but I had loaded up so much junk at the bottom of the first flight of stairs leading down that it was all pretty much jammed in and successfully blocking their way.

Some of them decided to climb over. I reached out immediately, grabbed the first one over, and flung him down the entire stairwell. It took a few seconds, and then I heard the wet splat of his body as it hit the ground over the screams of all the zombies reaching for me through my barricade.

"This is one of those stairwells that have the winding stairs with an open center?"

Exactly, that's how I was able to look over earlier and see if they were following me.

"I understand. Could you see how many zombies were blocked behind the barricade?"

I was trying really hard not to…but yeah. There were a lot, maybe a hundred…maybe even more.

Others started climbing over the barricade. I made a last frantic search in the side pocket of my backpack, and found the matches just as a zombie was closing its hand around my neck.

I struck the zombie in the face, and then I struck the match…it broke. I was too frantic. I tried it again, and the zombie reached out for me once more. I lit the match and then I lit the barricade.

It caught in a loud 'whoosh.' I had to jump away from the sudden heat. The zombies on top of the barricade jumped, and twisted their way off the fire. At least two of them fell down the stairwell and slapped the ground floor.

I took a moment to relax. That one had been way too close. They were all staring at me but none of them dared to cross through the flames. Some reached out, but the heat made them instantly pull their arms back. They screamed their rage out towards me until I was forced to leave the stairwell. It didn't take me very long either, zombies can be pretty loud. I went back two more times and filled the stairwell all the way up to the door with trash, and waited a brief moment before it went up in flames.

I slammed the old metal door with a satisfied grunt, and then I even threw more debris in front of the door for when the fire went out.

Merrick was looking at me as if I'd gone insane.

Oh well, at least we were going to be safe for a while.

"Weren't you worried about the hotel catching fire?"

I was fortunate, like most of the stairs I've seen in hotels and buildings with multiple floors, this one was also made of metal and brick. Not things that you have to worry about catching fire.

"What happened with that flickering light you saw?"

I was just getting to that. As soon as I was free and clear to investigate my surroundings and find a way out, my first thought was that flickering light. It should have been to find another stairwell, but the curiosity was just too much for me, and yes I know the saying about it killing the cat.

I crept down the hallway as quietly as I could. It wasn't difficult to cover up my noise. The screams and moans from the barricaded stairwell were rattling the walls. Anyway, maybe it's better to say that I approached the flickering light as cautiously as I could.

The light was coming from beneath a door to one of the many, many rooms. I was positive it was the light of a fire. I felt the door; it wasn't hot to the touch. Merrick gave it a sniff and wagged her tail. That wasn't something she'd do if there were zombies lurking behind the door. I tried the handle; it was locked so I gave the door a hard kick and broke it down. There was a chair propped against the, now broken, door and it flew across the room to hit the opposite wall. The door itself flew off its hinges. I was standing before a group of terrified teenagers. Against the wall was a laptop that was connected to the Internet; it was logged on to the EPUA website.

"I assume I don't need to introduce myself," I said.

Chapter 5

CALVIN

Calvin wasn't hard to spot. He was the young man surrounded by bodyguards. That isn't why he was so easy to spot though. He's been on countless talk shows, and news reports. In his own right, he's as famous as the General, just not in the same way. As I just said, he looked young, very young, but he's as outspoken and articulate as someone twice his age. He won't place himself anywhere near the General, but he did agree to meet me outside of town in a small coffee shop. He was wearing a dark suit despite the heat, but didn't seem bothered by the weather.

Personally, I'm rather shocked that you asked to meet with me.

"Why would that be?"

Well, it's pretty common knowledge that I'm the General's biggest detractor.

"Well, when I decided to write this book, I decided to tell the entire story. There are people that believe in him, and there are people that don't. I need to hear both sides in order to be as accurate as possible."

Does he know that you're interviewing me?

"Yes."

And how did he take that information?

"He didn't seem to care."

You see; that's just like him. If you were writing a book about anyone else in the world and went to interview their enemies, they'd be nervous. This guy is so full of himself that he invites such an action, and has no fear of it whatsoever. It's arrogance.

"I see. Do you really consider yourself his enemy?"

Not in any physical sense, but yes. I don't think his actions should be sanctioned. I believe, if anything, he should be placed in prison. Now tell me, are you a fan of his, or do you sit on my side of the fence?

"Actually, I must admit that I'm a fan. I've seen, and spoken with thousands of people that he's rescued, and I've seen the famous fifteen minutes of footage."

Ah, the famous fifteen minutes of footage. Yes…the footage that turned a violent man into a hero. Well, I knew him a little bit before that footage came out, and let's be honest…it is the footage that really made him a superstar. Anyway, I knew him a little bit before that, and I can tell you that I had an instant dislike for him the moment I laid my eyes on him.

"Why don't you tell me about that first time you laid your eyes on him?"

That's what everyone wants to hear. Instead, I'll take a moment to explain how we all got stuck in Downtown El Paso in an abandoned hotel.

Being younger, we had, all of us, been raised on horror movies. It wasn't hard to figure out what was going on. The dead were coming back to life, and they were hungry.

There were six of us in the beginning, Rachel, Rebecca, Jen, Heather, Thomas, and myself. We had gathered at Jen's apartment for a little bit of swimming. We had the volume on the radio up pretty loud, so we heard the exact moment the local news started to report the outbreak.

Rachel and Rebecca were both in their early twenties, with almost identical light brown hair. They were as close as sisters. Rachel had just acquired a new job at a daycare where Jen had been working for the past year. The two of them became fast friends. Jen was a redhead, and smoked way too many cigarettes. Her friend Heather was incredibly tall, and had straight blonde hair. Thomas was Heather's brother. He was also tall, but he had dark brown hair.

The radio reports kept getting worse and worse, so we turned on the television and saw the rampaging dead for the first time. Right then and there, we decided to leave town. Rebecca wanted to bring her father with us, but he wasn't answering his home phone. It didn't take her long to remember that he had previously mentioned something about doing a little shopping at a military surplus store Downtown.

I was against going Downtown. I thought the safest thing to do would be to leave El Paso immediately. Obviously, no one paid me any attention.

We loaded up some supplies into some backpacks and hopped into Heather's truck for the trip Downtown. I've never liked this part of town—despite being where all the lawyers are located—it was dirty and filled with poor people. It just wasn't of my taste. Regardless, if Rebecca wanted to find her father, everyone but me seemed willing to help. I jumped on the bandwagon, of course. What else could I do? I was dating the girl.

It took three hours to get there, and in doing so, we drove through the worst kinds of hell I'd ever seen. We saw the freshly made zombies. It was still early on, and the Westside (where we were) was just beginning to break out, but we still saw more than a few of them.

The moving corpses were, more often than not, covered with blood, and running down Mesa (one of the main streets on the Westside) in search of someone to eat. Sometimes they ran from car to car trying to see if any of the doors were unlocked. More than once, a wet dead thing rattled the latches on my side of the truck. They had the hungriest eyes while they did this.

Everyone's heard that zombie scream. Well, we were right there and stuck in traffic as it sounded out all around us. We were terrified, but we didn't leave the truck. Others did, and we saw them fall, and sometimes rise back up in search of living flesh.

Finally, Heather couldn't take it anymore. She drove onto the median, and left the traffic jams behind. Other people tried to follow her example, but there were too many of them and they formed yet another traffic jam on the median. We were just lucky it was behind us. The freeway wasn't very crowded when we hit it. Everyone was headed in the opposite direction, which was away from the biggest outbreak. We were headed right towards it. Of course, we didn't know at the time how fast it was spreading.

Eventually, the Downtown traffic jams became so bad that we had to abandon the truck. I knew it was a bad idea, but everyone else was in support of finding Rebecca's father.

"Look around," I told them all. "Look at how many people are running around over here. It's like finding a needle in a haystack."

I was right, of course. We never found the man. There were thousands of people rampaging through the streets. Some were looting the stores; others were just running for what appeared to be no apparent reason. Then, suddenly, everyone came to an almost abrupt stop. I didn't know why, somebody must have heard something. It became so quiet you could have heard a pin drop. That's why we finally heard it…somewhere in the distance…a scream.

The streets and sidewalks were packed shoulder to shoulder with people. The scream came from farther down the street, somewhere behind us. Every head turned in that direction. I don't know who saw what, or if anyone actually saw anything, but one thing was for sure…a fear had set in all of us.

It was pandemonium after that. A free for all that involved every living soul seeking shelter. The six of us managed to hide in a small, cheap, clothing store on one of the many streets. The owners of the store let us in after we pounded on the door for a good five minutes. It wasn't safe by any means, the entire front of the store was made of glass, but it was better than nothing.

A few minutes after that, we saw the first zombie run by. It brought down a woman, and began to tear at the flesh on her leg with its dull teeth. Jen got sick. The rest of us froze in place as we watched the zombie chew into what must have been a major artery. The gushing blood spread out over the sidewalk. We couldn't turn away. Some idiot, who obviously wasn't paying attention, ran right by the zombie, the zombie left the woman in exchange for chasing down the idiot.

In seconds, the woman rose to her feet, and spotted us. She charged head first into the glass front of the store. The impact knocked her off her feet, but she got right back up, and pounded the glass with her fists.

Her frenzy attracted other zombies, and very soon the front of the store was littered with the fresh undead. They wanted in. They wanted to eat our flesh. Their fists became bloody pulp while they pounded and pounded.

The glass wouldn't hold forever, in fact it was already beginning to wobble dangerously in the metal frame.

The owners gave us a case of bottled water and we left them in the store as we exited out the back. I'll never know why they refused to come with us. They only spoke Spanish, and I'm afraid that I've never mastered that language.

We ran from street to street looking for a safe way out of the area, but it seemed that in every direction that we tried to turn, people were running in the opposite direction. None of us thought it would be a good idea to run in a direction that hundreds were running away from. It was chaos, hell. I knew it was a mistake to come Downtown. I knew it, and none of them listened to me. Well, they were all ready to listen after they saw everything that was happening.

We began to see the zombies. More and more of them were making an appearance. Their numbers were growing as ours were dwindling. There were certainly a lot fewer people on the streets.

"All right," I said. "We aren't going to be able to leave the area, it's too dangerous. We need to find a place to hide. Somewhere where there aren't a lot of idiots that will give away our position."

"I saw an empty building by the McDonald's we ran past a little bit ago," Rachel said.

So, off we ran in that direction. It was good that they were finally taking my advice. People need to be led. Without a leader, they'd wander around in circles until one of these corpses bit them on the leg.

That was exactly what happened by the way.

On the way to this empty building, we passed this parking lot, and it came running out after us from the backseat of one of the cars. We ran…but Rachel fell behind. I looked over my shoulder, and I saw a zombie grab her by the hair, and pull her to the ground. She screamed and screamed. Rebecca tried to run back and help her, but I caught her by the arm, and dragged her away.

"There's only one of them," she screamed at me. "We can help her."

"No," I shouted back. "We'll end up just like her if we go back."

It didn't take long to find the building Rachel brought to our attention. It was perfect, completely abandoned, and had been for years. We all climbed through a broken window in the rear of the building. I had Thomas and Heather do a quick search of the first floor. They both came back in under twenty minutes. The place had indeed been closed up tight with the exception of the broken window we all just climbed through. I had Jen and Rebecca seal up the window with some of the many boards scattered around the floor.

"Now, let's all just sit tight, and wait for help to arrive."

They all just stared at me.

"What kinds of supplies do we have?" I asked, ignoring their stares.

I knew that I hadn't carried any supplies but the rest of them had their backpacks.

"I only brought my laptop," Jen said.

"I brought a little bit of food, and I still have the water that they gave us at the clothing store," Heather said.

"I just have water," Thomas added.

Rebecca said nothing.

"What do you have, Rebecca?" I asked.

She still said nothing.

"Rebecca," I shouted.

"We could have saved her," she mumbled.

"She was beyond help, sweetie. There was nothing we could do."

"There was only one of them. We could have…"

"No Rebecca," I told her. "We lost her the moment you dragged us all Downtown. We should have left the city like I wanted to."

"No…" she stammered. "You wouldn't let me…it's not my fault."

"Yes, Rebecca," I told her. "It is your fault. If I have any blame, it's in letting you bring us down here."

The shuffling footsteps put an abrupt end to whatever she would have said in reply. We heard the noise clearly, but none of us could pinpoint the direction.

With all the windows boarded up, the only light that was coming into the first floor was the little bit filtering through the cracks in the boards. It wasn't nearly enough; there were too many shadows, and dark corridors.

The vagrant came out of the hallway farthest from all of us.

He froze in his tracks when he saw us all there staring at him. From what I could see of his clothes, they were mangy and covered in that dirty grease that bums tend to accumulate on all their belongings. His long hair was matted down with sweat against the back of his neck. I could smell him from way across the room.

"Hello there," Heather said.

There was no reply.

The vagrant merely continued to stare at us.

"You doin' okay over there, buddy?" Thomas asked.

As if to answer, the vagrant began to shamble towards us.

I didn't like this one bit. All the hairs on my arms were standing on end.

Rebecca walked right over to him. She was a foolish girl.

"Sir, are you okay?" She asked. "Would you like some water?"

The vagrant didn't answer until she was a mere few feet away. I probably should have stopped her from getting close to him, but she'd probably just tell me how rude I was.

It's my belief that the vagrant crawled through the same window the rest of us had, only we weren't bitten like he was. I'm guessing he died very soon after he made it through the window.

He screamed in Rebecca's face and tackled her to the floor.

His face was buried in her neck before the rest of us could react. I ran in the opposite direction. Heather, Thomas, and Jen ran to help Rebecca.

As I rounded the corner, I realized I was alone. I headed back and watched as the three of them pulled the zombie off of my dying girlfriend. Of course, there was nothing they could do. All they accomplished was aggravating the zombie.

It started to grab at them wildly. I realized why it never ran at us. It had been bitten quite severely on the lower left leg. All it could do is shamble around at a rather slow pace. It would be easy to outrun.

I shouted at every one to follow me, and once again, when everything had gone to hell… they listened.

"What about your girlfriend?"

Look, this is where I get into a lot of trouble. I have a different belief system than people that grew up on comic books. In my view, the greatest thing we could do was survive. I had no idea of knowing whether or not this outbreak would spread out of the city. The world didn't need heroes, the world needed survivors.

"When you're referring to heroes, can I assume that you're speaking of the General?"

Of course I am. I died inside when I saw my girlfriend get attacked, but there was nothing I could do the minute she was bitten. If I tried, I would have endangered myself needlessly.

Now the General, this is a guy that got lucky and survived his first encounter, and then it all went to his head in one of the greatest power trips the world has ever seen. This man is nothing special; he's just a guy that left his friends (whom he should have been protecting, and keeping safe) over and over for glory. In doing all this glory searching, he also endangered the people he brought with him on his little adventures, not to mention all the property damage he caused.

"So you believe that he should not have risked himself to save others?"

Correct, the smartest thing any of us could have done was to stay somewhere safe and hidden. The minute we stopped doing that we endangered those that were already under our protection, and who's to say that all those people needed him? Who's to say that the government wouldn't have eventually come in and saved everyone?

"Well, the government said that."

At the time the government said that they wouldn't go into the outbreak due to the risk of spreading the infection. I understand that, but what people need to understand is that the government said that during the *initial phase*. No one knows what they would have said, or done, later on. I believe public outcry would have forced their hand.

In other words...we didn't need the General.

"Okay, let's get back to your story. What happened after Rebecca was attacked?"

We ran like hell.

That's the simple and straightforward answer. I didn't grab a weapon, and defend everyone by risking all our lives. I led them to safety.

We headed to the stairwell and made it to the twelfth floor. As soon as we exited the stairwell, I heard the first zombie scream from Rebecca. It was a hard moment for me. I froze at the stairwell exit. Thomas, Heather, and Jen were waiting for me. It wasn't easy, but I forced myself to forge ahead.

The windows weren't boarded up on the upper floors. The sunlight was shining through in the dusty hallways. I found us a room that looked decently habitable for the foreseeable future.

I barricaded the door behind us.

"Rebecca's still out there," Jen said as she lit a cigarette. "We need to do something."

"She was bitten," Thomas said. "I don't think we can do anything for her."

"We can put her out of her misery," Heather said.

"No," I replied. "There's nothing we can do but wait for help."

Everyone looked at me but none of them said a word against me. After all, I was right; the risk was simply too great.

It wasn't long before Jen took out her laptop, and found EPUA. We all took turns reading the posts. I knew that eventually, this nasty outbreak would be taken care of. It was just a matter of time.

What came instead was something different. I don't remember how many days had gone by but it was Jen that saw the first post from the General. He was bragging about how many of the dead he had slain. He was immediately searching for attention. When he signed off, others took over the bragging for him. His legend was spreading like some sort of disease in the human body. I don't blame the survivors; they wanted a hero in their time of need. I don't blame them at all. I blame the General for taking advantage of the situation.

Jen, Heather, and Thomas were immediately members of his fan club. Like all the others, they were searching for someone to believe in. I kept my opinions to myself, even when others began to describe his battles, which they just happened to see with their own eyes. His trip to meet all the survivors at Lowe's was especially repulsive to me.

You are aware that he posted messages summoning all the survivors to join him at Lowe's, correct?

"Yes, in fact he personally told me the story?"

Good…and you are aware that 172 survivors gathered together under his summons?

"Yes."

So, if 172 people made it to him, how many people do you think died on their way?

"What do you mean?"

I'm saying that if only 172 survivors actually made it to Lowe's, I then have to wonder how many people were killed trying to get there.

"I see…I don't believe there are any numbers for that."

How convenient.

So there we were, gathered around that little laptop. The days wore on and on. Our water supply was getting somewhat low and even I was beginning to wonder when, or if, help would arrive.

It wasn't long after the General blew up some apartment complex that we were reading about how he was headed to the Downtown area in order to see how bad things had gotten down there.

Of course, my three companions were elated. They were positive that their salvation was on the way. I tried to calm them down. After all, how lucky could one man get? I was sure that he'd turn tail and run once he saw the state of Downtown El Paso.

"What was the state of Downtown El Paso?"

Every evening, more and more zombies would arrive. They tended to stay low in the bright light of day unless something caught their attention, but at night they wandered the streets. We carefully watched from our windows as the zombies claimed the outside world. Thousands of them would pass the street that connected to the alley beneath our window. It was frightening. Their moans and screams would sound out and echo off the many buildings. Every now and then, a scream from a living being would join the undead screams and we would know that another soul was forever lost.

"It must have been terrible?"

You have no idea. The sheer number of zombies that passed our viewpoint was staggering. Waves and waves of them would pass by our alley, followed by fifteen minutes of nothing, and after that another wave that could last for hours. We had to crane our heads to the right a little bit to see the street, so we all had sore necks. It wasn't long before we stopped watching altogether. The sheer volume of the dead was just too disheartening.

"Did you ever consider making a run for it? Try and escape the area?"

We wouldn't have made it past the corner of the first street. It would only take one of them to spot us, scream that wretched scream, and thousands would be chasing us down. We were safe where we were, trapped of course, but safe nonetheless.

It was late in the evening when we saw the lights of the vehicle reflect off the window. At first even I was elated. It wasn't long after that we heard a door smash from far below on the ground floor. Someone had entered our building. The rain began to fall from the sky. It was Thomas, who was looking out the window, who first saw the two men and the dog.

"There are people leaving our building," he shouted.

Everyone ran to the window. We watched the quick life and death struggle that occurred in the alley. We watched as they entered the McDonald's. We waited for them to return but it was only the one man and his dog. No zombies had entered the McDonald's; of that, I was positive.

Anyway, he had stirred up a hornets' nest. The dead were well aware of his presence, and they were eager to make his acquaintance.

"It's the General," Jen said. "It has to be. Who else could fight like that?"

"We need to get his attention," Heather added.

"Stop it, all of you!" I ordered. "It very well may be the General, but he's leading all those zombies straight into our hotel."

"Then we need to let him know that we're here," Thomas said. "We need his help to get out."

"No," I said. "If he knows we're here, that glory hound may lead them straight to our room. Let's just be quiet and hope that he leads them all through the hotel and back onto the street."

"This could be our only chance," Jen said.

"And which one of you would like to go down there and look for him with all those zombies streaming into the hotel?"

Of course, none of them were very eager to leave the room, and I sure as hell wasn't going to do it.

It wasn't long before we heard the sound of the stairwell door being slammed open. Shortly after that, we heard noises in the hallway…sounds of banging, sliding, and crunching.

"This is when the stairwell barricade was being made?"

Yes. We could hear the dead screaming out for him. The idiot had led them right to our floor. We were all in danger because of him.

The whump of a sudden fire echoed through the halls. We heard him slam the stairwell door and pile rubbish up in front of it.

We heard the doorknob of our room rattle and we heard the dog sniff underneath the door. None of us moved. I don't believe my three companions knew how to react but I knew…I was hoping that he'd go away, and leave us in peace.

Instead, he kicked the damn door off the hinges.

"I assume I don't need to introduce myself," he said. The arrogance was amazing.

Now, if you're thinking that some knight in shining armor showed up at our door with a white pony to save us, you are sadly mistaken. The man was a beast. He certainly didn't look like any hero I'd ever heard of. He looked as if some hell-bound gladiator just time-traveled straight out of a Roman Coliseum into our hotel.

The General's probably just a shade less than six foot, but he's a wide man. His shoulders are immense; they remind me of a silverback gorilla. He was wearing black clothes that were ripped, and torn. His skin was dirt smudged, and pale. His hair was very short, and there was stubble on his cheeks. It must have been days since he last shaved. His eyes were fierce. It's not that the green in them was brilliant or anything…it was more about the stare. He looked as if he were about the rip us all apart.

All in all, he wasn't a man who other men would bother. Whatever mold that created him came from the past. It was a mold designed for killing machines; a mold that was once needed to win wars, but no longer had a place in our modern times.

His dog was no better, a pit bull. An animal designed to fight. This creature was, at best, unpredictable. I was afraid to get anywhere near it.

"Are you the General?" Jen asked. She was in awe. I could tell what she was thinking…if anyone could save us, it had to be him.

"Call me Jax," the General said.

"It is you," Heather added. "I knew it had to be you. We saw you in the alley."

"Let's cut the chitchat," the General said. "We need to move, that barricade won't hold them for long."

"Who says we're going with you?" I asked.

At this point, the man stared at me long and hard. We were two leaders sizing one another up. I won.

"You're free to stay if you want," he said, "but those things will be coming right for you as soon as the flames I lit die down."

"We aren't staying," Heather said.

I looked over at her. I tried to give her one of those looks, but she refused to meet my gaze. I wanted her to shut up. Unfortunately, it was too late. The damage was done. One idiotic voice influenced the rest of them.

"Is there another stairwell?" The General asked.

"Yes," Jen answered. "I saw one down the hallway when we were looking for a room."

"There are other zombies in the hotel," Heather added. "We were running from them."

"How many?" The General asked.

"At least two," Heather answered. "We didn't see anymore."

This man wasn't even trying to create a plan. He found it perfectly acceptable to lead us all straight into danger, and hope for the best.

"What happened to the man that was with you in the alley?" I asked.

He gave me one of those wild stares again. He looked like he wanted to rip me into pieces. I was hoping my companions could see what I was seeing. The man was a violent animal.

Unfortunately, I set him off. Before I could even blink, his hand shot out and grabbed the front of my shirt. Then he shoved me hard against the opposite wall. The plaster around me crumbled.

"I'm not going to play games with you," he said. "You can stay here or you can come with me. If you choose to come with me, then you need to shut the hell up."

I valued my life, so I kept my mouth shut for the time being. I firmly believed that violent man would kill me if I said another thing to upset him.

"Are you now aware that he had to kill the man you were just asking about in self-defense?"

I had a pretty good idea even back then. As far as him saying that it was self-defense…well, that's debatable, I'm sure. After all, it's very convenient that there were no witnesses.

"Do you think a man who has dedicated his life to saving others would be able to kill another man in a situation that didn't involve self-defense?"

He had just thrown me into a wall. Yes, I believe that he's quite capable of ending another human being's life without much provocation. Like I tried to tell you earlier, the man that broke down our door was the personification of rage and violence.

As I looked at him, I could tell that he meant what he said. I don't believe it's just a dislike for the General that has caused him to speak out (though there is definitely a strong dislike). He actually believes the General is a dangerous human being.

We were all off, and tearing down the hallway in search of Jen's stairwell. She didn't remember exactly which hallway she saw it in, and it was a lot brighter the last time we were outside our room. The search took too much time.

At last, she found it.

The General carefully opened the door and peered into the darkness with his flashlight.

"Looks empty," he said. "I'll go first just to make sure. All of you stay close behind me and keep quiet. I want to be able to hear if anything's creeping up behind us."

Just then, we heard pounding on the door of the barricaded stairwell.

"The flames must have died," the General said. "Run."

He started shoving us down the stairwell into the darkness. It was dangerous. Anything could be lurking just beyond the beam of the flashlight, which he had handed to Thomas.

"I forgot the laptop," Jen said.

"Oh shit," Heather added. "We may need that."

With that she was off and heading back towards our room. The General reached out for her and missed. In just a brief moment, she had rounded the corner, and was out of sight.

"There's not enough time," the General shouted after her, and then to us he added. "Stay here, and don't fucking move."

Things happened in bright flashes of horror after that.

The General broke off at a dead run for Heather just as I heard the stairwell door give way. I could hear the zombie screams as they flooded through the door, and past the hastily erected barrier.

Just as the General reached the hallway corner that Heather had taken, he was met by what looked like thousands of zombies pouring into the hallway.

He slid to a stop in slow motion. The zombies screamed that hellish scream and then they charged.

He ran back towards us with the dead hot on his heels.

He barely made it to us, they were that close.

He was closing the door when undead hands reached in through the crack, and scratched at his face. The blood they drew caused them to go into an even greater frenzy.

They were screaming and pounding and shoving, at the door. Jen and Thomas began to help push it closed as the General hacked at the reaching, and clawing hands with his tomahawk.

Blood began to spray in our little area before the stairs.

At last, they were able to close the door just as we heard Heather begin to scream.

The zombies had found her.

For a moment we all just stood there listening.

Thomas was the first to break the silence.

"That's my sister," he shouted as he reached for the door. The man clearly wasn't thinking. If he opened that door, we'd all be goners.

I jumped on top of him and pulled him to the ground.

"Don't open that door," I shouted as he struggled beneath me.

The General separated us easily and held Thomas against the wall.

"It's too late," he said. "I'm sorry but it's too late."

Thomas began to sob, and clutch at the General's shoulders. Jen was just standing there in shock. Heather wasn't screaming anymore.

"Let's go," the General said. And with that he pounded away down the stairs. We had no choice but to follow him.

We reached the ground floor in no time at all. The General paused before opening the stairwell door.

"Be ready for anything," he said.

Slowly, he opened the door. It creaked very loudly. Anything around surely knew where we were.

We stepped out slowly, and cautiously. The vagrant zombie that killed Rebecca had been waiting for us. From behind the door, it shambled towards the General.

The man had no fear; he whipped out a knife, and slammed it into the zombie's temple as it reached for him.

"That's the one that got Rebecca," Jen said.

"Then I should have let one of you do it," the General answered.

"We should take Rebecca's body," Thomas said. "I don't want to leave anybody else behind."

"Her body isn't here anymore," I answered.

Calvin went quiet for a moment.

"She had turned?"

Yes, she turned. I was already looking for her remains before Thomas suggested we take her body with us.

I did care about her, you realize. I just knew it was too late to do anything.

"Let's go," the General said without any concern of the pain we were all going through. "I have a Jeep waiting outside."

Rebecca came tearing out from behind the front counter as we headed towards the door. Most of her mid-section was missing. A few pieces of organs were trailing out of the large hole. The scream that came from her mouth was nothing that could ever have come from her when she was alive.

I froze. I didn't know what to do. I just froze.

The tomahawk went flying past my head with tremendous force. It landed in the middle of Rebecca's forehead with a disgusting, wet, crunch.

The General had no remorse. I had just seen my girlfriend die for the second time, and he merely walked by me, stuck a foot on Rebecca's throat, and yanked the tomahawk out of her skull.

"Let's go," he said.

He walked out into the wet night without looking back. The rest of us were in shock. We had never seen a man kill so carelessly. I know he was only killing zombies, but there wasn't even the slightest bit of hesitation. There was also no consideration for what the three of us were going through.

"Did you follow him outside?"

Yes, we had no choice.

The black Jeep was waiting right in front of us. The rain had slowed down to a soft drizzle. A man was waiting inside the Jeep and another was standing by the corner. Scattered between them were the remains of at least ten zombies. When they saw us emerge, they came running towards us.

"Kingsley, put Merrick up with you. These three can take the backseat; I'll balance in the trunk by the tailgate," The General said.

"Dudley got bit," Kingsley said in reference to the other man.

The General grabbed the young man's arm, and removed the piece of clothing that was serving as a bandage.

"Fuck," the General said in a quiet voice. "That's deep."

"Yeah," Dudley answered. "Burns like hell."

"Keep it covered," the General said. "I'll take a look at it later."

With that, they started getting into the Jeep.

"Wait a minute," I shouted. "He's going to turn. That's what happens when you get bitten. He's going to turn into one of them."

The General went insane.

"Shut up," he shouted as he pulled a pistol from his belt, and walked towards me. "Shut your mouth. Not another fucking word." He pushed the barrel against my forehead. "You got that? Not another word."

I put up my hands in surrender.

He walked away, and started firing the weapon wildly into the front door of the hotel while screaming out profanities.

"Jax," Kingsley said. "We need to go."

The General seemed to calm down for a moment. We could hear screams echoing from between the buildings. His outburst had been heard. The dead were coming for us.

"All right," the General said. "Load up."

We didn't wait a second. We all just hopped into the Jeep. As Dudley turned the ignition, the General walked to the back and stepped into the area between the backseat and the tailgate. He held the roll bar for support. His dog wanted to be next to him, and she whined in protest as Kingsley held her to his chest.

"Find us a safe place, Dudley," the General said. "We need to talk."

I think I'm the only one who noticed, but there were tears in the man's eyes.

"You saw this?"

Yes.

"So you can at least admit that the man cares about others?"

I can admit that he is capable of caring about a few people. I didn't see him shed any tears when we lost Heather.

Dudley drove around the maze that is Downtown for just a little while when Kingsley spotted a dark-looking alley. Dudley turned the Jeep around and entered the shadows.

As soon as we stopped, he fell out of the vehicle. His skin was as white as a sheet. A sickly sweat was pouring from his forehead.

"It fucking burns," he said as he ripped away his makeshift bandage and shoved his arm in the dirty water of a rain puddle.

"That water is dirty," the General said in a concerned voice.

"But it's cold. I need to take away some of the burn," Dudley answered.

No one said a word as we watched the dying man soak his arm in dirty water. None of us even knew what to say.

It was a shock when he suddenly started screaming.

"Ah…fuck…it feels like my skin is ripping."

"What?" The General asked.

"It hurts like hell," Dudley groaned.

"Let me see," the General said as he yanked Dudley's arm out of the dirty puddle. He studied the wound for what seemed an eternity, and then he began to laugh.

After looking at his wounded arm, Dudley began to laugh as well.

"What the hell?" Kingsley asked.

Dudley responded by holding his arm out. The wound had stopped bleeding.

"You're like Jax," Kingsley said.

"Kind of…I think. Not as fast though."

"Who gives a shit," the General said. "You're gonna be fine. Keep soaking it."

"I thought I was a goner," Dudley said.

"Fuck no. You're too gay to go out that way," the General answered as he patted Dudley on the back. Kingsley began to laugh.

We waited around in that dark and dangerous alley for another fifteen minutes before the pain of the wound settled down. Dudley eventually pulled his arm out and the bite looked to be about a week old.

In truth, it probably was. I think…no…I believed that it was all a lie.

"You don't believe that he was bitten?"

Yes, I believe that he was bitten. I just don't think the wound was recent, and no, I didn't get to see his arm until after he had pulled it out of the puddle.

"Do you think the wound was made by a zombie?"

Of course not, it's just all part of the show.

"Pull out the map, Kingsley," the General said. "I want our next location."

"What do you mean, 'our next location,'" Jen asked. I myself wasn't about to open my mouth again.

"There are two groups of mercenaries setting up explosives to blow apart the entire Downtown area," the General answered. "We need to stop them."

"I thought you were taking us to the Safe Zone."

"Just as soon as I keep all the other survivors from getting blown up," the General said.

He then turned back to the map without another word of explanation.

"Okay," Kingsley said. "This is where we are, so that means that the closest target for us would be in this bank."

"All right, let's go," the General said.

They loaded back up, and off we drove. It took some time to get to the bank due to all the abandoned cars on the route Kingsley had chosen.

We were also rushed by a sizeable group of zombies. After the sounds of gunfire had died off, I simply couldn't take it any longer.

"What if we just leave," I asked. "Can we do that?"

"Of course you can," Dudley said with a shocked look on his face. "But why would you want to? It's pretty fucking deadly out there."

He was right. I couldn't leave just yet. It wasn't safe but as soon as it was, as soon as I found a safe place to wait it out, I planned on taking it.

"I'm not going anywhere without them," Jen said.

"Are you serious?"

"Yes. We won't survive without them."

I gave up on the idea immediately. She had obviously fallen too deeply for their act. Thomas was also a lost cause; he'd do whatever Jen said to do. There was no getting the two of them away from the madness. Yet, if the opportunity came, I'd certainly save myself.

"If you wanna leave now, Calvin, I'd be happy to toss you out of the Jeep," the General said with a laugh.

I ignored this; we had finally made it to the bank. There were no zombies in sight.

"I'll take Merrick inside with me," the General said. "Dudley, stay in the Jeep with our passengers. Kingsley, you wait outside the Jeep and keep them covered. Remember…no guns."

I don't know how long we waited, probably about twelve minutes or so, before the General came back outside with a frown on his face. Fortunately, we hadn't been attacked while we waited around for him, but we did hear gunfire coming from a few streets down.

I also found it rather convenient that we had to wait outside, in danger of being attacked, while he was able to go inside the relative safety of a bank.

"You don't think it was dangerous inside a dark building where zombies could be hiding around

every corner?"

Calvin pointedly ignored my question and continued with his story.

"There were seven survivors inside," the General said.

"Are they going to be safe in there?" Dudley asked.

"They're all dead now…bullet holes; it's pretty fresh."

"What happened?" Jen asked. Thomas was still quiet, still in shock.

"Gamma team killed the survivors to get them out of the way," Kingsley added.

"Was this one set up by Gamma team?" The General asked.

"I think it was."

"I was hoping that they'd still be here."

"Well, they can't be far. There are too many zombies around. They'd have to clear out an area before they could set up a bomb, and we just happened to hear shots from not very far away."

"Fuck it," Dudley said. "Let's just take them out. That way we won't have to chase them around for another eleven charges."

"Now you're talking," the General laughed. "It's not gonna be easy though. These guys are armed and trained."

More shots began to ring out in the night. The General paused to listen for a moment, and then continued.

"Does the gunfire sound nearer or farther away now?" He asked.

"Sounds about the same as it did when you were in the bank," Dudley answered.

"All right, hopefully they've been pinned down, and with all the shots they're firing off, they probably have half the undead in the city boxing them in."

"Then we could just leave them there, right?" Kingsley asked.

"That might be possible," the General answered. "I just want to make sure."

It didn't take a rocket scientist to understand that these three men had just decided to kill their fellow human beings.

Chapter 6

JAXON

I had to wait a while for this third meeting with the General, which took place in a bar just out-side of Tombstone, Arizona. Supposedly, there had been recent reports of an undead outbreak in the area. When he finally entered the room, he was holding two beers. He offered me one of them while he grabbed a seat across from me at the table. He seemed tired.

"I've just finished my interview with Calvin."

I'm sure that was insightful. How far did he take you?

"He took me all the way to where you come out of the bank, and decide to go after Gamma team."

Ah, yes…I remember that.

"Is it true that you decided to kill those men?"

The short answer is, yes. Those guys were trained killers, and there was no way they were gonna just surrender because I asked them nicely. They were intent on blowing up the Downtown area. I was intent on stopping them. One way or the other they were going to be stopped.

"Would you have taken another option if it were possible?"

I was prepared to take any option available.

"Is it true that you put a gun to Calvin's face and threatened him?"

Hell yeah, the guy's a dick and a coward. There were moments when he could have saved peo-ple; instead, he chose to run. He thinks only about saving himself. I have no respect for him, and when he started crying about leaving my nephew behind, well…I just wanted him to shut up.

"He views you as a dangerous and violent man."

I am a dangerous and violent man. I make no apologies for that.

I couldn't help but laugh a little at his honesty. He was a man who simply did his job. It's not his job to impress others or try to get into their good graces, and he apparently had no intentions of trying to do so.

"What were you thinking when you saw that your nephew had been bitten."

I don't know that I was thinking. I just kind of went numb. There wasn't a single part of me that was willing to believe I was going to lose him.

"So you were ignoring the situation?"

No. I just froze. It was too much to handle. Family is family. There's nothing thicker than blood. If it turned out that I lost a friend or a family member…well, I don't know if I could handle that.

It's not something I like to think about. It's not a situation that anyone would be comfortable thinking about.

"So what happened after you came out of the bank?"

We heard the gunshots. Actually, the boys were hearing the gunshots before I even got out of the bank. We decided that both Gamma and Alpha team needed to be stopped.

"Was that an easy decision to make, considering you might have to kill them?"

I'd just walked out of a bank where they massacred seven people.

"Tell me what happened."

The bomb was easy enough to disarm; it was just…seeing those seven people who probably thought help had arrived…it wasn't easy.

I also realized the commitment to the mission Martin's entire group must have had. If they were able to execute innocent people, in addition to using them as bait to achieve their goals, were they going to stop just because we disarmed their explosives?

They weren't. Their callousness was evident.

"What do you mean?"

I mean that if we chased them around, and disarmed all the explosives like we had originally planned, we were just delaying them, not stopping them. They would eventually just re-arm the charges after we left the area. They weren't going to give up just because their bombs didn't go off when they pushed the button. They'd go see what went wrong, and fix whatever wires I pulled. The only way to stop them would be to face them, and force them to stop.

"So what did you do?"

I told everybody to wait by the Jeep and I went for a walk with Merrick.

We took the alleys for the most part. I was smart enough to bring their little radio with me. It was a heavy sucker to be lugging around but I managed.

It didn't take me long to pinpoint where Gamma team was holed up. They were in an auto salvage yard that had a chain link fence around the front, and high buildings on either side. Inside the salvage yard they had a large military truck loaded with the same explosives I'd been trying to disarm. Apparently, they weren't able to accomplish much of their mission before getting themselves surrounded. I'm guessing they had made too much noise.

There were hundreds of zombies surrounding the fence. To keep them from climbing over, they had ignited a wall of flame along the length of the fence, but the flames wouldn't last forever.

"So, they were in trouble?"

Possibly, it was hard to tell from my vantage point, but I could see that one guy was assembling what appeared to be one of those high powered machine guns (the kind they use to take out aircraft) on top of a little wooden shack. The shack must have served as the office for the salvage yard, and the other guy was setting himself up on a pile of wrecked vehicles with what looked like a grenade launcher.

Whatever they were planning, Mr. Grenade Launcher was waiting patiently for Mr. Machine Gun to get his weapon prepared. I don't think they'd originally planned on using it, because half the weapon was still lying in pieces in the crate.

Every zombie around was focused on Gamma team. So it was easy enough for Merrick and I to force our way into the three-story building across the street, and make our way to the roof. Once there, I had a perfect view of Gamma team and the zombies surrounding them. If the guy with the grenade launcher started shooting grenades into the group of zombies and blowing them to bits, it might just be easy enough for his teammate to finish off whatever was left standing with the machine gun.

I used the radio.

"Gamma team…can you hear me?" I asked.

"I can hear you, ya bitch," Dudley whispered.

In an effort to not look like a pussy, I can assure you, I only jumped about a foot.

"You asshole," I snarled. "You're lucky I didn't kill you in a reaction."

"You couldn't kill me in a dream. Now, what the hell are you doing?"

"I'm going to talk to Gamma team," I said. "Why aren't you with the others?"

"It's boring over there, and I'm getting sick of you wet nursing me."

"Whatever, don't cry to me if they get attacked and you start feeling bad because you were responsible for all their deaths."

"I'm pretty sure every zombie in the neighborhood is on its way towards these noisy bastards," Dudley said with a laugh. "Still, I wouldn't mind if that little Calvin guy took a few bites."

"Not a big fan of Calvin?"

"Mother fucker wanted to leave me…and he cries too much. He was sitting there whining about how you were endangering us all. He wanted to leave you behind, and head for the Safe Zone. To hell with all the survivors trapped here."

"Maybe we should have told the little weasel they plan on heading to the Safe Zone after they finish here," I said with a snicker. "So, what did you do?"

"I punched him in the face and followed you."

"Nice one," I laughed. Now maybe he'll…"

"This is Gamma, who is this?"

We'd forgotten about the radio. Dudley and I looked at each other as if we'd been caught doing something wrong in science class. Finally, I shrugged.

"Who do you think it is numb-nuts?" I asked with a smile. I couldn't help pissing the guy off.

"Is this Gerald?" the guy on the radio asked.

Dudley peered over the lip of the roof to see who we were talking to.

"It's the guy with the machine gun," he whispered.

That was good news. I wanted to delay him as much as possible.

"Look Gerald," Mr. Machine Gun continued. "We can't raise Martin, and we're surrounded. Nothing we can't handle, but it's going to take us some time."

"Gerald's dead ya toad sucker," I said. "And if you don't agree to give up the explosives, you're going to join him."

There was a few seconds pause as my words bounced around the guy's head.

"You just made my hit list, pal," he said. I guess he knew who he was talking to. A loud crack and boom of thunder echoed in the skies above us. The rain began to pick up once again. Things were certainly headed in my favor.

"Last chance, Rambo," I said. "Agree to give up the explosives or I rain down hell."

"As soon as we're done here, I'm coming after you."

Mr. Machine Gun then turned off his radio.

"Did you really think they were going to give up?" Dudley asked.

"Not really," I answered.

"You got a plan?"

"Yup, see how the rain is starting to put out their fire?"

"Yeah, when that goes, they'll be crawling in zombies," Dudley answered.

"Not if they get that machine gun set up. The other guy on top of the cars has a grenade launch-er."

"Yeah. I can see that," Dudley said. "So what's the plan?"

"The chain link fence."

"What about it?"

"Watch."

I picked up my rifle, which I had propped up against the lip of the wall, and took aim. I fired once, and believe it or not, I missed.

Mr. Machine gun spotted our little hiding spot on the roof immediately and returned fire with the automatic weapon strapped to his chest. There was a little bit of good in this, because instead of assembling his weapon, he was wasting his time on us. There was also some bad, because we were now being shot at. I grabbed Merrick's big fuzzy head, and pulled her down under the lip of the roof with me.

"What the fuck are you doing?" Dudley shouted.

"I missed. Gimmie a freakin break," I shouted back.

"You shoot as bad as Georgie?"

"How about you go fuck yourself."

"Hey, check it out," Dudley said in an abrupt subject change while motioning towards Gamma team.

Even from across the street I could hear the two men arguing. I chanced a peek, and saw that Mr. Grenade Launcher must have noticed that the flames around the fence were dying down in the heavy rain, and Mr. Machine Gun hadn't fully assembled his weapon. The zombies were getting excited; they'd soon be able to climb over and chow down.

I took a glance at the unassembled weapon. Progress had been made; it finally looked like a machine gun. That made me a feel a bit rushed, so I took aim once again, and fired just as Mr. Machine Gun tried to take off the top of my head. My aim was true. I hit the lock on the gate.

The flames around the fence had died down considerably. One zombie braved what few flames remained, and pushed against the gate. It swung open freely. Gamma team was swarmed within moments. Mr. Grenade Launcher managed to launch a grenade. The explosion shook our building, and took out a decent number of zombies, but that barely slowed the mob down.

Dudley and I sat back and listened as both men screamed their last screams.

"Well," Dudley said. "You did try to warn them."

"Yeah," I answered. "Let's go find Martin."

Truth be told, I was a bit distracted. I expected to feel some sort of remorse. I had just killed two more people. However, I didn't feel bad about it at all. That sort of bothered me. I wasn't sure I wanted killing to be easy for me.

I never mentioned that to Dudley, by the way. I just grabbed the radio and led the way back towards Kingsley and the Jeep. We were at a good jog when we reached the final turn and something felt wrong. I slowed to a creep and peered around the corner of a building.

I saw the Jeep but only Thomas was inside of it. It looked like he had fallen asleep. I knew better.

"Where is everybody?" Dudley asked after peering over my head.

Our radio crackled to life.

"Mr. General, can you hear me, good buddy?" Martin asked. "Be a pal and try not to irritate my Gamma team if you don't mind? I still have three of your friends left, and I'd hate to have to shoot them as well. Tell me, was this Thomas a close friend of yours?"

"Don't say anything about Gamma team," Dudley said as I reached for the microphone attached to the radio.

"No shit," I retorted.

"Were you concerned? Or were you confident that you could save your friends?"

I was totally panicking is what I was doing. I normally just react. I don't plan too far ahead, so while confidence rarely enters the picture, panicking and I are old friends.

"Hey, Martin," I responded. "Do me a favor, and kick that Calvin in the balls for me as hard as you can."

To my shock, they did exactly as I asked for.

I hate to laugh at the suffering of others, but I laughed. The entire situation between the two men wasn't especially funny when I was hearing things from Calvin's point of view, but hearing things from the General…well it was a bit difficult not to become sadistic, and join in on the fun.

I could hear Calvin moaning and crying over the radio. I felt kind of bad for the guy, but to be honest it was something we all laughed about later.

"All right Martin," I said. "Tell me what I have to do to get my friends back…and Calvin."

"You can have them back when you turn yourself over to me, pal."

"And what happens when I turn myself over to you?" I asked but I already knew the answer. There were seven victims lying in that bank that just happened to get in the way of his men.

"Well, things aren't looking so good for you, I'm afraid. But once you're out of the way, I'll be sure to let your friends go free, providing they don't do anything to upset me."

"Gimme a minute," I replied.

The situation was about as fucked as fucked could get. I had no idea what to do. There was no way in hell I was going to let that crazy asshole put a bullet in my head, but for the life of me, I didn't know what to do.

I thought about storming the bank, I was pretty sure that was where they were hiding. There were, however, two problems with that idea. The first one was that they may not be in the bank, and the second was that even if they were in the bank, they might kill the hostages before I could bring them down…if I could bring them down.

"Well, you obviously didn't end up turning yourself in, because I'm sitting here talking to you."

Yeah. Like I said, that wasn't an option. If I turned myself in, he'd probably just kill everyone anyway.

"Does the bank have a backdoor?" Dudley asked.

"I have no idea. Why?"

"We could try to sneak up on them," he answered.

Now, to be honest, I thought that was a pretty bad idea. I mean…we weren't exactly trained soldiers, and I highly doubted that we possessed the skill to sneak up on a bunch of ex-military mercenaries.

Dudley could sense my hesitation.

"You got any better ideas?" he asked.

"Fuck it. Let's see how it looks," I answered.

I left the radio where it was and Dudley, Merrick, and I crept across the street and made our way towards the rear of the bank.

We encountered some zombies on way. They were milling around the back of the neighboring building.

Have you ever seen a startled zombie?

"I can't say that I have."

It's kind of funny. They aren't used to it at all. They tend to look up or turn their heads in this over-exaggerated kind of way. Then, they stare at you for a second as if they can't believe you just walked right up to them. After all that, they sometimes scream, but they always charge.

We were on top of them before they could scream. One of them was able to grab a hold of my leg before I pushed my knife through the top of its head. Merrick grabbed another zombie by the wrist, and began shaking it all over the place while Dudley swung at it with his machete.

"Don't hit my dog, asshole," I snarled.

"I'm not gonna hit your dog."

"Make sure you keep it that way," I retorted.

Ever since that time, I've always joked with Dudley that he should keep Merrick beside him in case he needs any help. She'll be more than happy to hold them down for him.

"Does Dudley find this funny?"

Not a bit.

Anyway, we got the drop on the zombies, so they weren't exactly a problem. Yet, there was no rear exit to the building.

We stood under an overhang on the building next door to get out of the rain. We were soaked to the bone. It was a cold rain, but it wasn't horrible; it was a break from that humid heat. "Let's move up the side of the building through that little alley," I said. "Maybe there's a side entrance."

Between the bank and whatever building was next to it was a little alley about four feet wide. It was littered with all kinds of rubble and extremely dark. I doubted that there would be an entrance but I figured that we might as well check and see.

Halfway through, we saw that a car ramp blocked off with a chain link fence that separated the bank from the alley. There was no way to get inside the bank.

We were now towards the front side of the bank, still in the alley, and crouching beside the car ramp. As luck would have it, and I do consider it to be sheer, dumb luck, I happened to see movement in the corner of my eye as I craned my head over the ramp in order to see the front of the bank.

The movement was coming from the window of an office building across the street from the front of the bank.

I had just found Martin.

It was a smart move not to be waiting for me in the bank, because that was where I expected him to be. Instead, he was waiting for me across the street, ready to come from behind when I entered the front door.

I motioned to Dudley and watched his eyes grow wide when he realized what I was looking at.

"I'm going to act like I think they're holing up inside the bank," I said. "I'll put my arms up and everything."

"What the fuck?" Dudley said, astonished.

"Just listen," I snapped. "After I go in the bank, one or both of them will come running out of that building and enter the bank behind me. They'll think they got the drop on me. All you have to do is follow them in and start shooting."

"What if I miss?"

"Then try again. If you miss, trust me that I'll be firing as well. We'll give them two targets, and they'll be trapped between us."

"What if only one comes out, and the other starts shooting the hostages?" asked Dudley.

"I don't really know," I answered with complete honesty. "You got any better ideas?"

"We could try going in through the rear of their building."

"It's an idea," I answered.

"It's what we were going to do if they were in the bank and the bank had a rear entrance," said Dudley.

"Because we had no other options...I don't really like going with the whole, I have no other options approach." I said. "At least this way, we're sure to take out at least one of them...hell, maybe even both of them, and if not, maybe the other one will give up when they realize they're the only one left."

"I'm just worried that they'll end up shooting our buddy, or that Jen chick."

"Maybe we'll get lucky, and they'll shoot Calvin first."

We had a brief laugh once again at Calvin's expense. It was brief, because we had to do something soon. Martin was probably getting very antsy since we weren't communicating with him anymore.

"Let's do it," I said.

Dudley nodded his head in agreement, and I left the alley with my rifle held up high over my head. Merrick wasn't happy, but for some reason she stayed with Dudley.

The minute I reached the street and began to walk to the bank's entrance, I felt eyes upon me. Worse than that, I felt that ugly feeling of having a rifle pointed at me. I got just a little bit nervous they'd shoot me down in front of the bank instead of coming out and getting me. I was hoping that Martin was sadistic enough to want me face to face when he pulled the trigger.

Just as I reached the glass entrance of the bank, I heard movement behind me. They were making their move.

I guess they didn't want to wait for me to get inside the bank. Martin's man had been waiting behind a car on the side of the road for me to make my appearance.

"Stop right there," he shouted.

I froze in my tracks.

"Keep your back to me and back up," he shouted.

I did exactly as he said.

I turned my head a little bit to the right, and I saw that he was still crouched behind the car. Dudley didn't have a good shot.

"Don't turn your head," he screamed at my back. "Keep walking backwards. Turn your head again and I'll fire."

I took his advice, and continued to walk backwards.

"Stop right there," the man shouted when he was satisfied with the distance between us. "Where's your friend?"

"I have no friends," I answered. "Nobody likes me."

"Did you really say that?"

Trust me, I've said a lot worse in worse times than that.

"I'll bet you have."

"You wanna be a wiseass?" snarled the man as he stepped out from behind the car, and began to close the distance between us.

"You got him covered?" shouted Martin. It sounded like he was at the front door of the office building.

And then Martin began to scream out a warning, just as the sound of a gunshot echoed up and down the street.

He must have seen Dudley stand up and take aim, but his warning came too late. Martin's final man took a straight shot to the head. He was dead before he even realized he'd fallen into our trap. I felt his blood mist against my back. It was a warm feeling that fought against the cold of the rain before finally dropping its temperature and joining the wet drops in a final embrace.

Martin was pissed. He spun immediately, and sprayed automatic fire at Dudley. Dudley however, must have the reflexes of a cat, because he wasn't even scratched before he was safely out of sight behind the cover of the concrete car ramp.

Martin immediately turned back towards me, (luckily he wasn't still spraying bullets everywhere) but it was too late. I already had my pistol aimed at his face.

He lowered his rifle immediately.

"You really think you're something, don't you?" he asked. Dudley came out of hiding with Merrick just about dancing around his feet. He joined me in aiming at Martin's face.

"Well, my wife likes to think so," I answered. "Throw down the rifle."

He did as I asked.

"I don't mind throwing down my weapon," Martin said. "But I don't surrender. I don't think you have the stones to shoot an unarmed man."

"I think I do," I told him. After all, it wasn't like he wouldn't do the same thing.

"I have a better idea," Martin said with a bit of a desperate whine in his voice. "Why don't you drop your weapon and face me man to man."

To be honest, it was just about the stupidest thing I've ever heard. Why in the world would I drop my rifle and fight this guy? I mean, I won fair and square didn't I? If the situation were reversed, I'd already have a bullet in my head. There was no way in hell I was gonna give up my advantage and fight this asshole.

"So what did you do?"

I handed my rifle over to Dudley, like an idiot, and told him to hold onto Merrick.

"Why?"

Because I didn't want to shoot an unarmed man in the face, and there was no way that I could let him go. Also…I just kinda wanted to kick his ass.

He rushed me immediately. I let him take me down; I wanted him close. He was faster than I expected, but not by much. His elbow came down on the ridge of my brow and opened up a deep cut. I felt the hot blood begin to flow.

I grabbed a hold of the offending arm before he could do anymore damage to my face, and used it to flip him over onto his back.

The cleansing rain washed over my cut, and I felt it begin to knit itself closed. I brought my face close to Martin's, so that he could see it heal.

His eyes went wide as realization set in. I wasn't a normal man. He wasn't going to win this fight.

I let him have it. I hammered both of my fists down on his face until it was unrecognizable. It felt good to do him damage. He deserved it for all the bad things he'd probably done in his life and all the bad things he had planned.

After his face was pummeled and his body had gone limp, I got off of him.

"Go ahead and get Kingsley and the others," I told Dudley.

"No problem," he answered, and ran off towards the office building with Merrick hot on his heels.

Just as he went inside the door, Martin made his final move. He pulled a gun from who knows where, and fired one shot at me. The bullet skimmed against my bottom rib. I felt the burn, but I was already in the motion, returning fire with my pistol.

I pumped two in his chest, and Martin was dead.

Dudley and friends came out of the office building just as the bullet wound healed itself up in the rain. For some reason or another, Kingsley had a military duffel bag slung across his shoulders. All of them (except for Dudley) had the red marks left from bindings around their wrists.

I wanted to ask Kingsley why he had the duffel bag but Dudley broke my train of thought.

"What happened?" Dudley asked.

"He pulled a gun and shot at me. I shot back."

"Sure he did," Calvin said.

"Go fuck yourself," I said.

"Kingsley found the detonator," Dudley interrupted, before Calvin said something stupid.

"Where is it?" I asked.

"I tore it into pieces and threw it in the trash," Dudley said as he held up a radio. "But I brought their radio with me."

"Can we leave now?" Jen asked.

"Yeah," I answered. "Just as soon as we convince most of the zombies in the area to chase after us…it shouldn't be too hard."

"Well, we better get moving then," Dudley shouted, and suddenly began firing his weapon down the street. Apparently, our shots had attracted the attention of many eager, and hungry, zombies.

"How many?"

It looked like at least a thousand from where I was standing. They were coming out from every alley, and side road from the opposite direction of the street. Fortunately, we were headed in a direction that was still clear, and I won't even tell you how fast we made it into my Jeep.

"What about the other radio, the one that you left on the corner before you went after Martin?"

We picked it up just as we were tearing off. It almost cost us big time though. The zombies were right on top of us.

"So your plan of playing pied piper was off to a good start?"

I would have preferred some time to map out a route to take but yeah…I guess you could say that we were off to a good start. We certainly had a lot of company. All we had to do was zip around until we got the rest of the Downtown zombies to chase after us.

I had Kingsley crank up the Jeep's CD player just to attract more attention, and what do ya know, it worked. The dead just kept on coming. They began to pour out after us from everywhere, buildings, more alleys and side roads, Dumpsters…you name it.

"What were you playing on the CD player?"

Johnny Cash, of course.

"I heard that you were a fan of his."

Something cool about that man.

"Sorry to jump off subject, I just had to know."

No problem.

So, if I really put my mind to thinking about it…I believe that the zombies had been tracking us ever since we left the courthouse. We had just changed locations so often that they were never able to pin us down. There were also some decent distractions from Martin and his men, but all in all, we were very fortunate that we hadn't been cornered by a group of this size.

"I guess the battle outside the bank gave them enough time to pinpoint you and catch up?"

That's my guess. We were also fortunate that the opposite end of the street was pretty empty. There was no way we would have been able to reach the Jeep if we had to go through the thousands of zombies that were running after us.

"Well, did the plan work? Were you able to get more zombies to follow you?" Were you able to lead them to the freeway?"

Yes, yes, and yes. It wasn't easy. I can't even count how many times we almost drove into a dead end street, or ran into a road that was just about blocked by abandoned cars.

It also wasn't easy to maintain a decent speed in the rat maze of Downtown. We had to go fast enough to keep them at a distance (in case we ran into some sort of road block) and we had to go slow enough to keep them following.

If the entire episode were a scene in a movie, it would have been quite hilarious. Dudley was steering the Jeep all over the road. Thousands of zombies were chasing after us, with hundreds upon hundreds joining the mob every second. Everybody was screaming directions over the blaring CD player, and every now and then Dudley would randomly shout out "fuck" at the top of his lungs when he got too confused.

It was only funny in retrospect though…at that moment it was scary as hell. We weren't able to leave until we drove through all the main areas of Downtown. We had to make sure we had most of the zombies following us.

When I was satisfied that we had the bulk of them in hot pursuit, we headed towards the freeway.

"About fucking time," Kingsley shouted over Johnny Cash. "I'm pissing my pants over here."

Dudley began to laugh just as a zombie ran out from a building, and almost collided with the side of the Jeep. I was able to pop him in the head with my pistol before he grabbed a hold of the vehicle.

Things were getting to that point now. I doubt it was intelligence that told the zombies to head us off, we were just attracting too many of them. Because of that, it was inevitable that they'd start coming at us from all sides. It wasn't much of a problem earlier, probably because they were a little shocked at our audacity. They stood there and stared for a second before running after us. They weren't shocked anymore, however. We had been playing this game way too long. They were getting used to the noise. They probably heard the music from a few streets away, and began to actively look for us. As soon as we were in their sights, they charged. Occasionally, it was from the front and sides. Things were getting dangerous.

To make things even worse, they were also starting to close the distance between us from behind a little bit. Something about the vast numbers must have enabled them to gain some speed. Maybe they were competing with each other. I don't really know, but every now and then I'd have to shoot one down that was getting too close.

"I can't imagine the kind of fear and tension you were all under."

I guess it kind of comes with the territory, but let me tell you. Having that many zombies running after you…it's not something you'll ever forget. The screams, the smell, the fear…it all gets burned in your memory.

Anyway, we were getting out of there while the getting was good. We decided to hook a turn at the Abraham Chavez Theater, because from there it would be a straight shot to the freeway.

"What's the Abraham Chavez Theater?"

It's just a huge building where they hold conventions, and theater productions, and things like that. Has its own underground parking as well. So it really is a big, big, place.

As soon as we roared on by the Abraham Chavez Theater, even more zombies came rampaging out after us, and in the middle of this massive horde of the undead…I saw the strangest thing yet. At least I thought I saw it.

"What was that?"

I thought I saw a woman who was chained by her foot to a spike that was pounded into the concrete, right there in the front of the Abraham Chavez Theater.

"Really?"

I know, it sounds weird. Let me set this up. There is a large paved patio area in front of the Abraham Chavez Theater. This area has walkways, and places to sit. It's really a pretty decent size. I went to a tattoo convention there once, and they even had a live band playing inside this patio area.

"Okay, I'm following you."

Well, the part of the patio towards the front doors of the Abraham Chavez Theater has a few steps, and at the top of these steps…I thought I saw a chained woman.

"What about all the zombies?"

They were all over the place. About as many as we had following us, probably even more. The noise alone could make you deaf.

"Not to sound morbid or anything, but wouldn't the zombies be eating her?"

You would think so, but they weren't. They weren't even paying her any attention. As soon as they saw us pass, they all ran right by her and after us, as if they didn't even care about her.

"Could she have been a zombie?"

No. Of that I was certain. There was nothing corpse-like about this woman. In fact, she was rather attractive. I mean…I only got a quick look before I lost sight of her, but she also seemed kind of sad.

"What was she wearing?"

A black dress.

"Did she wave or motion to you…or anything when you drove by?"

No but she definitely saw us. I saw her lift her head up, and just kinda look in our direction.

"What did everybody else say?"

I was the only one who saw her, and I wasn't about to tell anybody about it. They'd have thought I lost my mind. There was also nothing I could do for her. We had a couple of thousand zombies running about eight feet behind us.

Like I said though…I only saw her for a second. I could have been mistaken, so I filed it away under "what the hell was that?" and focused my attention back on the situation at hand.

Dudley made a left at the freeway and hit the gas.

"Slow down," I told him. "We need to lead them a little bit more."

"Damn, Jax," he answered angrily. "This is getting crazy."

He was right. Looking behind us at all those enraged, once human faces…yeah, what we were doing was pretty damn crazy, but I knew that if we hit the gas and left them behind they might lose interest and head back Downtown.

I needed them closer to the Westside before we hit the gas. That way, it wouldn't be long before they caught wind of the Safe Zone and headed there, but…damn those faces…their expressions weren't even close to human anymore.

"Yeah, it's a pretty frightening picture."

Tell me about it.

"Just thinking about one little Jeep leading thousands of zombies down the freeway…wow. I don't know how you kept so calm. What if the Jeep broke down or ran out of gas?"

We'd be dead. There's no doubt in my mind, we'd have been swarmed in seconds.

As luck would have it though, the Jeep didn't break down or run out of gas. We made it to the UTEP (University of Texas at El Paso) area, which is kinda the beginning of the Westside, and hit the gas.

In no time at all, the zombies were so far behind us we couldn't even see or smell them anymore. We could still hear them though, the screams and moans weren't happy. I think they were just a little bit upset about losing their meal.

We let the music play for a bit. Don't know why. Maybe we were finally able to enjoy it. I even saw Dudley begin to bob his head with the beat a little bit. Kingsley was finally relaxing, I could tell by the slump of his shoulders. Merrick had the top half of her body on Kingsley's lap and appeared to be napping. Jen was looking around everywhere as if she thought another zombie horde would bear down on us at any moment and Calvin…Calvin was crying like a baby.

The rain had stopped about the same time as we got on the freeway. I think the heat of the approaching dawn chased it away. The sun was just peeking over the mountain when we finally hit the gas.

It was that special time of the morning when it isn't too hot and it isn't too cold. The light was just getting rid of the gray tones, and the smell in the air was fresh and clean. Later on, the day would become one humid cesspool of nasty discomfort. Typical El Paso weather in the summer, but in that moment, it was almost peaceful.

Eventually, we turned the music off. There were still zombies after all. A few of them heard the music, and charged after us, but nothing too difficult to take care of quickly.

"Did you run into any large groups of them?"

No more than twenty or so. The large group was way behind us on the freeway.

"Now how many do you believe were in the group that came from Downtown?"

Around ten thousand by the time we passed the civic center.

To be honest, I was a bit speechless. That amount of zombies chasing after them is an image that just takes on some kind of frightening life of its own.

"Wow."

You should have been there. We were pretty fucking shocked. It was more than we had anticipated, even though we were warned that the mass was in the thousands. I guess we were just hoping the survivors were exaggerating.

"They've never gotten the exact numbers of just how many zombies were running around inside the city of El Paso."

No, but they believe that around two hundred thousand people survived, either by escaping before they closed the borders, or finding shelter after the borders were closed. Georgie estimated that around seventy thousand found shelter. Anyway you look at it...that leaves the potential for three hundred thousand zombies.

"Do you think there were that many?"

Close to it, but obviously there were some that were killed and never turned.

"You mean eaten?"

Yeah.

"How large of an amount?"

I don't think we'll ever know, but I can tell you that the horde we'd led to the Westside was one of the largest hordes I've ever seen.

"Really?"

Yeah, but there were still many, many zombies all over the city that had never made their way to the Downtown area, so who knew if there was another even bigger crowd just waiting to form?

"Was that something that you were thinking about? All those zombies scattered throughout the city?"

Vaguely. I knew there was a hell of a lot more, but I was trying to take one step at a time. Right at the moment, my goal was to get back to the Safe Zone and get the people there ready to move.

"Yeah, let's get back to that. Are you still on the freeway?"

Yeah, still on the freeway, still feeling somewhat good about ourselves, and still headed for the Safe Zone.

That's when we saw the military helicopters way in the distance. Let me be up front about this...I know next to nothing about helicopters from the military, but we saw two high tech looking, black helicopters. I was assuming they were military because they had missiles under their wings. Also, we could not hear them. I've seen and heard helicopters before. They make a lot of noise. These things made no noise. I didn't think they were civilian.

Anyway, one of them was cruising around the border between El Paso and Las Cruces, and the other seemed to be around the El Paso and Santa Teresa border (both Las Cruces and Santa Teresa were parts of New Mexico). Occasionally, we'd see bursts of machine gun fire from the helicopters. The machine guns must have been silenced as well, because we couldn't hear them.

"You think the government is finally helping out?" Dudley asked.

"Looks like it," Kingsley answered.

"Don't count on it," I said.

"Why do you say that?" Kingsley asked.

"They aren't leaving the borders. My guess is that they are traveling back and forth between two points, and blasting any zombies trying to cross out of El Paso. There are probably copters all over the city doing the same things these two are."

"So they are just keeping the zombies from spreading outside the city?" Jen asked.

"That's what I think."

"Still," Calvin said. (I hate Calvin). "They are now publicly doing something. Maybe it's just the early stages of a full blown rescue."

"I'd like it if you didn't speak anymore Calvin," I said testily.

It didn't take us very long to reach the Safe Zone after that, and I can't remember any more conversation. I think I probably depressed everyone. Still, I didn't want them to get any false hopes.

The gates of the Safe Zone were littered with zombie corpses. I couldn't tell you how many, I didn't bother to count. I just wanted to get away from the smell as soon as possible.

The guards opened the gate for us, and the survivors began to cheer. I stepped out of the Jeep, and waved my arm at everyone. In return, they crossed their right arms over their left breasts and nodded their heads. It was some kind of salute. A few of them had given it to me before but never all of them at the same time.

"Well, you saved a lot of lives. Those people respected you."

Yeah, made me blush.

Georgie and Tito ran up to us immediately. Georgie gave me a huge hug.

"What the hell kept you so long?" he asked.

"It was pretty bad over there," I answered. "I'll give you the details later. Let's have another meeting at sunset."

"I think you better say something to them," Tito said. "I've tried to keep things quiet but everyone's getting restless. Maybe you should let someone else be in charge since you aren't here a whole lot."

"I'll give it some thought," I said with a smirk. "Now, why are there so many dead zombies outside the gate?"

"We've been getting attacked pretty heavily," Georgie said. "It's just started to let up when the sun came out."

"Any serious problems?"

"No, it was rough for a while. We now have exactly four hundred and thirty people in here, so it's a little cramped."

"Four hundred and thirty?" I asked.

"Yeah man, they just kept coming."

"And the zombies came with them?"

"Yeah."

"How were you able to get them through the gates with all the zombies out there?" I asked.

"I had me some target practice," Georgie answered proudly.

"Anybody infected?"

"It's been dealt with," Tito said.

I wanted to ask more, but I decided against it. I didn't want to hear the details.

"Were you concerned?"

Yeah, I was, but at the moment there were too many people patting me on the back and shaking my hand. Some of them were even trying to take pictures with me. I didn't want to hear the details of how they dealt with the unfortunate infected. The end result is always the same.

"Death."

Yeah, death…I'd had enough death for a little while. It was time to relax. It was time to prepare for the next stage. There was also bound to be more death in my future. Maybe even mine.

"So you relaxed until sunset?"

I tried, wasn't much relaxing to be had. Mostly, I just hung out with all the survivors, and had a couple of beers.

"What happened with the others that were in the Jeep?"

Merrick, Dudley, and Kingsley went back to Georgie's and crashed out. Jen disappeared with I don't know who. Calvin and Tito started talking. I almost warned Tito about Calvin being an asshole, but I figured Tito would figure it out on his own in a short while.

Sometime before sunset I changed my clothes to jeans, a white t-shirt, and some combat boots. I didn't have much choice in the whole changing clothes thing. My previous clothes were filthy, smelly, and torn all to hell. I left all my gear at Georgie's except for my rifle, and headed over to the gates for some target practice.

I would have liked to have had a shower, but a sudden wave of zombies came rushing at the gate. Time for a shower would hopefully come later; at least that was what I was hoping.

It took the rest of the day, but as soon as we handled the zombies at the gate with some help from the guards, Georgie and I headed back to his house to have that meeting.

It was kinda cool being on the gate and shooting the zombies. A pretty big crowd had gathered to watch. Every time I brought one of them down, a massive cheer rose out over the Safe Zone. Georgie and I had a competition over who could bring down the most.

"Who won?"

I did, by five.

"How did it feel to have all those people cheering for you?"

I felt like a rock star. I've never had a run in with fame before. It was kinda fun. I mean…I wish it was under more pleasant circumstances and all, but it was still kinda fun.

I think Georgie was enjoying the run off as well.

"Run off?"

Yeah, since he and I have been pals for over ten years, he was getting a lot of attention as well. Also, Georgie can be a pretty funny guy most of the time. He's not always the pain in the ass that I described earlier. Most of the time, he'll have you in stitches.

Both of us were somewhat reluctant to head back to Georgie's house, but the meeting needed to be held.

"Who came to the meeting?"

Georgie, Merrick, Tito, Dudley, Kingsley, Ivana, Lucy, Jen (for some reason), and I. Calvin tried to get in the meeting with Tito, but Dudley grabbed him by the collar and tossed him out the front door.

"Because you didn't like him?"

Nobody liked him.

Once again, the bully in me joined in on the laughter.

"What happened at the meeting?"

The first thing I did, with a little help from Dudley, was tell them everything that happened Downtown. They weren't happy to hear about all the zombies headed our way.

"I can imagine they weren't. What did they say?"

Just what you'd expect.

"Why the hell would you lead them to us, Jax?" Tito asked.

"Because, by the time they get here, we aren't going to be here," I answered. "We're leaving tomorrow."

"That's impossible," Georgie said. "I did the research you asked me to do. Every exit in and out of El Paso is now fenced in with a ten-foot high chain link fence that runs a mile wide on each side of the road. After that, the military has patrols moving in Hummers around all the open areas. They're ordered to shoot anything trying to move out of El Paso between the fences."

"How many Hummers?" I asked.

"A lot, enough to cover the open areas and then some. They aren't taking any chances. There haven't been any escapes either. Rumor has it, that a lot of civilians have been shot as well."

"I don't doubt it," I mumbled. "It wouldn't only be the zombies trying to get out, I'm sure that some of the survivors tried to make a break for it as well. There's a lot of desert between the borders, they probably thought they could make it without being discovered."

"Well, they didn't," Georgie said. "The military has a lot of toys that can detect that sort of thing."

"How does the public feel about all this?" Dudley asked. "Hard to believe they aren't freaking out."

"They are…but they can't prove anything yet. So far, the military has kept all civilians far away from the borders and the open space in between. Only a few reporters have managed to get any kind of footage."

"What kind of footage?" I asked.

"One that was real bad was a woman at the fence begging to be let in and getting a rifle shoved in her face as an answer. There was also another that showed something trying to cross in the desert. Whether alive or dead…it was shot to hell."

"How upset would you say the public is?" I asked.

"On a scale of one to ten…I'd say about ten," Georgie answered. If they were upset before, they're good and pissed now. Riots are breaking out in Washington. Smaller riots are breaking out around the fences. People are really up in arms. It's all the news is talking about. Even other countries are going nuts over the way we are dealing with our own people. It's so bad, that the military brought in some helicopters to patrol over the open spaces with the Hummers. They're worried about some kind of underground railroad thing starting up."

"Well that explains the helicopters that you saw."

Yeah it does, and I was glad that the civilians were causing problems. It was nice to know that the people outside of El Paso cared about those of us stuck inside.

"How many civilians are gathering around the gates?" I asked Georgie.

"About a hundred, they aren't really at the fence though. The military keeps them about a mile away. None of the civilians and none of the reporters are allowed any closer than that."

"This is good," I replied with a smile. I had a plan…kind of.

"Tell him how famous he is," said Lucy.

"Yeah…Jax, you're getting pretty popular out there in the real world."

"What do you mean?" I asked.

"Everyone's talking about you, man. You're all over the news. We've been watching online. Your reputation has spread. Some of them are hailing you as some kind of savior, a few of them think you're just a redneck with a rifle, but most of them think you're make-believe."

"It's important that you don't start believing the hype Jax," Tito added. "We don't want to follow you if you're going to do something risky."

"Whatever," I replied. "How popular would you say I am Georgie?"

"Whenever they mention the zombie outbreak, they mention you right along with it. Like I said, they're curious about who you are and if you're real or not. There have been some artist renderings of what you must have looked like during some of your battles. I even saw an entire cartoon play out that showed how you saved Ivana."

"You're bigger than Mickey Mouse," Lucy said with a laugh.

"This is very good. I wanna meet my fans," I said with bravado. "Let's make that happen. You said there were about a hundred people at the fences…lets increase those numbers. Get on the computers and start typing. I want thousands of people at those fences by tomorrow afternoon. I want them to storm past where the military is keeping them, and I want them right at the border."

"How are we going to do that?" Tito asked.

"You're going to get on the Internet, and ask them to go there," I replied. "Duh."

"Why would they go and do that?" Georgie asked. "They'll get arrested."

"They'll do it, because we are going to meet them there," I said with no trace of a smile. "It's time for us to leave. This is our stand. We are going to those gates, and the military is going to have to choose whether or not they are going to shoot us or let us out, and they're going to have to do it with the entire world watching…so make sure the reporters have their cameras."

"Shit," Dudley said. "That might work. With the world watching, they may be forced to let us out. We should also post that we will voluntarily allow ourselves to be quarantined for the safety of others. It will make the military look real fucking bad if they don't let us out."

"It won't work," Tito said. "If we move everyone here, we'll attract the wrong kind of attention. Even if we make it to the fence, that entire horde of zombies will be right behind us. The military wouldn't be able to open the gate even if they wanted to."

"I guess we'll have to split them up." I answered. "We'll divide into two groups. I'll take most of the fighters with me, and someone can take all the non-fighters in another group. My group can make a lot of noise…get the bulk of the horde to follow us. As soon as the non-fighter group is safe, my group can zig and zag until we lose the zombies, and then we can head for the border as well."

"That would work, Dudley said. "It's not exactly difficult to get them to follow. We could even have the non-fighters head for the Las Cruces border, and the decoy group can head for the Santa Teresa border after they ditch the zombies."

"Everyone in favor of this plan, raise your hand," I announced.

Everyone but Tito raised their hands.

"Something on your mind, Tito?" I asked.

"I don't like the way you forced us to take action. You took it upon yourself to make certain decisions that led us to this point. I would like to have waited for outside help. Now, I have to make a run for it. I agree that it's the only plan available, I'm just not happy that I wasn't more involved with the decisions that led us here."

"We knew that we'd have to leave eventually," Georgie said. "Now's as good a time as any."

"You could always stay here in protest, Tito," Dudley added.

We all laughed at this. Tito didn't appreciate it but we couldn't help ourselves.

"I want you all to start raising hell on those computers," I ordered. "And don't stop till we hit the road tomorrow morning."

"What are you going to do?" Tito asked.

"I'm gonna make a speech," I answered.

The survivors were waiting for me when I got outside. Tito and Georgie were right behind me instead of working on the computers. I hopped up on top of a pickup truck, and everyone surrounded me. Merrick began to whine, and someone lifted her up to join me. I looked out over the sea of faces, and for a moment, I froze. I couldn't think of a thing to say. I finally took a deep breath and began.

"By tomorrow afternoon this Safe Zone will no longer be safe. It will be crawling with the dead, and they number around ten thousand." The crowd gave an almost collective gasp. They even turned their heads around to look at one another as if they weren't quite sure that I said what I just said. I waited for a moment, and just let the panic and urgency sink in. "The good news is…we will no longer be here. Tomorrow morning, we make our move. Tomorrow morning, we make a run for the gates with the entire world watching. The military will be either forced to let us pass, or they will be forced to shoot us."

"How did the crowd react to that?"

Some of them began to cheer. Others began to panic.

"Listen to me. I'm not forcing anyone to follow me. If you want to make a run for it on your own, that's your choice. But the dead are coming. Eventually, they will find you. There is no long-term solution if we remain in this city. Eventually, we will die. Now is as good a time as any to take our chance. The world is outraged at us being abandoned, and forced to stay in this city. The military will have to let us out. I know that some of you came here so that you wouldn't have to run anymore, and I know that some of you came here in search of a safe place to hide. Unfortunately, there is no safe place in this city. Our only chance for survival is to leave. This is our moment, this is our time, and this is our chance. Tomorrow morning we will show the world that we have had enough. Who's with me?"

This time, there were a lot more cheers. They were afraid. Who in their right mind wouldn't be? Yet, they were with me. That was the important thing. They were with me.

"Did you expect them to be with you?"

I didn't expect anything. I didn't know what they would say. It would be fair of me to point out that not everybody was happy. In the world we live in, that's relatively impossible. Some of them were far from being happy.

I let Tito go over all the details. I had nothing left to say. Tito likes that kind of thing anyway. Maybe he'd even smooth things out with those who were upset, or maybe he'd just add fuel to the fire and agree with them that I'm an asshole. Who knows? It did make me a little nervous that he was hanging out with Calvin.

"Was Calvin trying to turn the survivors against you?"

I wouldn't have put that past him, but the way I figured things, people had to do what they felt was right. I don't believe in forcing others to do what I think needs to be done. I simply do what I think is right, and those who want to follow me are more than welcome. If the survivors all chose to do something else, I wasn't about to try and stop them. I would simply continue with my plan without them.

I was never able to grab that shower, or grab any sleep. I spent the rest of the night helping others prepare.

"Mentally or physically?"

Both. Some of them needed help with their weapons. Some of them need help packing. Some needed words of encouragement. The worst of them were the kids without parents. They were scared to death. I tried to give them a little pep talk, and find them a family to hook up with so they wouldn't feel so alone.

"It sounds somewhat draining."

It was.

He didn't elaborate; he didn't need to. It's obvious that the man was worried, and along with that worry was a very serious dose of self-doubt. It's probably the same reason that he didn't force his ideas upon anyone. He wasn't completely sure he was right. Of course this is just conjecture. It's nothing he ever said. It's just the vibe I got from him on occasion.

As the night wore down, I pulled Dudley off the computers to help Georgie, and I arranged the two groups. It didn't work as well as we had hoped. In fact, our plan went out the window almost immediately. We wanted the fighters in one group and the non-fighters in another, but there were only about fifty fighters with experience in firearms, and some of these men and women had families. We couldn't ask them to split up.

It took hours to sort it out. In the end, we still had two groups, split as evenly as we could make them. The fighters were also divided almost equally in both groups.

"Didn't that ruin your plan of using your group to distract the zombies?"

Not really. We just put a few nimble vehicles to the side and I let Georgie take charge of the group I was going to lead. The vehicles we pulled aside consisted of my Jeep and two small trucks with four-wheel drive. Our job was to distract the zombies while both of the main groups headed for the borders.

"So the job of the three vehicles was to provide a distraction while the main groups reached the border gates, and after they were safe you'd ditch the zombies and join them?"

Exactly, it wasn't our original plan, but for all I knew it might even work a little better. At the very least, it gave a greater number of people a chance to make it to the border gates without being attacked by a large group of zombies.

"Who did you pick to drive the Jeep and two trucks?"

Dudley, me, and a guy named Jack, who also happened to own one of the trucks. We put an experienced shooter in the back of each truck. They alone had orders to fire whenever they felt it was needed. My copilot was Merrick. I was hoping that she'd bite anything that grabbed onto my Jeep.

After all that was organized, Tito came up to me. He'd been supposedly working all night in his efforts to smooth over any problems people were having.

"Problems with you?"

That's what he said when I'd asked him. He was supposed to eventually find his way to a computer and help the others broadcast our escape plans, but instead he informed me that some of the survivors were still upset, and the best way he could help would be to smooth things over.

"Was Calvin with him?"

Yeah, they were pretty close together whenever I saw them.

"Were that many survivors upset?"

Not one single person came to me with any problems. I'm sure many of them were nervous, but nobody was complaining. I'm not sure what Tito was dealing with. From where I was standing, I definitely had enough support.

"What did Tito tell you?"

He said that a lot of the survivors had trust in him and he wanted to be the one that led the second group.

"How did you feel about that?"

I didn't really mind. Like I said, I didn't see anyone with problems but just in case, I figured he was as good as anyone else. I really didn't think Calvin would play into any of this.

"Did Calvin end up...causing problems?"

I've never talked to Tito about it, but my guess is that he did.

"So what happened the next morning?"

The sun broke early and before we knew it, the morning was already getting hot. There was zero humidity in the air and not a lot of clouds. Personally, I prefer the humidity. I know that it makes you sweat some kinda nasty but at least the sweat somewhat cools you down. This dry desert heat made me feel a lot like I was beginning to cook. I hated it.

Kingsley wasn't happy. I didn't know if it was because he wasn't in my group or he was just nervous. He was sitting in a truck and chain smoking. I think I caught him drinking during the night. It looked a lot like the signs of an alcohol binge.

Jack, Dudley, and I were the first out of the gate. There were no zombies in sight but I was nervous. Not for myself mind you, I was just hoping that my plan was going to work. Too many lives were at stake.

I should also mention that I had a touch of the shakes. I guzzled an entire thermos full of coffee. I couldn't remember that last time I got any sleep and I was really dragging my ass—at least until I drank all the coffee. After that I was slightly more awake but damn near vibrating.

Tito led his group off towards Las Cruces and Georgie's group held back somewhat while my three vehicles scouted ahead. My mind was on the Santa Teresa border. I was hoping that the people would show. Everything depended upon the people outside the borders. If they brought their support, the military would be forced to let us through. Without them, we were screwed.

I thought of my wife. It was something I forced myself not to think about until that moment. I knew she was safe. That had been enough for me. Now, if I were able to leave the city, I would see her. I knew she'd be worried. I knew she was going to be pissed that I'd put myself into so much danger.

My wife has the biggest smile I've ever seen on a woman's face before. I think she reserves it only for me. It's the kind of smile that brightens up the worst kind of day. I wanted that smile. I knew she would be at the gates. I knew that smile would be waiting for me.

I was on my way. Damn, was it hot. Damn, I was tired.

I think that moment was the scariest part of the entire ordeal. The fact that we were moments away from safety and freedom and any number of things could ruin it for us. There was no way to deal with this kind of anticipation. All we could do was charge headlong into whatever destiny lay in wait.

There weren't any sightings of massive zombie hordes in the direction of Las Cruces. We figured that Tito's group had a straight and easy shot. As long as they kept moving, they shouldn't have had any major problems. Then again, it was a guessing game. Nobody really knew what either group would encounter.

"Were you shocked later to find out about what happened?"

I think devastated would be a better word. There weren't a lot of homes in that area (it was mostly open desert), that meant they shouldn't have to worry about any massive hordes of undead attacking them. If they kept moving, they...

Well, we kept the plan of two different groups just because we didn't want all our eggs in one basket. Four hundred and thirty people means a lot of cars. Moving that many cars is a slow business; way too slow when zombies are involved. Splitting into two caravans made traveling a little bit faster, and if one group failed for whatever reason, another group would hopefully succeed. Hopefully, both groups would succeed. Anyway, the three distraction vehicles stayed with Georgie's group. We knew for certain that there were hordes of undead in his direction (we led them there in the first place) and there were also a lot of homes. I figured they'd need my help the most.

"But it was all just a guessing game?"

Yeah. Who could say what either group would run into?

I can remember telling Tito almost those exact words. I told him that I didn't know what he'd run into, and that no matter what he needed to keep pushing forward towards the border. I told him not to stop for anything. Just keep moving forward.

Jaxon was quiet for a moment after saying this. It was just a moment and then he resumed as if nothing had happened.

Anyway, I had the one of radios that we took from Martin in the back of my Jeep. Georgie had the other one in his vehicle. The three decoy vehicles scouted ahead, and when I gave the all clear, Georgie moved forward.

We avoided places like the supermarket and Lowe's. I figured that even though it took a little more time because we weren't going the most direct route, it would be better to avoid the large hordes for as long as possible.

However, it was only a matter of time. Somewhere out there was a group of ten thousand zombies, and I didn't think it would take too long to find them…or for them to find us.

The caravan moved pretty slowly. I was glad we ended up keeping the two different groups. I didn't want to imagine how slow a caravan twice that size would be moving. Still, I guess moving slowly was better than pedal to the metal.

"Why is that?"

Car crashes. As it was, the people were having a lot of small fender benders due to the tightly packed caravan. It made sense. They were scared. There's no shame in it. I was pretty scared as well. If we were going pedal to the metal…wow. Instead of small dents in the bumpers, we'd be dealing with rolled over cars. Not a good idea.

"I see your point."

We had asked everyone in the caravans to refrain from shooting until I gave the order that shooting was necessary. Now, I didn't plan on giving this order unless we were being attacked by a larger horde. However, when people get a bad case of the nerves, and they're holding a weapon in their hand, they tend to pull the trigger.

Twenty minutes into our journey, the shooting began. It was a small group of four zombies. A man, a woman, and two kids. I'm guessing they were probably a family. Anyway, they came running out of a small brick house and headed straight for the middle of the caravan. Even though I was a little bit ahead of the group, I heard a woman scream. Then there was a pause and after that all hell broke loose.

"What do you mean?"

Sounded like everybody with a gun started shooting at the same time. It was bad, and it was loud. I didn't want loud; loud attracted zombies. Loud was not a good idea.

I jammed the Jeep in reverse and peeled the tires on my way towards the trouble. The four zombies had all hit a large station wagon that was packed with people. They were banging on the windows and climbing onto the hood. The people inside looked terrified. The folks with the guns were still firing. It didn't take long for bullets to start punching into the side of the station wagon. It was a miracle nobody inside was hit.

I yelled for a ceasefire and got out of my Jeep. Somebody actually heard me yell and they repeated the command. It didn't take too long for the shooting to stop. I walked over to the station wagon just as the mother zombie noticed me and charged. I took off the top of her head. The man and the two children zombies didn't notice me until I pulled them off the car. The man took a swing at me, which I ducked. I kicked him back to gain a little space and dropped the tomahawk into his forehead when he charged again. The two children were easy, at least in the physical sense.

I started to walk back to my Jeep and I felt it in the air. At first I thought it was just everyone staring at me. They were all staring at me by the way. Maybe they just hadn't seen any action up close and personal before. I'm not sure but they stared at me like I was some sort of monster. Maybe it was the two zombie kids.

Anyway, the feeling I felt, it wasn't all the people staring at me. It was something else. They had made too much noise. We had trouble headed our way. I was way too exhausted for this kinda thing.

I went to Dudley's truck.

"Do you feel it?" I asked.

"I feel something," he answered.

Then the slight breeze shifted just right and we smelled the rot. It would take a large number of zombies to cast out that kind of smell. We definitely had trouble headed our way.

"They know we're out here," Dudley said.

"And they're headed our way," I answered.

"You think they're running or walking?"

"It was a lot of noise," I answered after considering for a moment. "They're probably running."

I gave the order to move just as we heard the first of the moans.

I got on the radio.

"Georgie," I said. "Did you hear that?"

"Yeah, the zombies are coming."

"It's time to go to work. Lead them straight, let them shoot, and don't go too fast."

He replied but I wasn't listening anymore. I was rushing towards the smell. I was rushing towards the moans. I was rushing towards all the zombies that we had led out of the Downtown area. I wasn't looking forward to it.

Unfortunately, it didn't take very long to find them. They were moving up Mesa Street at a run. There were so many of them that they blocked the entire road. It was indeed the massive horde that we led out of Downtown. They'd moved a pretty impressive distance since I'd seen them last. I think I even recognized a few of the decaying faces...or at least some of the clothes.

"Did this group pick up any of the zombies that were already in the area?"

I imagine that they did. It's impossible to say for sure, there were just so many of them. However, single zombies tend to join up with larger groups for some reason.

The biggest problem was that they were running towards a head on collision with Georgie's caravan. You see, Mesa eventually just becomes Country Club road. There's no turn off or anything but as soon as Mesa hits the railroad tracks it then becomes Country Club.

"Okay."

Well the Santa Teresa border is at the end of Country Club. It's one straight road into the New Mexico border.

Our decided route led all over the place in order to avoid any large population of zombies that we knew about but eventually the caravan would hit the railroad tracks right at the end of Mesa and the beginning of Country Club.

"Georgie was leading the survivors right into a mob of ten thousand zombies."

Hence, the collision course.

Dudley and Jack pulled up next to me. They saw what I was seeing and neither one of them looked like they enjoyed the view.

"We need to get them to follow us," I shouted.

"Yeah," Dudley answered.

"Follow me, when I honk my horn have the guys in the back start shooting."

I took off once again. I was headed straight for the horde. Of course, they saw me coming, and just in case they happened to be blind, the hungry screams made sight rather unnecessary. The vast horde knew that food was heading their way.

Dudley was right behind me. Jack was not. I searched the mirrors but I couldn't find him anywhere.

I let Dudley pull up next to me. We were getting closer and closer. I think I was doing about fifty mph. About forty feet from the horde, I hit the brakes and yanked the wheel. The Jeep spun dangerously, but after a couple spins the wheels caught, and I floored the Jeep in the opposite direction.

I was only hoping to turn the Jeep around, the spins allowed the zombies to get dangerously close before I regained control. I was too tired and it was too hot. I was making stupid mistakes. Luckily, Merrick was up to the challenge. She nipped at any and all fingers that grabbed onto the Jeep.

I was supposed to honk the horn, but in a surge of nervous energy, I blared the damn thing.

Dudley, after seeing me spin all over the road, eased off on the gas before he turned. Still, his turn was wide and he went over the median. His shooter almost fell out of the back of the truck but somehow he managed to hang in there.

They both must have heard me blare the horn because Dudley began to blare his as well, and his shooter began to fire round after round into the rushing horde of the undead.

It was close, way too close, but we made it. The zombies were following us. Even though they probably smelled the caravan of survivors off in the distance as they moved through the streets towards the border, visual confirmation of our two little vehicles proved to be too much for them.

I guess it was just good luck, if you can call being pursued by that many zombies good luck.

With our adrenaline pumping so much, we created a little bit too much distance from the zombies. We had to stop and let them catch up a bit.

"What happened to Jack?" I asked Dudley after he pulled next to me.

"The pussy took off after he saw the zombies," Dudley answered. "He didn't even say a word to me. He just took off as fast as his truck could carry him. He knocked his shooter right out of the back of the truck as well."

That's when I noticed there were two shooters in the back of Dudley's truck. One of them was lying down; the other was on his knees over him.

"What's wrong with him?"

"I think he broke his leg when he fell outta Jack's truck."

That was all the time we had for chit-chat. The zombies were coming, and we were off again.

"How bad was it to once again to have that many zombies chasing after you?"

I don't think that it's describable. I mean…we kept our distance; there was really no danger. Yet, it really sucked to know that there were that many zombies trying to eat you. I tried earlier to explain the sheer numbers but I think that it's really impossible to describe the scope. We were on a four-lane road with houses on either side. The zombies took up all four lanes, and most of the front yards of the houses as they tried to outrun each other. Yeah, it was bad.

I radioed Georgie after leading them away from Mesa and Country Club for about a half an hour.

"Georgie," I asked. "You read me?"

"I'm here Jax. What's up?"

"We've got the zombies following us. Where are you?"

"We just turned onto Country Club. Ran into a little trouble but the shooters finally took care of things."

"Can you see the border gates?"

"Oh yeah, I see 'em."

"And?"

"Looks to be thousands of people."

"Radio me back when you get to the gates so I can head over there myself."

We led the zombies farther and farther into the suburbs. We took turn after turn, and pulled a little bit farther away from them each time.

Dudley pulled up next to me and shouted through his open window.

"What the hell is taking Georgie so long?"

"I should hear from him any moment now, I think."

"Have you noticed that there aren't as many zombies following us anymore?"

To be perfectly honest, I had not noticed that.

"Huh?" I asked.

"We've lost about half."

Georgie picked that moment to radio me.

"Jax, are you there?" Georgie asked.

"Yeah, what's up?"

"They won't let us through."

"Even with all those people?" I asked.

"The people are getting pretty angry over it but the military brought in reinforcements to keep them in order. Also, there were signs right before the bridge that said they'd open fire on any vehicles that cross the bridge, so we left our cars and went on foot."

"Wait up a minute, what are they telling you at the gate?"

"Major Crass is telling us that we have to wait for the decontamination units to arrive before they'll let us in," Georgie answered.

"Well that's not exactly bad news Georgie. They're gonna let us through, we just have to wait."

"Yeah well, the bad news is that we're sitting out here in the open in front of these gates, about five hundred feet from our vehicles."

"Just keep cool Georgie. Most of zombies are pretty far away, so I can be there in a few minutes."

"Jax, there's something else…"

"What's that?"

"Skie is here. She's safe behind the gates. I've talked to her."

"That's your wife."

Yeah.

He took another moment before he began where he left off.

"She's okay?" I asked.

"Yeah man, she's fine."

"I'm on my way," it was all I could say. I was choking back tears. She told me she was safe, I believed that she was safe but to hear someone tell me that they'd seen and spoken to her… I can't tell you the relief that was flooding through me."

He didn't need to either. I could see his eyes begin to well up just from thinking about it. He loves his wife.

I gave Dudley the thumbs up and we tore off towards Country Club. We tore off towards the gates that separated El Paso from Santa Teresa.

I thought about Tito. I wished we had another radio. I wanted to hear that he was safe and sound. I'd find out soon enough though. I'd find out that the other half of the survivors made it safely into New Mexico. It had to be that way. It had to be, because we took the dangerous route and we were almost free.

Most of all, I thought about Skie.

We hit Country Club road a little bit before where the caravan was parked. We took more than a few side streets to get there, we didn't want to take a straight shot and lead any zombies to our people. If any dead things happened to give chase, we certainly lost them with all of our twists and turns.

We left our vehicles on the side of the road by the end of the caravan. Nobody saw us pull up, or if they did no one said anything. Merrick and I hopped out of the Jeep, and walked over to Dudley's truck. I was running on empty. Just trying to walk at this point was an ordeal. Merrick seemed happy enough to be out of the Jeep.

Dudley was helping his shooter take the man with the broken leg out of the back of the truck. The wounded man had an arm around both their shoulders and was bouncing on one leg as the four of us and Merrick began to walk towards the gates.

It was odd to walk past the caravan of empty vehicles. It reminded me too much of all those deserted cars filling up all those empty streets. It wasn't like that now; these people were going to make it. We were all going to make it.

After we passed the cars, we saw the gates. The fence was impressive, as were the guard towers looming up high behind them. There were a lot of guard towers. It looked like they were spaced out about every one hundred feet or so. Inside each tower were two men with large machine guns. I wonder if they took that idea from our Safe Zone.

He chuckled at his own little joke and then continued.

As we reached the bridge over the Rio Grande, I could finally see just how big the gathered crowd actually was. It made our band of survivors seem extremely small in comparison. They were gathered behind the fence in a massive army, while our group was right at the entrance of the gate before them.

They were chanting.

"What were they saying?"

"Let them in. Let them in. Let them in."

All the helicopters had been grounded, and I could see that the military presence was scattered among the crowd. I don't think they planned it that way. I think the people just stormed past their designated spot, pushed their way to the fence, and the soldiers were now surrounded and a little bit confused as to what to do.

I looked off the side of the bridge. The Rio Grande was still high and the waters were moving just as fast as that long ago day that Dudley and I watched as the zombies waded in after us and got swept away in the current.

I heard movement off to the side of the bridge where the concrete hit earth and the bridge ended. Kingsley and another man walked up the side of the embankment and waved at me. I wasn't sure what they were doing under the bridge but I was too tired to ask.

Slowly, the chanting began to die down.

One by one, every single face on both sides of the fence turned to look at us.

"It's the General," a voice shouted.

The announcement was repeated by someone else, and then someone else, and then someone else all the way into infinity.

I stopped dead in my tracks. Dudley and the two shooters stopped right behind me. It was a nerve-wracking moment. I began to wonder if all these people were going to try and stone me or something.

And then they began to cheer.

I laughed in that tired sort of way where almost no sound comes out except for an exhalation of air. The people from the caravan rushed over to us. They clapped me on the back, hugged me, saluted me in that right fist over the heart thing that people do to me all the time. The crowd behind the fence was going nuts. The soldiers looked a little nervous.

It took awhile but I finally made my way to the fence. The fence was beginning to bow a little bit from the force of all the people trying to get next to me. Georgie, Ivana, and Lucy were waiting at the entrance gate. Georgie was smiling from ear to ear.

"Where is she?" I asked.

His smile got even bigger and he motioned with his head towards the cheering crowd.

The cheering began to die down almost immediately and the crowd began to part. Beyond the fence someone was making their way towards me, but there were still people in the way and I couldn't make out who it was. In the next second, I saw her.

It was Skie.

She was only ten feet away from me. She was wearing a little blue dress. Her big brown eyes were filled with worry. I took the few steps that were left between me and the fence and grabbed the chain link. I smiled at her and she smiled back. I saw the tears begin to fall as she ran to me. We were separated by the fence but her little hands reached out for my fingers through the holes.

"I want to hold you," she whispered. Her voice was choked. She was fighting the sobs.

"I want to be held," I said.

She began to laugh and sob at the same time. The crowd began to cheer all over again. The noise was deafening. The fence was wobbling as the many people shoved their way to a better look.

I barely even noticed them. I was with my wife. I had survived, and so had the people under my care. My legs felt weak and I began to lean against the fence as if I could push back the weight of all those cheering people.

"I've got you, baby," Skie said. "Don't you worry anymore, I won't let go."

"We're getting there aren't we?"

Getting where?

"The footage."

Yeah.

Before this moment at the fence, the General was an almost mythological character. It's easiest to think of him as some sort of modern Robin Hood or Zorro. The majority of the survivors trapped inside of El Paso believed that he existed. They believed in him without any hard evidence whatsoever, and some of them even left whatever protection they had in order to find him. They had the hopes of their survival pinned on this great man who refused to surrender to the horror. In truth, they simply wanted to believe. They wanted to believe that someone was out there fighting back. They wanted to believe that someone could stop the monsters.

However, a great many of the people who were safely outside of El Paso didn't believe that he was anything more than myth. Some thought he was simply a fairytale being passed around in an effort to give heart to the trapped survivors; some legend that would fade in time after nobody stood up to take the credit. Others believed that he did exist but his tales were greatly exaggerated. They thought him simply an ordinary man on the run that maybe got lucky a time or two, and helped a few people. Most of the people gathered at the fence that day came to find out what the truth really was. They wanted to see if the legend was real. They were about to see the truth of it all…in spades.

I've heard that most of the people gathered on the safe side of the fence were there to find out whether or not I was real. I mean—I'm sure that a lot of them came to help any survivors that managed to reach the fence but I don't think they really believed anyone would.

Regardless, I don't think any of them would have shown up at all if they didn't believe that they were safe.

"You don't believe that the people who came that day expected anything to happen?"

Exactly, they weren't ready for it. Nobody even noticed the lone truck sputtering its way towards the caravan. They were too busy cheering and clapping.

They did however notice when the air filled with the smell of rot.

I noticed it as well. I also noticed the lone man abandoning the failing vehicle, and running across the bridge. It was Jack, the man that ditched us when we were trying to distract the zombies from the caravan.

The look on his face told me everything.

Jack is not the man's real name. Nobody seems to know his true name. In fact, nobody seems to know much about the man at all. What we do know, or more accurately, what we can piece together, is that after abandoning Jaxon, Dudley, and the two shooters, Jack got lost on his way towards rejoining the caravan. In his search for his fellow survivors, he somehow attracted the attention of at least five thousand zombies. It probably wasn't long before the man's truck began to run low on gasoline and started to stutter, thus making it easier for the zombies to pursue him. It also isn't known what Jack was thinking when he led the zombies to the border gates and trapped his fellow survivors between a massive horde of zombies and a fence that they weren't allowed to cross. Perhaps, he was seeking aid. Or perhaps, Jack merely got lucky and finally found his way. We'll never know for sure; the man known as Jack disappeared after the events that were about to transpire.

I knew it was coming; the hell storm was on its way.

I could feel it deep down inside the pit of my stomach. I looked at Skie. I saw the confusion in her face. The cheering was dying down once again. It was almost as if everyone could sense the danger, and the vileness, headed our way.

I went completely selfish at that moment. All I wanted on this earth was but a few more precious moments with my wife. Just time enough to hold her close. Time enough to feel her warm embrace, and hear her tell me that she loves me, that's all I wanted. Then I could fall back into hell.

For a brief moment I held her fingers and refused to look away from her pretty face. I thought about ignoring everything. I thought about staying right where I was and letting someone else stand up and play hero.

Instead, I pulled my fingers out of her hands.

"Where's that major guy that Georgie told me about?" I asked Skie.

"Why?"

"We need to be quick, Skie. Where is he?"

"I'll go get him," she answered as she quickly disappeared into the crowd of people.

The onlookers knew something was going on. They were talking amongst each other. The noise was elevating once again as voices competed over voices in an attempt to be heard.

I saw Jack running towards us. He was shouting something but nobody could hear what he was saying. I didn't have to hear the asshole. I knew exactly what he brought to our doorstep.

Skie returned with the major just as Georgie, Dudley, and Kingsley came forward to stand next to me. Merrick was getting agitated. She was letting out little growls with each breath.

"You're in charge here?" I asked.

He was one of those middle-aged fellas that always seemed to have some sort of chip on their shoulder.

"What do you want?" He demanded.

"You need to get those helicopters in the air right now," I shouted motioning my head towards the aircraft. "And you need to let us through this gate." I said.

"I don't need to do a God damn thing," he answered. "You aren't the one calling the shots around here, boy."

"They're coming," I shouted. "Can't you smell them?"

"You deal with it," he answered with a smug expression on his face. "This is what happens when you try to tell the U.S. military what to do."

With that, he walked away.

The first of the screams began to sound off.

I motioned for Skie to come towards me. She lifted her hands and grabbed my fingers through the fence once again.

"I want you to run," I said. "Run as far away as you can. If you have a car, get into it and drive as fast as you can."

It was hard to hear her over the screaming. I knew the zombies had come but this moment was for my wife. I wouldn't look at them until I knew she would be safe.

I saw her eyes grow wide as she looked over my shoulder and saw what I knew was the advancing horde.

"Skie," I shouted. "Don't look at that, look at me."

She did as I asked. I could see the panic in her face. Around us…utter chaos. Everyone was screaming. On the safe side of the fence, people were running in circles, colliding with one another and trampling others. A few people managed to run off but smaller fences had been erected all over the place behind the main gate, and getting out wasn't easy.

"I need you to run, Skie. Can you do that?" I asked, trying to fight the desperate tone that flowed into my voice.

"No."

I was floored.

"You need to come with me. You need to be safe with me. You've done enough. You need to leave with me right now," she said.

I had no words for her. What could I say? How could I expect her to understand? She had just gotten her husband back and now she was faced with losing him once again. It wasn't fair, not to her and not to me.

I saw Jen, the redhead that I saved, along with that idiot Calvin, begin to climb the fence. She was half way up before one of the soldiers shot her in the head.

The chaos before was nothing compared to what it was after that shot.

The military was not going to help us. They were going to watch us die. They were going to sit back and protect their stupid fence and watch two hundred and twenty people literally be torn apart and eaten.

Skie was tightening her grip on my fingers.

"Georgie," I shouted.

"I'm right here," he answered.

I saw him out of the corner of my eye. He was facing the rushing horde of zombies, not even looking at me.

"We're fucked, Jax. What the hell are we going to do?"

"Get the shooters in a line in front of everyone else."

"I can't. They took our guns when we got here. They made us pass them through the fence."

Fuck. My mind was going over a hundred miles an hour but I couldn't find a solution.

"I have a rifle and a pistol in my overnight, I didn't hand it over," Georgie said.

Kingsley interrupted us.

"I got it covered Jax." He shouted over all the voices. "Me and this other guy rigged up the explosives I took from Martin to the bridge just in case these assholes didn't let us in."

"So that was why he had a duffel bag with him when he came out of the building."

Yeah, he thought we might need it so he grabbed it. He also grabbed a spare detonator. What comes later gets all the attention but if it wasn't for Kingsley rigging up that bridge…well…we'd all be dead.

"Is it ready to go?" I asked.

"You're damn right it is," he answered.

I didn't let go of Skie's fingers but I looked behind me and I saw the zombies that were rushing towards us for the first time.

It wasn't the entire horde that we brought all the way from Downtown but it was at least half of them.

They were running as fast as their dead legs could carry them. It was way too fast. I could hear their weird screams and snarls. They were just about to reach the abandoned vehicles of the caravan.

"Wait till they're halfway across the bridge," I told Kingsley.

I looked back towards Skie. I had no idea what these explosives would do. I had no idea how much of a boom they'd make. All I knew, I knew from looking into Skies eyes. She was terrified. Terrified for me, terrified for herself probably, and she wasn't about to let go of my fingers. It was just as well, I wanted to be between her and the blast.

BOOM!

It was loud, but not as loud as you might think though. It was kind of muffled from the water, and the weight of the bridge.

I turned away just as Kingsley hit the button. Dust and concrete flew into the air but we were far enough away. I could smell the water from the Rio Grande in the air as well. The wet splatter of the river fell like raindrops as I finally looked back.

The blast stopped the panic. Everyone began to calm down. They began to feel just a little bit safer.

I couldn't see anything just yet, the kicked up dust and concrete formed into an almost mushroom cloud that blocked my view.

People began to cheer once again.

"Can you blame them? Look at everything they witnessed. Look at everything they'd seen. On both sides of the fence, people suffered."

Of course they did.

"It's over," I said to Skie.

For a brief moment she looked into my eyes and smiled. Then I watched the smile slowly vanish as she looked over my shoulder.

I followed her gaze, and I saw the dead rise up on each side of the broken bridge from the river's embankment.

Some of them blew towards us in the explosion. It turns out there was some sort of delay in the detonation after Kingsley hit the button. Around two hundred zombies were blown towards our side of the river, almost as many as the survivors still under my care.

They were stunned by the impact of the explosion but that wasn't going to last very long.

There was no screaming this time; the soldiers had pushed their way to the front of the fence in order to guard the people on their side. I knew better than to expect them to help all of us on my side.

The survivors, all two hundred and twenty of them, began to crowd around me. Sound in general began to slip away. I could only see my wife's face as she looked into my eyes.

"I have to do this," I told her.

"Don't you dare leave me, Jax," she said. "You just stay right here; don't you dare leave me."

She clutched at my fingers as hard as she could.

"I love you very much," I whispered to her.

She frantically grabbed at my fingers as I gently pulled them away.

"No Jax, don't you do this. You've done enough."

I turned away from my wife.

"Get everyone together," I told Dudley. "Grab whatever weapons you can find and be ready for whatever gets by me."

"I'll go with you," Dudley said.

"No, you won't," I answered.

I walked to the middle of the street, and out in front of everyone. Merrick was right next to me. She growled at the growing mass of zombies. Everything went into slow motion.

A zombie screamed at me from the distance. In answer, I pulled my tomahawk and knife clear from my belt.

I was tired but the pumping adrenaline gave me temporary strength.

In front of me, about two hundred zombies that were hungry for human flesh, behind me, two hundred and twenty survivors that depended on my strength for their survival.

The mass charged me.

I charged them.

We met together in a fatal embrace of blood and steel.

I fought like I had never fought before. Their numbers were staggering but I wouldn't surrender. They struck at me, and I felt the impact and pain of their blows but still I kept fighting.

I swung and stabbed and chopped and slashed. I kicked and punched and twirled and fell. Their bodies began to drop all around me. Their corpses, no longer animated, littered the ground. The ground itself became slick with blood.

They growled at me. They screamed that blood-wrenching scream at me, but still they fell. I could see the hunger and rage in their eyes. Their stupid little brains couldn't comprehend why they couldn't simply rip into me.

I was growing weaker by the minute. They were so many of them, and they just kept coming.

I began to stumble and fall more often from their blows. Each time I did, it was that much harder to get back up. The zombies began to pile on top of me. It was unbelievably hard to shake them off and strike them down. I felt as if I couldn't move fast enough. I could no longer keep them at a distance.

Merrick did not abandon me. She bit and crunched bone at random. As they came for me, she came for them. She fought like a Tasmanian Devil from an old cartoon. They kicked and slapped at her, I saw her stumble and slide but, like me, she wouldn't give up.

One of them hit me on the back of the head so hard I saw stars and my vision began to cloud. The world began to sway and I once again fell to my knees. The zombies dove at me. Their sheer numbers were bringing me down and holding me underneath their crushing weight. For a second, a brief shining second, I almost gave up. I almost fell into that painful surrender of being ripped apart and eaten.

Something inside of me clicked.

Something inside of me snapped.

Everything became a blur of violence after that. I'm not exactly sure what happened. Yet somehow, I kept on fighting. Despite the exhaustion, despite the pain, I somehow fought them off. I stopped them from rampaging into all those people huddled together against the fence. I just…don't know…how I did it.

I only remember Georgie was suddenly standing next to me, and yelling for me to get up. He was firing round after round into the scattered remaining zombies as they rushed towards us.

I was tired, more tired than I had ever been in my entire life. I saw my tomahawk on the ground by my feet. I couldn't see my knife anywhere.

I picked up the tomahawk, and struck out at the twenty or thirty zombies that were still left.

It was hard to move. It was hard to keep my balance.

Merrick helped me. She rushed at them with no fear whatsoever. As she tangled them up or knocked them over, I struck them down.

In moments, it was over.

There was nothing left to fight.

I looked around and saw only blood and lifeless corpses.

I heard the screams and snarls of the rampaging dead coming from across the broken bridge over the Rio Grande. There were thousands of zombies reaching out for me—the lucky ones (if you could call a zombie lucky) that weren't on the bridge when it blew.

I walked to my end of the broken bridge and stared at them. They were enraged, hungry, and they desperately wanted to get at me. Some of them were even rushing into the water after me but the current was too strong and, just like they did on the day all this began, they were washed away down the river.

They screamed at me.

In defiance, I screamed back.

I wanted more.

My legs gave out. My body finally succumbed to the exhaustion. Georgie and Merrick were there. Georgie helped me to my feet.

I looked at my body; I was covered in bite marks.

I was too tired to freak out, even though I could feel the poison trying to spread through my system.

Using Georgie for support, I walked back to the fence. I walked back to my wife. Kingsley, Dudley, and Ivana met us halfway. They were all helping me walk. Everyone on both sides of the fence was staring at me.

I saw my wife. I saw Skie. Her face was puffy from crying. The gate was wide open. She was there waiting for me. Why in the hell was she holding a rifle?

I was the first one through.

"You walked through that gate, and you stepped into legend. One of caravan survivors had a camera and filmed your entire battle. Fifteen minutes, you fought for fifteen minutes, and no matter how badly you were injured, you never gave up. You became a hero almost overnight. The world knew your name. The world knew that you were real."

I never thought about any of that. I just did what I had to.

"Were you afraid?"

Of course, but action eliminates fear. A part of my mind told me to jump the fence. Use my new strength to hop over before the soldiers could shoot me down. A part of my mind told me that if I fought, I would die.

I hate being told what to do.

"Did you have any idea how famous you were?"

No. I mean, I knew people were talking about me…that had been going on from the beginning. I couldn't even begin to anticipate what things would be like after I got out of the decontamination unit.

"How long were you there?"

Georgie, Lucy, Dudley, Kingsley, Ivana, Merrick, and I were only there for a little while…I think. Skie never left my side. I slept through most of it, so I don't remember much. I only remember some elderly woman pouring water over my bite marks until the skin healed.

The next thing I knew, we were free to go.

Skie, Merrick, and I walked out of the room into a crowd of people. They were all giving me that salute thing they like to do.

My friends were out there as well. They too were saluting me. They just had bigger smiles than the others.

Skie was laughing.

"You did it baby," She said. "You saved everyone. You're a hero now."

I didn't reply.

I saw Major Crass a few steps away. There were soldiers trying to lead us to a helicopter, but I needed to know about Tito. I walked over to Crass.

"What happened to the other caravan of survivors?" I asked.

He gave me the nastiest look I think I've ever received.

"Don't come over here asking me questions, boy. Now get in that chopper and out of my sight before I have you thrown in the worst kind of jail you'd ever think about."

Spit was flying out of the guy's mouth he was so angry.

"Move, God damn you," he shouted again when I just stared in shock.

I didn't say anything; I was too tired. So I let Skie lead me away. The blades of the chopper were already spinning when I climbed inside. It was the first time I ever rode in a helicopter. As it lifted off the ground, I looked at my friends. They all looked as exhausted as I felt. I had no idea where we were even going, and I didn't much care.

It wasn't until later that I found out what happened to Tito.

Chapter 7

TITO

Arranging an interview with Tito wasn't easy. It took months. He wasn't easy to track down, and upon finally locating him, I was asked to not reveal his current whereabouts. He has never before made a public statement. He has never before done an interview. Upon his release from the decontamination unit, he simply vanished from the public eye until this moment. He is generally viewed as the worst kind of traitor, and the comparisons to Judas have not sat very well with him. Tito looked somewhere between nervous and angry as I sat across from him at the table. He was dressed in a dark suit and tie. His dark hair has gone mostly grey. When he speaks, he does so in a quiet voice.

Why would you want to hear my side of the story?

"A great story filled with great people has never fully been told. I want to be the person who finds out what really happened. I want to be the person that tells how it really was through the eyes of the people that lived it."

I guess you also want to tell about the greatest of mistakes as well…if you're talking to me.

"Is that how you see things?"

I'm very well aware of what I've done. I am also very well aware of what my pride has cost others. I'm no idiot; it's just that there's nothing I can do to change what I did. I wish there was but there isn't.

"Have you ever spoken to Jax about this?"

No, we haven't spoken since that morning.

"Which morning is that?"

The morning we left the Safe Zone. I've thought about trying to contact him…I'm just not ready yet.

"Why is that?"

I'm not sure that I want to hear what he has to say to me.

It was about as honest an answer as I could hope to get. To tell the truth, I myself am not sure what Jaxon would say to his one time friend.

"Can you tell me about it?"

Yeah, where should I start?

"Why don't you start with what was happening in the Safe Zone when Jax was in the Downtown area."

I can do that.

Well, while Jax was out causing trouble Downtown, I was left in the Safe Zone with everyone else. It wasn't easy, people were scared…no, they were terrified. I did my best to talk to them. I did my best to help them relax but they didn't want me, they wanted the General.

"Was that difficult for you?"

Yes, I was inadequate. It isn't easy to live in his shadow. He was always the popular one, he was always the adventurous one, the person every girl wants to know just a little bit better. It breeds resentment. If a person hangs with him long enough, that person will eventually resent him.

"Why?"

Because you will never be the one. No matter what you do, he will always be better than you. I think most people want to be him. After getting a taste of the life that he lives, they eventually get tired of being a sidekick and begin to desire the life of a hero.

The problem is…there's only one Jaxon.

"And you fell into this trap?"

Most certainly, I've always felt that I was in his shadow but when I was at the Safe Zone, and all those people were looking at him like some sort of hero…it was just too much for me. I wanted the fame that he had. I truly believed that, like so many times in the past, he was just in the right place at the right time. I wanted them to look at me like they looked at him.

"If he was just in the right place at the right time, what were your thoughts on how he rescued you?"

Before he got there, I was terrified. I was sure that I was going to die. I didn't think he'd come for me. It was a suicide mission; but then he was there. The world erupted into chaos as it so often does when he's around. He got me out with these simple ideas that anybody could have done. There was no magic involved, anyone could have done it.

I was angry with myself for needing to be rescued. I was angry for being afraid of the zombies. He wasn't afraid of them. I looked weak compared to him and I hated that. I took my anger out on him. I wanted to question everything he did. I wanted others to realize that he wasn't some great man. I wanted them to know that I was just as important.

"Did Jaxon ever do or say anything to put you down or make you feel this way?"

No, that's not his way. He's arrogant to a fault, but he never puts others down. In fact, he almost encourages others to have a higher self-esteem. It's just that no matter how high our self-esteem becomes, we still aren't Jaxon.

"You said he was arrogant. I've heard that before."

He has no doubts. If he wants something, he truly believes that he can achieve it. Most of us mere mortals are grounded in reality…Jaxon isn't. Truth be told, he doesn't have to be either, he does accomplish all his goals. I've never seen him fail at anything. People often want him to fail. He knows this and I think it's one of the things that give him the strength to succeed.

It's hard being around someone like that. It makes your flaws very apparent, if to nobody else but yourself.

"You said that you wanted to question everything that he did so that others realized that he wasn't so great. How did that work out?"

It worked out very poorly. Jaxon would just look at me like I was some sort of idiot. He knew exactly what I was doing. He probably even expected me to do it. That's another thing about Jaxon. Give him enough time to prepare, and he's a genius. He had an answer or a way to deal with everything.

"When did you meet Calvin?"

It was at the Safe Zone. Jaxon brought him and some redheaded chick out of Downtown. Calvin was told to "fuck off" as soon as the Jeep was safely inside the zone. I've known Jaxon for years, longer than any of his other friends. I could tell right away that he didn't like Calvin. Jaxon isn't normally that rude to someone unless they piss him off big time.

With Calvin, I found a kindred spirit. I found someone else that hadn't fallen under Jaxon's spell. Calvin saw him as an egomaniac and a dangerous one to boot. I now know better; I now know that Jax was only concerned about helping all those people, but when I spoke with Calvin, when I listened to him bash my friend and take away the fame…it felt…it felt good.

"You liked the fact that you found someone who didn't feel that the General was some sort of hero?"

Exactly, and when he began to talk about how the two of us could run things better than Jaxon, it was all I needed to hear. It was what I wanted to hear. I found someone who was thinking the exact same thing I was thinking.

I realize now that Calvin doesn't dislike Jaxon because he views him as a dangerous man. Calvin truly dislikes him…because Calvin is jealous. Jaxon is fearless, he's a leader, and people will follow him. Calvin is a coward. Nobody follows a coward.

"What happened the evening before you left the Safe Zone?"

I didn't want to be stuck inside and working on the computers, so I told Jax that some of the people were having some problems with his decisions.

"Is that true?"

No, I said that to bother him. I said it in an effort to cause him some doubt.

"Did it cause him to doubt himself?"

Not that I saw. He was more concerned with organizing everything with the caravans. He barely even paid me any attention.

"So if you weren't helping smooth over problems between Jaxon and the other survivors, what were you doing?"

Calvin and I were trying to cast some doubt into the minds of the other survivors. It wasn't like that at first, well at least for me it wasn't. I just wanted to know how they felt about Jaxon's plans to escape, but when everybody kept supporting him…I don't know…Calvin and I started to point out some of the faults we saw.

"What sorts of faults?"

They were only faults that we found in his personality. It doesn't really matter. What does matter is that nobody changed their opinion of him. They were ready to follow the General straight into all the valleys of hell if that was where he chose to lead them.

It was Calvin's idea for me to lead the second caravan. Actually, he wanted both of us to lead, but he knew Jaxon would probably smack him if he ever had the nerve to suggest it. Therefore, we decided that since Jax trusted me, I should be the one.

It wasn't difficult, I just told him that the people trusted me, and therefore they'd feel better with me in charge.

"What did Jaxon say to that?"

He agreed immediately. He even seemed rather relieved to hear me volunteer.

"How did you feel about the responsibility?"

Both Calvin and I were ecstatic. It was a chance for fame; it was a chance to prove that we were just as capable as Jaxon, and the best part about it was that we were taking the safer route with no known concentration of zombies. We would be the ones in charge out there on the road to Las Cruces, no longer under the General's shadow.

"Tell me about it."

It's not easy for me. It's still after all this time very difficult but I need to do it. I need to admit my wrong doings, and ask for forgiveness.

He paused at this point for about five minutes with his eyes closed before he began his tale.

Okay…my group left the Safe Zone first. I was angry that Jax felt he had to warn me to keep moving forward. He didn't want me to stop for anything, no matter what. I told Calvin what he had said to me.

"It sounds to me like he doesn't want anyone else getting any kind of recognition. Man, that guy's an asshole."

"Tell me about it," I answered.

We probably said a few more words on the subject but it wasn't anything of significance. Mostly, we sat in silence, thinking to ourselves. Both of us wanted that touch of fame. Both of us wanted to be the hero. We wanted to steal what Jaxon had. After all, neither of us believed that he had done anything extraordinary. Everything he accomplished, we could do just as easily.

The zombies came running out at us from the houses that we passed, not very many of them, at least not enough to worry me. We didn't stop. I knew that if we did, even more would undoubtedly be attracted by the noise. Later on, the houses would thin out until there was nothing left but open desert on both sides of the highway.

Still, I gave the order to shoot any zombie that gave us chase. It was something that I knew Jaxon would never allow me to do, because it made noise and noise attracted zombies. However, I didn't see it as a problem. We were moving forward, and we'd be long gone before any large hordes of the undead could track down the noise.

Calvin and I were laughing as the members of our caravan took shots at the pursuing zombies. The survivors ran through round after round with their guns, and missed so many times it bordered on ludicrous.

As we began to leave civilization behind and enter the desert we began to talk.

"There's still about ten of them chasing after us," Calvin said. "I can see them in the distance."

"Yeah, I can see them to."

"We should do something about it," Calvin said.

"Like what?" I asked.

"I'm not sure yet, but it might not look good if we lead them to the Las Cruces border."

"We're gaining distance on them," I answered.

"Yeah but I'd sure like to get some payback. Think about it. Wouldn't you like to blow away a group of zombies? Wouldn't you like to make a stand? Show everybody how it should be done."

It sounded good to me. It sounded like something that would get my name in the papers. I knew that I could lead these people. I knew that I could obliterate the zombies following us.

"See those small mountains way up ahead?" I asked even though they were kind of hard to miss. They were the last things we could see before the road curved behind them.

"Yeah, I see them," Calvin answered.

"Let's wait till we pass them, it's far enough away from suburbia that there won't be any surprises. Then, we'll make our move."

Calvin agreed readily. The road we were currently on led in an almost straight shot right to the New Mexico border just beyond the small mountains. At that point, we'd be about ninety percent of the way there. I thought it was a great idea. If all else failed, we were still close enough to the border to seek safety.

We plotted our course of action. It wasn't going to be extremely easy; we weren't able to coordinate with the other vehicles very easily. When we did tell them something, we had to shout out the windows and hope that they heard us.

After we passed the small mountains, we planned on turning a half circle in the road and aiming our SUV right back at our pursuers. Then we planned on having the other vehicles pull off to the sides of the road, one after another. We'd get the people out of the vehicles, and have them fall back behind our SUV. We didn't want them in the way when the bullets started flying. Finally, we'd get all our shooters, and have them line up across the road in front of our SUV. When the zombies rounded the small mountain, we'd blow them to hell.

I was nervous. Actually, I was scared to death. It's not easy to face down things that don't or shouldn't exist. Most people can't do it. Most people would rather run. I've heard of some people that just curled up into a ball before they were devoured. I kept telling myself to be strong. I only had to do this one time, and there was no way we could lose.

There weren't enough zombies chasing us. We had men with firearms. The minute the zombies were in range, it would be over, and I would be the one that lead everyone to victory.

Still, my legs were shaking violently. I don't know how Jaxon stood up to this kind of hell on such a regular basis. I began to wonder how he could make it look so easy, and I was damn near pissing my pants.

I assumed that it was frequency. That must be it. He did it so often and so many times that it became easy. If I had done this as much as him, I wouldn't be freaking out so much now.

I can do this. I can do this. I can do this. I kept telling this to myself as we got closer and closer to the small mountains. I didn't even have a gun; I wouldn't even be one of the men who were shooting.

My visions of greatness began to fade. I clung to the last one I had. It consisted of me raising up a hammer, and crashing it down on the head of the very last zombie. This zombie had been wounded from bullets and could only crawl towards me. It was an easy kill, but after I brought about its destruction, I would turn back to my fellow survivors with my arms raised in triumph. To a man, they would applaud.

When we finally passed the small mountain, we could no longer see the zombies that had been following us. We had plenty of time, and that was a good thing. Arranging the cars and the shooters was a hell of a time.

Calvin enjoyed being in power as much as I did. We gave out orders and, reluctantly, the people followed them. They weren't happy to be leaving their cars and trucks. We had to explain to them that they might not let us pass the border with zombies on our tail. It was a lie; it was a flat out lie. The zombies were so far behind us; whoever was at the gate probably wouldn't even see them until we had long since reached safety.

I think the people knew we were full of shit. They tried to argue but Calvin and I just ignored them and continued to give out orders. It took over a half an hour to get all the people behind our SUV.

The shooters weren't even lined up when the zombies rounded the small mountain. Their numbers had multiplied. Thinking back now, I guess there were about fifty zombies. All of them were running at us as fast as their undead legs could carry them.

For a moment, we did nothing but panic.

"What do you think happened?"

One of two things happened, or…maybe both. We made a lot of noise getting everyone to pull over and get into position. Some of the people were even honking their horns, and yelling out the window. They didn't want to fight. We made them. Also, a group of zombies in pursuit will attract other zombies. They were screaming and yelling as they chased after us. That's like a dinner bell.

Then again, maybe there's another reason. Maybe the extra zombies were just responding to all the noise we had made earlier when I ordered everyone with guns to start shooting at whatever gave us chase.

Regardless, it was bad. It was as bad as it could get. I shouted for anyone who had a weapon to start firing. To their credit, the survivors started shooting. They started shooting into that great mass of fifty zombies, and I'm not sure that they even dropped five of them.

As the zombies got closer, the people panicked. I panicked. Calvin ran off towards the border. He abandoned everyone. I tried to help people; I tried to get them to run…some of them listened. Some of them tried to get back into their cars. The cars were packed too tightly. They couldn't squeeze out. The sand on the side of the road gave them no traction to push their way out. The zombies literally fell upon them, and ripped them from their vehicles. I can still hear their screams in my head every night as I try to sleep. I can still see that fountain of blood spray from their necks as the zombies bit into them. I can still hear the way the sounds of their screams changed when the vocal cords were chewed through.

Eventually, I ran. I tried to stay as long as I could. I tried to get more of them to run but they wouldn't listen to me. There was just too much chaos, too much blood on the road, too many screams. It made things easy for the zombies.

As I was running, the zombies were chasing, and they were gaining. They don't seem to get tired and fall prey to exhaustion like the living do. They charged head long into the fleeing survivors and tackled them to the street. So many people fell around me, it was nightmarish.

There was more blood. There was more screaming. I began to scream as well. I gave up encouraging them to run. Panic filled my very veins. All I could think about was surviving. All I could think about was how much it would hurt if they began to chew into my stomach and devour me while I was still alive. It scared the hell out of me.

I began to scream for help as well.

I saw women and children brought down all around me. I saw them torn apart. I didn't try to help them. I just kept running.

Somehow, I escaped. I don't know why. It should have been me out there that died that day. It should have been me instead of them.

I was in charge of two hundred and ten men, women, and children. Only eight of us survived. Two hundred and two people died because I tried to grab some piece of glory for my fragile ego.

When I finally passed the gates, the weight of my mistakes rained down upon me. I crumbled to the ground under the realization of what I had caused. The soldiers had to carry me to the decontamination unit. They probably thought I was exhausted but that wasn't it at all. It was the shame. The zombies couldn't catch me but the shame brought me to my knees.

One thing, and one thing only, began to replay over and over through my mind as I lay there in the decontamination unit awaiting my release. Jaxon had warned me not to stop. He told me to keep moving forward no matter what. I didn't listen to him. I should have listened to him. I made a horrible mistake.

I've been in counseling since that day. The government pays for it. They pay for all the survivors of El Paso who need counseling. It took me a long time to be able to admit my guilt aloud but I can do it now. It's my fault. I accept all the blame. I won't speak for Calvin; he's an asshole just like the General thought he was.

I used to resent Jaxon for getting all the glory. I used to resent him for being the hero. Well, let me tell you…the man is a hero. He may have a gigantic ego but he saves lives. He puts himself in harm's way to protect others.

I don't envy him anymore. The things he faces…and I've heard that he's faced far worse since that day…but those things…are the stuff of nightmares.

However, I wish…I wish I could join him. I wish I had the courage to speak to him. Because if anyone needs to be there by his side, it should be me, I have a lot to make up for. I have a lot to apologize for.

Tears began to slowly slide down his cheeks and Tito turned his head away as if to hide them. His shame was so painful to watch, I began to cry along with him. I feel bad for him. I really, truly feel bad for him. The man had the gall to stand up and flat out tell me, and therefore, the entire world that he accepted full responsibility for his actions. It's impressive, and it's also probably a bit too late. However, I wish him peace. He's suffered enough.

On a side note, I tried to once again speak with Calvin in a follow up interview, but after hearing that Tito had broken his silence and spoken to me, he has since cancelled all his public engagements and interviews.

To this day, he will no longer speak to the press.

Chapter 8

SKIE

Skie is, by all accounts, tiny. She's maybe a couple of inches over five feet tall, and that's if she's lucky. She was wearing a light green dress that she proudly announced was of her own design when I complimented it. She smiles often, and when she does, I've noticed that it tends to make others smile as well.

What I didn't know from watching the short videos that I've seen of Skie is that she loves to talk. From the minute I entered the house where she and Jaxon are staying, her mouth was moving a mile a minute. Obviously, she has a talent for spreading cheerful happiness with more than her smile, because she had me laughing within three minutes of having met her.

Finally, I managed to get her to sit down and do the interview.

So, you want me to tell you about my husband.

"I'd like that. I can't think of a better way to get to know the man behind the legend than speaking to his wife."

Well, what would you like to know?

"Tell me what he's like. Tell me what kind of man he is."

Jaxon is different than any man I think you'll ever meet. I'm sure you've heard that he's arrogant right?

"I have heard that yes."

Well, it's true. He's pretty arrogant but what people may not have told you is that he's never arrogant in a way that puts others down. He just lacks pretty much all self-doubt. Maybe it's one of the reasons that he can go out and do the things that he does. He never imagines that he'll fail. He might believe there'll be some setbacks but in the end he truly believes he'll win.

That however, is nothing new to anyone. What I'd like people to know about my husband is that he's one of the sweetest people I've ever met. He truly does care about the well being of others. When I first met him, this protection mostly centered on his friends. That's probably why they are such a close group of people; they're attracted to his morals, his loyalty to them, and his, often childish attitude (which is more often than not very entertaining). During what happened in El Paso, his care and concern spread to others. It's probably much simpler to him; he can help people, so that's what he does.

He can be rude. That's something he probably doesn't even think about. He often says whatever's floating around in his head, but he usually doesn't mean to offend anyone. When strangers meet him, they'd probably note that he's quiet, and somewhat guarded, until he gets to know them. That's normal for him. He just doesn't always do well with strangers. It unfortunately also adds to his reputation of being rude, but give him time, and you'll probably like him just as much as the rest of us.

When he's on the job, he's very different from when he's at home. At home, he's all about having a good time. He'll laugh and joke from the time he wakes up to the time he goes to bed. He likes to read, he loves movies, and he's always playing the Xbox. When he's on the job, he's a leader. People die if they don't listen to him. He doesn't tolerate anyone interfering. He'll be rude, he'll be dismissive, and if things still don't settle down, he's likely to smack someone over the head.

"Has that happened before?"

I've heard about him smacking more than a few folks that were standing in his way when he was trying to save people. I've also heard about him taking on an entire police force once when they wouldn't listen to him. That's why the President gave him his badge.

"So that's true? Can you tell me about it?"

Of course I can, it's no secret. The badge basically grants him the power to override and/or take control over any police force or military body when a threat to the public is possibly underway. He uses it often; it allows him to cut through any red tape and start saving lives immediately. The police and military leaders don't normally like it very much but the men under them seem rather relieved whenever Jaxon shows up and takes over. At least that's what everybody tells me.

"I can see why, he does have a reputation of saving lives."

Yeah, he's good at it.

"How do you feel about what he does?"

I understand that it's necessary. I understand that people need him. However, I hate it. I've grown used to it. I've grown used to sitting up all night and waiting for him to come home. I know that when he gets called in, it's because something evil and monstrous is killing people, but if I could, I'd take him very far away from all of that. He's my husband. I love him with all my heart, and I truly wish that it were someone else that was chosen to be the Guardian and not him.

"Chosen to be the Guardian?"

Yes, Miriam believes that he's a sort of chosen guardian against the bad things that harm people. There's a lot worse than zombies out there. Jaxon has beaten everything down but it's really scary sometimes.

"Who is Miriam?"

Miriam is someone who works for the government in a kind of advisory capacity. She's an expert on the things that Jaxon fights. Don't bother trying to get an interview though; she'll never do it.

"How did you meet her?"

She showed up at my house in the middle of the night the evening before the outbreak with about twenty soldiers. They were banging on the door until I woke up. She was looking for Jaxon but he wasn't there. She started asking me about a million questions about him and then all of a sudden one of the soldiers got a call on his earpiece, and ordered everyone to fall back and retreat. Miriam took my two kids and me with them. At the time, she wasn't sure that Jaxon was going to be the Guardian but, just in case it did turn out to be him, she wanted him to be able to concentrate on his job without worrying about us.

"That must have scared the hell out of you?"

Of course it did. I was woken up in the middle of the night by some elderly lady and a bunch of soldiers and then taken from my home.

"Where did they take you?"

A Motel 6 in New Mexico. Major Crass (the guy in charge) had commandeered the entire motel and the military was using it as their command center. I was placed in a room with my kids and I had to wait for about three hours before Miriam came and knocked at the door. I let her in and she told me that zombies and other monsters were real, and all the signs and visions she was getting led her to believe that my husband was going to become some sort of hero. Miriam's a witch by the way, Gypsy ancestry and everything. She's also around three hundred years old. I'll explain more about her later when she actually meets Jaxon.

Anyway, it's not very easy to believe that your husband is supposed to become some sort of hero. By all accounts, Jax does show leadership qualities but he normally uses them to be a pain in the ass. Jax likes to have fun; he's creative, but he's often irritating, and always mischievous. People, for whatever reason, put up with him and he can also often talk them into participating in his pranks. I love him, but I'm not exactly sure how any of those qualities translate into him being a hero.

For the longest time I thought everyone around me was insane. The next morning, it happened. One minute nothing and the next…the outbreak was in full swing. The dead were everywhere, and it was spreading like wildfire. It was really scary.

Major Cross shut down all forms of communication very quickly. He wanted to track the General's movements and make sure no one was planning any sort of escape from the city that could spread the outbreak. It was Cross that set up EPUA but for the longest time there was no Jaxon. This really infuriated Cross. He provided only one form of communication and Jaxon wasn't using it. Another thing about Cross, he didn't believe in Jaxon either. He was put in charge of the situation and told to contain and cooperate with Miriam. If he had his way, he'd have simply nuked El Paso. Miriam was the one who stopped him. She gave the much-needed time for a hero to make his presence known. Cross would never have sent any of his men into El Paso. If no hero had ever stepped forward, he would have eventually destroyed the city.

Days went by and still no sign from Jaxon (I was allowed to email him once early on but he never responded to it). I began to fear the worst and hope for the best. I was hoping that he was either safe somewhere, and if that wasn't possible, I was hoping that he was running late and never even made it back into El Paso.

It was hard to have any hope at all with all of those poor people dying.

There was a large screen in a conference room of the motel. This screen was connected to the EPUA website twenty-four hours a day. I watched it as much as I could. Everyone watched it as much as they could.

One morning, Miriam came to my door. She told me to go look at the screen. Everyone was talking about the General. They were telling all these stories. At that point, my heart sank. Jaxon never had anything to do with the military. It couldn't be him calling himself the General.

Miriam laughed at me in a motherly sort of way and assured me that it was my husband.

I watched EPUA for hours and hours. Finally, after the sun had set, Tito began to ask for help. Somehow, he also believed that Jaxon was the General. He wrote a little bit more; I think he was talking about why he knew the General had to be Jaxon. I don't really remember all I remember was that the General answered him. He told him something about sitting tight and being safe. He told Tito that he was coming.

At that point, I believed. It was such a "Jaxon" thing to do. He would risk everything for one of his friends. Don't ask him to help you move into a new house but, if you had a major problem, he'd be there.

The site crashed with all the responses. So many people were calling out to him. So many people needed his help. Cross threw a fit. He blamed the crash on Jaxon. He started yelling at Miriam that this Guardian business was a waste of time and he'd be happier when the man was dead. I started yelling at him at that point. Miriam calmly stepped between us, and told him to follow his orders.

"Why was major Cross so against Jaxon?"

He hates Guardians. He doesn't believe that there are things out there in this world that can't be handled by soldiers. Supposedly, there used to be another man named Mr. Hardin that was in charge of these things but that man had retired a few years ago. They were currently looking for this man so he could take over and fix all the damage caused by Cross.

Anyway, Cross was pretty pissed off about Mr. Hardin's eventual return. He wanted to start exterminating the entire city. He thought it was an incredible danger to simply keep things contained.

The next morning, Jax struck again. He was on the move. He was fighting back. Others were joining him. Crass started laughing. He thought it was all just an ugly coincidence.

Miriam just patted my arm in response. She whispered to me that if she knew her Guardians at all, Crass was in for a big surprise.

That's how things went for the longest time. I followed his movement's every day and every evening until I could no longer keep my eyes open. At any given moment, there were always people talking about him.

"What was it like for you to be reading about your husband, to be sitting there and reading about him becoming a hero to all those people?"

It was terrifying and exciting all at the same time. I was proud of him, yet I was so worried about him. I would scream and cheer whenever he won something or accomplished something. At first every soldier in the room with me would just stare at me like I was some sort of crazy woman, but eventually I think they began to believe in him as well. They would hug me or pat me on the back when he was in danger. They also began to cheer right along with me when he was safe.

Eventually, the day came when Jax announced to the world that he was leaving El Paso. He asked everyone to meet him at two entryways into New Mexico.

Major Crass stared at the screen like he couldn't believe what he had just read. He stared, and stared, and kept on staring when that same message started repeating itself over and over from different people in the Safe Zone.

He then flew into a rage.

He started screaming and yelling. He was demanding that the website be shut down. He started yelling for the soldiers to shoot anybody trying to cross the fences. He started screaming at Miriam that her stupid beliefs were about to kill the entire country. He huffed and he puffed and he huffed and he puffed.

And then the phone rang.

Crass shut up immediately. He answered it in a quiet voice. I'm not sure who it was but Crass started speaking with a whole lot of respect. The conversation was quick, and after he said his respectful goodbye, he cancelled all his angry orders and left the room.

I laughed my butt off.

"Why?"

Because that course of action was so typical of Jax—give him enough time, and the man's a genius.

"I've heard something like that before about him."

Yeah, that's because it's true. His mind never shuts off. He's always coming up with new ways to attack whatever problem he's facing and normally, whatever solution he comes up with is most certainly going to seriously piss off whoever is causing him problems.

He did it once again.

I was so proud of my baby. I wasn't sure what was going to happen next but something told me that he'd just taken a big bite out of Major Crass's ass.

A few hours later, I learned that they were ordering decontamination units. The military was going to let them out. The world was going to learn that the General was not some made up myth, he was a real man, and I was for damn sure going to be right there at the fence waiting for him.

Miriam agreed to take me to the fence. She was going there as well, unfortunately so was Crass.

As the sun peeked out over the mountain, we arrived at the fence. The soldiers were already in place. The helicopters were grounded for some reason. Others were arriving. The Generals legions of fans were coming to see if their hero was indeed real. The military didn't even try to keep them away from the fences. Miriam said that someone higher up gave Crass orders to simply keep the people safe but to otherwise not interfere.

Crass marched over to Miriam and me.

"Any sign of trouble and I'm not opening that gate," he told Miriam with a smile on his face.

"Any trouble comes toward my husband and he sure as hell won't need your help," I answered with my own smile.

I'm not sure how long it took before I saw the caravan. I was waiting on pins and needles. I could barely contain myself. Then I saw Georgie and the rest of my friends, but no Jaxon. I ran to the fence just as Crass was telling them to hand over their weapons.

"Where's Jaxon?" I nearly screamed to Georgie.

"He'll be on his way. He was just creating a distraction so the rest of us could make it here without any problems," he answered. "That Crass guy said we have to wait for the decontamination units to arrive before we can cross."

I had learned all about those plastic box rooms the night before from Miriam. They weren't anything great, just portable safe areas designed with different glass walled rooms. They were going to be used just in case anyone was infected.

"How long were the survivors supposed to stay in these units?"

Two weeks. If they were still alive, they were released, because anyone still alive in two weeks time was obviously not infected. Two weeks was also a rather exaggerated amount of time, but better safe than sorry. If anyone was infected, the scientists and doctors on staff could study them and provide medical assistance to ease their suffering, if needed.

The decontamination units were currently being erected a few hundred yards to my left. They were almost finished, but somehow I knew Crass was going to drag his feet.

Georgie was carrying a portable radio. He began to speak to someone on the other end; it took me only a few seconds to realize who the person was. It was Jaxon. It was my Jaxon and he was on his way. In fact, he would be arriving in just a few minutes.

I looked towards Miriam and she smiled at me.

The crowd on my side of the fence began to chant at the top of their lungs.

"What were they chanting?"

"Let them in."

"How did Crass feel about that?"

I'm sure it pissed him off, but I wasn't paying any attention. I was just enjoying the fact that my husband would soon be in my arms where he belonged. Even the soldiers were somewhat lax about everything. They were there in the crowd but they had no orders as of yet and were just kind of enjoying the party.

"It was a party?"

It was. I mean, I know everyone was chanting and making their demands, but the entire atmosphere was very excited. Until Jaxon showed up that is.

You could feel the change in the air. The chanting began to die down slowly as everyone noticed the approaching men. The crowd pushed as close as they could for a better look. I lost my place in the shuffle. I tried like hell to get it back but there were just too many people in my way. Someone shouted out, "It's the General," and the rowdy crowd silenced completely.

I started jumping up and down for a better look, and finally caught a glimpse of him. He looked tired but he was smiling. I didn't even try to stop all the tears that were pouring out of my eyes. I can't help it; I'm a big crybaby.

After the very brief shock of seeing Jaxon for the first time, the crowd erupted into cheers. The excitement was tremendous. It was everywhere—even the soldiers were clapping. I knew this was probably embarrassing my husband. He's not too good with too much attention. I was laughing out loud now as he approached Georgie. He still hadn't seen me. Georgie motioned with his head and Jax walked over to the fence.

Everyone began to stare at me and I got a small taste of that embarrassment that Jax was going through just moments before. I don't know how they knew it was me—that I was his wife—but they began to move out of the way.

My husband could now see me clearly. I ran to the fence, and grabbed his fingers through the links. My baby was exhausted. I could see it in his face, and I could see it in the way that he carried his body.

I said something romantic to him and Jaxon, being the complete unromantic man that he is, said something stupid right back to me, but it made me laugh. He always makes me laugh. My body and mind began to argue over what I should be doing, crying or laughing. I must have looked ridiculous, but I didn't care. I had my husband back.

He leaned into the fence and I held his fingers even tighter. It was my turn to be strong now, and I told him so. I told him not to worry. The crowd was cheering so loudly I could barely even hear myself think. It was incredible. It was a relief that I had waited for. It was an exhalation that had been way too long in coming.

Something wasn't right.

I could tell from the way Jax was looking at me. Something was going on, and he was worried. The smell of the dead tainted my nostrils.

He pulled his fingers from my hands, and asked for Crass. I ran to find the man. I was in a panic. I didn't want to leave Jax but I did as he asked.

It wasn't easy to get Crass to come with me but he eventually did. I think he couldn't keep his morbid curiosity under control. Some sick part of him wanted to meet his self-appointed enemy.

Jax tried to warn him. He tried to ask for help, but Crass refused. I remember the look on my husband's face. He couldn't believe that Major Crass would sit back, and do nothing. He couldn't believe that, after getting this far, the military would refuse him.

Jax rebounded quickly. He came towards me at the fence and put his fingers back through the holes. I grabbed onto them as hard as I could. It was almost as if I were about to attempt to pull him right through the holes in the chain in order to keep him safe. I would have if I could.

People began screaming at some point. I'm not sure when, even though I heard them. I was stunned. This should have been our reunion. This should not have been happening.

Jax was telling me to run. He was telling me to leave the area as fast as I could. Actually, he was screaming at me. I could see the worry in his face. I wasn't exactly paying any attention. Over his shoulder, I caught a glimpse of what was headed our way for the first time.

Nothing on the face of this earth can describe the terror of that many zombies rushing towards you. They don't think. They don't feel pity. They are simply evil things that were once human. They will never stop until either you are dead, or they are dead. They were coming for my husband and all of those innocent people he had tried to protect.

I noticed the complete panic that was going on all around me in a vague sort of way. People were still screaming. They were running around now, most of them in circles. They didn't know how to get around all the little blockades the military had erected. They were like mice caught in a maze.

Jaxon told me to run once again. I told him no. I told him a great many things actually. I believe all of which dealt with him getting his ass over that fence and leaving with me. There was nothing anyone could do. At the very least, I could save my husband. He needed to come away with me. Enough of this Guardian shit…just run away with me and be safe.

Not far away from us, a redheaded girl tried to climb the fence. A soldier shot her dead in front of everyone. He was following orders from Crass; he was doing what Crass had ordered him to do in order to protect the rest of the country. It was wrong. She wasn't infected. None of them were.

Everything around me went even crazier. Everyone was so scared. I felt bad for them. I squeezed my husband's fingers as tightly as I could. I refused to let him go.

At some point Georgie came over to us. I paid him no attention. I know they were talking, but I have no idea what they were saying. I think Jaxon was trying to come up with a plan. I didn't care. As far as I was concerned, there was no acceptable plan unless it dealt with my husband killing all the soldiers, and making his escape with me by his side. That might be shocking, but to hell with them all if they weren't going to help my husband and the people he was protecting, I really didn't care if all the soldiers were killed.

Suddenly, Kingsley was there. I began to pay attention somewhat, because I heard him say something about explosives. Jaxon smiled. He said something to Kingsley, and for the first time, he looked away from me and gazed upon the advancing zombies.

I looked at the zombies as well. They were rushing down Country Club road. It was frightening. Jax told Kingsley to blow the bridge when they were halfway across. Then, he stood closer to the fence. I knew what he was doing; he was shielding me with his body.

We heard the click of the detonator, and after an odd pause that seemed way too long, Jax turned to watch the explosion. It was loud. It was scary loud, but apparently Jaxon had experienced worse. He didn't even flinch. The bridge blew up into the air, and then came back down with a crunch and rumble that shook the ground where I was standing. Dust and water and pieces of asphalt flew into the air.

The people all around us immediately went quiet. The storm of debris blocked out everything around the bridge. Everyone thought it was over. They began to regain some of their composure. Some of them even began to clap and cheer. Those people must not have seen that poor redheaded girl get shot down from the fence. I myself couldn't find anything to cheer about.

Jaxon told me that it was over. I gave him a smile, but then the cloud of dust began to drift away. I saw the dead rising slowly to their feet. There was a delay in the detonation. Something like two hundred zombies had been blown towards our side. They were unsteady and damaged after the explosion, but that didn't stop them. They wanted to get to the people, and already they were moving.

I immediately looked into my husband's face as he slowly turned his head back towards me. Our eyes met and he didn't have to say a word. I knew what he was going to do but he said it anyway.

"I have to do this," he said.

"Don't you dare leave me, Jax," I replied. "You just stay right here; don't you dare leave me."

I grabbed at his fingers frantically. If I could just keep him with me, everything would be okay. Someone else would have to stand up and play the hero. Someone else would die. Someone other than my husband; it didn't need to be him. He had done enough. He didn't need to die.

"I love you very much," he whispered, and gently began to pull his fingers from my grasp. I screamed at him. I screamed for him not to leave me. I screamed every single thing I could think of that might make him stay with me, but he wouldn't be stopped. Slowly, as if in a dream, my husband turned away from me and turned to face what I just knew would be the death of him.

I noticed Merrick for perhaps the very first time. She looked up at me and then over to Jax. She gave a little huff and trotted off after him.

As I watched my husband pull his knife and tomahawk from his belt, once again I noticed how very tired he looked. He didn't want to play the hero anymore. He wanted to be safe with me. I think that's what really defines him as a hero. He doesn't enjoy it. He does it because no one else can.

On both sides of the fence people stared quietly in disbelief. The General was making a stand against impossible odds, but he was making it nonetheless. It was a sacrifice meant to buy enough time for the decontamination units to be finished and the gates to be opened. You could have heard a pin drop.

Miriam came over to me. The shock on her face was evident. She couldn't contain the disbelief.

"What the hell is he doing?" she asked. "There's too many of them. He can't win. This is stupid. Get him back."

She had lost all the composure that she normally held onto with the grace of a queen. I had no words for her. I simply couldn't take the time to explain that my husband was sacrificing his life in order to give these people a chance. That is, of course, if Major Cross would ever open the damn gates. Yet, something told me that he'd have no problem letting everyone in once Jaxon was dead.

In a flash, the battle was engaged.

Jaxon and Merrick ran straight towards the unsteady zombies that charged towards them. They collided with a bone jarring impact that I could hear all the way from where I was at the fence, something like five hundred yards or so away. It was a sickening sound. I didn't like it. I wondered what kind of damage and pain that must have caused his poor body.

For a moment I couldn't see him through all the zombies that had surrounded him. Then, I saw the arc of the tomahawk as he brought it down in a powerful swing. Jaxon was incredible. He fought like some kind of demon. The dead fell all around him. They rushed forward, only to be brought down almost as soon as they reached him.

In my entire life, I've never seen such wanton destruction. Skull after skull was cleaved and crushed beneath his tomahawk. His knife stabbed into eye sockets and temples. He ducked and rolled, slashing tendons and crippling enemies. His white t-shirt was very quickly soaked in blood. The street became a literal pool of gore.

Still, the zombies came. Some eventually rose up off the street where the explosion had blown them, and others clambered up the embankment that lead to the rushing river. They were covered in hideous and severe injuries, but they were still coming, their very numbers making them a danger no man could overcome.

Jaxon was taking damage. His injuries were mounting up. I lost count of how many times he fell. I lost count of how many times my heart dropped into my stomach. I was screaming inside for this to be over with. How much could he take?

However, despite his suffering, I didn't want it to end. Instead, I wanted him to overcome the impossible and win. I wanted him to stand triumphantly in victory over his hellish enemies.

He fell. Eventually, there were just too many of them. Eventually, he just became so exhausted that he could no longer fight. I tried to keep from screaming. I watched zombie after zombie pile on top of him. Merrick was still fighting. She was still attacking them even when Jaxon could no longer be seen. She wouldn't give up.

It wasn't easy to hold back my screams.

The pile of zombies bit and tore into one another in an effort to grab a hold of my husband. The pile itself must have been six feet high. There was no sign of Jaxon. There was nothing moving in there that was human.

Time went by. Second after second ticked away on a clock I didn't possess. That scream was still inside of me. It needed to come out. I had just lost my husband. I hated them. I wished for a weapon. I wished for the power to fight them, to make them suffer for killing the man I loved.

I opened my mouth to scream obscenities at them. To curse them, to say hateful things as if my words could damage them as much as they had damaged me, what came out was something different entirely.

"GET UP JAXON! GET UP!"

People looked at me with pity in their eyes, as if I was some poor little woman who couldn't accept the fact that she just lost her husband.

They were right.

What they didn't know is that Jaxon really, really hates to lose. What they didn't know was just how incredibly tough Jaxon truly is. It comes from something inside of him that I will never truly understand.

The man is no quitter, and I truly think he heard me scream.

The pile of zombies rose up two or three feet, and collapsed once again. Then…it exploded. Zombies flew ten feet in all directions.

Jaxon stood alone.

He was covered in gore. Merrick walked over to stand next to him. He puffed out his chest and screamed at his attackers. They screamed right back and charged again.

He met them with a beautiful violence. It was beautiful because for the first time, I thought he might actually be able to win. Violent because all the carnage, blood, and sickening noises that came forth when steel met bone were something out of a nightmare.

I loved it.

I loved that he was breaking them. I loved that he was crushing them. He was exhausted, injured, in severe pain, and he was winning.

No one could believe what they saw. The people on both sides of the fence stood transfixed. They held their collective breaths since the battle began, and I had yet to hear them exhale.

"We need to get the gates open or all this will be for nothing," Miriam said. "We can't lose Jaxon. Look at him; he's been bitten. If he doesn't heal soon, he could die."

How the hell I was going to get the gates open was beyond me, but that didn't mean I wasn't going to try.

I ran to the decontamination units, and screamed into the doctor's face.

"What the hell are you doing? Cross won't open the gates until these things are finished."

"They've been finished for awhile now, lady," the doctor answered. "Crass doesn't seem to care."

That son of a bitch was dragging his feet, just like I thought he would. I had had enough. He wanted my husband to die. That was something I refused to allow. I don't know where I got the courage, I don't know where I found the strength, but I found a piece of metal pipe that was discarded by the side of the decontamination unit, and brought it down on the head of the first soldier I found.

Of course, I had only hit his helmet but when he spun around in pain and surprise, I hit him again in the face. He fell to the ground unconscious, and I picked up his rifle.

Jaxon and Georgie had taken me shooting a few times. It wasn't anything that I really enjoyed but I knew how to flick off the safety. Crass wasn't hard to find. He was by the fence, watching my husband fight for his life. Crass seemed to be enjoying the show. He had a smile on his face right up until the moment I jammed the end of the rifle barrel into his face as hard as I could.

He staggered a few steps back, and then glared at me with furious eyes.

"Open those gates or I'll blow your fucking head off," I told him.

It only took him a moment to realize that I was serious. He walked with me right behind him over to two soldiers guarding the entrance. The soldiers looked at me but did nothing. I find that odd considering I had a rifle leveled at the back of their commanding officer. Maybe they were glad the ass was finally getting what was coming to him.

He ordered the gates open.

That's when the oddest thing I think I've ever seen happened (not counting reanimated corpses of course). Nobody moved. All those survivors did not rush forth to safety. They stayed transfixed as my husband fought for their lives.

Jaxon had fallen once again. It wasn't from any blow, or maybe it was from the hundreds he had already received. The zombies rushed to close in on him. He struggled with his own exhaustion to rise and meet them.

Out of the blue, Georgie entered the battle. Apparently, he hadn't given up all his weapons. He had a pistol, and he was shooting down every single zombie that neared Jaxon. Georgie was on fire. It was as if he couldn't miss.

Then, he was standing next to Jaxon. Jaxon rose to his feet. He moved slowly, but soon had his tomahawk back in his hand. He'd lost his knife. He wasn't going to be happy about that.

Georgie, Merrick, and Jaxon fought, and fought, until all the zombies were destroyed. It didn't take them long. It didn't take them long at all.

Jaxon was covered in blood and gore. He was also apparently not finished. He shambled towards the edge of the bridge. The zombies on the other side reached and screamed for him. Some of them even tried to brave the rushing waters, only to be swept away in the current.

Jaxon screamed back. He screamed out his challenge with everything that was left in his body. Like I said, my man is no quitter.

She laughed at her own little joke, but I knew she was right. I've seen the footage. The entire world has seen the footage. Every now and then, you can still see it being played on the news. Every now and then, you can catch a one-hour special on TV that analyzes the man, and the footage.

"What happened next?"

His strength finally gave out. Jaxon fell, and Georgie immediately helped him to his feet. The two of them, along with Merrick, slowly walked back to the fence. Some of our friends went towards them to help Georgie with Jaxon. He was pretty out of it, dead on his feet, so to speak. I think he was even going in and out of consciousness.

When they neared the fence, the crowd parted to let him through. Everyone was reaching out to touch him. Some of the people even began to pray for what they thought was their fallen hero. They saw the bites. They saw the tears in his flesh. Any normal man would have turned inside of an hour.

Jaxon is far from being a normal man.

Miriam immediately went into action. She was barking orders at everyone. Jaxon was now completely unconscious as the poison spread throughout his body.

"He's been bitten too many times," Miriam said. "He's also exhausted himself. I need to get to work immediately."

When Miriam gives orders, people listen. In seconds he was brought to the decontamination unit and stripped down. Georgie took his tomahawk and held it for him. Jaxon would want that back.

Merrick snapped at anyone who tried to keep her away from my husband.

Miriam began hosing Jaxon off with a water-hose-like thing that was attached to the wall, kind of like one of those moveable showerheads. The wounds were already yellow and rimmed with puss. The water actually hissed when it hit the damaged areas, but the worst of the infection was literally being washed away right before my eyes.

After that, she had him placed in some sort of muddy bath. I was shocked at first. I couldn't believe that that was all she or they or anyone was going to do for him.

"Mother earth will heal her chosen son," Miriam said with a smile on her face. "It will work; your man is strong...very, very strong."

All of our friends were watching through the glass wall. None of them would leave until they were sure Jaxon was going to be all right. When they heard the good news, their cheers were simply thunderous.

All in all, I think Jaxon was unconscious for about three days. Georgie, Lucy, Dudley, Kingsley, Ivana, Merrick, and I never left his side until the moment he woke up. When that happened, the others went outside to give us some time.

He smiled at me. There was a billion dollars in that smile, and I hugged and kissed him, despite all the mud and muck.

He wasn't about to stay there; he immediately got out of the mud bath, toweled off and dressed.

Nobody tried to stop him. I think they were all just baffled that he was moving around. Miriam waved the doctors and scientists away from him.

Together, along with Merrick, we stepped out of the decontamination unit and Jaxon stepped into fame.

Everyone was there, and they were all saluting him. Jaxon was too stunned to really react; he just hugged me to him a little bit tighter.

I remember that I was laughing. I was as happy as could be. My husband was safe, and we were finally leaving this nightmare behind.

"You did it baby," I said. "You saved everyone. You're a hero now."

He didn't reply. He had seen Crass, and despite the soldiers trying to usher us to the waiting helicopter, Jax rushed over to him to ask about the other caravan that was led by Tito.

Major Crass, being the asshole that he is, refused to answer Jaxon's question. Instead, he threatened to have my husband arrested if he didn't leave immediately. I felt bad for Jaxon. He had no idea how much Crass hated him. He was dumbfounded at the animosity. Which was probably a good thing for Crass; Jaxon normally wouldn't stand for being treated like that. I led him gently away to our friends and the waiting chopper.

He fell asleep the minute we were in the air.

My husband only woke up when we began to descend. A clearing had been made in the thick pine forest of his parents' front yard.

"Can you tell me where that is?"

New Mexico. Ruidoso, to be exact; Jaxon's parents own a big cabin up there. He likes to ride his bike around in the mountains, so we're always going up there.

I saw his parents on the front porch waiting for the chopper to land. They looked worried, and they also looked relieved. I wasn't allowed to make any phone calls during this entire ordeal. In fact, I had only this very morning been able to contact my own parents. I wasn't too worried, they live outside of El Paso, and I had no real reason to be worried but—man, oh man—were they worried about me.

My kids came running out of the woods. They had been taken to the cabin earlier in the day. To say the least, they were happy enough not too cramped inside a motel room any longer.

As we left the chopper, it immediately rose back into the air. It was then I noticed our many bodyguards. They had sent at least ten soldiers to the cabin to make sure we were safe and sound, or maybe they were here to make sure Jaxon didn't leave.

No chance in that. My husband was exhausted. He barely said a word to anyone. He immediately went straight to the shower, and spent over two hours scrubbing. When I finally went to check on him, he had just finished shaving, and was in the process of dousing his body with cologne.

"I can't get the smell out of my nose," he told me.

He wasn't right. Miriam had warned me about this. She said that he would eventually go through some kind of post-traumatic stress. It's a byproduct of all the killing he was involved in. As a matter of fact, she told me that most Guardians are eased into the violence. Jaxon was put in a sink or swim situation. There were bound to be some negative effects. Still, she told me that it wouldn't last long.

I helped him find some lotions, and hair products, that smelled pretty. It wasn't enough. He jumped back into the shower, and began scrubbing furiously. Afterwards, he slept for two solid days.

I would check on him every few hours or so but he never stirred. Nobody could tell me when the last time he slept had been. Merrick, for her part, was perfectly happy being with Jaxon's parents. She loved his mom, but she would sneak into his room and check on him almost as much as I did.

When Jaxon finally woke up, he had a glass of Pepsi and went right back to his room for another shower. I was worried that he hadn't eaten. His entire body looked different, not only slimmer but somehow stronger. It's hard to explain, but my husband had changed.

Five days after we had come to the cabin, Georgie dragged Jax out of the bedroom to watch something on the TV. The rest of us had known since our first night at the cabin about the fifteen minutes of footage, but this was the first time Jaxon had seen it.

He watched it for about three minutes, and then left the room with a dull expression. Georgie felt pretty bad, and began to worry that he caused even more harm on Jaxon's psyche.

That evening when we went to bed, Jaxon began to have the nightmares. Miriam had warned me about this as well. All the Guardians went through this. It was pretty much where they learned to fight, and they learned about the kinds of things they would have to fight. Jaxon would wake up in a cold sweat.

Another evening, he heard a noise outside the cabin, and tore off into the woods with his tomahawk. It was just a deer, but he almost killed it anyway. He couldn't sleep for the rest of the evening. I had no idea how to help him. He sat looking out the window until the sun rose in the sky.

Another week went by, and everyone was worried about him. He rarely left the bedroom. His mother wanted to take him to a shrink. This definitely wasn't the Jaxon we all knew and loved. All of us were careful about even talking to him. The slightest thing could set him off. The look of anger that would come into his eyes was frightening.

When Miriam finally arrived at the cabin one morning, I almost cried I was so relieved.

"You warned me that he would have a difficult time, but I'm really worried. He's not acting right; he can barely sleep, he barely eats, and he won't talk to anybody about it."

"Well, how would you act if you went through the things he went through?" she answered with a motherly pat on my head. "It's time that he learns about his destiny."

I called Jaxon into the kitchen, and gave him a cup of coffee as I introduced him to Miriam. He shook her hand politely, and settled in to drink his coffee and ignore her. Miriam wasn't about to put up with the silent treatment.

"Having a rough time of things, Jaxon?" she asked.

"Are you a shrink?"

"Not really, but I have had to listen to enough problems over the years. Actually, I'm sort of your guide."

Jaxon immediately turned to me.

"What's she talking about?" he asked.

"If you have questions about me, I would appreciate it if you asked me yourself, young man."

The look Jaxon gave her as he turned his head was terrible. It should have come with a snarl.

"All right, who the hell are you, and what the hell do you want?" he asked in a low voice. His friends and family (who were scattered about the living room) all turned to see what was happening between the two of them, they were certainly more than a little worried when they heard his voice.

"First of all, I don't like the attitude, so drop it," she answered rather bravely. "Second of all, you are the chosen Guardian. It happens; deal with it. If the world can harbor, and create, things like zombies, it makes a certain sense that the world can create something to combat the zombies. That would be you."

"Really?" Jaxon asked. The sarcasm was practically dripping from his tongue.

"Yes, really, and you better get used to it, because there are a lot worse than zombies in your future and you need to be prepared. So stop feeling sorry for yourself, and get ready to be the hero everybody thinks you are."

It was the wrong thing to say, and Jaxon was certainly in the wrong mood to hear it. Obviously, Miriam had no idea how much my husband was willing to put up with, and she was definitely pushing her luck with the disrespect.

"Are you fucking serious lady?" Jaxon asked. "You really want to come into my home and run your mouth off at me?"

"Well, it obviously needs to be done by someone," Miriam answered. "Because that's what seems to be needed to get you to stop acting like a coward."

Jaxon's fist hit the table so hard his cup jumped into the air. I'm actually quite surprised that the granite of the counter didn't crack. I tried to stop him, but he was too fast and too strong. He grabbed Miriam roughly by the arm, and dragged her to the front door. Then he unceremoniously shoved her out the door, and slammed it in her face.

After all that, Jaxon simply went back to his room, and slammed that door as well. I went outside after Miriam who was straightening her rumpled clothes.

"What the hell is the matter with you?" I asked. "Why would you speak to him like that?"

"Relax dear. He needed that to get his motor running. You'll have your husband back in a few days, and then I'll come and talk to him again."

"What are you talking about?" I asked. To be honest, I was furious with her. I expected her to help him, not piss him off and belittle him.

"He needed someone to vent on; I let him vent on me. Didn't take very long though, he has a bit of a temper. Well, no matter. Now that he got it out of his system, he should be right as rain in a few days. It's how they all work."

"What are you talking about?" I asked once again.

"Dear, he went through a horrible ordeal. He's hurting inside, but all the Guardians tend to freak out in the beginning. They need something to vent on, something to get them over the shock. I gave him that something. Now it's out of his system and the healing will begin to take place. After that, we need to work on getting him to believe that he really is the Guardian, and that there really are people out there who need him."

"You've been through this before?" I asked.

"A few times, yes," she answered somewhat sadly.

"So he'll be okay now?"

"He might rant and rave for a few hours, but yes, he'll soon be okay. It's how the Guardians work. It's in their genetic makeup. They simply cannot be stressed out, depressed, or bothered by anything for long periods of time."

She was right of course. After she left, and I went back inside to check on Jaxon, he did indeed rant and rave for about three hours. After that, he told me to leave him alone, and gently ushered me out the door of our bedroom.

That evening, he finally came out and watched a movie with us. He didn't talk and he didn't eat, but he actually spent time around us.

A day or so later, Harley Davidson sent him a new motorcycle since his old one was still in El Paso. They apparently found out he was a Harley lover, and wanted to do something nice for him. He was still rather quiet. The old Jax would have been jumping up and down with excitement. However, I could tell that he loved it. Fortunately for Georgie, who also enjoys riding motorcycles, they had a spare and let him keep that as well. The two of them began to spend their afternoons riding the hills of Ruidoso. It was a start; a start on the road to recovery.

"Were you more optimistic about him returning to normal?"

I'm a wife and a wife worries about her husband. I had obviously noticed the improvement, but I also knew that he just wasn't the same. The laughter and the orneriness weren't there. That's a big part of Jaxon's personality. He's always causing trouble and getting away with it.

He began running again. That was good; he was always running before the zombies. He'd wake up early in the morning, and just go at it. He was also taking walks in the woods with Merrick. Another improvement because Jax, if anything, is extremely curious. He loves an adventure.

I'm not sure how it happened. Somehow, they had all gathered on the porch of the cabin one morning, drinking coffee and enjoying the view (the cabin has a wonderful view of the hills and valleys around it). I was watching out the window. I had taken to doing that kind of thing. I was always keeping my eye on him. Anyway, he wasn't saying anything, but of course Georgie was talking a mile a minute. I think Georgie is the only person that I've ever met that can talk as much as me.

"It's a good thing those zombies never actually made it to the Safe Zone," Georgie said. "At least for them it is. I would have brought them all down with my superior firepower."

"Let me see if I get what you're telling me here," Dudley said. "You actually think that you could bring down thousands of zombies all by your lonesome with one of your rifles."

"Yeah, that's what I'm saying," Georgie said, after contemplating it for a while.

That's when I saw it. Jaxon smiled.

"Well, it's too bad you were too chicken shit to leave the Safe Zone until the very end," Dudley retorted. "We could have used your mad skills all those times we risked our lives."

"Well, fortunately I was able to show everybody my skills at the very end when I saved Jaxon."

"What the hell are you talking about?" Kingsley said. "You can't hide while everything that went on, went on and then act like a bad ass at the end because you were the only one with a gun."

In answer, Georgie lifted his leg and farted.

Everyone started laughing, even I was laughing. Most importantly, Jaxon was laughing and he was laughing pretty hard. I started jumping up and down I was so happy. Jaxon's mother came over to see what I was so excited about. When she saw her son laughing, she started jumping up and down with me.

And just like that, Jaxon was better.

That evening, with a full security detail, we went into town and had dinner at a Chinese restaurant. It was a buffet and Jaxon did it some serious damage. His appetite was back with a vengeance. The boys laughed and joked all through our meal. It was great. I had a blast. My husband was back.

"I have a question. When did he hear about what happened with the other caravan, the one that Tito was leading?"

Oh, I forgot about that. Actually, I try not to think about it. Jaxon heard about that early on. It was all over the news. I think it was his father who told him.

"What did he say when he found out?"

I don't know if he said anything at all to his father, but later that night when we were alone he said something to me.

"I don't understand why he didn't listen to me."

I had no response. I had no idea at the time what it was that Tito ignored. Jaxon never brought it up again. I'm not sure how he feels about it now; I've never heard him speak about it to anyone. I have heard the others speak about it in great detail.

"What did they say?"

It wasn't good, and I don't think I'll repeat it here. Whatever choices Tito has made are choices that I truly hope he can find peace with.

"Now that Jaxon was back to normal, what were things like?"

Things were great. Things were back to normal. We laughed, we played, we went for rides on the motorcycles, and all of us would explore the woods together.

"Were you aware of what was going on inside of El Paso?"

Yes. Every night we would all gather and watch the news. The situation had not changed in the slightest bit. The gates were closed immediately after the caravans went through and nobody had dared to approach them. The survivors still trapped in the city were still asking for help, and the military was still doing nothing but containing the zombies.

"How did Jaxon feel about this?"

It made him angry. He had a strong dislike for Major Crass. He thought the man should be taken out and shot for incompetence. It really bothered him when the people still stuck in the city asked for the General to come and save them. He normally left the room when something like that happened, and it happened a lot. He never even tried to look at the EPUA website. The news was bad enough just mentioning it, and I could only imagine how many people were asking for his help there.

Miriam eventually came back.

I went out to see her on the front porch.

"Did it work?" she asked.

"It did," I answered.

"Good. We need to get down to business. There are a lot of people that need him right now."

"No," I told her. "It took too long for him to come back to me. I don't want you to say anything to upset him again."

"Sweetheart, if Jax doesn't embrace his destiny, he'll regret it for the rest of his life. Aside from that, there's no one else that can save all those trapped people."

"Find someone else," Jaxon said from over my shoulder. "I've thought about what you told me that day, and I don't believe you. I don't believe that I'm anything special. I almost died. Those people need the military to stop acting like a bunch of cowards and do their jobs. I'm a false hope. I got lucky."

"The military is frozen right now," Miriam said. "They were put on hold until Mr. Hardin gets here to take charge. They've just located him by the way, he'll be arriving in a week or so, and he's going to need you Jax."

"Well," Jax replied. "Whatever crazy shit it is that you're selling, I'm not buying. Tell this Mr. Hardin to go fuck himself. I'm done."

"I'll relay the message, but Max is still out there somewhere in that city and, until he's stopped, there will be no brighter day for all those people trapped in the crossfire."

"Who's Max?" I asked.

"He's the former—"

"He's nobody," Jaxon interrupted. "Get out of here lady. Don't talk to my wife anymore."

"Jaxon, he's going to come for you," Miriam said.

"Whatever," Jaxon grumbled before he walked inside the cabin.

"What's going on?" I asked Miriam.

"Ask your husband," she answered before she too started walking away. After just a little bit, she turned back and looked at me. "And by the way, the Guardians always have four less powerful assistants. Since Tito has disappeared, you should probably be expecting company."

"What about Merrick, doesn't she count?" I asked.

"Merrick has been touched by the Guardians power, but that's a lucky side effect. Expect a friend of Jaxon's to show up sometime soon. This man will be drawn to him and his duty."

With that, Miriam left.

I went inside to find Jax, and found him downstairs playing poker with the boys. He seemed to have forgotten all about Miriam.

"Jaxon, are you going to tell me what Miriam was talking about?" I asked.

"I'm not sure what Miriam was talking about," he answered.

"Can you tell me who Max is?"

"Never met him," he answered.

I wasn't about to leave it at that. Also, Kingsley and Dudley immediately perked up upon hearing the name.

"Just because you haven't met him doesn't mean you haven't heard of him," I announced.

"You may be right."

"What have you heard about him?" I asked.

"Nothing worth repeating," he answered.

"Jaxon, if you don't tell me who this person is…someone else will and that someone else will receive some Dunkin' Donuts as a reward."

Dudley perked up immediately. His addiction for Dunkin' Donuts was well known. In fact, it was the only non-healthy food he allowed himself to eat.

"He fought zombies back in 'Nam," Dudley blurted. "We heard about him from some mercenary. They called him a Guardian or something."

"If he's a Guardian, why would he be coming for you Jaxon? I thought the Guardians were the good guys?"

It took Jaxon awhile to answer. He was busy glaring daggers at Dudley.

"To be honest, I don't really care," he finally answered. "I'm done with the violence and the fighting. I don't have it in me. I'm not the guy they think I am. C'mon Skie, let's not talk about it anymore…okay?"

"All right," I answered.

As long as Jax wasn't interested, I was happy. I didn't want him dragged back into the nightmares of El Paso. That part of our life needed to be over. I was thankful to Miriam for saving me and my kids. I was also thankful that she helped Jax. Now, we were done.

Two days later, one of the soldiers guarding us announced that there was a man here to see Jaxon. Jax went out to see who it was, and came back with Javie, an old friend of his.

"I brought an Xbox," Javie said when everybody came over to hug him.

Javie is a great guy. He's always happy and he's always funny. Not in the pick on people kind of way that Jax is. Javie more or less makes fun of himself. Miriam predicted that someone would come by to join up with Jax. Javie's sudden arrival made me kind of nervous.

Fortunately for Javie, he wasn't in El Paso when the outbreak occurred. The man loves to travel, and he was lucky enough to have been in New Orleans at the time. However, he now had no home to come back to. Thinking the bunch of us might be at the cabin, Javie ventured on over to see for himself.

Now there were five.

That made me nervous. Jaxon had his lieutenants. Still, it was hard to think of Javie as a violent man. He just wasn't that kind of person. He was the most gentle of the bunch. Of course, Jaxon and Dudley were the only ones that actually looked like they could fight. Georgie however, was really good with guns, and Kingsley had at some point in his life been a marine.

I didn't like the way things were transpiring. It was almost as if some cosmic power was trying to force this group of men to become warriors. I knew if Jaxon decided to go out and play hero, the boys would all follow him. I was pretty sure that none of them wanted to, who in their right mind would? Yet, I knew they were waiting for Jaxon to decide what to do.

All was not lost yet. For the time being, and it looked like it might even be for eternity, Jaxon had no interest in fighting. I was glad for that, Lucy was glad for that, and Ivana was glad for that.

"Jaxon said that he didn't believe he was the Guardian. Did you believe he was the Guardian?"

I had no doubts in my mind that my husband was the hero they were looking for. I saw with my own eyes the power he wielded when he let go at the fence. It was amazing. No mere human being should have been able to do what he did. I also saw the way he healed from all those bite marks he received when only one of them should have killed and turned him. In addition to all that, I had read the posts on EPUA almost religiously, so, I knew some of what he did when he was trapped in El Paso. My husband was no normal man, for whatever reason, he was the Guardian. He was the chosen protector.

It was inevitable I suppose, he had the kind of personality that made people want to follow him. It made people want to root for him. I always knew he was made for something greater…but I sure as hell didn't think it would be this.

"Promise me that it's finished," I asked Jaxon one night. "Promise me you won't go back there and fight, no matter how hard they try to talk you into it."

He looked at me in a strange sort of way.

"I won't go back there," he finally answered. "I've done my part. It's up to the military now. I just don't understand why they don't get off their asses and do their jobs."

"You have done your part, you realize?" I asked. "Nobody else risked their life to save everyone. You did that. You took your chance, and played your part, now it's over. You made it back to me, and now it's done."

"What are you so worried about, Skie?"

"Because I can see it in your eyes…you feel guilty. Some part of you thinks that there's something you could be doing."

"Skie…I'm afraid to go back. I hate admitting it, but I'm terrified. You don't understand what it was like for me; and it's not only that I'm afraid for myself, I'm also afraid that I might make a mistake, and others will die. I don't know how to face it. So even if I wanted to and yes, you're right, there is a part of me that wants to…I simply can't do it. I don't know how."

"Then I'm glad that you're afraid," I told him. "If that's what keeps you and all the other guys safe, I'm glad for it."

"Then what's bothering you now?" he asked.

"I've never seen you afraid of anything. I'm not sure how it's going to sit with you. I'm not sure you'll be able to be afraid of something without fighting back."

"I don't understand what you're saying."

"I'm worried that the fear will at some point make you angry," I said. "If you get angry, fear itself isn't enough to hold you back. You'll go out and fight. I just don't think you're the type of man who can avoid facing your fears head on."

"I've been doing pretty well so far," he said. "Besides, I can't leave you to go out there to fight. I know how worried you are about me. That, in itself, is enough to keep me away from any danger. I don't want you to have the kind of life in which you're worrying every night about whether or not your husband is going to come back alive."

"Good," I said.

With that, I changed the subject. I was satisfied that he was not only safe, I was also satisfied that he was going to stay that way.

I never for a moment thought that I was the one in actual danger.

Chapter 9

JAXON

Once again, I had to wait for my meeting with Jax. The team had gone into battle. The outbreak (according to them) was small. There were no casualties. The fight was over in moments. I was actually able to watch from the top of a building as about one hundred zombies strolled into town. For me at least, it was terrifying. Not only the zombies but the casual violence the General was capable of unleashing. One thing was for certain as we sat down and began our discussion, if I ever needed rescued; I would want Jaxon to be the man who did the rescuing.

So, you want me to talk about my last evening of living a normal life?

"Yeah, just start off where Skie left off."

No problem. I had assured her that I wasn't going to fight anymore. I had a bad case of the nerves. I'm not sure if it was the fight by the fences or just the aftermath of everything, but the thought of facing zombies again turned my blood cold. Some Guardian I turned out to be.

He made light of his problems with a little laugh and an uncomfortable shift in his seat, before reaching down to scratch Merrick behind her ears. I was pretty sure he was going to clam up on the subject, but I just wasn't ready to quit yet.

"Does it make you uncomfortable to discuss what you went through after you left El Paso?"

It does. I know I'm being ridiculous, but I just feel embarrassed about it. Skie was right though. She knows me very well. I can't stand to be afraid of anything. It won't be long before I confront whatever it is that's giving me the nerves.

In this case, I had a little push.

The conversation Skie told you about was right before we went to bed; I was sitting by our bedroom window listening to the rain falling. I like the sound it makes when it hits the metal roof of the cabin. Then again, I've always loved the rain. Skie hates it. She's like some kinda weird solar battery. Give her lots of sun and she smiles, but put out a rain cloud and she's liable to be in a mood.

"I think it's perfectly normal to be afraid after what you went through."

I had to tell him that. This man should in no way be embarrassed about what he went through internally, after all the times he risked his life for others. It fell on deaf ears. He simply continued on with his tale, and it wasn't long before he had me captivated.

I fell asleep thinking about how wrong she was to be worried about me ever endangering myself again. My time was done. Thanks for the fame. Thanks for the good times. I'll leave you with the bill, but my ass is going home.

I'm guessing it was around two in the morning when I woke up. To this day I have no idea what woke me up, I certainly never felt Skie leave the bed. Something just didn't feel right. Merrick was still asleep next to me; I could hear her snoring.

Once Skie falls asleep, nothing ever really gets her out of bed until morning, so I went to go see if she was all right. She wasn't in the bathroom, so I went upstairs to see if she wandered over to the fridge for a late night snack.

She wasn't upstairs, but across the room, under the light of a soft lamp was a young man sitting in my father's La-Z-Boy. He was rather wet, so I took it that he had recently just come out of the rain. He had long, tangled black hair that fell to his shoulders. He wore dirty jeans and black combat boots. He had no shirt on.

I knew who he was of course. At least I had an educated guess. I just didn't know what the hell he was doing in our living room reading one of my books.

He finally found me worthy of attention, and glanced over at me.

"I realize this must be rather odd meeting me like this," the young man said. He couldn't have been over twenty. "I just really felt it important that we meet, and I noticed you weren't coming back to El Paso, so I came to you. My name is Max."

I was right about who he was, but I wasn't really patting myself on the back. I was staring at his face, or actually the left side of his face, around his jaw. There was no skin. His cheek had been torn off, and drool was occasionally dripping down to his chest. It was pretty disgusting.

"Hi Max. Have you by any chance seen my wife?" I asked.

"She's safe. I can't exactly tell you where, but I can tell you where she's going to be. All you have to do is come and get her."

"Max…I'd rather rip you into pieces than play games."

"That's the spirit," he said. "I was hoping you wouldn't disappoint me. You know I saw another Guardian once…a long time ago. It was in France. Man, that guy could fight. It took me about a half an hour to convince him to die."

"What do you want?" I asked. Because to be perfectly honest with you, I had no idea what this freak was after.

"I want to fight you. I want to kill you, and I want Major Crass to know it was me," Max said casually. "My boys are currently paying him a visit in order to cover that last part by the way."

"Yeah great. So if I fight you, I'll get my wife back unharmed?" I asked.

"Yes."

"Let's get it over with then." I said with a snarl in my voice. My adrenaline was pumping overtime. I was prepared to rip this man into pieces for involving my wife into whatever problem he had with me.

"Not yet," Max said as I took a few steps over to him. "If I killed you now, everyone would think I gave you a great big sucker punch. I certainly don't want that. I want to kill you fair, and square."

"Why are you doing this?" I asked.

"Revenge," he answered. "That idiot Crass put me out to pasture. Now I'm going to show him what a mistake that was. The second I turned bad, I knew another Guardian would be chosen, and I'd heard Miriam mention that he was more than likely going to come from El Paso. I can't tell you how difficult it was to cause an outbreak. I mean, once it all got going, all I had to do was sit back and watch, but getting that fucking Gypsy off that island was a major pain in the ass. We had to kill a few of those little soldier boys in order to pull that one off."

"You did all this to get even with Crass?" I asked. I sincerely doubt I kept the astonishment out of my voice.

"Of course I did. I've been fighting evil since 'Nam. All of a sudden Mr. Hardin decides to retire, and a few months later Crass dismantles my entire team. I had a purpose. I had a cause. I had power. Crass left me with nothing."

I couldn't believe that this guy actually enjoyed being a Guardian.

"I'll kill you just to prove that help no longer exists, but I started the outbreak just to show him how useless he was without me. Of course, outbreaks happen all the time, but I needed a big one. One that hit hard and fast…there are only a few places you can go to find that kind of potential."

"Well, you're officially a psycho," I said. "Congratulations on that."

I rushed him. I'd learned all I needed to know. Now, my plan was to break one of his bones for every second he refused to give me back my wife.

I can't tell you how shocked I was when he answered my charge with a backhand that I barely even saw. I flew across the room, and through the banister of the bottom floor stairway. I ended up somewhere around the middle of the stairway, flat on my back.

Max strolled over to the edge, and peered down at me.

"Come back to El Paso, little Guardian. Your wife will be waiting for you."

With those words, Max pulled a pistol from the back of his jeans and shot me four times in the stomach. It hurt like hell. My blood was gushing out all over the stairway.

I looked back towards Max, but he was gone.

I only had a few moments before I bled to death. I fought through the pain and crawled down the remainder of the stairs. It took way too long; I was getting weaker by the second. I could hear the commotion from upstairs as everyone began to wake up.

I figured someone would come and help me, but then I heard the gunshots coming from outside the cabin. All my friends and family went outside to investigate. By the time they got back, I'd be dead if I didn't make it to the bathroom.

So, I crawled. Merrick found me, and began to paw at me as I slowly pushed myself forward. I didn't have enough strength left in me to tell her to stop it.

When I finally reached the tub, I cranked on the water. I didn't much care about the temperature. I just needed that well water. I mean, any water would do, but well water was probably the best. I almost couldn't haul my broken body up over the lip of the claw-footed tub, but I did it.

I felt the sting as the water hit the bullet holes. I felt the push as the bullets were expelled from my stomach. It hurt almost as bad as the gunshot itself. Slowly, my body knit itself back together.

It took about an hour.

Of course, everyone eventually found me. They just happened to find me in my boxers, lying in a tub full of blood.

One thing great about the way my body heals. When it's over, it's over. There isn't any weakness or pain left. When the healing is done, I'm as good as new.

I heard from everyone that our bodyguards were all dead. I informed them about what happened to Skie and my encounter with her abductor while I was healing.

Then I was finished.

I practically leapt out of the tub and dashed into my bedroom. I dressed quickly in jeans and a t-shirt while yelling at everyone else to do the same.

I grabbed my tomahawk and stood in front of the mirror while everyone went about getting dressed. I studied the edge of its blade. I ran my finger along that edge, and looked at myself in the mirror.

I was going back into hell.

Georgie, Kingsley, Dudley, Javie, Merrick, and I were ready in less than five minutes. When we reached the front door, Miriam was waiting.

"I came as soon as I heard about the attack on Crass's outpost," she said. "What's your plan?"

"I'm going back into El Paso after my wife."

"I'll take you to the outpost so you can get some weapons," she answered.

"Then move," I told her.

A hug from my mom and dad, and we were driving through the nighttime streets at a furious pace. For an old lady, Miriam was a freaking mad person behind the wheel. She got us to the airport in less than five minutes. Of course, the airport isn't far at all from the cabin.

There was a Blackhawk helicopter waiting there for us.

In another few moments we were airborne. I can't even begin to describe the rage that was coursing through my veins as I waited to reach our destination. My anger was a palpable presence in the chopper. Nobody said a word.

Dudley was looking out the window. Kingsley was looking down at his hands, Georgie was cleaning a pistol (it wasn't easy for him to get away from his wife by the way, but he refused to let her convince him to stay behind), and Javie was looking right at me. I could see the worry on his face.

"You really don't have to come with us, Javie," I said to him.

"Yes I do," he answered back. No jokes, no nothing.

We landed in the parking lot of a burnt down Motel 6. Soldiers were everywhere. Stretchers and bodies and ambulances were carrying the dead and wounded away from the destruction. I'm not sure that the word "destruction" can even accurately describe how bad this place was. Max's boys really leveled the place.

"How many men does Max have?" I asked Miriam.

"He has four, just like you," she answered. "Guardians always have four lieutenants, not counting animals."

"Does he have any animals?"

"No, you're the first Guardian in centuries to have an animal that's been touched by the power."

After that, we were off running towards the rear of the motel towards some bunkers that had been (from what I could tell) erected rather recently. We entered one of them and were greeted by about five soldiers with M16s aimed at our chests.

"The major would like a word with Jaxon," one of the soldiers said.

Georgie and I were disarmed (we were the only ones with weapons) and then all of us were led to a small office building down the road. Apparently, Crass had taken over this place as well. There were soldiers and military vehicles everywhere.

As I was being led to Crass, I had that feeling you get when you know things are going to go bad. I was still keeping quiet, just waiting for the other shoe to drop. What happened now was going to be entirely up to Crass.

"Obviously, you thought he was going to stop you from going into El Paso. What were you going to do if he did?"

Well, at that point I had no idea. I was just going with the flow, but I can admit that I was seeing everything through a veil of red that began to cover my eyes when Skie was taken, and was now turning about a hundred shades darker from being delayed.

I was going to rescue my wife and kill the bastard that took her…end of story.

Soldiers everywhere were staring at me. Some of them even gave me the 'General salute,' but whenever a soldier did that, another soldier told them to stop. Things were not going to turn out well at all.

Everyone was told to stay in the waiting area while I was led to Crass's office. He was waiting there for me with a smug smile on his face.

"Don't bother sitting down," Crass said. "You won't be here that long."

"I need to get back into El Paso," I answered.

"You really screwed up this time," Crass said. "You should have stayed off my radar. I was after you from the beginning. I hate your type. You have no respect for those of us that have earned our power. You just come in swinging and defy us at every opportunity. I was actually hoping you'd die back there at the fence, but your bitch of a wife…well; let's just say that I've now been relieved of this command. I've been in charge of it for the last three years, I was about to become classified and now…"

"I need to get back into El Paso," I repeated. I didn't give a shit about his life, or what he thought of me at the moment, however…when he referred to Skie as a 'bitch,' I almost snapped.

"That's really too bad for you. You see, Mr. Hardin is on his way here. He's been located, and he's going back on the active status. The old man is actually taking my job. However, in the meantime, I'm still holding down the fort so to speak. And since I'm still currently in charge, I'm shipping you out to one of our less reputable prisons. I have no doubts that Hardin will release you as soon as he finds out, but arranging for your release will eat up a whole lot of time; time that should have been spent on rescuing your wife.

"I need to get back into El Paso."

"You need to take your medicine, boy," he answered.

I snapped. I admit it freely. What was I prepared to do if Crass delayed me? Well, I was prepared to kill him, and everyone else that stood in my way.

My wife is special to me. There is nobody on the face of this earth that reserves the right to keep me away from her.

I grabbed Crass's borrowed office desk, and threw it across the room. It made a hell of a noise. The thing was huge. After that, I grabbed his neck, and lifted him up from his leather chair. I slammed him against the wall hard enough to crack the plaster. My face was very close to his, and I could finally see the fear creep into his eyes.

Crass had crossed the line with me more than once. He was lucky I was busy trying to save lives the first time, and he was even luckier the second time when I was in a funk and he threatened to have me arrested.

Now, I was all me.

I worked him over a bit. He really didn't enjoy meeting the walls with his face, but he certainly deserved it. I was surprised that the wall gave out before he did, and suddenly we were standing in the waiting area with the rest of the gang.

Georgie tried to stop me; he went sailing across the room. I didn't actually shove him, I just never stopped going after Crass after I threw him through the wall. Miriam said something, but I'm not sure what it was or who it was to.

I heard a group of soldiers running towards me. One of them had my tomahawk. I picked up Crass's limp form and threw him at the soldiers, and then I was on them as well.

We ended up in the hallway leading to the office when everything was over. The white walls had quite a bit of blood on them. There were ten soldiers in all. They lasted less than a minute against me. I didn't kill any of them, but I wasn't completely against such an action if that was what I had to do to rescue my wife.

"Let's move," I shouted to my friends. "Doesn't look like Crass wants to help, and now we're gonna have to fight our way in."

They all just stared at me.

I heard the footsteps before I actually saw the next group of soldiers. Bad luck for them I had my tomahawk back in my hand.

They rounded the corner of the hallway, and came to an abrupt stop. The hallway was dusty with all the broken and cracked walls, and I was standing in the middle crouched low and ready to lunge when a voice came out from behind me.

"Stop," the voice said, and believe it or not, all the soldiers stopped dead in their tracks.

I chanced a glance at the owner of the voice, and saw a man in his mid fifties. He wasn't wearing a military uniform; he was dressed in jeans and a black, long sleeve button-down shirt.

"You must be the man I'm looking for," he said.

"Bad luck for you then," I replied.

"Not at all son," he said. "Looks like I got here just in time. I'm Mr. Hardin."

I sized him up and relaxed just a little bit as he dismissed the soldiers, and sent them out to find a medic for all the injured men lying around. My group was crowding around Mr. Hardin. It looked like they had finally got in the game, and were wondering whether or not to jump him.

"Hello Miriam," Mr. Hardin said when he finally noticed her standing there in the background. "You're looking well. I guess I should have kept in better touch with you."

"You're here now," Miriam answered. "That's what matters. These ravens are ready to fly."

"Well, follow me then. Let's have a brief chat and see what we can do."

All of us followed Mr. Hardin into an even bigger office with plenty of seats. I didn't sit down. I was ready to go. Patience has never been one of my strong suits.

"First of all," Mr. Hardin said as he sat down at the office desk. "I'd like to apologize. I really take full responsibility for everything that's happened. I should never have retired. Max has always been unstable and I've been the only one who can control him. I've been doing this for about eighty years or so, and figured it was time I gave myself a break. Enjoy life, have some fun, take a break from fighting evil. There hadn't been anything major happening in a few years, so I chose Major Cross as my successor, and hit the high road."

"You chose that asshole?" I asked. I couldn't believe someone would choose Cross for anything. He'd be the last guy that I'd pick in a game of dodge ball.

"Unfortunately, I did. I had no idea that he was harboring resentments towards Max. It's actually his dismissal of Max that led to all of this. Cross thought he could handle anything that came along without the help of a Guardian. Max showed him just how wrong he was."

"I've heard that much already from Max when he kidnapped my wife," I said. "And by the way, how in the hell have you been doing this for eighty years?"

"Miriam," Mr. Hardin said with a shocked look on his face. "Haven't you explained anything to him?"

"Not really," she answered. "He doesn't seem to like to listen."

"If you're gonna start chatting, make it quick," I said. "I'm low on patience at the moment and my wife needs me."

Miriam went on for a while, and I finally listened. She told me about the secret history of the Guardians, and how there has always been a Guardian around since the dawn of man. She told me that nature can heal my wounds. She explained how my friends were also more durable, and could also be healed by natural elements. Finally, she explained that I, and those around me, basically, no longer aged, We'd all stay our current age until I was killed.

There were a lot of things that she didn't know, like the whole 'why?' of everything. Why were there Guardians? How are we chosen? Who does the choosing? Why are my friends involved? Why are there five of us (six including Merrick)? And why are others infected with a lack of aging?

She touched on the scarier things, like zombies aren't the only things out there that people need saving from. I won't go into it now. No reason to make people nervous until they need to be nervous.

All in all, it was rather interesting. At the moment however, I planned on going after my wife. I could always ask questions about this stuff later, but she needed me now. This is where Mr. Hardin came in.

"There's a secret military island near Hawaii," he said. "It's where we keep the unfortunate souls that have been cursed. It's a small island, never really gets noticed by anyone, and it houses around forty civilians and twenty soldiers."

"What are they cursed with?" I asked.

"They make zombies," Mr. Hardin answered. "They don't do it on purpose, it's not their fault, but whenever someone in a close enough radius dies around them, that same someone will rise up as a zombie. It's real horror movie stuff. In earlier days, they actually tried to kill these cursed people only to find that the curse would travel down their family tree, and attach itself to one of their relatives."

"This is what Max meant when he started babbling about getting some Gypsy off an island." I said.

"Exactly," Mr. Hardin answered. "He waited for the right moment and attacked. He took a young woman named Clara, brought her to El Paso, and basically waited for the curse to take effect. It worked in about twenty-four hours. Even caused an outbreak on the island after they shot up two soldiers, but we had that under control almost immediately."

"Max must really hate Cross to being causing all these problems," I said, basically because I couldn't think of anything else to say.

"Cross took away his purpose in life," Mr. Hardin answered. "Max took it very hard; it drove him over the edge you might say. From what I've learned so far, Major Cross seems to have developed some problems with Max. Actually, it seems that he has an incredibly difficult time dealing with anyone unwilling to follow his every whim and wish. Power can rot a man to the core. Crass has been rotted, and he was ill equipped to deal with the supernatural side of life without Max around, which is exactly what Max set out to prove. Regardless, Major Crass will be dealt with legally after he gets out of the hospital. Unfortunately for you, yours, and everybody in El Paso, you just happened to get caught in the middle of all their drama."

"Crass seems to have a more personal problem with me than just being unlucky enough to get caught in the middle of him and Max."

"Well," Mr. Hardin replied. "You are the new Guardian. He'd rather have handled things without one. I understand that he may have even hired some mercenaries in an attempt to destroy the city against orders. Regardless, he was unable to, and as a result we have our current situation in El Paso. You were destined to be the next man to come in and take away his power. From what I've been briefed on, you were already stealing most of his thunder while you were still in the damn city, but all that's over now son. Let's get to the part where we save lives."

"First, let's talk about saving one life in particular. I want my fucking wife back."

"You're putting me in an awkward situation here, Jax," Mr. Hardin said.

Oh boy…I knew this guy was too good to be true. I'd been waiting for the other shoe to drop, and I had no interest whatsoever in whatever he was going to say.

"If you plan on telling me some sort of reason as to why I can't go to my wife," I interrupted. "Please understand that I'm going to beat the living shit out of you just like I did to Crass. I'd also like you to understand that I'm prepared to break anything that stands in my way."

Mr. Hardin didn't look the least bit shocked.

"Well, of course you are," he said. "That's what the problem is. If I try to stop you, you'll attack me, and everyone else that gets in your way. If, on the off chance, we can stop you, all that will do is result in the death of your wife, and give me another Guardian as an enemy."

"What's the problem then?" I asked impatiently.

"The problem is…Max is going to kill you."

"I'll take my chances."

"Of course you will. What you don't understand is that Max has been around for a long, long time—probably longer than any other Guardian—and in that time, his sole purpose in life was fighting. He's more powerful than you, and he's got a hell of a lot more experience than you. I don't see how you're going to beat him."

"Well, he's obviously lost before," I answered. "Just look at his face."

"Sorry to disappoint, but that happened to him in the war before he became a Guardian. It might be one of the reasons he's so unbalanced. That wound will never heal."

"Once again," I replied. "I'll take my chances."

"And I'm not going to stop you," Mr. Hardin said. "But have you thought about how you're going to find him? Crass was hoping to do exactly that, and it didn't work out too well for him. Hell, if Crass could have managed to locate him, he wouldn't even be a problem anymore. Crass would have just dropped a few bombs on his head, but being smack dab in the middle of zombie territory has given Max a pretty decent hiding place, which probably explains the mercenaries, if you can't find the needle in the haystack…destroy the haystack."

"What about the Gypsy?" I asked.

"Clara," Miriam corrected.

"Yeah," I said. "Won't Max be somewhere close to her?"

"Most certainly," Miriam answered. "He'd keep her pretty close to make sure he doesn't lose her. It's part of his revenge. Anywhere he takes her, she'll cause another outbreak the minute someone dies. He could effectively destroy the entire country if he wanted to, but nobody knows exactly what his plans are after he's ruined Crass."

"He's at the Abraham Chavez Theater," I said. "I've seen Clara chained on the steps."

"You can't be serious?" Mr. Hardin asked.

"Will the zombies attack Clara?" I asked.

"No," Miriam answered. "The cursed ones are never attacked by the undead."

"Then Max is at the Abraham Chavez Theater," I said.

Mr. Hardin immediately spoke into the phone, and a few seconds later a nerdy little soldier guy came running into the office. Mr. Hardin told him that he wanted schematics on the Abraham Chavez Theater brought into the war room immediately.

"Well, we have a location now," Mr. Hardin said once the nerd had left. "Do you have a plan?"

"I never really have a plan. I just kinda go with the flow, and hope for the best," I answered.

"I wish I could change your mind about this," Mr. Hardin said. "I don't see how you can beat him. He's just too good at killing."

"How about his buddies, how good are they at killing?"

"They're incredible at it," Miriam answered. "However, Max has apparently done some experimenting with them in the last few years. We'll probably never know why he's done what he's done to them. Maybe they weren't keen on following him anymore? Anyway, whatever he's done to them…Let's just say they aren't exactly operating on all four cylinders."

"So they're stupid?" Dudley asked. Everyone kind of chuckled at that.

"They can follow orders from Max to the letter," Miriam answered. "But yes, they're rather stupid now."

"Well at least we'll have an easy time," Dudley replied. "Jax is fucked, but we'll make it through a bunch of morons rather easily."

"Once the fight is on and they're coming after you," Mr. Hardin said. "Whoever has the bigger IQ won't make much of a difference I can assure you. His men are excellent warriors. Just look at what the four of them did to Crass's complex up the street."

"How were you feeling with all that you had just learned?"

Well, I wasn't happy with the way things were, that's for sure. It didn't make much of a difference though, I needed to kill Max in order to save my wife, and that's what I was going to do.

"What about the Gypsy girl…I forget her name? Did you have any plans for her?"

Not really, I mean…we certainly didn't want her dead. That would just spread the curse to one of her relatives somewhere, and this entire outbreak of zombies would start all over again somewhere else.

"What happened next?"

Ah, we went to the war room. This is where Mr. Hardin actually became an asset. The first thing he did was hand out 'bite suits'. These things are probably the greatest invention ever. A zombie can't bite through them. They're somewhere between a green and grey color, and they feel rough and light, like a soldier's normal uniform. If you look at the texture though, they are actually made of these little millimeter sized squares all bunched together. It's weird.

We all pulled on the fatigue pants and shirts with this strange material, along with combat boots, utility belts, and a thick utility vest with a wide, high collar that came almost to our chins. These vests were also very light, and the collars would keep our necks protected. All of us but Georgie turned down the helmets.

Next, we got a look at the weapons. This was my favorite part, since I had lost everything but my tomahawk. I still have the tomahawk by the way, I mean; I passed by a row of new high tech tomahawks, but for some reason I stayed with my old faithful. I did however find a couple of neat clips to hold it to the back of my belt in a horizontal placement. I also found another SOG Seal Pup knife and went for that immediately. Miriam surprised me at that point by handing me my old sheath complete with my Swiss Army Knife still in the front pocket. That went on my left hip, complete with the brand new knife.

I picked a silenced Glock to go on my right hand thigh. In fact, except for Kingsley, we all chose silenced weapons. I didn't grab any rifles, I saw another .30-30, but decided against the noise it would make. Georgie grabbed a silenced .50 caliber sniper rifle, and Kingsley chose a sawed-off shotgun just in case.

I spent way too much time trying to replace the folder knife I had lost, but eventually found a Cold Steel Ti-Lite. It's a fighting folder with a four-inch blade, and just looks like it was made to cause damage in a fight. I loved it immediately. To this day I carry one as my backup's backup.

"Can I see it?"

Immediately, the General pulled a knife from his pocket. The quills that formed a cross guard between the handle and the blade snagged on the pocket as it was being removed, and flicked out the blade. The motion happened all too fast. It was then that I realized that was the point. Jaxon leads a violent life. His weapons are chosen with deadliness and survival in mind.

As we walked to the helicopter, Mr. Hardin was still complaining about us not being ready. He was complaining about how we were headed for trouble. Obviously, we ignored him. He wasn't happy about letting us go, but he never once tried to stop us. He basically said that his job was to make sure we succeeded in our goals and came back alive. It wasn't his job to stand in our way.

I was beginning to like that man, but I wasn't sad to leave him behind since he was acting like such a negative Nancy.

We were in a nice black chopper this time. It made very little noise, and had none of those running lights. We had all grabbed these little radio ear pieces so we could talk to one another if we split up after the chopper. We could also speak with headquarters as well. They were small, and looped over our ears, so they didn't annoy me.

Everyone was arguing about where to land and what to do. I was trying my level best to ignore them all as I tried on a pair of half-fingered leather gloves that I found inside the chopper. One thing about doing what I do…I get the coolest stuff for free.

Suddenly it occurred to me.

It came as I was thinking about all the free stuff I had just received. Immediately, I tapped my earpiece to turn it on.

"Mr. Hardin," I asked. "Can you hear me?"

"I can hear you perfectly Jaxon," he answered almost immediately. "What's up?"

"Is Max familiar with these bite suits?"

"Certainly, both he and his men have used them regularly for the last ten years."

"How many do you have on hand?"

"I think there's about twenty left," Mr. Hardin answered.

"Turn around and go back," I told the pilot.

It took less than five minutes to return to base, pick up the suits, and get back into the air. The ride was quick; everyone was waiting for an explanation. I ignored them and enjoyed the quiet. Suddenly, we were over the Abraham Chavez Theater. I told the pilot to take us five streets away, and land on top of the biggest building he could find.

I made Georgie and Javie carry the suits as we left the chopper. I grabbed some rappelling rope and so did Dudley.

"Did you rappel out of the chopper?"

No, I just wanted the rope.

The sun was coming out as we looked over the edge of the roof, and the morning air was rather cool. The building was only two stories high, and we'd already attracted attention. The zombies had apparently managed to find their way back Downtown. Then again, I'm not exactly sure if it was the same group of zombies that we led away from Downtown, or an entirely new group, but regardless, there were hundreds of them screaming up at us from the street.

"Why'd we land so far away from the Abraham Chavez Theater?" Georgie complained.

"I thought it might be a good idea to keep Max from knowing exactly when we're coming, if that's okay with you?" I replied.

Everyone had a nervous little chuckle at Georgie's expense and we were off.

It was easy enough to shoot out the lock on the door leading into the building. It was more difficult to find our way to the first floor. The building was a maze of offices. It took about fifteen minutes. I began to curse up a storm. Georgie began to complain loudly about carrying the bite suits. The helmets were clanking around together in his arms. If I hadn't been so worried about my wife, I'd have been laughing my ass off.

Finally, we were out of the building and shooting at all the zombies that were in the alleyway that we'd just left. I'd chosen the clearest side, but when you're dealing with that many zombies…well, no side is exactly going to be easy going.

It took awhile, but we made it into the next building, through the following building, and across the street. It was a mad sprint down the road and to the left a few more blocks. Suddenly we were inside a small, shabby building that was facing the Abraham Chavez Theater.

Outside of the building, the zombies that were able to follow us were banging to get in but we had sealed up our entrance tightly, and they weren't having any luck. There were even more of them now than when we first landed. This was actually a good thing for once. I was going to need those zombies…or at least some of them.

"Jax," Georgie said. "What are we going to do if they get in here?"

"You mean what are you going to do?" I answered. "We aren't going to be here. Now get your ass on the roof."

The building wasn't that big. If I remember correctly, it was only three or four stories. I put Georgie on the roof, and told him to shoot anything that needed to be shot. Then, I went back down to the others who were waiting on the next floor down. We spread out the schematic of the building, and took a look at where all the security cameras were located.

It took a long time, but we finally figured a route that would get us where I wanted to go.

"But Jax," Dudley said as he pointed to our destination on the schematic. "If we head there, we'll be trapped. If we move around the corner, the next camera will catch us."

"That's fine," I answered. "We're not going to that next corner; we're going up on the roof."

"Ah," Kingsley said. "That's why we brought the rope."

"Part of the reason," I answered. "Go ahead and attach the grappling hooks to the ends of the ropes. After that, it's going to be your job to carry them. Javie, it's your job to carry all the bite suits since Georgie is staying here."

Kingsley wasn't happy and grumbled something under his breath. Javie made a funny gesture to complain about carrying the suits, but it wasn't really serious.

"All right, on our way over there, only use the silenced pistols. No shotgun, Kingsley. When we get to our target area, start throwing the grappling hook up to the roof, as soon as the hook is secure, start climbing. Can you climb with all those suits Javie?"

"It's kinda heavy," he answered.

"No problem, we'll help pull you up. Just don't drop the suits."

Just like that, we were fighting through all the zombies gathering at our building, and heading towards the theater. We approached the building from the side, in an effort to avoid the cameras. When we were close enough, I saw that the cameras were indeed moving. That was a good thing. I wanted Max's men to be watching out for our approach.

The bad part of the run was how much ammunition we wasted just getting there. The zombies were everywhere. The stink of them filled my nostrils and my pistol was all too soon emptied. My tomahawk came out immediately and I started having flashbacks of the fence as I hacked our way to our destination.

The very thought of ever having to confront more zombies had filled me with dread from the moment I was safe at my parents cabin right up until I met them on the street at that very moment. The second I began killing them, it once again became sort of like second nature to me. My nerves were gone. I was vaguely aware of how odd that was, but didn't have the time needed to think about it. In retrospect, I think it had something to do with confronting that which was terrifying me. I think Skie was right when she said I was the type of man who needed to face his fears head on.

Anyway, enough of that. The point is, I was back to being me.

As soon as Georgie had a clear view of our progress, he started shooting. He had a lot of ammunition, so I wasn't worried about him running out. Dudley and I ended up taking out all the zombies in our way, and Georgie took out all the ones that came too close to our flanks.

I can't tell you what a beautiful sight it is to see when a bullet from a .50 caliber sniper rifle meets a zombie. It looks like a bursting water balloon that someone filled with red liquid. I loved it. Sometimes, he even took out three or four zombies with one shot.

With Dudley and me in the front, and Kingsley and Javie bringing up the rear with the suits and rope, we made it to our target area in less than three minutes. Kingsley was gasping for air. He's a smoker unfortunately, and I was worried about whether or not he could make the climb to the top of the building.

The Abraham Chaves Theater, from where we were approaching, has a large dome kinda thing, and I wanted to be on top of it. You know how all those modern theaters tend to have those odd designs that would be ugly as hell on a normal building, but end up looking kinda cool on a theater?

"Yes, I get what you're saying."

Well, I'm guessing it's about three stories high. Quite a throw for the grappling hooks, but I was confident I could do it. The trouble would be getting there.

"Wait a minute…before you go any further, I have a question."

What's that?

"What happened to Merrick?"

Oh yeah, I left her with my parents. It was going to be awhile before more security details were going to arrive. Miriam had told me that it could take up to an hour, not long, but long enough that I wasn't going to leave family alone without some protection. My dad went and loaded his gun, and I left Merrick to play watchdog. She didn't like it, of course; she hates being left behind, but she really makes a great watchdog.

So anyway, we zigged and we zagged all through the front of the theater. There were steps, low walls, and patios everywhere. We kept low when we had to, but my worry was that we'd meet too much opposition from the zombies before we could arrive at our hidden wall.

I was finally able to pop another magazine into my Glock. That made things easier, but as I looked over the low wall we were all crouched behind, I saw what looked like thousands of zombies headed down a side street towards our destination. They hadn't seen us yet, so they weren't running. They were probably responding to the screams of their comrades, and possibly our smells.

Wow, and I mean wow. We really had to make it to our destination before they figured out where we were.

Finally, we reached a spot where we had to sprint the rest of the way, because once we left the shelter of the staircase we were using for cover, we'd all be in plain sight—and the horde would charge.

Dudley tapped me softly on the shoulder as I drilled a zombie in the head with my pistol. I turned to look where he was pointing and saw the sad pretty girl in the dress. She was still chained to the ground, but this time she was sitting. She didn't look very well at all, but she was watching us with a very still face. Like she was curious about what we were doing, but too tired to do anything but watch.

Dudley went to toss her his water bottle, but I grabbed his hand and pointed to a camera that was facing her. It would alert whoever was watching those cameras to our presence if their captive Gypsy girl was suddenly drinking out of a water bottle she shouldn't have.

I reached out towards Kingsley and he handed me my grappling rope. I nodded to everyone; we watched as Georgie took out a group of zombies coming from behind, and then we bolted towards our destination.

I moved so fast, I had to put out my hand to stop myself from colliding with the wall. I threw my grappling hook and missed. The second time, it hooked solid. Dudley was successful as well, but Kingsley and Javie were having trouble. The pounding feet of the rushing, screaming, and advancing, horde of zombies was making the ground shake. They saw us just as quickly as I thought they would. My adrenaline kicked into overdrive as I grabbed the ropes from both of them and started throwing. I caught Kingsley's immediately, but I had to calm myself down before I was able to get Javie's hook to stick.

I snapped at Dudley to get his ass up the wall as I tied the end of Javie's rope around his waist and told him not to drop the suits.

I scrambled up my own rope, and made it to the top of the theater in just a few seconds. Dudley was right behind me. Kingsley was trying, but he kept slipping down the wall. The guy was exhausted. Here's a little tip for all would be zombie fighters…don't smoke. I told Dudley to help him, and I began to pull Javie up the wall.

Javie did his best to climb with his feet, but his hands were too full to offer much help. The zombies hit the wall with a loud thud. Javie and Kingsley were only inches away from death when the wall vibrated with the force of their impact.

A few moments later and all of us were safe on the roof of the Abraham Chavez Theater.

We took a few moments for everyone to calm down and get their strength back. We didn't have to worry about cameras on the roof because they were all pointed downwards, so we were able to walk around as we pleased. I actually encouraged this, because I wanted as many zombies as we could get to gather on the ground below us.

I ordered Kingsley to start making nooses out of our ropes. I rummaged through Dudley's backpack until I found his duct tape, and waited until Kingsley had all the ropes finished.

"All right," Dudley said. "What the hell are you planning?"

"I'm planning on taking out Max's men," I answered. "He messed with them somehow, and now they're kind of stupid right?"

"Yeah," Dudley answered.

"Well, I'm going to use that against them. Max is expecting us to try and sneak in obviously, so he has a man in the control room watching the camera monitors. I'm guessing that the other three are located at the not so obvious entrances. Don't count the front entrance or the rear entrance... those are too obvious. I'm talking about the one in the parking garage, the one on the side of the building for deliveries, and the one on the other side of the building."

"Sounds feasible," Dudley said.

"Well, I'll rappel to the control room, and take out that guy. Then, we'll release some captured zombies wearing bite suits wherever his other men are, to distract them. My guess is that because they're so stupid, Max gave them simple orders like 'take them out when you see them.' When they go after the zombies, you guys can come up behind them."

"Won't we have to deal with all the zombies afterwards?" Kingsley asked.

"No," I answered. "Just shoot Max's man, and then relock the door."

"Did they agree to your plan?"

They agreed to it, but they didn't really like it. I have to admit, it was a little off the wall, and it certainly wasn't going to be any fun catching all those zombies and dressing them up like us.

"But you wanted Max's men to think you were coming in through those entrances correct?"

Exactly, let them chase after some zombies in our clothes while we come up from behind.

So, off we went to the side of the building with our nooses. We selected the best zombies we could find. By the best, I mean that we selected the least decayed of the zombies we could find. This wasn't easy. Most of the zombies that were gathering had been dead a pretty long time. Add the blaring sun, and the sudden rain showers that they'd been living in, and the crop of zombies to choose from was pretty gross.

When we had a zombie selected, we'd just drop a noose till it settled over its head, and pull it up by the neck. It was rather easy. They just stood around at the bottom of the building reaching up for us and screaming. They barely even noticed the noose 'til they were yanked off their feet.

Once we had them on the roof, we taped up their mouths, cut off their clothes, and put them in bite suits. After that, we taped their hands behind their backs, and taped their legs together. Then, we'd go after the next one.

We stopped when we had fifteen zombies taped up, and dressed like us. On a plus side, we also received proof positive that the bite suits actually worked. One of the zombies managed to take a quick snap at Javie as we were taping it up. Scared the hell out of him, and he said it pinched like a mother trucker, but no blood was drawn.

Everything was now ready. It was my turn. I was just hoping that Max wasn't in the control room with his pal. That could put a serious damper on my plan.

"Did you have a backup plan if he was in there?"

I was gonna spray as many bullets through the window as possible. I doubt that would be enough to keep him down long, but hopefully it'd keep him down long enough for me to bury my tomahawk in his head.

I took one last look at the schematics, but I already knew where I had to go for the control room. The guys were waiting for me by the taped up zombies as I scrambled across the roof towards the edge over the control room window.

I found a nice pipe to tie the rope on, and began climbing down. When I was beside the window, I took a peek inside.

It was the wrong damn window.

I cursed and growled, and made my way back to the roof. I then ran back to the guys and told them the problem. We once again all looked at the schematic. I was definitely at the right window, but for some reason the control room must have moved.

"Mr. Hardin," I asked after a quick tap to my earpiece. "You there?"

"I'm already on it," Mr. Hardin answered.

"How do you even know what's going on?" Kingsley asked.

"I can hear everything with your earpieces," Mr. Hardin answered. "There's also a camera in each earpiece, so I can see everything as well."

We all kinda stared at each others' ears for a while looking for the camera like a bunch of morons. It was Javie that finally found the little dot the size of a pen cap.

"Jaxon," Mr. Hardin said. "It seems that the schematics you have are a few years outdated. The control room has been moved to the third floor. Unfortunately, there are no windows to that room."

"Well that's fucking great, isn't it?" I demanded to no one in particular.

We sat around for a little bit wondering what to do. I really didn't want to lead my friends into a gunfight with experienced killers. Somehow, I just didn't think those odds were going to turn out in our favor.

I finally sat back against a large air duct made of flimsy metal. It made a slight indentation when I put my weight on it. When I took my weight back off, it popped back into the right position with a soft 'bonk' noise...I had a plan...hopefully.

"Hardin," I said after another tap on the earpiece. "Do the air ducts lead to the control room?"

"I'm checking right now."

It took some time, but Hardin finally came back with the good news. The air ducts did indeed lead to the control room. In fact, they led directly over the control room, and they were big enough for me to fit in.

I pulled my Swiss Army knife out of my sheath, and started unscrewing the screws around the duct opening. It was going to be a tight fit but I was determined to make it work.

"Do you think they know we're here?" Dudley asked suddenly as he peered over the edge of the roof at all the zombies.

"How could they know?" Kingsley answered.

"They know," I answered. "There are too many zombies around the building now. They're just waiting for us to make a move."

Kingsley threw his arms up in disgust. His nerves were getting the better of him. The situation was pretty freaking tense.

I grabbed a small flashlight, and squeezed into the air duct. It didn't take long to squirm my way to the control room. Mr. Hardin was giving me directions through the earpiece the entire time. The only difficult part was keeping the noise I was making in the flimsy metal tunnel as low as possible.

As I neared the vent that Mr. Hardin said would drop down into the control room, I turned off the flashlight and inched myself slowly closer to the opening. I peered down into the room, and was shocked to discover there were four men in the room.

Three of these men stood with their backs to the wall with a vacant look in their eyes. The final man was seated before a computer terminal with five different monitors. I could only see the back of his head from my position, but his head was moving back and forth in a robotic fashion as he searched through the cameras in an attempt to locate us.

He was clearly agitated, because he was flipping through different images rapidly. He concentrated on the areas that had the largest concentrations of zombies. The dipshits weren't smart enough to even think about us being safe and sound on the roof.

Then I got a look at Max's handiwork. Each of his four men had their heads shaved. There were metal plates attached in places that should have had skin over skull. Whatever else he'd done to them, he obviously played around with their brains. Worst of all were their faces. Their jaws were all clamped shut with metal brackets that ran in and out of raw and infected holes in their cheeks.

I tried to scoot back so they wouldn't hear me when I radioed back to my friends, and the stupid air duct made a loud pop that echoed in my ears.

I immediately froze.

Then I began to panic. There was no way they didn't hear the noise. I expected them to start spraying bullets through the ceiling, but nothing happened. I waited and waited, and still nothing happened. Finally, I crawled back towards the vent and took a peek. None of them had moved.

I thought about it for a second, and then lightly tapped the inside of the air duct. Still no response, so I hit the wall of the air duct harder. They never moved. Whatever Max had done to them, they'd ended up deaf.

"Jaxon," Mr. Hardin asked. "What are you doing?"

"Relax," I answered somewhat confidently. "These guys are deaf."

"Are you sure?"

"I am now, because I'm sitting here talking to you in my outdoor voice," I answered. "Can the rest of you guys hear me?"

They all spoke up into the earpieces that they could indeed hear me.

"All right, I was wrong about these guys being at the entrances. They're all right here in the control room waiting to be sent out. So, take five of the zombies, cut their tape, release them at the delivery entrance, and let's see what happens."

They radioed back that they understood, and were doing what I asked. So, I waited about half an hour, and watched the monitors over the man at the computer terminals shoulder. Eventually, he found the zombies in our clothes. They were being dropped off the roof.

At that moment, as I watched the last two zombies free fall to the cement, slowly pick themselves off the ground, and limp around looking for something to bite, I began to truly believe that my plan sucked big time. This was so unbelievable it was almost laughable. Nobody would face plant on the cement in order to gain access to a building. Nobody could survive a landing like that.

The most amazing thing was that these guys were so dumb the plan actually worked. The guy at the computer reacted immediately. As soon as he saw our decoys, his fist shot up into the air. One of the other guys approached him, and after a few signals, he ran out of the room. The guy at the computer never even acknowledged that our decoys were dropping out of the sky and landing on their faces.

"We're good," I radioed to everyone. "The retards took the bait. Get the next group ready to drop by the parking garage entrance. It might take them a while to wander in front of a camera, and make it quicker this time. I want this done in five minutes, not thirty."

I heard the grumbles over the radio but I just ignored them. I wanted all the pieces in place before we took action.

The second they told me that the zombies had entered the parking garage I had them drop the remaining group of five off by the side entrance, and I sat (or rather, lay) back and waited.

The side entrance zombies were the next to be discovered. I saw it on the computer screen a split second before the control room fellow did. He raised his hand, he was approached by Max's thug, they went through a series of hand gestures, and the thug was off and running towards the side entrance.

I wanted to make sure that all of Max's men were in the places I wanted them to be before I sent in my guys. I didn't want them to run into one another in a hallway. I wasn't sure that would end up being a situation my guys could win. Dumb or not, these guys took out Crass's headquarters. Shooting them in the back would certainly be the safest way to finish this.

I was really becoming impatient as I waited for the zombies in the parking garage to be seen on the cameras. It seemed like it was taking forever. Not good. I debated taking out my pistol and trying to take out the remaining thugs, but in the close confines of the air duct I couldn't reach my hand down to the weapon.

"Then how did you expect to shoot the remaining man if you couldn't reach your pistol?"

To be perfectly honest, I hadn't thought about that one yet. I was too concerned with getting the others in position.

Finally, one of our zombies crossed in front of a camera in the parking garage and the remaining thug was sent out. I was alone with the remaining man. I waited around five minutes before I sent out my friends to go deal with Max's thugs, and I could hear them break through the door on the roof from where I was in the air duct. I was nervous about Max hearing the noise, but there wasn't much I could do about that at the moment.

I debated through more than a few ways of taking out the computer guy, but in the end I just smacked the vent cover to the floor with a hard whack, and dropped myself into the room behind it. It was a bad move; Max's thug was on top of me the minute I landed. Luckily, he didn't shoot, but he had a big enough knife in his hand.

I twisted and turned out of the way of the swinging knife, but I had almost no room to maneuver and no time to grab one of my own weapons. I was rolling left and right and left and right, before I was finally able to get in a quick finger poke to the thug's eye. It bought me enough time to get to my knees, but still not enough time to reach a weapon.

The thug recovered rapidly and charged. From my knees, I lunged in for a takedown, and had the man flat on his back. The knife almost got through the fabric of my suit. I could feel the tip of the blade working for penetration as I grabbed the man's arm.

I broke the arm with a quick twist and snap. The thug was making the freakiest noises that I've ever heard. I guess that without being able to hear, they didn't know how fucked up they sounded when they were in pain.

With the knife out of his hand, I kept him on his back with all of my weight, and spun to the side when I was ready, so that he could now get to his knees. He should have known better, as soon as he rose up, I had my arms around his neck. I began to squeeze with all my strength. He made some choking noises while he still had some air but that quickly ended. The choke I was using cut off both his air and the blood supply to the brain. These guys were tough. I could feel his strength as he fought me, but the struggling rapidly turned to simple twitches from the arms and legs. Finally, the man was dead. I rose to my feet, and shot him in the head to make sure.

I went to the computer, which had thankfully survived our struggle. It took a minute, but I was finally able to figure out how to work the cameras. I watched as Kingsley, Dudley, and Javie shot Max's men in the backs. It would have worked flawlessly, but the thug that Kingsley was after had actually entered the parking garage, and Kingsley had to follow him there to take him out.

The zombies in the garage were already after the thug when Kingsley arrived. The thug was shooting them down, and because he was distracted, it wasn't too difficult for Kingsley to get behind the man and drill him in the back. The problem was that Kingsley still had to get out of the parking garage and back into the building while the remaining zombies were chasing after him.

He probably should have turned and fought. There were about ten of them, but instead he tried to make a run for the door. The zombies had gotten too close (he's a smoker remember) and he wasn't able to close the door behind him.

The zombies were in the building.

"What did you do?"

I ran from the room and began to search for my wife.

I no longer had a lot of time. Very soon, the entire building would be crawling with zombies, and I wanted my wife to be long gone before that happened.

"What were you going to do about Max?"

I was going to kill the prick. I didn't exactly know how, but I figured that I'd figure something out when the opportunity presented itself. It only took me a few doors before I found the entrance into balcony of the theater itself.

I quietly entered the theater, looked over the railing, and saw that Max had done some redecorating. Pathways had been created through the seating area. The seats normally covered the entire floor of the theater, the back seats being higher in altitude than the front seats, and it used to resemble a movie theater with only walkways on either side. Now, seats had been crushed, and swept to the sides all over the place, creating little walkways.

Above all these little walkways, and the stage itself, I saw chains hanging from the ceiling. Many, many chains were just hanging there. It was rather weird in the dim light to be seeing chains hanging from the ceiling, but whatever. I was already distracted. My wife was sitting, or rather, tied to a chair in the middle of the stage. Max was relaxing just a few feet away from her with his legs hanging off the edge of the stage.

"They're right behind me," Kingsley shouted in my earpiece. "I'm gonna have to use the shotgun, my pistol is out of bullets."

Everyone started jabbering into my earpiece after that, so I figured it was time to make my move. Max was going to be on alert when he started hearing Kingsley's shotgun, and I wanted to hit him unawares.

I stood up proudly behind the metal railing of the balcony.

"Hey Max," I boomed out in my most arrogant voice. "Welcome to El Paso."

He had just enough time to drop the book he was reading, look up an me, and give me an equally arrogant grin that said, "I'm going to rip you apart" before he saw my tomahawk thundering through the air towards him.

I've got to give credit where credit is due. The man was fast. He managed to lose his grin, and move just enough to prevent my weapon from burying itself in his face. It hit his shoulder with a tremendous amount of force instead. In fact, the tomahawk bit into his shoulder so deeply, it went right through the collarbone and buried itself to the wood of the shaft.

Max gave a nice little girlie scream, and spun off to the side of the stage.

I laughed a little bit, hopped over the railing, and landed on the floor of the theater. From where I landed I had a straight walk to the stage, thanks to Max's renovations. I avoided the chains hanging from the ceiling in case they were some kind of lame booby trap, and headed for my wife.

"Jaxon, look out!" Skie shouted as I climbed onto the stage.

Unfortunately, her warning came just a little bit too late. Max wasn't down for the count. He spun to his side, brought up some sort of little machine pistol, and sprayed bullets right at me. I managed to duck and roll, but I took a few in my left leg, and a couple more in my stomach.

Still, I managed to draw my own pistol and returned fire. I hit him dead center in the chest but somehow, even as I fell…Max crawled to a group of those hanging chains…studied them for a second, and pulled one.

A gentle cascade of water poured forth from the rafters and drenched him completely before drawing to a trickle. The bastard was healing himself. Well, two could play at that game. I immediately crawled towards the group of chains nearest me, and pulled one for myself. A cement cinder block fell down from the rafters, and smacked into part of my head and my right shoulder. I saw stars, then lost most of my vision, and fell to my knees. I could hear Max getting to his feet, but it was almost impossible to move. I heard my friends babbling in my earpiece as they tried to keep the zombies from overtaking the theater. I had to move. I rose up, just as Max let loose with another spray of machine gun fire.

I dropped behind a pile of what used to be seats, but was reduced to just a pile of debris, and found that the mess made a decent cover. I was in complete agony. My head was gushing blood, my right shoulder was probably broken, and I had at least five bullets in me. Not a good day. This guy was kicking my ass, and we hadn't even fought yet.

I willed movement back into my legs, and I willed my vision to clear as Max began to rant and rave.

"You were off to a pretty good start," he screeched. "I don't know why you didn't press the attack while I was injured. Now look at me, I'm almost completely healed. You can have your tomahawk back by the way."

My tomahawk thudded into the wall closest to me. Max wasn't stupid enough to try the direct approach. He knew that I was still armed. Instead, he was using his irritating voice to distract me, while he kept low and made his way to the side of the room. If he succeeded in getting there, he'd have gotten around my cover.

I needed to do something and I need to do something fast.

I was getting frantic. I had about zero good ideas coming to mind. Still, I refused to let that defeatist voice that was scratching at the back of my mind come forth. Dudley was screaming in my earpiece. The zombies had overtaken the bottom floor. My friends were trying to organize a defensive. Obviously, they knew where I was, but they couldn't help me. They had their hands more than full, and Kingsley was separated from the rest of them, never having made it out of the bottom floor.

Things were going badly.

Things were going very, very badly.

Suddenly, everything clicked together in my mind.

It was like someone had just flipped a light switch. I peered over the debris of broken seats and watched as Max made his way around my cover, always keeping himself behind something.

I could see where he was going. He was trying to make it to one of his renovated open spaces where a bunch of those tricky chains hung from the ceiling. I waited patiently. Or at least as patiently as I could…I've never exactly been known for having a lot of patience.

"Jax," Mr. Hardin said in my earpiece. "You need to do something, and you need to do something quick. If Max gets to that open space, he'll have a clear shot at you." There was a clear note of panic in Mr. Hardin's voice, but he wasn't telling me anything I didn't already know.

His words made Dudley freak out. He started asking over and over again whether or not I was all right. I couldn't answer him; I was busy. I wanted to chance a look at Skie as well, but I couldn't do that either. No distractions.

Finally, Max entered the clearing.

Before he could even think about shooting me, I opened fire at the ceiling. I couldn't make out my targets; it was way too dark up there. Instead, I shot rapidly in wide groupings. Max was confused for a moment, and didn't return fire. It was his mistake. I finally hit something, and clear fluid poured from the ceiling.

For a second, my heart skipped a beat. I thought I hit another water source. That's all I needed at the moment…to give the bastard another boost of healing. Then the liquid landed on his head. He screamed for all he was worth. He screamed, and clutched at the skin literally melting off of his skull.

It was acid. I got what I wanted; I dropped one of his own booby traps on top of him. I think I chanced a little bitty smile as I watched him writhe around on the ground for a while. It didn't take him long to master his pain. Not long at all. Before I would have thought it possible, he was moving again, crawling towards a certain chain.

I waited till he found the right one and pulled. I was worried that my body might not respond to my commands when I willed it to move, but I was lucky. Despite all the blood loss, the will to live was as great as ever.

As soon as Max pulled the chain, and water began to heal him, I had dropped my empty pistol, tumbled over the debris of my cover, and limped as fast as I could right towards him. I was lucky that he was either in so much pain or blinded, because he didn't even notice my approach until I grabbed a hold of him around the ribs in a crushing bear hug.

The only thing is, the bear hug wasn't an attack…I was just trying to hold on as the water began to pour over me as well. I could feel my wounds closing up. I could see the skin re-growing on Max's ugly face.

Then, he realized what I was doing. He realized that I wasn't attacking. He realized that I was getting stronger. He tried to throw me off, but my grip was too strong. He tried to knee me in the balls, but I already had my leg twisted in front of me to block him.

This wasn't a gentle cascade like the first water source that he had used to heal himself. This one seemed to have tapped into the water main of the building. It was like taking a shower of health. I loved it. Max however, did not.

He tried a head butt, but I was expecting this as well. I lowered my head just enough that the impact broke his nose. He screamed, and became frantic to injure me. Too bad for him, I was feeling a lot better.

I speared my fingers into his right eye, and before he had even finished screaming, he managed to kick me square in the jaw. Under the pouring water, I barely even caught the tiniest hint of stars before they vanished, and my sight became clear. We began to punish each other, trading blows and kicks, neither one of us bothering to block. Under normal circumstances, the damage we were inflicting would have brought either one of us to our knees, but the water was still pouring, and we were still underneath it. He was healing as soon as I was damaging him, and likewise for me.

Finally, we both shoved each other out of the water at the exact same time.

I slid backwards about five feet using my hands and knees on the floor to keep my balance. As soon as I came to a stop, I rose fully and faced my opponent. As soon as he had finished rolling backwards in a controlled somersault, he rose to his feet as well. We stared at each other for a moment. He was about to say something, and I dove for his legs. A perfect takedown, now I was on top of him, and the water was behind us...I began to pummel his face with bloody results.

"I'm confused...I thought he was better than you. I thought he was faster than you. How were you able to dominate and abuse him like that?"

Typical military arrogance, Max was faster than me, and stronger, and certainly better at using his powers. What most folks in the military never seem to realize is that they don't have the necessary skills to defend against a trained ground fighter in an unarmed fight.

"Ground fighter?"

Someone that will take an opponent off of their feet and attack them on the floor...I excel at this type of fighting. The military doesn't train for this type of fighting, except for the basics, and they don't really need to; they have guns. However, as an instructor that deals mainly in ground fighting, I've worked with soldiers before. I know for a fact that this is their weak area.

"You were hoping to take the fight to the ground."

I was hoping for a chance to compete my skill against his strength and speed. I never bothered to mention it to anyone, because you can never tell someone from the military that they lack ground-fighting skills—they'll just argue with you—but I was really hoping to get my hands on him. I knew if I could do that, I'd bring the fight into my world.

I could also tell from the shock on Max's battered face, that this knowledge was new to him as well. He looked as if he couldn't believe what was happening. I wanted to laugh at him. I settled for breaking his arm.

I rolled away when I saw him pull out a Bowie knife with his good arm. I wasn't happy about it; I wanted to punish him, and he still had plenty of bones left. At least his gun had fallen from his hands when the acid hit his face, so it wasn't like I was in danger of being shot anymore. I hate being shot.

He growled his rage at me, and rose to his feet.

I pulled my knife and we charged each other.

He was good with the knife. He managed to slice me about three times before I severed his femoral artery. This shocked him as well. I don't think he actually thought I knew my way around a blade.

"Have you had training with a knife?"

Almost an entire life's worth. I've been training with knives since I was a little kid. It wasn't until much later that I learned there were actually martial arts styles based on the use of a knife. As soon as I found out though, I happily started studying the art. I think I was in my mid twenties.

Max threw me away from him in a flood of rage. He was definitely strong. I think I flew about fifteen feet before I smacked into the nearest wall.

Before either of us could make another move, the sound of gunshots echoed through the corridors outside the many doors of the theater.

"Looks like my soldiers found your friends," Max said with a grunt as he began to tie off the wound on his leg with a piece of shirt.

"Your men are dead, jackass," I replied. "That's the sound of suppressing fire."

Max listened again as the gunshots boomed from beyond the doors of the theater.

"I'm going to kill you."

"Not likely," I answered.

The dipshit had thrown me right next to where my tomahawk had been stuck in the wall. I watched him hobble over to where the water was still pouring from the ceiling, and right when he was about to get wet, I threw the tomahawk.

The tomahawk flew through the air like a spinning missile. Max was barely able to duck out of the way. For the first time, I saw fear in his eyes.

With my friends still screaming in my ear, I charged him like a runaway freight train. His knife pierced my side. I lost my own blade as we fell to the ground…but I once again had my hands on him.

I worked on his still broken arm. It was his weak point. He screamed out loud as I taught him how to suffer. I twisted his injured arm into new and exciting positions as he screamed and screamed. It almost looked like he was about to give up, but he suddenly remembered his Bowie knife still sticking in my side. He gave it a twist, and this time I threw him into the wall purely on reflex.

It wasn't a great move on my part. I just gave the bastard some distance. It was what he wanted. It was what he needed to win the fight, but fortunately I had a pretty good idea what he was going to do before he resumed his attack.

I can't tell you how happy I was to be right.

"He went for the water again didn't he?"

He sure did, and I rushed forward to meet him.

We collided like rams underneath the pouring water. He pulled his knife from my side, and once again tried to drive it into me. I blocked the swing, and drove my fist into his armpit. He screamed, and then he laughed. The water was healing him too fast to inflict any major damage without a weapon. I also believe that he healed faster than me, so add that up to another reason for why this was so freaking difficult.

I grabbed his head with both of my hands and brought it down to meet my knee. I nailed him like this about twice when I discovered that not only had his broken arm healed, he also managed to switch hands on his knife.

It caught me by surprise. I was still worrying about the other hand. He buried the blade into my ribcage. I dropped to my knees in shock. He took a small moment to gloat, and slowly raised his Bowie knife with both hands above his head for the deathblow.

As soon as he began the motion of bringing the knife down, I went for my new pocket knife. As I pulled it from my pocket, the blade engaged. I stood up inside the arc of his swing where it was safe, and stabbed him in the throat.

He made a choking sound, and staggered backwards. I pulled him to me again, and slid the blade back and forth across the soft skin of his throat. His eyes went wide in shock and fear. His body went rigid as I quickly ducked low, and severed both of his femoral arteries before piercing his navel and dragging the blade up to his sternum.

For one second, we eyed each other, and before the rushing water could heal the vast amounts of damage I had just inflicted, I kicked him away.

I watched him flounder around for just a moment as I stood under the rushing water and let the last of my injuries mend together. He didn't struggle very long. The damage was too severe. The blood was literally pouring out of his body.

He tried to rise, fell back down, tried to rise once more, fell back down, and just as quick as that, it was over. Max was dead.

I rushed towards Skie, and cut the ropes holding her to the chair. She grabbed a hold of me instantly, and began smothering me with kisses.

"I thought he was gonna win," she gasped. "When he stabbed you that last time…I thought he was gonna win."

"Well, next time leave the thinking to me," I answered with a laugh.

"Jerk, how about I kick your ass?" she squealed.

"Later, right now I wanna get the hell out of here."

I took her hand and made my way towards my fallen tomahawk and knife. After picking those up, I gave my earpiece a tap.

"Mr. Hardin," I said. "How about sending a chopper to come pick us all up, I'm in the mood for a cheeseburger."

"I'm already in route Jaxon," he answered. "I should be there in about five minutes. Light a flare on roof for the pilot, please."

Just then, the doors burst open, and Dudley charged in spraying bullets everywhere. I shoved Skie to the floor, and hopped on top of her just in case any strays found their way towards us.

"Stop shooting, Tex," I shouted.

Fortunately for us, Dudley did as I asked.

"Did I get him?" Dudley asked.

"Sure," I answered as I picked up my discarded pistol and reloaded. "Good thing you came when you did. I don't know what we would have done without your well aimed and excellent shooting."

"Oh, I get it," Dudley responded in a temper tantrum. "I fight my way all the way over here, just to help you out, and you wanna be a smart ass about it. How about you bite me? How about that?"

"I'll settle for getting out of here," I answered. "Have you guys found Kingsley yet?"

"Sure did, he was hiding in a broom closet. It took him a while to figure out how to use his shotgun."

"Are you serious?"

"Yeah, he couldn't figure it out. So after his pistol ran out of bullets and he went for the shotgun… Well, let's just say that the zombies were so close, he had to hide in a broom closet till we came to get him."

"Tell me it wasn't the safety button," I demanded.

"I'm not saying anything," Dudley answered with a laugh and a nod.

I retrieved my pistol just in time for both of us to draw and aim our weapons at Javie and Kingsley as they burst through the same door Dudley had just come from.

"We gotta go," Kingsley said in a breathless voice. Damn that boy needs to quit smoking. "They're coming up right behind us."

Without another word, we ran to the stage and through the doors in the back. Kingsley was in the rear, and just as he was about to enter the door, the zombies began to flood into the theater. There were hundreds of them, all screaming for our flesh.

Skie began to panic. I felt her tense up next to me as she heard their howls of rage, and smelled their decaying skin.

"Don't worry," I shouted. "We've been through this more than a few times. Just don't freeze up."

I didn't hand her a gun. I didn't want her shooting any of us. Instead, I kept her right next to me, and hauled ass through the maze of corridors until we could back track our way to our exit point.

The zombies were right behind us the entire way. I certainly didn't like the situation. There was no room to maneuver, and I definitely didn't want to let Skie out of my sight. So, we shot over our shoulders, and kept on moving forward.

It took much longer than it should have, but in our defense, we weren't exactly familiar with the building… Anyway, we finally made it back to the control room with all the computers and the dead body of Max's thug.

Skie screamed when she saw him.

"Forget about him," I shouted while I closed the door behind us. "Get up in that air duct and start moving."

"Is that the same air duct you used earlier to gain access?"

Yeah, but getting out of there wasn't going to be that easy. Javie and Kingsley barely fit through the opening. I actually had to pound and bend the metal with my fists to make it wider for them.

Kingsley was barely through when the door burst open and the room was filled with zombies.

Fortunately, they couldn't reach the air duct or they would have been crawling after us. However, when we finally got to the roof...either Dudley, Javie, or Kingsley had forgotten to close the access door behind them and we had company waiting for us.

"Oh no, it never seems to stop."

When it rains, it pours. I pulled Skie out of the way of the nearest zombie and shot it in the head. Javie popped off a flare. Fortunately, the chopper was already in the area, circling.

We fired and fired the few rounds we had left as it landed far away from the zombies. With Skie at our backs, we pulled our blades, and fended them off as we backed up towards the chopper.

Their screams brought reinforcements, and in a few moments the roof was covered with screaming zombies. I can't tell you what a relief it was when the gigantic machine gun of the helicopter started mowing them all down. The roar of the spinning barrels was deafening, but damn, it was just about the nicest sound I'd heard in a good long while.

I was the last in the chopper, and more than a little shocked to see Clara, the Gypsy girl, sitting shotgun with a smile on her face, but I figured I'd hear about that later. I had a more important question at the moment.

"What took you so long to start shooting?" I asked Mr. Hardin who was manning the machine gun.

"Had to figure out how to work the damn thing," he answered.

Everyone started laughing. Well, everyone except for Kingsley, but he managed to crack a smile when we had to turn around and go back for Georgie after we were about halfway to the base and remembered that we had left him behind.

Georgie wasn't happy to be forgotten. I however, thought it was hilarious. Especially after he told me that he had lost his earpiece over the side of the roof, while he was peering down at all the zombies gathering on the street around the building. Poor Georgie was waving his arms like a madman trying to get our attention as we flew off into the bright blue sky and towards a land without the rampaging dead.

Epilogue

SKIE

For all practical purposes, the story has ended. Of course, Jaxon has found his way into the news many times since those early days. Someday soon I would like to tell those tales, but this was his first taste of the blood and violence that would become his life. This is the complete story of what exactly happened when El Paso was under attack. This is the origin of the General.

I'm now taking a rather unique opportunity, and jumping forward about ten days after Skie was rescued. There's something that I found…interesting. It would be easy enough to ask Jaxon, or one of the boys to narrate this tale, but for some reason I wanted to hear it from someone outside the group. I chose Skie. I wasn't disappointed.

I went back to the house where she and Jaxon are staying. Skie laughed hysterically about my reasons for seeing her again.

I can't believe you want to hear about the first time Jaxon spoke to the world. What a day! I can't believe he did what he did.

"To be honest, I don't think anybody can believe what he did."

True enough. Well, for days we argued. Like I said before, I didn't want my husband playing hero anymore. Obviously, I relented. I don't really think I had much of a choice. It wasn't something Jaxon wanted to do; it was something he had to do. Denying him this would be denying a fundamental need.

"Still, it couldn't have been easy."

It certainly wasn't, but I got over it.

Anyway, let me tell you about their name. Obviously they needed a name. But it was Mr. Hardin that told Jaxon to come up with one. He figured that since they were already in the media, they should have a name for the team. That way Kingsley, Dudley, Georgie, and Javie, would have the same kind of respect that Jaxon had when they were on missions. Also, it would be a team that was officially sanctioned by the government with many, many privileges.

"Is this when Jaxon received his badge?"

Yeah, they all have one. It lets them override all the red tape, and the idiots who enjoy getting in their way. We've spoken about it before; it lets him take control over any police force or military body, etc. when a threat to the public is possibly underway. It also prevents him from being detained or arrested at any time. There was a lot of debate about that in the news.

"Tell me the name they chose?"

They called themselves the Regulators. It's off of a group in the late eighteen hundreds who fought during the Lincoln County war. Billy the Kid was a member.

"What happened next?"

Mr. Hardin scheduled a press conference in New Mexico. They chose the college in Las Cruces for the event. Jaxon wasn't happy about it, he hates public speaking, and no amount of bribery on anyone's part was able to convince him to wear a suit for the event. That really drove me insane…I wanted my husband to look nice for his first public speech.

"What did he wear?"

Jeans and a t-shirt…oh, and his black boots, and after he dressed that way, all the Regulators followed suit. I wasn't happy. Everyone else was, but not me.

We were all driven to the press conference in one of those large Hummers. The boys passed the time by picking on the driver. Jaxon kept telling him how Jeeps were better for off-roading than a Hummer could ever hope to be. The driver wasn't happy and kept arguing back. It was actually a fun time. Nothing serious, everything light hearted. In fact, when we got out of the Hummer, the driver even asked for Jaxon's autograph.

"Why were you driven to the press conference in a Hummer?"

Protection, all of Las Cruces was packed with people trying to get a look at Jaxon. There were literally thousands upon thousands of people screaming out for us the minute we entered the campus, so we were also provided with a police escort. It was like we were rock stars or something. They even had the National Guard present for crowd control.

The walk to the building was more than a little wild as well. They had cordoned the sidewalk off, so we could walk to the building without being molested, but each side of the sidewalk was lined with people reaching out for Jaxon. Everyone wanted to touch him, to take a picture with him, to shake his hand, to tell him that he saved a friend or relative. It was surreal. Jaxon and the rest of the Regulators were having a blast signing autographs and letting young girls kiss them on their cheeks.

Ivana, Lucy, and I were hanging back from them, and just laughing at how popular they were. Some girls were even throwing their bras at them. It was a crazy time. It was fun. We even got to sign some autographs as well…I loved it. I loved that people were being so nice. I loved that people appreciated what everyone had gone through. I loved that they were getting the rewards of heroes. They deserved it. They earned it.

That's when Jaxon got the news.

"And what news was that?"

Calvin, who had been up and down the country since the moment he was released from the decontamination unit, telling anyone who would listen what an animal my husband was, and how he was responsible for the loss of more lives than he could ever hope to save, was also going to be there, and he was speaking after Jaxon.

"Why exactly was that?"

I never asked. Obviously, whoever planned the press conference didn't know my husband. Mr. Hardin was also furious, but he was reluctant to do anything about it since the press had already been informed that Calvin was going to speak.

"Should I ask about how furious Jaxon was?"

Very, he was thinking that Calvin was going to try and turn things into a debate. Calvin was an experienced public speaker. Jaxon was not.

Jaxon was fuming as we went inside one of the bigger buildings. We had our own waiting room. He got even angrier when we passed Calvin's name on a door at the end of the hallway; the jerk had his own room as well.

"What the hell did he do to deserve that?" Dudley asked. "Aside from crying like a baby and abandoning his friends to the zombies. He should be arrested and these assholes gave him his own room."

Mr. Hardin dropped us off at the waiting room, and went to see what could be done about preventing Calvin from speaking. That was a good thing, what wasn't a good thing was the fact that

Jaxon and Dudley never made it into the waiting room. I thought they were right behind me, but to my surprise, they were nowhere to be found.

"Did the rest of the Regulators know where he was?"

Probably, but they weren't talking.

When Mr. Hardin came back to the waiting room, he also had no idea where Jaxon and Dudley had gone off to. We began to wonder if the two of them had just up and left the press conference.

"But they hadn't left, had they?"

Unfortunately, they had not left. They returned to the waiting room about ten minutes after Mr. Hardin. Both of them were disheveled and grinning like Cheshire cats.

Mr. Hardin had exercised some muscle, and had two choices for Jaxon. Either Calvin would be prevented from speaking, or the Regulators could abandon the press conference all together. I really began to worry when I heard Jaxon's answer.

"I think every man deserves to be seen and heard," Jaxon said. "So don't do anything."

With that, we were lead to the conference room on the fifth floor. It was a huge auditorium with large windows running the length of the wall opposite the podium. At the moment; automatic shades had been lowered along all those windows, blocking what would probably have been an excellent view of the campus.

After a brief introduction, Jaxon found himself at the podium in front of everyone. I'll never forget that moment. He became the General. The laughter and whatever mischievous schemes he came up with on a regular basis had all disappeared. He was a leader of men now, and every one of the thousands of reporters who had gathered in the auditorium was ready to listen.

"I'm not much for public speaking," Jaxon said. "But, I wanted to inform everyone about our decision."

Jaxon paused before continuing to speak. Flashes of light bounced around him as photographers snapped his picture.

"In ten days time," Jaxon continued. "I'm declaring war on the undead of El Paso. Tell your friends, tell your family members to hold out for ten more days. Help is coming. I have the man-power. I have the weapons. I'm coming for all of them. I plan to eradicate the threat of zombies from my city, and the assault will commence in ten days."

After that, he answered questions for about a half an hour. He did really well. He wasn't entirely comfortable, but he got through it easily enough…and then, things became…entertaining.

"That's one way of putting it."

Right…anyway, right before he left the podium, Jaxon took the opportunity to introduce the next speaker.

"The man speaking after me has become quite popular as of late. As far as I know, he has be-come my biggest detractor. I'm not especially fond of him. In fact, he reminds me of something I'd likely scrape off the sole of my boot. I found him to be the worst kind of coward, and I hold him personally responsible for a number of needless deaths. Regardless of that, I believe that everyone deserves fifteen minutes of fame. Ladies and Gentleman, I give you the biggest douche bag I've ever had the misfortune to meet."

With that, the shades were drawn on the opposite wall. What I thought would have been an excellent view of the campus, was marred by a completely naked, and hogtied, Calvin. He was hanging upside down outside the window, suspended by a single rope, and dangling out over five stories of empty air. His mouth had been gagged by what I believe were his own socks.

There were gasps of horror, followed by the flashes of hundreds of cameras. The noise in the room became deafening as the reporters started shouting out questions to Jaxon. He was already surrounded by the other Regulators, and every single one of them was too busy laughing to answer anything.

I chanced a look at Mr. Hardin who was standing there in shock. Our eyes met, and he gave me a look that spoke volumes. He was worried that this was the typical behavior he should be expecting from my husband and his friends. I didn't have the heart to tell him that it was.

"It was pretty bad public opinion wise that they did that to Calvin wasn't it?"

Not as bad as when the laxatives kicked in.

THE
REGULATORS
BOOK 2 OF THE GUARDIAN INTERVIEWS

BY MICHAEL CLARY

Chapter 1

JAXON

After The Guardian was published, I was happily sitting on top of the world and, to be honest, I truly felt I deserved it. I alone had managed to piece together a series of interviews that told the complete, true story of how the Regulators were formed. I had covered all the events that led up to the famous fifteen minutes of footage. I had even managed to cover the aftermath that led to the kidnapping of the General's wife and the battle between the past and present Guardians.

I was pretty happy with myself.

I had accomplished something that no one else had been able to do, and when it was all over, I went on my merry little way. The interviews, the talk shows, and the meet and greets... I loved every bit of it. It was nice to be famous. It was nice to be thought of as the reporter that gets the job done.

But did I get the job done? I certainly thought I had found out everything there was to know about those terrible dark days.

It turned out, I was wrong.

It began with an email, one single email with a short, little command. It said to dig deeper. It told me to ask about the Battle of the Sun Bowl. I didn't know who the sender of the email was, and I didn't have much interest in pursuing events that had been covered by other reporters like the Battle of the Sun Bowl had.

I blew it off.

Three days later, the mysterious writer of the email contacted me again. He sent me a video of a grown man having a nightmare. It was a scary thing to watch him thrashing about in his bed, but it was the one word he shouted out after he had woken up screaming that really captured my attention.

One word.

It took months to arrange the interview; the General is a busy man. But in a small compound, near but separate from Fort Bliss Army Base in El Paso, Texas, I once again found myself waiting for him.

I didn't know if he had read my book, so I wasn't sure if he would be altogether happy to see me. I never embellished the story. I had that going for me, but some of the story isn't exactly flattering. The General has his detractors.

So, as I sat there patiently waiting to meet with the General, I was just as nervous as the first time I had ever spoken with him.

He finally walked into the room as if he were without a care in the world. Before me was a man totally at ease with his surroundings. Nothing seemed to bother him. I couldn't help but stare. His shoulders were still immense, and I could see the muscles of his large arms moving underneath the flannel of his shirt. He's not extremely tall, but he's certainly not short. His hair was a sort of light brown. He had it cut just as short as before, almost as if it would be a nuisance any other way.

I didn't know exactly what it was, but the man was imposing. At least until he cracked a smile that shattered his normal scowl and pulled up a seat across from me.

This was a surprise; I would have thought you'd be sick of me after hearing me ramble for so long during all those interviews.

"On the contrary, I was amazed by all the things I learned."

Amazed or horrified?

"Both actually, it's amazing to hear what happened back then. It's also rather horrible to hear how bad things were."

And yet you're back for more.

"I am. I'm not sure that the story is finished."

Hmm, perhaps you need me to elaborate on something?

"I was hoping that you could walk me through the 'cleansing' of El Paso."

The military already did a pretty good job of keeping the media informed of those events. Why don't you just go through some old newspapers?

"The media does indeed have a great supply of information about the military's involvement of those events, but I would be much more interested in hearing about what happened with your team."

Care to tell me why?

"Care to take a guess?"

I was taking a risk by being coy. The General wasn't a man to play games with. Just ask those three intoxicated men who tried to give him a hard time at a restaurant in New Mexico. Their hospital bills were staggering.

However, I was hoping that by keeping things fun and light-hearted instead of confrontational he might be at least slightly amused and tell me what I was there to find out.

I've been wrong before.

When he narrowed his eyes and sized me up, I almost bolted out of the room. His green eyes were piercing. They had seen things that would cause me to have nightmares for the rest of my life.

There was a clock on the wall. In the silence I could hear the second's ticking off. I was just about to apologize when he finally spoke.

Where do you wanna start?

"Take it from the beginning."

The beginning is kinda boring. It would take us back to five days of meetings as Hardin, my team, and a bunch of nerds tossed around different ideas about how to take El Paso back from the zombies.

"In the end, you made different teams that basically went from house to house saving and evacuating people. Is that correct?"

Sort of. Extracting the survivors was our first goal, but we didn't go to every single house, just the ones that had the survivors in them.

"Did you use EPUA to track down where the survivors were?"

Yeah, that website was very beneficial in helping us find survivors. It's just that not all the survivors were hooked up to it. You would be surprised at the amount of survivors that never even had an Internet connection, but Hardin was pretty damn good at finding them anyway. There has been a lot of talk about whether that was the right way to handle things or not, but from our end...it was the only way.

"Why is that?"

I guess we just wanted to get those people out of there. It wasn't exactly an easy thing to do, but it needed to be done. Our thinking was that once the survivors were all removed from the city, we could then go in and destroy all the undead with larger teams.

At no point did we ever want to go in and just start dropping bombs. If we did that before we removed the survivors, we would end up killing innocent people. If we dropped bombs after they were removed, there wouldn't be a city left to return to.

We also considered using large armored vehicles and driving around neighborhoods with a loudspeaker. The thought was to call out the survivors, load them up and drive outta dodge.

"That would probably attract a lot of unwanted attention."

Exactly. No matter how many guns we had firing, the masses of the dead would eventually overrun us. It would have just been a matter of time.

We tossed around a ton of ideas, but in the end...the only viable option was to go in quietly with small teams. That way, we could hopefully avoid large-scale detection and try and save some lives.

"All while putting down any zombies you encountered?"

As long as we could do so without attracting undo attention. We also had the benefit of air support if the shit hit the fan. That was definitely an added plus. A .50 cal machine gun ripping and roaring from a low flying chopper can do massive amounts of damage to large groups of zombies.

"Couldn't you have just sent helicopters to patrol the city and shoot down all the large groups of undead?"

We did. We had all the large groups that could be seen from the air decimated before we ever motored in. It worked great for the gigantic hordes. The only problem was that not all the zombies were walking around in big bunches. Many of them had wandered into stores, buildings and homes. A street might seem deserted, but one loud noise and a zombie scream later and you would have a pretty decent mob running you down.

Another interesting tidbit about the choppers is that the zombies learned that a flying helicopter was dangerous to them, but a landing helicopter was a meal ticket. Therefore, once we gathered the survivors, we couldn't just call in a chopper and air lift them away. We would have gotten mobbed the minute the chopper started lowering from the air. To deal with that problem, Hardin and his people had to find relatively safe places that we could defend and then escape after the survivors were lifted away.

"How many teams went in?"

There were four teams including the Regulators, one team for each major section of El Paso: the Northeast, the Eastside, the Westside, and Downtown. These teams came from all over. We had Rangers, Green Berets, SEALs and even some SWAT members all on the teams together. All of them were volunteers. The amount of people on each team was different, but started at around five; sometimes there were more if there was a particularly hostile area they needed to clear. Sometimes there was less depending on what was needed. People who had never dealt with this before often needed a break after seeing so much nasty.

"Did the Regulators ever take a break?"

Not very often and certainly not when we were still on the Westside, but towards the end sometimes one of the guys would take a weekend off to go visit his family. That kind of thing was entirely acceptable. Hell, it would have been acceptable to me if they just needed a break, but my boys are troopers. For the most part, they stuck with it. Georgie was even going through a divorce.

"Georgie divorced his wife while the Regulators were cleaning out El Paso. How did that affect his job?"

It didn't. Lucy wanted the divorce the second she heard he was going back in. It wasn't because she was worried about him; it was because she was selfish. She didn't want to spend that much time alone. He knew it was coming. He had already recognized that she changed somehow; maybe it was because of all that happened...I dunno. The funny thing was that the judge couldn't even make him show up for court. Our job takes precedence over any of that stuff.

I actually knew many of the details of Georgie's divorce, at least as reported by the magazines. Aside from Jaxon's wife, most of the women that the Regulators date don't last very long. As a result, it would get difficult to keep track of who had a girlfriend and who didn't. The gossip magazines, however, seemed very interested in those statistics. The divorce stuck with me because, for a while there, it felt like Lucy was one of the most hated women in America.

"The reporters tried very hard to dig up information on what part you played during all the

extractions, but the military wasn't very forthcoming for the first few weeks or so, at least until the Battle of the Sun Bowl. Is it safe to say that you were in the trenches with the other Regulators, and there were no problems?"

I wouldn't say that there were no problems. We were in hostile territory fighting to save lives. There were problems every day, but you could definitely say that I was in the trenches.

"I was actually wondering if you had any problems within your team."

Yeah, I know what you're getting at; we lost a teammate. The military released that information in a press conference so it's not exactly a secret. I was surprised you didn't mention it in your book or ask me about it in our last set of interviews. I think what you're really wondering is how we lost him, and why the military refused to release any information about the Regulators during the first few weeks.

"I didn't cover the loss of your teammate because it wasn't part of the story I was covering. I was covering your origins. I felt that there was already enough information out there about your return trip, but if my sources are accurate and no one is pulling my leg, there's a whole new story that the media never knew about...and...well, I'm not sure if it's an incredible story or a terrifying one."

Go for incredible; it will help you sleep at night.

I thought about his words. For a brief moment, I wondered if I wanted to know the truth. Maybe it would be easier to live my life in ignorance of the dark and scary things that go bump in the night, but then I looked over at Jaxon. He was smiling. It was a slight smile, but it was there nonetheless. I realized in that moment that I shouldn't worry, because the man sitting across from me had but one purpose in life and one purpose only.

He killed those dark and scary things, and he was very good at his job.

"Take me back to when you first reentered El Paso."

We went in the same way we got out, Country Club Road and the border between El Paso and New Mexico. Those locations were part of the Westside if you remember correctly. I chose the Westside for my team just because that was the side of town I knew the best. I also chose to take it without any kind of backup, so it was just the Regulators.

"Can you give me the names of your teammates just to make sure I'm on the same page?"

It was the same team that went in to rescue Skie. It consisted of Dudley, Kingsley, Javie, Georgie, and me.

At that moment, there was a scratching on the door to our room. Jaxon turned his head towards the sound and began to chuckle. When the noise level increased to the point in which I thought the door would break apart, Jaxon went over and opened it up. The large black pit bull gave a snort of irritation and strutted into the room.

I shouldn't have left out Merrick; she gets a little irritated when I do that, but of course she was with us.

The dog was intimidating, to be sure, but as soon as she came over and placed her head on my lap, I realized that she remembered me from our last set of interviews. I patted her head and scratched her behind the ears before she turned her back towards me and settled herself by Jaxon's feet.

"Your bodyguard?"

Got that right.

"Okay, I'm confused...I thought that you guys blew up the bridge on Country Club Road when you left the city the first time?"

Oh yeah, Kingsley took that thing out big time. However, a military construction crew had erected a drawbridge kinda thing by the time we got there. They lowered it for us to cross and as soon as we were back in the city, they raised it back up.

We were driving two matte black Jeeps that had been armored up and customized for battle. Georgie was driving the second Jeep with Javie riding shotgun and Kingsley in the back with his weapon. I was in the lead Jeep with Dudley driving, Merrick riding shotgun, and me in the back with an HK MP7.

Let me tell you about this gun, because it's an excellent weapon. It's small and lightweight; it has a collapsible stock and it even comes with a holographic sighting mechanism that puts a dot on the target while still in the optical. It eliminates the red laser, which is something that might give away our position. Georgie and I picked them out for everyone; we just headed out to a range and tried a ton of guns till we found the ones we liked. We also had silencers put on all of them, because a gun is worthless around zombies if every shot you crack off brings a mountain of corpses down on you.

"*Can I interrupt very quickly before you get too far ahead?*"

Sure.

When we interviewed before you made sure to tell me about the weapons you used. In fact, you were very descriptive about them. Did you still use any of the same weapons or had they all been replaced by the MP7?"

Well, I still had the Cold Steel Ti-lite in my pocket. It worked so well in my last fight I wasn't about to part with it. I also added a Cold Steel Recon 1 folder with a tanto style blade. It was just a monster of a knife and I couldn't pass up a chance to try it out.

"*Were you still using the bite suits?*"

Yes, all of us had bite suits. They look like normal fatigues, except they feel a little rougher to the touch, and the zombies can't bite through them. All of us were also using tactical vests with built in backpacks and high bite proof collars to protect our necks. Georgie was still the only one of us that wore a helmet.

"*Any other weapons?*"

I traded in my Glock for a Sig Sauer P226 with a silencer. No real reason—they are both great guns, but the Sig has a hammer release that I thought was kinda cool and it fits really well in my hand. The other guys had various firearms. Dudley was once again using the .45 he 'liberated' from Georgie.

"*I'm actually wondering about a certain weapon that you used quite often in your earlier battles.*"

Ah, my tomahawk. Yeah, that I didn't change at all. It was resting in the small of my back on my utility belt. I had some special loops added so that I could fit it in there sideways and draw it out quickly. Now that you mention it, all the Regulators carry some sort of chopping weapon as a backup. It just pays to be prepared; we learned that from the last time. Bullets run out, but a good knife or tomahawk never lets you down.

"*Excellent, just what I wanted to know. Now, did you enter the city during the day time or at night?*"

We entered well after midnight. Our plan was to lay low while the sun was up and work our asses off after it had gone down.

"*Was it safer to work at night?*"

Yes and no. We would be able to sneak around a lot easier, but the shamblers would be harder to spot as well.

"*Shamblers?*"

Ask Dudley; it's his new word for zombies.

So there we were, cruising at around thirty miles per hour. It was weird driving past the line of cars we had used to make our escape. We had a moment of silence as we remembered all that we went through.

"Looks different in the dark," Dudley said. "Never realized what a scary road this is with all those trees."

"Maybe you're just a pussy now," I replied. You probably just lost your nerve after we rescued Skie."

"I don't think that's it."

"Well, it could be. Maybe you just need to take a deep, long look at yourself. You might just be able to see your inner pussy trying to shine its way to the surface."

"Speaking of being a pussy, have you spoken to Kingsley today?"

"I haven't," I answered. "Why do you ask?"

"It kinda seemed like he was having a bad case of nerves. He's been a grumpy bastard these last couple of days."

"I don't blame him if he is having a problem with his nerves. We gotta be crazy to be coming back here."

"You're the moron that announced to a room full of reporters that we were coming back to save everyone," Dudley said very calmly and clearly.

"Well I'm regretting it now," I answered in an equally calm voice. "Next time, tell me to shut up."

All joking aside, he was right. It was kinda scary. For whatever reason, there aren't many streetlights in the Upper Valley area. Everything was dark and quiet. There were shadows everywhere. Every now and then, from somewhere off in the distance, we could hear glass breaking or other random and unknown sounds.

El Paso had become a nightmare town, and we had no idea what was around the corner. We didn't go down Mesa (a main street on the Westside). Instead, we turned immediately down the side streets and the winding roads of all the neighborhoods.

We were hoping to avoid any battles our first night back. We just wanted to get somewhere safe and get our bearings before things kicked off the next evening. Now, we had no reason to believe that these neighborhoods and side streets were any safer than Mesa. We were just hoping that if we picked up a large group of shamblers, we'd be able to lose them in the maze.

To be honest, I was beginning to wonder why we hadn't run into any trouble. I knew we hadn't blasted away enough zombies from the helicopters to make too much of a difference when we were on the ground.

Not that I was complaining. I just don't like the anticipation. Halfway to our destination, I heard Hardin's voice in my earpiece radio.

"What's up?" I asked to let him know I was listening.

"We just got an SOS from a house in your immediate area," Hardin said.

"What's the address?"

"They don't know the address, but the street is Oveja," Hardin said. "They heard the sound of your engines as you passed them by."

"I'm on it."

The entire team heard the conversation; we all had the same earpiece radios. Kingsley wasn't happy about it.

"I thought we were gonna start this shit tomorrow night?" Kingsley said in his radio.

"What do you suggest," I asked. "Leave them here until we're ready?"

His only answer was a heavy sigh and a small bit of grumbling. All of which had a somewhat negative tone. I could tell that even through my earpiece. He was right of course; we were supposed to begin the next evening. I just couldn't leave them behind.

I gave my radio another tap.

"What's up?" asked Hardin.

"Did they mention if there were any undead in the area?"

"I was just about to let you know. We lost contact with them. We don't know the amount of survivors in that location and we don't know if they are in any immediate danger."

I heard Kingsley curse in my ear. We were idling in the middle of the road as everyone awaited my decision. It wasn't exactly the safest place in the world to be. There were a few streetlamps around, but they only gave off a teeny bit of light and ended up casting everything in an eerie yellowish glow.

From the passenger seat, Merrick let out a soft whine.

I strained my ears listening for any sounds of the undead. I couldn't hear anything. Everyone was staring at me.

I honestly didn't know what to do.

Oveja is a decently sized street. There were houses on both sides. I had no idea where to even begin looking for any survivors.

The night air was rather cool. There wasn't even the slightest bit of wind. I still couldn't hear anything.

Merrick let out another whine.

I was just about to leave when someone threw a small rock onto the street in front of us.

"What the hell?" Dudley grumbled as he jumped about a mile in his seat.

I was out of the Jeep immediately and scanning the houses from where I thought the rock had been thrown.

Merrick was right behind me and suddenly so was Georgie.

"Georgie," I whispered. "It's not exactly brilliant when the driver leaves the vehicle. What if we need to get out of here quick?"

With that suggestion, Georgie tapped his ear and asked Javie to take his place as driver.

"Use your head, dumbass," I said.

"Bite me," Georgie replied. "Did you see where it came from?"

I motioned quickly with my weapon at my best guess.

"I'm thinking it was from one of these houses, but I can't be sure."

"So what do we do?"

"Hell if I know," I answered. "I know what I don't want to do. I don't want to have to search five or six houses looking for a survivor, but I think that might be our only option."

I could hear Kingsley let out another exasperated sigh all the way over to where we were standing. In return, I shot him as nasty a look as I could manage. Maybe Dudley was right. Maybe he was having a problem with his nerves. Regardless, I didn't want any noise; even the soft engine rumble coming from the two Jeeps was beginning to make me feel uneasy.

I trotted over to Dudley and told him to kill the engine and keep a look out. I told Javie the same thing at his Jeep and informed Kingsley he would need to come with Georgie and me. He didn't like that at all.

"Why don't I stay?" Kingsley said. "I banged my leg on the drive over; I'm not sure how fast I can move."

"Because you drive like an old lady. The zombies can crawl faster than you can motor."

He was pissed, but he got out of the Jeep. Then he started limping around like a little girl with a thorn in her foot. I could hear Dudley laughing quietly from the other Jeep, and when I saw the look of anguish on Kingsley's face, I couldn't help but snicker right along with my nephew.

"Just go back to the Jeep," I said before heading back towards Georgie.

The situation sucked. We could have used another guy to help us search the houses. I had no idea what was going on with him.

"*I remember from before that Kingsley was a big help when you went on previous missions. Were there problems that you didn't mention during those interviews?*"

Not really. I mean he drank a lot. He was prone to panic during some of the meetings, but he was always ready to go. His behavior was a bit of a shock. At that moment, though, I just didn't have the time to give it a lot of thought.

Georgie gave a weird look towards Kingsley and rolled his eyes.

"So where do we start?" Georgie asked.

"Let's take it like a book and go from left to right," I answered.

If Kingsley had joined us, I would have teamed him up with Georgie and searched one end of the houses while they searched the other, but this was the first time Georgie had ever really been in the thick of things. I didn't want him to panic if something came running out at him. So, we were sticking together.

"*Wasn't it Georgie that ran to help you after the bridge blew up and you made your escape out of El Paso?*"

Yeah, it was, but a one-time moment of bravery only makes a temporary hero. I had no idea what he'd do if the shit hit the fan and I wasn't going to risk his or my life finding out.

We carefully and quietly made our way to the first house. We avoided walking over the rock and gravel yard and instead stuck to the paved driveway and walkway that led to the front door.

I tried the knob. No luck, the door was locked. I gave it a soft tap with my knuckles and waited to see if anyone would answer. No luck again.

"You want to go inside?" Georgie asked.

"No, I don't."

The other homes gave us the same results. The doors were all locked and nobody was answering.

Merrick gave another whine and I left the front porch of the final house and sniffed the air. I could smell rot. It didn't smell too close, and I didn't know if it was there before or not.

I didn't like the situation. In fact, the situation was pissing me off. It didn't make any sense; somebody chunks a rock at us, and then they hide while we are trying to save them. We aren't back in the city for thirty minutes and strange happenings were already afoot.

"Fuck this," I said.

I walked off back towards the Jeeps. Georgie was right behind me, just as confused as I was. I hated leaving, but now wasn't the time to go kicking in the doors. I didn't know what was around, and I didn't want to find out. I figured that the best bet would be to wait until they made contact again.

We were ten feet from the Jeeps when the guy screamed out.

"Don't leave us! Don't leave us! We need help!"

Everyone turned and looked at the same time. Georgie reacted to the noise the quickest. He started motioning for the guy to shut up. In fact, he was motioning like a madman for the guy to be quiet, but of course it was too late.

We heard the first zombie scream come from inside one of the houses across the street. Soon, it was followed by others. The dead were in the houses. I wasn't sure how many, but from the noise level it seemed like there were a lot of them.

"Here we go," I muttered as I flicked off the safety on my MP7.

Dudley, Javie, and Kingsley tumbled out of the vehicles as a wave of zombies exited the houses and rushed towards them. I began to fire into the horde as my teammates regrouped behind me. I didn't panic. I aimed and fired calmly but rapidly. I did not miss. I dropped shambler after shambler.

One of them actually got to within three feet before I brought it down with a shot between the eyes. I had to stop its tumbling body with my combat boot or it would have slid right into me.

Georgie finally began to fire as well. Dudley and Javie were right behind him. Kingsley had set his MP7 down as Georgie and I walked back towards the Jeep. He didn't have time to grab it again before he bailed out of the Jeep with the others. He pulled out a Glock and started shooting rapidly. The problem was he forgot to put the silencer on the damn thing.

"Shut the fuck up," I growled in his direction. "Fall back and kick the damn doors open on that house."

Because our weapons were silenced, we were able to hear one another despite the growls, snarls, and screams of the zombies moving in on us.

"Back up towards the house," I ordered everyone else.

We began to back up immediately, but the wall of lead we were dishing out to keep the zombies at bay wasn't going to buy us enough time to get secured inside the house.

So, I did what I had to do to save my buddies. I waited till I heard the crunch of a door being broken down and I ran straight for the shamblers. I let go of my rifle in mid-run and yanked my tomahawk out of my belt.

I heard Dudley shouting my name, but it would have been too late for me to turn around even if I had wanted to. The zombies were just too close.

My actions had the desired effect: our attackers stopped charging immediately. They didn't know quite what to make of my attack. Before they could figure it out, I was on top of them and hacking my way through.

How many zombies were coming towards your team?

I didn't exactly have time to count, but I'm guessing that there were more than a hundred. They were literally pouring out from all the houses across the street. We had the misfortune to stumble upon a seriously nasty nest of vipers.

Kinda typical for us if you really stop and think about it.

Chapter 2

DUDLEY

I waited for Dudley in the same conference room I met the General in. He arrived twenty minutes late with a salad in one hand and a protein shake in the other. He was still wearing those tight t-shirts, but he seemed to be a lot more muscular.

He didn't say a word when he walked in the room; he was too busy setting down his meal and answering a text on his phone, both at the same time. When all was finished, he pushed his Elvis style sunglasses up on top of his head and smiled at me.

Your hair is different, little lady.

"Do you like it?"

Pretty nice.

"Did Jaxon tell you why I was here?"

He said you're fishing, but I'm thinking that what you are really interested in is a spin off story all about me. I'm sure everybody would love to hear tales of me wrestling with gorillas and slaying dragons and stuff.

I had to laugh at this. Dudley didn't really join in, so I cut it off quickly. He was more interested in stirring his protein shake.

"Well, why don't we just start off like we did the last time. Jaxon was telling me about how you were all attacked on a street named Oveja shortly after your arrival."

Yeah, that was a fucking blast. I knew something was wrong from the get-go. What kind of asshole throws a rock to get our attention and then hides? It was bogus, but there you have it. We tend to meet some seriously deranged individuals in our line of work, but back then…we had no idea how badly fear can jack somebody up.

"Is that what happened? Was the man afraid?"

He was terrified. He saw movement in the windows of another house earlier in the day, that's why he dragged his family to the roof. He wanted to be out of the way in case they came over to pay him a visit.

We didn't know that at the time of course. All we knew was that we were under attack and the enemy was flowing towards us like a giant wave from hell. I could smell the barest hint of rot in the air when we stopped, but it was nothing like the smell that assaulted our nostrils when they all came running out at us.

We were firing like hell to keep them back, but those things know no fear. They just kept coming. I was afraid we were gonna run out of ammo, and the shamblers just kept getting closer and closer as they climbed over the dead and down.

"That reminds me, where did you get the name 'shambler'?"

If you look at them, they're a freaking mess. They are, literally, in shambles...but for whatever reason, the decay doesn't seem to slow them down any.

"Okay, I get it...Please continue."

Muffled shots were popping off, and zombie screams were sounding out. It wasn't a very long moment, probably less than a couple minutes. Jaxon was quick to act. He probably saw the outcome of that situation way before the rest of us.

The next thing I knew, he was barking out orders and I heard a door break behind me. This all happened from somewhere far away. All my attention was concentrated on the gang of rapidly approaching undead.

Jaxon charged right into them.

He gave no warning; he just attacked. I saw the tomahawk come out. I saw dark blood and skull fragments flying in the air as he carved his way right through the center of them.

And then he was gone.

They closed in around him. I called out his name. In shock, I took a step forward and then another. I felt arms close around me. They were pulling me backwards towards the house. I tried to explain. They must not have seen what happened. We had to get to my uncle. My uncle was in the middle of that shit storm.

Next thing I knew, I was inside the house.

Kingsley slammed the door shut. I don't know why he bothered. The mass lost interest in chasing us as soon as Jaxon charged them. We were safe. Javie was peering through the curtains. It was the only source of light in the room.

Georgie was still holding me. I could have pulled away; I'm a lot stronger than Georgie. Instead, I collapsed. I was exhausted, or maybe it was shock. I couldn't believe what had just happened. I had just lost my uncle.

"Jaxon's running," Javie said.

"What?" Georgie asked.

"He made it through. He's leading them away from us. Merrick is with him."

I tapped my earpiece.

"Jax," I said. "Are you there?"

No answer.

"Give him time to lead them away," Georgie said. "That's what he's doing; he's leading them away from us."

I began to calm down. My breathing became more regular. It was then that it finally dawned on me that we were in a dark house and we had no idea if it was safe or not.

"Get ready," I ordered.

Everybody jumped and brought their weapons up. I was on my feet and reaching in my backpack for a flashlight.

"We have no idea what's in this house," I said. "So don't drop your guard."

It took a bit, but I finally found my light. I attached it to the front of my weapon and waited for the rest of the team to follow my example.

"Room by room then," Georgie said.

"Georgie and I in front," I added. "Kingsley and Javie will cover the rear."

Nobody said anything, they just moved into position and we searched the house as quietly as possible. We quickly realized that the back door was wide open, but other than that there were no threats. The only sound I heard was Kingsley's labored breathing.

Do you smoke, little lady?

"Not since college."

Good, it's a bad habit, and if the downstairs wasn't empty, you could be sure that his dirty mouth air would have alerted whatever was lurking in the dark to our presence.

If it weren't for my uncle's idiot move of charging a horde of the living dead, I would have laughed a lot sooner than I did. I held it in for a long time, but when we all paused at the foot of the stairs...I let out a little chuckle.

"You let out a chuckle?"

Yeah, I couldn't help it. I think it was all the tension. Everything was quiet except for Kingsley's Darth Vader breathing. I kind of lost it...so did Georgie...so did Javie.

Kingsley was pissed.

I was about to apologize, but suddenly there was a figure at the top of the stairs. It was what appeared to be a teenage girl in a summer dress. One minute there was nothing and in the next minute...she was just there.

I slowly moved my light up her body to her face. She charged us when my light got about halfway.

I reacted on pure instinct and fired randomly. My weapon was on auto fire, but I missed. Georgie fired as well, but Georgie always misses so that's not a big shocker.

She jumped the last few stairs and screamed that undead scream.

I caught her in the air. She smelled horrible. I rolled her to the side and kinda flipped her off of me. She barely weighed anything, so she flew across the room. As soon as she came to a stop though, she snapped back up and charged again.

I didn't miss on her second charge. I dropped her just a few steps into it. I never got a clear look at her face. I'm kinda glad about that.

"Heads up," Georgie said in a panic.

The upstairs had suddenly come to life. About fifteen members of the undead club poured down the stairwell after us. The smell of decay was horrendous, I'm not sure how I didn't notice it until they were rushing us, but we handled it as quickly and quietly as we could. The only scare came when Javie suffered a bite on the arm. It didn't go through the bite suit, but it was a sobering experience.

Things were looking pretty bleak. I almost got chomped on by a teenybopper zombie, and we shot up half the freakin' house taking care of only fifteen attackers. I was the ipso de facto leader if Jax wasn't around, and I was not handling things very well. My arrogant ass uncle made this shit look easy.

"Ipso facto."

Beg your pardon?

"You said ipso de facto. What you meant to say was ipso facto."

I think you probably heard me wrong.

"That must have been it. Please, continue with your story."

I didn't hear him wrong; it's just well known not to argue with Dudley. If he thinks the sky is purple, then even a blue sky over his head isn't going to change his mind.

Good idea. Where was I?

"I believe you were getting to the part where you were now in charge and not handling it well."

I don't like it when you say it. It sounds so much worse.

I had to laugh at this, and this time he actually joined in with me. It's very hard to tell when he's joking, because he has such a dry sense of humor. It's very different from Jaxon's, because Jaxon seems only concerned with humoring himself, so he's quick to laugh even when nobody else gets the joke.

I was saying that he can make the crazy decisions and throw himself in front of the bus a lot easier than I can because he heals so fast. He doesn't have to worry so much about getting killed. If zombies charged down the stairs at him, he would have charged right back.

"From what I hear, the entire group has some pretty amazing recuperative abilities. Wasn't it you who recovered from a bite?"

Oh yeah, we do, but it's not on his level. He's the Guardian; we just help out. He was born to lead, and he doesn't give a rat's ass whether or not people get pissed at his decisions, or the way he talks. It works for him. The rest of us aren't so lucky.

Anyway, I realized I was doing a piss poor job. So I decided to sack up and act like a man. I was the first one up the stairs. The boys were right behind me, but I was determined to bring our bad luck around.

As soon as I took my first step, Mr. Rock-Thrower himself called to me through the window.

I almost shot him in the face.

"Are they gone? Did you get them?"

As soon as my heart stopped trying to jump out of my throat I answered.

"Yeah, it's cool."

"One of them actually managed to turn the doorknob on the back door. Fortunately, I had already taken my family to the roof before they came inside."

"What's your name?" I asked.

"My name's Adam," he answered. "You're not the General. Where's the General?"

It was a pretty fuckin' good question. I was curious about the answer myself.

"Well, Mr. Dipshit, since you decided to let the entire neighborhood of shamblers know our position, he thought it would be a good idea to lead them away from here."

"I'm sorry. Those things were in the house. I couldn't go down and meet you...and earlier today, I saw one of them moving in the house across the street...so I hid."

"Why didn't you just throw another rock at us?" Georgie asked.

"I was out of rocks. I couldn't find anymore."

"Why are you still outside on the balcony. Why don't you come in?" I asked.

"It's my family; they're still on the roof. I need help bringing them down."

"Why do you need help bringing them down?" Georgie asked. The distrust was damn near dripping from his mouth.

"They're hurt."

Georgie let out a long breath. Javie was quiet; he doesn't really talk much during tense situations. Kingsley slumped against the wall. We all had an idea why he needed help with his family. We just didn't have Jaxon here to handle it for us.

"*His family had been bitten.*"

Yup, we learned since the Safe Zone that a person won't tell you that they have a contaminated family member. Instead, they tell you they have an injured family member. It's hard for them to face the truth...and the truth is their family member needs to be put down. I think that they're hoping the loved one will recover, and they need to protect them from people like us until they do.

A lot of people have died believing that. It's unfortunate, but they always turn. There is no cure; it's a death sentence, unless of course you're a Regulator.

Don't think we're lucky though. "Lucky" would be living up in Alaska, far away from this shit and watching it on the TV.

"Let's take a look," I said.

I climbed out the window after him. Georgie went with me. Javie and Kingsley stayed by the stairwell to make sure nothing snuck up on us. If they were turned, I was hoping Georgie would put them down instead of me. I didn't want that on my conscience.

Once on the balcony, we had to shimmy up the chimney to get to the roof. It wasn't too difficult, but I put some scratches on my MP7. Georgie, being the gun nut that he is, looked at me like I was an idiot.

There was an indention on the roof between two skylights. Two figures were there covered in blankets. One of them was moaning and twisting around. I approached her and saw that it was a little girl. She was as white as a ghost even in the dark of night. She had a bandage on her arm from where she was probably bitten and had a gag in her mouth to keep her from screaming. It looked like she had died just a few hours ago.

"I didn't know what to do, so I tied her up. I don't think she's gone all the way. Sometimes she stares at me like she remembers who I am."

For a second, I almost lost my shit. This scene was playing out very close to my not-so- distant past. A scared-to-death little girl with Jaxon, Kingsley, and I, praying that she wouldn't turn from her bite. I was carrying her when she turned. I haven't forgotten that one. Maybe I won't ever forget any of them, but that one really bothered me. I was carrying her when she died, and I didn't even notice until my uncle shot her in the head.

Georgie put his hand on the man's shoulder. The poor guy started to cry. He did it quietly, but I could see his shoulders bobbing up and down as Georgie hugged him.

"You're not the General," said the woman next to the child.

"No," I answered. "The General would know what to do."

"Adam won't let her go," she said, "but I don't want this for her. I can't even hold her anymore. My baby is gone."

The woman was damn near as pale as the child, but even though she looked pretty weak, she was still all there.

"Were you bitten?" I asked.

"Yes," she answered.

"When?" I asked.

"A few days ago. We were hiding in a house a few streets over. I was in the kitchen by the window when something broke through the glass and dragged me out. It pulled me up on the roof and started biting me."

Now that was odd. A bite to the neck should have turned her pretty quickly.

"Let me see the bite," I said.

She obliged by turning her head, moving her hair, and showing me the bandage.

"If you get the sudden urge to eat me, give a warning," I said as I pulled back the bandage.

Underneath, was a nasty ass bite, but it didn't look infected. Zombie bites normally fill up with pus and turn all sorts of nasty colors within about twenty minutes after the attack. This bite just looked like an injury.

"Were you attacked at the same time as your daughter?" I asked.

"No, my daughter was attacked today. We left our last hiding place because we kept hearing footsteps on the roof. We thought it might be the same zombie that had bitten me. After I was attacked, Adam boarded up all the windows. The thing on the roof seemed like it was looking for a way in. After a couple nights of it returning over and over again, we decided to find a safer place. Adam carried me the entire way. We only wanted to keep our little girl safe."

"Of course," I said. "What else could you do? It's not your fault, so don't ever go and start thinking that way."

She started crying.

"I'm not sure what to do. Let me talk to my teammate," I said. When in doubt, I figured that I might as well be honest.

The Regulators have a strict policy when someone gets bitten. We absolutely do not put them down until they turn. I had no problems pulling out the father, but there was nothing I could do for the mother and daughter because we also had a strict policy about not extracting infected people. Well, I take it back; there was something I could do for them. It just wasn't going to be easy.

I pulled Georgie into a brief conference. He agreed with me about evacuating the father and putting down the daughter. However, he absolutely did not want to be the one to do it. He had a daughter of his own and the very thought of shooting a child was too disturbing for him. As far as the mother was concerned, we were gonna wait for her to turn and put her down as well.

We gave them some space to say their goodbyes, but we kept our eyes on them all the same in case they did something foolish in their grief. It was a pretty emotional scene. I don't really want to get into it, but it deeply affected both Georgie and I.

After their farewells were said, Georgie helped Adam move his wife back inside the house where Kingsley and Javie were waiting. Though she seemed rather weak, she had none of the joint pains that other infected people seemed to acquire very shortly after being bitten. I had no idea what to make of the situation.

Finally, I was left alone on the roof with their child. I wanted to do it quickly and be done with it. I rushed towards her and raised my rifle, but I couldn't fire. It was a child. I didn't want to shoot a child. Yet, I had to do it. I had to do the right thing by that little girl and her parents.

It took a while, but I finally mustered up enough courage and put her out of her misery. There was no loud bang, just a muffled thump as the bullet traveled through the rifle's silencer. Her life was over.

"*Her life was over when she was bitten.*"

Yeah, that's what Jax always tells us.

Anyway, I was a little sullen after that. I needed a moment by myself before I rejoined the team, so I just sort of sat there on the roof for awhile and waited for the sun to start trying to peek out over the mountains.

It wasn't long before Hardin was talking in my ear.

"Dudley, are you okay?"

"Yeah," I answered.

"I saw everything. You did the right thing."

I always forget that our earpieces also have small cameras. I made a mental note to remember that the next time I had to pee.

Then all of a sudden it hit me.

"Where's Jaxon?" I asked.

"We lost contact with him as soon as he charged the horde. We have air support tracking the mass right now."

That's when I realized that I completely forgot about my earpiece radio. I hadn't tried contacting my uncle since we first entered the house. I needed to quit making mistakes; people were depending on me.

"Why don't you have the choppers open fire on the horde?" I asked.

"Because we aren't exactly sure where Jaxon is in the mass; it's jumbled and chaotic; they are moving fast and traveling through alleys, backyards, and homes. We could end up hitting Jaxon by mistake."

"So what are you going to do?" I asked.

"We are hoping that he will lose his pursuers and find a way to contact us."

"I want you to keep me informed on this. In the meantime, I have an extraction. It's a man and woman—the woman is infected, so we'll wait that out and take care of it. It probably won't take too long."

"Right, we're on top of it. We've already located the nearest extraction point."

I forgot about the damn cameras again.

"All right, we're going to stay here until tomorrow evening, just in case Jax makes his way back."

I finally went back inside the house as the sun rose in the sky and had everyone gather up in the living room. The poor girl's parents were filled with grief. I had Kingsley and Javie move all the corpses we'd shot up to the front and back exit of the house in an attempt to mask the smell of the living people inside. I wasn't sure it would work, but they smelled pretty bad to me. Hopefully if a shambler happened to walk by, they wouldn't be able to sniff us out.

Those things have some serious nose power.

When all was said and done, we all settled down to rest. The team took turns on guard duty. Fortunately, nothing exciting came our way, and we were able to relax a bit. I was even able to get some food and liquids into Michelle.

"*Michelle is the girl's mother?*"

Yeah, Adam's wife; I finally got her name. She was actually starting to look a lot better. I couldn't explain it; I thought for sure she was a dead woman. I was seriously out of my depth here, so after examining her wound again and applying some antibiotic cream, I gave my earpiece a tap.

"This is Miriam."

I was expecting Hardin. To be honest, I really didn't know Miriam all that well and I'm not sure if we had ever even spoken.

Dudley is well known to be very quiet around people he doesn't know. However, that all changes once he becomes used to them. When that happens, well, everyone tells me that they need some earplugs if they expect to get any sleep.

"I was looking for Hardin," I said.

"He's taking a break. Is this about Jaxon?"

I had been pestering them all morning for information about my uncle. They were probably getting pretty tired of me, and I was getting pretty sick of them not having anything new to tell. That last decent bit I heard came shortly after sunup, and all they knew for certain was that the large group of undead in pursuit of my uncle had broken up and begun to disperse.

"There was no sign of the General?"

None. He seemed to have vanished, and the zombies were going back to doing whatever it is that zombies like to do when they aren't chasing and eating people. On the plus side, when the sun came up enough to see clearly, the helicopter was able to fire into the remaining groups of shamblers and start dwindling down their numbers.

"Were you worried?"

A little bit, but I knew he got away. If he got caught, they would have seen that massive horde come to an abrupt stop when they ripped into him. They don't need to positively identify someone to know whether or not they are being devoured.

My worry was how he was going to find his way back in hostile territory. When the horde finally began to disperse, they were miles and miles away on the opposite side of Mesa towards the Sunland Park Mall. Go ahead and feel free to insert a number of mall-related zombie jokes.

I'm sure everyone will get his reference, so I'm not going to explain it.

"It wouldn't be very original if he hid inside a mall would it?"

Absolutely not, and if Jaxon is anything, he's original.

This, however, wasn't about Jaxon. This was about Michelle…and me being out of my depth.

"No, it's about this woman with the bite," I told Miriam over the radio.

"Is she getting worse?" Miriam asked.

"No, it's the opposite. She seems to be getting better."

"Dudley, there is no getting better from a zombie bite. The onset of symptoms varies depending on the severity of the bite, but the conditions will only worsen."

"Okay, well what about some kind of remission?"

"No such things with a zombie bite, things just go from bad to worse."

Now, just to give you a little back-story, Miriam knows what she's talking about. She works with our team in a sort of advisory capacity.

"I've certainly heard of her. Yet I've never met her or even seen her. If I remember correctly, Skie told me that she's a three hundred-year-old witch. Can you tell me in what sort of way she advises the team?"

She's an expert on the scary stuff. She knows all about what's out there going bump in the night. In other words, she knows stuff about monsters.

"I get it."

Awesome, so we're on the same page?

"Yes we are."

Then you can understand how confused I was, because right in the next room was a woman that seemed to be improving after being bitten by a shambler.

"Here's the thing," I said. "I just looked at the bite mark and it really doesn't look too bad. It actually looks like it might be healing. On top of that, the woman herself seems to have a lot more energy, and she's taking foods and liquids."

"Really?" Miriam asked.

"Yeah," I replied.

"Are you sure she's not faking. The poor woman is probably scared to death."

"I guess she could be faking the whole feeling better part, but I'm not sure how she could be faking a healing wound."

"Do me a favor and put the camera close to the wound, so I can see it this time," said Miriam.

I did as Miriam asked. I went back over to Michelle. I took my earpiece off and held it close to her bite mark for a few seconds. After that, I placed the contraption back on my ear. I think my actions kinda freaked out Michelle, but the woman didn't get emotional or anything. That actually impressed me. I remember when I was bitten. I was freaking right the fuck out, and I would have probably freaked out a lot worse if I had started to feel any major symptoms. The sigh of relief I breathed out when I realized I could heal was enormous.

I tapped my radio for Miriam.

"Well, what do you think?" I asked.

"I'm not sure what to think. That bite doesn't seem to be showing any of the normal symptoms that a zombie bite typically shows. I need to do some research on this. I will let you know when I have something. In the meantime, do the evacuation as soon as possible...and get that woman on the chopper. I want to talk to this person. That is, if she's still alive by nightfall."

"Gotcha, as soon as the sun goes down we're outta here."

Adam wanted to know what was going on. I didn't blame him a bit. I just didn't exactly know what to tell him. How do you explain to someone that the so-called experts are actually stumped? At that point, I was really wishing that Jaxon were with us. Then again, Jaxon isn't exactly the emotional type and I can't really even picture him being in my situation. He'd probably just tell the guy to go talk to Kingsley.

I was a mess. I had no idea what to say to him.

"*Dudley, do you realize that you've become somewhat popular around the world?*"

I may have heard that once or twice. Are you gonna hit me up for my autograph?

After a polite chuckle, I answered him. It somewhat crosses the line with unbiased journalism, but I'm pretty sure most people would agree that I already crossed that line during the first set of interviews.

"Unfortunately, I'm not going to ask you for an autograph. I'm going to pass on a little secret that you haven't seemed to grasp just yet."

Really, what's that?

"*You among the other Regulators (excluding the General) have become popular...because you are so very human.*"

After seeing his look of confusion, I went ahead and elaborated.

"*The General is a walking legend. He goes out and does these very brave things, but he seems somewhat distant and cold. Don't get me wrong, Jaxon is a hero; he saves the day, but he isn't personal. You, however, are affected by the things you see. You feel bad for people; you care.*"

"*It's just something I've noticed. Obviously, a lot of other people have noticed your humanity as well, or I don't think you would be quite so popular in those Internet chat rooms.*"

Uh huh...are you trying to say that I'm a crybaby?

That time, I did laugh.

"*Not at all. I'm just saying that your emotions are what set you apart. That's a good thing.*"

So not knowing what to do is a good thing according to you?

"*Being a human being is a good thing, because in spite of how things affect you, you still go out there and try to help people. So what did you tell Adam?*"

He paused and looked at me for a bit, shrugged his shoulders and continued.

I think I'd rather just be a badass know it all, but regardless of that, I told Adam the truth. I told him that his wife's bite mark was confusing us and that unless she took a turn for the worse, we were going to evacuate her at nightfall.

This of course gave both of them a dangerous thing; it gave them hope. I tried to explain that getting their hopes up might not be such a good idea, but I had lost total control of the situation and just kept my thoughts to myself as I wondered how badly they would hate me when things turned ugly.

Turns out, things didn't turn ugly. Michelle just kept on eating and drinking. Her cheeks were flushed with the joy of leaving. Shortly after the sun had finally set, we were on our way.

Hardin was back in the control room at this time so I was able to talk to him.

"We're moving out," I said after tapping my earpiece.

"We have a new extraction point; the previous one has too much activity at the moment. The chopper will be there within the next thirty minutes."

I was the first out the door, followed by Georgie, then Adam and Michelle. Kingsley and Javie made up the rear. There were bodies all over the street. This was just a bit shocking. I knew our gunfire had brought down a bunch of shamblers before Jaxon charged them, but from inside the house I wasn't able to see all the bodies that Jaxon must have dropped as he led them away.

Once again, I was somewhat amazed by my uncle's ability to bring forth so much destruction. I was glad he was on our side.

That's when something caught my eye.

I motioned everyone to the Jeep and went forward to investigate. As quietly as possible, I ran up the road and investigated the object that had caught my interest. It was Jaxon's earpiece. He must have lost it when he attacked the horde. I would have grabbed it for him, but it looked like it had been stepped on about a dozen times, if not more.

Further up the road, I noticed something else. It was Jaxon's vest and MP7. Why he would ditch his neck protection and weapon I had no idea, but I picked it up for him anyway.

Within seconds I was back in the Jeep. It was a tight fit cramming everyone inside one Jeep, but I wanted to leave the other one for Jaxon. I figured he would make his way back to this location with hopes that we had left a radio for him to make contact. I didn't want to disappoint him.

Georgie was driving, Javie was riding shotgun, Adam and Michelle had the backseat, and Kingsley and I were on either side holding onto the roll bar for dear life, and that's not an understatement with the way Georgie drives.

Javie had already called up our extraction point on the dash-mounted computer. It showed a little map of the Westside with a red dot on our destination. It looked like we were headed to the top of the Coronado Tower, which was located on Mesa.

"*What's the Coronado tower?*"

Oh yeah, you don't live in El Paso. It's just a tall building on Mesa. It might actually be the tallest building on the Westside, but don't quote me on that. At the moment, however, I can't seem to think of anything taller. It also has a nice restaurant on the top floor. I heard it's pretty delectable, but I've never actually eaten there.

Also, just in case you didn't know, Mesa is one of the main streets on the Westside of El Paso.

"*I actually remembered that. Please continue.*"

Well apparently the zombies that Jaxon had led away from out location were all in the process of returning. It was evident the minute we hit Mesa and random corpses starting charging the car and belting out those nasty screams.

It was almost a game between Kingsley and me as we tried to pop off headshots before they could scream. It wasn't an easy game by any means. There were too many deserted cars and blocked routes on the street and the shamblers were coming from all directions.

I really don't know how to accurately describe something running out at you from behind an abandoned car. Their decaying yellowish faces, their slimy bone-like hands. It's nightmare material. Some of them were limping; others just bolted towards us at a dead run.

Still, we did a decent job. We kept all of them from approaching the Jeep. Unfortunately, we weren't able to keep all of them from screaming. More and more of them were attracted by the screams and headed our way. My main concern was that they were going to mass around the Coronado Tower once we made our way inside.

"Hardin, there's too many shamblers out here," I said after I gave my earpiece a tap.

"I think you're okay, Dudley," Hardin replied. "The dead are pretty spread out in your area. Just to be safe, instead of doing the extraction at the top of the tower, let's pull this off in the large parking lot behind the building."

"That'll work," I replied.

It was a relief to all of us. Nobody wanted to go to the top of that building. We had no idea what we would encounter and didn't want to get stuck if the exits got surrounded.

The parking lot behind the Coronado Tower also was a bit of a challenge. It was an open area with pretty much zero cover. According to the plans that Jaxon and Hardin came up with, we weren't supposed to hang around when a chopper came to pick up survivors, because a landing chopper is pretty much a dinner bell for the undead. The idea was for us to leave the survivors in a safe place, while we retreated to a decent cover where we could provide protection in case the survivors needed it.

There was no safe place for us to place Adam and Michelle for extraction. We would need to be right next to them in order to provide security, and that pretty much left us fucked when it came time to remove ourselves after the extraction.

I wanted to explain this to Hardin, but I didn't want to look like a pussy. Man-pride won out in the end. I said nothing.

When we reached the location, I had already figured out a plan. We parked the Jeep on one of the adjoining streets and left Georgie with the Jeep. Then we pretty much covered the compass by using Coronado Towers as south. Javie took north in an area where some construction was going on. Kingsley and Georgie made up east and west. Georgie had the Jeep for cover, but Kingsley found a group of cars in which to hide himself fairly well.

Everything was far from ideal, but we made do. There were a few zombies in the area. I popped off some shots to bring them down as I walked Adam and Michelle to the center of the parking lot. Both of them were terrified, but Michelle seemed to have more energy. She was walking without any aid from Adam, only holding his hand.

As soon as we hit the center, I tapped my earpiece for Hardin.

"We're in position and the position sucks, so get that chopper here now."

I felt a little uncomfortable barking orders at him like that; the guy was pretty hardcore. I've seen Jaxon bark at him a bunch of times, but Jaxon barks at everybody when he's in a mood. Fortunately for me, Hardin didn't get all emotional, and he ignored my tone of voice. It would have sucked if he decided to tell me off over the radio or, even worse, delay the chopper, but the man's a professional.

The helicopter arrived within moments.

So did the dead.

It was an immediate firefight as soon as the chopper started to descend. Everyone was firing to keep us from getting overwhelmed. That is, everyone except for Kingsley. There were no shots coming from his direction. I had to cover myself, and anything moving towards us, from the area he was supposed to have been taking care of.

My nerves got the best of me. I started to miss my targets. When that happened, I started to fire more shots. It was a losing situation. We would soon be overwhelmed. Things got real bad when I fumbled my mag change.

I had some serious shakes when I was finally ready to start firing again; the zombies were just a few feet away. I sprayed that damn weapon like a fire hose and, fortunately, dropped all the shamblers that got past Javie and Georgie. I even had a moment of fear go lancing through my head about Kingsley. Why wasn't he shooting?

Suddenly, the chopper pilot was speaking in my ear.

"Sir, I can't land here. There's too many of them."

"No shit," I replied. "Do it anyway."

The pilot started crying about this and that and how he was going to get himself killed if he brought her down any farther. I don't blame him. How many sane people do you know that would place themselves in that kind of danger? I just didn't care. I needed to get Adam and Michelle on that helicopter yesterday, and I needed to get the team outta the damn area.

"The pilot refused to land?"

Yeah, he took one look at the situation and panicked. Even Hardin was yelling at him to land. There was just no reaching the guy. With all the bricks he was shitting, I could have built a house. Finally, after hovering over us for way too long, he started gaining altitude. At this point, I was barely going to be able to get myself out of the area. There was no way I was going to be able to pull Adam and Michelle out as well.

Luckily for everyone, Ivana was in the helicopter. She really shouldn't have been. Jaxon kept her well away from any danger, and if he found out that she was joy riding over El Paso, he was going to have a fit, but it was fortunate for all concerned that she tends to ignore him. She didn't like the situation one bit. I could hear her screaming at the pilot, and the chopper began to hesitate. Suddenly, a rescue line and harness were thrown down. I immediately dropped my weapon to hang around my chest and prayed that Georgie and Javie could keep me from getting eaten for just a few moments.

I hurriedly stuffed Michelle into the harness and told Adam to hold on tight as the helicopter began to ascend once more. Georgie and Javie succeeded in keeping the zombies off of me for a few moments, but those few moments were over.

I waved a goodbye to Ivana and focused my attention back on my surroundings. About fifteen or twenty rancid corpses charged in my direction. I pulled out my machete while random pictures of Jaxon charging headlong into masses of zombies fired around in my brain.

I glared at my oncoming attackers. For just a brief moment I pictured the battle that was about to go down. Then I mumbled, 'fuck it' and ran like hell.

I could hear the muffled thumps as Georgie and Javie fired on my pursuers. I was worried that I was going to end up taking a bullet due to Georgie's shitty aim. Luckily it didn't happen, but I was still worried.

My escape route was planned from the beginning. As soon as Georgie saw me retreat, he would fire up the Jeep, pick up Javie, and then come around to pick up Kingsley and me. The only problem was that Kingsley might have been hurt, or worse. Regardless, if he had been able, he would have cleared me a path. My retreat didn't have a safe exit, so I was hacking every shambler that got in my way. I think I brought down at least five of them. I just remember goo dripping down my blade and onto my gloved hands. I squeezed the handle as tight as possible to keep from losing the weapon.

When I finally reached Kingsley's hiding place, I couldn't even find him. I did a real quick search under and between the cars and was about to give up due to my pursuers, when the door of one of the vehicles opened and he stepped out.

His eyes were giant orbs of fear as he looked over my shoulder.

"You led them right to us," he managed to stammer.

I turned and followed his gaze. The parking lot was worse than I had realized. It was flooded with the undead, and all of those zombies were headed right for us.

"Move," I shouted out.

I grabbed Kingsley by his weapon strap and began to run. At first I had no idea where I was going to go, but then my brain began functioning once again, and I headed us towards Javie's direction in the hopes that after Georgie picked him up, we would be able to catch him on the way to our appointed spot.

Of course, if I was wrong and they were somehow delayed, we would probably be swamped and eaten. Not a great thought.

Behind us, the situation was pretty grave. The horde of undead was rapidly gaining on us. Kingsley just wasn't a fast runner. I could hear him huffing and puffing behind me as I dragged him along.

I could have ditched him, but that's not my style. I'm a Regulator. If my fellow Regulator goes down, I'm going down with him, and I'm going to fight until the bitter end. I could feel my MP7 bouncing about on my chest. I wondered briefly if I should drop the machete and grab the rifle. I had just enough time to consider how much ammo was left in the weapon when I saw the lights of the Jeep turn a corner and head our way.

I poured on the speed.

"Let go of me," Kingsley growled as he slapped my hand away from him.

I dove into the back of the Jeep as Georgie came to a screeching halt. Kingsley was suddenly on top of me, and I felt the air leave my lungs when his weight slammed against me. Kingsley is a big, big, boy. My face was buried in the fabric of the backseat and I had to fight to lift my head.

I wasn't happy with the view.

Standing there in the glare of the headlights were the snarling and decaying faces of a couple hundred zombies.

Georgie and Javie looked like they were about to piss themselves. Kingsley and I already had. We knew this situation from before. They might be temporarily confused, but it wasn't going to last long and then they were going to charge.

"Kingsley," I said. "Get your legs inside the Jeep. Georgie hit the top."

Georgie was frozen solid. I can't blame the guy. He wasn't exactly an old hat at this game. Especially since his candy ass never left the Safe Zone.

I had only a few moments to act.

Slowly, just as slowly as possible, I leaned forward to reach the lever on the floor of the Jeep next to the four-wheel drive stick.

I couldn't reach.

I shifted my legs just a little bit in order to get a better angle. I was using Kingsley's shoulder to hold myself steady. I ended up over-reaching and my MP7 clattered on the floor of the Jeep just as I lowered myself beneath the dash.

The sound was rather loud.

I heard the scream, but I wasn't sure if it was coming from Georgie or one of the shamblers. All I knew was that I needed to hit that lever or we were all going to end up a bowel movement from an undead stomach.

"*Lovely.*"

Not really.

I heard the first of them slam into the hood of the Jeep. I couldn't resist, I raised my head above the dashboard. Through the glass of the windshield, I was face to face with a member of the undead club.

It's actually a pretty horrible sight when you're that close to one of those things. Its eyes had gone a milky white. It was missing most of its nose and part of its lips. The teeth were scum colored brown and its hair was a mass of dirt and tangles.

I hit the lever just as its hand smashed into the windshield.

I shouldn't have hesitated.

The face in the windshield wasn't the only zombie that charged us. It was just the only one I noticed in that brief second. It turns out that all of them came at us and if I had been a second later on hitting that lever, well, it would have been a pretty crappy evening.

I was able to hit the lever in time though, and believe me it was *just* in time. The armored top of the vehicle shot up through a bunch of different slots at what seemed like warp speed. The pieces clicked, snapped, and slammed together so fast it actually took the head off of one of the shamblers just as it leaned forward to take a chomp out of Kingsley.

We were enclosed in an armored vehicle courtesy of some military genius that figured an armored, transformer-like top would probably come in handy some day. I was gonna kiss that guy if I ever figured out who the designer was.

Georgie was still screaming.

Kingsley was cussing up a storm.

Javie was still frozen stiff.

The inside of the Jeep was covered in gore. Apparently, some other zombies also lost some limbs when the top assembled.

Georgie was still screaming.

With a smile on my face, I got to do something that I've wanted to do many times since meeting Georgie: I bitch-slapped him. His scream stopped immediately.

"Everybody calm down," I said. "We're safe in here."

Georgie was quietly hyperventilating, and Kingsley had stopped cursing. There was no change from Javie, though. He was still staring out the window. All of the zombies were pounding away and scratching at the Jeep in an effort to get to us. It was pretty loud.

"Georgie," I said. "I need to switch seats with you. I'm going to get us out of here."

In acknowledgement that he actually heard me, Georgie bobbed his head up and down. We both moved by each other at the same time. It shouldn't have been easy because Jeeps aren't exactly roomy, but we were both covered in slime and chunks that acted as lubricant, and we just kinda slid into our new seats.

Right then Javie came out of his stupor.

"MOTHERFUCKER!" he shouted.

It was unfortunate he chose to shout, because it made the zombies begin attacking the vehicle with renewed frenzy, and the Jeep began to rock back and forth with their onslaught. At some point, I actually froze for a second. I'm not sure if it was Javie's exclamation that did it to me or when we ended up on only two wheels.

Regardless, I felt it was prudent to get our asses out of Dodge. I cranked the starter. I can't even remember when the Jeep stalled out in the first place. The engine roared to life as I revved it up. I slammed the shifter in reverse, and punched the accelerator.

I heard the nasty thumps and crunches as I backed up into the mass of undead bodies behind the vehicle. When I had created just a bit of space, I slammed the shifter into first and punched through the crowd in front.

The Jeep bounced up and down as zombies were pulled under the heavy-duty front bumper. Still more shamblers pounded on our doors and windows. I couldn't even tell where I was going; the pile was that thick. I suddenly jerked the wheel to the left and punched it again. A few more bumps and slams, and suddenly, we were free. The way ahead of us was clear. Behind us was pretty much a hornets' nest, but we had a way out and believe you me I took it.

It didn't take very long to lose our new friends. I took the first road I could find that led away from Mesa, and we soon lost our tail in the maze of suburbia. We were all glad to be out of danger, because the inside of the Jeep really reeked, with all those nasty zombie bits all over.

I pushed the lever to retract the top, and we all breathed deeply of the cold night air.

"Where are we headed?" Kingsley asked.

"I say we find a carwash and spray this bitch out," I answered.

It didn't take long to find one. Those self-serve carwashes are just about everywhere. As soon as I pulled up, we all bailed out of the vehicle. Georgie did the cleaning and the rest of us took up defensive positions.

When he was done, Georgie was in shock that there wasn't a single dent on the Jeep. I started laughing.

"What part of armored did you not understand?" I asked him.

"I thought it was some sort of code word for you being an ass-hat, to be honest with you. I didn't think it would actually work."

"I'm just glad you stopped screaming," Kingsley added. "My ears are still ringing."

By this time, we were all laughing.

"My favorite was Javie," I added. "He's all quiet and frozen then all of a sudden he belts out this loud 'MOTHERFUCKER.'"

"That's so you bitches know I'm serious," Javie said.

I could barely breathe, I was laughing so hard.

Hardin must have thought we were having a little too much fun. He was suddenly in my ear once again.

"You boys having a good time?" Hardin asked.

"Hey, nice job with the extraction," I replied. "Could you have picked a worse fucking place? You almost got us all killed."

"My mistake," Hardin said. "The area looked clear enough. I didn't expect all of them to run out of the nearby buildings. It won't happen again, and you guys all got through it. How's Georgie? Has he stopped screaming?"

"Barely," I answered. "So what do you need? I think we might be done for the night."

"We found another survivor," Hardin said. "I think you guys might want to take this one."

"Is he in any immediate danger? We still don't have Jaxon with us, and since you haven't brought him up, I'm assuming that he's still missing."

"Yes, Dudley, we have not had any contact from Jaxon, and no, this survivor is not in any immediate danger. However, I was thinking that you might still want to jump on this now instead of tomorrow."

"Why is that?"

"This guy is rather disagreeable, so it might be that he's telling the truth, but I have no way to tell since he won't give us his name. Anyway, he says that he knows you guys and he's stuck inside your old Safe Zone. According to him, he arrived not long after Jaxon led all the survivors out of the city, and he's been there ever since."

We left for the Safe Zone immediately.

Hardin said that the guy was disagreeable. That's what got me thinking he might actually be a pal. Jaxon has a lot of friends that are sort of rough around the edges. Most of them don't have criminal records that I know of, but I don't keep up with all of them.

The other thing that had me jumping was that he was in our old Safe Zone. That place has a special meaning to those of us that were fortunate enough to have been there. If this guy went looking for us and somehow wasn't able to make it in time for our departure, he deserved our help, and he deserved it immediately. Also, it would give us a pretty decent place to spend the day if it was still secure.

We were there inside of about ten minutes. I let Georgie drive after he promised not to start screaming again if he saw a zombie. The front gate was locked up tight. I took that as a positive sign and leaned out of the Jeep with my MP7 and started taking shots at the ten shamblers gathered around it.

It didn't take long to bring them all down, but we made noise. It wasn't a lot of noise, but it was noise nonetheless. I was worried that we were going to have more company so I wanted to get inside as fast as possible.

"Georgie, go hop the fence, and open the gate."

"But I'm driving," Georgie said.

"I'll drive, just go do it. I never paid attention to how you guys rigged everything up."

Watching Georgie climb over the fence would have been pretty damn amusing if I hadn't had to divide my time between laughing at him and being paranoid about an attack. It seemed to take him forever to slide open the gate; and when he did, he made a lot of noise.

I drove through as soon as he had the gate open far enough. I almost ran over his foot in the process, but better that than have another massive fight in the same night.

I tapped my earpiece for Hardin.

"Which house is it?" I asked.

"He's in Georgie's old house," Hardin answered.

That was good news; I was beginning to hear screams echoing around in the nearby neighborhoods, and Georgie's house was right in front of us, on the left hand side of the street.

"Georgie," I said. "Use your keypad to open the garage door. I'm going to back in the Jeep to keep it out of sight. Everyone else follows Georgie to keep him covered."

We were all safely in the garage by the time the screams got louder. I wasn't too worried about the zombies massing around the gate. There were plenty of elevated stands to shoot from if it came to that, and they'd probably drift off by themselves anyway if they didn't see anyone outside.

From the garage, we entered Georgie's house. All the lights were off except the one in the kitchen. I was leading the way with Georgie right behind me. We held our weapons at the ready in case the place was occupied by anything nasty.

We were entering the kitchen when something came hurtling from the darkness beyond the bright kitchen light. It narrowly missed my left ear, but it nailed Georgie right in the forehead, bounced off, and shattered on the floor.

All of us immediately ducked for cover. Except for Georgie, he just sort of sat down after he got hit.

For about thirty seconds nobody moved.

Then we heard the laughter coming from the shadows. I looked back towards Georgie and the broken glass all around his still form. The fucker had nailed him with a beer bottle, and by the sound of our attacker, he thought that was pretty damn amusing.

"If I had a gun, I could have shot all you pussies," a voice I immediately recognized said.

I wasn't happy. I was not happy at all. He was gonna be a pain in the ass. The guy was a habitual line-stepper.

"Well, we weren't exactly expecting you to start chunking beer bottles at us, now were we?" I said as I stood up and motioned everyone else to do the same.

Our attacker followed my example and stepped out from the shadows and into the kitchen light. He was grinning from ear to ear. I heard Georgie moan and Kingsley groan as they realized who it was.

"What the hell are you pussies doing here?" Nick said. "And where in the hell is Jaxon?"

Chapter 3

NICK

Nick is a very large man. I realized just how large the minute he walked into the room. I've seen him in photos before, but photos simply do not do his size justice. He makes all the other team members look rather small. According to Dudley, he's even taller than Kingsley who tops out close to 6'2". His arms are massive and his legs are just shy of tree trunks. He has black hair and a somewhat boyish face that carries a ready smile.

He offered me his hand immediately. His skin was soft and somewhat clammy.

It's about time you decided to interview me. You should have talked to me last time.

"I was doing a story about the General and how he came to be."

Came to be?

"I was doing a story about his origins and how things started in El Paso."

Yeah, yeah, I knew what you meant. I've seen you before, ya know? When you went and interviewed Jax the first time. You were looking all nervous. It's a pretty good look on you. I tried to get him to introduce us, but he never did.

"Uh huh, well I've certainly heard about you. Make no mistake about that."

Really, what have you heard?

"I probably shouldn't say."

Go ahead.

"Well, I heard about you from Jaxon."

Never mind, I don't wanna hear it.

"He said that you're a wanton man whore with no quality control. Shall I go on?"

He's an asshole sometimes.

"He told me that you'd say that. He also told me to start off my interview by mentioning your quality control problems. He thought it might help you focus."

Well, I guess when we are all finished here, I'll have a few things to bring up with him.

"He said you would go there as well. Would you like to hear his response?"

He actually took a moment to think about his options before he decided to ignore my question completely and changed the subject.

So what did you want to ask me?

"I've been speaking with Dudley; he took me all the way to the moment he met up with you at Georgie's house. Do you think you could lead me up to that moment as well?"

Did he tell you how I pegged Georgie in the head with the beer bottle?

"Yes, he did."

That was pretty fucking funny. I didn't mean to actually hit the dumbass, but it was still pretty funny.

"So what were you doing in El Paso? I understand that you don't actually live there."

I went to visit a friend of mine.

"I'm curious as to why Jaxon didn't come and rescue you like he rescued Tito from his apartment."

That would be because I don't need someone to come and rescue me, and also because none of them even knew I was in town. I was visiting a lady friend.

"Did she make it out?"

No clue. I really don't know her that well.

"I see."

No, no, don't look at me like that. It's not like I ditched her or anything. She went to work the day things started to go bad. I was in my motel room because she didn't want her husband or kids to find out about me. Whatever. The point is: I was nowhere near her. If she had been with me when the shamblers came, I would have protected her. Unless she slowed me down, then I would have just pillow snuffed her.

I was completely floored that he actually admitted that and said it so casually.

He started laughing at the expression on my face.

Gotcha.

"You were making fun of me?"

I was. The reason I did that is because after talking to Jaxon, you have some preconceived notion that I'm this dumb asshole. I could tell by the looks you were giving me, and I don't think that's very fair. I may be rough around the edges, and I may have some personality conflicts with certain people, but I'm still a Regulator. I still go out and save people with the rest of the team. Besides that, have you ever even seen Jaxon in polite society? He's rude. He's like the rudest person I've ever met. I'm at least nice to people when I meet them. All in all, I'm a pretty good guy.

I was a little shocked by all that he said. I was indeed thinking of him as a sort of dumb brute. It was surprising that he seemed rather intelligent.

"You're right; I wasn't being very fair to you. Let's start over please."

Much better. Now what kind of panties are you wearing and how do I get them off?

Once again, I was completely floored and speechless.

So anyway, I was in my motel room when the fucking zombies came. I was staying at the Camino Real. Jaxon would probably call that pretentious, but I like to stay in nice places. If he wants to slum it, he's more than welcome.

It's a pretty tall building. I forget what floor I was on, but I was up there pretty high and I was able to see all the mayhem on the streets below from my window when it finally came my way. It wasn't a pretty sight. It wasn't a pretty sight at all. People were attacking and eating other people.

The idea of fighting back didn't even cross my mind. I was concerned with self-preservation. At that moment, nobody was thinking about fighting back. Everyone was running. They were even trampling each other in their haste to get away.

I was safe in my room when it started, but I knew I wouldn't be able to stay there forever. I ran into the hallway towards the vending machine. I used a well-placed kick to break the glass and snagged every single food item it held.

After that, I went to another machine that held bottled water and sodas. It took a few trips from there and back to my room, but I was able to empty it out. There were a few other people hiding out on my floor as well. I shared with the ones I met in the hallway.

After I was back in my room, I pushed a large wooden dresser in front of the door to make sure I was safe.

I guess I ended up staying in that room for a few days. It was pretty lonely. I had no contact with the outside world; then again, that was kind of the point. The outside world had gone to shit. I could see that much from my window, and I had no intention of getting any closer.

My truck was waiting for me in the parking garage if I ever decided to leave, but where would I go? For all I knew the entire world had been overrun by those things. I watch movies; I know about zombies. They multiply pretty fast, and from what I had seen out of my window, El Paso was overrun with them.

The only problem I had was food. After those few days of being locked up in that room, I was almost out of it. I still had plenty of fluids, and the water in the bathroom still ran, but I was going to need a new food source. I didn't relish the idea of leaving the safety of my room, but I figured that the hotel kitchen would have enough canned goods to last me a pretty long time.

I left my room the day after I ate the last bit of crackers. My stomach was grumbling as I pushed the heavy dresser away from the door.

I opened it just enough to peek out.

I looked from left to right. The hallway was deserted. I wondered what had happened to the people I saw when I raided the vending machines, whether they were still somewhere on my floor, perhaps hiding behind a locked door.

I'm a hunter. I own a variety of different types of firearms, from pistols all the way to rifles. I'm also a pretty damn good shot, unlike Georgie. However, I had no weapon. All of them were back at my home in Laredo. I didn't even keep a pistol in the glove box of my truck.

That was the worst part, knowing that I could defend myself really well, and not having the means to do so. I hate that useless feeling. When you are dealing with zombies, you need a weapon. That's pretty much all there is to it. I mean, I've been in plenty of street fights—I was no stranger to beating people up, but you can't punch out a zombie. You can't even hurt those damn things unless you destroy the brain. As hard as I can hit, I can't hit that hard.

When I left the safety of my room, I was completely defenseless.

I thought about Jax at that moment. He always has a knife on him. I would have loved a knife in my hand. It wouldn't be much and I wasn't exactly a knife fighter, but it would have been better than nothing.

I chose the elevator instead of the stairs. I had no idea what the doors would open up on, but I didn't want to be all tired from taking the stairs.

I figured the kitchen would be located on the first floor somewhere near the bar and restaurant. The elevator still played music as it descended; I remember that much. I also remember just how terrified I was that the door was going to open onto a room full of zombies.

I watched the floors count down on the electric panel.

I was damn near pissing my pants.

Finally, the doors opened. The way was clear. I crouched low, just in case I needed to duck behind something and made my way forward. Fortunately, the lights were all on so I wasn't lost in the dark. Unfortunately, I could see all the carnage.

The dead had been through here. There were at least eight bodies lying about in the bar area. Those bodies had been devoured so completely that they weren't able to rise back up. It was nauseating. I felt the bile rise in the back of my throat and swallowed hard to push it back down. Retching would make noise. Noise would attract the attention of the dead.

It took awhile, but I finally found the kitchen. The lights in the room were off, and the smell of spoiled meat hit me like a closed fist. That didn't bother me too much though. It was much more pleasant than the foul odors of blood and internal organs reeking off the unfortunate corpses I had just passed.

I went to the pantry. Inside were enough canned goods to keep me going for a good while. I had brought pillowcases with me in order to carry supplies. I filled them up as rapidly as I could, making sure to grab a can opener as well. I also found some trash bags. I filled those up as well. I wasn't going to starve anytime soon.

When I was finished, I had two large trash bags and two pillowcases stuffed with food. It was more than I could comfortable carry, but I didn't want to come back down here before I needed to. It was a dilemma, but common sense told me to stay away from the ground floor. The dead could easily enter there. It might be clear at the moment, but that might not be the case when I needed to come back.

I was taking all of my loot. It wasn't far back to the elevator, and I could drag the trash bags with one hand and sling the pillowcases over my shoulder with the other.

I had barely gotten back to the bar when I heard the tin sound of music coming from a set of headphones. If my head was turned in another direction, I probably would have missed it, but my head was exactly where it needed to be to pick up the quiet sounds.

It was so quiet that I wasn't alarmed. I was, however, curious. I scanned the room in the direction of the music but saw nothing. I let go of my bundles and took a closer look. I found the source of the music underneath a booth.

It was a child. He was probably ten years old. I have a son close to that age.

"You have a son?"

Actually, I have three children—two girls and a boy. The boy is the middle child. The oldest is a teenager.

"You're divorced correct?"

Twice divorced, but I'm still very, very, close to my kids. I was worried about them. I spent hours every day in my room just praying they were okay, that somehow they were someplace safe, and nowhere near this hell.

"Being cut off and secluded, you didn't realize that the situation had been contained inside El Paso?"

Nope, for all I knew, the entire planet had gone to shit. As for that boy, I wasn't going to leave him behind. I was hoping that maybe he had a parent or parents hiding somewhere nearby, and I could reunite them. Maybe he even had a single mom that would be very grateful to have her son back, if you know what I mean.

I was almost beginning to respect his sleazy honesty. It seemed that since I already knew he was a man whore, he offered up no further attempts to be anything but his normal self.

I knelt down under the table and whispered to the terrified kid.

"What's your name little guy?"

"Jason," he answered after removing his headphones.

"Are you here all alone?"

"No," he answered.

"Are you with your mom?"

"She's not here."

"Then who are you here with?"

"My dad," he answered.

"Where's your dad at now?"

"Behind you," said Jason as he pointed with a shaky finger.

It was one of the corpses I had passed earlier. Most of its torso had been eaten away. Silly me, I thought that was enough to keep it from coming back. Still, it seemed to be having a hard time standing upright without all the necessary muscles. It was leaning heavily on the bar as it made its way over to us.

I had never seen one of those things up close and personal before. I was lucky enough to be safe inside my room and looking out at them through the window. Now, the thing was a mere five feet away from me. I couldn't help but take in all the gory details and wonder how it could keep moving.

It was a young guy. I could tell that easily enough, because his face was completely intact. He must have died not very long ago. There was no sign of decay on his face at all; it wasn't a normal-looking face though, make no mistake about that. It was filled with hatred and all twisted up in blind rage.

The chest and arms were also intact, but his button-up shirt was savagely ripped away from his stomach area. I say 'stomach area' because his stomach seemed to be missing, along with whatever other vital organs were normally in there. His legs seemed unmolested, but ropes of torn intestines hung from his stomach cavity down to his kneecaps, and smeared gore all over his khaki pants.

Without warning, he screamed at me.

It was the first time I had heard a scream up close. It sent a surge of adrenaline straight into my body. I reacted immediately and jumped straight to my feet while swinging my fist straight into the side of the zombie's head.

He went limp as soon as I connected. His body slammed into the bar behind him and then crashed to the floor amid a smattering of barstools.

He was back on his feet almost instantly.

I picked up one of the barstools and swung it at his head. I hit him square, but unfortunately it was the cushioned part that connected. When he dropped, I brought the barstool down on his head once again.

He tried to rise as soon as I stepped back.

I brought the barstool down on his head again and again. The barstool broke apart after about three more hits, so I picked up two legs from the pieces and hit him over and over again. I hit him until my arms felt like lead, and his brain was a smashed puddle on the floor.

I was about to throw the gory wooden legs of the barstool away from me in disgust, when I heard another scream coming from down a hallway to my right side. I reacted without thinking and grabbed the kid. I ran back to the kitchen. It was about the worst place I could have chosen. It was a dead end, but like I said, I wasn't thinking.

I gave the kid a shushing gesture and wondered if the new monster would leave if we stayed quiet. I guess I was hoping it would get bored if it didn't spot us immediately and leave the area without trying to find us.

It searched the room, found the gory remains of the kid's father and made a beeline for the kitchen.

How this one knew where we were hiding, I had no idea at the time. Obviously now I know that they have a great sense of smell when it comes to humans, but at the time I didn't have a clue.

I was able to get a good look at the creature's face as it peered at me through the circular window of the kitchen door. This one had its lips torn away from his mouth. It was missing one eye, and it looked as if some of the skin on its forehead had been peeled away.

The kitchen door was one of those doors that swing forward and backward. I braced my body against it as the zombie slammed himself forward in an effort to get inside the kitchen. I'm a strong guy. I'm a very strong guy, but I was having a hell of a shoving match with this thing and I only had a flimsy wooden door to separate us.

I scanned the room behind me and noticed that a stainless steel oven wasn't very far away. I told the kid to open the oven, and move off to the side of the room. When he did as I had asked, I moved away from the swinging door just as the zombie gave a final charge of fury.

The walking corpse flew into the room and cracked his shins on the open oven door. The impact didn't seem to faze him, but it did trip him up, and he sprawled over the door. I quickly ran behind him, grabbed him by both legs and pulled him backwards until only his head remained over the open door.

I slammed the oven door shut on his head and neck. He squirmed and fought for freedom, but I had all the leverage and I used all of my remaining strength to push that door against his head and neck. I'm not sure what gave out first, but I heard the crunch and saw his body go limp.

I was beat. I slid to the ground right beside the zombies still form. I knew I should grab the kid and get the hell out of the area, but I was exhausted. I just wanted to sit there and get my breathing back under control. I wanted to shake the lead out of my limbs. My legs felt as though I had just run a marathon.

I didn't get my wish.

I heard the pounding in the distance. It didn't sound very far away. I grabbed the kid by the arm and pulled him along behind me. I stopped in the bar just long enough to grab the two trash bags of food, but I left the pillowcases behind.

I couldn't lead the kid anymore; my hands were full. My left hand gripped the ends of the two trash bags, and my right hand carried one of the bar stool legs. I passed the second bar stool leg over to Jason and told him to keep right behind me.

I still heard the pounding. It was coming from outside. It was louder now and more frantic. I was pretty sure it was coming from an area of large windows. At least, it sounded like a bunch of fists pounding on glass. I had seen that area before, I just couldn't remember when. Still, it was in the back of my mind somewhere. I think I must have seen it when I arrived at the hotel.

I had a vague recollection of where those windows were and avoided them by taking a longer route back to the elevators. I wasn't exactly sure where we were going, but I figured that it was best to stay away from any windows.

Eventually, we passed some offices and I felt Jason tug at my shirt.

"My mom's in there," he said.

Acidic fear dripped into my stomach.

"Is your mom still alive?"

"She was trying to find a phone or a computer," he answered with a confused look on his face.

I realized that Jason probably didn't understand that it was his father's corpse that attacked us. In his eyes, if his father was walking around, and making noise, he must have been alive. There was also the possibility that his parents kept the truth about what was happening out there from him in order to keep him from panicking. The poor kid was shaking violently. It was a miracle that he hadn't run away from me screaming after he saw me beat on his father. Still, he didn't look very well, and I briefly wondered if he was going into shock.

"Is your mom angry like your dad?"

"No, she was really scared."

That sounded much better, but I wasn't going to take any chances. I had my bar stool leg held high and ready. I went into the small waiting room of the main office. The stench rose up like a fist once again and punched my face. It was awful. I found myself fighting to control my gag reflex.

When I calmed down somewhat, I dropped my trash bags and motioned for Jason to hide behind a desk. I didn't want anything eating him while I checked out the closed door just beyond the waiting room.

I tightened my grip on my weapon as I tested the doorknob. It turned easily and quietly. The smell was worse beyond the door. It was creeping out from under the space between the door and the floor.

The floor.

I don't know why I missed it when I walked into the room, but there was a nasty slime trail as if something oozing came into this office and then closed the door behind it.

Ah fuck it, I thought.

I threw the door open in a rush and prepared to nail whatever lurked inside. I saw nothing, but that wasn't very shocking. The room was pitch black. I heard a scratching noise.

The growl came at once. It was low in volume, but that somehow made it even creepier. I felt the chills crawling up my spine as I fumbled for a light switch.

Click.

The room was instantly bathed in fluorescent lighting. Beyond the main desk was a closet. The door had been closed on the sleeve of a pitiful looking zombie. The beast was once a woman, but she was now missing the lower half of her body. She even lacked the hanging entrails of Jason's father.

She also happened to be missing her left arm and lower jaw. Her face was hideous. It was in an advanced stage of decay. The nose was missing, the ears were barely nubs; still, the look in her eyes was unmistakable. It was rage.

It was her trapped arm making the scratching noise on the door as her fingers clenched and released only to clench again in frustration.

I brought the bar stool leg down on top of her head in a muffled crunch.

After making sure the disgusting corpse wasn't getting up, I knocked on the door.

There was no answer.

I knocked on the door once again.

"If you are alive in there, you better let me know!" I yelled. "I don't want to hurt you, but I'm coming in swinging if you don't answer."

"I'm alive," she said from behind the door.

She sounded like she might be sort of sexy.

I opened the door and pushed the corpse out of the way. Luck wasn't on my side; she was just sort of average looking.

"At a time like that, you were concerned about her looks?"

So?

"What about her well being?"

I saved her didn't I?

"I guess you did."

Whatever. You're judgmental. It's not like I looked at her and left her ass there. I even offered her my hand and helped her to her feet.

Together, we walked back into the waiting room. Jason took one look at his mom and ran into her arms. I let them have their moment as I gathered up the second bar stool leg that Jason had just dropped.

I told Jason's mother, her name was Katie, to pick up the trash bags and I led the way to the elevators. It was a struggle for her to carry the weight, but Jason helped her and I needed to have my hands on my makeshift weapons in case we met any other hostiles.

We were near the elevators when the glass finally shattered from the continued onslaught. I heard the sound very clearly. I fought off the temptation to run away in a blind panic. I couldn't leave Katie and Jason behind. I needed them to carry the food so we wouldn't starve once we reached the safety of my room.

I can't tell you how freaked out I was when we reached the elevator and the doors did not immediately open after I pushed the button. There must have still been more people in the hotel and one of those dumbasses had used my elevator.

I could now hear the sounds of running feet, combined with growls and snarls. We were going to have company very soon, and it sounded like there were a bunch of them.

Just a moment later, I heard that stupid scream they make. I roughly shoved Jason and Katie behind, me and prepared to fight the two zombies that just rounded the corner.

Then, two became ten, and ten became thirty.

I lost count after that because none of them stood still. They just saw us and charged. I knew I was going to die; I just wished I could smack the motherfucker that stole my elevator in the head before I went down.

I wasn't going to go without a fight, however. To hell with that. I was preparing to charge them right back when the doors suddenly opened behind me. I felt Katie's hand on the collar of my shirt. She was pulling me backwards into the elevator when the first two zombies reached the door.

I started swinging like a madman. I was screaming as loud as they were. In no time at all, the rest of the large group had joined them. I was swinging and swinging in an effort to keep them out of the elevator, but it wasn't easy. My arms were getting tired fast, and I was only slowing them down.

"Close the fucking doors!" I screamed. "Close the fucking doors!"

I was pounding away when Jason hit the button and the doors began to close. I was still pounding when the doors came to a sudden stop on one head and a bunch of reaching arms. I battered at them as well. I battered, and pounded, until the head and arms were forced away and my blows began to fall on just the metal doors of the elevator.

I had cleared the way. I had survived. I crumpled to the floor. I couldn't get my breathing under control. I began to scream. That's all I really remember, just laying there on the floor of the elevator and screaming my head off.

I came back to myself hours later in the bed of my hotel room. I didn't remember telling them what floor and what room, but I was finally safe in my room once again and I had even managed to save my new friends.

"Were things different with Katie and Jason with you?"

It wasn't just Katie and Jason. Somewhere along the lines, we picked up some more people. I was introduced to a chubby guy named Ruben, who was a janitor for the hotel. A teenage girl named Martha who watched her entire family be devoured, and Charlie, a businessman who happened to be staying in the hotel when things went down just like I had been.

They were all pretty impressed by my performance. Jason couldn't stop talking about how I fought off all the zombies. I could tell he was terrified. It was probably just his way of dealing with things.

"What do you mean?"

Well, he was acting like I was some sort of hero. I think that maybe in very bad times it helps to have a hero. I didn't feel like much of a hero. In fact, I felt pretty scared. I just wasn't going to let anyone know that.

Ruben was smart enough to freeze the elevator on our floor, so it couldn't move. He was also smart enough to seal the stairway. Somehow, Martha, Ruben, and Charlie, had been together since the dead came back. I kind of tuned out when they were sharing their stories with Katie. They had holed up a few floors below us, but when they saw the elevator move on our return trip they decided to go investigate the floor it landed on.

They used the stairway to reach us, and it was a good thing they did it when they did. A few moments after Martha, Ruben, and Charlie reached our floor, the zombies found the door to the stairs on the ground floor. They flooded into the stairwell within moments.

From the noise levels echoing through the walls, ceilings, and floors, the only safe place in the entire hotel was probably the floor we were currently occupying.

We were trapped.

Fortunately, they had more food with them. Even better, we now had some weapons. Ruben had a Smith and Wesson .38 Special, and Charlie had a baseball bat and a big fireman's axe. I chose the axe. I wasn't a fan of the large red handle, but the black coating over the metal blade looked pretty cool.

I would rather have taken the .38, but no amount of bribing could make Ruben part with it.

"How long did the six of you stay there?"

It was kind of hard to keep track of time, but it was a few weeks at least, maybe more. The only reason we left is because we ran low on food.

"Did anyone know about the EPUA website?"

Martha had heard about it. She probably got her information from the TV before the stations went off the air. All of us were curious about it. None of us knew what was happening outside the floor of our hotel. We could see things from the windows, of course, but they weren't pretty things.

"What did you see?"

We saw an army of zombies. We saw blood on the streets and rotting corpses. I once spent most of a day watching a zombie with two broken legs crawl down the sidewalk.

It was depressing. We were basically just waiting to die. Eventually, the time came when we were so low on food that it became necessary to replenish our supplies. Someone would need to leave the safety of our sealed off floor.

I volunteered.

I knew where the kitchen was, and I knew where I had left the pillowcases full of canned food. Ruben agreed to come with me, just in case I got turned around. He also knew where the hotel manager kept a laptop. We were all anxious to find out what was going on in the world.

I watched Ruben engage the elevator, and down we went.

The trip was over way too quickly. I wasn't at all anxious to run for my life again while fighting off what was now, more than likely, hundreds of zombies.

The situation was terrible. I wasn't convinced that starvation was worse than being eaten.

When the doors opened on the ground floor, my heart was threatening to burst out of my chest. Fortunately, the hall was deserted.

I followed Ruben as he led me down the quickest path to the pillowcases full of food. I jokingly whispered to him that he didn't even need me; and for all the good I was doing, I might as well just wait for him in the elevator. He laughed at that and squeezed my arm.

"You're the hero here, my friend," he said. "I may know the way to the food, but I may also need your muscles to get us there."

I didn't like the idea of everyone seeing me as the tough guy. Like I said before, I wasn't feeling very tough. I gripped the handle of my axe very tightly. I was determined not to let him down, no matter how I was truly feeling.

I used the axe four times in order for us to get to the food. In all four times, we were lucky and had the element of surprise. Therefore, there were no screams. We didn't want them to scream—screams led to more zombies. Too many zombies, and Ruben and I were going to die.

After the food was gathered up, we headed to the manager's office. Ruben pulled the laptop out of the desk drawer along with a power cable. All of it and some of the manager's personal items were safely secured in a nylon case complete with a shoulder strap. I carried the laptop along with most of the food.

"*Did you gather more food along with the pillowcases full of cans?*"

Yeah, we were pretty set. We gathered up enough to last us about a month, and maybe more if we rationed them properly. After those ran out, we were out of luck. At that point, the kitchen was empty.

The attack came when we reached the elevator.

Ruben and I were busy marveling about how easy things had been. We were amazed at how much food we had gathered. We were just happy to have succeeded.

The corpse came at us as soon as Ruben stepped into the elevator behind me. He was joking around and pretending that he was having problems dragging the large trash bag he was carrying through the door.

The zombie was moving so fast he collided with the one side of the elevator doors before he fell on top of Ruben and tore into his stomach.

Ruben screamed. I will never forget the sound of that scream. I will never forget the way he reached out for me as if I could help him. Once the bite punctures the flesh, it's all over.

There was blood all over the floor by the time I managed to pull the zombie off of him. I threw the corpse against the wall opposite the elevator. It was a young man, probably in his early twenties. There wasn't a mark on him except for the bite on his hand.

He screamed and charged at me. I swung my axe and took him off his feet. I stomped on his neck in order to retrieve my weapon. I enjoyed the crunching sound the weapon made as I pulled it free.

Three more zombies responded to the call. They were rushing down the hallway as I stepped back inside the elevator and closed the doors.

Ruben died on the ride back to our floor. Later that night he came back, and I killed him again.

Up until that moment, they had all been faceless and unknown to me. It's a different feeling when you know them. It's not a good feeling. I liked Ruben. I liked him a lot.

Nobody ever asked what happened. Nobody said a single word the rest of that day. I threw my clothes away; they were covered in Ruben's blood.

It took another week or so before we even remembered the laptop.

"*Is that when you first heard about the General?*"

Yes, but we didn't pay much attention to the rumors at first. We were more concerned with how the rest of the world was dealing with things. Imagine our surprise when we realized it was only in El Paso. On one hand, it was great news. If we ever got out of here, we would be safe. On the other hand, we had the misfortune to be stuck at ground zero when the "undead bomb" went off.

The people on the website were really nice. They patiently answered all our questions, and were genuinely happy that we were alive. Some of those people were trapped just like we were. Some were undiscovered and had nowhere to run to.

"Don't worry," they wrote. "The General is real."

"He's going to save everyone."

"He's ten feet tall."

"The zombies are afraid of him."

"I've seen him; he drove by my house."

"I know his real name, but I'm not telling."

"He's just a legend. He isn't real."

So many random thoughts kept scrolling along the page. At first, I ignored them. I was only interested in having my many questions answered, but the people just kept writing about him. They never stopped.

Day in, and day out, they never stopped.

I began to wonder if such a man truly existed. I wondered how he found the courage to stand up to these things and fight back. I mean I'm not a weak man, by any means. I couldn't even tell you how many fistfights I've been in during my life. I don't scare easily, but these things...these things... they're monsters.

I read about his Safe Zone. I knew the location. Georgie's house was right in the middle. I wrote to Georgie, but with so many messages scrolling by, it was no surprise that he never responded.

"When did you first realize that the General was Jaxon?"

When he and Dudley went and rescued that punk-ass Tito. There was no lead up or warning—none of that shit. He was suddenly there, on the EPUA website, asking Georgie how to blow up a stove or some shit. I recognized Georgie's screen name. He hadn't bothered to change it since college.

It took a bit, but I made the connection. The General was rescuing Tito and blowing up a building in the process. Georgie's house was located inside the Safe Zone. Jaxon had to be the General. Who else knew both Tito and Georgie and also had enough balls to do the kind of shit that he was attempting.

"So your old college pal was the General. What were you thinking?"

It was unbelievable. I mean, back in the day, Jax was more interested in getting laid than being any kind of leader. I realize that other people who met him later have different opinions, but many, many girls will tell you the same thing. Back then he was only interested in having a good time.

"Why do you think other people feel so differently?"

Probably because he's so damn famous. I mean, don't get me wrong. Undoubtedly, he's highly intelligent. He outsmarted just about everybody. He just tends to use his intelligence to play practical jokes and to harass his friends.

"So you saw him mainly as a pretty smart guy that liked to have fun and joke around?"

Yeah, but those were really my initial thoughts. I could also see him as a fighter. That was another thing he got involved in on a somewhat regular basis. It wasn't in his personality to back down from a fight.

He was also fiercely loyal to his friends. Their problems were his problems. He wasn't the type of guy to let his buddies down.

I started remembering these things, and everything slowly started to click together. The guy I knew in college, my fraternity brother if you must know, had all these gifts and personality traits even back then. They were the same traits that would one day assist him in his role as a hero. Of course he wasn't making any beneficial use of his gifts and personality traits back in those days, but they were there. They were just waiting for him to grow up and become a leader. It's those aspects of his personality that make him so effective.

Still, I was floored.

I had to laugh at that. I heard a roughly a similar story from Ivana. It's nothing new, but it is entertaining to hear people tell me what Jaxon was like before he became the General.

"After all that you just told me, why were you still floored?"

I guess it's just weird to think that you know the guy everybody was talking about. Hell I knew all of the Regulators. Jaxon, Georgie, Tito and I all went to the same college. I knew Dudley since he was a kid, and I met Javie and Kingsley through Jaxon before I moved away. Jaxon and I kept up with each other after I moved as well. It wasn't like I hadn't seen him in a long time. If I came into town, we would hang out, and he was always talking smack to me over the Internet. We even went to his parent's cabin in Ruidoso one weekend so I could take my son skiing. My son and Jaxon got along famously, by the way. It's funny, because Jaxon normally doesn't relate very well to kids.

I guess it was when he blew up Tito's apartment complex that things really sunk in for me. I just remember going to the nearest window that faced the Westside. Everyone in my group followed me. I guess we all wanted to see what would happen. They were all pretty excited when I told them I knew the General and that he was about to do something crazy.

All of us crowded by the window. I told them where to look and we waited. I never told them what was going to happen, I just told them to watch.

BOOM!

We could see the mushroom cloud rise up into the sky. It was a beautiful sight. All of us started dancing around. That explosion meant something to us. It meant that the General was real. It meant that all of us could once again dare to hope. To hope for a rescue, to hope for a way out. You name it, we could once again dream it.

It meant that we were no longer just waiting to die because, and this is important, there's one other thing I forgot to tell you about Jaxon. He's a stubborn guy. He's so stubborn—he just doesn't know when to quit. I knew he wasn't going to stop fighting. That explosion was a declaration of war, and Jaxon was going to win.

Once again, Nick had managed to shock me. His eyes began to well up, and his voice began to crack as he told me this last bit of information about his friend. I didn't think he was the type of man to get emotional, but I have long since realized that Jaxon's deeds can often have emotional impact for even the hardest of people.

I gave him a few moments to get himself together. I could tell he was embarrassed, but he wasn't the first to become emotional when discussing those days.

So where were we?

"You were talking about the Jaxon that you knew in college and how . . ."

Yeah, whatever, I wasn't crying so don't think that. I was never able to get through to him or that idiot Georgie. There were too many people asking for help. I got lost in the shuffle. I tried pretty hard, but in the end, no luck.

We followed EPUA almost religiously as the days went by. Everyone was excited when Jaxon came Downtown. They thought he had come to rescue everyone.

"Everyone?"

Oh yeah, we were far from being the only group of people who were trapped. We used to communicate with different buildings by blinking our lights. It was nice to know that there were others.

It also gave me a fair amount of hope. There was a decent chance that one of those other buildings held some good-looking women.

I didn't, however, harbor any hope of being rescued by Jaxon. One look out my window and I knew those odds would prove insurmountable for him. There were just too many zombies on the streets, and they were always on the move. One day we would only see about twenty, but on the next day there would be hundreds down there.

Jaxon himself wouldn't be able to clear out that area. There was no way. He was coming for a look. He wanted to see how many zombies were in the area. He would probably be driving his Jeep. Jax only drives two types of vehicles, by the way, and those are Harleys, and Jeeps. Regardless, neither one of them were big enough for any kind of rescue mission.

There were gunshots when he was in the area. We knew it was him even before we saw the square taillights of his Jeep. We also saw the enormous legion of zombies he led out of the area. At the time, I literally thought he was crazy. I mean, what was he trying to accomplish? Leading zombies around like that was crazy.

"He was trying to reduce the numbers of undead, so the people trapped in the area would have a better chance."

You're right, and he certainly gave me a better chance. The minute I saw that mob moving away from the area I was in action. I was gathering up the little bit of food we still had left, which wasn't very much mind you. A pretty decent amount of time had passed between when Ruben and I had gathered up the food till the time Jax led the zombies out of the area.

I quickly informed everyone of my plan as I packed. They thought I was crazy. Charlie wanted to wait for help. I told him that help had just arrived and we were going to take advantage of it.

With much respect, I grabbed Ruben's .38 special. I loaded the gun rapidly and pocketed the extra box of ammo we had found in his few belongings.

I pretty much shoved everyone into the elevator. I wanted to be moving. I didn't want to give them any time to think about what we were going to do and begin to panic. We took the elevator all the way down to the parking garage.

They were on us as soon as the elevator doors opened.

There were probably about twenty or so of them just wandering around down there. They screamed at us and charged. I chopped and chopped with my axe. Charlie swung his bat; even Martha and Katie did their part with my old bar stool legs. We kept Jason safe. That was the important thing. Not one of those suckers could get near him.

I dragged him behind me the entire way. That was the basic idea behind my plan. We would never stop. No matter how many of them came at us, we were never going to stop. We would just keep pushing forward until we reached our destination.

The screams brought more of them. I could hear them in the distance: the screams, the moans, and the sounds of running feet slapping against the concrete. If too many of them reached us, we weren't going to make it.

Martha was the first person we lost. I can't really tell you how it happened. There were just too many of them. All it took was one to grab a hold and drag her down. She screamed for help. Charlie tried; he really tried. By the time he fought his way to her, she had stopped screaming.

So we ran.

I swung my axe at anything stupid enough to get in my way. I can't tell you the elation I felt when I saw my truck. My key ring was wrapped around one of my fingers. I was ready to go. Thank God the battery wasn't dead when I remotely unlocked the doors.

I remember Jason and Katie diving in the cab as Charlie and I held off our pursuers. I remember trying to shove Charlie in as well and the look he gave me as the last of the zombies fell to the ground.

Time froze still for just a brief moment. Charlie should have been happy. We were almost home free. Instead, he looked miserable. His eyes left my face and moved down towards his hand. I followed his gaze and saw the bite mark. I don't know when he was bitten; I didn't see it happen.

At that moment, another wave of zombies entered the parking garage. There must have been hundreds of them. Charlie looked over at all of them as they rushed towards us. Then he looked back towards me with the saddest look on his face.

"We almost made it, didn't we?" he asked.

I knew what he was thinking, and I knew what he was going to do.

I punched him right in the gut and threw him into the cab of my truck.

"Day ain't over," I said.

Now Jaxon may prefer his Jeep, but I'm a big fan of Chevy trucks with big ol' V-8 engines. I can't say that I plowed through the zombies because that would have damaged the vehicle. I can't say that I crawled over them either. I'm not sure how to describe my pace. All I can tell you is that I went fast enough to not get trapped by them, and slow enough that I didn't damage the vehicle and trap us all.

In just a short time, we were free and headed to the Safe Zone.

We were reaching Sunland Park Drive when Charlie started getting sick. His bite was worse than I thought. The garage was pretty dark, but as the sun rose in the sky I could see just how bad the damage was. Two of his fingers were barely hanging on. He was in a lot of pain, and the wound was already infected. Actually, that was an understatement: the wound had just about the worst infection I've ever seen in my life.

I pulled off on Sunland and drove up to an old house I used to rent with my first wife. It didn't have a lot of windows, and the few it had were small. The place would be pretty secure.

I backed into the driveway, hopped out of the truck, jumped the fence and broke down the back door. I then ran into the garage and opened the automatic garage door by pushing the button on the side of the wall.

After the truck was safely hidden inside the garage, we carried Charlie into one of the bedrooms. Katie did her best to clean the wound, while I ransacked the house looking for painkillers. Luck wasn't with me. Poor Charlie would have to suffer.

Katie wanted to check the EPUA website, when we remembered that Martha had been carrying the laptop. It was gone, and I wasn't going to go back for it.

We spent the rest of that day keeping Charlie quiet. He was turning; it was just taking a long time. I couldn't stand seeing him in so much pain. It was horrible. The thought of making it to the Safe Zone was still there, but to even consider moving Charlie was unthinkable.

By the second day, his breathing had become labored. He wasn't able to take in any fluids, and he was in so much pain he could barely talk.

"You need to leave me," he said when I went to check on him.

"I can't leave you like this Charlie."

"I don't want you to," he said.

"What do you mean?" I asked.

"I'm not going to get any better. I don't want to turn into one of those things. It hurts, Nick. It hurts a lot. Be a pal."

I knew immediately what he wanted. For a moment, I thought I wouldn't be able to do it. Then I realized I was being selfish. I was only thinking about myself. My friend was suffering, and he needed me.

I pulled the .38 out of my waistband and covered it with a pillow. The gunshot was muffled, but it was loud enough to bring Katie running into the room.

"What happened?" she asked.

"I couldn't let him suffer anymore," I answered.

Then I began to sob.

Like I said before, I'd been in plenty of brawls in my time, but I had never before given anyone a serious injury. I was having some trouble coping with what I had just done. Was it the right thing to do? I don't know. All I know is that Charlie was suffering terribly, and I did what he asked me.

It took another day before I was able to function again.

"*You missed everyone leaving the Safe Zone didn't you?*"

Yeah, the bastards left without me. We had no way of knowing they were going to storm the gates and demand their freedom. I figured we had all the time in the world. It was my fault. I just needed time to recover.

The fences were closed up tight when we arrived. There were no zombies in sight. However, there were no living people in sight either. I had no idea what was going on. I got the fences opened; I pulled my truck inside the Safe Zone and parked it on the side of the street. There was plenty of food left behind, not just in Georgie's house but in others as well.

I started using Georgie's computer. We found out that everyone had left the area not long before we arrived at the gates. We had no other choice but to sit and wait for help. As soon as it was announced that the Regulators were coming back into El Paso in order to rescue all the survivors, I started announcing our location.

I'll be the first to admit that I was more than a little pissed off. Talk about bum-fucking luck. To go all that way and find the stupid place deserted. To add insult to injury, I'm announcing our location over and over and still getting lost in the shuffle of all the other survivors who were also announcing their locations over and over.

By the time someone responded to me, the first thing I told them is that I was a friend of the General.

"*And then help arrived?*"

About two hours later and it wasn't Jaxon. It was his little followers. After I outmaneuvered them, and when they were through pissing their pants, I brought out Katie and Jason. I had kept them hidden upstairs in Georgie's bedroom just in case something went wrong. Not that I thought anything would go wrong; I just wasn't going to take any chances with their lives after everything that happened.

Once again I asked the question.

"So where's Jaxon?"

"We kind of lost him," Dudley said.

"You did what?"

"We lost him. I'm sure he's fine, but we're waiting to make contact with him."

"No wonder you assholes ignored me the first time I asked," I responded.

By the time everything was explained to me, the sun was coming up, and it was too late to make an extraction. We decided to wait out the day in Georgie's house and head for the extraction point come sundown.

Georgie made a pretty decent fuss about not getting to sleep in his own bedroom, but when I threatened to toss another bottle his way, he grumbled off into his daughter's room.

"Were you relieved when they showed up?"

Yes, and no. I mean I was relieved that Katie and Jason were going to get out of that hellhole, but at the same time I was kinda worried about Jaxon, and I could tell that the others were worried as well.

I wasn't sure I was going to be able to leave the situation in the hands of those guys. Dudley is a pretty cool guy, but the others aren't exactly considered tough guys under normal circumstances if you know what I mean.

I wasn't able to sleep. Part of me wanted on the next train out of there, but the other part was telling me to stay and help Jaxon. I wasn't exactly a huge believer in him being all "special" at the time. I figured the guy just had a mean set of brass balls. I was a little surprised when Georgie put his face under the faucet and the bruise I gave him kinda melted away, but it still wasn't enough to convince me these guys were going to have the kind of stones needed to find Jaxon.

An hour after sunset, all my worries were alleviated. Jaxon found us, kind of.

We were inside the garage getting ready to hop into the Jeep. I was arguing with Georgie because I wanted to drive. Georgie said I wasn't part of the team. I told him to stick his team up his ass. Dudley told me to get in the back. I told him to get in the back. For a moment, it looked like he was going to shoot me, and then the call came in.

"Jaxon, is that you?" Dudley said into his earpiece. "What's happening...we're in the Safe Zone... yeah, we'll be in the watchtowers."

"What's going on?" I asked.

"All right everybody, listen up," said Dudley. "Jaxon is on his way to us. He's in some kind of trouble. I don't know exactly what it is, but he was shooting. So, we're arming up and setting up on the two watchtowers on either side of the gate. Once we see him drive up, we are to open fire on whatever is chasing him."

"What's chasing him?" Kingsley asked.

"I don't know; there was a lot of background noise, but something's after him. Now let's move because he gonna be here any minute."

I sent Katie and Jason back inside Georgie's house. I wanted them safe and out of danger. Then, I grabbed the assault rifle in the back of the Jeep.

"How do you work this thing?" I asked Georgie.

"You should get inside the house," Georgie answered. "This is Regulator business."

"How 'bout I just aim it at your balls and pull the trigger till it fires?"

"Dudley!" he screamed like a little bitch.

Dudley eyeballed the situation.

"Fuck it," he said. "Show him how to use it and give him some ammo."

The gun was a pretty simple weapon to use. I just wished I had taken a few moments to look it over myself before asking Georgie. I was going to help my buddy Jax no matter what any of them said, and I really didn't want to give them an opportunity to think otherwise.

It was pretty cold up in the watchtower. The slight bit of wind had just enough bite to make me miserable without forcing me to go back to the house. The others seemed comfortable enough with their olive drab colored suits and gloves, but all I was wearing were a pair of jeans and a button-down shirt.

I was in the same tower as Dudley. Georgie, Javie, and Kingsley had a tower to themselves. I was glad Georgie wasn't here with me; I might have been tempted to throw him off.

We sat for a while and watched the empty street with our weapons held at the ready. I was a little nervous being on top of the tower. It didn't exactly seem very sturdy. I had time to think thoughts like this because the wait was a long one.

"How far away was he?" I asked.

"Be quiet," Dudley responded.

"Just answer the fucking question," I replied.

"I don't know. Now shut up."

Since he was being an ass, I stopped trying to talk to him and focused my attention on the street. There were a couple of street lights, so visibility wasn't going to be a problem, but sitting there and waiting was completely nerve racking. I felt like one of those little villagers waiting for King Kong to show up after they tied that chick up as a sacrifice. You know what I'm talking about?

"*I do.*"

Then we heard the engine. It was loud, so that meant that Jaxon was hauling ass. Just a moment later, we saw the headlights and then the Jeep was turning up the road and heading right towards us. I couldn't see beyond the glare of the headlights. I began to panic and started shouting at him to turn off his lights.

Dudley smacked me on the arm.

"Shut up," he growled.

The Jeep wasn't slowing down. I began to worry that it was going to collide with the gate. If that happened and the gate fell, the two watchtowers would probably go with it.

"Dude, tell him to slow the fuck down," I told Dudley.

"Nick," he growled without taking his eyes off the road. "You're going to be in a fight very soon. If you can't stop acting mental, then just duck down out of sight, and I will let you know when it's over."

With just enough room, Jaxon hit the brakes, squealed his tires in a wicked slide that put the passenger door almost at our gate, and faced the driver's side door down the open street. The Jeep had been beaten all to hell. I immediately thought that he must have driven it through a big bunch of zombies, and I started wondering how many were going to show up hot on his trail.

Jaxon stepped out of the vehicle with his pistol aimed down the road. I could have recognized him even without the heads up from Dudley. There's just no mistaking those big ass shoulders of his or the scruff on his chin. He was wearing the same olive drab fatigues that the other guys were wearing, but his were a hell of a lot filthier and his left sleeve was completely torn off. Accompanying all of this was the black Harley Davidson cap over his light brown hair that, as always, was turned backwards so that the bill was over his neck. He was tense. I could tell that from his posture. He was rapidly moving the gun from left to right as he desperately searched for something to shoot.

I looked from Dudley to the morons in the other tower. They were all watching Jax and looking pretty confused. I decided to watch the street instead of Jax. I was hoping to find a target before anyone else, that way I could give them hell later.

The nighttime air was deathly quiet. The only sound around for miles was that of the crunching gravel under Jaxon's shoes. It was a weird silence. It didn't feel right. I'm not really sure how describe it.

A young woman in a white dress climbed onto the rooftop about six houses down. I knew she wasn't a zombie just by looking at her. She just didn't move like a zombie. It was obvious that she also didn't want Jax to see her by the stealthy way in which she hid herself in the shadows of a chimney. I wasn't sure why she was being so sneaky, but her white dress was filthy and her hair was shaggy enough to confuse a person. I was worried that Jaxon might take a shot at her if she came out of her hiding place.

I was about to warn everybody not to shoot at her when I realized that she was looking right at me. I'm not sure how she managed to find me, the streets weren't bright enough to provide that kind of visibility, but I was positive she was looking right at me.

Then, she placed her finger to her lips and gave me the 'shush' gesture as if I were about to ruin a big surprise.

"JAXON," I shouted. "DON'T SHOOT THAT CHICK ON THE ROOF!"

Jax turned at the sound of my voice.

Everything began to happen all at once.

The woman in the white dress ran freakishly fast towards the edge of the roof. Jaxon spotted her immediately and began firing off shots. When the chick reached the edge, she leapt out into the darkened sky. I was worried she was going to kill herself when she landed, but instead she sailed through the air this incredible distance, and landed lightly on her bare feet.

Jaxon kept shooting at her. I could see the little flashes of light from the barrel of his gun and I could hear the muffled thumps even with the silencer. She hit the ground running and rapidly began to close the mere twenty feet that separated her from Jaxon.

She ran in a zigzagging manner, as if she were trying to avoid all the bullets Jaxon's pistol was spitting out in her direction. When she reached him, she swung out her fist and knocked him from his feet and into the side of the Jeep so hard it damn near shifted about a foot from where it was parked.

That was enough for Dudley; he drilled her right in the chest with five rapid-fire shots. I actually saw the bullets make little puckers in the skin around her collarbone, and I saw the black ooze of what must have been blood mingle with the other stains of her dress.

She took a few backwards, stumbling steps from the impact. Then, she lifted her head towards Dudley, opened her mouth, and roared at him.

"*She roared at him?*"

I don't know how else to describe it. The sound was earsplitting. It wasn't a scream; it was more like a sound of fury, almost like she was telling us to mind our own business.

"*What happened next?*"

Jaxon was on his feet again. He rose up right in front of her. At the time, I was shocked. I mean that bitch hit him hard. The impact with the Jeep alone should have broken some ribs, but he just stood right back up as if the punch and the slam against the Jeep didn't bother him at all.

He had his tomahawk in his hand.

I saw the thing's eyes go wide.

She barely had enough time to lift up her arm in a defensive gesture. The blow was intended for her head, but instead the tomahawk buried itself deep into her forearm. I heard the crunch as the blade met bone. Yet, the arm didn't sever. I saw more of that black ooze as Jaxon yanked his blade out of her arm, and pulled back to swing again.

The woman just about vanished from the street.

"*She ran away?*"

It was more than that. She moved fast, almost too fast to be real. She also ran straight up the side of the nearest house and disappeared over the rooftop.

All of us stood there in a sort of stunned silence for a moment before Georgie started babbling.

"Did you guys see that shit with her mouth when she shrieked at Dudley?"

"See what with her mouth?" I asked.

Of course I knew what he was talking about. I was just trying to pretend I didn't. It's kind of funny, but I was hoping that by acting like I didn't see it, then maybe I wouldn't have to be worried about it, but Georgie is a dick.

"Her mouth was filled with fangs," Georgie said.

Chapter 4

JAXON

My second meeting with Jaxon started out very differently than the last one. Both of us were having trouble focusing through our laughter.

I told him about Nick's reaction to being called a "wanton man whore with no quality control". Jaxon didn't really think I'd be brave enough to repeat his words. I proved him wrong. It also turns out that Nick went and asked him about the incident in front of the other Regulators They all began to laugh like crazy when Nick told them what had happened.

It's a strange feeling to be joking around with this man. Every time he walks into a room with me, I feel just a little bit intimidated, every single time.

Eventually, we laughed ourselves out, and I was able to continue the interview.

"So tell me, what took you two days to rejoin the other members of your team? I've been dying to know."

Do you want me to start from the moment I charged into the horde?

"Yes, please."

Well, there really didn't seem to be any other option. We weren't going to shoot down enough of them to make it inside the house so I charged into them. Unfortunately, they were so close that I wasn't able to build up as much momentum as I would have liked and ended up having to hack and slash my way through.

It wasn't pretty.

"Now, the entire world saw you fight an even larger group when you and the other survivors left the city. Why didn't you stand your ground and fight?"

Well, for starters, when I fought that large group of undead that was caught on those fifteen minutes of footage, I had no other choice. They wouldn't open the gates and allow us to get to safety. Also, those zombies had just gone through a pretty decent-sized explosion. They weren't exactly in top condition, and it still almost killed me.

The gang of shamblers I was charging into were in as good a shape as zombies can hope to be, and by that I mean that they were all functioning at high levels.

"So they were all trying to eat you?"

Exactly, but before they could eat me, they had to catch me. That was the trick to the whole thing as far as I could figure. If I let any of them grab on to me and slow me down, I was a goner. I mentioned last time that I dropped my rifle. Well, it was still connected to me by the shoulder strap. The zombies grabbed it almost immediately. There I was, hauling as much ass as I could, right through the middle of them and all of a sudden I felt the yank around my neck. I had to cut the strap with my Cold Steel Recon 1 knife.

After that, I began to hack and slash my way through them once again. Yet the damage was already done. They had managed to slow me down too much and I couldn't build up any more speed.

The next thing I knew, they had grabbed a hold of my backpack, which was attached to my tactical vest. I didn't want to lose my tactical vest, especially under those circumstances; it had that wonderful little bite collar to protect my neck. I just didn't really have much of a choice. I undid all the buckles in rapid fire and let the dirty bastards yank it off of me.

All during this, I never once stopped moving forward. They may have slowed me down considerably, but they were never able to stop me. Those cold dead fingers kept on reaching and grabbing, but I kept on moving. Somehow, I even retained my hat.

When things got bad enough, when the zombies were so thick that I was no longer able to push forward, I abruptly changed direction. I stopped charging into them, and instead—after ducking low and taking out the legs of the few shamblers on my left—I headed up the road instead of across. It was a brilliant move on my part. I wish I could say that I planned on doing it from the get go.

Regardless, it worked. The way ahead cleared up almost immediately. The horde was so determined to run me down that they completely forgot about my teammates. I ran for all I was worth up the road. I had plenty of cardio to give this group the chase of their lives, and then leave them in the dust when they were far enough away from my buddies.

And then I just about froze in my tracks.

I felt the icy grip of true fear crawling up my spine. I had left Merrick behind. She was right behind me when I charged the mob, but as soon as I was free I couldn't find her.

I had gained about half a block when I realized this. The zombies were closing the distance rapidly as I stood there like a jackass and wondered what to do.

I was just getting ready to charge back into them when I heard her bark.

"*You were going to charge back into them for your dog?*"

Wouldn't you?

Anyway, I didn't have to. I heard her bark and then I saw her emerge right through the middle of the crowd. She must have gotten confused like they did when I changed directions. I started to run again, and she was able to catch up to me easily.

Together, we rounded a corner and made an immediate left on the first street available. I was doing my damnedest to shake them off our tail, but for some reason I was suddenly not feeling very well. I kind of felt like how a person feels when they start catching the flu, everything began to ache and my entire body felt sort of weaker.

In any case, I figured I had given the boys more than enough time to load up the survivors into the Jeeps so I reached up to tap my earpiece. I wanted to let the team know I was going to head back after I lost the zombies. The earpiece wasn't there. I must have lost it when they were all trying to grab a hold of me. To make matters worse, my hand came away bloody.

I always wear fingerless gloves when I go on missions. It just feels more natural when I have some bare skin on the trigger. In my mind at least, it also gives me a better grip on my weapons.

I felt the wetness of the blood on the bare skin of my fingers immediately. I frantically began to search the area between my shoulder and my ear for an injury. It wasn't an easy thing to do while I was running, but I found the small wound on my neck. I felt the sting of it when my finger came into contact with the torn skin.

I had been bitten.

It must have happened after I lost my tactical vest complete with bite collar. I was probably so pumped up on adrenaline I never even realized I was being bitten.

I was already feeling the effects.

It wasn't horrible yet, but I was feeling them, and they seemed to be worsening. I was rather alarmed by all of this and did my best to stay calm and in control while I came up with a plan. As things stood, I had lost contact with my team; I was bitten and starting to get sick; and I had a few hundred zombies about fifty feet behind me.

"*A few hundred?*"

Yeah. The group was growing due to all the noise they were making, not to mention the screaming.

All in all, I had cause to be alarmed. I needed to take care of my bite wound immediately, but healing required a natural element. Water and a hot bath in one of the many empty houses would take care of that. I just needed to lose all of my rotting friends despite my waning strength in order to get there. Outrunning them and regrouping with my team was no longer an option. I wasn't sure I could move fast enough for that anymore, let alone have the strength to get back to the guys if I did somehow manage to lose the zombies.

I had no idea how long it would take before I weakened to the point I could no longer run, and I didn't want to find out. The only option left to me was to find a hiding place and heal myself.

"*You can't be killed by a zombie bite correct? It can only sicken you?*"

Incorrect. I can most certainly be killed by an untreated bite. I can also be turned by a zombie bite. It would take a lot longer to fuck me up than your average bear, but if I can't let nature do its work and heal me up, I'm just as dead as anyone else.

I ran straight into the nearest house. I damn near shattered the flimsy front door with my shoulder, but after stumbling around the house for a few moments I was breaking through the back door as well and racing across the small yard.

At the rear of the backyard, was a ten-foot high rock wall. I picked up Merrick and tossed her over. I made a jump for it. And missed. I jumped again. And missed. Merrick was barking at me from the top. I'm not sure if she was just pissed because I tossed her or if she was telling me to hurry up. Regardless, on the third jump I hooked my tomahawk over the edge and pulled myself up.

It was a jump that would normally be no problem to me. I was getting weaker and weaker. The zombies came through the house and filled the yard just as I scrambled over the edge into another backyard. They were climbing over one another in an effort to pursue me.

I paused for a moment to catch my breath and then I was on the move again.

There was no reason to go through this house so we ran towards the side gate and made our way to the front yard.

No luck. A troop of shamblers was already turning the corner of the street to our left. It was a pretty bad situation. I knew I wasn't going to have enough energy to outdistance them. The zombie toxins were spreading through my system way too fast. I decided to crash through house after house and lose them that way.

Merrick and I bolted straight across the street and through the front doors of the closest home. We had a pretty good head start on our pursuers, but they had the numbers and their screams would only add to those numbers.

We charged through the house and headed straight into the backyard. I could hear the sound of an approaching helicopter from somewhere in the distance. I didn't bother looking for it. It would never be able to pick me up because it would be swarmed upon landing.

We hopped over the backyard wall. Fortunately that wall wasn't as tall as the previous one, and we ended up in yet another backyard. We went around to the side of the house and out the gate. The chopper was closer now, but I still didn't pay much attention to it. I was heading down this new street and through another new house.

"*Do all the homes in El Paso have rock walls in their backyards?*"

Pretty much. I'm sure there are a few odd balls, but for the most part everyone on the Westside uses a rock wall to separate their yards and give themselves some privacy. The only thing that varies is the height of the wall.

The rest of my evening went pretty much the same way; in a house; out of a house; through a yard, and then down the street. I was getting slower and slower. My muscles were starting to cramp up hideously. I found myself having to take breaks in order to catch my breath.

There were plenty of times when I thought I finally lost them, only to be suddenly surrounded all over again. Fighting my way out of those situations was becoming hazardous in my weakened state. At some point, even swinging my tomahawk became tiresome, and I drew my Sig out of its holster and screwed on its silencer. It was a lot easier to shoot than chop.

The moments when they caught up to me were the worst. I had to start all over again in order to gain some distance. The zombie virus was having a grand ol' time with my body during all of this. The cramps in my legs and arms were horrible. I was sweating profusely, my nose was running, I was freezing cold, and my stomach was in knots.

My body was about to fail me. In that, I had no doubts. The only thing that kept me moving was my own stubborn refusal to die. Every now and then, the helicopter would get close. I remember hearing it, but I never bothered to look up. For all I knew, it was right above me and then I would lose it along with the shamblers whenever I ducked into a new and random house.

"This went on until dawn?"

Just about, but don't get me wrong here, there were plenty of breaks. I found little hiding places often enough. Sometimes it would be in a house and sometimes in an abandoned car. Sometimes I was even able to rest for a good half hour before the zombies would roust me out.

It was really bad, as it got closer to the break of day. I was losing consciousness, and stumbling around, instead of running. I don't remember crossing Mesa. I don't remember taking refuge in a house that belonged to an old high school friend of mine.

Suddenly, Merrick was tugging on my sleeve, and I was awake. I had no idea where I was and no idea where my pursuers were. I was just sitting in a dark hallway inside an even darker house.

I could barely breathe. I was dying.

If Merrick hadn't wakened me, I probably would have just died in my sleep.

I couldn't run anymore. In fact, I was barely able to drag myself to the nearest window and peer down on the street. Somehow, I had managed to find a two-story house and even climb up the stairs to the second story. I didn't recognize the neighborhood below. I saw a lot of zombies running around, but they had nowhere near the numbers they had had earlier.

It looked like I was safe or at least safe from being eaten. I had actually managed to give them all the slip even though I couldn't remember doing it. When I think about it now, it must have been pure dumb luck. I must have slipped into my old buddy's house at just the right moment, when there were no searching eyes around to give me away.

Of course I didn't know it was my old buddy's house at the time. I was half-dead after all, and all I knew was that I had to heal myself. That became my new pressing concern. I needed a water source.

There was actually blood, or some sort of bile, leaking from my eyes, ears, and nose, as I crawled from room to room in search of a bathroom. I knew a running sink and a toilet weren't going to be enough, so I passed the first bathroom I came upon and continued to the last door in the hallway.

As luck would have it, the door led to the master bedroom and inside the master bedroom was an enormous bathroom complete with a large sunken tub. It was a good thing. At that point, I was having problems focusing. I never would have made it down the stairs in search of a tub or shower on the lower floors.

I vaguely remember pulling myself into the tub; then I must have passed out. Merrick's high-pitched barking woke me up. I couldn't have been out too long; the sky in the window was still a nighttime sky. I needed to turn the water on, but the pain in my joints was incredible. I could barely move my arm to the faucet.

I tried to lift my back from the bottom of the tub in order to reach the knobs, but the pain actually made me cry out in agony, and I fell back almost immediately. I could no longer move enough to reach out and turn on the water. I just couldn't lift myself, but Merrick's whiney and high-pitched bark kept me conscious.

I was just staring at the knob. It was so close and yet so far away. Maybe I even laughed a little. My head was the last thing to drop. The strain on my neck was just too much, and I could no longer hold my head up. The thud my head made when it hit the porcelain actually hurt my ears, and I remember doing just one final thing before I died.

I angrily kicked at the damn knob.

"You died?"

I might of. It sure felt like it, but that's not the important part. The important part was my temper tantrum. My kick actually managed to lift up the knob. The tub began to fill up around me. I didn't actually recognize that I had achieved my goal, mind you. I was pretty much dead to the world at that point.

The sun was out when I finally opened my eyes. Merrick was whining again. She hates getting wet, and the tub had overflowed a long time ago. I sat up immediately and turned off the water.

I sat up.

It took a moment to realize it, but I had actually managed to heal. I started laughing. Then, I looked at the water and realized it was an ugly brown color. It was also pretty damn cold, so I drained it out, cleaned up the tub and refilled it with hot water.

I was far from being healed completely. My entire body was on fire, and my head was pounding. Yet, I was still alive. I was on my way; I just needed more time.

As the tub was filling up, I was able to take off my clothes and drape them over an open window to dry in the morning sun. I went downstairs to see how secure the house was. The front door was wide open, as was the back door. I quietly closed each door and locked them up. There were a few shamblers in the backyard, but they didn't see me. When I was satisfied of my security, I headed back upstairs and hopped back in the tub while Merrick played watchdog for me.

It felt good to let the water do its magic. I was hurting pretty bad. The funny thing was I've taken some pretty serious injuries, and recovered rapidly, once I came into contact with water or something green and growing. The sheer amount of time it was taking to fix me up gave evidence to how narrowly I escaped being turned.

It wasn't a pleasant thought.

I kept wondering if there was something I'd done wrong. I was wondering why the situation had gotten so badly out of control so rapidly. The street was completely empty and then it was suddenly filled with the dead. It was almost as if the zombies were hiding from us and laying in wait for our arrival, but zombies don't hide or lay in wait. Zombies mindlessly charge and attack. Well, if the zombies were relatively brainless, that meant someone else came in and set a trap for us, and we walked right into it.

A trap!

We walked into a trap!

I sat straight up in the bath. I was royally freaked out. Nothing was amiss except for the panic attack I had just given poor Merrick. I was still safe. I lowered myself back into the water and continued to heal.

"A trap?"

Yes, it had to be a trap. Someone had to have led all the zombies into those houses and kept them there somehow, at least until we were far enough away from the cars that driving away wasn't an option. Someone must have also gotten those survivors to the same street; either before, or after the zombies were secured in the houses and backyards.

It was the only thing that made sense. If the zombies had just happened to be in the neighborhood, they would have charged us immediately. They wouldn't have waited for some of us to get out of the Jeep and look around. We had walked into a trap.

"Okay, so you just realized that someone set up a very deadly trap. Obviously, they wanted to kill you. What were you thinking when the shock of the situation wore off?"

I was thinking that someone was going to get his or her ass kicked.

However, the first thing I needed to do was recover. I needed time for that. When the water finally cooled, I left the tub feeling much, much better. I wasn't perfect, and I was pretty much exhausted, but most of the pain had receded.

The first thing I did was clean off my weapons. I had somehow managed to unclick my utility belt before I climbed into the water. I didn't remember doing it, but I was glad I did. Wet ammo wouldn't exactly help me out of a tight spot. Still, the belt was lying on the same floor that got soaked by the overflowing tub. I dried the belt and weapons off as best I could, laid the belt itself near the window to dry, and climbed into the large bed in the master bedroom. I had my Sig in my hand as I drifted off to sleep. Merrick hopped up as well and curled up close. She put her head on my lap. It's probably a pretty common thing that dogs do, but at the moment it was reassuring. I knew it was safe to close my eyes because she would watch over me. I slept like a baby.

It was dark when I woke up.

I took another bath to finish the job, and was rewarded by a vast amount of energy. I felt good. It had taken some time, but I was back to normal. I put on my clothes and gear next. They were a little stiff, but at least they were dry.

I had no idea where I was.

I went downstairs and out into the backyard. There were still some zombies there. I shot them immediately, before they could let out a scream. I didn't want to spend the rest of the evening running again. After they dropped, I went to the rock wall and took a look at my surroundings.

I was a stone's throw away from Sunland Park Drive. In a bit of confusion, I looked back at my temporary lodgings, and realized that it was the old home of my high school buddy. The interior was different, but the exterior was unmistakable. I laughed at the situation, and wondered idly whether or not I had sought refuge in a slightly familiar place, or if I had just stumbled in here by pure coincidence.

Then I realized just how far I was from the rest of my team by foot. That sobering thought wiped the smile right off my face, before I realized there were abandoned cars all over the place. I didn't need to walk back: I could freakin' drive back. I went back into the house and entered the garage. In there, I kid you not, was an actual cherry condition 1977 Firebird Trans Am. I was in love. All I could think about were those old *Smokey and the Bandit* movies I used to watch when I was a kid. I was in geek heaven. This thing still had the bird on the hood. I was going back to my team in style.

I quickly checked the dash; there were no keys in the ignition. I ransacked the house for about an hour before I finally found them in a kitchen drawer. The car rumbled like a thunder god when I revved up the engine. I buckled Merrick into the passenger seat, hit the button for the garage door, and squealed down the driveway.

I was loving life.

Then I saw a brief glimpse of a woman in a white dress. I hit the brakes immediately. I was still in front of my old friend's house, but I saw her directly across the street. It looked like she jumped from the roof of one house onto the roof of the next house and then vanished down the backside of the roof.

I looked over at Merrick as if she could explain what I had just seen. Her tail began to wag excitedly. She was just happy to be in a car.

I briefly wondered if I still had some zombie toxins coursing through my veins. Neither healthy humans, nor zombies, could make a jump that far. It was easier to believe that I imagined it, but I knew deep down that I hadn't.

Trouble was coming. Hell, trouble already paid me a visit. I was positive it had something to do with that rooftop-bounding freak.

"Why were you so positive?"

I guess it was because there's only so much weird shit you can chalk up to coincidence. Someone set a trap for us, and now I'm suddenly seeing a woman jumping superhuman distances on the rooftops of houses.

Nah, I had no idea what she was, but I knew she was up to no good. I just didn't know what her game was.

I was about to find out.

I drove slowly enough to scan the rooftops as I hit Sunland Park Drive and drove towards Mesa. I didn't see anything, but from somewhere up in the distance, I heard the familiar sound of a zombie scream.

I wasn't alarmed. It was too far away to be screaming because of me, and even if it was, I was in a Firebird Trans Am. It wasn't as tough as my Jeep, but it was a hell of a lot faster. Regardless, I slowed my pace. I didn't want to slam into a shambler and jack up my new ride. That sort of thing could end up ruining my fun and making me walk back after all.

The intersection of Mesa and Sunland was blocked by cars, and there was no way to get through it. There were also a number of shamblers, but they were headed away from me and down the street.

Well, I was going to join them. There were a number of different side streets that would get me back to Mesa. As I was back-tracking to one of those side streets, I heard the unmistakable sound of bumpers colliding and bending metal. Why I was hearing the sounds of a car crash minus the squealing brakes I had no idea, but I was hearing it rather clearly, and I was also hearing more of the zombie screams.

I turned up a street called Thunderbird. It was the first street I came upon that would lead to Mesa Street. Imagine my surprise when I saw all the abandoned cars blocking my way. Some of those cars were rather smashed together. I kept thinking back to when we led the survivors out of El Paso. I remembered that those of us playing decoy had used Mesa, but I couldn't remember a bunch of smooshed cars blocking the intersecting streets.

There were more shamblers here as well, but none of them had eyes for me. They were headed farther up Mesa towards the sounds of grinding metal and smashing vehicles. The sounds were too clear this time to make me question what was going on. Someone or something was blocking my access.

My thoughts drifted to the woman in the white dress; I couldn't imagine why she would want to cut me off from Mesa. It just didn't make any sense, but I knew the zombies weren't doing it. I squealed the tires as I made a violent U turn and headed back the way I had come.

In behind a small shopping mall is an actual alleyway that led through the mall to a large parking lot that bordered Mesa. It's tiny and maybe not a lot of people use it, but I had used it many times when I was too impatient to wait for the lights at the intersections that were now blocked.

I drove through the opening in the chain link fence behind the shopping mall and made my way towards the alley as quietly as the rumbling car would allow me. When I reached the alley, I was pleased to see that it wasn't blocked. After the alley was the fairly empty parking lot, and not much else between Mesa and me. I was almost there.

I headed through it slowly, on the lookout for any danger. When the nose of my car began to inch its way free of the alley, I heard the screeching sound of tires on asphalt and the immediate response of a car alarm. All of this happened just before a small truck was shoved in front of the open end of the alley. The truck slammed into the curb, and a light post, right after it clipped the front of the Firebird. I wasn't sure what was worse, the cosmetic damage on my new vehicle, or the fact that someone was fucking with me.

I thought about how long this game of blocking my access to Mesa could go on. I quickly realized that it could continue until the cows came home, or until it attracted so many zombies that passing Mesa would prove impossible, even if I did manage to get around the blockades. With great reluctance, I unbuckled Merrick, and jumped out of the vehicle. I pulled my pistol out of its holster, just in case I could get a shot off at my annoying stalker.

Merrick crawled under the truck while I climbed over the bed. Once on the other side, I scanned the area and found nothing to shoot at. The area was free and clear. Hell, there weren't even any zombies around. They had all been led away farther down the road.

I was getting pissed.

Merrick and I bolted across the parking lot, reached Mesa Street, and managed to find some cover behind a group of abandoned cars just as a horde of shamblers flooded into the parking lot in search of prey.

I had the grim satisfaction of reaching my destination, despite my adversary's attempts to prevent me from doing so. Then, I thought about how far we'd have to hoof it, and I realized that my adversary didn't care about me reaching Mesa; she just wanted me out of the car.

"*How did you get to that conclusion?*"

I just thought about the situation. The blockades were only going to stop my car. None of them were going to present much of a problem if I was on foot. Also, I was pretty far from where I had last left my team. There was a lot of walking distance and a serious amount of danger between where I currently was and where I was headed.

I was being hunted.

"*You were being hunted?*"

Yeah, and I'd be easier to follow on foot.

"*And you thought it was the woman?*"

I sure did. She was just too much of a coincidence to be ignored. Yet, I didn't really care about that; I was more annoyed to be playing someone else's game. I needed to turn things around, and play my own game. I've always hated playing by other people's rules. This was no exception.

My hunter wanted me on foot. I understood that well enough. She also probably wanted me out in the open so I'd be easier to pick off when the right moment came.

It was time to screw up her game.

Merrick and I bolted from cover to cover until we passed the burnt remains of Tito's old apartment building. We went around the rubble and came once again to Thunderbird—this time on the opposite side of Mesa. It was the same side of the street Dudley and I took, back when we rescued Tito. Anyway, Merrick and I didn't head toward the desert this time. Instead, we turned left on a street called Westwind.

"*You were headed back to your friends?*"

I was headed in that direction. My hunter was probably expecting it, and I didn't want to disappoint. My guess was that the attack would come when I reached the spot I left my team. I wasn't positive of this, but I had spent an entire day pretty much out of commission and nothing tried to kill me, so she had to be waiting for something. Also, there were no attacks while I was traveling. There were plenty of opportunities, but no attacks. Here I was, all alone and out in the open, and I was, as of yet, unmolested. She had to be waiting for something.

Another thing I should mention is that travelling this distance was really very time-consuming. Merrick and I had to duck and hide constantly to avoid being detected. There were that many zombies wandering around. Mostly it was a lone shambler, but one scream and we'd be in some serious trouble. One time, we had to hide and wait in a darkened office building as a herd of hundreds made their way past us. That alone took the better part of an hour.

The second we hit Westwind, we broke into a serious run. I felt eyes on me, and I didn't like it a bit. I was positive I was being followed. I didn't see anything, I didn't hear anything, but I knew it. I was being followed. I was being hunted and toyed with.

We ran for a pretty long time. I had to constantly remind myself that just because there was a new player in the game didn't mean that the old players were any less dangerous. The zombies still needed a respectful amount of attention. I didn't want another bite to deal with.

I made my move on a street called Tarascas. We broke right and hauled ass to the first two-story house we found. Once there, I tried the front door, and, to my surprise, it was unlocked. Merrick gave a low growl as soon as we entered.

I pulled my pistol.

Clearing a house is never my idea of fun. I hate any kind of situation in which something can jump out at me from the dark. I think we even previously had some sort of conversation about this.

Anyway, I didn't want something to jump out and bite me on the ass while my attention was elsewhere, so I went from room to room as rapidly as possible. There were three zombies in one of the downstairs bedrooms.

As soon as I got close to the bedroom door, the door flew open and all three of them rushed out at me. I backed up as rapidly as I could and tapped them in the head, one after the other.

The upstairs held the last of the home's inhabitants. It was a pretty nasty customer; let me tell you. It was an old fat man in a nightgown of some sorts. The rot was evident; it always is. I think I've gotten somewhat immune to how nasty these things look. So it wasn't the rot in his face that grossed me out. It was the rot on his legs that did that. For whatever reason, this particular zombie had been spending his time in the half-filled bathtub of the master bedroom. The skin on his legs was literally peeling off as he scrambled out of the tub and came at me. I shot him in the head immediately and then threw a blanket over his legs so I didn't have to look at them anymore.

After that, we went out on the balcony. From the balcony, I climbed to the roof. Merrick wasn't happy to be left behind, but I didn't want to heave her heavy ass over my shoulder and make the climb. Once I was on the roof, I took cover behind a short wall that marked the boundary of the rooftop.

After that, I waited.

As time went by, I began to get a little nervous. Maybe my plan wasn't going to work. Maybe I had already lost my opportunity. Clearing the damn house had taken around fifteen minutes according to the Luminox watch on my wrist. Fifteen minutes would have been more than enough time to travel through the area.

I saw movement.

I wasn't exactly sure from where, but I saw movement on the rooftops. Yes, there it was again—a shaggy head peeking up over the rim of a building across Westwind—the lady in the white dress. Not that I was very surprised.

I couldn't see her too well. It was dark, and she was pretty far away on the opposite side of Westwind. It looked as if she were sniffing the air.

Suddenly, she was bounding across the roof. She was moving way too fast to be human. It was pretty unbelievable watching her move, and that's coming from a guy that kills zombies for a living.

When she reached the edge of the roof, she didn't even slow down. She just vaulted through the air and came down upon another rooftop. From rooftop to rooftop, she traveled with amazing speed, and then she came to a street called Cresta Bonita. If she turned left on that street, she would be headed in the direction of Oveja.

"Oveja is where you left the team, correct?"

Yeah, and I think it's also where she wanted to have our little showdown, but I must have lost her somewhere along the way. She certainly looked like she was trying to make up for lost time.

She turned on Cresta Bonita.

I stood up from my hiding place so I could continue to track her. She was a few houses down the street when she suddenly came to a sliding halt. She froze. It looked like she might have been sniffing the air again, but with the distance between us, I couldn't be sure.

She ran to the edge of the roof and jumped over to the next house. I believe she was sniffing the air once again. Then she went to each side of the house and peered down below. She punched a brick chimney in frustration and hit it so hard brick pieces flew through the air.

She backtracked over and over again, at each new house sniffing the air and peering off each side of the house. Yes, as she got closer and closer, it was clear she was sniffing the air.

It was almost dawn when she stood across from me on the other side of Westwind. I watched her look towards the sky, and stomp her bare feet in frustration. She went to each side of the roof and did her sniffing test. She must have caught my scent because she stared down at my street for a long moment before she turned on her heels and began to walk away in the opposite direction. It looked like she didn't want to continue the hunt during the daytime. I guess it was because I could spot her easier with the sun on my side.

Suddenly she stopped.

I knew she sensed me, but I didn't know how. I had ducked back under the low wall the moment I saw her retracing her steps. Somehow, though, she knew I was there. She knew I was watching her.

She slowly turned around and walked to the edge of the roof that faced my direction. I stood from my hiding place, and her eyes caught me immediately. I'm not exactly sure how I knew this, maybe it was the slight movement of her head in my direction, but we stood facing each other for the first time.

The moment was frozen. I had caught her by surprise and she didn't know quite what to make of me. So, she decided to try and mock me. She gave me an over-exuberant and very theatrical bow. I repaid her idiotic gesture with a gesture of my own. I flipped her the bird.

"You gave her the finger?"

The middle one to be exact, and it pissed her off. I could see that in the sudden movement of her shoulders. I could tell she wanted to charge me, but something stopped her. Instead, she looked beyond me to the mountains in the distance. The sky had begun to lighten there. She had lost her element of surprise.

Instead of rushing me, she gave me a nonchalant wave of her hand and vanished down the far side of the roof.

Game on.

I was moving immediately. I had an idea, but I needed some stuff to pull it off, and I had no idea how long it would take to find it. I gathered up Merrick and ran to the backyard of the neighboring house. Once inside, we gave it a rapid search, came up empty handed, and moved to the next house.

All in all, I have to admit I was very disappointed. We searched through some twenty-five homes before I found what I needed, but in the final place I looked, in the final house we searched, I found what I had been looking for: a hunting rifle.

I needed a weapon that could take a long distance shot. I needed something with a scope in which to make the long distance shot. I just couldn't believe it took all morning to find the damn thing. El Paso is a part of Texas and in Texas we love our freakin' guns.

It was there waiting for me in the back of a closet. I recognized the hard plastic carrying case immediately. I remember hoping when I opened it up it would be something I could use. I wasn't disappointed at all. The case held a beautiful Remington 700. Next to the case, I even found a box of ammunition. I wasn't sure whether the owner used this gun for hunting or sniping, but .30-06 ammunition packs a hell of a punch.

The rifle also had a large scope. It looked big enough to cover a pretty decent distance, but the lack of a maker's mark made me a little nervous. I needed to test fire the rifle, to make sure the scope was zeroed in and could cover the distance that was required.

"Have you ever done any long distance shooting?"

A little bit, but it didn't really matter. As part of the whole 'Guardian' thing, I get these weird dreams at least once a week, and in these weird ass dreams I learn how to use all sorts of different weapons. I don't remember many technical terms, but I can sure make the guns go bang.

The only problem was that if I fired off this rifle it was going to make a really loud noise. A really loud noise was going to attract company. I certainly didn't want any company. I already had to clear out a ton of them while I was searching all the homes.

I needed to get some distance from my current location. So, once again, I went through all the homes looking for a working automobile. I was not in luck. Every time I found a car, I couldn't find the keys. If I happened to find keys, I couldn't find the car they belonged to.

"Did you happen to run across any computers or laptops you could use to make contact with your team?"

I did. I managed to sign onto the EPUA website and left a message, but due to the sheer volume of people writing on that thing, I didn't have a lot of hope in being rescued. To be honest, I don't even remember asking for an extraction. I think I just announced that I was alive and well. The situation had become rather personal to me. I wasn't about to turn tail and run until I got some payback.

It was mid-afternoon before I found some decent transportation. It was a pretty beat up dirt bike, but someone must have done some kind of maintenance on it because it started on the second kick.

I strapped the gun case over the rear fender, left Merrick in the backyard, and zipped up the street. The bike was a little too loud and certain to attract the wrong kind of attention. It was also rather smoky in the exhaust department. There was a slight chance I was wrong about it having had maintenance.

I put some distance between Merrick and myself just by driving around the different neighborhoods. When I felt I was far enough away that the shamblers wouldn't end up near the homes on Tarascas, I pulled over, grabbed the rifle, and entered the nearest house.

Inside the house, I grabbed a vase, a computer screen, and a large clock. I hefted these things in my arms and ran to the end of the road. I placed them strategically at different levels. The computer screen went in the middle of the road. The clock went on someone's porch and the vase went on a nearby roof.

When the items were placed, I ran back up to where I had left the bike. I could barely see the computer screen in the middle of the road. I climbed to the roof of the same house I had entered to gather my targets. I crawled to the very edge of the roof and peered through the scope at the computer screen in the middle of the road.

The scope was excellent. I could very clearly see my target. I dropped a round in the chamber and slid the bolt all the way home. I took aim very carefully. I controlled my breathing, and held my breath. On the next inhale, I squeezed the trigger until the bang actually surprised me.

My aim was true, and the scope was accurate. The computer screen just about exploded. I retracted the bolt and dropped in another round. I took out the clock with no problem. The vase was even easier. The rifle was awesome. It was going to work perfectly.

Zombies began to pour out of the nearby homes.

I didn't even notice it since I was still staring through the scope, and my vision was limited, but I did hear the screams.

I pulled out my tomahawk the minute I hit the ground. There were about five of them waiting for me. I took the top of the nearest zombie's head off with my first swing. The second swing met my next attacker in the kneecap. I was being as careful as possible not to bang the rifle around too much. I didn't want to screw up the accuracy.

I ran the short distance to the dirt bike before the others could grab a hold of me and placed the rifle back inside its case. I could see more zombies in the distance. All of them were headed right towards me.

I pulled out my Recon 1 knife with my left hand. Then I took out the three I had just avoided, by stabbing one, and chopping the other two with the tomahawk. The shambler whose knee I had destroyed was crawling my way, but not yet close enough to be a danger.

It was the thirty-some screaming gang from farther down the street that worried me. I stashed my weapons in their holsters and jumped on the bike. I gave it a kick. Nothing. I gave it another kick. Still nothing. I could smell gas. The engine must have flooded.

I hopped off the bike, grabbed the handlebars, put my left foot on the left foot peg, and ran the bike down the road in the direction of the screaming shamblers. I needed speed to pull this off, and fortunately for me, the street I was on had a pretty decent downward slope. I would have preferred the slope to head away from the advancing horde of zombies, but beggars can't be choosers.

As soon as I started picking up speed, I pushed with my right foot to gather some more. I was about ten feet from the zombies before I felt I had gathered enough speed to pop the clutch. The bike roared to life instantly, and I spun it around as fast as I could, but not fast enough to avoid the furiously grasping hands. The bite proof material of my clothes protected my skin from being ripped open from the many jagged nails scratching for a grip, but I did take a pretty decent strike to the kidneys before I was able to get up to speed and leave them behind me.

Overall, it was a good lesson for me. I now knew I only had enough time for one or two shots. If I hung around after that, the area would become infested.

I rode that crappy ass bike all over the place to confuse all the shamblers. I took so many twists and turns; I almost got lost myself. At the top of Tarascas, I killed the engine and coasted down the hill. The first thing I did was pick up Merrick. She did her normal little dance of greeting for me. I raided some of the homes I had previously entered and managed to scrounge the both of us something to eat. It wasn't great, and I'm a picky eater.

Afterwards, the two of us walked higher up the road to the tallest house. I was pretty sure it would be tall enough for my purposes, but there was only one-way to find out. I climbed up to the roof with my rifle. When I found a pretty comfortable position, I sighted down towards the roof of the home I used to identify my pursuer. I could see the entire roof perfectly. There wasn't a single corner that would block a shot. The distance was a bit far, and I was a little nervous about that. There just wasn't anything I could do to get closer and still retain an unobstructed view.

The next thing I did was walk back to the target house and turn on a bunch of outside lights. I figured if I turned on the lights during the daytime, zombies wouldn't be attracted by the sudden appearance of light later on.

The final thing I did, before I began my rest, was to prepare my exit strategy. Even with only firing one or two shots, I would need to get the hell out of Dodge pronto. It was late afternoon when I finished turning on all the lights. I simply didn't have time to look for a new vehicle, so I stashed the crappy dirt bike against the side of my new house after I strapped a hard plastic laundry basket to the back of the seat and the back fender.

Everything was ready.

All I had to do was wait around until the shaggy-headed woman in the white dress showed up—if she showed up. I was pretty sure she would. She would want to follow my trail and take up the hunt again. Besides, she was probably more determined than ever after I gave her the finger and pissed her off.

Merrick and I took a nap in the upstairs bedroom of the new house. I can't say it was the best sleep I have ever enjoyed. In fact, it was rather restless. I was worried that my hunter would come before sunset. I kept telling myself that she would wait for darkness because she was a predator, and most predators like to hunt in the night. Still, what the hell did I know?

As soon as the sun had started to set, I was on the roof.

The waiting game began. The hunt was on. Except this time, I was going to be playing the role of the hunter. To tell the truth, I was almost having fun.

It wasn't long before she made her appearance. I was once again shocked at how fast she could move. She leapt from house to house until she reached the roof of the home she had spotted me in at the end of the previous evening.

I knew she would come back there. She needed to pick up my scent again, and that was the last place she had seen me. All the lights I had turned on managed to create just enough of a glow that I could see most of the rooftop.

I sighted her through the scope and watched as she walked around sniffing the air and peering down over the sides of the roof. Eventually, I caught sight of her face, and the scope brought it up close and personal. Her skin was an odd, grayish color. It might have been a trick of the light, but I couldn't be sure. It was her mouth that bothered me the most. There was a black stain all around her lips. Hell, even the backs of her hands were stained. It was pretty gross, especially when I realized where the stain came from. She was a drooler, and the drool was black. Her hands carried the stain from when she would wipe at her mouth. Other than that, she looked rather normal, possibly even attractive, if you took away the black drool and brushed her hair.

She turned and looked right at me.

How she managed to find me again, I have no idea. I was beginning to really dislike the woman. So I shot her. The crack of the rifle in the quiet evening was loud as hell, but my aim was true, kind of. The bullet punched a nasty hole in the right side of her chest, and spun her around so that her back was facing me when she dropped to her knees. The exit wound pretty much took out her entire shoulder blade.

I heard the familiar zombie screams echoing out from a few streets over in response to the gunshot. I would have company very shortly. Too bad I wasn't going to be there for them. I had a smile on my face as I stared at the crumpled form of the woman-thing that had been stupid enough to try and hunt me. I can't even begin to tell you how satisfied it made me feel when I shot her, as morbid as that sounds. In my defense, however, let me remind you that she led my entire team into a zombie-filled nightmare trap. She blocked off the roads and dinged up a beautiful car, and last, but certainly not least, she had been hunting me. She probably wanted to eat me. I didn't know that for a fact, but she certainly wasn't human.

She stood back up.

I don't know how she did it. The damage should have been fatal enough for three people, but she stood back up. I shot her again. This time my aim was a bit better, and I nailed her right in the spine. I knew the wound had severed her spinal cord, at the very least. She just rag-dolled onto the rooftop. I watched as long as I dared, but there was no further movement, and I could hear the sounds of pounding feet from farther up the street.

I left the rifle on the roof and jumped down to the side of the house where the dirt bike was waiting for me with Merrick sitting grumpily in the basket. I grabbed the handlebars and ran the bike to the street.

The zombies were a just a house-length away from us, and there were a whole bunch of them. Not that I stopped to count how many; I was too busy running down the street while they got closer and closer to catching me. The zombies must have been just a few feet away when I jumped on the bike and popped the clutch. None of them even managed to tag me. I was too fast on the bike, and I didn't need to spin around. It was a straight shot down the hill.

I heard a chilling scream just as I rounded the turn and sped off down Westwind. It wasn't a zombie scream. It was something different, and if you can believe it, the scream sounded angrier.

Whatever, I wasn't sticking around. Things had gotten way too hot for me on Tarascas. I flew down Westwind and slid around the first turn I came to. I don't remember the street name, but it wasn't really important. I grew up around that area. I didn't need to know what street I was on. I would find Oveja just by heading in the right direction.

"You were still going back to where you left your team. Even though you believed you walked straight into a trap the last time you visited that area. Did you believe the team would still be there?"

I doubted they would still be there. It's not good to stay in one place very long when you're visiting a zombie occupied city, but I was hoping that they'd left me some sort of message as to where I could find them.

Imagine my surprise when I rounded the last turn with my craptastic bike and found my super Jeep waiting for me, just as pretty as you please. I can't even begin to tell you how relieved I was. The Jeeps we were using would plow through just about any roadblock my shaggy-haired, drooler friend could come up with.

"Speaking of her, did you believe you had killed her?"

I wasn't sure if I had killed her or not. That scream I heard didn't sound zombie-like at all. However, if the scream came from her, I was pretty sure that I'd given her enough damage to keep her off my ass.

At least, that's what I was hoping.

Whatever the case, I was certain that once I reached the Jeep, I'd be safe enough from anything until I could reunite with my team. So, I dropped the craptastic bike right in the middle of the road, set Merrick down in the back seat of the Jeep, and hopped behind the wheel.

The keys were waiting for me in the ignition. There wasn't a note telling me how to locate them, but the vehicle did have a computer with a direct link to Hardin. It took a moment to figure it out, but I finally got through to him.

"Jesus! Jaxon, is that you?"

"Yeah, it's me," I answered as I turned the key in the ignition and revved up the engine.

"We've been worried sick about you," Hardin said. "Where the hell have you been?"

"It's a story to tell," I said. "But right now I need to find my team."

"Yes," Hardin said. "I think that would be a pretty good idea. Miriam has found something that is worrying her. It has to do with a bite mark on one of the survivors the team extracted while you were missing."

"Yeah," I answered loudly in an effort to cut him off before he really started going. "Just tell me where they're at."

When he told me that they were at the Safe Zone, I started laughing and clicked off the computer before he could start blabbing in my ear again.

"Why were you laughing?"

Because I spent the last couple of evenings knee deep in shit, and those assholes were hiding out in the relative safety of the Safe Zone. That was kinda funny to me. I had every intention of picking on all of them mercilessly.

I was about to drive off, when a thought occurred to me. I backed up a bit to one of the houses the zombies had poured out of two nights ago. The windows had been boarded up. I hopped out of the Jeep and walked up to the front door of the house. The door was reinforced, and the wood along all the locks had burn marks where it had been cracked and broken. Further investigation showed me small shards of some unknown plastic lying on the floor.

"The locks were blown, weren't they?"

I'm no explosives expert, but that would be my guess, and I bet if I checked out those other houses,

I'd find the same kind of damage around the locks. I was now certain. We had walked into a trap.

I just didn't understand the why of things.

When I was about halfway back to the Jeep, Merrick gave a little warning growl. In response, I pulled my pistol out of its holster. I didn't see any sign of danger on the road, but just in case I moved as quickly as possible to the Jeep.

As soon as I was in the vehicle, I hit the lights and saw her standing in the middle of the road.

I was really beginning to hate this woman. I tore off with a very serious attempt to run her down, but as soon as I was about to hit her, she leapt onto the hood of the Jeep, stepped over to the roll bar, and dropped over the back.

She waved to me as I drove off.

Then she started to chase after me. I didn't realize it at first; I was watching her in the rear view mirror of course, but I took my eyes off of her for one brief moment to avoid some shamblers in the road, and when I looked back she was gone.

The zombies were beginning to swarm on the area. There weren't too many to make me nervous, but that was going to change rapidly. Fortunately for me, I wasn't going to be there, but it made me wonder if my new friend left the scene to avoid the zombies.

Merrick began to whine as soon as I hit open road. I looked back in my rearview mirror and there she was, running behind us. I freaked out a bit and hit the gas, but even full throttle she was gaining rapidly.

As soon as she reached the back left corner of the Jeep, she rammed it with her shoulder. Merrick and I spun around at least twice before I managed to bring the vehicle under control once again.

I didn't waste much time looking for her as we came to a stop. There were zombies all around the vehicle. I'm not sure where they came from; I had been too busy dividing my attention between the road, and the evil bitch chasing us down.

It sorta freaked me out.

I stopped the spinning, tried to grab a quick breath of air and suddenly there were a bunch of decaying hands grabbing at me. Merrick began to savage the first zombie that tried to crawl over her as I smacked away some hands, put the Jeep in gear, and tore out of there like a bat out of hell.

There was a zombie clinging to the back of the Jeep. I pointed him out to Merrick, and she gleefully hopped into the back seat and tore chunks out of its hands until he fell away.

I looked into the rearview and saw her once again. She was tearing right through the mass of zombies. She was like a force of nature. Anytime one of them got in front of her, she just smacked them out of the way like a little kid knocking down a stack of dominos.

It wasn't long before she reached the rear corner of the vehicle once again. This time, however, I was ready for her. When she rammed the side of the vehicle, I counter turned just right and kept the Jeep from spinning.

This must have pissed her off, but I've been driving Jeeps since the day I turned sixteen. She wasn't about to make me lose control again. I responded to her attempt by hanging my left arm out of the side of the vehicle and giving her the finger again.

She punched the side of the Jeep in frustration. I had a laugh at her expense, but I also noticed the dent she just added to my armored vehicle and the damage to the rear left corner where she'd been ramming me.

The evil bitch was strong. She was also running up farther along the Jeep towards my open window. I waited till she reached out for me, and I felt her hand scratch along my sleeve. The crushing grip of her fingers was agony. I shot her point blank in the face.

"Bastard!" she cried as she tumbled away on the street.

I took the brief moment her fall had provided to contact Hardin on the computer and tell him to connect me to Dudley.

As soon as he was on the line, she was back again. I was shooting at her even as I spoke with Dudley to make sure my team was still in the safe zone. I continued shooting at her as I told them all to wait in the watchtowers and be ready to shoot anything they saw chasing after me.

Right when Dudley clicked off, she was at my side again, and my pistol was empty. She grabbed at my arm, and I backhanded her in the face. She reached farther into the Jeep and began to claw at me. I lost control of the vehicle. I felt the bumps, bangs, and the eventual crash, as we collided with something and came to a stop.

I saw none of this, though, because my attacker had shoved me out of my seat and onto the floor of the vehicle. Most of her body was inside the Jeep. She was scratching at my chest with her ragged nails. She was banging my head against the metal flooring.

I reached towards my utility belt and felt for my knife. It seemed to take forever before I actually felt it in my hand. I briefly saw Merrick biting at her head as she attacked me. I plunged the knife into the side of her neck, and she screamed. Black blood erupted from the wound. It was an impossible amount of blood; it sprayed all over the interior as she thrashed and jerked on top of me.

Suddenly, her weight was gone. She had pulled herself out of the Jeep and was stumbling and thrashing on the road. There were shamblers running towards us; I heard their pounding footsteps and their screams.

I hit the lever to the armored top of the Jeep. Protection erupted around me at an alarming rate. I was safe inside the Jeep as the zombies began to swarm on top of my pursuer. They brought her down in seconds. I saw her fighting against them as one after another began to pile on top of her. Eventually, I couldn't even see her underneath the pile of bodies. All of a sudden, the pile erupted.

She was standing there, holding her neck, and swinging at all the zombies that rushed towards her. She looked horrible. There were bite marks all over her body. Chunks of flesh and muscle were missing from her arms and legs and that black syrupy blood was leaking freely from her many wounds. Most importantly of all, the wounds weren't healing. Or at least they weren't healing rapidly.

I started the Jeep. The crunching and the impact I had felt were the collision of my vehicle and an abandoned car. The Jeep was fine. I doubted the front bumper even had a dent. Jeeps were made to be tough, and the ones we were using were reinforced and armored to be tougher still.

She glared over at me when she heard the rumble of the engine and then took off in the opposite direction.

"*Just like that it was over?*"

Just like that. I hadn't managed to kill her, but I succeeded in causing her enough damage she gave up the chase. The knife attack had hit a major artery. She lost a lot of blood, way too much blood if you ask me. That stuff just kept pouring out of her. The other wounds I had given her barely bled at all before they closed up.

I knew she was going to be back. I had no misconceptions about that, but my guess was that a significant amount of blood loss would fuck up her healing. I didn't know for how long. I didn't know much of anything to be honest with you. I just knew major blood loss should slow her down.

That was the good news. The bad news came to me as soon as I tried to reverse the Jeep. My bumper was stuck tight to the abandoned car. I couldn't free myself in reverse, and I was afraid to make the situation worse by trying to plow forward.

The shamblers were, of course, all over the Jeep. They were banging on the windows and scratching at the doors. I kind of felt like a sardine in a can. If they managed to open the can, they were gonna have a nice dinner.

"*You were safe in the Jeep though, right?*"

Yeah, I mean, it's not like we had a lot of time to test out the armor. I really didn't know what kind of force could rip it open, or shatter the windows. I was surprised when the evil bitch started denting it all up. Then again, from the looks of things, she hit like a freight train.

So, yeah, I was safe for the moment. It didn't look like the zombies could pound through the armor. I was still worried about their numbers though. More and more of them were approaching and attacking the vehicle. I had no idea if they could break in if enough of them banged on it.

My other worry was that my stalker would come back. She healed herself pretty rapidly when I shot her. I was pretty sure she could tear through the armor easily enough.

Merrick was going insane beside me. The screaming and pounding were getting her all riled up. Hell, there were even a few zombies on the hood and roof.

Then they started rocking the vehicle.

"On purpose?"

No, it was simpler than that. Zombies don't have enough brains to come up with any kind of plan. Sure, they can sometimes manage to turn a doorknob, but that's about it. This was more like zombies on one side of the Jeep pushing and the other side zombies responding by pushing back. Regardless, the Jeep was rocking. It only lasted for a brief moment, but I heard a grinding noise through the metal of the vehicle.

I tried to reverse once again. It didn't work. I was still attached to the abandoned car. I tried to rock the Jeep from the inside in order to get them started once again, but it didn't work. Merrick thought I was a lunatic though. She actually stopped her furious barking just long enough to give me that look that dogs often give people: the one that makes you feel like a complete idiot.

"I've seen it before. I adopted a pit bull after our first interview."

Best dogs ever aren't they?

"I agree, but tell me what happened next?"

Well, I was stuck. I think I was there for about a half an hour, maybe more. I wasn't exactly looking at the time. I also didn't bother to call for help. There were too many zombies to pull me out safely, and I was also a little embarrassed to be stuck in that situation.

Then, my evil bitch stalker made another appearance.

She was on the roof of a nearby school. I only saw her briefly; there were too many zombies blocking the driver's side window for me to get a good look. I didn't think she could see me at all through the corpses, but if she could have, I would definitely have given her the finger again.

"Have you ever read a Spiderman comic?"

Yeah.

"Well, Spiderman constantly taunts his foes in an effort to make them frustrated because if they get all crazy mad at him, they will make mistakes he can capitalize on. I only bring it up because you seem to go out of your way to annoy your adversary. Were you doing this in an effort to frustrate her into making a mistake?"

No, I was doing it because I was pissed.

I laughed at this, actually we both did. It was amusing that someone like the General could be irritated enough to retaliate in such a way.

The funny thing was there were too many zombies surrounding the Jeep for her to get close. She couldn't do anything but watch. A few times, she vanished and large sections of shamblers broke away from the Jeep and charged off down the road. I figured she was trying to lead them away so that she could get to me, but too many of them stayed behind. I guess most of them were just too close to a meal to give up and chase after her. Plus, they were really driving each other into a frantic sort of craziness with all the pounding, screaming, and moaning.

It was a bad situation for everyone if you really look at it. The zombies couldn't get to me because of the armored Jeep. My stalker couldn't get to me because of all the zombies. I couldn't get away from any of them because my Jeep was stuck to an abandoned car.

A group of them began to push against the front of the vehicle. I'm not sure why they did it. I guess they were just so excited they were pushing against anything they could push against. I felt the shudder of grinding metal. I started honking the horn in an effort to encourage them. Maybe it worked, and maybe it didn't. All I know is some of them climbed onto the hood, and others kept on pushing against the front of the Jeep.

The sudden lurch from the right side of the vehicle meant the zombies on the right side started to push as well. They must have been concentrating their efforts on the rear of the Jeep, because the Jeep began to rotate on the street. I guess they were responding to movement like they did earlier with the rocking, or maybe they thought they could somehow crush the armor that was holding them back. I really have no clue.

The nasty screech of metal against metal could be heard over their screams. It was the sweetest sound I had ever before heard.

I punched the gas.

The Jeep shook and shuddered, but I was still stuck. I slapped it into four-wheel drive and tried it again. This time the shuddering was even more violent. I could smell the burning rubber, over the scent of decay, as the tires sought a purchase on the road.

Then I was free.

I violently plowed through a bunch of decaying bodies as I gunned the Jeep in reverse. When I had room, I slammed the stick into first gear, and bull dozed right through any of them that got in my way.

It was a rough-ass ride for about fifty yards or so, but the Jeep made it through easily enough. If I ever harbored any doubts about what type of vehicle I'd prefer in a hostile situation, I sure as hell didn't have them anymore.

All the windows were slimed over with zombie residue, and I could barely see out of them. The front windshield wasn't much of a problem. I just sprayed the water and hit the wipers, but the rest of the windows were beyond nasty. As soon as I was free and clear, I hit the lever and collapsed the armored top.

It was good to be able to breathe clean air again. The interior of the Jeep reeked of whatever that black blood gunk was that came out of my stalker's neck.

"Speaking of your stalker, what happened to her?"

That was another reason I wanted the filthy windows out of the way: I wanted to see her coming. I scanned everywhere I could while also driving as fast as I could go. I didn't see her anywhere, but I knew that she hadn't given up.

The attack came hard on the right side of the Jeep.

I barely even caught a glimpse of her as she darted into the road and charged me. Fortunately, a glimpse is all I needed to prepare for the impact. I was still moving forward.

There were a few assaults after that. One time I even braked hard when I caught her sneaking up on the rear. She slammed into the Jeep. It knocked her on her ass, and I tried to back over her, but she rolled out of the way just in time.

The situation was so tense I didn't even breathe a sigh of relief when I reached Georgie's neighborhood. I lost sight of her once again when I turned onto his street.

I could barely make out the outlines of my team in the watchtowers as I rushed towards the fence, but I knew they were there. That was the important thing. I now had more than a pistol, a tomahawk, and a knife to defend myself with. I finally had some backup.

I hit the brakes and spun the wheel at the very last moment. The Jeep came to a sideways rest in the middle of the road right next to the gate. I jumped out of the Jeep with my newly loaded weapon drawn. There were some streetlights on the road, but I could still find no target.

I scanned the road. I scanned the yards. I was just beginning a scan on the right hand side rooftops when I heard a loud voice warning me not to shoot at some chick. I didn't recognize the voice, but it did sound disappointingly familiar.

I immediately spun to my left and saw her jump from the roof of a nearby house. I started firing at her before she even left the rooftop. I was still firing on her when she landed on the road and raced towards me in an erratic manner. I was shooting at her right up until the point she slugged me off my feet and into the Jeep.

The punch was bad. The collision with the Jeep wasn't as bad as the punch, but it still managed to crack some ribs. I needed to get on my feet, and I needed to do it fast, but I'd lost my gun.

I heard the muffled thumps of a machine gun at just about the same time that I saw a hail of bullets punch through her chest as she advanced towards me. The impact of the bullets nailed her pretty hard. She actually backed up.

The roar that came out of her sounded like a mix between a lion and a movie dinosaur. It was loud, and eerie as hell. I gave up looking for my gun and climbed to my feet with my tomahawk in my hand instead.

I have to give credit where credit was due. The woman was fast. She somehow managed to block my swing. Instead of crunching down on her head, the blade of my tomahawk buried itself into her arm. Underneath the sound of breaking bone, I heard her whimper.

I was shocked that my weapon didn't go right through her arm and still find her head. Her body was somehow denser than that of a normal human being. I yanked the tomahawk free in order to take another swing, but as soon as the blade was removed she took off.

There was a moment of quiet stillness.

I took stock of my injuries. Things weren't too bad, nothing that wouldn't heal right up. The most shocking part was that she somehow managed to rip off a sleeve of my bite proof shirt and tear through the same material around my chest and stomach. Without the suit, she probably would have eviscerated me.

Georgie was babbling about something in the high voice he gets when too excited. Then, I heard the new voice answer him in an angry tone. I didn't pay much attention to them. I was more concerned with finding my pistol.

"Jaxon!" Dudley shouted. "Are you alright?"

"Barely," I answered as I picked up my pistol. "What the hell took you dumbasses so long to shoot?"

"She looked like a normal woman," Dudley answered.

"A dirty, nasty, woman," the unknown voice answered.

"Shut up, numb nuts. You were the asshole screaming for Jaxon not to shoot her."

"No I didn't," the voice answered.

Suddenly, I had a mental picture to go along with the person talking. I dismissed it immediately. There was no way that my luck was that bad. It had to be someone else. It had to be.

The screams began to echo around the neighborhood and for a brief moment, we all froze.

"Open the gate," I shouted as I dove back into the Jeep.

"*Damn.*"

I really didn't mean to say anything. The word just sort of popped out of my mouth. Jaxon smiled and laughed at my reaction.

Yeah, those were pretty much my thoughts exactly. When it rains it pours, I guess.

Well, they got the gate open for me as rapidly as possible, and I drove my battered Jeep over to Georgie's driveway, and parked it as they were closing the gate behind me.

We were all safely inside of Georgie's house when the dead began to run up the street. Thankfully, they didn't see any of us. That meant they weren't likely to hang around very long. If they had seen us, they would have torn at the fence until we put them all down, or they got in and ate us.

I went into Georgie's kitchen and immediately began to ransack the shelves until I found some crackers. Merrick deserved a treat for being a good girl and staying in the vehicle like I'd told her. I caught a glimpse of Nick as we entered the house. I tried to pretend I didn't see him, in the vain hope he would vanish if ignored.

"So you glad to see me or what, fucker?" Nick asked.

"Or what," I replied.

"Jax," Dudley interrupted. "What was that thing? It looked like a girl, but that was no girl."

"Ask Hardin," I answered while stuffing my mouth full of crackers.

Dudley gave his earpiece a tap. I motioned for Kingsley to hand over his earpiece and stuck it on my ear just as Hardin answered.

"We think we know what you boys are up against. Miriam had her suspicions ever since she took a look at the bite mark on Michelle. The fight I just watched through everyone's earpiece confirms things for us. It's time to get you boys out of the area."

"Why the hell would we leave the area?" I asked.

"Because, for whatever reason, this thing is hunting you, Jaxon. In the past, whenever we came near a creature as dangerous as this one, we made an immediate retreat. There are some things out there that are just plain foolish to play around with, and this thing is one of them."

"Well, you told me what you wanted to do, but you didn't tell me what we are dealing with."

"The fact is, we really don't know very much about them. They're too deadly to study. There are stories of course—way before my time—but most of the Guardians that went up against these things were killed. It became a sort of policy to retreat if we thought one was in the area."

"Hardin," I grumbled. "What the hell is it?"

"You're dealing with a vampire, Jax."

Chapter 5

GEORGIE

My first meeting with Georgie was probably the funniest interview of my entire career. There was something hilarious about the man. He wasn't overtly funny, cracking jokes or making witty comments. That wasn't it at all. I think it was the way he tried to be so serious and professional. I should just tell what happened when he entered the room. That should kick things off in the correct direction.

I was waiting for Georgie in the same room I had previously been conducting interviews for this piece. He was forty minutes late when the door finally opened. In walked a man clad from head to toe in black padded leather. He had a helmet over his head as well. The helmet had a black visor, so not even his face was visible.

He closed the door behind him as quickly as possible, but I could hear the unmistakable sounds of Jaxon's cackle from the hallway. Slowly, he took off his gloves and his helmet, which he placed on the table. He then offered me his hand.

Hello, my name is Georgie.

"It's nice to finally meet you, Georgie. I've heard a lot about you."

Yes, I'm sure you have. Where would you like to begin?

I was beginning to get a little worried. Georgie actually sounded more like a robot than one of the Regulators. Every other member of the team had a definite personality. Georgie, on the other hand, seemed as if he had lost his in one of the battles.

"Jaxon took me to the point in which you had just found out that you were dealing with a vampire. Could you continue where he left off?"

I'm not sure that you are authorized to receive that information.

I was trying to think of a response, or possibly a way to remove myself from the room, when Dudley burst through the door, took one look at Georgie, and started laughing. I had no idea what he was laughing about, but Georgie looked more than a little upset about it. A moment later, Jaxon joined Dudley, and they were both laughing at an angry looking Georgie.

It was when Jaxon and Dudley began to poke and pull on his leather pants that I realized they were making fun of the way he was dressed. I honestly tried not to laugh along with them, but, in the end, I lost it. It started with a smile, but in moments I was laughing hysterically along with them.

Apparently, anything more than a helmet and leather jacket when riding a motorcycle is some sort of faux pas. In between chuckles, Dudley explained to me that Jaxon always laughed about the way Georgie dressed when riding his motorcycle, but Dudley had never actually seen it until that very moment.

Jaxon asked me if the interview was going well. I said that Georgie wasn't being cooperative. Dudley then walked over to Georgie, pinched and twisted his nipple, all while demanding that he whistle if he wanted to be released. Georgie was unable to produce a whistle, but Dudley released him anyway, after he promised to cooperate fully and answer all my questions.

Dudley and Jaxon were still laughing when they left the room.

Okay, what was your last question?

"I was wondering if you could continue where Jaxon left off."

I can do that, yes.

"Before we get into that, I'm wondering, do they act like that a lot?"

Dudley and Jaxon?

"Yes."

All the time. We all act crazy and immature. I think it comes with the job. The minute the stress is over, we live it up. Because sooner or later we are gonna be put back into those dangerous situations again.

Then again, those two have always been assholes. Just don't tell them that I said that.

We laughed for a moment, and suddenly a new person started to emerge. He was surprisingly very funny as he told me stories of the antics the team often got caught up in. It was a fun time. Georgie is an excellent storyteller.

When the laughter finally stopped, Georgie became a little serious again.

It was pretty rough. At the time, I didn't know everything that Jaxon had gone through, but it was rough on him. He looked worn out. I was a little worried about him after I saw the damage on his arm with the torn sleeve. Even through his tattoos, I could see the bruises.

You see: it's the team's job to worry about Jaxon, because he never worries about himself. He'll often throw himself into the most dangerous situation. It makes us pretty nervous to tell you the truth, but that's Jax. He's the hero. If he didn't act that way, I don't think he would have been chosen to be the Guardian.

If a vampire had been hunting me, I would have pissed myself. Jax isn't like that. He's just wired differently. He took the news from Hardin with barely a shrug of his shoulders.

"So how do we kill it?" Jaxon asked.

"Jaxon, you are not listening to me," Hardin answered. "We don't know how to kill it. We don't even try to kill it. We evacuate you from the area until it goes away."

"Yeah, yeah," Jaxon replied. "I've heard it before. Weren't you the one that told me the last Guardian was going to kill me? What happened there?"

"This is different, Jaxon. Even the last Guardian was evacuated if we thought there were vampires in the area. It's not safe."

"I'm not running. So why don't you figure out a way for me to kill that thing, and get back to me. Also, I need some new gear. Javie will give you a list."

With that, the conversation with Hardin was over.

After Jaxon told Javie everything that he needed, Javie vanished into another room in order to relay Jaxon's request in relative quiet. The kitchen was getting rather loud as Jaxon related his story of the last couple evenings. Nick's new friends, Katie and Jason, even joined in on the fun. It probably wasn't the type of story the kid should have heard, but he stared up at Jaxon with a vast amount of hero worship.

Jaxon pretty much ignored the kid.

When the tale was told, we all sat around in amazement. Things had become even more difficult. It was one thing to rescue people from zombies, but what the hell were we supposed to do about the vampire that was trying to kill us?

"I imagine it must have been more than a little upsetting."

It was, but Jaxon tried to break the tension. At least, I think that's what he was doing. For all I know, he might have been serious. It's often hard to tell with him.

"So, Nick," Jaxon said. "Why are you here, and how do I get rid of you?"

Nick sort of just looked at him for a moment as if he wasn't sure how to respond. That, by the way, is a normal reaction when people aren't sure if he's joking or not. Nick eventually decided to laugh it off, and even threw in a few expletives for revenge. Jaxon kept looking at him as if he were some sort of weird insect never before classified.

I relaxed a bit when Javie returned with the news that Jaxon's gear would be parachuted in within the next half hour. That was when Kingsley began to question Jaxon.

"Are you sure about this, Jax? Should we be continuing this? I mean, a vampire? What the hell do we know about vampires? I think you're in over your head."

"What did we know about zombies until we were stuck in the middle of an outbreak?" Dudley asked. "It's not like we can choose which battles we want to fight. What do you expect us to do, turn tail and run every time something wants to kill us? If we plan on killing evil monsters for a living, we had better get used to evil monsters wanting us dead."

"I agree with Dudley," Nick said. "That bitch ain't got shit on us. We can take her out easy. All we need is to do is fill her up with bullets whenever she comes around looking for Jaxon."

"I'm still wondering why you're even here," Jaxon said to Nick. "And Dudley is right. Regulators do not run. We didn't come back to El Paso just to run away when things get rough. There are people out there that need us, and nothing is going to stop me from helping them. Anyone that wants out, feel free to catch the next chopper out of here."

"Here, here," I added. "Only pussies run from sparkly vampires."

"Shouldn't you be long gone then?" Nick said.

"Jax was wondering why you're still here," I replied.

"How about I hit you with another bottle?" Nick asked.

"Jax," I said. "Will Nick be leaving when we extract Katie and Jason?"

"Yes," answered Jaxon.

"What the fuck?" Nick roared. "Are you off your rocker? You would really want a pussy like Georgie and a candy ass like Kingsley fighting next to you instead of me? Look at Kingsley. He's terrified. He doesn't even want to be here, and Georgie has always been a wimp."

"I'm not a pussy when I have a gun in my hand," I replied.

Jaxon had also taught me some hand-to-hand. It wasn't something I wanted to rely on when facing either zombies or vampires, but I really wasn't that big of a wimp.

"What the hell do you want to be a part of this for?" Jaxon asked.

"I don't know," Nick answered. "I spent so much time being terrified, and so much time trying to survive, I guess I feel bad for anyone else going through what I went through. It feels like something that I need to do."

Nick started getting a little teary-eyed. Jaxon looked at him for a long moment and then shrugged his big ol' shoulders once again.

"Whatever," Jaxon said.

"*What did that mean*?"

Basically, it meant that Jaxon wasn't happy about it, but he was still going to give Nick a chance. Javie then announced the gear was being dropped, and we all rushed to the front of the house to see how this was going to go.

The helicopter was already headed home when I looked out my front door. I was impressed with how quickly they were able to deliver the new gear, but I had no idea where it was.

It was Dudley that first noticed it. He pointed his finger up into the nighttime sky and after a brief moment, I located what he was pointing at. There were three large canisters silently floating down towards the street beneath black parachutes that weren't big enough for a person but suited the canisters perfectly.

The only problem was that they landed in the middle of the street.

We all looked at each other and then as one gazed down the road towards the fence. There were about a hundred or so zombies wandering aimlessly at the gate. They hadn't seen us, so they weren't trying to break in, but the noise we made from the brief fight with the vampire girl had attracted them.

Left alone, these zombies would probably just wander off eventually, but if they happened to see a living person inside the safe zone, they weren't going to go anywhere, and their screams would only attract more of their friends.

"Oops," Dudley said.

"Send Georgie out to go get them," Nick said.

"How bout no, bitch," I responded.

"Sounds like a job for the new guy if you ask me," Jaxon said.

"I agree," Dudley said. "Go get those canisters, tough guy."

"What the hell?" Nick sputtered. "There are zombies out there."

"There sure are," Jaxon said. "But a big, tough guy like you isn't afraid of a bunch of shamblers. Hell, you should have seen all the zombies Dudley and I had to deal with back when we blew up Tito's apartment complex."

"Good times," Dudley said.

"Pussy," Jaxon whispered.

Everyone was starting to snicker at Nick's expense.

"Here pussy, pussy, pussy," Dudley whispered while tapping his legs as if Nick were a dog, and Dudley was trying to call him forward.

"Oh, you guys are funny." Nick said.

Even the little kid was starting to laugh.

"Let's just wait until that crowd wanders off," Kingsley said. "They won't stick around if they don't see any people."

"Well duh," Jaxon said. "But where's the fun in that?"

Everyone began to laugh, but the funniest part was the look of relief on Nick's face when he felt confident Jaxon didn't really want to send him out to retrieve the canisters.

"It wasn't so much the zombies that were making me nervous," Nick said. "I just didn't want to run into that vampire all by myself out there."

"Regulators are never by themselves," Dudley said. "We have each other's backs, or we don't survive."

"What about when Jaxon charges a horde of zombies and then disappears for two days?" I replied.

"Jaxon's special," Dudley answered.

"You trying to say I'm short bus special?" Jaxon asked.

"Of course not," Dudley said.

"Because you had a definite tone," Jaxon added.

"I'm not sure what you're referring to," Dudley said.

"Well, maybe if you removed your head out of your ass, you would understand things a bit better."

"Keeping my head in my ass is the only place I have to get away from you."

"Well, maybe I should..."

"Would you guys stop fucking around," Kingsley shouted. "There are zombies at the fence and a freaking vampire somewhere out there, and you guys are joking around like our lives aren't in serious danger."

"Now who's a pussy?" Nick asked. "It's not me."

Kingsley became angry at the comment and stormed off up the stairs to the bedroom he always used when he crashed at my house.

It was the last time I saw him alive.

Javie was the one that went to go check on him. The rest of us were eating in the kitchen. I remember the look on his face when he told all of us Kingsley wasn't in the room. He looked like he already knew we had lost a teammate. I also remember getting angry at the look on his face. I wasn't ready to write off one of our guys until I saw the body.

All of us ran to the bedroom.

The window was wide open. Cold air was gently blowing into the room. There were blood spots on the windowsill. Jaxon approached cautiously and peered outside. "There are broken shingles on your neighbor's roof," Jaxon said. "She must have grabbed him and carried him off."

"How do you know it was the vampire?" Nick asked.

"Because I don't think Kingsley can jump thirty feet to the neighbor's rooftop," Jax answered.

"Yeah, but what if…" Nick said before Jax cut him off with a wave of his hand.

We'd lost a teammate. We'd lost a dear friend. It hit the entire team pretty hard. So hard, in fact, that none of us really spoke the rest of the evening.

"*Nobody went after him?*"

How could we? The vampire traveled over the rooftops. Plus, there were zombies out there and we couldn't let them see us, or we would never get out of the safe zone. It was a bad situation. All of us wanted to go after him; it was just impossible at that moment.

"*I'm sorry. That was insensitive of me. I should have realized you would have done something had you been able.*"

Well, I didn't say we didn't do anything. We just had to wait until daylight.

"*Why daylight?*"

Daylight is when the zombies finally drifted away. Jaxon stayed up the entire night waiting for them to leave. It finally happened when the sun rose over the mountains.

Jaxon and Dudley ran out the door, gathered the canisters, and returned to my house in a matter of seconds. It took us a bit to figure out how to open the canisters, but as soon they were opened, Jaxon changed into a new bite suit and vest.

The new vest was pretty cool. It had a skull and crossbones design on it. Except that instead of crossbones, they were musket pistols, and the skull had a bandana over its mouth like an old western bandit. He also got a new MP7 to replace the one Nick had commandeered. Nick had wanted the vest with the skull and crossbones, but that was never going to happen.

The big oaf wasn't left out, however; Jaxon had gotten him a bite suit and gear as well. Both of them also had new earpiece radios. The rest of the gear consisted of backpack supplies like food and ammo.

When the ammo had all been divided between us, Jaxon asked if I was ready. I had no idea what he was talking about.

"Am I ready for what?" I asked.

"You, me, and Merrick, are going to go look for Kingsley," Jaxon said.

"What do you want us to do while you're out?" Dudley asked.

"Just stay here and keep our survivors safe," Jaxon answered.

"Jax," I said. "It's daylight. Why are we searching for him in the daylight? What about the zombies? They could spot us."

"Because we need the daylight to follow any signs or tracks left behind. In case you're wondering why I'm taking you, it's because you are the only hunter in the room with tracking experience."

"I can track," Nick answered.

"Anyway," Jaxon said. "Get your gear, and let's get going."

Jaxon was on my neighbor's roof when Hardin contacted him. It was easy enough to listen in; Hardin was using the open frequency.

"Jaxon, can you read me?" Hardin said.

"Yup," Jax answered.

"You already lost one teammate. Let's get you boys out of there before you lose anymore."

"Not gonna happen," Jax answered.

"I was afraid that you were going to say that. Come this evening, I'm going to pull out the other teams until this mess is over and done with. I don't want to risk good men."

"That's your choice. What kind of information have you found out about vampires for me?" Jax asked.

"All we really know at this point is sunlight will kill them," Hardin answered. "I have Miriam and Ivana going through the old, old records. Maybe they will come up with something new, but I doubt it."

"So, if we found out where this thing hides during the day and drag her out into the sunlight, she'll burn?"

"I believe so, yes."

"All right," Jaxon said. "I'll contact you later."

A few moments later, he was standing next to me.

"She didn't stop on that rooftop as far as I can tell. I think she kept on going up the hill. There are scuffmarks on the edges of the roof where somebody scraped against the stucco. I'm guessing she was dragging Kingsley, and he was putting up a fight."

"Makes sense to me," I answered. "Kingsley is a big boy, and she's a somewhat small woman from what I could tell. He'd definitely have enough length on him to scuff up against some things."

"What's at the end of your street? I've never been up there before."

"There are a few other streets that intersect, but if you continue going up it's just desert and then mountains."

Jax appeared to think about this for a minute while he knelt down and scratched Merrick behind the ears.

"I doubt a vampire would want to be stuck in the desert come sunrise," Jaxon said when he was ready.

"Not if a suntan is fatal," I replied.

"Let's grab a Jeep and take a drive up towards the mountain and see if we find anything near the desert."

We didn't bother to stop back in my house and let everyone know what we were up to. Instead, Jax just tapped his earpiece and let Dudley know where we were going as we drove off in the Jeep that wasn't so beaten up.

We didn't see any zombies. The bastards still weren't very active in the daylight even though it was rather cool outside. Well, at least as cool as El Paso can get during the day. It's the nights that get pretty cold during the winter months. Zombies apparently dislike the sun and not the heat, at least that's my belief. The sun won't stop them from charging if they see you, but they are certainly more active at night.

This is a much-debated topic. Some people think zombies prefer to avoid the sun, while others feel they seek shelter to avoid the heat of the day.

The ride to the desert didn't take very long.

Once there, the three of us left the safety of the Jeep and began to walk along the edge of where the desert began. We were looking for footprints in the sand, or anything else that would tell us there had been recent activity in the area.

I thought we were pretty much grasping at straws. The odds were against us. From what I understood, the vampire preferred to keep herself off the ground. She liked the tops of houses and buildings, that way she could swoop down like some demented bird of prey and attack.

Imagine my surprise when Merrick found footprints.

I mean, don't get me wrong, I would have found them myself. It wasn't like they were hidden or anything. Merrick just happened to be walking about ten feet in front of us so she was the first one to find them. Leave it to Jax to be an asshole.

"Wow," Jax said. "Makes me wonder why I even brought you."

"I would have found them," I answered.

"One of these days," Jaxon said with a smirk, "you are going to need to prove to me you're actually good at something."

"I'm going through a divorce," I said.

It probably wasn't the right time to bring it up. I just, for some reason, blurted it out.

"I know you are," Jax said. "I didn't want to ask you about it. I figured you would come to me if you wanted to talk."

"I don't know that I want to talk about it," I said. "I just wanted to tell you myself."

"That's fine," Jax said. "I'm here if you need me, and if you don't, well, that's okay too."

I changed the subject again as we approached the tracks.

"What do you think?" I asked.

The tracks were obvious. In fact, they seemed a little bit too obvious. They even had an evident drag mark.

"Too early for me to tell," Jaxon said. "We might as well follow them. Not much chance of anything sneaking up on us during the day in the open desert."

We followed the tracks for about two hours. They led us in a straight path with no deviation. I was actually beginning to feel a bit warm under the sun when we finally came to a small scrub brush covered hill. The tracks went around the hill. We followed them and came upon a grisly scene once we reached the opposite side.

There were two different sets of tracks in the sand. One set of the tracks was the barefoot tracks that we had been following. The other set belonged to very large combat boots. There was blood everywhere, along with massive amounts of disturbed sand. Kingsley had fought back.

There was a large mound of sand off to one side that called our attention. Something had been buried there, and it didn't take a genius to figure out what. Jaxon knelt beside the grave and gently put his hand upon the sand. I was quiet. No, we were both quiet. We had just found the grave of our friend and teammate.

Merrick gave a little bark off in the distance. Jaxon went over to her. She had found Kingsley's pistol. We didn't look for the rest of his belongings.

The walk back to the Jeep was a long one. I didn't want to break the silence. The look on Jaxon's face was rather intimidating, but I couldn't take the quiet any longer.

"Are we just going to leave him there?" I asked.

"For now," Jax answered. "But we'll be back for him someday. He needs a proper funeral, in a proper place. I won't leave him there forever."

We continued on in silence for another half an hour when Jaxon suddenly stopped.

"I don't get it," Jaxon said. "I just don't get it."

"What don't you get?"

"Why here?" Jaxon said. "She could have killed him anywhere. She could have killed him on your neighbor's roof if she had wanted to. Why drag him all the way into the desert, and why bury him?"

"I don't know," I answered. "I guess when you think about it, it doesn't make much sense. Maybe she just wanted to take her time with him."

"She didn't have to come out here to do that. No, I'm missing something. I don't know what, but I'm missing something."

"I don't know, man, maybe she's just messed up in the head."

"I'll tell you one thing," Jaxon said. "I'm going to kill her. I'm going to find her and I'm going to rip her into pieces."

Jaxon wasn't going to break down and fall apart. He's not that type of person. He's the type of person that can actually push emotions aside and do what needs to be done. He would mourn the loss of his friend someday, but it wasn't going to be any time soon.

"*Has Jaxon always been like that?*"

Yes, he's never been a very emotional guy. He has emotions, of course. I realize that a lot of people out there say he's pretty cold hearted, but he's not. He was hurting, hurting very badly, but he wasn't about to fall apart. There would be time for that after he got his revenge.

We walked in silence all the way to the road where we first saw the tracks. Merrick had gotten there ahead of us and she was staring down the road at the nearest house.

When the two of us reached her, Jaxon began to stare off towards the house as well. Merrick even gave a small little growl. I was completely clueless as to what they were doing.

"What's going on?" I asked.

"I'm not sure but something."

"Is it that house?" I asked.

"Hold on a second," Jax said.

I waited quietly as he stared and stared at the house. I was still at a complete loss.

"There," Jax said. "Do you hear it?"

"Hear what?" I answered.

"There's a pounding noise coming from that house."

"Are you sure?"

"I'm pretty sure," Jax said.

Without another word, he and Merrick took off towards the house in question. I was left trying to catch up to them. It wasn't a situation I was very comfortable with to be totally honest. Jaxon had the ability to survive in this environment indefinitely, but I didn't. I didn't even like leaving the vehicle, if you want me to be totally truthful, but Jaxon thought nothing of it.

I was slightly out of breath when I caught up with them at the front door of the house. Everything was eerily quiet. Something in the air just didn't feel right. I didn't want to say anything and end up looking like a pussy, but something was wrong. I knew it.

"Do you hear anything?" I asked.

"No, it's completely quiet in there now."

Jaxon was giving me a dirty look because I was still breathing heavy after my run.

"What do you want to do?" I asked.

Jaxon didn't answer me; he just clicked his earpiece.

"Hardin," Jaxon said. "Are there any known survivors around our current location?"

"Negative," Hardin said over the radio. "We haven't received a single distress call in, or around, your current location. It's a no man's land out there."

I completely agreed with Hardin. The neighborhood around the house had a very ghost town sort of look to it. All of the windows were boarded up—which is what normally happens when people are trying to survive a zombie invasion—but there was also sand all over the road and sidewalks. The area seemed very deserted.

"Thanks," Jaxon said.

"Not a problem," Hardin replied before clicking off.

Jaxon backed up to the mailbox and gave the house a thorough scan. Apparently he arrived at the same conclusion I had, because he shook his head and motioned for me to come over to him.

"I must be hearing things," Jaxon said. "Maybe I was just hoping…"

He didn't finish his thought. He didn't have to.

"You wanna head back to the Jeep?" I asked.

"I guess so."

Jaxon gave out a quick whistle to get Merrick's attention. She was busy sniffing around the side of the house, but she bolted to Jaxon's side immediately after the whistle and the three of us set off towards the Jeep.

I heard a thump.

Jaxon didn't hear it. He was lost somewhere in his own thoughts, but I heard it. It was a dull, muffled thump, and it was indeed coming from inside the house. One thought raced through my mind. Could it be Kingsley that was somehow trapped somewhere inside, and he was banging on something in the hopes that someone would help him?

"Jax, I just heard it."

"You heard what?"

"I just heard a thump."

I was scanning the windows, but I couldn't see anything since the shutters were all closed. Jaxon walked back to the house, and he too began to scan the windows, but he was much closer as he attempted to find an angle in which he could actually see inside.

"I can't see anything," Jax said.

"What do you want to do?" I asked. "Kingsley could be in there."

"How do you figure that?"

"The scene in the desert was just a diversion," I answered. "What if she actually trapped him inside this house somehow? You said yourself what we saw in the desert didn't make sense."

"That's a pretty big stretch; I dunno."

"We owe it to him to at least check out the house," I said.

Jaxon nodded his head and the two of us walked over to the front door. Merrick began making weird little growls from the yard, but she came with us. I put my hand on the doorknob and gave it a turn. The door wasn't locked, but it did vibrate a little, which I thought was sort of weird. I pushed it open, but after about five inches the door bumped into something soft and would move no farther. I pushed and I felt some give, but then the door pushed back, and the zombie screams started.

It was a trap. Again.

I vaguely remember hearing Jaxon start to scream orders at me. I think he was telling me to close the door, but his voice was drowned out by all the zombie screams. It sounded like there were a lot of them in there, and they sounded very hungry.

I was trying to pull the door closed when I saw all the decaying hands grab through the space I had created and begin to pull against me. It was a tug-of-war. I was trying to close the door and they were trying to open it.

Jaxon was still screaming at me, and I couldn't figure out why he wasn't helping me close the door. When I heard the muffled thumps of his MP7 from behind me, I wanted to turn around and see just what the hell he was shooting at, but I couldn't. I was afraid to divide my attention.

Suddenly, I felt Merrick's teeth around my ankle, and it hurt like a son of a bitch. The shock of being bitten by Jaxon's dog distracted me from the door, and I felt it being yanked from my hands.

The house was jam packed with shamblers.

"Why weren't you able to hear them before?"

If we had come by during the evening, we probably would have. As it was, they were probably in that lazy state they tend to get into when the sun is out, and nothing is capturing their attention.

They all surged for the door at the same time, and that's the reason I'm still alive. They got in each other's way.

I backtracked immediately. I didn't even bother turning around; I just went as fast as I could in reverse.

I almost collided with Jax.

I turned to grab him and that's when I realized the street had filled with zombies. That's why Merrick grabbed my ankle, by the way. It wasn't a bite. She was trying to lead me away. I froze at the sight of all the zombies, but Jaxon kept firing. I remember being completely impressed by how calm and cool he seemed to be as he fired off shot after shot. I remember thinking that if I had a gun I could probably help him out. Then I recalled I did have a gun. I also possessed an MP7, and it was currently hanging uselessly off the sling around my neck.

I grabbed the gun… Oh wait, I'm sorry. It's actually a rifle. I brought the rifle to my shoulder and began to bring them down one at a time.

"To your right," Jaxon snarled.

I had forgotten about the zombies that were still in the house. They were flooding out of the open door right towards us. I swung the barrel in that direction, and began to fire at them. As soon as I had nailed all the shamblers outside the door, things got a little bit easier for me. The instant I saw them appear in the doorway, I brought them down. The bodies began to pile up around the door, and that slowed them down even more.

I paused to reload. While doing that, I took a look over towards Jax. He was in trouble. Hell, we were both in trouble. There were zombies everywhere. They were literally pouring out of the nearby homes. He was doing his best to hold them back, but it was obvious we were going to be overwhelmed.

"Let's make a run for it!" I shouted to be heard over the screams and moans.

"I'm right behind you," Jaxon yelled back.

I took off as fast as I could move. I wasn't going to win many races, but I hoped it would be fast enough to stay ahead of the zombies. I heard Jaxon screaming something from behind me, but I couldn't make out what it was.

Suddenly, Jaxon was right beside me, and then he was in front of me, reaching back to grab a hold of my arm, and drag me along at an even faster rate. I couldn't take it for long. I managed to round the corner of the road and get about another block or two before my breathing became loud enough to block out the sounds of our pursuers.

Jaxon was shouting at me to hurry up. It felt like he was going to yank my arm out of the socket, he was running so fast. I could hear them behind us. It was terrifying. I pushed and pushed myself, but my legs felt rubbery and weak. I couldn't even remember the last time I had gone running.

I felt the pull on my arm rapidly change direction. I looked up and realized that Jaxon was cutting through a yard. We ran to a backyard gate and fortunately for me, Jaxon didn't jump over it. He took the time to lift the latch, let me in, and closed the gate behind us.

The next thing I knew, he was breaking down the rear door of the house and shoving me through. After he closed it behind me, I was left alone and gasping in the shadows of an empty house. I stumbled to a window just in time to see all of the shamblers flood into the backyard.

It took me a moment to locate Jaxon. He was waiting for them on the edge of the rock wall farthest from the house. The zombies spotted him immediately, and charged towards him. He waited until the last possible second and jumped ten or twenty feet into the neighboring yard behind the house I was hiding in.

Jaxon was gone.

I was all alone in an extremely hostile environment. Something scraped against my leg and I almost screamed. It was only Merrick. She was pawing at me for attention. Jaxon had pushed her into the house as well.

The backyard was filled with zombies. Some of them were dropping off the wall in an effort to continue the chase, while others wandered around aimlessly.

Jaxon was gone.

I tapped my earpiece.

"Jaxon," I whispered. "Where are you?"

"I'm not exactly sure," Jaxon said with a little laugh.

"What do I do?" I asked.

"Just wait there," Jaxon said. "After I lose them, I'll be back to get you."

He clicked off after that. I tried to ask a few more questions, but he continued to ignore me. I sat on the floor of the kitchen for around thirty minutes. It took that long before I was breathing normally.

I drank some water out of my backpack. I wiped the cold sweat from my forehead and finally got to my feet. My legs were still shaky. It wasn't a good feeling at all.

I heard a noise from somewhere in the house.

I was afraid to use my MP7. Even though it has a silencer, it still makes a muffled thump. I didn't want any of the zombies outside the house to hear it so I pulled out my large bowie knife. Jaxon insisted that all of us carry some sort of bladed, backup weapon. I chose the bowie knife because it looked mean as hell. It was a Cold Steel knife, so Jaxon approved of my choice, since he believes they are the best fighting knives available.

I had to laugh at this. Jaxon was definitely the man to seek approval from when it came to edged weapons. He might even be considered a bit of a knife snob, but then again, he needed the best. His life often depended on his weapons.

I crept into the next room as quietly as I could. Once again, I was breathing heavily, and the noise made me worry. Jaxon began jabbering in my ear, but he wasn't talking to me. He was asking Hardin to send a chopper over his location. The radio chatter made me nervous as well. It seemed to be way too loud. I tried to find the volume on my ear, but I couldn't so I ended up shutting the earpiece off.

I was terrified. That may come as a shock to you, but I didn't exactly have a lot of experience in those sorts of situations. When everything went down before, I was in the Safe Zone, right up until we left the area.

"Weren't you the one that went out to help Jaxon during those fifteen minutes of footage?"

Yeah, that was me, but that doesn't really count. Things just happened, and I just sort of reacted. Besides, Jaxon had already done all the hard stuff. I just kinda helped bring things to a finish.

"Later on you went with them to rescue Skie, correct?"

And my involvement in that little operation consisted of sniping out targets while I was safe and sound on a rooftop. To be honest, I think Jaxon knew I was pretty worried. It's hard to say with him. He often takes care of people without really telling them he's taking care of them.

There was nothing in the next room, just a darkened living room. There was a sofa, a nice TV, a recliner but nothing out of the ordinary. I was hoping I was hearing things. I was hoping the house was empty…I was hoping for a lot of things actually.

I heard the noise again.

I followed the sound. It sounded like someone rattling a doorknob. I went down the darkened hallway. I wanted to use my flashlight, but I was afraid it could somehow be seen from outside, and the area around the house was infested with shamblers.

At the end of the hallway was a sturdy wooden door. I didn't want to open it. I really, really did not want to open that door. Under normal circumstances, I wouldn't have turned that knob for all the tequila in Mexico, but if there was a zombie in the house with me, it would be better if I took it out quickly. If I tried to ignore the problem and it got out of the room and found me, I might not be able to kill it before it let out a scream. A scream would be fatal for me; there were just too many of them outside.

I turned the knob and opened the door.

It was a suicide. Dudley was correct in saying those are often the worst things to come upon. It was a middle-aged woman who had hanged herself. On a side note, I said hanged. I did not say hung, because that would be incorrect. Way too many people would make the mistake of telling you the woman hung herself. When, in fact, the woman had hanged herself from some pull up bars that were attached above the doorframe of the bathroom. It was a sad sight to see.

My guess is she chose to end her life after she had been bitten. She probably didn't realize she would come back as a zombie. She should have destroyed her brain. Anyway, it was her twitching foot that made the noise as it bumped against the doorknob of the open bathroom door.

I began to relax somewhat when I realized I wasn't in any immediate danger. Unfortunately, my eyes drifted to the bed. There was something under the covers. I needed to make sure whatever it was wasn't going to jump up and try to eat me so Merrick and I entered the room and quietly closed the door behind us. Then, I pulled back the covers with the point of my knife.

I looked into the rotting face of a middle-aged man. There was a bite mark on his shoulder. The woman hanging was probably his wife. She had probably committed suicide after killing her husband. The man had a bullet hole in his temple. It's a shame she didn't kill him before he had taken a bite out of her. Then it would have been a situation of rescuing her instead of putting her out of her misery.

I approached the twitching body. She couldn't scream, the rope didn't allow enough air for that. Yet, she became visibly excited as I approached her. Those rotting hands of hers began to reach out for me. I felt them graze against the top of my helmet.

I didn't know how to put her down. The ceiling was unusually high and I wasn't anywhere near tall enough for a head shot with my knife. Fortunately, the chair she probably used to hang herself was nearby.

I wheeled the office chair in front of the poor woman and climbed on top of it. I was now level with her head. I wanted to put her down with one swing, so I waited until she pivoted at just the right angle and I pulled back for a swing.

She grabbed a hold of the strap on my helmet.

I freaked out completely, and the wheeled chair went flying out from under me. It's a very natural instinct to reach out when you're falling down. Unfortunately for me, my natural instinct led me to reach out and grab onto the rope by which the woman had hanged herself with.

Her head was cranked back at just the right angle, so her biting me wasn't a problem. No, that wasn't my worry at all. My worry came from the razor sharp knife that was still in my hand: the very same hand that had instinctually grabbed for the rope around her neck as I fell. There's something to be said for Cold Steel knives: they are sharp as hell. Believe it or not, the knife cut through the rope, and both of us landed on the floor in a heap.

Unfortunately for me, the woman landed on top of me. At that point I realized her neck was no longer craned backwards. She was free to bite me.

I struggled. She struggled. Her jaws came towards my face with a ferocious snap. I barely saved my nose from being removed. I had my free, gloved, hand on her neck, but the hand that held the knife was trapped between us. Her breath was horrible. I was gagging as I struggled against her.

She finally changed her position on top of me by lifting her upper body. The good thing about this was that it freed my knife hand. The bad thing was that she had moved in order to strike me. Her fists began to rain down upon me, one after another. Fortunately for me, most of them ended up on my helmet.

It was hard to keep my wits about me under the onslaught, but my hand found her neck as she came down in another attempt at my face. The skin of her grayish neck started to peel away under my glove.

The second attempt to bite me actually worked in my favor. It gave me the brief moment I needed to gather my senses and go on the attack. I started to stab at her side, beneath the ribcage. I realized it wouldn't kill her, but I was hoping to distract her enough to allow me a chance to escape.

It didn't really work.

The zombie woman barely even registered the fact that I was stabbing her. The fluids in her body began to gush out of the wounds I was creating. Following all the fluids were a number of internal organs as well. No doubt they were pushed out due to the pressure in her abdomen from the bloating. It was a disgusting mess. The handle on my knife was becoming rather slippery

When she pulled back to start punching at my head again, I finally saw my best chance. I pulled my blade free of her side and grabbed the rope around her neck with my free hand. I pulled her back towards my face. The sudden motion knocked her slightly off balance as she came towards me, and I brought my knife up under her chin.

The kill was instant. My weapon went in under her chin and penetrated all the way into her brain. The poor woman collapsed on top of me.

I pushed her off immediately and got to my feet. Adrenaline was coursing through my veins. My legs felt weak, and my hands were shaking. Actually, my entire body was shaking.

I didn't know whether to let loose with a triumphant Tarzan-type yell or rush to the bathroom and get sick. The situation was just way too close.

I almost died.

I guess it's one thing to shoot them from a distance, but another thing entirely to lock yourself into mortal combat with one of them, and emerge as the victor. I made up my mind. I felt sick. My head began to swim, and I sat down on the edge of the bed.

That's when I noticed Merrick sitting there, as proper as you please, not far from the remains of the zombie. She had been attacking the woman's legs as I struggled with her upper half. Merrick had done about as much damage as I had. The woman's right leg had pretty much been severed at the knee, and her left was badly mangled. She must have been making a lot of noise as she savaged the woman's legs. Merrick always makes a lot of noise when she attacks, but I never even heard the smallest growl.

"*Why do you think that was?*"

I think I was so caught up in trying to survive I just pretty much blocked out the world. I ended up sitting on that bed for hours. I was still sitting there when the sky began to darken outside. I hadn't heard from Jax, or anything from anyone. I was alone in hostile territory. I could still hear the moans of the living dead echoing around from outside the house.

I wasn't terribly safe. Jaxon had broken the back door to the house. For all I knew, there were already some unwanted guests entering the home in search of a living meal. The room was pretty dark when I heard the creaking of the back door. The only light available was coming from a window in the bathroom.

I didn't know where my knife was.

I didn't want to use my firearms. The noise was way too loud even with silencers, and I didn't carry a 9mm on my hip like Jaxon. I carried a .45. It was a hell of a gun, but it didn't silence anywhere near as well as Jaxon's Sig. I needed my knife.

I frantically began to search the floor. Merrick was wagging her tail as her gaze shifted between the door and me. She knew we weren't alone. I felt the icy chill of fear begin to crawl up my spine. My stomach began to churn acid as I searched, and searched, for my knife. It was the only weapon I could even begin to fathom using. I needed my knife.

I heard footsteps approaching me.

I heard the soft click as the doorknob was gently turned. Merrick began to whine, and suddenly, my hand closed upon the handle of my knife. I could feel the smoothness of the wood through my glove. I could feel the metal of the guard, and finally I felt the heft of the weapon as I lifted it in my hand.

This is funny, but I really remember this quite well. I stood up with that big knife in my hand and felt like I had just pulled Excalibur out of the stone. I felt that powerful. I finally understood why Jaxon was such a bladed weapons buff. They made you feel like a warrior. I knew my blade was good. I knew my blade would not fail me.

I had finally become a warrior. Was I still afraid? Yes, I was, but not as much as the enemy lurking behind the door was going to be.

I moved across the room as the door pushed slowly open. A crouched figure entered the room. I would destroy it easily. I could destroy it easily. My enemy was only one lonely figure, and it would take legions to bring me down.

I swung my blade towards its head.

I have no idea what happened after that. Suddenly, my entire arm was numb. An almost electric pain was jolting around near my armpit and I was swung violently forward and turned around all at the same time. My back should have slammed into the wall, but I was stopped inches before the impact. Again I was driven forward until I fell forward onto the softness of the bed. I had a brief moment of confusion as I awaited the final act that would surely end my life, but it never came. Instead, I felt powerful legs wrap around my torso and I felt the snakelike squeeze as those same legs tightened around me. Finally, I heard the familiar laughter as my attacker began to spank me.

"I'm sorry, did you say spank?"

Oh yeah, Jaxon was having a great time. He had me face down on the bed underneath him and he was spanking the hell out of me while cackling the entire time. I knew it was him the moment he clenched his legs around me. I've wrestled with him before. He said he was teaching me how to defend myself, but in reality I think he just enjoyed bullying me.

I found myself laughing out loud at poor Georgie's expense. All the suspense lead up to a massive spanking. I felt bad. I really did. I just couldn't help but laugh.

I'm sure it sounds pretty funny to hear, but if you were me during that situation, well, it wasn't really funny. The spankings only stopped to be replaced by drumming on my helmet as the bastard continued to laugh at me. The real insult came when I felt Merrick begin to hump my leg.

"Okay," I complained. "Okay, I'm done. Let go of me."

"Hold on," Jaxon said. "Merrick isn't finished."

Fortunately for me, he was joking. He released me and scooped up Merrick into his arms.

"Did Georgie take care of you baby?" Jaxon said to his dog. "He better have, or we'll beat him up again won't we?"

"Where the hell have you been?" I asked. "Do you have any idea what I've been through?"

Jaxon didn't even look around the room as he answered me. He had probably taken in the entire scene within a second of entering.

"My first guess is some weird type of orgy," Jax said. "But I'm going to be just fine if you never share the details with me."

"Oh, that's lovely," I snarled. "Now where have you been?"

"I was leading the zombies away from your hyperventilating ass, or did you already forget how I totally saved you earlier?"

"You left me here."

"Because you couldn't run anymore. I thought you were going to have a heart attack on me. Hell, I thought you were already dead. Why didn't you answer your radio?"

"Nobody called me on it."

"The hell we didn't. I must have called you a billion times. I was very worried about my poor

Merrick being left with your candy ass. Then again, I thought you might need a bodyguard."

I then remembered I had turned off my earpiece. I wanted to turn it back on, but the humiliation would be more than I could even think about bearing. I would wait to turn it back on when Jaxon wasn't paying attention.

"What happened to the helicopters?" I asked. "I heard you radio in for them."

"I just needed them to point out a clear escape route. Man, this area is seriously hostile."

"I don't get where they all came from." I said. "That was another trap, wasn't it? One second the street was deserted and in the next second we were swarmed."

"Yeah, we walked into another trap. There were zombies stuffed in houses all up and down that road. I don't even want to guess how our little friend accomplished that one, but it's the second time I fell for it. There won't be a third."

"So the tracks in the desert..."

"Were probably part of the trap. She knew we would go look for Kingsley, and she probably wanted us to be near that house so we could hear some noise coming from it. Not sure about the burial in the desert, but I'm pretty sure the tracks were a plant."

"She probably knew we would head off in that direction," I thought out loud. "Where else could we go?"

"Yup, and she probably has traps like that all over the place. We just happened to step right into one of them."

"Maybe this is out of our league," I said. "This chick is smart. Eventually, she's going to either take us out one by one, or we're going to step into another one of her booby traps and finally get caught."

"I don't think Kingsley is dead," Jaxon said.

"Come again?"

"It doesn't make any sense to kill him. I didn't think the desert burial made any sense to begin with, but if this vampire is hunting us, wouldn't it make better sense to keep Kingsley alive?"

"No, why bother? It would be a lot easier to kill him off and, yeah, why would she bother to bury him? That doesn't make sense. Then again, why would she keep him alive?"

"If you plan on setting a trap, you're going to need some decent bait."

It made sense. Maybe it was too good to be true, but it made sense. There was a chance Kingsley was still alive. It didn't mean he was going to stay that way, especially if we didn't rescue him sooner rather than later, but at least we had a chance.

"How are we going to find him?"

"No idea," Jaxon said. "We're going to have to wait for the vampire to make the first move. Until then, I think we need to play things as if we actually believe he's dead. That'll cause her to show some cards."

"Then we need to get out of here," I said. "Let's call back those choppers."

"Why call back the choppers?"

"You don't hear all those shamblers out there?"

"So?"

"We're kind of trapped here," I said.

"Nah," Jaxon said. "While you were having your little slumber party, I already went and picked up the Jeep."

Getting to the Jeep wasn't exactly the easiest thing I've ever tried to do in my life. There were still way too many shamblers outside the house. That we actually made it to the Jeep is all that's important. Jax had Merrick and me get into the vehicle while he took out all the zombies that had gotten close enough to make him uncomfortable.

He made it look easy.

As soon as I started the engine, he hopped in the back seat and started popping off shots while I drove us out of the area.

"Are we headed back to the Safe Zone?" I asked.

"No, we are going to meet up with everyone else at that mountain church off Westwind."

"The church all alone on that big hill?" I asked.

"Yeah, they are extracting that lady and the kid Nick saved. If we're lucky, Nick will get on the helicopter as well."

"That church isn't off Westwind by the way," I said.

"Well, you can see it from Westwind so we can figure it out from there, asshole."

"I don't need to figure it out. I know how to get there. I was just wondering if you did."

"I could find it," Jaxon said. "Does that bother you?"

"Does what bother me?"

"My awesomeness," Jaxon said with a smile. "I understand that a lot of people are put off by my awesomeness. So, when you pointed out that the church wasn't actually on Westwind, I assumed that maybe you were trying to make yourself feel a little bit better."

"Well, I am better at directions than you are."

"So are a lot of people, but that doesn't make them awesome."

"What's your definition of awesome?" I asked.

"I don't need a definition. I'm the living embodiment of awesome. Don't waste your time with definitions, you geek. Just pay attention to the things I do, and possibly you will be fortunate enough to one day understand.

"Do you actually believe that shit, you arrogant prick?"

"Only if it irritates you."

"I'm immune to you," I replied.

"I don't think you are," Jax said.

"Too bad for you then, because I am."

"What about if I tell everyone how you hid in some house like a little girl while I whooped undead ass all around the neighborhood?"

"I would actually be more shocked to find out that you hadn't already told everybody I was hiding in that house."

Jaxon started laughing.

"You already told them didn't you?"

Jaxon started laughing harder.

"I'm not liking you right now. I want you to know that."

Jaxon then tapped his earpiece.

"Dudley," Jax said. "Tell Georgie what you said about him hiding out in the house."

"Not right now," Dudley said.

Suddenly Jaxon became very serious.

"What's up?" Jaxon asked.

"Nick set off another booby trap. We're in a bit of a jam."

"What about the extraction?" I asked.

Jaxon looked at me questioningly. I knew he was wondering why my earpiece was suddenly working again.

"The extraction has already been completed. Now how soon can you get here?" Dudley asked.

"Very soon," Jaxon answered.

I hit the gas, and we moved.

I made it to the long road that leads up to the church in just a few minutes. In the middle of the road was the other Jeep. Fortunately it was empty, because there were about fifty zombies passing by it as we pulled up.

"Kill the engine," Jaxon said.

As soon as I killed the engine, we could hear the zombie screams and muffled shots coming from further up the hill. They were already in the middle of a fight. The zombies running up the hill were just going to be the topping on the cake.

"Get to the top of the hill and stop," Jaxon ordered.

I started the engine once again and floored the gas. We hit the top of the hill and the entrance to the church's parking lot mere moments after the group of zombies. Dudley, Javie, and Nick were across the parking lot at the entrance to the church. Nick, and Javie, were shooting at the zombies coming out of the church while Dudley was firing on the zombies we followed up the hill.

Jaxon was already out of the Jeep and charging into battle. He moved so quickly it was almost frightening. The tomahawk and knife were in his hands, and Jaxon was screaming for all he was worth. He was trying to get the zombies to focus on him. If they managed to reach Dudley and the others, they would be smack dab in the middle of a small horde, and that could only be fatal.

I started screaming as well. It wasn't working, the zombies were still charging towards Dudley even as Jaxon reached the rear of the pack and started chopping them down. I started blaring the Jeep's horn. It was way louder than I could scream. It actually worked. The zombies slowed their pace immediately, and turned around to see Jaxon in their midst.

The group began to separate. Some of them went after Jax, and the rest continued towards Dudley and the others. The next thing I knew, Nick turned around and joined Dudley in firing into the advancing zombies.

Meanwhile, Jaxon was a demon. I don't know how else to describe it. I could hear the bones breaking and skulls crunching from all the way across the parking lot. Obviously I had seen him in action before, but it was something I had a difficult time getting used to.

I shook off the shock and jumped out of the Jeep. I told Merrick to stay put, and I started firing on the zombies that were outside Jaxon's slaughtering circle. Then I noticed that Dudley was yelling something at Nick, and Javie was yelling something at Dudley. At that point, I ran around the parking lot and away from the violence. My goal was to reach Javie, because I had a pretty good idea of what had happened.

I was being followed.

A few of the zombies had broken off from the main group and chased after me as I had passed them. I stopped, slowed my breathing and caressed the trigger. One. Two. Three. I nailed all of them.

Jaxon was still in the middle of the group and fighting for his life when I finally reached Dudley. I was correct in my assumption. Nick had abandoned Javie to go help Dudley and Jaxon with the advancing group of zombies. The only problem was Javie wasn't enough to keep back all the zombies trying to exit the church.

The situation had become critical by the time I joined him at the doorway. The zombies were literally right on top of him. I fired, and fired, as fast as I could. It only took a few moments, but the surge towards the door had been stopped.

"You got them all?"

Not yet, but we managed to keep them from escaping the church in a great big wave. Then I heard Dudley screaming at Nick again. I turned slightly to see what the next problem was going to be and saw Dudley reaching out for Nick just as Nick pulled out his fire axe and charged into the group of zombies.

"He jumped in to help Jaxon?"

I guess so, but Jaxon doesn't really need help. Even if Jaxon takes a bite, he'll be okay if we can get him healed. Nick, however, is a regular guy. We didn't even know for sure if he could recover from a bite. If Kingsley was still alive somewhere, then Nick may not have been touched by the Guardian's power. There are only supposed to be five of us, but none of us really knew if that was a hard rule.

"Javie, can you handle this?" I asked.

"I got it," Javie answered.

I turned around immediately and joined Dudley.

Jaxon looked like a scene out of a comic book. Every move he made caused damage. Every blow he struck was on target and devastating. Nick, on the other hand, looked clumsy. He would swing his large axe and miss. He would get swarmed, and end up running backwards to avoid getting bitten.

All in all, he caused a lot more harm than help. He was actually breaking up the crowd and spreading them out. This made it a lot harder for Dudley and me to get a good shot, because targets are a lot easier to hit when they are closer together.

In the end, Jaxon had to save Nick from being overwhelmed. He didn't do it kindly; he sort of shoved Nick out of the way, and finished off the five zombies that were trying to eat him.

Again, he made it look so easy. He ducked the first attacker, and slashed his kneecap before swinging his tomahawk sideways into the temple of the next zombie that came for him. As the third charged, Jaxon brought up his knife at the last second, and the zombie actually impaled his own head on the weapon. The fourth met another swing of the tomahawk: the weapon buried itself in its face. The fifth actually managed to grab Jaxon by the waist in a tackle, but before he could accomplish anything, the knife was slammed into the top of the zombie's head.

Nick was stunned from what had just happened. Seeing Jaxon work seems to have that effect on people, but he recovered enough to chop the head off of Jaxon's kneecap victim. He then smiled a shit-eating grin and raised his hand up high for a high five. Jaxon ignored him, and walked over to Dudley.

"What happened?" Jaxon asked.

"We came in and checked out the perimeter," said Dudley. "Everything looked good, so we situated Katie and Jason in the parking lot while we backed off farther down the road. I figured it would be the best place to provide any needed backup, and still give us an escape route after the chopper left. It was a good plan. I mean there's only one road up here. Any approaching zombies would need to get by us.

"It was a good plan," Jaxon agreed. "So what happened?"

"Nick thought it was taking too long. He left the Jeep and went back to the parking lot. After that, I don't know what happened."

"Nick?" the General asked.

At this point, Nick was helping himself to a serious piece of humble pie. His entire attitude seemed to have changed the second Jaxon refused the high five.

"Just like he said, Jax, I was worried about them, so I went back up. When I got there, Jason said he was thirsty, so I tried to open the front door of the church. I figured there was probably something to drink in there that he would like."

"Let me guess," Jaxon said. "You opened the door and found out the church was filled with zombies."

"That's right," Nick said. "I screwed up. I should have listened to Dudley when he told me to stay in position. I did my best to close the door. I even held back the zombies until the rest of the team could help me out."

"It was close, Jax," Dudley said. "We got there right before the chopper landed. If we'd have been just a little bit later, they'd all be dead. If you hadn't of shown up when you did, we'd be all be dead. I don't want him here anymore. He doesn't listen to orders. He's a liability that's going to get people killed."

"Like I said," Nick said. "I screwed up. It's not a mistake I'm going to make again. I think… I think I really screwed up."

With that, Nick held up his hand for everyone to see. The bite mark was small, but it was still there. Nick had been infected.

"Shit," Jax said. "When did that happen?"

"I don't even know," Nick answered. "I only realized it was there when I tried to high five you. How bad is it?"

I personally couldn't tell how bad it was. It didn't seem very deep, but it was difficult to tell because the wound was bleeding steadily. Nick was trying very hard not to panic. His skin had gone chalk white, and his hand was beginning to tremble. I didn't blame him a bit. I would have been crying like a baby.

"We need to wash it out and clean it up," Jaxon said.

Dudley and Jax both grabbed Nick by the arms and dragged him into the church. Fortunately, the bathrooms were close to the front door, so after wading through a bunch of corpses, they managed to get Nick to the sink. Javie and I kept watch at the bathroom door as Dudley began to wash out the wound with water from the sink and soap from the dispenser. Nick sort of collapsed into a wooden chair by the sink. Dudley wasn't being gentle with the scrubbing and there was a look of pain on Nick's face as Dudley worked. Jaxon quietly watched all this from a distance. It seemed as if he were waiting for the inevitable bad news.

"Jaxon," Dudley said. "You need to see this."

Jaxon let out a big sigh and approached the sink. Nick didn't even bother looking up at him as he came near. Instead, he kept his eyes focused on the floor. Jax stared at the wound for a long time and finally let out another sigh.

"Is it okay?" Nick asked.

"No," Jax said. "It's not okay."

"Oh fuck," Nick mumbled. "What am I gonna do?"

"You're not going to do anything," Dudley said in a sad tone. "It's too late."

"I'll do it," Jaxon said as he pulled out and snapped open his folding knife.

Nick's eyes went wide with fear.

"No," Dudley said as he pulled out his machete. "He's closer to you than he is to me. I should be the one that does it."

"I don't want you to have to carry that burden for me," Jaxon said. "I can make it quick. He'll barely feel a thing."

Nick apparently couldn't take any more. He jumped out of his chair in a frightful panic and started backing away from Jaxon and Dudley.

"FUCK YOU GUYS!" Nick shouted. "NOBODY IS STABBING ME! THIS IS BULLSHIT! I DON'T WANT TO GO OUT LIKE THAT! IT'S NOT FAIR!"

Jaxon and Dudley just looked at him in a sad way.

"He's right," Dudley said as he pulled out the pistol he stole from me. "He deserves better than that."

"Maybe," Jaxon said. "But, what if your hand shakes and you only wound him? I still think I should be the one to do it."

"Why would my hand shake?" Dudley asked.

"Because you like the guy," Jaxon said. "You might freak out when it comes time to pull the trigger."

"I don't like him that much," Dudley said.

"YOU ASSHOLES AREN'T LISTENING!" Nick yelled. "NOBODY IS GOING TO KILL ME! WHY AREN'T YOU LISTENING?"

"Well, you like him more than I do," Jaxon said. "I had enough of him in college."

"I do not," Dudley said. "I barely like him at all."

"Bullshit," Jaxon said.

"It's not bullshit," Dudley said. "I'll prove it right now."

With that, Dudley aimed his gun right at Nick's face. Naturally, Nick went into a full on panic. He backed up past Javie and I and screamed out a slew of obscenities while Jaxon and Dudley just stared at him.

Outside the bathroom and in the hallway, Nick found a plush recliner and picked it right up into the air and held it before his chest as if it were a shield that could stop a bullet. He carried his recliner shield all the way out into the parking lot and he never once heard the snickers and eventually full on laughter of Dudley and Jaxon.

"Wait, what?"

Nick was fine. The water had healed up his hand. He wasn't infected.

"So Dudley and Jaxon were just messing with him?"

Correct.

"That's mean. That's so mean. I can't believe they did that."

I was completely shocked. I was laughing, but I was shocked. I guess it was one of those things that are funny when it happens to someone else, but it wouldn't be funny at all if it happened to you. It was a really mean thing to do.

Yeah, it was a pretty rotten thing to do, but then again Nick did just endanger everybody's life.

"Were you and Javie in on the joke?"

Not at all. We didn't have a clue. Even when they started laughing, it still took us a moment to figure it out.

"How did they tell Nick they were just messing with him?"

That was even funnier. They both walked to the door and just watched him shouting obscenities from the middle of the parking lot. Nick was so freaked out he didn't even realize they were laughing at him. Then Jax gave out a shrill whistle, and Merrick bounded out of the Jeep, ran up behind Nick, and bit him in the ass.

At this point, I was laughing heartily. In fact, I was laughing so hard I was actually crying and having problems catching my breath.

She didn't bite him hard, mind you. She just gave him a nasty little nip. Nick freaked out even more and dropped the recliner on his foot. Now all of us were laughing hysterically at the poor guy. It was just too funny, and to be honest, Nick sorta deserved it.

He finally noticed we were laughing at him. He didn't know how to react. Finally, he looked at the clean wound on his hand and then he got pissed.

"Oh, you guys are funny." Nick said. "That's just a riot!"

Everyone else was still laughing, but I knew Nick from way back in college. I knew better than to push my luck. The dude got scrappy when he was pissed.

"That was not okay," Nick said as he walked over to us. "I don't know why you're laughing: that wasn't funny."

The smile vanished from Jaxon's face, and he moved forward to meet Nick in the parking lot.

"Actually," Jaxon said in a sinister tone. "It was funny. It was also deserved. Your actions jeopardized my team and could have cost someone their life. This isn't a game and it sure as fuck isn't the Nick show. I make the rules around here, and if I happen to be absent, Dudley is in charge. You can accept it...or you can do something about it."

They were now face to face. Well...Nick is a lot taller than Jaxon; so let's just say that they were up in each other's grill. I truly began to get a little nervous. Neither of these guys were the type to back down. I simply could not see how a fight could be avoided.

"Would it have even been a fair fight?"

I don't know. Nick is a huge guy, but Jaxon knows how to fight and let's not forget he is the Guardian. Then again, Nick punched out a lot of drunks back in college. I don't really know who would have won, but it would have been a bitch to break them up.

Luckily, instead of throwing a punch, Nick mumbled something quietly to Jaxon. Jaxon began to mumble something back, and Merrick started to wag her tail. The tension lifted. I'm not exactly sure what they were talking about, but it consisted of a lot more mumbling from Jaxon, and a lot of head nodding from Nick. When Nick offered his hand and Jaxon shook it, I knew all would be well.

"You never found out what they were saying?"

Knowing Jax, it was probably very straightforward. I'm guessing he let Nick know who the boss was and what the rules were. If Nick didn't like it, he was free to leave. If he screwed up again and someone got hurt, well, I'm sure he explained some consequences for that as well.

Life, however, wasn't even close to getting better for me. As soon as they came back to the doorway of the church where the rest of us were standing, Nick waited for everyone to get distracted, and promptly hit me in the balls with the handle of his axe.

"I saw you laughing asshole," Nick said as he smiled at me.

I didn't have a chance to respond. I'm not sure I would have even if I had a chance. I wish I could have just shot him in the leg or something, but I'm not sure Jaxon would appreciate that too much. Anyway, Hardin chose that very second to radio in. He was speaking to Jaxon, but it was an open communication, and all of us could hear what he was saying.

"Jax," Hardin said. "We've got big problems."

"What's going on?" Jaxon said.

"We have two teams down, and we've just lost contact with the third."

"I thought you were removing the teams from the area?" Jaxon asked.

"That was the plan. The Northeast team wanted to do one final extraction on their way out. I gave permission. It ended up being another one of those traps. There were no survivors. The Eastside team got attacked by your vampire friend, shortly after sundown. There were no survivors. This is rapidly turning into a cluster fuck."

"Wait up," Jaxon said. "What's going on with the Downtown team?"

"I'm thinking it's another trap. They entered an abandoned hotel for a final extraction as well. Something attacked them, but I couldn't get a clear visual before communications were lost. I believe they have lost some men, but I'm not sure how many."

"So there could be survivors?" Jaxon asked.

"These are elite teams," Hardin said. "I'm actually surprised we already lost two of them, but they just aren't used to fighting a supernatural being."

"So there could be survivors?" Jaxon repeated.

"It's possible," Hardin answered.

"Jax," I said. "We need to check it out. If we keep hunting the vampire, we may find a lead on Kingsley."

"I agree," Jaxon said. "But we still need to extract the rest of the survivors."

"What do you mean find a lead on Kingsley?" Javie said.

"We didn't see a body," I answered. "We found a grave. We probably should have checked it out but we're guessing it was probably just a lead up to a trap we fell into. We were also thinking that live bait would work better than just killing him."

"So Kingsley could still be alive?" Dudley asked.

"It may be wishful thinking," Jaxon said, "but there is a chance."

"So what do you want to do?" Dudley asked.

"I want to see if I can track this bitch down and find my friend," Jaxon answered. "And this possible trap is the only crappy lead we have right now. I'll take Nick with me and check it out. Dudley, you take the rest of the team and continue with the extractions. Take Merrick as well; she'll be a good bodyguard for Georgie."

"Should we be splitting up?" I asked.

"I would like to look for Kingsley," Javie said.

"I'm sure everybody would," Jaxon said. "We just can't forget about all of those trapped survivors while we search for our friend. I'm taking Nick with me. I want to make sure he's learned to be a team player. The rest of you can keep on with the extractions."

Just like that, it was over. Our jobs were given and we set out to do them.

"Were you disappointed you weren't going out after the vampire?"

It wasn't the vampire we were concerned about. We just wanted to find Kingsley, but yeah, I think everybody not going was disappointed. Kingsley was a teammate and a friend. We wanted him back.

Chapter 6

SNAKE CHARMER

It was quite a journey to reach the man I can only refer to as "Snake Charmer." I can't actually reveal where it was I met with him, but I can tell you that it was overseas. I have also been asked to not give too detailed a description, other than to say he is tall—though not as tall as Nick—has a muscled body, and a thick beard.

Snake Charmer works in one of the most elite sections of the military; again, I cannot reveal which one. His job description has only been explained to me as one that allows him to save and take the lives of others. He is a very intelligent and well-trained man.

When he walked into the room, I could immediately tell he was very different from the Regulators— before me stood a professional. He didn't possess the humor or the carefree attitude I was used to seeing. Before me was a man who chose his line of work because it appealed to him. He wasn't chosen like Jaxon.

These differences are why I worked very hard to get an interview with him.

Ma'am.

"You are a rather difficult man to meet. Um, should I call you Snake Charmer or Mr. Snake Charmer?"

You can call me Snake, ma'am. That's what my team calls me.

"Okay, that sounds easy enough. I've been briefed on what information is classified, but as far as I know, your involvement in one of the extraction teams is fair game. Am I correct?"

Yes, ma'am. I have been instructed to cooperate, and answer any questions you may have concerning that mission.

"Okay then, take me back to when you first got the assignment."

It wasn't much of an assignment, ma'am. My team had just finished a mission and was called into a briefing. At the time, the contents of the meeting were considered top-secret, but I have been given permission to explain it to you.

"Please do so."

We were briefed about certain aspects of the supernatural world that have been kept a secret from the public since the dawn of men fighting monsters. We were told that a large zombie outbreak in El Paso Texas had just blown the lid off the secret supernatural world. We were informed that special men were chosen as Guardians to fight these supernatural creatures. We were also advised that certain parties were awaiting a Guardian to be chosen from inside of the city of El Paso.

"What else were you told?"

We were told the zombie presence in El Paso was of a particularly bad nature, and if the Guardian failed, the entire country would be at risk.

"Were you asked to intervene?"

No, ma'am. The situation needed to play out. We were only asked to provide two volunteers if things went south. I volunteered immediately as did another teammate you may refer to as Scalp Hunter.

"Okay, as it turned out things didn't go south. A Guardian was chosen, and he eventually led a large group of survivors out of the city. What happened next for you?"

Well, we watched the situation unfold. I won't speak for Scalp, but I had a lot of difficulty believing zombies were rampaging through some city in Texas. It just didn't sound believable. At the most, I expected to see a few twitching corpses. I wasn't really prepared when I saw the first piece of footage that had been leaked through the Internet.

"What did you see, and how did it make you feel?"

I saw bodies, with injuries so severe they should have been dead, attacking living people and devouring them. I don't really know how to describe how I felt. I've seen some pretty terrible things in my line of work. I'm no stranger to violence, but that footage actually made me sit down and catch my breath.

It wasn't long before a man named the General came forth and through a series of events and probably some pretty tall tales, led that group you mentioned to safety. Suddenly, our mission changed. Things were working out the way the higher ups were hoping for. I didn't really understand this. I believed that a strong military presence should have entered the city and destroyed the zombies. The higher ups wanted the situation to be handled by the General.

When the General gave that speech and announced he was going back into the city after the survivors, Scalp Hunter and I were immediately shipped to a temporary base in the outskirts of Las Cruces, New Mexico. Once at the base, we were sent to a large warehouse that was filled with men like us.

"You mean military men?"

Not just men from the military. I believe there were some SWAT team members as well. Where they came from didn't seem to matter as much as them being proven in battle. The men in the warehouse had all been in some serious action. They also had serious talents.

We were informed that small teams were being formed to extract survivors. These teams would be responsible for whatever area they were chosen to work in. The job was simple enough. We would get directions to a survivor. We would extract the survivor. We would place the survivor in a safe place for pick up, while we retreated far enough to escape, but close enough to protect the survivor if need be.

No one ever explained to us just how hostile the environment actually was.

I mean, we didn't expect it to be a cakewalk, but we just...Well, I just don't think someone can truly prepare himself for what we were sent into. I mean, don't get me wrong, I'm glad I went. Those people needed help and I was glad to offer it. It's just, wow, it was terrible. It was easily the worst situation I had ever, or will ever, be put into.

Not everyone was assigned to a team. Most of the guys in that room were marked down as backup in the event that a team went down. None of us actually thought such a thing was possible. We were surrounded by some of the most dangerous men in the country. All of us were highly trained warriors. It was pretty ludicrous to think an enemy that couldn't even fire a weapon would give us any problems.

Scalp Hunter and I made a team. We were assigned to the Downtown section of the city.

"What were your opinions about the General?"

He was a joke.

"Would you care to elaborate?"

Let's just say that the men in that warehouse were given years of training. When things go bad, guys like us were the people that got sent in. All of us were from different branches, but that didn't matter much. We all knew that each and every one of us could be counted on.

"You didn't feel that the General could be counted on?"

Of course not, he was an untrained civilian. We had absolutely zero respect for him. He had no business being anywhere near any one of us. It was almost offensive that this guy was leading his own team. Don't get me wrong; it was a great thing that he did when he led all those people to safety, but now the grownups were ready to take care of things.

"Did you happen to see the 'famous fifteen'?"

Is that what they are calling it now? Yeah, we got to see it. The General took on a shit ton of zombies. It was impressive, but it was somewhat misleading.

"How was it misleading?"

When the men in that room saw the General fight, we automatically assumed we could do a whole lot better. Guys like me, unfortunately, come with a bit of arrogance. We watched an untrained civilian go to town on a bunch of zombies, and we in turn…well, we made assumptions.

"What kind of assumptions did you make?"

The footage led us to believe that the zombies are vastly inferior to the average man. It was pretty stupid of us to assume that, but hindsight is twenty/twenty. The zombies weren't at all inferior. Those bastards are lethal. It would have been better if the higher ups could have clarified that the zombies had just come through an explosion and were somewhat dazed and damaged.

"So you didn't believe what you were told about the General being a chosen Guardian?"

Did I believe that some random man was chosen to defend humanity against the forces of darkness, and that he was gifted with special abilities in order to combat supernatural threats? Hell no. Nobody was ready to believe that shit.

"Well, obviously somebody believed it."

Not the troopers. The people that believed in that crap certainly weren't in our warehouse. I had heard a few rumors over the years, but it was never anything I paid much attention to.

"What kind of rumors?"

I know I had heard rumors about a Mr. Hardin. Supposedly, everything about the man was black ops and classified. It was said that he was associated with a team that dealt with monsters. In other words, he eliminated nonhuman threats. Like I said, it was mainly nonsense stuff. I never saw the man and neither had anyone else as far as I knew.

"Mr. Hardin wasn't at the warehouse?"

No, he wasn't there. And let me tell you, the guys in charge didn't believe in the General either.

"At what point did you realize that Mr. Hardin was actually in charge of the operation?"

Take off.

"What do you mean?"

He spoke to us through our earpieces en route to El Paso. I think it was sort of getting around that the men in the warehouse weren't too convinced with all that we'd been hearing. He came on the radio to let us know differently.

"What did he say?"

He basically told us that if we underestimated our adversary, we weren't going to make it out alive. I'm not sure it was completely necessary. I mean, we were literally the best in the business, whether we were believers in the Guardian or not. We weren't exactly going to go easy on the zombies. I think he just wanted us to know the shit was about to hit the fan.

"Did his words have any effect?"

Any man that would tell you he wasn't nervous before he entered a city full of zombies is a bold faced liar. It doesn't matter how easy you believe those suckers will go down, you are about to fight something that shouldn't exist; something that has already taken over a city. So, his words didn't make us take our mission any more serious, but it did let us know that he was in fact a real person, and that he'd been facing threats like this for a very long time.

"How did you get into the city?"

We took a plane to our designated drop zone and parachuted from high altitude. Once we touched down, we were supposed to secure our own transportation and radio in for the first extraction.

"*How did that go?*"

It went fine. We all touched down and regrouped behind an old building without any problems or zombie sightings.

"*How many were on your team?*"

There were five of us. I was team leader. Scalp Hunter was there as well as a guy named Voodoo, one guy named Fox, and another guy named Pitt.

"*Okay, take me through the next few hours.*"

After regrouping, we immediately set out for a truck that Pitt had spotted as he was coming in. We figured that it would handle anything we needed. There were still no signs of anything hostile, even as we hotwired the vehicle and removed the two corpses from inside of it.

"*There were corpses in the truck?*"

Yes, ma'am. It was a mother and her son.

"*How did that affect you?*"

It didn't. I've seen far worse things than that. Unfortunately, it's a part of my job. In order to function and still do a job like mine, you have to really deaden the parts of you that will break up when you view an atrocity.

"*I understand. What happened after you got the truck running?*"

We radioed in to find our first target. It wasn't very far. We ended up leaving the truck. We figured the engine sound might be too loud, and it would be safer to hoof it.

We found the family in an empty clothing store. There were four of them in total, a father, a mother, and two young boys. They were half-starved, and the mother had a twisted ankle. Fortunately, none of them were infected.

Scalp was at the door covering us as we assessed how difficult it would be to move the family. Voodoo radioed in for our extraction point, while Pitt provided first aid for the mother's ankle. The situation was rather calm when Scalp gave out a low whistle.

I went over to him immediately and took the opposite side of the window he was looking out from. He pointed a finger in the direction he wanted me to look, and I saw the enemy for the very first time.

It's a lot different when you aren't seeing them on a video feed. There's something evil about them. It actually made the hairs on the back of my neck stand up straight. I tried to repress a shiver, but I must have failed, because Scalp noticed my discomfort.

"I had that exact same reaction," Scalp said.

I didn't respond. I didn't have the words. We both stood and watched the zombie make its way along the street. It was a woman. She was wearing a business suit and missing one of her shoes. Her hair was matted into a gory clump and stuck to the side of her face. Her face was rotted and it seemed as if the skin had actually constricted tighter over the bones. The way she walked really freaked me out. She walked slowly, but not slow enough, despite missing a shoe. It seemed as if she was more than capable of a sudden burst of speed if the occasion required it.

Mr. Hardin's words started to echo through my mind. These weren't slow moving corpses. They weren't hindered by death or decay. It was quite the opposite. These things were in better than prime condition, when you include the fact that they don't slow down or get tired.

"Take her out," I said to Scalp.

He gave a nod of understanding and went to the entrance. He cracked the door just enough to poke his MP7 out, took sight, and popped off a muffled round into the zombie's brain. The dead woman went down with an almost noiseless thump.

Unfortunately, she wasn't alone.

There was a pack of them around the corner. They must have been pretty far away because we never heard them. We would have never even of known they were there, but one of them ran over to investigate the fallen corpse.

It was the weirdest thing. They really have a very low intelligence, but seeing the zombie woman collapse must have piqued his curiosity in some way. I guess they are capable of being curious when something different than their norm occurs.

Regardless, the new zombie came running over to investigate. It had probably been a young man, judging from his clothing that consisted of a t-shirt and jeans. His hair had been cut rather short before he was turned, and I could see a tremendous laceration across his scalp. I'm not actually sure what happened to his nose, but it wasn't there.

He stood over the fallen zombie woman, and sort of stared at her. Then he lifted his head and began to look up and down the road. Going with my best guess, I would say that this zombie had probably seen other zombies get shot and drop. Possibly he learned to associate zombies dropping with humans shooting guns. It's just a guess, mind you. I really don't have a clue as to why a zombie does anything.

Scalp began to move towards the door once again. I motioned for him to stand down. If there was another zombie, there could be even more. I felt the hairs on the back of my neck begin to stand up again. I didn't like the feeling.

I went over to the father of the family.

"How many of them are in this area?" I asked.

"There are a lot of them. That's why we couldn't leave the store. Every time I look out the window, I see them out there. If they see you, it's all over."

I had heard about how dangerous the zombie screams were. I had no desire to bring down a bunch of them on top of us, but I also didn't want to be stuck in that store. Reluctantly I gave the order.

"Take him out Scalp," I said.

Scalp obliged me and stepped to the door. The door made a creaking sound and alerted the curious zombie to his presence. The scream echoed up and down the road. It was answered almost immediately, and suddenly the area became a hot zone.

All in all, I think there were about fifty or sixty that rushed towards us. It was a valuable lesson. Strictly speaking, we had never faced anything like that before. Most of the time when I shoot at someone, they don't want to be shot. These things don't care if they get shot. Also, two in the chest doesn't work. We had to adjust our aim for headshots. Anything less than a headshot, and we'd be lucky if we even knocked them off their feet. It was a different way of fighting. Of course, we were informed about all that. It's just a bit of a challenge when we're used to putting holes in center mass.

It got pretty close, but we made it through. It's a real test to actually remain calm and stay on target when they keep getting closer and closer. After the dust settled, so to speak, things got a lot easier. We hoofed it to the truck, radioed in, and located our extraction point.

We were lucky to be Downtown. We kept our extraction points on the rooftops of tall buildings. Two of us would lead the survivors to the top, while the rest of us set up shop on a nearby rooftop. That enabled us to snipe out anything stupid enough to come up after the survivors when our team members left.

It worked pretty well for us. We just made sure to choose extractions points as far away as possible from the ones we'd previously used.

"So you figured out a pretty good routine while you were there?"

Yes, I was satisfied with the results. We were highly successful in our extractions. That's why it came as a surprise when our Colonel radioed in that we were being pulled out of the area.

"It wasn't Mr. Hardin who told you?"

No, each team had their own set of advisors working behind the lines. Mr. Hardin oversaw everything, but he only dealt with the Regulators on a personal basis.

"Were you told why you were being pulled out?"

We were told that a new player had taken the field, and there were too many unknowns for us to remain. We really didn't know what that meant, but our extraction was scheduled for the following evening.

"When did you hear about the other teams?"

The following evening on our way to our extraction point, we were told that the Eastside team had been attacked. Halfway to our destination we got a call involving children at an old hotel. They left the extraction up to our discretion, but informed us that the Northeast team had been overrun on an extraction they tried to handle on their way out. They also said that it might have been a trap set up by the mysterious new player.

I put it to a vote. We opted to at least check the situation out. None of us wanted to leave any kids behind. The hotel in question was only a few blocks away, so we got there pretty quickly. The building was a brownish, dirty, color. The windows were all boarded up on the first floor. The front door was completely missing, and a large piece of plywood had been nailed up in an effort to keep out any trespassers.

It would have been easy enough to knock down the plywood door, but we were worried about the noise levels. Instead, we went around to the back of the building and discovered a loose board on one of the windows.

I was the last one in.

Once inside, we brought out our NVGs. That's short for "night vision goggles". The room was some sort of dining room. The place seemed to have been classy at one point, but it was obvious nobody had been there in a very long time.

Some of the tables still had tablecloths draping over them. There were dusty wine glasses on a few other tables. My team spread out immediately in order to make sure the room was clear. I went to a light switch and gave it a flick. The chandelier above the center of the room sparked and flickered a few times before bathing everything in a soft glow.

I was pretty shocked that the place had power, but there was still some sort of problem judging by the weak amount of light.

"Weren't you worried about the light attracting zombies?"

That really wasn't a concern. Like I said earlier, the windows were all boarded up. Not much light was going to be able to escape the interior of the building. Also, we were looking for a group of children. I was hoping the light might make them feel safer and possibly come out to investigate, rather than run and hide when they heard us moving around.

After the dining room was a long hallway with a tan and paisley carpet. There was dust everywhere. The hallway lights worked as well, but it was still the soft glow instead of a bright light. I would have preferred the bright light, but the soft glow was better than nothing, and we no longer needed our NVGs.

We weren't too worried about being rushed by any zombies lurking around inside the hotel, the boarded up windows should have kept them out easily enough. Still, we proceeded with caution. Scalp had taken point, and I was bringing up the rear.

The hallway opened up into the lobby.

My team spread out to clear the room. It was empty, but Voodoo found a place where the dirty carpet met a wooden staircase. There were dusty footprints on the staircase, and judging by the size of the prints, they were made by a child. None of us even noticed the child wasn't wearing any shoes until Pitt pointed it out.

We followed the footprints to the landing in between floors.

There were more prints on the landing. Judging by the new prints, there were at least five or six kids running around the hotel. All of them were barefoot, and some of them were very small.

Pitt was the first one to notice the bodies at the top of the next floor. There were ten couples lying side by side along the hallway. The soft light on this floor was flickering on and off rather badly. I wasn't sure how long it would hold, so I told everyone to have flashlights handy just in case. I figured that the flashlights would be better than the NVGs if the lights suddenly came back on.

I shined my light at the corpses. It wasn't hard to tell the cause of death. All of them were covered in savage bite marks.

"They haven't been eaten," Fox said.

"No, but they've been chewed on," Pitt said.

"That's not the point," Fox said. "Zombies don't just take a bite out of someone. They devour their victims. Whatever did this just took a bunch of bites out of them."

"Maybe they were all bitten and infected yet somehow escaped and came up here to die," Voodoo said.

"If that was the case, we'd be dealing with ten zombies instead of ten corpses," I said. "Somebody check for head wounds."

Fox immediately took up the task of manipulating the bodies in an effort to search for any damage to the heads. There wasn't any, but that wasn't surprising. What was surprising was how light and brittle the bodies were.

"It feels like they're hollow or something," Fox said.

The lights finally went out.

All of us immediately lit our flashlights. That's when we noticed the little girl in the nightgown standing at the other end of the hallway. She couldn't have been older than six years old, and her dark greasy hair was covering most of her face. The most disconcerting thing was the odd way in which her back was arched forward and her hanging arms were absolutely still.

"Little girl," Pitt said. "Don't be afraid. We're here to help you."

"I want mother's milk," the little girl responded in a voice much too low to come from a child.

Pitt began to approach her, but I didn't like the situation at all and told him to pull back.

"She's probably just traumatized," Pitt replied as he slowly walked to the little girl.

"I want mother's milk," the little girl repeated.

At that moment, there was an urgent voice shouting into my earpiece. I couldn't understand what they were saying at first, but they were definitely upset about something. It was our Colonel, I could tell that much, but he was shouting, and the higher decibels caused a static over his words.

"Repeat that," I said after tapping my earpiece. "Lower your voice. I can't make out what you're saying."

The lights came back on. Pitt was right next to the little girl and bending down to look her in the face.

The Colonel's voice came through my earpiece once again. I could tell that he was forcing himself to remain calm and deliberate.

"Make a full retreat," he said. "That hotel is a trap. It's filled with hostiles."

"I read you," I replied. "We'll grab the girl and boogie."

"Negative," the Colonel ordered with that same strained voice. "She's a hostile."

"What?" I asked.

"She's a vampire."

For a second I thought I was the victim of a cruel joke. A vampire? You gotta be kidding me. Then I realized I was in a city overrun with zombies, and suddenly the idea of a vampire wasn't too farfetched.

I looked over towards Pitt. I wanted to shout out for him to get away from the little girl, but her dead eyes locked onto mine as a black bile leaked from her mouth and she reached out for Pitt to pick her up. She wasn't human. My warning, when it finally came, was way too late. Her jaw actually unhinged just as she wrapped her skinny arms around his neck. Her mouth was filled with fangs—horrible, jagged, nasty fangs.

The lights went out.

In a panic, I fumbled for my light. I heard Pitt scream. I heard a deep-throated growl echo up and down the hallway, and then I heard other voices. They were the voices of children.

"I'm thirsty."

"Mother's milk."

"Come play with us."

"Mother's milk."

"I don't want the light to come back on."

"I get to drink first."

The lights flickered on before my panicked hands could turn on my flashlight. The little girl had fastened herself onto Pitt's neck. He was thrashing around the narrow hallway in an effort to get her off, but it wasn't working. I didn't have a clear shot. I could do nothing but pull my knife, and run to his aid.

Worst of all, behind the two combatants, at the other end of the hallway, were the children. They were slowly pouring into the hallway from the T-intersection at the other end. All of them had the same lifeless eyes.

The lights went out.

I heard the footsteps—they were moving fast. I again reached for my light. This time I found it, but not before one of my teammates found his own. Pitt was down. He was no longer struggling. He was surrounded by a troop of tiny bodies. I could hear the slurping sounds as they drank his blood.

The lights came back on.

There were more children. They were rushing past Pitt's body. All of them were barefoot. All of them had that black bile leaking from their mouths.

The lights went off.

I heard sounds on the walls and ceiling. We aimed our lights in that direction. Some of the children began scaling the walls on all fours in an effort to pass the children up front. They were actually competing with each other to be the first one to reach us.

I started firing.

I was shooting them off the walls. Scalp was next to me; at least I think it was Scalp. He was firing at them as well.

I heard a child's laugh come from above my head.

I raised my light towards the ceiling and looked up. Above me, clutching to the ceiling with his little baby hands and feet was a child even younger than the little girl that attacked Pitt. He was smiling while his bottom jaw distended far beyond the reaches of anything even remotely human. He then launched himself on top of me.

I dropped my light.

The hallway became a cacophony of screams and roars. I fought like hell. I couldn't even reach my weapon. In order to do so, I would have had to let go of the evil child clawing at the bite proof suit I was wearing.

I just wish we all had our vests zipped up all the way. If we had, Pitt may not have had his throat torn out.

I don't know how I did it; I really couldn't see shit, but somehow I threw the child away from me. After that, I ran down the hallway. I had no intentions of leaving my team. That's something guys like me just don't do, but I needed space in order to regroup and get back into the game.

The lights came back on as I reached the T-intersection. Scalp and Voodoo were somehow right behind me. I turned around and prepared to fire. Fox was pinned against the wall by about ten of the children. They had already ripped through his bite suit with their teeth and claws. He wasn't moving.

I began to fire at the children. I was even able to knock some of them off of Fox. It was a bad move on my part. I had gotten their attention, and they rushed towards the three of us in response. It was a pretty horrible sight watching all those little bodies crawling on the walls and ceiling. I doubt I will ever get that image out of my head.

We had no choice but to leg it out of there.

Unfortunately, we had gotten twisted around, and instead of heading towards the exit, we had no choice but to run deeper into the hotel. They were on us and in between us so quickly that Voodoo got lost in the chaos and ended up running the opposite way from us down the stem of the T-intersection hallway.

Most of the demonic children followed him for some reason. Scalp and I were finally able to lose the two or three that trailed after us by shooting and running.

Eventually, we made it up to what I believe was the third floor. Both of us had lost our earpieces, and Scalp had even lost his helmet. Both of us had zipped up the collars on our vests in order to protect our throats, but from what I'd seen, I doubted the collars would hold up for very long.

Scalp was trying different doors. He wanted to find an unlocked one. Breaking down a door would give the little bastards an easier time if they chose to come in after us. About the eighth knob he turned, he found what he was looking for, and we both just about tumbled inside.

"What the hell are those things?" Scalp asked.

"Vampires," I answered. "The Colonel told me right before everything went to shit."

"We need to find a way out of here," Scalp said.

I went to the only window in the room. It had bars on the outside. Why a window this high up would need bars on the outside, I had no idea.

"Well," I said. "We can't go down. We'd never make it out. My only idea is that we try to go up and get to the roof. Maybe we can figure out a way down from there."

"Sounds like a plan. Do you wanna go now, or do you wanna wait for things to die down a bit?"

"Let's wait it out and see what happens," I answered. "We may actually end up hoofing it out of the city if we don't find a radio."

"We've been through worse," Scalp said, but the truth of the matter was that we had never been through worse.

Fox had carried a computer and GPS, but Fox was down, and his body was surrounded by our enemy, who was immune to our gunfire. Things were indeed looking bleak. I was trying to think of something. I was trying to plan something; I'm not sure what. I guess I was hoping to figure out a way to make contact with our people and arrange a pick up.

Anyway, that's what I was doing when Scalp headed into the bathroom. I heard his low whistle and joined him at once. The bathroom was dark so I hit the filthy switch on the wall and a garish light bathed the room at once.

Scalp pointed towards the tub.

The pale green bathtub was filled with watery blood. It was a pretty nasty sight made even worse by the pale little arm floating at the top. We couldn't see the rest of the body because it was submerged in the bloody water, but what we saw was more than enough to make us nervous.

"This might be a food source," I said.

"Think we should leave?'

"Might be a good idea," I answered.

I turned off the light and both of us headed towards the door of the room. Outside the door we heard footsteps running up and down the hallway. Judging by the voices, it sounded as if the vampire children were playing a game of hide and seek with each other.

"We can't go out there," I said.

"Hell no," Scalp replied as he listened to one of the children counting down from one hundred.

"We're gonna be screwed if one of them tries to hide in here," I said.

"We're gonna be screwed if one of them gets hungry and comes in here looking for a snack," Scalp said.

Just then we heard a gurgle come from the bathroom and both of us became immediately quiet.

"We should check that out," Scalp said.

"I agree," I replied. "But I have a feeling I'm not going to like what comes out of that bathtub."

"Then let's get it before it comes out," Scalp said as he drew his combat knife.

I drew my knife as well. I didn't exactly want to get that close to one of those things, but I knew bullets had little effect, and I really had nothing to lose by trying a blade.

I hit the bathroom light just as we walked into the room. Nothing had changed outside the bathtub, but the bloody water inside the tub was gently sloshing about. The pale arm was still visible. Fortunately, it appeared the same.

"We can either wait," I said. "Or you can reach in there and drain the water."

"Are you fucking kidding me?" Scalp asked.

"How about pull the arm and see what comes up?" I asked.

"Waiting sounds like a pretty good idea to me," Scalp said.

We didn't have to wait long. It was maybe five minutes before we saw the arm twitch and heard another gurgle. A few seconds after that and the little boy that owned the arm erupted out of the bloody water. He was a vampire obviously. His dead looking eyes convinced us of that immediately.

The boy was young, maybe about four years old. He was wearing droopy SpongeBob underpants. He seemed confused as he looked from Scalp to me and back again.

"Where's my mama?" the little boy asked.

"I'm not sure," I answered. "Why don't you just wait here while we go and find her?"

I don't know why I didn't just attack the boy, by all rights I should have. I think it was the confusion in his eyes. That and his lack of aggression towards us just made it too difficult. Instead, Scalp and I backed slowly out of the room while the kid stood in that filthy water just staring at us with those lifeless eyes.

As soon as we were out of the room, I slowly started to close the door. I looked back towards Scalp, I was telling him something, but I don't remember what. I just remember his eyes going wide and when I turned back towards the door to see what had startled him, I was shocked to see the little boy at the door.

"I'm thirsty," the dripping child said.

"I'll go look for your mother," I replied. "I just want you to stay in the bathroom and be safe."

"You smell good," said the boy.

My heart probably skipped a beat or two when he said this. Whatever innocence the child still possessed after waking up in the bloody bathtub was rapidly vanishing. The nature of the beast was beginning to take over.

"Pick me up," the little boy said as he reached out his arms.

I wasn't anywhere near stupid enough to let him get that close so instead I started to try and close the door. I'm pretty sure I began to mutter some weak excuses as to why I couldn't pick him up, but they seemed to fall upon deaf ears.

The boy looked hungry.

His little hand shot out and grabbed the door. He was strong enough to prevent me from closing it any further.

"Why do you smell so good?" the boy asked.

"I just need to close this door while I get your mother," I answered.

He began to moan. It sounded as if he was in pain and his dead eyes were locked on mine. I tried to calm him down. I once again don't remember what I said. I just remember the way his moaning got louder and his lower jaw began to distend.

I reacted when I saw the fangs that filled his little mouth.

I kicked him straight in the chest. It was a hard kick. It probably would have sent an adult male to the hospital with a broken sternum. Being that he was so small, the kick actually sent him flying back against the cabinets under the sink.

He cracked the wood of the cabinets and lay very still for just a moment before he popped up onto all fours and snarled through the fangs.

"I'm thirsty," he shrieked before leaping on top of me.

He was so fast; I barely had time to raise my arm to defend my face.

Scalp had, fortunately, reacted much quicker than I had. The minute the boy sprang from the floor, Scalp swung his long knife. The blade caught the vampire child right on the side of the head. The impact, as hard as it was, didn't get him off of me. The knife even dislodged from Scalp's fingers and ended up hanging from the side of the kid's head.

It worked out in my favor, regardless. I was able to use the knife to keep his head away from my neck. The child was in pain from the wound. It didn't make him any weaker, but black blood began to ooze from the wound as he screamed and screamed.

Suddenly, he let go of me and dropped to the floor. I backed away immediately. He was glaring at Scalp. The hatred in his stare filled the room like a venomous shadow. I found my own knife, which I had dropped onto the floor while I was struggling to get the kid off of me.

It was a grotesque sight when the vampire, still glaring at Scalp, began to remove the knife from his head. I almost don't want to describe the back and forth motion he used to try and remove the knife, but it wasn't easy to watch. Maybe that's why I chose that particular moment to finally get in the game.

As the child was distracted with the knife in his head, I swung my own blade as hard as I could into his tiny little neck. Surprisingly, my blade didn't go through. Yet, I did enough damage to cause his head to flop at an unimaginable angle. These creatures were denser than a normal human being. I figured that out when Scalp's attack didn't slice off the top of his head. For that reason, I was able to retain my grip on the knife.

The kid turned in my direction as his black blood began to spurt all over the room. He began that awful moan once again. The moan was different this time, though. It was filled with anger as well as pain, and it ended in a shrill scream as he rushed towards me.

Scalp grabbed at his knife when the vampire turned his back on him. He twisted and yanked at the handle until it came free from the boy's head. I swung at the child's neck as soon as Scalp was out of the way. It wasn't until my fourth strike that the head finally separated from the body. Black blood was everywhere. I was, literally, drenched in it.

The creature was finally finished. We should have been happy. We figured out how to kill them, and we thankfully survived the experience. We weren't happy at all. The experience sickened us. Regardless of what that boy turned into, he used to be a child, and we had just committed an unspeakable act of violence upon him.

However, we were on our feet immediately when the door broke off its hinges.

In the doorway was the man of the hour himself, the famous General. Things had gone from bad to worse.

"*You weren't thankful to receive help?*"

We would have been thankful if we were truly receiving some real help. We wanted trained professionals. Instead, we received a liability. As far as I was concerned, keeping this guy alive had just been added to the list of things Scalp and I needed to do. Like I explained earlier, we had zero respect for the man, and being face to face with him only made things worse.

Let me describe my first impression and maybe you will see what I'm talking about. As far as appearances go, the General isn't as tall as I would have expected—he's probably a shade less than six feet, but he has pretty large shoulders. He looked like he could fight. The man was dressed head to foot in bite suit protection, including the vest and high collar. So the only difference between us was the different colors. Our suits were black while his was a sort of olive drab, and on the chest of his vest was a large skull with a western bandana around its mouth crossed with old timey pistols. He wasn't wearing a helmet. Instead he had a backwards Harley Davidson cap on his head.

It wasn't the way he was dressed that made me really doubt him, though; it was more about his mannerisms. His hands rested on top of his MP7 instead of holding the weapon in a ready position. He had a surly expression on his face as he sized up the room. He also seemed too calm, too assured of himself. It was as if he was mentally taking control of the situation without saying a word. That sort of arrogance could get a man killed. He didn't act like a professional.

"You, boys, having a rough night?" he asked, with a slight drawl.

It was the wrong thing to say to guys like us. We're not used to needing rescue. We normally act alone without anyone around to pull our asses out of the fire if things get hot. We especially didn't want someone that we have no respect for acting like he's doing us a favor.

"What are you doing here?" I asked.

I didn't like the way he sized me up and grinned when I asked him a question.

"The nerds lost communication with you," he answered. "We figured you might be in trouble."

"How did you get in here?" I asked.

"Loose board on a window out back," he answered in a tone that suggested I was an idiot.

I walked past him to close the door. I didn't want any unexpected visitors joining our little chit-chat. As I did, I noticed for the first time that he wasn't alone. Behind him was an extremely large man with a boyish face, making sure nothing attacked from the rear.

I motioned them both inside immediately, and then Scalp and I set about propping the door back onto its frame, and barricading it with the weight of the bed.

"Isn't that going to make things a bit difficult for us to leave?" asked the General. "Or do you plan on having a slumber party?"

I ignored his jabs and continued barricading the door. It wasn't great and it probably wouldn't keep anything out without us pushing up against it, but it was all that we had thanks to that idiot kicking in the door.

When we were finished, I finally turned to have a few words with the General.

"Let's get something straight right off the bat," I said. "I don't buy what you're selling. I'm not sure how you got up here without being attacked, but now you're my responsibility, and I don't appreciate it. From now on, you don't move or speak unless I tell you to. Pay attention and stay behind us, and maybe we can get the two of you out of here in one piece. Jeopardize us in any way, and we'll leave you behind. Got it?"

He didn't actually 'get it'. He wasn't actually even paying me the slightest bit of attention. Instead, he was kneeling over the body of the vampire child we had just killed.

"How many of them are there?" he asked.

"Are you listening to me?" I demanded.

"Not really," he answered. "How many of them are there?"

"There's about thirty to forty from what I could count," Scalp answered.

"Rotten luck," the General said with a sigh. "You, boys, are lucky to be alive."

"You've dealt with these things before?" Scalp asked.

"Just one of them," the General answered. "It was an adult though, nasty customer."

"All right, enough of this," I said. "You need to radio in for a rooftop extraction so we can get out of here."

The man moved across the room impossibly fast. He might have been as fast as those damn vampires for all I knew. I didn't expect it. I also didn't expect the slap he landed on the top of my helmet. I've been hit many, many times but never that hard. There were stars in my vision as I watched Scalp go for his weapon to back me up.

Scalp was too slow, or maybe the General was too fast. He had a Sig leveled at Scalp's face before the man could raise his weapon.

"I think we got off on the wrong foot here, boys," said the General as he re-holstered his sidearm. There was a smile on his face.

The meaning behind his actions was crystal clear. He could have killed both of us in an instant if he had desired to do so. I have to admit, I was impressed. I think he got lucky and caught us with our pants down, but I was still a bit impressed.

Even his backup guy was ready. He had what looked to be a fireman's axe in both of his hands, and he certainly looked like he was ready to swing that thing at us, and not regret it in the morning.

"Listen," I said. "You guys don't have the training…"

"Let me stop you right there, before you make a bigger ass out of yourself," the General said.

Then he motioned for his pal to turn around, and after fishing in his backpack for a while, he came out with two spare earpieces that he promptly tossed to me and Scalp. As soon as we had them on, the General tapped his own.

"Hardin," he said. "I'm taking control over the Downtown team. Make sure they know who the boss is."

It was only a few moments before the Colonel was relieving me of command over my team and placing the General in charge. I wasn't happy about it, but in the military you learn to follow orders.

When the General saw the look on my face, he actually chuckled.

"Now, now," he said. "Don't go pulling a stomp and pout. I have no interest in hanging out with you a minute more than I have to. I just don't want you getting all chewed up on account of me."

"What do you mean on account of you?" I asked.

"Some vampire bitch is after Jaxon," the big guy said. "He probably dated her or something."

"Yeah," said the General. "I might have dated her once upon a time, but anyway, she's set up a lot of booby traps around the city. Normally it's a bunch of homes filled with zombies, and when we turn the doorknob or something like that, all the zombies get released and fill up the street. This is a bit different, but it's still her work."

"So what are your plans for getting out of here?" I asked.

"Getting out won't be the problem," the General said. "I'm more concerned about leaving a bunch of little vampires alive. How long will it be before they decide to leave this building? I'm thinking our best chance is to deal with them all while they are still in one place. In addition to that, I'm looking for a missing teammate, and I want to make sure he's not stuck in this building somewhere."

"We lost more than half our team not very long ago because we tangled with those things," Scalp said. "They aren't like zombies. Zombies go down with a headshot. These things are hard to kill."

"Yeah," the General said. "I agree with you, but it also looks like you guys figured out the winning formula."

The General walked over to the headless body and nudged it with his boot.

"Not many things can keep kicking without a head," I said.

"Exactly, so let's put away the pop guns and get ready to handle things up close and personal."

"I don't think you understand," I said. "It took both of us to take out just one of these things with our blades."

"I don't doubt that," the General replied. "You're using some piss poor pig stickers."

"It's not that," I retorted. "These things are plenty strong and their bodies are dense. It was hard to cut through."

"Well," the General said. "I guess I'll just swing extra hard."

The General had no problems moving the bed out of the way of the door. After that, he was in the hall with us behind him. I'm not sure when the noises of the playing vampires had stopped, but I'm guessing it was when the General entered the building. It was completely silent.

"Why are the lights so dim?" the big guy asked.

"I think the electricity is faulty," Scalp said.

The General walked over to the nearest wall sconce and unscrewed the bulb. It wasn't easy for him to do, he was wearing fingerless gloves and he kept burning his fingers on the hot bulb.

"Low watt bulbs," the General said as he bounced the hot object from hand to hand before screwing it back on the sconce.

"This place was prepared then," I said. "Someone must have gone around and replaced all the light bulbs."

"Yeah," the General said. "I don't think vampires are overly fond of bright light. Let's start in that hallway where all the bodies are, and then we'll go door to door and see what happens."

"That's where we were attacked," I said.

"We noticed," the big guy said.

The light was still blinking on and off as the General searched for his missing friend among the bodies. The hallway smelled horrible. Human and vampire blood was splattered all over the walls. The bodies of my fallen teammates were almost unrecognizable.

"He's not here," the General said. "Let's start kicking down some doors."

"I have a better idea," I replied. "I can pick the locks. I can do it quick, and it'll make a lot less noise."

I reached into my pack for my little kit, but the General interrupted me.

"I wouldn't bother. They already know we're here. When they want to find us, they won't have any problems. It doesn't matter how quiet we are."

"So what are we going to do when they come?" Scalp asked.

"I'm going to kill them," the General said as he shouldered open the first door he came to.

It was, to say the least, a very ugly situation for Scalp and me. Being that we knew what the vampires were capable of, we also knew that our odds of surviving were relatively low. The General proved he could fight, but the odds weren't in our favor. Unfortunately, there was nothing we could do about it. We had our orders.

"*It must have been a very difficult situation for you to be in. Being forced to follow orders from a man you don't believe in couldn't have been easy*".

Don't get me wrong. It's not like I've never followed orders from a jackass. I'm in the military for crying out loud. It's just that, well, let's just say that it's been a while since I had to follow orders from someone I did not have complete faith in.

I could also tell from the signals Scalp was giving me that he agreed completely. When they came for us, Scalp and I would do what we were told, but if the General went down, we were going to get our asses out of that building as quickly as possible.

Going from room to room didn't take as much time as I had thought it would. There were only about ten rooms per floor and we swept and cleared each of them in less than two minutes apiece.

It wasn't long before we had reached the stairs for the top floor of the building.

"Did you find anything of interest in the search?"

Just bodies, lots and lots of bodies. The General searched every single one of them, but he still hadn't found his missing friend. Some of the rooms had blacked out windows and no bodies. I'm guessing some of the vampires slept in those rooms during the daytime, but I can't be sure.

"What do you call something like this?" the big guy said.

"Something like what?" the General asked.

It amazed me that they were actually capable of having normal, everyday conversations while they were smack dab in the middle of a very dangerous situation. The big guy looked a little nervous, but the General was calmly sipping water from his canteen and leaning against a wall as we took a short break.

Another thing that surprised me was that the General never seemed to notice how cold it was in the building. Everyone else began to shiver every time we stopped moving, but not the General. I even remember rubbing my hands together in order to make sure that they'd worked properly when the time came.

"A building full of vampires, what do you call it?"

"Let's go with lair," the General said. "How's that sound?"

"How about a nest?" the big guy said.

"I like lair, but what does it matter?" the General asked.

"It matters because I might freakin' die here and I want it to sound cool."

"I wouldn't worry about it," the General said. "I don't think people will remember you."

"Fuck that," the big guy said. "I'm part of the team now."

"Yeah, but you just joined up. Nobody knows you exist yet. Maybe after all this is done people will learn your name, but being that you might not even make it out of this building, I don't think it's that important."

"So can we call it a nest?"

"Yeah, that's fine."

After that, the conversation was over.

We were about to get into the thick of it once again. We had searched the entire hotel, and we had not seen a single vampire. That meant that they were all waiting for us on the top floor. I didn't like the situation one bit. The only positive aspect was if we were fast enough, we would be able to retreat all the way to the street without anything blocking our exit.

"You knew this because you cleared all the floors below you?"

Exactly.

"We ready?" the General said.

All of us nodded that we were. For the first time, the General removed the tomahawk from the back of his belt. It was a little foreboding to see him go for that particular weapon. Through all the previous floors, he had simply carried a black folding knife in his hand.

As soon as the General took his first step into the hallway, the dim lights came on. He looked back at me and smiled. He really is an arrogant bastard.

"Why did he smile at you?"

It was his way of saying I told you so to our earlier discussion when I wanted to use the lock picks, and he told me the vampires knew we were there and being quiet wouldn't help us out any. The lights turning on when we reached the top floor proved that.

The little girl in the nightgown once again stepped into the hallway. The chills shot up my spine so fierce, it was almost as if someone were pouring ice water down my back. Her walk was strange; it was almost aimless as she made her way towards us. She was playing a game. Black ooze dripped from her mouth as she looked at me and smiled.

"You found me," she said.

I'm not sure why she said that, but I'm guessing it was in reference to the game of hide and seek they were playing. I don't think I will ever find out either. The quietness of the building was interrupted by a *whump*, *whump*, *whump*, sound as the tomahawk flew through the air and split open her forehead.

The General wasn't waiting to see the results. He was right behind the tomahawk, and immediately after it connected, the knife in his hand slashed twice and the vampire's head fell to the ground before her body followed it.

"No mercy," the General said. "These aren't children anymore. They look like children, but they aren't. No mercy and no hesitation."

I was stunned into silence and immobility. These aren't things I'm used to mind you. I'm used to taking charge and acting. My team, my job, and my life often depend upon my ability to act intelligently under duress. However, the General succeeded in killing something that was entirely way too deadly for a normal man to kill, and he made it look easy. It was the suddenness that did it to me, the sudden and immediate destruction. I never before saw a man move like that.

Snake Charmer steps into some familiar territory at this point. I've heard many times from many different people how shocking it is to see Jaxon in action. The way he moves and the devastation he causes are apparently quite alarming.

I don't know if it makes sense to explain. Maybe it's something you need to see in real life instead of just hear about it, but the guy is scary good. He fights like no man should be able to fight. I'm sure I've said it before, but I'll say it again anyway. I've seen a lot of violence and action in my time, but he makes the things I've seen seem amateurish.

He was just getting started.

Once again, the little girl was followed by the entire nest.

The General didn't retreat. He didn't hesitate as they rushed towards us. He wasn't stunned by the speed of their movement. He wasn't concerned as they crawled across the walls and ceiling.

He eagerly met them in a deadly embrace.

His tomahawk twirled in his hands, and his black knife flashed up and down, as he took them out one by one. It was really something to see. He didn't normally kill them with one hit, but he at least injured them enough to render them temporarily harmless. He seemed to have complete situational awareness. Even when they came from behind, he knew. He knew, and he reacted before they could grab a hold of him.

I'm a believer in zombies because I saw them and killed them. I'm a believer in vampires as well for the same reasons. Despite that, I wasn't a believer in the whole Guardian business until that very moment. Because for the very first time I was seeing a man do something in a fight that I was simply not capable of.

I was watching a master at work.

Maybe that's wrong.

A master is a mere human at the height of his skills. The General is by no means a mere human. Human beings are not capable of doing the things he was doing.

All this happened very quickly. It's not like everyone else sat back and watched. No, we were fighting as well. The General was in the middle of the hallway. Scalp and I were at the far end. The big guy moved in between us, racking up his own tally.

The General met the charge, and the big guy attacked whatever got behind him with that big axe of his. Scalp and I attacked whatever got behind the big guy. It wasn't easy. The fighting was vicious, and it wasn't the type of fighting I was used to. I normally fought with guns and intelligence. If I was in a firefight, I followed the tactics I was trained in, and improvised when I needed to. Rarely did I ever need to go hand to hand. This type of fighting brought me out of my element. It was almost medieval.

We were bringing them down. We were succeeding. It was difficult. More than a few times I felt claws scraping against my vest. I heard the material tear from a far off place that wasn't anywhere near the fighting.

I was getting tired. Scalp was getting tired. The big guy was breathing pretty heavily, and his suit had multiple tears. The General must have noticed this.

"Do you have any flash grenades?" he shouted.

I yelled back that I had one and he told me to set it off in front of him. I pulled the pin and tossed the stun grenade just a few feet in front of him. It went off with a loud bang and an extremely bright flash of light.

We all had time to cover our ears and protect our eyes, but it still played havoc on our senses. The General got it the worst. He was down on one knee and using the wall to get back to his feet. Yet, all of us, though banged up, were recovering just fine.

The vampires didn't fare so well.

The light must have been extremely painful to their eyes. They were all screaming and clutching at their faces. They were running around blindly and slamming their small bodies into the walls of the hallway.

They weren't interested in attacking us anymore. They simply wanted to retreat, to go back to whatever dark place they felt safe in. I was shocked that they retreated so easily. Then I remembered that they weren't adults. Whatever they were now, they still had a child's mentality. We hurt them, and they ran away. An adult might have fought through the pain and continued the attack, but children don't think that way.

"Well, that sucked," said the General. "I was hoping to take out a few at a time since some of them have already fed. I didn't expect to deal with the whole nest."

"What the hell are we going to do?" the big guy asked.

"I'm not sure yet," the General answered. "But I'll figure it out."

I realized something about the General immediately. He wasn't experiencing any adrenaline surge. The rest of us had our hearts pounding in our chests. Our adrenaline was so high at that moment our hands were shaking. He was completely calm as if he had just woken up from a peaceful nap.

What does that mean?

Well, an adrenaline surge is your fight or flight response. It can help save your life, but it also causes a loss of hand and eye coordination. That's why a lot of gun battles use so much ammunition. The adrenaline surge ruins their aim, and they end up missing shots they would normally hit very easily.

There have even been some studies that were conducted to find out just how badly it can affect a person's performance. It also applies to martial artists. Sometimes their coordination suffers in the beginning of a fight, and they can take unnecessary damage.

I have a theory that a lot of the successful gunfighters from the old west somehow controlled their adrenaline. This made them extremely lethal because their aim was never off. My guess is that the General somehow manages this as well. His aim with the tomahawk was absolutely perfect.

So what does it mean?

It means he's completely lethal. He doesn't have a fight or flight response. Instead, he has a fight response without an adrenaline surge to damage his chances of success. Or maybe he does experience an adrenaline surge, but somehow he's hardwired in a way that it doesn't mess with his coordination, but I doubt it because he was way too calm after the vampires made their retreat.

His earpiece went off. It was a private message, so the rest of us couldn't hear the conversation. The grin was back on his face.

"We need to get to the roof," he said. "Miriam finally turned up something with her research, and they are going to drop off a present for us."

It was a relief to hear they finally had something that would hopefully give us an edge because, despite how well the General could fight, the odds were seriously stacked against us. The only problem at the moment was how we were going to get to the roof in one piece.

The General already had a plan for that.

It wasn't really very much of a plan, mind you. It consisted of him holding off as many vampires as he could, while the rest of us retrieved whatever was about to be dropped onto the roof, and then rush back to help him.

Of course, the plan was based upon us being attacked by the entire horde. There was a small chance we'd receive a moment's respite from their attacks due to the flash grenade.

We weren't going from door to door either. Our goal was to find the way to the roof as quickly as possible and then come back to mop things up. It didn't take but a moment for us to figure out the right direction. The way we needed to go was down a long hallway that led up a short flight of stairs to the metal door of the roof.

We could hear the hungry moans and the sounds of the vampires whispering to one another as we searched for the rooftop exit. We could also hear the sound of a helicopter coming from outside the building. The sound of the chopper was a relief, but the childlike whispers of the vampires were nerve wracking. The attack was coming. We just didn't know when.

"*What were the vampire children saying?*"

"Mother's milk."

"They don't play right."

"I hate them."

"Let's go find them."

"That man hurt me."

"I don't like the light."

"I'm thirsty."

Simple things like that. They weren't exactly capable of any deep thoughts, but it was a relief when we finally started down the long hallway. The sound of the helicopter was already fading into the distance, which meant that whatever they sent us had been delivered to the rooftop.

The General brought up the rear as our group rushed towards the metal doors. It was good that he chose that position. The attack was fast; much faster than anything we had previously seen before. It came from an older kid; possibly he was in his teens. I'm not really sure, but he was way too fast and way too strong.

He crawled along the ceiling leaving claw marks in the plaster as he rushed towards us. His bottom jaw was already elongated and that black ooze was smeared all over his chin. The fangs were what really caught my attention. They were much longer than those of the smaller children.

"Come back here!" the kid screamed at us. "Come back here! I want to talk to you."

When we reached the small set of stairs leading to the metal door, the General told us to keep going as he turned to face the incoming monster. I saw the tomahawk flash through the air and bite deeply along the vampire's back. I saw the vampire drop from the ceiling and land on top of the General, and then I was through the door and slamming it shut behind me.

Scalp was rushing towards our package. It wasn't hard to spot. The small black parachute was floating in the cold wind. Attached to the parachute was a medium sized plastic box. Scalp cut the parachute free, and the big guy opened the box.

It was cold in the open night air, but nowhere near as cold as the dim hallways inside the building.

I stood by the door with my knife just in case the vampire got past the General. I could easily hear the drama unfolding from behind the metal door. The battle was furious. I could hear bodies slamming against the wall. I could hear bones shattering as the tomahawk crunched against them. I could hear the vampire screaming.

Then I heard the screams of others.

They weren't the hungry moans. No, they were screams of rage. More vampires had joined the fight. No doubt, they were attracted by the teenager's boldness and the sounds of the fight. I knew the General would be overrun. It was the inevitable outcome.

I didn't want to go back in there. I didn't even like the guy, but I wasn't going to let someone like him die in a dim hallway when he was capable of so much more. I was reaching for the doorknob when the big guy was next to me all of a sudden and pushing a bunch of magazines into my hands.

It took me a moment to understand the situation. At first I couldn't understand why he would be giving me more ammo when we all knew that normal ammunition was useless. The keyword there was 'normal'. I saw a glimpse of the ammunition in the mag before I slapped it into my rifle. The bullets were a strange blue color. I'm not talking about the casing mind you. That was regular brass, but the projectile that actually shoots out from the gun was blue.

I had seen that type of blue before.

The big guy opened the door, and we saw a rather nasty scene. The General had killed about five of the vampires, but they just seemed to keep coming at him. There were also three more teenagers.

He was fighting them, but the sheer numbers gave them too much of an advantage. They were trying to surround him, and he was attempting to prevent it from happening.

"Get down," I shouted as loudly as I could.

The General took a quick look at us. I saw the confusion on his face for a brief moment, and then I saw a flash of teeth as he smiled and dropped flat on the floor.

We unloaded on the vampires.

The effect was less than spectacular. The vampires barely reacted to the bullet penetrating their bodies.

"Aim for their chests," said a woman's voice through my earpiece.

I believe the voice belonged to the woman named Miriam, but I never asked anyone. I just listened to her advice, as did Scalp Hunter, and the big guy. The results were instant.

I plugged one of the teenagers right in his center mass. For a brief moment he tried to take a step towards us then came to a complete stop and looked down at the wound in his chest. I shot him twice more just to be safe. He face planted on the hallway carpet, and I found another target.

The next one was one of the smaller vampire children. I took her down with only one shot. When the bullet impacted with her body, she just sort of sat down, looked at me with the saddest eyes, and dropped over on her side.

The vampires were falling.

For the first time we had the upper hand, and the three of us turned that hallway into a slaughterhouse. The General was doing a rapid crawl towards us when another teenager went for him. The big guy made a mistake and drilled a hole in the vampire's forehead instead of shooting him in the chest.

The General couldn't stand up and defend himself with all the bullets flying over his head, and the teenage vampire was rapidly gaining on him. I was just about to take aim on the teenager, when the big guy finally nailed him in the lower chest. The vampire took a step back and then roared at the big guy. On his next step forward, the big guy shot him again.

"STOP THAT!" the vampire screamed. "It hurts!"

The black ooze started to leak from his eyes as he dropped to his knees. The big guy shot him a final time and it was over.

When all was said and done, we brought down seventeen of the vampires.

"What the hell kind of ammo did they give us?" the General asked.

"I've seen it before," I answered. "This coating was used to make poison darts. It dissolves on contact with blood, so after the dart enters the body, the coating dissolves leaving only the poison to kill the victim."

The General then grabbed a single bullet and dipped it in some of that black vampire blood. The coating dissolved immediately, leaving behind a hollow pointed wooden bullet.

"You gotta be kidding me," the big guy said. "A wooden bullet won't mushroom out; it will splinter."

"I think that's the idea," the General said. "The splinters puncture the heart in several places, and it drops the vampire. It might take a few shots to get enough splinters in the heart, but apparently the old stake through the heart trick actually works."

"But a wooden bullet wouldn't actually shoot very well," I added. "That's why they coat it in that blue gunk to make it denser for distance, and to also keep it from breaking apart when it exits the barrel."

"Load up then boys," the General said. "We're going back in."

It was when we walked past the dead vampires that we realized they weren't actually dead. They were frozen, and immobile. They were in obvious pain, but they weren't dead. Some of them had even started a low whimper. Others had started a low moan. A few of them had the black tears running down their faces.

The General tapped his earpiece.

"Are you seeing this?" the General asked.

It was a private conversation, so the rest of us weren't privy to the details, but when it was over the General let out a deep sigh.

"Research indicated that wood through the heart was effective," said the General. "The research did not say how effective it was—only that the heads were always removed after the staking."

"I guess we now know why," I added. "The stakes probably just immobilized them and hurt like the devil, but they don't kill them."

"Sunlight and fire are also supposed to work," the General said as he once again pulled out his tomahawk.

It would have been easy to let him do the dirty work himself. I really didn't want to participate. Once immobilized, the vampire children lost all aspects of their true nature and appeared only as terrified children. In the end, we all assisted in the task. It's something I try not to think about too much.

When we were finished, we broke down the rest of the doors.

We hunted down the vampires. There was no place that was safe for them. We shot them down in closets and pulled them out from under beds. We found them in the shadows, and we destroyed the nest.

One thing we noticed was that the older the child was, the stronger and more lethal they were as well. The oldest among them required a lot more bullets to the chest before they went down.

"You said the vampire hunting you was an adult?" Scalp asked after all of us unloaded our weapons on the last of the teenagers and chased him down two flights of stairs, before he finally dropped.

"That's right," the General answered. "An adult female, and from what I can tell, she's a lot tougher than these little ones."

"I don't envy you at all," Scalp said with a laugh.

"That's okay," the General replied. "I don't envy me much either, but that doesn't mean I'm not gonna kill her."

After that it was more room searching and shooting. It took a fair amount of time even with all of us firing, but eventually we cleaned the entire hotel. We even went down to the basement. It was clear of vampires, but it held some bodies. Scalp and I found what was left of Voodoo. None of the bodies belonged to the General's friend.

I could tell he was worried, but he didn't say much about it.

Since the hotel was cleaned out, Scalp and I radioed in for our extraction. We were leaving by way of the rooftop.

"After going through what you went through, you were still being extracted?"

Those were our orders. The higher ups wanted none of the special teams on the ground until the vampire threat was neutralized. I didn't have any ill feelings because of it either. The vampires we dealt with were more than a match for us. I heartily agree with what Scalp said about not envying the General. I'll take human threats any day of the week and twice on Sundays.

When the helicopter came, Scalp shook the General's hand and thanked him for the assist. After I thought about it for a moment, I realized I wouldn't have made it out of the building without his aid and offered my hand as well.

He shook it immediately, and I leaned forward to whisper in his ear.

"What did you say?"

I told him I still owed him for slapping my helmet, and one of these days I was going to give him some payback.

"What did he say to that?"

He said I should feel free to look him up anytime I wanted to get my ass kicked.

Chapter 7

JAXON

Jaxon was tired when I next met with him. The entire team had started their morning with a long distance run. As always, good cardio seemed to be very important to him. After the run, they worked on hand-to-hand combat and completed their morning at the shooting range.

This isn't anything new to the team. Every member spends countless hours in training. If they aren't fighting, you can bet they're busy training to fight. Most of them don't mind the long hours. They are working hard on skills that will save their life, or the lives of their teammates.

"So, I spoke to Snake Charmer."

Wow, I'm shocked you were able to track him down. You must have some important friends.

"*I've been meeting some interesting people, that's for sure. He said you smacked him over the head and then drew on Scalp Hunter.*"

Yeah, that's true.

"*Can you tell me why?*"

He was acting like an asshole. I mean, I could have just radioed in to Hardin and taken over his team, but he never would have respected me. By proving that I could take both of them out let them know what I was capable of. My actions made me credible.

"*You wanted to intimidate him so he would follow your orders?*"

Not at all. I wanted to prove to him I was legitimate. He didn't believe in me; he thought I was a joke. I showed them my reputation was deserved and that I had even more right to be in El Paso than they did.

"*What if one of them had shot you?*"

I've been shot before.

"*Yes, I guess you have. Well, what was it like working with highly trained fighting men?*"

I prefer working with the Regulators. Don't get me wrong, those guys have skills, and if I needed to rescue a hostage or take down a terrorist, they'd be the guys I wanted with me, but I fight monsters. I fight nasty, biting, and scratching monsters that can disembowel a man with a simple backhand. I want the boys that are most experienced with fighting monsters at my back. It just so happens that my team is probably the most experienced in the world right now.

Guys like Scalp Hunter and Snake Charmer aren't exactly trained for the kinds of things we take on. To be honest, we aren't always trained for the kinds of things we take on. However, we adapt quickly. We haven't been rigorously trained in the regular methods of fighting. We make our own rules. Sometimes it looks like we're bumbling, but that's the thing, we go in loose and adapt to whatever jumps out at us from the closet.

"So basically, they are good for real life threats, but the Regulators are good for supernatural threats that don't follow the normal routines of men?"

There ya go.

"Okay, I'm very anxious to find out what happened after Scalp Hunter and Snake Charmer were extracted from the rooftop."

Immediately after the helicopter took off, I radioed to Dudley. I wanted to see how things were going for him.

"And how were things going?"

Excellent, those guys had managed to pull off one extraction after another. Plus, they had collected their own supply of wooden bullets, courtesy a helicopter drop off arranged by Hardin. It was also a relief to hear they hadn't run into any more booby traps, but I was pretty sure there were still plenty of traps out there, just waiting to be sprung. I told him to be careful and to be ready to back me up if I called him.

"To back you up?"

Yes, I had a feeling things were coming to a close with my vampire stalker. The reason I felt that way was due to the nature of the trap. All the other traps were zombie traps. We touched a doorknob and zombies came after us. This trap, however, was a vampire trap. The hotel was a nest.

I figured this trap was more important to her than the others because of the vampire children. Also, I put myself in the mind of a hunter and realized that if I set a trap, I would want to see the results when it was sprung. For all I knew, she might want to check on the vampires in the nest. They didn't seem keen on leaving the hotel, so somebody must have been bringing them victims.

I was guessing, or maybe I was hoping…I don't know, but I was guessing or hoping she would turn up before dawn to see how things had gone down, and dawn was only a couple of hours away.

"So what's next on the agenda?" Nick asked.

"We prepare a little welcome home surprise," I answered.

Nick followed me back into the hotel and into one of the rooms. I had left a couple of the vampires alive.

"What are you planning?" Nick asked.

"I'm planning on setting my own trap," I answered.

"They're just kids. We should put them out of their misery," Nick said.

"They stopped being kids when my stalker turned them into monsters," I answered. "My goal is to stop her from doing this to anyone else, but in order to do that, I need to get my freaking hands on her."

"I don't like it."

"Neither do I," I answered, "but I'm out of options, and she has a friend of mine captive. So unless you have a better way of bringing her in, hush up and grab a hold of its legs."

To give Nick some credit, he actually stopped grumbling and picked up the vampire's legs. We carried the paralyzed vampire to the roof and went back to get the next one. Once we had both vampires on the roof, I wrapped their feet up with some rope out of my backpack, and tossed them off the edge.

They fell about ten feet on each side of the building; the trap was set.

"Can you explain the details of the trap for me?"

Sure, I took the two remaining paralyzed vampires and hung them off two different sides of the roof. Across the street from each hanging vampire was a tall building of the type my stalker seemed to prefer, since she travels by rooftop.

My hope was she'd swing by before dawn to see what had happened with her booby-trap. When she approached the building, she would see one of the paralyzed vampires. If she circled the building, she'd see both of them.

After that, she'd have to make a choice. She could rescue the vampires or she could let them burn in the sun.

"*Wouldn't she know it was a trap?*"

Yeah, it was a pretty obvious trap, but if she wanted to save those vampires from burning in the sun, she'd need to do something anyway.

All Nick and I had to do was wait.

"*Were you certain sunlight would kill them?*"

Yeah, my stalker never bothered me during the daytime. Also, Hardin said earlier that sunlight would take them out.

So that was that. We just hunkered down beneath the lip of the roof and waited to see if she'd show. It was shortly before dawn when she finally made her appearance. Nick noticed some movement on the side he was watching.

"Jax," he said. "I think I saw something."

"What do you think you saw?" I asked.

"I saw movement on the building across the street," he answered.

I rapidly crawled over to him and looked over the lip of the roof.

"I don't see anything," I said. "Are you sure?"

"Just keep watching," he answered.

After what felt like a long time later, I finally saw her. She was in between what looked like brick support columns, about midway up the building across the street. She had also changed her clothes. For some reason, she was wearing a white tutu and unitard. It was an odd choice of clothes, to be sure, but I doubt vampires are very much in touch with fashion.

She was pretty much level with the vampire we had dangling off of our roof, and she was making a bunch of odd clicking sounds in its direction. I could see the black drool dripping off of her chin.

I removed my tomahawk from my belt.

Nick readied his MP7.

All she had to do was get close enough for me to pounce on her.

I expected her to jump to our roof, but instead she crawled up to the top of her own building and crouched on the edge. We watched as she paced back and forth. Suddenly, she jumped to a neighboring building and then proceeded to hop from building to building until she had made a complete circle around the hotel.

We waited patiently and merely watched.

She knew it was a trap. That much was obvious when she slammed her fist down on the edge of the roof and sent pieces of brick down onto the street below. She was frustrated, but she wasn't taking the bait. She didn't want to walk into danger.

We waited silently.

She began to pace back and forth once again. She examined our rooftop from every conceivable angle, but she never once saw us because we had moved away from the lip and ducked low under a billboard sign.

Dawn was less than an hour away.

She finally made her move.

The leap carried her from her building across the street all the way to the top of our building. If she'd stopped to sniff for us, she would have found us easily. However, she seemed to be extremely nervous and instead of checking her surroundings, she immediately went to the rope and began to pull the helpless vampire back onto the rooftop.

We made our move.

Nick unloaded on her, and just as she turned to face him, I buried my tomahawk deep into her chest. She reacted violently, grabbed the collar of my vest, and slammed my head onto the edge of the rooftop, before dropping the rope holding the immobilized vampire and rushing towards Nick.

It took me just a moment to clear the cobwebs from my head and shake the stars out of my vision. I unloaded a burst from my MP7 right before she could get her hands on him. She arched her back in pain and spun in my direction.

My tomahawk was still embedded in her chest. She grabbed the handle, wrenched it free, and threw it back at me. Much to her surprise, I caught the weapon by the wooden handle and threw it right back at her.

The blade of the tomahawk embedded itself into her collarbone and slashed open her carotid artery. The black blood began to gush forth, and she screamed so loud I had to cover my ears.

When she finally stopped, I noticed to my dismay that her jaw had elongated and filled with fangs. She was laughing at me as she pulled the weapon out of her collarbone and held it in her hand. I drilled her with another full auto blast from my machine gun. The impact spun her in circles, and Nick connected a solid, crunching, blow, to her spine with his fireman's axe.

I had no doubt that we owed our success to the wooden bullets. They weren't bringing her down, but she was definitely getting weaker.

The bullet holes were not healing, and black blood was leaking freely from the wounds. Her neck was still gushing, and she was trying to staunch the flow of blood with her hand as she ran away from us to the edge of the roof.

She hesitated, as if she was worried about making the jump in her injured state.

"Bastard," she said in a low voice as she turned to face me.

I shot her again.

She ran towards me, and Nick immediately started shooting her in the back, but she wasn't stopping. When she was close enough, she swung my own weapon at me, but I managed to duck under the blade, and slash out with my folding knife. She was getting slower. My blade was able to sever the connective tissue of her left arm, and she dropped my weapon as she ran past me towards the metal door of the building.

She was still scary fast.

The metal door slammed shut behind her with an extremely loud bang.

"Are you hurt?" I asked Nick.

"She never touched me," he answered. "How's your head?"

"Hurts like a bitch," I answered.

"It's no wonder," Nick said. "You're bleeding pretty badly, probably ruined your cap."

"I'll worry about it later," I said as I rushed towards the metal door.

She'd jammed it into the frame, and we wasted precious moments figuring out how to get through. In the end, Nick's fireman's axe was able to get in between the door and the frame and pry it open. I made a mental note to stop picking on his lame weapon.

The bodies in the hallway had been disturbed.

"I think we're in trouble," I whispered to Nick.

"Fuck that," he answered. "We've got this bitch on the run. Let's go finish this shit."

"Get behind me," I ordered.

Fortunately, Nick listened. It was then that I heard the laughter. I couldn't tell where it was coming from. It seemed to be echoing around the entire floor.

Nick and I both froze in the hallway.

The situation was bad. I didn't want to get stuck in an empty hotel with a bloodthirsty vampire without an avenue of escape. The situation would have been so much better out on the street where we could get away from her if things went bad. I had the distinct feeling I was a fly walking right into a spider's web.

"I don't get it," Nick said. "Despite her wounds, she's still a bad ass. Why's she hiding?"

I didn't answer. Nick talks a lot when he's nervous. It's best to just ignore him, because nothing else really makes him shut up.

I heard a noise coming from one of the rooms, and I rushed forward with my MP7 in a ready position. I kicked open the door to find my suspicions confirmed. The vampire was feeding off of the corpses of all the vampire children we had killed.

She had used their blood to jumpstart her healing.

As soon as I broke down the door, she stopped her feeding and hurled the corpse at me. I ducked out of the way, but Nick wasn't so lucky. The impact took him off his feet. I unloaded an entire magazine on the vampire as she streaked around the room in an attempt to avoid taking too much damage.

She was screaming so loud I wanted to cover my ears, but I couldn't ease up for even a moment, or I ran the risk of her healing completely. The cut to her carotid artery had already closed over, but her skin was a sickly pale color—and that's saying a lot, because she was already grayish to begin with. There were even dark circles under her eyes, causing her face to have an almost hollow appearance. She definitely wasn't in top shape, but she was still very dangerous.

In less than a second, she had grabbed a hold of me once again. This time I was ready for her, and as soon as she was close enough, I flashed out my folding knife and opened up her neck. She reacted violently and threw me across the room into Nick, who was just getting to his feet.

The black blood was spraying everywhere as she raced past us towards the stairs.

We collected ourselves as quickly as we could, and followed after her. The only problem was that in addition to my head wound, I now had a pronounced limp that was slowing me down considerably. I tore something in my knee when I slammed into Nick, and the stabbing pain traveling up my thigh told me it was probably serious.

I didn't have time to heal myself. If I took the time, we'd lose her. Then she would heal herself completely, and come back for us at a different time. It was now or never. I took the stairs two at a time, just trying to close the distance.

It wasn't until the final flight of stairs that my knee gave out entirely, and I tumbled the rest of the way to the landing. I came up on my good leg immediately and wiped the blood away from my eyes with my free hand.

Nick was staring at me in amazement.

I tried to take another step, but I only fell down again.

Things were looking bleak. I had lost the vampire. I had no idea where to look for her outside of the building.

Nick was trying to help me back up and restrain me at the same time when Dudley radioed in.

"Jaxon, you there?" he asked.

"Yeah," I answered. "I'm here."

"Are you still hunting after that vampire chick?"

"No," I answered. "I blew it. We had her wounded, and I screwed up and lost her."

"Well, I wouldn't worry about it," said Dudley. "I think I just found her lair."

"It's her nest, asshole," Nick said after clicking his earpiece.

"What?" Dudley asked.

"Never mind," I interrupted. "Give me directions."

Dudley was on a street called Baltimore. It was pretty close to UTEP; that's University of Texas at El Paso. I'm sure I mentioned it before, but it's the local college. I actually graduated from there.

How did Dudley find the nest?

Well, they were seriously kicking ass on the extractions. They had pretty much cleared out the remaining survivors while we were busy fighting vampires. The calls for help had become almost nonexistent— for lack of anything better to do while they waited for Hardin to find another survivor— they were just sort of heading down Mesa in order to shorten the distance between us, in case I needed backup.

As they neared UTEP, Hardin finally found more survivors. Luckily enough, the team was pretty close to their location, and they went immediately. The house was pretty old, but it was well maintained. A lot of the area by Baltimore is part of the historic district.

Anyway, Dudley and company went inside and searched the darkened house, but they didn't find anything. At least, not until Javie walked into the dining room and almost fell through the floor when he stepped on a rug.

They moved the rug out of the way and saw that a hole had been dug about ten feet into the ground. In this hole were seven survivors that had been chained to the wall—four women and three men. The vampire had been feeding on them. There were also about five corpses she had drained completely. The corpses were still chained to the wall.

From my understanding, one of the remaining survivors wormed her hand free and started going through the pockets of the corpses near her. She was lucky enough to find a cell phone that had Internet access and sent out a call for help.

Georgie was trying to break the chains as Dudley was telling me the story. I ordered Georgie to stop trying to free the survivors.

"Why?" Dudley asked.

"Because the vampire is wounded and she's probably heading your way. I want you and Georgie to jump down into the pit and pretend you are two of her captives. Have Javie and Merrick wait in one of the bedrooms."

"What do we do if she shows up?"

"Fill her with holes," I answered.

After I was done talking to Dudley, I reached into my backpack and grabbed some duct tape. Then I used my tomahawk to chop up a little end table from the lobby. I shoved my kneecap back into the correct position, placed two pieces of the end table on either side, and taped everything up. It certainly wasn't perfect, but it immobilized my knee just enough to allow me to move.

"*You shoved your knee cap into the correct position? Didn't that hurt?*"

It hurt like a bitch, but it takes time to heal, and time was something we didn't have. I didn't want to leave the team to face an angry vampire while I nursed a boo-boo. I still had a nasty limp, and my leg was shooting out sparks of pain, but I made it all the way to the loose window board and outside to the rear of the building.

The Jeep was parked across the street and down the road a bit.

I was using Nick's shoulder for support as we came around the building and started to cross the street. There were zombies there. They must have been attracted by all the noise but were unable to pinpoint exactly where the noise had come from, so they were just wandering around the street.

This is the same mistake I kept making. I got so caught up in the vampires that I forgot about the zombies, and every time I did that, it came around and tried to bite me on the ass. There weren't enough zombies coming towards us to freak me out, but I was far from top condition.

It was a little bit funny to see Nick's eyes go wide as he saw them rushing towards us. I would have laughed, but my knee was really killing me, and it sort of felt like it had slipped out of the correct position again.

Both of us began to fire on them as they came nearer and nearer. I didn't even think about using my knife or tomahawk. There was no way I'd be able to go hand-to-hand with my leg jacked up the way that it was.

I fired and fired, but then the worst possible thing that could have happened, did.

One of the zombies screamed.

It was a real nasty one too. For whatever reason, all of the skin beneath its nose was missing, and it seemed to have a permanent smile, as it looked at me and screamed. Both Nick and I stopped firing for just a moment as we waited to see just how much trouble that scream was going to bring.

We heard answering screams echo around the city in response; a lot of answering screams.

We needed to get the hell out of there, and we needed to do it fast. The current zombies were bad enough. If mobs of them showed up before we made ourselves scarce, we would have to waste time losing them in the Jeep before we could meet up with Dudley, or we'd end up trapping ourselves in the house.

The problem with taking time to lose large mobs of zombies is that my nephew and the rest of the team were waiting to ambush a hungry vampire, and they were going to need our backup.

Over the moans and screams, I told Nick to go get the Jeep while I handled our noisy followers. I figured we would be able to leave the area faster if I stopped slowing him down and allowed him to bring the Jeep to me instead.

"Dude," Nick said. "Are you serious? How are you going to fight with your leg all fucked up?"

"It's not a debate," I replied.

Reluctantly, he left me. Thankfully, he could move really, really fast for such a big guy, which was good for him, since the zombies were only about fifteen feet away. I was shooting and shooting, but

I wasn't fast enough to take them all out before they closed the distance.

When the first one reached me, I smacked it away with the barrel of my weapon just as the second zombie grabbed a hold of my shoulders, and attempted to bite through the bite proof collar of my vest.

I responded instantly by dropping my MP7—it was stuck between our bodies—and reaching for the Sig on my side. I pulled the pistol quickly, shoved the barrel under the zombie's chin, and popped off a shot straight to its brain.

As that zombie fell, the first zombie I had smacked away, dove for my legs and wrenched my bad knee. The pain was incredible, and I think I even screamed out as I fell to the ground. Somehow, I managed to work my left hand under its cold and clammy chin, and pushed its head back away from my neck. After that, it was easy enough to put a bullet through its forehead.

The next zombie, literally, dove from about five feet away and landed on my chest. He was trying to bite into my stomach, but my bite suit prevented penetration, and I was able to fire a round through its temple.

After that, there were more zombies trying to pile on top of me. The situation royally sucked for me because my wounded leg made getting back to my feet extremely difficult, and every time I tried, another zombie dove on top of me.

I think there were about four of them smothering me when I heard the sweet rumble of the Jeep, and the muffled shots of Nick's MP7. After pushing the corpses off of me, and using the Jeep to get back to my feet, I became aware of Nick screaming at me to hurry.

I really didn't want to look back down the road and see what he was so upset about, but damned if I couldn't help myself. One glance was all I needed. The road was filled with zombies, and the gang was getting bigger and bigger.

I dove into the Jeep as Nick hit the gas pedal.

The zombies were so close a bunch of them were actually able to grab a hold of the Jeep and begin to pull their decaying bodies inside, before I managed to sit up in the passenger seat and fire off a bunch of headshots.

The worst had happened. We had a horde of hundreds of zombies following us, and we'd need to waste precious time losing them before we could meet up with the rest of the team. Nick was laughing.

"What the hell are you laughing about?" I asked.

"I totally saved your ass back there."

"As opposed to all the times I saved your ass?" I retorted.

"When did you save my ass?" Nick asked. "I'd like to hear when you saved my ass, because that's news to me. Maybe you're just upset that you actually had to rely on someone other than yourself. You saved my ass? Bitch, please! I'm the hero in this vehicle."

I was ignoring him. Somewhere in the middle of his rant, I looked down at my leg and realized that everything below the kneecap was twisted and bent at the wrong angle. I had no idea where the pieces of wood I'd been using to keep my leg immobilized had fallen, but they certainly weren't stuck to my leg anymore. All that remained was a wad of stretched out duct tape.

The worst thing about it was it didn't hurt.

I simply couldn't feel a thing from my kneecap all the way down to the tips of my toes. I wasn't sure which was worse, my seriously fucked up leg or the battalion of zombies twenty feet behind us.

"Can you heal that leg?" Nick asked, when he saw how bad the damage was.

"Yeah, but it will take time, and I need water or something natural," I replied.

"What do you mean something natural?"

"Something living, like a plant or grass," I answered.

"Does it hurt?"

"No, I think I might be going into shock or something. I'm not sure."

"How can you not be sure if you are going into shock?" Nick asked.

"I'm not sure because I never went into shock before, you douche bag! Have you ever gone into shock?"

"No, but if I was going into shock, you can bet I'd know it," he snarled back at me.

"Whatever, just figure out a way to lose the zombies. We don't have time for this shit. We need to meet up with the team."

Nick started to laugh.

"What?" I asked.

"You just sit back and rest your pretty little head. I got this shit covered. I know where to go. Maybe you'd know as well if you ever left the Westside. "

I honestly didn't have the energy to waste arguing with him. I didn't have much energy to do anything, other than attempt to keep my limp body from sliding off the seat onto the floorboards of the Jeep. The stars that were starting to dance around in my eyes told me that very soon I was going fail at that attempt as well.

In retrospect, I'm glad I passed out as Nick flew around the city, because what I actually managed to see of his driving was nothing short of terrifying. He would charge straight at a car parked on the side of the road and wait until the very last second before he veered around it. I couldn't count how many times he bounced over a curb. If I hadn't buckled myself into the Jeep, I'm pretty sure I would have bounced out.

I'm not exactly sure what he did, but I came to when we began to slow down. I realized that he had somehow gotten behind the horde of zombies. I watched with heavy eyes as they ran up the street and away from us.

I wanted to ask what was going on, but Nick motioned for me to be quiet as he reversed the Jeep into some sort of enclosed area. After that, he got out of the Jeep, and closed some sort of metal door on a track, and we were hidden from the street.

"You got any quarters?" he asked when he finally came back.

When I didn't answer, he snorted through his nose and vanished. Less than five minutes later, I felt hot water spraying down on me from above. The water was invigorating. Instantly the dancing stars in my vision vanished, and I was able to sit up straight.

"I used to work at one of these places," Nick said. "I managed to jam it on 'spray' so you can fix your leg. You look like hell."

I ignored Nick as I pulled up the leg of my pants and exposed my purple and black knee to the spraying water. It hurt even worse than the first time, but I shoved my kneecap into the correct position as I straightened out my leg under the water.

I'm pretty sure my kneecap would have placed itself in the correct position if I'd simply waited, but I was in a rush to speed things along. Still, the pain of the slow healing process was making me grit my teeth.

"Is that shit working?" Nick asked.

"Nick," I growled through clenched teeth, "one more word and I'll to shoot you."

I waited only a few moments. I wanted to get a grip on the pain before I collected my thoughts.

"How long were we driving around?" I asked.

Nick did not answer.

"NICK!" I shouted. "How long were we driving around?"

"You told me not to talk, asshole," Nick said.

"What are you, twelve?" I asked while he started laughing.

"Damn, you're a moody bastard," Nick said. "We were only driving around for like five minutes. I told you not to worry."

He'd lost them in five minutes. I could barely believe it, but the lack of light coming through the open spaces around the door confirmed it was indeed not yet daylight outside.

There was still time to meet up with Dudley before the vampire got there. I mean seriously, how fast could an injured vampire move?

Nah, don't answer that question. It's not really important. What is important is how fast we tore out of that carwash the second after I pulled some metal brackets off the wall and attempted to tape them against my leg. I was hoping they'd last a bit longer than the wooden table pieces, but I wouldn't have bet any money on it.

"Your leg isn't fixed yet?" Nick asked.

"Do you think my kneecap is normally the size of a grapefruit?"

"How bad is it?"

"It's pretty fucking bad, dumbass," I answered. "Not as bad as it was, but that's sort of relative I think."

"Will you be able to walk on it?"

"I think I will be able to limp on it. Everything seems to be in the correct place, but I doubt the connective tissue has gotten a real firm grip. Then again, I'm not a doctor, so how should I know?"

"Maybe you should sit this one out. I can take up your slack."

"You think so?" I asked. "You think you can do some of the things I did in that hotel? They ought to write songs about my awesomeness. I doubt they would do the same for you though. Nothing really song worthy about hiding out in the Camino Real."

"I wasn't hiding. I was plotting. I was devising a plan that would allow me to destroy all my enemies, and for fuck's sake, how the hell do you close the top on this thing? I'm freezing my ass off."

Fortunately, I hadn't even noticed how cold it was until he started complaining. Cold weather didn't seem to bother me much anymore. Once he pointed it out, I realized that it was cold, but it still didn't bother me much.

The cold air wasn't slowing him down any. The man was hauling ass. It's a really nerve-wracking experience, being in a vehicle with that guy when he's in a hurry, but I wasn't about to complain. He was making excellent time. The sky was just starting to brighten up when we finally made a wild left turn on Mesa. You would have thought Nick would need to slow down somewhat and pick a course through all the abandoned cars on the street, but he didn't.

Instead, he floored it. He slammed the brakes. He shoved cars out of his way, and he even jumped the curb and tore off on some sidewalk when he got frustrated.

"I've always wanted to do this shit," was all he said when he caught me staring at him.

On the plus side, he had at least begun to lighten up and relax a bit. He seemed just a little too tense when we were back at the hotel fighting the vampires. I was beginning to get a little worried he wouldn't be able to handle the stress.

It seemed as if he'd somehow found a way to adjust.

"Are you gonna kill this bitch, or are you going to try and capture her?"

"I'm going to kill her," I answered sharply.

"If you kill her, how are you going to find out anything about Kingsley?" Nick asked.

I didn't have an answer for that. I hadn't even thought about it, and now that I was, I still didn't have an answer. I wasn't too sure we would be able to capture her. She was scary tough. If we went in with anything less than lethal intent, she'd probably tear us apart.

In the end, I had to go with extreme violence. If the opportunity to ask questions arose, I'd take advantage of it, but I was by no means expecting that opportunity to arise. It wasn't like she was exactly talkative whenever we got up close and personal.

"If you weren't going to get any information out of her about Kingsley, what were you going to do to find him?"

Tear the damn city apart.

I didn't doubt him for an instant. There's nothing about the man that would even lead me to believe that he was being anything less than brutally honest. His dedication to his friends has no bounds. There simply isn't enough danger in the entire world that could make him give up until his friend was safe and sound.

It's hard not to respect him even more.

"What happened when you got to the house on Baltimore?"

We drove through a nice park and stopped right next to where Dudley had left his Jeep. The idea was to not let the vampire know we were waiting for her to show, so neither of the Jeeps were directly in front of the house. It wasn't like we had hidden them extremely well, but dawn had arrived, and we didn't have time to fuck with it. The first rays of sunlight were peeking over the mountain and repelling the darkness away for yet another day.

I was betting she'd be in such a hurry to find a quiet and dark hiding place that she wouldn't even notice the two Jeeps.

I used Nick for support as we moved hurriedly through the park, across the street, and to the front yard of the house in which we were setting our trap.

Maybe I was just imagining things, but the house felt sinister. It gave me the heebie-jeebies. There was something evil in that house, something that shouldn't be there. I don't know how else to describe it. The house didn't want us to enter.

I think Nick felt it too. He came to an abrupt halt the second he stepped foot into the yard. Yeah, I'm positive he felt it. The house was a place of pain and death.

Then, we heard the muffled thumps of silenced automatic fire coming from inside.

I was the first one in despite my wounded leg. At first, I saw almost nothing. All the windows had been blackened out with a dark paint.

Then, I heard a vampire screaming.

I also heard Georgie screaming.

I was too late. Somehow, despite her injuries, the vampire had beaten me to the house. I hobbled in the direction of the scream and saw the shoved aside rug. I heard more silenced gunfire.

As soon as I approached the pit, the vampire leaped out. She was covered in bullet holes, but her throat had closed once again. I watched as her face registered shock at my being in her lair and then anger that I had discovered her hiding place.

I slammed my tomahawk straight down on the top of her head.

In response, she gave me an open handed slap that—even though I managed to partially deflect it with my arm—still sent me sailing across the room. My arm was sprained from the blow, but fortunately I managed to not land on my bad leg.

"I'll kill you," she growled as she followed me across the room with my tomahawk jutting from her skull.

I responded by drilling her in the chest with my MP7. Then Nick appeared and opened fire as well. Dudley was slowly climbing out of the pit. He looked injured, but he also began to fire upon the vampire.

She twisted and turned under the storm of wooden bullets, but she still wouldn't go down. Instead, she leapt to the ceiling and began to roll around on it as we pelted her and pelted her. I'm not sure when Javie and Merrick arrived on the scene, but Javie began to shoot at the windows.

It took but a second to realize just how great of an idea he had, and I ordered Nick to join him.

"Which windows?" Nick asked as he avoided a clawed hand.

"All of them," I answered.

The room was filling up with smoke and dust from the bullets tearing up the walls and ceiling, when a beam of sunlight finally entered the room and the screams of the vampire came to an abrupt stop. Then we heard the loud whack of a body hitting the tiled floor. It was hard to see through all the dust, and my eyes were beginning to water, so I couldn't make out where the vampire had fallen.

"Did we get her?" Dudley asked.

"I'm not sure. I can't find her."

The soft tapping on the back of my shoulder should have alarmed me, but for some reason I thought it was one of my teammates.

It was the vampire. She was smiling at me and dangling my tomahawk by the blade between two of her fingers. Somehow, she had managed to find the one patch of shadow in the entire room and was safe and sound.

For the moment…

I reached out with all my might and grabbed her by the throat while at the same time shoving her against the wall. My actions had the desired effect, and she never noticed I had dropped my MP7 and flicked out my folding knife.

She easily removed my hand from around her neck, but the look on her face as my knife opened her throat was priceless.

The blood began to gush, and I was able to slash her neck a few more times before she was finally able to overcome the shock of my attack and kick me across the room.

She didn't even try to advance on me. She didn't get a chance. Dudley had begun shooting out the windows behind her, and for the first time, she kissed the sunlight.

The effects were less than impressive.

She didn't burst into flames. She didn't roll up into a ball of agony and simply burn away. She just sort of melted. Nothing incapacitating, nothing like that at all, just think of nasty sunburn, and multiply it by about a thousand.

Her flesh did bubble and crisp, and smoke did rise from the exposed flesh, but I was pretty disappointed that she didn't explode.

Well, on second thought, she did sort of explode. She exploded right out of the room and down the hallway to what seemed to be the bedrooms.

"Did you see that shit?" Dudley asked.

"Yeah, I saw it. Where does that hallway lead?"

"It leads to the bedrooms, but which one did she enter?"

Even through the dust I saw what he was talking about. There were at least five rooms at the end of the hallway, but only one of them had a shattered door.

"Let's finish this," I said to no one in particular.

I began to slowly walk towards the hallway when Nick started shouting.

"We got company," Nick said. "Lots and lots of company."

Right after he said that, I heard the moans. Fortunately none of them were screaming yet, but that was only a matter of time. They tended to be a bunch of noisy bastards whenever something aroused their curiosity.

"Hold them off," I shouted back. "Don't let them get into the house."

"I'm on it," Nick said. Then he and Javie began firing out the windows at the zombies flocking towards us.

"Dudley," I said. "You're with me and... and...where the hell is Georgie?"

I was beginning to panic. Both Dudley and Georgie were in that pit and only Dudley had emerged. I didn't waste a moment limping to the edge of the hole. When I got there, he almost shot me in the face.

Georgie was fine. In fact, he didn't seem to have a mark on him. I would have laughed, but the moment really wasn't there.

"Georgie," I said. "Stop being a pussy and do something useful. Get those survivors out of those chains, and do it now."

I'm pretty sure he nodded, but I didn't wait around. I immediately set off towards the room with the broken down door. Dudley was right behind me, and I almost jumped out of my skin when he started tapping me on the shoulder.

When I turned around I saw that he was handing me my tomahawk, I breathed a sigh of relief and muttered my thanks. I was going to need that particular weapon.

When we entered the room with Merrick, the stink of vampire hit us like a slap. It's a nasty smell I can't even begin to describe. It's not as bad as the smell of zombies, but it's close.

The dark room seemed to be deserted, but the smears of blood along the walls gave it a sort of lived in appearance. Merrick began to sniff around the floor, and I walked over for a closer inspection of what she had found.

She was sniffing at some drops of some type of liquid, but in the darkness I couldn't tell if the liquid was vampire blood or human blood. Dudley had walked past us towards the bathroom as I studied the drops, and he returned from the empty room with a confused look on his face.

I pulled out my flashlight and shined the beam on the drops. The bright light lit the floor up in a wide circle, and I was able to see the black drops of vampire blood that Merrick had been sniffing at.

I got down on all fours and searched for more of the vampire's blood. I found what I was looking for on the side of the bed.

"Is she under the fucking bed?" Dudley asked as he backed away.

In order to answer his question, I grabbed a corner of the bed and flipped the entire thing out of the way. There was another hole beneath it. It was barely wide enough for me to fit through.

"Are we going down there after her?" Dudley asked.

"I guess so," I answered.

"I need to find another line of work," Dudley mumbled.

I didn't respond. In fact, I agreed with him.

I jumped down the hole and made sure to land on my good leg. All in all, I'd say it was about eight feet deep and it opened up into an eighty by eight room with a ceiling made up of many different sizes of wooden boards so low I had to duck my head. Dudley almost landed on top of me when he jumped down. As I looked around the room, I noticed that the dirty plywood walls had bloody smears all over them.

Merrick began to bark from the top of the hole.

"Maybe we should take her with us," Dudley said. "She can track the vampire."

"No," I answered. "I don't want Merrick getting too close; she might get hurt. Besides, I can follow the vampire's trail."

"Well, where are you going to start? This room has no exits."

He was right about that. There were no clear passages leading out of the room. I was thinking there had to be a hidden door somewhere so I aimed the beam of my flashlight downwards and started searching the dirt floor.

It took awhile, but I finally found a drop of black blood, and two feet away from that one, I found another one. The blood drops led me across the room to a corner with a hairline crack in the wood. I tapped on the area near the crack and was rewarded with a hollow echo.

I then punched the area and the piece broke free, revealing a tight hidden passage in the corner of the wall. Dudley and I were going to have to crawl through it. It wasn't a very pleasant notion.

The little tunnel led another eight feet under the house and we emerged into a room very similar to the one we had just left, complete with a wooden ceiling consisting of different sized boards and plywood walls. The only exception is that this room held a coffin.

Dudley let out a deep breath when he emerged from the tunnel and saw the wooden coffin. We had come to the end of the line. The tension in the air was thick enough to cut with a knife. Also, there was the presence of evil. It felt wrong to be in that room, but I couldn't leave. I had a job to do. I had a duty to perform, and I wasn't leaving until accounts were settled.

I quietly approached the coffin. I could no longer hear Merrick barking from the bedroom. I could no longer hear the muffled sound of gunshots as Nick, and Javie, kept the approaching zombies from entering the house.

The moment seemed to drag on and on. The coffin was by no means modern. It was one of those old western style jobs: bare wood and cheaply made. It looked as if it would crumble if I stomped on the lid. That's when I noticed the hinges. This coffin wasn't the kind that gets nailed shut. It had hinges on the side so it could be opened and closed.

I held my breath as I reached out and grabbed a hold of the corner of the lid. I put myself in a position that would allow me to dive out of the way if she came flying out at me, and I began to lift the lid. The hinges creaked loudly, and I jumped away causing the lid to slam down with a loud crack.

Dudley jumped about a foot.

Then he started to snicker.

"Maybe you should lift it up," I said. "That way I can nail her with the tomahawk if she grabs a hold of you."

"Good luck with that idea," Dudley said.

I opened the coffin.

It was empty, just a little bit of dirt on the bottom.

"There must be another tunnel that we missed," said Dudley.

"There wasn't another tunnel," I replied. "I followed the blood drops. She had to have gone this way."

Dudley came away from the tunnel we had used to get into the room and stood next to me beside the coffin. I thought for a moment and once again began to search the floor for blood drops with the beam of my flashlight. Perhaps there was another tunnel leading out of this room we had missed in the darkness.

Dudley began to search as well. We looked near three of the four corners but came up empty handed until Dudley began to search the dirt floor near the final corner of the room.

"Jaxon," Dudley said. "I think I found something. It might be a blood…"

He didn't finish his thought. A pale hand came down from between two ceiling boards and grabbed him by the hair. We never looked up. The new tunnel was above us in the ceiling. It was plain as day, and we never even noticed it.

Dudley twisted and turned as the hand tried to pull him up through the boards and into the new tunnel. His frantic movements saved his life. The vampire couldn't pull him into the hole. Given a few more seconds, she might have been able to do it, but I wasn't about to give her those few seconds.

I swung the tomahawk into her outstretched arm and damn near severed it. Actually, I was somewhat shocked that the arm didn't come flying off, but vampires are built pretty damn tough. Still, the wound deadened the arm. It went immediately limp, and I shoved Dudley out of the way and sprayed automatic fire into the hole.

I was rewarded by a crumbling noise above my head, and I had to step out of the way as the vampire fell from the hole onto the dirty floor.

She looked horrible. Her skin was as white as paper. Her tutu was smeared with black blood and slimy dirt. The skin on her face and arms was burned horribly, and worst of all, the tomahawk wound in her head had not yet closed, and I could see a sliver of her brain.

"Wait," she gasped as I walked towards her with my tomahawk.

I paused for just a moment, shocked that she was actually asking me not to attack her. I couldn't remember her doing anything other than threatening me or insulting me.

"You win," the vampire said. "I'll leave. Just go away, and I won't bother you anymore."

For the very first time, I could see the actual fear in her dead eyes.

"Where's my friend?" I asked. "What did you do with him?"

The only answer I received was a quiet, dry laugh. So I pulled back my tomahawk and prepared to deliver what I was hoping would be the final blow of the fight.

"Leave me alone," the vampire said as she suddenly slammed into me and ran from the room and into the tunnel leading back to the bedroom.

"Fuck me," Dudley said. "How the hell can she still be moving?"

"Beats me," I answered. "But did you notice how much she's slowed down?"

Dudley didn't bother to answer. Instead, he followed me back the way we had come. I could just see her feet disappear up the hole under the bed as we entered the first room. I limped in pursuit and had just started to climb the hole when I heard the sound of Merrick attacking and the vampire screaming.

I climbed to the top of the hole just in time to catch Merrick out of the air as the vampire threw her away. I quickly set Merrick back down on her feet and then straightened up to face the vampire.

She stood in the corner of the room. She was crouched and waiting for just the right moment to pounce on me.

"Leave me alone," she whispered. Her voice sounded like a little girl.

"Not a chance," I answered.

She found her moment when Dudley poked his head out of the hole, and I briefly looked in his direction. What she didn't realize is that I wasn't really distracted. I just gave her a fake out because I wanted her away from the wall.

To her shock, I met her charge, and before her good arm could close around my body, I ducked down and picked her straight up into the air by her legs. I didn't try to flip her over or slam her down onto the ground. Instead, I never stopped charging forward. I ran with all the speed my wounded leg could muster, right to the blackened bedroom window, and I dove head first through the painted glass into the bright morning sunlight of the backyard.

I felt the wet drip of blood from a dozen small cuts on my face from the broken glass as I tumbled and rolled on the cold grass. I felt my knee pop, and threaten to explode. Yet I managed to find my footing and locate the vampire.

She had tumbled from my grasp, but not very far. She looked me straight in the eyes for just a moment, and then she began to scream as the smoke rose from her body and her skin began to blister and crack. Dudley emerged from the broken window and started to pepper her chest with bullets whenever she tried to crawl away.

A burning vampire is a difficult thing to watch. They seem all too human as they twist and contort in agony. The smell is nauseating. The end is almost too far away. Her features had been burned away completely when I finally took pity on her.

I swung my tomahawk with all my might, and cleaved through her neck. The screaming stopped instantly, and I began to notice the bright and clear morning for the first time. It was almost beautiful if I looked away from the melting corpse at my feet. I'd never been much of a daylight person, but at that moment I was certainly grateful.

Dudley and I watched the corpse sizzle and pop, until there was nothing left but ash. The flames never came forth. I think I was a little disappointed at that. I was hoping to see a much more impressive death. Instead, what we got was a slow and torturous end.

Then we heard the sounds of muffled gunfire, and the screams of many zombies. I'm positive the battle with the zombies had been raging on all along as we watched the vampire dissolve. It was only when we were satisfied she wasn't coming back, and Dudley had kicked away the largest pile of ash with his boot, did the realization begin to hit us.

We were trapped.

I leaned on Dudley and we hobbled to the back door of the house. Merrick rushed forward from the bedroom, and jumped into my arms. Now that the vampire was dead, she wanted her fair share of attention. I gave her a quick scratch and joined Nick at one of the front windows.

The zombies were everywhere.

I radioed immediately to Hardin and told him to drop off a shit-ton of ammo. Then I looked towards the survivors. All of them were emaciated and weak looking. They wouldn't be able to make a run for to the Jeeps.

"We'll make a stand here," I announced. "I need some time to come up with a plan."

"Not a problem," Dudley said. "The house doesn't have a lot of windows. We can board things up and give you some time to repair your leg and head."

"Dude, get off me," Nick said. It was the last thing I heard as I slid ungracefully into him, and passed out.

"*You passed out?*"

Right on top of Nick. One second I was standing there, and then I wasn't.

"*Why did you pass out?*"

I'd taken some serious damage since I got to the hotel. My messed up leg was the worst of it, but I'm pretty sure I had a concussion and possibly some broken ribs. I was also exhausted.

"*You had all that going on?*"

Yeah, vampires hit hard.

"*Why didn't you tell anybody?*"

Who am I going to tell? It's not like anyone could have done anything. Besides, I can put most problems to the side and get on with my job. The leg was the only thing giving me trouble.

"*I've heard from more than a few people that you are relentless in a fight. They sort of think it's a little spooky. Would you agree?*"

I would agree. I have no problems with that one. When it's time to fight, I'm going to go balls to the wall until I can no longer do so. I guess it seems a little spooky, but I am the Guardian, after all. I can absorb more damage than the average person, and continue to function.

"*How long was it before you woke up after passing out on Nick?*"

I think I was out for about ten hours or so. I could have shaved maybe five or six hours off of that if someone had woken me up, but the boys thought I needed the rest.

I woke up to the sounds of screaming.

One second I was nestled firmly under a layer of sleep, and then I began to hear the screams. They were distant at first, but they soon became louder and louder. The muffled thumps of silenced weapons came next.

I opened my eyes.

I was in a bathtub full of warm water. My clothes were cleaned, and folded, on top of the sink. My weapons, boots, and backpack were stacked in a pile next to the clothes. The only thing I had on was my underwear and my wristwatch.

I looked at the time and realized it was only a few hours until dark. The screaming began again. It sounded like Georgie. I wanted to tell him to shut the hell up because he was irritating the hell out of my headache. Then I realized I no longer had a headache. My leg was all healed up as well. In fact, I felt pretty damn good.

I stood up in the tub and grabbed a large towel to dry off with. When I was dry, I caught my reflection in the mirror. I was looking pretty healthy and energetic, as far as I could tell. Nothing to complain about until Georgie barged through the door.

"Jaxon," Georgie shrieked. "We're in trouble. They're breaking through our barriers."

Fortunately, at that point, I had my pants on.

"Did you forget how to knock?" I asked. "Or are you trying to sneak a peek at my awesomeness?"

"What?" Georgie asked before it dawned on him that I was just joking around. "Seriously, we're in trouble."

I could see the panic in his eyes, but to be honest, I wasn't really impressed. Georgie tends to panic on a somewhat regular basis.

"They're inside the house," shrieked out another voice, and this one actually caused me some alarm. It was a female voice, and I didn't recognize it at all.

I threw on the rest of my gear, shoved my Ti-Lite folding knife into my pocket, checked that my Recon 1 folding knife was on my belt, threw my blood stained Harley Davidson hat on top of my head, and ran out of the room.

Things were bad.

Even the backyard was full of zombies. When the backyard is full of zombies, you can be sure the entire house has been surrounded. I immediately ran up to the first woman I saw. She was one of the survivors from the pit.

"Where are they?" I asked.

She pointed a shaky finger towards the kitchen, and I went running. I didn't like what I saw when I got there. Merrick had a zombie by the back of the neck and was shaking him around the linoleum floor. There were two others headed right towards me and even more attempting to climb through the broken window.

I took out one of the zombies with my tomahawk. It was easy enough. The first hit is always pretty easy. The zombies never see it coming. It was an angled cut to the forehead. The blow just barely sliced the brain, but since no momentum was lost upon impact, I was able to swing the tomahawk all the way around in a wide arc and miss my second target.

The bastard had ducked and grabbed me around the waist. It was a wasted effort. I was too healthy and full of energy. I shattered his nose on my knee, and then elbowed his temple to smack him loose. While I was doing that, I ordered Georgie to fire on the broken window so no more of them got inside the house.

I finished off my second zombie as he was climbing back up to his feet. It was a simple chop to the back of his head. After that, I told Merrick to release her new toy, and I chopped that zombie as well.

Georgie was in full panic mode as he fired aimlessly towards the window. He wasn't being very effective, so I told him to go find some nails and something we could use to board it up, and I took his place.

Shooting a hole through every head that popped up into my sights was pretty much the easiest job I'd had since I returned to El Paso. Merrick was even wagging her tail happily as I fired away merrily.

Eventually, I realized that I could, in fact, do two things at once. I tapped my earpiece and asked for Dudley.

"What's up?" Dudley asked.

"Oh, I'm just curious about how long we've been under attack?" I asked nonchalantly.

"We had some problems in the morning," Dudley answered, "but it only started getting really bad about forty minutes or so ago."

"What happened forty minutes ago?"

"Damned if I know," Dudley answered. "They just started coming out of the woodwork. We've been keeping them out, but more and more are showing up. Maybe we should call for an extraction?"

"We would never make it to the chopper with the house being surrounded," I answered. "Besides, only pussies call for extractions. How are Nick and Javie holding up?"

"Everyone is holding up pretty well except for Georgie," Dudley answered. "I could hear him screaming for help all the way on the other side of the house. I was about to go help him when one of the survivors told me you were up and about. How are you feeling by the way?"

"I'm peachy," I answered. "How much ammo do we have?"

"More than enough," Dudley answered. "And the survivors are making sure we have fresh magazines when we need them. Maybe you should try and help us figure a way outta this mess?"

"Yeah, let me think on it for a bit."

At that moment, Georgie came back into the room with his arms full of what seemed to be a broken table. He hesitated just a second before he went to work on securing the window. It was fun to watch the biggest piece of wood—which he had placed over the hole—buck and tremble as he tried to nail it to the wall. I was tempted to help him more than a few times, but the scene was just too funny.

"Georgie," I finally said when he had the situation somewhat under control. "Maybe you should find a different line of work. You seem to be a little bit too much of a pansy for this job."

"I'm no quitter," Georgie said.

"Yes, you are."

"Well I'm not quitting this. It's something I should be doing. I just know it. So fuck off."

I laughed. Georgie always makes me laugh. I used to call him my best shittiest friend, but I still hung out with him because he always made me laugh.

"What does that mean, 'best shittiest' friend?"

It means he's a shitty friend, but out of all my shitty friends he was my favorite. I guess that still doesn't make much sense, so let's just say he wasn't a great friend, but since he made me laugh I still hung out with him. There are actually some very positive factors with having a best shittiest friend by the way.

"Do tell."

I can laugh at their expense and never feel bad about it.

It was when Merrick and I started to leave the room that Georgie did the oddest thing.

"Jax," Georgie said. "I'm glad you're feeling better."

It was odd. So odd that I didn't bother to respond because I didn't know what to say. I just gave a nod and went to see for myself how everyone else was doing. Some of the survivors tried to talk to me, but I sort of ignored them.

"You ignored them?"

I did. I had other things on my mind that were probably more important. I wanted an escape plan. I was starting to get a bit claustrophobic and the only thing bouncing around my head was to take everyone underground into the vampire's tunnels and wait until the zombies got bored and left.

It was by no means the best plan I had ever come up with, but I couldn't find an easy way out. If we made a run for it and pushed through the horde, I'd lose people. That wasn't going to work for me. I wasn't about to commit to a plan in which I knew I was going to lose people.

I also didn't think I would be able to make a run for it by myself, in an effort to lead the horde away, as I had done in the past. There were too many of them surrounding the house. They would swarm the door as soon as it opened. Even if I fought my way out, I don't think the team would have been able to get the door or window sealed up again.

It was a bad situation all around.

Nick was guarding the front of the house. If an arm came through a boarded up window, he was quick about hacking into it with his fireman's axe. The look of focus on his face was actually pretty impressive. I couldn't remember having seen him so focused before.

Javie took the rear of the house. He was mainly using his pistol to keep the dead from gaining entry. He was shooting every face that came into view between the boards at point blank range. He was making quite a mess. It was odd seeing him dishing out so much violence, but he seemed to have everything under control.

Dudley was at the farthest end of the house, opposite Georgie. Things were pretty busy for him. He hadn't managed to board up all the windows by the time the zombies started to attack. Some of them must have gotten in. The bodies on the floor gave evidence to that.

The screams of the dead were loud on his side of the house. The moaning, growls, and snarls joined the screams in a cacophony straight from hell. The fists pounding on the outside walls made it difficult for me to think. I didn't want to begin to imagine how many were out there. Certainly it wasn't the biggest horde I've ever encountered, but it was probably the largest horde that ever had me trapped.

I pulled my tomahawk and began to hack at the zombies as Dudley completed the job of boarding up the windows. He managed a smile for me as he once again picked up his machete and hacked away at any limbs daring enough to come through his barrier.

We weren't going to be able to keep up this pace forever.

Not nearly as important was what happened forty minutes before that caused the entire ruckus. Yet, it was still in the back of my mind. I knew we had company before I passed out, but according to Dudley, the house had been really swarmed only forty minutes ago.

"Duds, how bad were things before the house got swarmed?"

"Not bad at all," Dudley answered. "I'm not even sure there were any out there. Then suddenly, the house was rushed."

"What about before that?"

"It was pretty bad right about the time that you passed out, but it wasn't anything we couldn't handle. That's why we decided to stick it out and give you some time to heal. We finished off most of them by the afternoon while we boarded up the windows and reinforced the doors. After that, there would be just a few of them on the street every now and then."

"There has to be something going on outside the house that we aren't aware of," I said. "Something must have led the horde here if things had been quiet before the attack."

"I was thinking the same thing," Dudley said. "But it's not like I can stick my head out the window and take a look up the street."

"All right," I said. "Keep up what you're doing and let me know if you need some backup."

Merrick and I went back to Georgie and watched him panic as he attempted to keep the zombies out of the kitchen. I even helped out when the water got too deep for him. Merrick helped as well. She almost seemed to be making a game out of catching the hands and arms that reached through the boards.

The battle raged well into the night.

We were under siege, and I couldn't find an acceptable way out that would benefit everyone. I helped out wherever I was needed, but I could see the fatigue beginning to set in on everyone's faces.

It was time to make some tough decisions. I tapped my earpiece. I wanted everyone to have a say.

"All right, folks," I said. "It looks like this crowd isn't thinning out anytime soon. The only idea floating around in my head involves all of us hiding out in the vampire tunnels until the zombies get bored and go away. What do you guys think?"

"Dudley told us about the tunnels," Javie said. "If they find us down there and come in after us we'll all be trapped."

"We'll be trapped with a lot of ammo and a more defensible position," Georgie added. "I don't think we have many other options."

"What if we have the choppers open fire on the zombies out there?" Nick asked.

"Those zombies are pressed up against the house," I answered. Think about what a .50 cal will do to the walls. Wait a minute. Wait a minute. What if we go down to the tunnels and then have the choppers come in and thin out the horde?"

"I'm down with that," Dudley said.

"I'm still concerned about getting trapped," Javie said.

"I like the idea," Georgie said.

"We can hold them off until the choppers are in range and then drop into the tunnels," Nick said. "That way we won't have to worry about them getting inside the house before the helicopters show up."

"All right then," I said. "We have a plan. Everyone keep doing what you're doing while I get the survivors into the tunnels."

"I'm following everything," Hardin said into my earpiece. "I will have two choppers en route inside of five minutes. You radio in and let me know when you have everyone out of harm's way."

"Excellent," I replied. I still wasn't used to having Hardin paying attention to our conversations. I guess it did save us some time every now and then, and he rarely intruded until we asked him for something.

It didn't take me very long to lead the survivors to the hole in the floor of the basement. I can't say they were actually happy to be going down inside of the vampires sleeping quarters. Once I explained what was going to happen within the next ten minutes or so, they rapidly got over whatever problems they were having.

I did my best to lower them down. I didn't want any of them to twist an ankle or break a leg when they landed. I don't think I'll ever forget the look on each of their faces as I took a hold of their arms. They were afraid. They had every right to be, but they were also trusting. I could see it as plain as day in their expressions. They had complete trust in me.

I wasn't going to fail them.

The dead were still beating on the walls, and reaching through the boarded up windows. I hated the sound. I hated feeling trapped. I went to Georgie and helped him reinforce his barrier. I wanted him and everyone else to have a head start when they ditched their area and ran for the hole in the bedroom.

If the zombies were right behind us when we went down the hole, we'd then have a firefight underground and though the odds were in our favor, I'd just assume not have any zombies follow us down there.

After Georgie, I moved on to help Javie. When he was relatively secure, I moved on to help Nick. When Nick was good and ready, I moved over to the far side of the house to help out Dudley. Merrick was right beside me through all of this. She seemed to sense that something big was about to happen and was wagging her tail excitedly.

The shamblers were still pretty heavy on Dudley's side of the house, and it took some time to secure things enough to give him a head start when it was time to go. Merrick seemed to enjoy another chance to play her game of savaging all the hands and arms trying to reach through the boards.

"You ready to roll out?" I asked.

"Ready when you are," Dudley answered. "But maybe we should let Georgie go first. I don't want him to piss his pants being the last man to leave his post."

"Georgie," I said after I tapped my earpiece. "Are you secure over there?"

"I'm doing pretty good," Georgie said.

"All right," I said. "Get your ass down that hole."

After Georgie radioed back that he was safely underground, I radioed Javie.

"Javie, how are things going?"

"My barrier will hold for about five minutes, I'm guessing."

"Good, now move your ass down that…"

"Jaxon," Nick interrupted, "I've got movement over here."

"Of course you have movement over there," I answered testily. "The house is surrounded by zombies."

"No, asshole," Nick said. "Something just barreled into them and took a bunch down."

"Everyone hold your positions," I announced through my earpiece. "Georgie, get back into position and cover the kitchen again."

I sprinted through the house with Merrick at my heels. I found Nick kneeling by one of his windows, gazing out at the darkened street. He wasn't fighting off any zombies.

"There it is again," Nick said. "Check it out."

I dropped to the ground beside him and took a look out one of the many cracks between the boards. The zombies were no longer searching for an entry point on his side of the house. Something had distracted them, and they were all wandering around the front yard in search of it.

There were also a lot fewer zombies.

"I don't see anything," I said.

"Give it a minute," Nick said.

"I've got something going on in the backyard," Javie announced through his earpiece.

"What the hell?" I exclaimed to no one in particular.

I ran as quickly as I could to the back of the house where Javie was trying to look through the boards and avoid the grasping undead hands.

"What do you see?" I asked.

"Something dropped down on them and started ripping them apart," Javie said. "Then it vanished, but almost half of them are gone."

"Double what the hell?" I exclaimed.

"I'm getting help over here as well," Dudley said through his earpiece. "Not sure what it is, but it moves pretty fast."

"Jax," Nick said through my earpiece. "It's a dude. It's a dude in a gray suit and he's fucking up the zombies."

I ran over to Nick and just as I expected, whatever he had seen was no longer there when I looked between the boards. I would have thought they were all going crazy, but then I noticed that there wasn't any pounding on the sides of the house. When I looked out the window, I only saw about eight zombies when there had been maybe a hundred or so on Nick's side alone.

"I've got a woman over here!" Dudley shouted since he was too excited to use his earpiece. "She just took out about ten or fifteen shamblers."

"What about you, Javie?" I asked through my earpiece.

"I think there's a few of them," Javie answered. "It's hard to tell, but the horde is definitely thinning out."

"Jax," Nick said. "Take a look."

I took his advice and finally saw one of our secretive helpers. It was a man dressed in beige pants. He moved so fast I couldn't really tell where he had come from. He darted in among the zombies smacking them hard on their heads and scooping up their unmoving bodies before they hit the ground. He had gathered up three of them before he moved off quickly and disappeared from view.

"Hardin," I said after tapping my earpiece. "Keep the helicopters at a distance."

"Understood," Hardin answered.

I was just about to turn away from the window when I saw the man in the gray suit Nick had mentioned earlier. He dropped down from a nearby rooftop and proceeded to pick up where the other man had left off. I realized quickly that the slaps on the head were hard enough to kill the zombies.

"Fuckers are strong," I pointed out to Nick.

"Got that right," Nick answered.

I left him at the boarded up windows and went to check on Georgie. I found him at his post, looking through the boards. I was just a little surprised he actually went back to his post. Then again, there were no longer any zombies attacking his area.

"You see anything?" I asked.

"Not a thing," Georgie answered. "I heard a lot of thumping and crunching sounds before I made it to the windows, but I never saw a thing. You think we should go out there and help these guys?"

"Do they look like they need our help?"

"No, but it's the polite thing to do."

"I guess that depends on why they're helping us," I said before walking back to the front of the house.

It took about another fifteen or twenty minutes before the area was completely secure. Our saviors had not once tried to make contact with us. An eerie silence breathed over us when they were finished. Nobody said a word. It was almost as if everybody was waiting for the other shoe to drop; it lasted half an hour. Everyone stayed put and rested during the all-too-brief intermission.

Then a body dropped ungracefully from somewhere above, and landed in the front yard.

Nick and I could hear the wet slapping sound it made as it slammed into the dead grass. Icy fingers began to climb up my spine and the hairs on the back of my neck began to stand straight up. I wasn't sure what was going on, but I knew it wasn't going to be good.

"Why the hell can't they just be on our side?" Nick asked. "Why do they need to go and fuck things up?"

"Why throw a body at us?" I asked. "That doesn't make much sense."

"I knew they were too good to be true. I just knew it."

I wasn't really paying attention to Nick at the moment. I was studying the body. My brain wasn't giving me much of a clue, but something about the body seemed awfully familiar. I felt my eyes widen in my skull when I finally figured it out.

"Nick," I whispered. "He's wearing a bite suit. I think its Kingsley."

"No way," Nick replied.

"Yeah," I said. "I'm going out there."

"Listen up everyone," I said after tapping my earpiece. "I want you all up to the front of the house immediately. I'm going out there, and I want backup."

"So they just threw Kinsley's body onto the front lawn?"

That's exactly what they did.

"Why would they do that?"

I'm not sure. Maybe they wanted to get our attention. Or, maybe they just wanted to freak us out a bit.

"Was Kingsley alive?"

That's the million-dollar question, isn't it? At the time, we didn't have any idea. All we could see was a lump in the grass wearing our protective gear, complete with the tactical vest and the high bite collar. The lump wasn't moving.

"I don't think you should go out there," Dudley said after everyone had gotten a look out the window. "This seems like some sort of a setup."

"Yeah," I answered. "But that's our buddy out there, and he doesn't look so good. I want everyone to file out behind me but stay next to the door in case we need to make a hasty retreat back into the house."

I walked out into the yard slowly. I could hear Merrick whining behind me as Dudley held her by the collar. I stayed on the concrete path all the way to the sidewalk. I was scanning the area all around me. I looked above the houses, in the trees, everywhere.

As far as I could see, the area was clear.

Kingsley was in a heap to the left of the concrete path, just before the sidewalk. He still wasn't moving. When I reached him, I feared the worst. His skin was cold and clammy. His eyes were closed. I unzipped his bite collar and reached in his vest. I wanted to see if I could feel his pulse.

"Jax," Kingsley whispered. "Is that you?"

"Yeah, buddy," I whispered back through an ear-to-ear smile. "It's me. Now let's get you out of here."

I let my MP7 dangle by its strap and shoved my hands through the armholes of his vest in order to haul him to his feet. He felt lighter than usual. I was wondering when he'd eaten last. His arms went around me in a hug when he had both his legs underneath him.

"Jaxon," Kingsley whispered, in a voice too low.

"Yeah Kingsley," I answered. "I'm here. Let's get you moving."

"Jaxon," Kingsley whispered once again. His rank breath was on my ear. "Stop bossing me around."

I was about to ask him what he meant, but he didn't give me a chance. His arms tightened around me as if they were made out of steel, and he spun me around so that my back was towards the rest of the team.

I was in shock. I was speechless. I didn't understand what was happening. The punch came, and I didn't even see it. He hit me right under the jaw, and I went flying back towards the team. Suddenly, I understood: the violence and the power.

But I didn't like it.

I was crushed. All I could think was that I should have tried harder to find him. I shouldn't have killed the vampire. I should have caught her sooner and made her talk. I should have made her tell me where he was. I failed him.

I failed him, and she turned him.

Kingsley was a vampire.

Thoughts of protecting him raced through my mind. I wouldn't let anyone harm him. I wouldn't let Hardin or anyone else stake him or burn him...or...or...try anything to finish him off. He was my friend. I let him down.

I failed him.

I failed him.

"Kingsley," I said, through a mouth filled with blood. "Try and control it. I'm here for you. All of us are here for you. We can beat this thing. We can maybe even find a cure."

None of the team had moved, except for Nick. He had his MP7 up and ready to fire. If Kingsley made the wrong move, Nick wouldn't hesitate. I wanted to diffuse the situation before Kingsley got hurt.

"Nick," I said. "Lower your weapon. "Kingsley's our friend. He just needs a moment to get himself together."

"Is that what I need, Jaxon?" Kingsley asked. "You're telling me what I need now?"

I couldn't understand what was happening.

"I'm just trying to help," I answered. "It's not your fault that they did this to you. I want to help you."

"I don't want your help, Jaxon," Kingsley said in that low voice. "Nobody did anything to me I didn't ask for."

"What?" I asked. It was all I could say: one little word. I couldn't understand what I was hearing.

"I asked for this," Kingsley said. "I wanted it. I was tired of being weak and afraid. I was tired of being forced to endanger my life time and time again, while you played the hero."

"Who forced you to endanger yourself?" Dudley asked with an angry tone.

"HE DID!" Kingsley shouted while he pointed down at me with a clawed finger. "HE FORCED ME! HE FORCED ALL OF US! ARE YOU TOO BLIND TO SEE WHAT HE DOES TO PEOPLE?"

"He didn't force you to do anything," Dudley said calmly. "We do what we do of our own free will."

"Really?" Kingsley asked. "What do you think he would do if one of us tried to quit? What do you think people would say if I had quit? I think they'd be calling me a coward right now. I think people would be ridiculing me. I had no way out."

"Nobody would have thought anything like that," Dudley said. "Why would you...?"

"You're a liar," Kingsley interrupted. "Either that, or you don't know him like I do. He's controlling. He forced me to follow him back into this fucking city. Eventually, he would have gotten me killed. I was terrified, and I was sick of being afraid. Now, I don't have to be afraid. Now I'm the king of the mountain."

"No," Georgie said. "You're a monster that needs put down."

"Come and try it, Georgie," Kingsley said. "Try and put me down. All of you are now expendable. The Master doesn't care about anyone but Jaxon. He wants Jaxon all for himself."

"What are you talking about, Kingsley?" Dudley asked. "Your little Master is dead. Jaxon killed her this morning."

Kingsley began to laugh. It wasn't a pretty sound. It was more like nails on a chalkboard. I wanted to do something. The situation was rapidly heading towards the point of no return, but for the life of me I didn't know what to do.

So I sat there. Right on the sidewalk, still on my ass, with blood dripping down my chin from the tongue I damn near bit off when he nailed me with that uppercut.

"She wasn't the Master," Kingsley said with a triumphant smile. "She wasn't even close, not by a long shot, but the Master is coming. He's coming for Jaxon. He wants Jaxon to pay for what he did. Do you remember what I told you, Jaxon?"

I had no idea what he was talking about. I was still numb and in shock.

"I told you that you were in over your head," Kingsley continued. "You were just too stupid to listen. You have no idea how long I've resented you. You have no idea how much hell is coming for you. You have no idea how much I'm going to enjoy this. I can't wait to see your little self-important world come crumbling down upon you. When this is all over, you won't be anything more than a footnote in history. Nobody will even remember your name."

Somewhere in the back of my mind it occurred to me that Kingsley was rather talkative in that moment. He was normally a quiet guy. It probably wasn't the best thing to notice at the time, but it struck me as odd.

"I think you're going to be pretty disappointed, you fucking traitor," Dudley snarled.

"Right," Kingsley said. "I'm a traitor. I'm a traitor because I don't want to follow an egotistical man who will eventually get me killed. I can't be the only one here who feels that way. I know I'm not. What about you, Javie?"

"What about me?" Javie asked in a quiet voice.

"We've always been tight," Kingsley said. "Join me and we'll get away from here. We'll spend the rest of our lives traveling the world and living it up. Just me and you, what do you say?"

"Were Javie and Kingsley as close as he was implying?"

Yeah, they were pretty tight. I felt bad for Javie at that moment. He had been really worried about his buddy, and just when he thought things were going to turn out all right, he finds out that his friend jumped sides. Even worse than that, Kingsley was asking Javie to bail on the team and join up with him.

"You can't live any kind of life," Javie said. "You're dead and you're a monster just like Georgie said. I won't go anywhere with you, but I will do my very best to put you down."

The shock on Kingsley's face was almost humorous. He really truly expected Javie to join him, but the shock didn't last long. His face quickly turned to pure fury, and the black drool began to drip from his lips.

He went after Javie.

He was fast, but Nick had been waiting for him to make a move. The spray of wooden bullets stitched across Kingsley's chest, and he screamed out an inhuman wail. Then one by one, everyone began to drill him. He spun, twitched, and wailed across the yard before he found his feet and ran off down the street.

"I always knew that guy was an asshole," Nick said.

"Everyone back inside the house," Dudley said.

The team started moving. Well, everybody started moving but me. I was still sitting on the sidewalk, not even bothering to wipe the blood off my chin. Dudley noticed I wasn't moving and hauled me to my feet by my vest.

"Are you hurt?"

I didn't even acknowledge that he was talking to me. I was just—I don't know—empty. I was having a very difficult time accepting what had happened. I couldn't believe Kingsley had turned on me.

"Jax," Dudley said as he gave me a little shake. "Are you hurt?"

I shook my head that I wasn't injured.

"Let's go," Dudley said as he dragged me back into the house.

"This isn't the first time a friend turned on you. Tito betrayed you as well. I don't think I've ever

asked you personally, but did you feel the same way about Tito?"

I don't really think Tito betrayed me. I think he more or less betrayed himself and the people that were following him. It's not really the same thing. I don't think Tito would ever have wished me harm.

I thought about what he said for a brief moment before I realized he was right. When I spoke with Tito, he was filled with regret. He admitted that he did what he did because he was jealous. He never wished harm on anyone.

"What happened next?"

We were inside the house. Dudley had removed my canteen and was forcing me to drink. The water would heal up my tongue, and he was pretty worried about the amount of blood. Everybody was staring at me.

"Why are you all shocked?" Nick asked. "It was pretty obvious that guy had some sort of problem with you. Hell, I noticed he was kinda mental the minute Jax showed up at Georgie's house."

I was pretty sure he was looking at me, but I ignored him and sat down against the wall. To say the least I was defeated. Having a friend betray me was beyond my comprehension. It's happened before, of course, never to that degree, but it's happened. I'm sure it's something that happens to everyone at some point in time.

The thing is…I could never, in a million years, even conceive of betraying one of my friends. It's just something I could never do. To me, my friends are my family. That means something to me. Unfortunately, it doesn't always mean something to other people.

"What do you mean?" Dudley asked.

"I mean that Kingsley is a resentful bastard," Nick answered. "I could practically see the resentment drip from his mouth every time he said something."

"He did seem sort of nervous when we came back into the city," Georgie added. "I just can't believe he did what he did."

"I think he's fundamentally weak as a man," Javie said. "He wasn't man enough to let anyone know he was too chicken shit to come back. It was easier for him to just blame Jaxon for all his problems."

"The only problem with that bullshit," Dudley said, "is that Jax did a lot of shit for that traitor. Seriously, where the hell would Kingsley be if it hadn't been for Jax? He'd be dead, that's where he'd be. Think about it. Kingsley doesn't possess the drive or will to have survived the outbreak."

"You got that right," Georgie added. "He was even starting to come a bit unglued before we led everyone out of the city. I remember the way he started drinking and the angry comments he would make. We should have seen this coming. Kingsley was too weak to be a member of this team."

"It's just unfortunate that Nick is his replacement," Dudley said.

Everyone began to laugh. Well, everyone but Nick.

"Seriously," Dudley said as he offered me his hand to help me up. "You were good to him, Jax. You were a great friend. You saved his life. The villain in this story is Kingsley. The hell with him, all right?"

"Yeah," I answered. "The hell with him."

I think it was the support that snapped me out of it. I was still hurt. I still felt betrayed, but I realized I had done nothing wrong. I mean it's not like I'm a mind reader. To start resenting me because he was too afraid to speak up for himself, well, that kinda seems to be more of his problem than mine.

"Hardin," I said after tapping my earpiece. "Send in one of the helicopters for an extraction."

"Good idea," Hardin answered.

Everyone was looking at me once again.

"We need to get those survivors out of here, boys," I said. "We have some vampires to hunt."

Everyone began to cheer. Even Georgie, which was a bit of a surprise. I would have been less shocked if he would have sucked his thumb and pissed his pants.

It wasn't long before we heard the sound of a chopper above our heads. Georgie had led all of the survivors into the living room to await their extraction. The plan was to lead them to the helicopter and then hop into the Jeeps once it was back in the air.

As soon as the house began to vibrate, which meant that the chopper was descending, we led the survivors out to the front yard. We wanted to make the extraction as fast as possible. There may not have been any zombies in sight, but we weren't about to take chances.

Everyone was looking up as the helicopter lowered itself from the sky. The pilot was going to bring her down right in the middle of the street so all of us hung back in the front yard in order to give it plenty of space.

Something black streaked through the sky.

"Did you see that?" Javie asked.

I'm pretty sure everyone saw what he was referring to. It's just that nobody was exactly sure of what it was. To me, it looked as if a black shape zipped through the sky and landed inside the helicopter.

It was only a few moments after that when I had figured things out. The helicopter began to spin around wildly. The nose of the craft was lifting up and down in an erratic pattern. Then things got even worse: the chopper did a nosedive straight into the asphalt.

Right before it crashed into the street, I saw the black shape shoot from the helicopter, and streak across the sky to the rooftops of the houses further up the road.

I was amazed there was no explosion, but the crash was deafening, regardless. The sounds of tearing metal when the body of the aircraft crumpled against the ground were grotesque. The blades of the helicopter sliced into the street, sending chunks of metal and asphalt straight towards us.

I took down at least four of the survivors and covered them with my body. Dudley was on the ball as well, and he shielded the ones I couldn't grab. I could hear him grunt as he was pelted by debris.

When things finally settled down, I ran to the chopper. I knew it would be a wasted effort on my part, but if there was even the slightest chance the pilot or crew were still alive I was going to help.

Nick was right behind me. He was telling me to be careful. He was worried that the broken remains would explode. I climbed over the wreckage and investigated the bodies. The pilot was dead. I knew it before I even checked his pulse. Two of the soldiers were also gone, but the third soldier, he died in my arms.

I was pissed.

"It was a vampire that attacked the helicopter, wasn't it?"

It was, and that was the scary thing. The vampire children we put down in the hotel were pretty tough, but we managed. The female vampire that had been stalking me was about a hundred times more difficult to put down, and we barely managed. Whatever took out that helicopter was nothing I wanted to mess with.

Nick tapped me on the shoulder and pointed up the street. I took a look and saw that two female vampires were standing in the middle of the road about a block away. Reluctantly, I looked down the road in the opposite direction. I saw two male vampires, also about a block away, and they were slowly walking towards us. I cast my gaze towards the park on our side. There were another four male vampires walking through the overgrown grass in our direction.

"Dudley," I said after tapping my earpiece. "Get everyone back into the house immediately."

"Gotcha," Dudley said.

"I don't see Kingsley with any of them," Nick said.

"I doubt you will, either," I answered. "He's apparently not exactly big on fighting."

Nick laughed at my comment and the two of us slowly backed away from the wreckage of the helicopter to the front door of the house. We took our time. I didn't want to run and give them a reason to chase after us. That wouldn't have been good at all because they probably would have caught us.

I was the last one inside. My eyes were trained on the vampires the entire time. They all came together on the street in front of the house just as I closed the door. We were effectively trapped once again.

I had some bad news to deliver, but while I made myself ready to let everyone know how bad our situation was, I realized nobody was even looking at me. Instead, they were staring down the main hallway that branched off into the living room—a room that none of them seemed very keen upon entering.

I smelled fire. Someone had lit a fire in the living rooms fireplace. We had company, and judging from everyone's expression, it wasn't the good kind of company.

I walked past the huddled group and poked my head into the living room.

There was a man in a black suit stoking the fire. His suit was immaculately pressed, and so was the white shirt underneath. I found that rather odd because the suit was old and worn. It had small tears in the pants and jacket. The edges of the sleeves were frayed. Yet, there it was, nice and pressed.

The man wearing the suit had pale, grayish skin. He had the face of a man in his mid-forties, but his dark grey hair made him seem just a little bit older. His lips were black and his chin had smear marks from what seemed to be a constant wiping of his mouth. Even the ends of his white sleeves that peeked out of his jacket were stained by the black drool.

The worst thing about him was his eyes. They were white and filmy. If I had seen a human with those eyes, I would have assumed he was blind and in need of medical attention. No such luck with this vampire though. I knew he could see. It was the way in which his eyes darted around the room.

"Come in, Guardian," the vampire said with a motion of his clawed hand.

I moved my body into the room. Everyone else stayed more or less behind the wall. Yet the team was ready for action. I could hear them adjusting their weapons as I moved closer to the vampire.

He finally looked at me.

For what seemed like an eternity we simply sized one another up. Then with a smile and a sigh he began to speak.

"I felt her passing just as I began my slumber. It was as if my heart were breaking into a thousand pieces. I didn't want her to go. I was against the idea from the very beginning, but my daughter was a hunter, probably one of the very best hunters to ever walk among us. She knew things, even modern things, like explosives and weapons. She loved the hunt. She loved to toy with her food. She used her knowledge of all things modern when she hunted, but I would imagine that you already know that don't you?"

I just stared at him.

"She had always wanted to hunt a Guardian. It was her dream, but I always refused her. The last Guardian was much too experienced for her. It would be too dangerous. That was the excuse I used, but then you came along—a brand new, and inexperienced, Guardian. She begged me to let her hunt you. She came to me with tears in her eyes, and begged me for the ultimate hunt. I could refuse her no longer. It was my mistake."

I just stared at him.

"Once upon a time, I would have had no problem letting her go. We vampires always killed Guardians. Your kind is nothing more than a pest. Even a young vampire is stronger than a Guardian, but times have changed. Weapons have improved. A Guardian can pose a threat in this day and age. She was so young, my beautiful daughter—so very young—and all her hunter's skill proved inadequate. Tell me, did she die well?"

I just stared at him.

"ANSWER ME, HUMAN!" he screamed in a voice so loud that I heard someone back in the hallway whimper.

"She died screaming," I answered finally.

The vampires face contorted in fury. His clawed fingers dug into his palms causing the black blood to ooze. The black drool began to leak from his mouth, and then he was under control again. His face was calm, almost serene. He smiled at me politely and nodded his head in respect.

"Forgive me," he said. "I rarely lose control. I am almost ashamed of myself."

I just stared at him.

"I'm going to kill you," the vampire said. "I want you to know that. I don't want the fact that you are going to die to come as a surprise. I want you to be fully prepared, knowing that I am going to kill you."

I just stared at him.

"I could have my followers end your life, but that would cause me to lose respect. Vampires are, by nature, a rather violent species. The ones outside this home are under my control. They obey me, and I, in turn, allow them to exist in my territory. This beautiful land has been my territory for a very, very long time. I claimed this land for myself after I destroyed the previous Master in battle, and I've held it ever since. Such is our way."

I just stared at him.

"So you see," the vampire said. "If I fail to avenge my daughter's death, the others will see me as weak and will eventually attack me. I have no doubt I can destroy each and every one of them. That isn't the problem we're facing at all. It's much simpler than that. You see, I very much want to kill you. I want to end your life. I want your death to be slow, and I want you to suffer. Most importantly, I want all of the humans around you to see you suffer. I want your death to have an audience. I want the humans to know what happens when they cut down an immortal."

I just stared at him.

He gazed back at me, and the black ooze began to drip from his lips again. He slowly wiped his mouth with the back of his hand, but he never took his eyes off of me.

"Excuse me," the vampire said. "The fluid aids in our digestion, and it tends to flow heavier when our hunger is at its worst or our emotions are at their strongest. It probably seems rather revolting to you."

I just stared at him.

"You are a warrior," the vampire said. "That much I can tell; you aren't afraid of me. You know you can't possibly win, but still you want to attack."

My eyes narrowed.

"What are you waiting for, little Guardian?"

With the speed of a demon, I freed my tomahawk and let it fly at his face. It was a perfect motion. There were no slips or stutters. The action was so fast that no living, breathing person, on the face of this earth could have survived.

The vampire caught the weapon in mid-air. It reminded me of what I did to his daughter.

Then he moved. He was fast, unbelievably fast. He crossed the room in the blink of an eye and grabbed a hold of me. The team poured into the living room and took up positions. I could hear Merrick growling. He threw me into the lot of them.

I crashed, tumbled, and hit my head against the wall. The vampire was still moving. By the time I had gotten to my feet, with my MP7 pointed in his direction, I realized he had incapacitated the entire team. Even worse, he held Georgie by the throat in front of him.

I didn't have a shot.

Everyone was pretty banged up, but they were slowly coming back to their senses.

"That was almost impressive, little Guardian," the vampire said. "Ultimately, it was a futile gesture, but it was audacious, nonetheless."

"Squeeze any tighter on my buddy's throat, and I'll blow your mind," I snarled.

"Have no fears about that, Guardian," the vampire said. "Our time is not yet ripe. As I said before, I want your death to have an audience. Tonight, I simply wanted you to have a sample of the power you will soon be facing. Enjoy your stay of execution. Use the time to prepare for your final battle, but I warn you, make no attempt to leave this house, for if you do, my revenge will be terrible."

Then he hurled Georgie through the air as if he were nothing more than a ragdoll. I did my best to catch him. I partially succeeded, but we both sort of collided into Nick, and Dudley. When I turned back to have another go at the vampire, he was gone.

Merrick gave a soft whine and rushed over to cuddle up next to me. I reached over and began to scratch her behind the ear. Nobody said a word. I guess we were sort of shell-shocked.

"Well that fucking sucks," Nick said, breaking the silence.

I had to chuckle at his ability to sum an entire situation up with just four words. It wasn't long before Dudley joined in on the laugh and before I knew it, everybody was laughing heartily.

"I agree with Nick," Dudley said.

"Well I agree with you agreeing with Nick," I announced.

And we all laughed some more. I'm not sure why we were laughing. I think it was because none of us knew what else to do.

"Why did you have to go and kill his daughter?" Nick asked.

"I didn't like her haircut," I answered.

Everyone laughed even harder.

"That motherfucker whooped all of us in a matter of seconds," Nick said.

"He sure did," I agreed.

"And he was holding back," Dudley added.

"He did take us by surprise," Georgie said. "Next time we'll be ready for him."

"Take it from me, Georgie," Nick said. "If he can whip us that easily, it won't make much of a difference how ready we are. We could have a month to prepare ourselves, and he'd still kick our asses."

"Then what are we supposed to do?" Georgie asked.

Everyone looked to me.

"We gotta get the fuck out of Dodge," I answered. "The Master is out of our league. Add his followers to the mix, and none of us would even make it through the first round."

"What about all the survivors?" Dudley asked.

"I think you guys cleared most of them out of the Westside," I answered. "I'm sure there's still more, but they'll have to hold on until we can figure out a way to deal with the vampires. Maybe we can drop food and supplies to their locations. Give them enough to hold out until we can come up with a new game plan."

"It's a good idea," Javie said. "We need to get out of this alive so we're able to fight another day. If we hang around here any longer, all of us are going to get ourselves killed."

"We need better weapons," Nick said. "More powerful bullets might do the trick. Something that will put them on their ass with the first shot."

"I like the sound of that," Georgie said.

I was smiling. The team was already thinking about returning, and we hadn't even left the area yet. It was good to see they were all aboard, but I was still pretty unhappy about retreating. I hate running away from a fight. It's embarrassing.

"All right," I said. "We'll hang out here for the night because I don't want to endanger any more helicopters. Come sunrise, we'll fly out of here and figure out a better game plan before returning to deal with these bloodsuckers. Everyone agree?"

Everyone agreed.

"Hardin," I said after tapping my earpiece. "Hardin, are you hearing all this?"

There was no response.

"Hardin?" I asked. "Are you there?"

I tapped and cursed for about ten minutes before giving up and asking the others to try and see if they could get through. None of them could, but we kept on trying. In fact, we were still trying to make contact with Hardin when the sun finally rose up in the sky and the time for making some choices was at hand.

"Well shit," I said as I gazed out the cracks in the boarded up window at the empty street. "I'm not sure what's wrong, but it looks like we're on our own. The suns up, so we won't have any vampire problems. What do you say we just hop in the Jeeps and drive the fuck out of here?"

"Can we get through the gates around the city?" Georgie asked.

"I don't have this little badge because it looks pretty," I answered. "Besides, if the guards give us any problems we'll just kick their ass."

It didn't take long for everyone to agree. The alternative was to sit in the house and wait for the vampires to come back for us, and nobody wanted to go through that again.

It didn't take but a second for us to load up our meager supplies and head out the front door. The air was incredibly cold, so cold it actually made me shiver. The sky itself was a leaden grey. I guess if I thought about it, the weather had been turning colder and colder. There was a storm coming and it had been gathering its strength for a while now.

We crossed the street and headed into the park towards the Jeeps at a slow jog. It didn't take but a second of looking at the vehicles to realize they were trashed.

The armored hoods were tweaked and bent from being forced open. I knew it was going to be hopeless, but I looked at the engines anyway. They were torn to pieces. The metal was bent and twisted. Some parts were crushed and others had been ripped away.

We had no vehicles.

The team had spread out in a circle around the Jeeps to give me some time to check things out. The survivors were next to me inside the protective ring. I didn't know what to say to them as they all looked at me imploringly. Fortunately, Dudley came to my rescue.

"We have company."

"How many?" I asked without bothering to look up from the demolished engines.

"There are two of them," Dudley said.

"I'll take care of it," I announced as I rested my hand upon my tomahawk.

"They aren't zombies," Dudley said. "Not unless zombies have started carrying hunting rifles."

That got my attention immediately.

I went over to Dudley and the two of us began to walk towards the armed newcomers. I allowed Merrick to come along as well. Odds were that they were good people, but I wasn't about to take any chances. My MP7 was twisted around on its strap so that it was pretty much hanging on my back in a nonthreatening manner, but the Sig on my right side could be drawn, and fired, faster than most people could blink.

If one of them made a move, I was going to shoot both of them dead.

Both parties stopped about ten feet from one another in the middle of the park. Dudley seemed relatively calm. He'd seen me shoot before. I, on the other hand, was tense. I didn't like them being armed. I didn't like how they were the only survivors I'd seen walking around outside instead of hiding in a house and boarding up the windows.

The woman was the first to speak.

"Are you guys the Regulators?" she asked.

"That would be us," Dudley said. "What are the two of you doing outside?"

"We were gathering supplies yesterday, but when we opened a door on this one house, the street suddenly began to fill up with zombies. We were able to get out and hide in a house up the road, but the entire area was way too hot for us to try and leave."

"At least until you guys started clearing them out," the man added. "How the hell did you manage all that?"

"That wasn't us," Dudley said. "And trust me, you don't want to know about it. I wish I didn't."

Our conversation was interrupted by pounding footsteps. The man tensed up and raised his rifle just a little bit higher. I responded by inching my hand closer to my pistol. Merrick sounded off with a low growl. I didn't turn around to see who was running up behind us. I wasn't about to take my eyes off the man and woman. Dudley however had no problems checking it out for me, and since he seemed unconcerned, I assumed that it was probably one of my teammates.

"Joe? Claudia?" Javie asked. "Is that you?"

"Javie?" the woman asked. "You're a Regulator?"

"Yes," Javie said with a smile. "I can't believe you guys made it. This is freakin' awesome. Dudley and Jaxon, allow me to introduce Joe and Claudia. I know them from college and a school trip to England."

Everyone instantly relaxed. Javie was a pretty good judge of people. If these two were friends of his, then they certainly weren't a threat to me and mine. I immediately offered my hand along, and so did Dudley.

"So if it wasn't you guys that took out all the zombies," Joe asked. "Who was it?"

"Vampires," Javie said. "Jaxon and Dudley killed a Master vampire's daughter and now he wants to fight Jax and give him a slow death."

"Are you kidding me?" Joe asked.

"What?" Claudia laughed. "You can accept zombies, but vampires give you pause?"

We all sort of chuckled at that. It was sort of funny how easily I accepted that a Master vampire was hunting me. Before I became the Guardian, I probably would have thought anyone believing in zombies and vampires was out of their minds. Now it seemed even vampires were easy to believe in.

"Are they the scary kind or the teenage love story kind?" Claudia asked.

"Definitely the scary kind," Dudley answered. "They drool this black slime and everything."

"But they killed all the zombies?" Joe asked.

"Yeah," I answered. "They only did that to get them out of the way. After the zombies, they brought down one of our helicopters when we tried to extract some survivors."

"You guys are rescuing survivors still?" Claudia asked.

"That, and killing vampires," Dudley said. "You two can join up with us, and as soon as we find a ride we'll get you out of here."

"We can't leave," Joe said. "There are too many people in this city that need our help, but I bet we can hook you up with a car, and we can certainly make room for your survivors if you want to follow us back to the church. It's on Mesa, not very far from here."

"What exactly are you guys up to?" Dudley asked.

"Not us," Claudia said. "We just work for the priest. We gather supplies, and look for survivors, but it's the priest that arranges everything. He's the man in charge."

"Do you have other survivors at this church?" I asked.

"About five hundred," Joe answered. "It's a tight fit, but we manage."

"That explains why the team and I weren't super busy while you were at the hotel," Dudley said.

"I guess so," I replied. "It also means we won't be leaving the city unless we can get a hold of Hardin. I'm not leaving any survivors behind while the rest of us run for the hills."

"You think the vampires would attack the church?" Dudley asked.

"Don't you?"

"Probably," Dudley answered after considering it for a bit. "That'd be an easy way to make good on the Master's revenge. I'm sure they already know there are survivors there. I guess it's best that we don't take any chances. Maybe we can fortify this church and defend it."

"That's what I was thinking," I answered. I turned to Joe and Claudia. "So, who's this priest you mentioned? And how long has he been rescuing people?"

"He's been rescuing people since this all started," said Claudia. "And his name is Father Miguel Monarez, but everybody just calls him the Chainsaw Priest."

Chapter 8

FATHER MIGUEL MONAREZ
A.K.A. "THE CHAINSAW PRIEST"

I met with Father Miguel on a bright and sunny afternoon in a pleasant, quiet park. He was strolling along near a duck pond when I came upon him and introduced myself. Fortunately for me, he had read my book and had no problems speaking to me.

He seemed to be in his early thirties with a jet-black head of hair receding from his forehead. The most noticeable thing about him is his height. Or maybe it would be more accurate to say his lack of height. Father Miguel stands a mere 5'5". He's a slight man with a warm, contagious smile. As I watched him walking along the banks of the pond, strangers would come up to him at almost regular intervals and speak with him. He welcomed all of them with his smile.

I wondered how a man like that would fit in with the Regulators.

Tell me, my dear. What would you like to chat with me about? I doubt I have anything to say as entertaining as the others you've spoken with.

"I think I would like to hear your opinion of the General."

The priest gave me a somewhat confused look before he smiled shyly and slowly shook his head.

You came all this way to hear my opinion of the General?

"That, and some other things. I'm also curious about vampires."

Ah, now we get to the meat of your story. I'm just a little bit surprised the story got out. I was under the impression that certain important people were not too keen on releasing that sort of information.

I'm sure there are a lot of people that didn't want the world to know about vampires, but that doesn't seem to concern the General. I have his 'go ahead' to pursue the story.

No, I don't guess it would concern the General. He seems to follow his own path.

"He does indeed, Father. He does indeed."

You know, I've never given an in-depth interview about what happened in El Paso. I'm not sure where to begin. Shall I start with my schooling? I went to some very prestigious schools, you know?

"I'm sure that is all very fascinating Father, but I'm wondering if we could possibly skip ahead and discuss why they call you the Chainsaw Priest?"

Ah, now there's a nickname that will haunt me for the rest of my life. Just recently I've been told some company has begun selling t-shirts over the Internet that have an image of a priest holding a chainsaw. A few years ago, I never would have believed you if you came out and told me I would be popular with teenagers.

"You were there from day one Father. Tell me what you saw. Tell me what happened."

Very well, my dear, but please bear with me. I still need to talk about my education. It will help explain my state of mind, and perhaps allow me to bear some of the burden weighing down my soul.

"Very well, Father, please begin."

I was born from a moderately wealthy family. A family that knew the value of an education, and because of my family, I grew to be a studious sort of fellow. Therefore, it was no surprise to anyone when I was accepted into the best possible schools, but it was a shock when I entered the priesthood after receiving my doctorate. Everyone imagined I would enter a profession that would grant me fortune and great prestige.

You see, my dear, I'm moving along quite rapidly. I'm only touching on the important parts.

"Yes, Father, you are certainly moving quickly."

The where's and why's aren't the important part of the tale. The important part is that I was a highly educated and ambitious man when I decided to become a priest. You see, I had always been a believer. I had always been fascinated with the Catholic Church. And, despite my excellent marks, I was bored.

The priesthood was the only thing that held some fascination for me. Again, I dedicated myself to my studies. I was an ambitious scholar when I became a man of God. Have you noticed I've used the word ambitious twice?"

I shook my head that I didn't.

Ambition is the key to summing up my desires. I don't think I became a man of God to help people and teach them the ways of Christ. I believe I entered the priesthood for selfish reasons. I had too much ambition. I had dreams of how far I could go. I wanted the Vatican.

I received El Paso.

A man of my intellect and skills was sent to El Paso, probably because I spoke Spanish fluently. Of course, the church there was doing poorly. They told me that a man of my skills would have no problem turning it around. I truly believe I was sent to El Paso not to save the church, but because I spoke the language.

I detested El Paso. I hated the hot weather. A man could boil in his own skin just standing outside on a summer afternoon. I also resented the people. I never let on that I felt that way, of course, but I did.

I was an unhappy man, stuck in a thankless job, in a city that would do nothing to fuel my many ambitions.

Now, I believe that God sent me there for a reason. Why else would a man of my intellect be sent to such a place, if not for the will of God? I must sound rather arrogant. It isn't the most attractive side of me, but it's important to know. It was the cause of my psychological state—my very frustrated and unhappy state of mind.

Certainly, I did my duties, and I did them well. I brought up attendance in the church, made improvements. I did the work of God, but I would have abandoned all if the opportunity had presented itself. I longed to escape and dreamed about going on to bigger and better things. It never once occurred to me that such a young and inexperienced man was lucky to have been given the opportunities that I was given. I was on the verge of becoming lost in my own arrogance.

And then the zombies came.

It was a hot, humid day I will never forget. It's funny how people so easily believe the dead can walk, but they find the idea of El Paso being humid during the summer impossible. Well, others have told it true: El Paso can become extremely humid during the summer.

I never saw the news, or heard the radio reports. I'm not too interested in those things. What I learned, I heard from the worshippers pounding on the door of my church. There were four of them, all elderly, all terrified. I allowed them entrance immediately. I recognized them all, of course. They were regulars at my services.

"The dead have come back to life, Father!" one of them cried out.

"They are attacking the living!" shrieked another.

"What are you talking about?" I asked.

I simply couldn't believe them. The idea sounded preposterous. I was beginning to wonder if they were on drugs, or perhaps suffering some sort of mass hysteria. They tried to explain, but they were all so excited they began talking over one another, and I couldn't understand a thing.

One of the men began trying to close the door. He seemed positively paranoid about leaving it open. I put my arms around the man's shoulders and gently led him back to the others. He was in quite a state, I can assure you.

My church was on Mesa, not very far from the university. Now, Mesa is a high traffic road, and it took me just a moment to realize that something was wrong. Something was missing. It was the traffic. There was no traffic outside the doors of the church.

I took a look outside just to be sure, and sure enough, the street was empty. The only exceptions were some abandoned cars in the middle of the road. The emptiness was shocking. Then I began to hear the screams. They weren't anywhere close. They were off in the distance, but I could hear them well enough without the usual traffic outside the church.

I saw other people running down the street, and I called them over. The elderly man that tried to close the doors began to panic when I did so. He didn't want anyone else to come into the church. He believed I was inviting some great danger in by doing so.

"This is the house of God," I assured the man. "He will allow no harm to come to his children in this house."

For most of the morning I invited anyone I saw on the street to seek sanctuary inside the church. They all told me the same tale. The dead were attacking the living. Some of them even suffered bite wounds from the calamity that was going on out there.

I treated the wounded and calmed the frightened.

They had complete trust in me. I had resented them for so long and they all had such faith in me. It was heartbreaking. I felt completely ashamed of myself. I vowed right then and there to become a better man. I would become a man who deserved their trust and faith.

My new resolve was about to be tested.

The first of the wounded died. I had no idea why a bite wound on the leg would have caused the man to die, but I believed that possibly the mouth of his attacker possessed some type of toxin. At the time, I was still unable to believe his attacker was a zombie. I hate that word, by the way. It reminds me of a horror movie. It eliminates the suffering the poor soul went through when they became a zombie. I believe it's dehumanizing.

Still, it's the only word available, so forgive me for using it.

"*What about shambler?*"

I believe that one is even worse. I've heard that handsome, polite, young man named Dudley using it quite frequently. I've actually asked him not to use it in my presence, and he was kind enough to refrain. Well, I believe he made attempts to refrain. He possibly takes after his uncle too much to completely abandon his enjoyment of irritating others.

I found myself laughing at his assessment. Knowing both Dudley and Jaxon I wasn't shocked to hear it. He certainly wasn't trying to be funny, but it struck me as hilarious nonetheless.

"*They are quite the characters, aren't they?*"

They are indeed, my dear, but that isn't necessarily a good thing.

"*Tell me more, Father. Don't let me interrupt you.*"

Well, the man came back from the dead and attacked me. At first he went after his own wife, but I intervened before he could bite her. I grabbed his shoulders as she fought underneath him. Finally, I was able to spin him around and throw him off.

He tumbled to the ground and came up to his feet instantly.

As his eyes met mine, I knew the people were correct. The man was a walking corpse. The man was evil, or more accurately, there was something evil inside of the man's shell. Evil has no place in the house of the Lord.

I reached for the gold crucifix around my neck, and held it aloft. In that church, I commanded the power of the Lord, and the Lord would never allow a demon to endanger his flock in His own house.

I commanded the demon to abandon the body. I commanded the demon to leave the church, and go back to hell. Everyone began to panic. They were calling for me to run away. They were afraid for me. I was afraid as well. Yet, I held my ground and faced the demon. I called to God and asked him to banish the evil from His house.

The zombie charged me.

I was tackled to the floor. I didn't feel the hand of God. I didn't feel his love and protection emanating through the cross. I struggled with the zombie on top of me, but my mind was a million miles away. I felt that God had abandoned me.

I knew it was because of my ego and ambition. I knew it was because I entered the priesthood for all the wrong reasons. I was simply not worthy to be a man of the cloth. I was unworthy, and the Lord had abandoned me.

I couldn't accept my punishment. I just couldn't. Because, if I accepted his abandonment, the people I had brought into the church and promised safety would have no protection. I had promised them a refuge and I couldn't fail them.

I told this to God as I struggled with the zombie. I told him of my promise to be a better man, and I begged him for the opportunity to prove myself. Still, God did not answer in the way I was hoping for. No godlike power vibrated down my arm to turn the zombie clawing at my face to dust.

It would have made things easier, but the ability to banish the evil never manifested. Instead, I felt the Lord's strength. I have always been an active man. I have always enjoyed exercising and did my very best to stay fit, but this was something different.

I felt positively strong.

I realized in that brief moment, the Lord had heard my prayers. He was answering me. Not in the way I wanted Him to answer me, but He was answering me all the same.

I threw the zombie off of my chest and stood up. The thing was instantly on its feet again. This time when it ran towards me, I ran away. I led it away from the terrified people, through the sanctuary, and down a hallway through the back of the room that led to the offices. Right before I reached the offices, I left the church all together through the side exit.

The zombie followed me. It was unbelievably fast, but I had no problems maintaining my distance. Unfortunately, I had run into the church's garden. It was a square area enclosed by a high rock wall. The garden had only one exit, and for that I needed a key. I had trapped myself.

Aside from the flowers in the garden, there was a utility shed. I realized that it might offer me some sort of shelter, so I ran to the shed.

The zombie followed, but I was able to close the door behind me before the zombie could reach me. All was right as the zombie pounded on the thin wooden door. I had saved the people inside the church. I had led the monster away from them. It wouldn't take him long to break down the thin wooden door that separated us, but I saved the people I begged God to allow me to save.

Then I heard a shrill cry from inside the church.

The cry was unnaturally loud. I was able to hear it even through the pounding coming from outside the shed. I realized it wasn't human. I knew there were others still inside the sanctuary that had been bitten.

I became frantic. I was needed, trapped, failing miserably, and I desperately wanted to succeed.

I saw the chainsaw.

It was lying there among other pieces of equipment. I probably saw it a thousand times before, but never paid it any attention. The gardening I had been doing since I moved into the church never required the use of a chainsaw. I wasn't even sure it would work.

I picked it up, and noticed it was too light. There was an old and rusted gas tank right next to it. Quickly, I poured the gasoline into the chainsaw. The door to the shed was beginning to crack and splinter apart as I resealed the gas cap.

I could see the pale hands of the zombie reaching through the cracks as I pulled the starter cord. The chainsaw rumbled, but did not catch. I pulled again, and again, and again, and again. I pulled 'til

I was out of breath and thoroughly exhausted.

I pulled a final time as the door finally fell apart, and the zombie entered the shed with bloody fists. The chainsaw started. The dangerous chain whirled, and the loud sound of the little motor filled the room.

The zombie charged me.

That first battle was a bit of a lesson for me. I had to learn where my enemy was the weakest. How could I have known only damage to the brain would put a zombie to rest? In my ignorance, I unfortunately made a mess, but I emerged victorious.

I didn't have time to celebrate my victory, however; the screams were still echoing from inside the church, and I ran to meet them.

I had gathered about thirty or so people inside the church before the first man turned into a zombie. So, it was the twenty or so uninjured souls who saw me violently cut down, with the chainsaw, those that had been turned. Violence, by the way, was something I have abhorred my entire life, but I felt not the slightest bit of guilt as I cut down our undead attackers.

That, my dear, is how I earned my nickname.

"I'm sorry, Father. I had no idea."

Don't be sorry. I'm not sorry. I did the right thing. I felt bad that the people who turned were made to suffer, but I have never felt bad about killing a zombie. In some ways, I think I was born to do it.

"At what point did you hear about the General?"

We heard about the General around the same time everyone else did. He was becoming quite the celebrity. At the time, he began his rise to fame, I think my followers and I had rescued around two hundred and fifty people. Many of those people had laptops. None of them wanted to try and venture to the Safe Zone. They had no reason to do so. They were safe enough right where they were.

When the General finally took his group and escaped the city, we were happy for them. Yet, I personally couldn't conceive of such an idea. To leave the city, we would need to drive. The streets were hazardous and the church was made of stone. It would have no problems standing strong against a siege from the undead.

Still, I had hopes for an eventual evacuation. Not by a caravan, that was simply too dangerous, but if air transportation was made available, I would have jumped at the chance to see my people to safety.

"What about yourself?"

I wasn't about to leave. My place was inside the city. Until the last person was evacuated, I planned on staying and rendering what aid I could render. I also had twenty soldiers that felt the same way.

"Soldiers?"

Well, that's sort of a private joke. Twenty of the able bodied men and women who found their way to the church began to help me. We scoured the neighborhoods in small bands. We gathered supplies, and we found survivors. We also destroyed zombies when it was possible. We were very busy during those times. Our numbers rose, as well. I believe that the final estimate was well over five hundred, but we really never made a true effort to count everyone up.

"When did you meet the General?"

I met the General and the rest of the Regulators right before the Battle of the Sun Bowl. Are you aware of that particular battle?

The Sun Bowl is the outdoor football stadium of UTEP. It has a seating capacity of over 50,000. It was also used for concerts and different types of events.

"I know what most everyone knows."

Yes, well, what everyone knows isn't quite accurate. They know there was a zombie battle right before a mass extraction inside the Sun Bowl. What they never heard about were the vampires.

Earlier, you asked my opinion of the General. I can tell you without any hesitation whatsoever that my first impression was entirely unfavorable. He was extremely rude and entirely dismissive. I also felt that he was somewhat dangerous.

"I take it the two of you didn't get along very well?"

No, we did not. The Regulators were brought to the church by two of my soldiers, Claudia and Joe, a married couple who went out gathering supplies the day before. They were scheduled to return by sunset, but they never made it back. I was extremely worried, to say the least.

When they finally turned up the next day, they had the Regulators with them. The General was a beast of a man. I think you could have fit two of me inside his shirt. That's how large his shoulders were. The rest of him seemed of average size, but his shoulders were immense. He also hadn't seen a razor in quite a few weeks and his clothes were marked with gore that someone had apparently attempted to wash off, but had been relatively unsuccessful in removing the red and black stains.

I didn't like the way his eyes darted around the room as if expecting an attack at any moment. It made me uncomfortable the way his hand always rested near the tomahawk on the back of his belt. Most of all, I didn't like his dog. From all that I'd heard, pit bulls were an extremely dangerous breed. The dog looked menacing. Appearances are often deceiving, however, and I have since changed my opinions about pit bulls. In fact, I even own two of them now.

Of course, I was in the vast minority with my immediate opinions of the General. The survivors all gathered around to greet the famous man. Each and every one of them wanted to say something to him. Many of them even tried to salute him in that strange fist over the chest salute that became popular over the Internet.

He ignored them all.

He was a symbol of hope. He was a hero in the eyes of all of them, and he ignored all those who paid him homage. It was frightfully rude. Instead of a single kind word or a return salute, he simply walked by them and started barking orders.

I was angry. Who was this man who would come into my home and begin to make demands?

"Excuse me," I said testily. "Do you know how much these people look up to you?"

He ignored me as well.

He actually ignored me.

Well, I simply would not be ignored. I was much too angry. I was way too offended. I grabbed one of his massive shoulders, and I spun him around to face me. His dog gave a low warning growl at my actions.

"You have insulted the people living in this church, and you are now offending me!" I shouted. "Give me one good reason why I shouldn't throw you out!"

He simply shook my hand from his shoulder and continued giving orders.

"What were his orders?"

Well, he had questions, too. He wanted to know what types of building supplies we had. He wanted to know how many windows were in the sanctuary, things of that nature. His orders concerned the creation of a barricade, as if he expected an attack.

It was his nephew Dudley who apologized for his behavior. It was Joe and Claudia who explained what might happen in the near future. They told me about the vampires. I doubted the story, to tell you the truth. For a brief moment, I just couldn't believe them.

"What changed your mind?"

Zombies. The zombies changed my mind. I was living in a city full of zombies, and I battled with them nearly every day. If I'm living in a world filled with the living dead, it's not hard to make the leap from zombie to vampire.

I decided to take charge.

After all, I had been the one leading these people since the very beginning. Who was the General? I didn't even know the man. I understood that he had a small measure of success, but from what I understood at the time, nearly half his party died when they tried to escape from the city. I wasn't about to hand over the reins to someone with that sort of track record.

Father Monarez was referring to the caravan that was led by Tito. Most of them were killed on the way to the border when Tito disregarded Jaxon's orders and tried to fight. Father Monarez didn't know the full story at the time.

At the time I interrupted him, he was demanding to know what skill sets were of the people under my protection. I simply would have none of that. Many of those people were old or infirm. I wouldn't have them endangering themselves by following his orders.

I wanted to gather everyone and hide in the basement. It would be horrendously cramped, but if what I heard about the vampires was true, hiding would be our only chance for survival. The people were terrified. They weren't warriors. They thought the arrival of the Regulators meant an end to the nightmare they had been living through. Instead, they were quickly learning that the General had brought something much worse to our door.

"STOP!" I shouted at the General. "This will not happen. You are not in charge here. I lead these people, and I will not have them endangered by you or anyone else. We cannot possibly make a fight out of this. I'm taking all of them into the basement. If the beasts actually come for us, we will be safely hidden from danger. I, for one, am not even convinced that they will come. After all, their fight is with you, not us. Maybe you should leave. Yes, leave and take your vampires with you."

Everyone became quiet instantly. All eyes were upon us as the General and I faced each other in the middle of the sanctuary. I saw his eyes narrow as he sized me up.

"The vampires will come," he growled. "That's going to happen, whether you like it or not. If you aren't ready for them, they will break down your doors, find you in the basement, and tear you apart. They will do this whether I'm here or not. They will kill all of you because they are evil, and evil does nothing but destroy."

The tone that he used absolutely terrified me. In that brief moment, I saw the man as nothing more than rage and fury. He spent most of his days holding it all back of course, but it was always there, hiding underneath the surface, just waiting to come forth and destroy.

"These people are not warriors."

"Come tonight," he answered, "they will be."

I wanted to say something back. I wanted to defend everyone, and keep them from danger. I was at a loss for words. With the zombies, we always had the church to keep us safe. The stone walls were impenetrable.

My world was turned upside down. I could no longer rely on our home to keep us safe. No longer were we bringing the fight to the monsters: the monsters were now bringing the fight to us.

I didn't know how to help.

I didn't know how to protect everyone when our fortress could be breached. I had no choice but to let the man take charge. I had no alternative but to rely on a man I considered dangerous. Worst of all, I thought he was exactly the type of man we needed to make it through the night.

It was Claudia who led me away from the room. I was noticeably shaken. I was worried. I felt that I had failed. A threat was coming and I was powerless to stop it.

"*You shouldn't be so hard on yourself. It's not as if prestigious schools and seminary ever trained you for battle. Think about how many lives you managed to save. I don't know many people who could have handled what was coming your way.*"

In truth, you are certainly correct. I had at that point achieved far more than should have been possible, but at the time, I was a broken man. I was devastated by my perceived weakness. I had no idea what the General was doing. I merely sat in my office, and cursed myself.

In case you haven't noticed by now, failure does not sit very well with me. I'm not used to it. I am also keenly aware that if it weren't for the General and his team, I would not be sitting here today speaking with you. He was right about that basement. I would have led everyone to their deaths. Vampires are evil. I truly believe they would have attacked us regardless of whether or not the General was inside the church. They would have killed us all, just to upset him.

Of course, I knew none of this at that time. At that moment, I merely felt like a failure. It wasn't until the large one by the name of Nick came to visit me that I began to see things a bit differently.

"Can I have a moment, Father?" Nick asked after politely knocking on the door.

I didn't answer him, but he didn't let that slow him down at all. He walked right in and leaned a large axe on the wall next to the chair he dropped down on.

"Don't think too badly of him, Father," Nick said. "He has the weight of the world on his shoulders."

"He's a very unpleasant man," I replied softly.

"That he is, Father," Nick said. "Always has been, but he grows on you once you get to know him. Besides, I don't think I would want to follow a pleasant man into a fight like this. Jax knows what he's doing. I don't know how he knows, but for some weird reason, everything seems to work out for him in the end."

"I hope you're right, young man," I replied, "because I certainly don't feel comfortable entrusting anyone's safety to him at the moment."

"Of course not," Nick said. "You're a leader. You've led all these people to safety. But tell me, what does a priest truly know about killing vampires?"

I had no answer for him, of course, and he didn't seem to truly need one. Instead, he nodded respectfully in my direction and left me to ponder what he had said. His words had affected me. What did I know about killing vampires? The zombies were easy enough, but from what I heard, vampires were a different matter altogether. I was in over my head, or was I?

The moment things were about to turn bad, the Regulators appeared at our doorstep. Could it be? I had prayed for God's help in defending the people under my protection every single night, and just when things became dire, the General appeared.

Well, God does work in mysterious ways.

I had been horrible with the man. In fact, it was me who started the rudeness. Sure, he was rude to all the survivors that came forward to meet him, but Nick was correct. The man had the weight of the world on his shoulders. He was trying to find a way to save everyone.

At that moment, I realized I was acting rather immaturely. I had it in my mind that I would leave my office, walk over to the General, offer my hand in friendship, and apologize for my behavior. I could sit there and nurse my wounded pride, or I could walk out there and do something beneficial.

I chose to do something beneficial, and just as I rose from my chair, the General himself strode into my office and slammed my chainsaw down on the desk before me.

"If you're through with your stomp and pout," he said. "We're going to need every able- bodied person tonight."

Before I could reply, he stomped back out the door.

I grumbled to myself. I may have even cursed, but in the end I followed him. The sanctuary was a mess. There were odd contraptions being built above all the windows. There was a heavy looking and rudely constructed spiked platform at a ninety-degree angle above the front door. The pews had all been moved and stacked together in two large groups. It looked as if they had become some sort of protective wall, but I wasn't sure.

The noise level was something else. I was terrified at how much noise the people were making. The electric saws, the drills, and the sounds of hammering would attract every single zombie in a ten-mile radius.

I immediately looked out the window.

"Be careful, Father," the General said as he walked past me carrying one side of a pew with one hand, while pointing to the contraption above the window with the other. "Don't want to lose a hand, do you?"

"There are zombies out there," I stuttered while backing away from the window. "I'm going out there to take care of them before their numbers swell up any higher."

"Let them be," the General said before walking away to continue whatever it was he was doing.

"Jax isn't always good at explaining himself," Dudley said. "Makes him seem like an asshole sometimes, but he doesn't mean anything by it."

"I'll take your word for it," I replied.

"Look," Dudley said. "The zombies outside can't break the walls. We're hoping that they'll slow down the vampires a bit. At the very least, they'll be a bit of an early warning system. If they stop trying to get in, we'll know that the vampires are on the property."

"Why is that?"

"Vampires don't seem to like zombies," Dudley answered with a shrug.

The work went on and on throughout the day. Finally, an hour before sunset, the General was satisfied. The defenses were finished. The sanctuary became very quiet. Outside, we could hear the moans of the dead. We could hear the dry slaps of their hands as they pounded against the stone walls.

The General sat quietly upon the steps of the altar. He had taken out his tomahawk and was slowly running a sharpening stone against the blade. The sound of metal scraping against stone as he made slow passes over the blade echoed throughout the church. Everyone was watching him. He didn't seem to notice.

A half an hour before sunset, the very youngest and the sick were led into the basement. I was glad to see that at least some them were being placed far from danger, but I was terrified that those of us remaining in the sanctuary were their only line of defense.

It was a ragtag band, to say the least. Our numbers ranged from twelve year olds all the way up to seventy year olds. They all carried makeshift weapons or knives. They all looked terrified. I watched as the Regulators moved among them and chatted easily. They showed them the best ways in which to use the weapons, calmed their fears, and told them to stick together.

The General still sat upon the steps of the altar while his team moved among the people. The scrapes of the sharpening stone against his tomahawk were the only noise coming from his area. Even his scary, black, dog was quietly sleeping next to him with her head upon his lap.

There was a little girl under my protection. Her name was Mona. Her family used to attend services. She was a lovely, shy, little girl, and she possessed the most beautiful voice I've ever heard. She used to sing for the congregation. When the dead began to walk, her father had been lost, but the mother and daughter were able to escape and make their way to the church. They had been with me almost from the beginning.

I became rather uneasy when I saw Mona slowly make her way towards the General. I had noticed the girl watching him throughout the day and I warned her to stay away from him. If I had been any closer, I might have stopped her from approaching him. Yet, I was near the front door, and I would have had to shout to halt her progress.

When she approached close enough, the General looked up at her and stopped sharpening his weapon. Mona came even closer. She was completely undaunted by the dog which lifted its head from the Generals lap and sniffed in her direction. She handed the General a picture that I had seen her drawing earlier in the day as she watched him.

I watched the man politely take the picture from her little hands and whisper something to her that I was unable to hear from across the room. I don't know what he said, but it was undoubtedly sweet because Mona giggled and ran happily back to her spot behind the barricaded pews.

"Why is this story important to you?"

I honestly wish I knew. It was just odd to see the man do something nice. I had judged him on how abrasive he was. I found him to be a tad despicable, and I thought I had his measure. I even wondered why his team often rushed to his defense. Then, just when I thought I understood him, I saw a completely different side of him.

He has the weight of the world upon his shoulders. That is what Nick had told me. I began to wonder if that might not make a man forget to act politely around others and focus on saving them instead.

Aside from that, Mona had an important part to play later on, but I'd rather not rush ahead. Instead, allow me to take you all the way to the setting sun.

"Were you afraid, Father?"

I was terrified. I don't mind admitting that at all. There is something very frightening about creatures that come for you in the darkness. It's a primal sort of fear. The sanctuary was thick with its presence.

Everyone became quiet again. Even the whispers had hushed. Outside, we could still hear the moans and screams of the dead. There must have been hundreds of them out there.

"Turn the lights on," the General ordered when the room became dark.

The Regulators were spread throughout the room. Each of them looked tense, but ready. Despite what evil was headed our way, I knew they would stand strong. Their commitment was evident in their features and postures.

The sun had set.

Nothing happened for another hour.

Then the General stood up and cocked his head. He was listening for something.

"They'll be here soon," he announced. "Make yourselves ready."

"What are they waiting for?" I asked.

The General regarded me before answering.

"They're cleaning up the zombies that aren't around the church away from the neighborhood. They don't want the interference. When they've finished with that, they will come."

If I listened hard enough, I could actually hear what he was talking about. In the distance, there were the sounds of battle. I didn't pick them up before, because I wasn't too familiar with what the sounds of battle actually sounded like.

Eventually, the sounds became louder and closer. I could hear screams and wails in the night. Occasionally, I could even hear explosions. If I was frightened before, it was nothing compared to what I felt when I listened to the sounds of the vampires as they destroyed the zombies in the surrounding area.

Around four hours after sunset, the zombies outside the church stopped pounding on the walls. The vampires had arrived. Shortly after that, I could hear the sounds of bones breaking and skin tearing. I could hear the moans and screams of the zombies as they spotted what could only have appeared to them as an easy meal.

The crashing and thumping, the chaos outside our walls lasted only a brief moment, and silence reigned supreme. I watched as everyone's eyes darted back and forth between all the windows. None of us knew where the attack was going to come from. I watched Nick adjust his grip on his axe. I saw Dudley take deep, centering, breaths. I observed many of the survivors whisper quiet prayers.

The attack came from everywhere at once.

The vampires shattered the windows. The freezing air filled the room instantly. The front door reverberated with the sounds of impact. I could hear an unearthly laughter floating through the outside air. The very walls of the church began to throb beneath the violence being committed upon them. The noise was deafening. Some of the people in the sanctuary squeezed themselves lower under the barricaded pews. Some of the children began to cry. Someone else began to scream.

The General did nothing.

The man stood absolutely still in the center of the large room. He was waiting for something. I just didn't know what. I also couldn't understand how he could appear to be so calm. It was as if he expected everything that was happening to happen.

Everything came to an abrupt stop. It was silent once more.

"They can't enter the church," someone shouted.

"Why did they stop?" someone else asked.

The first vampire came crashing through one of the broken stained glass windows. He didn't make it very far, and I finally learned what the contraptions above the windows were. The General had found a few engineers among the survivors, and together, they constructed guillotines over all the windows.

As soon as the vampire came crashing through, he must have triggered the blade. I'm not sure what the blades were made from, but the church had been redesigned many times over the years, and a lot of materials were stored down inside the basement.

The blade sliced into the vampire's neck. It didn't sever the head, but it must have caused the creature an immense amount of pain. The way it screeched and wailed was completely awful. The black blood spurting from its neck and mouth almost reached the ceiling.

Everyone began to panic—but not the General.

He finally began to move, and when he did, I was shocked at his speed. He crossed the room instantly, and the tomahawk twirled in his hand. He brought the black blade crashing down upon the creature's neck. The creature wailed even louder. It thrashed even more fiercely. The General never paused, not even for a moment. He struck the vampire again, and again, until finally, the head rolled from the shoulders.

The General picked up the head and held it out for all to see.

"They can be killed!" he shouted. "They can be killed. All you need to do is stay strong. All you need to do is fight."

Everyone began to cheer. Everyone began to thump their weapons against the floor. I even joined in myself. All the problems that I had with the man were instantly forgotten. We all had the same goal: to help one another survive the night.

The next attack came at the front door. I watched as pieces of heavy wood flew across the room. I watched as the large spiked block came pivoting down upon the vampire, instantly impaling the creature through the chest. I watched the creature struggle against the wooden spikes. I watched its movements begin to slow, and I watched it cease moving all together.

"Take its head off!" the General shouted. "And board up that door."

Nick began to hack at the creature's neck while others set the front door back onto its thick hinges. The youngest brought hammers and nails. Others brought wooden braces. Soon, the doorway was strong once again.

The assault picked up with an even greater fury. The vampires outside the room began to tear at the very walls of the church. They began to throw rocks through the windows. The General paced up and down the main aisle telling everyone to be patient, telling everybody to wait until they were inside.

I personally did not want to wait for the vampires to enter the church, but I could see the logic. Inside the sanctuary we were strong. Inside, we had numbers on our side. The third vampire burst through the window with the already triggered guillotine.

The dark shape punched right through the flimsy metal of the makeshift blade and tumbled amongst us. In a flash, the General was after her, but the damage was already being done. The people froze as she charged through the barricade of pews and slashed out with her clawed hands.

It was horrible to see what the vampires were capable of. The devastation she caused was astounding. I watched as she ripped through clothing and flesh with ease. I saw the red blood of my fellow man splash the walls.

The General was upon her just as soon as her attack began. The tomahawk slashed through the air, and cleaved off a piece of her skull. The vampire screamed in pain and anger. The black drool frothed at her mouth, and she swatted the man away as if he were an annoying insect, and continued her attack upon the innocent people.

I became enraged.

Without thought I ran towards the vampire. I was determined that she would bring no further death to the people under my protection. I pulled the starter cord as I ran forward to meet her. I could barely hear the motor of the chainsaw as the instrument came to life in my hands, but I could feel the vibration. I also felt my strength returning to my arms and legs.

It was the same strength that had saved me on my very first encounter with the zombies. I slashed the chainsaw at her neck when I was close enough. The whirling blade ripped open her throat, and the vampire gurgled and tried to staunch the flow of blood.

The General was upon her back and hacking at her neck with a black knife. The damage I had caused on her neck increased with his slashes and I was covered in her vile, black blood. Still, she easily threw the General away from her. I felt the blood chill in my bones as she cast her dead eyes upon me.

The people attacked.

They came at her in a great mob. I watched her disappear beneath their violent hands and crude weapons. I saw Nick run forth, and swing his axe down upon her head with a sickening crunch. I watched the mob undulate as she struggled beneath them. I heard her screams. I heard her curses. I saw people fly through the air as she swatted them away.

But as soon as she got away, they pulled her back down. They were upon her, stabbing at her, and causing her pain. The black blood was everywhere. I understood how dangerous the creature was; how much damage they were capable of withstanding.

"That's why the General set the traps that he did, isn't it? He wanted to trap them, to immobilize them in order to kill them easier."

I would assume so. I never actually got the chance to ask the man, but I can attest that a trapped vampire is a lot easier to destroy than an unencumbered one.

Still, the violent mob brought the vampire down. It took some time, of course, and lives were lost.

But the vampire fell. She fell and I charged forth once again with my chainsaw and removed her head. It wasn't a difficult cut by the time I got another chance to attack. The mob had seen to that. When all was finished, she was barely even recognizable as a human shaped figure.

When my breathing finally calmed down enough to hear other sounds, I became aware of Dudley, and Javie, firing their silenced rifles outside the window in an effort to prevent more vampires from entering the sanctuary. The dog was tearing at a grey hand the grasped at the windowsill despite the machine gun fire. It wasn't until Dudley swung his machete that the hand disappeared.

We were withstanding them so far. We were still in our castle, so to speak. The battle had not yet been lost, but I knew we wouldn't last the night. The vampires were unstoppable. I remember looking towards the General and watching as he surveyed the damage. His face gave away nothing. It was just as cold as it had been when I first met him, but for just a brief moment I saw his great shoulders sag. I saw the way he slowly bent and retrieved his tomahawk off the debris-covered floor. I saw this and understood.

He expected us to lose.

He knew the strengths of our enemy, and he knew the chances of us lasting through the night were very slim. He knew it was just a matter of time before each and every one of us fell beneath the terrible claws and snapping fangs.

He knew all this and still he stayed.

It was all over in a moment mind you. I was the only one watching him at the time. I doubt anyone else saw what I saw, much less understood, what I did. Still, I wondered about him. I wondered about a man willing to stand with a group that was surely doomed. I even felt just a little inspired by him.

Everything was quiet outside.

The cold night air was penetrating my clothing, and I realized the only way to keep warm was to keep myself moving. It was uncommonly cold outside, but judging from the grey skies earlier, a cold front wasn't really surprising.

I aided the injured, and said prayers for those we had lost. It was hard to keep my spirits up. I had never actually seen battle-wounded people. It was hard to not simply sit down and give up. I did what I could. I even stitched up deep cuts across one child's back while he proudly announced he wanted to be a Regulator when he grew up.

Finally, when our wounded had been tended to, and our dead had been gathered up, I began to hear the moans of the zombies once again, coming from outside the church. I wasn't terribly alarmed because I knew they could never breech our walls, but the Regulators had all gathered at one window and were talking excitedly.

"I'm not exactly sure what I saw," Dudley said.

"Tell me one more time anyway," the General said.

"It looked like the vampires were carrying something," Dudley said. "That's all I know. They were moving pretty fast."

"How many of them did you see?"

"Four or five."

"Where were they going?"

"They were going to both sides of the church," Dudley said. "What do you think is going on?"

"That's what I'm trying to figure out," the General said.

"The moans," I announced and all of them looked at me. "Have you noticed that we can hear the zombies again?"

All of them tilted their heads and cocked their ears until they also began to hear the anguished moans coming from outside the walls. Then, I watched as each of them looked questioningly to their neighbor.

"I have no idea," the General said.

"Do you think they gave up?" Georgie asked.

"No," Dudley said. "I saw them carrying something."

"Could they have been carrying zombies?" the General asked.

"Why would they be carrying zombies?" Dudley asked.

"I'm not…"

The General wasn't given the opportunity to finish. The first zombie crashed through the window on the opposite side of the church and rolled right next to a young woman. She shrieked in alarm and tried to scramble away from the monster, but it was too late. The zombie had attached itself to her leg and began to tear off huge chunks of muscle right through her jeans.

I rushed over to help her. I bounded over the demolished pews scattered across the room as I pulled the starter cord on my chainsaw. I revved the motor and I struck out immediately when I was in range. The zombie was destroyed, but once the motor was cut off on my chainsaw I began to hear the sounds of breaking glass. I even began to hear the diabolical 'snick' sound as the guillotine blades dropped on bodies.

I turned and I saw pieces of zombies before three of the broken windows. I saw that the guillotines had been triggered. Then, I saw the flimsy blades break apart and fall to the floor as more zombies were thrown into the church.

"So the vampires were using zombies to set off the traps?"

Not just to set off the traps. They were using the zombies to attack us as well. Once a guillotine had been triggered, they broke it apart and began throwing zombies through the broken windows.

Glass began to break on both sides of the church. We were under attack from seemingly everywhere. I can't really say how the others fared during these moments. I lost myself in the heat of battle. I think that's probably the way it is sometimes. I was so concerned with killing the zombies that were rampaging inside my church that I don't really know what was happening around me.

Should I have paid attention to everyone else? Could I have saved lives if I had abandoned my weapon and tried to provide aid? I don't know. I believe that I did what I could. I believe that my actions, which were strictly offensive, must have saved lives, but I will never be sure.

I was everywhere, and nowhere. I heard a zombie scream and ran towards its source. I struck them down one by one. I heard screams all around me, both zombie and human. I felt the bitter chill in the air. I slashed and I cut. I made a path through the dead. Not a single one of them got by me. Not a single one of them escaped my attention.

Surely, others were also fighting. Every now and then, I could hear orders being given, and I could hear the sounds of metal colliding with flesh and bone. The church was a warzone. Our enemy was fearless, and so was I.

I had long since given up on fearing the zombies. They did not chill my blood even slightly. I had faced them many times, and every single time I came away triumphant. We were finally having a fight I could understand.

I was in the thick of things from the very beginning. I didn't mind at all. I was glad to finally have an enemy that I could destroy by myself. Or maybe that isn't completely accurate—I would like to amend my last statement—I was glad to finally have an enemy that could be defeated.

I don't know when the vampires began to enter the church.

I shouldn't have been surprised that they did. The zombies triggered our traps and even cut down our numbers slightly. The way inside was wide open and had no defenders. The vampires simply walked inside.

The only reason I noticed them was because I was soon fighting them. I went from zombie to zombie and from zombie to vampire. I didn't even have time to be afraid. The monster was simply before me. His bottom jaw had grown to enormous proportions. His savage teeth snapped at my face. His cold hands grabbed a hold of me. He easily swatted my chainsaw aside. I heard it clatter to the floor. As soon as the little motor died, I heard the screams all around me.

This time, the screams were only human.

The grip of the vampire was very similar to being caught in a vice. I could not escape as his horrific teeth came closer and closer to my neck. I struggled of course. I struggled for all I was worth. I couldn't get away. The General's dog came to help me. She ripped and tore at the vampire's leg, but to no avail. I was going to die and when that became apparent, I averted my gaze. I didn't want to see the lifeless eyes.

People were running in all directions. Not all of them were running away mind you. Most of them were actually trying to fight. It saddened me that, after all we had gone through, there would be no light at the end of the tunnel.

I had failed.

I felt the teeth begin to press into my neck.

"STOP!"

The voice...I didn't know where it had come from, but it penetrated every nook and corner of the sanctuary. It was a compelling voice. I wanted to listen. I felt the teeth pull away from my neck. I was released from the vise-like grip. I became aware of my surroundings and noticed that the entire sanctuary was still and quiet.

The vampires were withdrawing.

I watched the beast that almost ended my life join his own kind and walk through the shattered front door of the church back out into the cold night air.

I could hear the labored breaths of hundreds of people.

Nobody moved. We simply stood in our places and watched the broken front door. I assumed we were about to face yet another horror intent on ending our lives. I was wrong. The voice came again.

"Guardian," it called. "Guardian, come outside and meet with me."

"Go fuck yourself!" the General shouted in response.

"Guardian, I can't tell you how pleased I was to find you here. I thought for sure you had left the city. In turn, I was going to massacre all those you left behind, but imagine my surprise to find you waiting for me at the very first place we came to."

I watched as the General came forth from the crowd of people. He was covered in gore. Obviously, he had been fighting, and, as the gore was not his, I'd say that he had been fighting well. His team followed closely behind him. They were also gore-spattered.

Once the Regulators were in front of all of us, I saw the General motion for everybody but his team to fall back. He didn't want anyone close to the broken front doors. The crowd obeyed his wishes. All of us scrunched back towards the altar.

"Guardian," the voice said. "Come and talk to me. If you agree to my demands, I'll let all of the innocents live. You have my word."

I saw the General turn and look at his nephew. Dudley shook his head furiously. I watched the General sigh heavily, walk through the broken front doors, and out into the dark and frozen night. The dog wanted to go with him. It was Dudley who restrained her.

I'm not sure that I like the General. I find him rather abrupt, rude, and somewhat cold. However, I respect the man greatly. I regret that the people have a need for him, but I pray for him every single night.

And I'll tell you this as well: I believe in him. If I ever had a friend or a loved one in danger from some dark evil—whether it was a zombie, or a vampire, or whatever else lurks in the night—I would want the General to be the one trying to save them.

I believe in him that much.

Chapter 9

JAXON

My next meeting with Jaxon was a bit of a somber one as we discussed the events in the church. Despite the lack of options, it had been very difficult for him to accept the losses. In total, twenty seven-men and women had been killed by vampires or zombies. The wounded numbered forty-three, with varying degrees of severity, none of which were life threatening.

"Father Monarez told me about the voice that stopped all the fighting. Was it the Master vampire?"
Of course.

"What did he say to you when you went outside the church?"
He said he wanted to fight me. If I didn't agree to fight him, he was going to continue the attack until everyone was dead. He also informed me he was holding Hardin, Miriam, Ivana, and a bunch of other behind-the-scenes-type people hostage.

"Did you agree to fight him?"
Yes, I did. He wasn't giving me much of a choice. It wasn't exactly a fight that I wanted. I wanted to kill him, of course, and I would have done my best to do it even, but I certainly didn't want to fight him on his terms. That sounded a lot like suicide. I would have preferred to chase him down with some rocket launchers and flamethrowers.

"Where was the fight supposed to take place?"
The fight was to be held in the Sun Bowl the following evening. None of the remaining survivors were allowed to leave the church. All of them were commanded to stay put until the human foot soldiers of the vampires came to collect them. They were to become the audience that would witness my death. After the Master or I was dead, everyone would be allowed to leave peacefully, and Hardin, Miriam, Ivana and the others would be released.

"What about your team?"
My team was to leave the area at daybreak. The Master vampire did not want them in attendance because they may be tempted to help me.

"You actually agreed to all of this?"
I didn't have much choice. We were losing. I was watching people die. The fight was too stacked against us. They all would have been killed.

"Did you trust the vampire to keep his word?"

Hell no, but by accepting him at his word, I borrowed us some time to plan. I mean the boys weren't exactly happy when I told them all the news. In fact, they were downright pissed at me. I didn't give them a lot of time to yell at me though. There were wounded people that needed our help.

I kept catching Dudley giving me dirty looks as we all cleaned up and bandaged the wounded. I knew he wanted to have a word with me. I just planned on avoiding it as long as possible. I also had people boarding up the front door and all the broken windows. The place was freezing cold.

Finally, when everything had been cleaned up, and all the wounded had been taken care of, Dudley came over to me.

"What the hell are you doing?" he asked.

"I just gave us the best chance of survival we were going to get," I answered. "The vampires were going to tear us all apart. Now we have time to plan."

"What do we need to plan?" Nick asked, having listened in on us. "Regardless of whether you win, or lose, he's promised to release everyone."

"Do you actually believe that?" I asked.

"If you don't believe him," Dudley asked, "why did you accept his deal?"

"I accepted his deal to keep everyone from being torn apart," I answered. "And no, I don't believe him. I think he plans on killing everyone after I'm dead. That way, when the extraction helicopters show up, they will find nothing but a stadium filled with corpses. He will have sent a message to Hardin that vampires shouldn't be fucked with, and he will also have saved face with the vampires following him."

"Why doesn't he just kill Hardin if he's worried about Hardin fucking with them in the future?" Nick asked.

"If he kills Hardin," I answered, "Hardin will just be replaced. He doesn't want to deal with that, not when he can send Hardin a message that he won't ever forget."

"That makes sense," Dudley said. "If Hardin shows up to extract everyone and finds hundreds of corpses and a dead Guardian waiting for him, he'll think twice about letting the next Guardian fight any vampires." He turned to Nick. "Hell, he didn't want Jax here to fight any vampires to begin with."

"He also won't have any witnesses but Hardin and the crews in the helicopter," I added.

"So?" Nick asked.

"So a vampire doesn't want the world to know about vampires. If the world knew vampires existed, can you imagine the witch-hunts? Vampires are strong, but they can't fight an entire population. No, win or lose nobody is going to make it out of the Sun Bowl alive."

"All right," Dudley said. "There's a bloodbath coming. What's the plan? And don't you dare tell me that it involves you fighting a vampire."

"I need a needle and thread," I answered. "Also, have any of you been to the Sun Bowl in the last few years? I'm not very familiar with it."

"I'm familiar with the Sun Bowl," Nick answered. "I actually go to the games when I'm in town, instead of getting drunk in the parking lot."

"*Who was that shot aimed at?*"

Everyone.

"Is the grass real or fake?" I asked Nick.

"It's fake grass, why?"

"Just wondering," I answered. "Wondering, wondering, wondering. Did anyone find me that needle and thread?"

Georgie went off to go look for my needle and thread, and the rest of us retired into the little priest's office. I actually wanted to be alone, but the team wasn't about to let that happen. They wanted to discuss ideas. I sat alone in the corner of the room with Merrick, and let them talk amongst themselves while my mind went into overdrive.

The situation sucked. The fight sucked. The deck was stacked against me. I knew that I could come up with a plan. That wasn't the problem. The problem was that the plan wouldn't be optimal. We simply didn't have the weapons. Hell, I wasn't even allowed to bring anything to the fight but my knife.

Then again, what weapons did I have that would prove even the slightest bit effective against the vampires? The wooden bullets apparently had a very limited effect against older vampires. Cutting weapons did work, but you really had to hack the hell out of them. I just didn't have anything in my arsenal that would make much of a difference when things went from bad to worse.

I remember thinking that I needed a weapon that would cause massive amounts of damage to the vampires very quickly. I was stuck on that idea. It kept going over and over in my mind. It was annoying having the same thoughts circling around and around.

"I hate running," Nick said. "It makes me feel like Kingsley."

"Kingsley didn't exactly run," Dudley said. "He, more or less, mentally checked out and joined the other side."

"Well that's even worse than running," Javie added.

"I'm not leaving Jax," Dudley said.

I don't know why I tuned into their conversation when I did. I really don't, but the idea that had been bouncing around in my head suddenly slammed into the topic of their conversation, and the result was beautiful with promise.

"The topic of their conversation, do you mean Kingsley?"

Yes, it was something Kingsley used when we escaped El Paso the first time. It's something that I never forgot about, and even though I wasn't very practiced in its use, I kept a fair amount in my backpack just in case. I had forgotten it was even there, since it wasn't something I'd normally use.

"I've got it," I announced. "It's not pretty, but it's all we have."

I told everybody my plan. Dudley hated it. He didn't like the idea of me fighting the Master. The odds of me surviving weren't that great. I told him it was necessary in order for my plan to work. The alternative would be me running away. If I did that, too many people would die, and some of them would be people we knew. He calmed down a bit, but he was still pissed.

I can't really say that I blamed him. The Master was faster and stronger than me. I had no idea what on earth I was going to be able to do to him. The field wasn't even real grass. At least if it was real grass I would be able to heal a bit, because most natural things have that effect on me, but I didn't even have that going for me.

An idea occurred to me.

The field had artificial grass, but I couldn't help but think that vampires probably don't spend a lot of time watching football. Therefore, he probably didn't know what the field was made out of.

I had another idea.

I explained everything to my team as soon as Georgie came back with my needle and thread. Dudley was a bit happier, but happiness is relative. Nobody liked the idea of me fighting the Master.

I wasn't getting much in the way of confidence from my team. They were walking on eggshells around me as the night wore on, actually treating me as if I were a condemned man instead of someone that had a chance of winning. It was hard to take. It's not that I mind being the underdog, that's not it at all. I've been the underdog many times before, but I've always known what everyone else didn't: I knew I would win.

This time, things were different.

I didn't actually believe I could beat the vampire. I had a bad, bad feeling about the entire fight. I would try and hold out as long as possible in order to give everyone a chance, but in the end…well, things weren't looking too good.

I didn't want to die, of course. I wanted to win. I wanted to kill the vampire, but the odds of that happening were slim to none. Still, I wasn't going to give up. I knew that perfectly well. It wasn't in my nature to quit. I would fight until I could no longer fight.

It was going to hurt like hell.

I didn't spend much time on those thoughts, however. I didn't allow myself. Instead, I thought of ways in which I could win. I thought of strikes that would cause damage to the vampire. I spent hours going over and over different scenarios.

Everyone in the office was quiet until Javie found an old guitar and started strumming a tune. I caught what song it was almost immediately. It was one of my favorites. I was sick of moping and thinking, so I went over and stood by him as he sat there plucking out the correct cords to the music.

Before I knew it, he was even singing the song, and I was joining in with him. None of us can sing, by the way, but that didn't stop Georgie, Dudley, and Nick from joining in as well. We weren't quiet; we were loud, and we got louder.

Nick, of course, was the one that started going overboard. He was slamming a chair up and down in time with the guitar. After the chair, he attacked a desk. Nick may have been the one making the ruckus, but it was Dudley that brought out the bottle of Jack. He's carried one around ever since he discovered the Rat Pack.

Anyway, once the alcohol started being passed around, things went from bad to worse. The place became a madhouse. The noise level was deafening. Others started joining the party, and before long, the craziness had spilled out into the sanctuary.

It was a good night.

The music just kept coming. More alcohol was found and passed around. Everyone was singing. The little priest was playing tug of war with Merrick. People were clapping me on the back. They were sharing stories with me. They were asking me why I was so damn rude. Dudley did his famous "drunken monkey" dance. Everything was great. Nobody even once mentioned zombies or vampires.

And then Father Monarez ruined everything.

"What did he do?"

He asked me if I wanted my last rites.

"What did you tell him?"

I didn't tell him anything. I stormed off and went back into the office. This time, I only allowed Merrick to come with me. The priest tried to follow me, but Dudley headed him off and took care of things.

After that, the party was over.

I somehow managed to grab a bit of sleep in the office. I remember staring out the window with my head upon the desk. It had started to snow. That's a pretty rare thing for El Paso. We're normally lucky if it snows once or twice a year. I sat there watching the flakes fall lazily from the sky through the window. I remember thinking that it wasn't a bad way to fall asleep.

Once I woke up, the sun was rising in the sky and the team was packing up their gear. I went over some last minute instructions with them, and pulled Dudley aside. I gave him my tomahawk. I wasn't going to need it; rather, I wasn't allowed to bring it.

He asked me about my wife. Something about a worst case scenario, and he wanted to know what he should tell her. I didn't really answer him. I just blew him off. I couldn't allow myself to think along those lines.

I was going to see my wife again. I was going to see that smile that I knew so well and hold her close to me. I would do everything in my power to make it back to her.

I gave Merrick a big hug before everyone left. I ran my fingers through her short fur, and hugged her for all I was worth. In response, she gave a quick lick to my cheek. I walked her to the beat up station wagon the boys were piling into, and watched them drive away.

I spent the day in the office alone with my thoughts. Someone brought me food once, but I didn't have an appetite. I didn't want my last meal. I didn't like feeling like a condemned man. I was getting angry.

By mid-afternoon, the anger had turned into a black rage, and I could feel my upper lip begin to twitch involuntarily. I welcomed the rage. It took away all the negative thoughts. I let it wash over me. I wanted to shut down completely and become the machine that took on all those zombies at the bridge.

Outside the windows of the office, it was still snowing heavily. The sight of snow against the window did nothing to change my mood. The beauty of it was lost on me. I merely sat and raged.

I went from rage to straight-out murderous an hour before sunset. Father Monarez knocked politely on the door and informed me that the foot soldiers of the vampires had arrived and were preparing to escort everyone to the Sun Bowl.

A half an hour before sunset, there was another knock on the office door. I didn't answer it. I just sat there on the desk opening and closing my black folding knife. One wrong word and I was going to tear the intruder apart. The door opened slowly, and I saw for the first time what the vampires must consider a foot soldier.

He was a pale man with a broken spirit. I felt sorry for him immediately. It was hard to look at him. It was hard not to see the wicked wounds on his neck and wrists. I redirected my anger away from the innocent victim who couldn't even look me in the eyes, and I focused it back towards the vampire.

We drove to the Sun Bowl in a decent enough car. The foot soldiers never said a word, not to me, and not to each other, but I thought I could hear one of them crying softly in the silence of the vehicle.

When we arrived at the Sun Bowl, the sky was darkening and the snow was still falling. I was actually a bit shocked that it was still snowing. Like I mentioned before, it doesn't snow much in El Paso. I would have enjoyed watching the snow fall for a bit, but I wasn't given the opportunity. Once I got out of the car, I was immediately led to a locker room.

Once in the locker room, one of the foot soldiers quietly asked me to take off my vest and bite suit. I had a feeling that was coming so I didn't freak out. I just put my utility belt and clothes on a table while all the foot soldiers meekly looked away.

I had planned ahead for the event, and instead of being left in nothing but my underwear; I had a black pair of shorts on underneath my pants. I was also allowed to keep my fingerless gloves for some reason and, with the exception of the large black folding knife in my left hand, I almost felt like a professional fighter preparing for his shot at the title.

Except, I didn't stretch or work up a sweat. I didn't really do anything except sit on a wooden bench and fume.

"Why do you think they wanted you in only your shorts?"

Two reasons, I guess. First, the bite suit would offer some protection. Second, I think the vampire wanted the crowd to see the damage. Like I said earlier, it was going to hurt like hell. I had no delusions that I was going to go quick. He was going to be as cruel as he could possibly be.

I avoided those thoughts as much as possible. They kept creeping back into my head, of course, but each time they did, I shoved them away. I had a plan. It was a plan based on what I had learned from my other vampire encounters. I just had to stay alive long enough to enact my plan.

An hour after sunset, I sensed a change in the foot soldiers. They began to act a little nervous and started fidgeting around. I knew from their actions that the vampires had arrived. It was only a matter of time.

I did what I could to focus. I imagined myself winning the fight. It was hard to collect my thoughts, though, and I ended up listening to the sound of my heart beating inside my chest. It was like a great engine filling my limbs with energy.

The door to the locker room opened.

I was led through some hallways to a long dark corridor where I was abandoned. At the far end of the corridor, I could see the football field. The stadium lights had been turned on and the place was awash in a bright light. He was waiting for me out there. I could feel him, but I couldn't see him yet.

It was freezing cold and I had goose bumps all over my body. I was opening and closing my fingers as I walked through the corridor in an effort to warm up my hands. The walk was long, and I was alone. As I got nearer to the stadium, I could actually see the snowflakes falling against the stadium lights.

I could scarcely believe everything was happening so fast. It seemed like only minutes ago that we had entered the city to rescue survivors. I couldn't even begin to imagine how things had gotten so fucked up. Then I realized that I was afraid.

The rage came back.

I was no longer shivering because of the cold. I was shivering due to the massive wave of hatred that was flowing through my veins. I despise being afraid. Fear isn't something I'm at all comfortable with.

I walked on with murderous intent. I felt the power in my limbs. I breathed deeply and took one step into the stadium. The Master was waiting for me on the fifty-yard line. He was only wearing his black pants. He seemed rather skinny, like somebody that would normally be a cakewalk, but I didn't really believe he would be. I had seen how fast he could move. I had felt how strong he was. He had been holding back then and made his daughter look weak in comparison. He wasn't going to hold back tonight.

On my left side, closer to me on the field, were the survivors. They made up a large group. Every single person from the church was in attendance. On my right side, were all the foot soldiers. There were only about fifteen of them. They probably weren't very important to the vampires.

Along both sides of the field were wide PVC pipes. There must have been at least two rows of them inside the field, but it was difficult to tell with the light dusting of snow. All in all, it looked like a badly rigged irrigation system, the kind that should be below the ground instead of lying on top of it.

Mind you, I didn't really focus much on the pipes or the people. I just sort of saw them out of the corners of my eyes. My attention was focused on the Master, but I noticed when all the survivors began to salute me. They didn't make a sound; they simply all moved at once and crossed their right fists over their hearts.

I felt my upper lip begin to twitch, and I walked towards the Master. That's when I heard the little girl begin to sing. I don't know if you heard about her, but she drew me a picture before the battle at the church.

"Yes, her name is Mona."

Well, I guess she got through the first verse or so on her own before the others joined in on the chorus.

"Others?"

The survivors from the church.

"How many of them began to sing?"

All of them.

Instantly the tears began to well up in my eyes. It's just one of those moments. I felt more than a little embarrassed to be crying in front of the man. After all, he was the one going through everything. I couldn't even begin to imagine how he must have felt.

I don't know how to explain it, but I think it has something to do with all the support. Jaxon was going out there to fight for all of them. He was facing insurmountable odds, and there probably wasn't a single soul among the survivors who actually thought he was going to win. Still, they sang him on. They let him know they were there for him. He wasn't alone.

That was also something that I learned from Mona when I tracked her down and asked her why she began to sing. She told me that Jaxon looked lost and alone. She wanted her song to guide his way back to her and the others.

"I apologize. Please continue."

I was about ten feet away from the Master when their song ended. He began to talk. He was addressing everyone in the stadium. I have no idea what he was saying. I think he may have been asking me a question at one point, but I didn't come there to talk.

When I was about five feet away, I charged.

He didn't expect it. He wanted to play games for the crowd before we got down to business. I wasn't about to stand for that. I wasn't going to exchange back and forth banter with him. I charged him with my full speed and power. When I reached him, I ducked down and wrapped both of his legs with my arms.

I lifted him straight up into the air, carried him a few more feet, and slammed him down on his back. The look of shock on his face was almost comical. He couldn't believe that a human had just put him on his ass.

I didn't laugh at him though. I wasn't in a jovial type of mood. Instead, I immediately began to pound at his face with both of my hands. My left hand was the deadlier of the two. It was holding my unopened folding knife and the impacts were doing more damage.

I broke his nose in an instant. I saw the black blood run freely for just a moment before the injury healed. So I broke it again, and after it healed, I broke it once more before the vampire backhanded me into orbit.

I sailed through the air. I remember thinking that I was in some serious trouble before I landed hard on my back. I struggled to bring air back into my lungs, but the vampire didn't give me any time.

"YOU DARE!" he shrieked as he closed the distance between us, picked me up off the ground, and brought my face to within an inch of his own. "You'll pay for that."

I slashed his neck from ear to ear with my knife. The vampire threw me aside as if I were a ragdoll. His hands flew to his neck as he attempted to staunch the spray of blood that was darkening the light snowfall.

I stood up quickly and charged at him. I wanted to hit him while he was injured and in pain, but by the time I got there, he had healed. He was a lot stronger than his daughter. I didn't even see the slash of his clawed hand, but I felt my head snap back and I saw stars begin to dance at the edges of my vision.

His claws cut me all the way to the bone. He had opened up my face and the blood was freely flowing. I almost managed to avoid his next attack, but he still caught me on the chin with his fist. I'm pretty sure the blow shattered most of my jaw.

I fell to the ground. I was hurt, but I wasn't out of the fight. When he came for me again, I slashed open the inside of his right arm. The blood spurted out, and I rolled away from him as he shrieked in pain.

I charged him from behind and was able to open up the femoral artery in his left leg before the wound on his arm healed. Then he struck me in the stomach so hard I felt something burst in my abdomen. As I rolled on the ground in pain and attempted to rise to my feet, I noticed there was black blood all over the ground. I also saw that the Master was standing right beside me.

He grabbed at my neck with his clawed hands and dragged me to my feet. I tried to cut him again, but his grip was so strong I couldn't breathe. Instead, he rained blow after blow upon my face. I could feel the bones break. Everything went numb. I didn't have the strength to give him a serious cut so instead I put my knife in front of my face and let him slam his fist down on the blade.

The vampire screamed out his rage and again threw me away from him. I flew through the air and came to a rolling stop. I rubbed my face in the snow in an attempt to clear the blood from my eyes. The falling snowflakes were hissing into little puffs of steam as they landed on my body. Even the snowflakes were trying to heal me, but they weren't enough, not nearly enough.

My face was ruined. I didn't even want to guess at how bad the damage was, but still I climbed to my feet. I walked on unsteady legs to meet the vampire as he in turn walked towards me. He was rubbing his injured hand as it healed.

I ducked his clawed strike, reopened the artery in his left leg with a forward cut and made sure his right leg matched before rolling away from him. His hands flew to his injuries and he doubled over in an attempt to stop his precious blood from leaving his body. I jumped on his back and opened his throat once again.

In a blind rage, he reached behind himself and grabbed a hold of my left arm. He yanked me off of him easily, and slammed me into the ground. The impact drove the breath out of my lungs. As soon as he let me go, I tried to stand back up, but my legs were having a difficult time cooperating with my mind. I looked over at the Master to see why he wasn't pressing the attack while I was at a massive disadvantage. He was rolling around on the ground in pain. His blood was spraying everywhere. No human could geyser out blood like that. I don't think the average heart is strong enough to pump it that far.

I felt my lips pull back in a smile.

I finally got to my feet just as the vampire stopped rolling in agony. The slam on the ground had damaged my hip, so I limped over to him. He stood up before I could slash my knife.

He was smiling back at me.

He understood what I was trying to do. I could see it in his face. I wasn't necessarily trying to cause him pain. I wasn't trying to finish him off with one cut. I was trying to drain his blood and he knew it.

The wounds I had given him were still leaking. His neck was still torn open in places and black blood was seeping from the wound. He wasn't healing as fast as he had been when the fight started.

I tried to cut him again, but he was too fast. He dodged my attack easily and slashed open my chest. More of my blood began to flow freely from my body. The wound felt as if it were electrified. I heard a collective gasp rise up from the crowd so I knew it must have looked pretty bad.

He followed the chest gash with more slices and cuts. Two could play at the bloodletting game, and he was showing me just how good he was at it. I dove for his legs, but I couldn't budge him off his feet. I felt his clawed hand pierce my back and tightly grab my spine.

I can't even begin to describe how badly it hurt when he lifted me into the air by my spine and held me over his head. I heard him shouting something to our audience, but the words were lost to me. The wound was fatal. That much I knew. I could tell that by the pain. I could hear it from the crunching noises coming from inside of me.

But that didn't mean I was finished.

I spun around and slashed his wrist open. The blood didn't spray out this time, it just oozed. And the wound gaped and stretched open in the cold night air. In reaction, the vampire dropped me and clutched at his wrist. As I fell, I sliced open his stomach and when he doubled over, I sliced his neck.

The Master retaliated by kicking my stomach with his bare foot. I felt something else explode inside of me from the blow. I watched him with cloudy eyes as he stuffed his internal organs back inside his opened stomach. His entire body was covered in the black blood, and his wounds bled horribly. The organs wouldn't stay put. The wounds would no longer close. I had finally drained him.

Still, he fought through the pain, and approached me. I could no longer get off the ground, and judging from the numbness in my legs, I probably had damage to my spine. He easily grabbed my left hand and crushed my fingers as he tore the knife from my grasp.

I think I may have cried out as he crushed my fingers. After that almost everything was a blur as he stomped and pummeled my body. I tried as best I could to defend myself, but I was too slow and too injured to stop him. He easily broke most of my ribs and cracked my hipbone with the violence of his attack, but he wasn't doing very well himself. He still had some serious strength, but his movements were also slow and he seemed rather clumsy as if he couldn't fully control his body.

It wasn't long before he'd exhausted himself with his efforts, and his organs began to slip from his body cavity. I could barely see through the blood, but I could hear his ragged breaths as he stood there, swaying back and forth in front of the bright stadium lights. He fell heavily to the ground right next to me.

I watched him slowly climb back to his feet, and I willed myself to move against him. Pain was etched across his features as he held his wounded stomach. He was looking down at me. He wanted to finish me off, but he was too injured. He was too weak and could barely stand. He couldn't heal. The bloodletting had done its job. My plan had worked. I stayed alive long enough to drain him.

I wiped blood from my right eye with a numb hand and saw him turn his gaze away from me and cast it instead upon his foot soldiers. He motioned them to come forward as he swayed on his feet. He cursed aloud when they refused to move. He took a shaky step in their direction and managed to stay upon his feet. His second step was just as shaky as the first. I knew what he was doing. He wanted their blood. If he fed upon them, he would heal. If he healed, I was a dead man.

I played my ace in the hole.

I reached my right hand down towards the bottom cuff of my shorts and pulled free my Cold Steel Ti-Lite folding knife.

"Is this the same knife you used to finish off the former Guardian?"

Yeah. I used the needle and thread to sew it on the inside cuff of my shorts. I figured the Master would eventually attack my hand if I kept cutting him, so I made sure to keep the blade in my left hand. I'm actually right handed. As soon as I had the blade in that hand, I threw my entire body to the side, and slashed the vampire's Achilles tendon.

He fell to the ground instantly. I crawled slowly over to him as he looked at me in fury, and I cut the Achilles tendon of his other foot as well. The Master could no longer walk, but he slowly began to crawl away from me.

I was finished. I could no longer move. Cutting his Achilles tendons took the last of my strength. My breathing was wet and sloppy. Something was rattling inside my chest. I wanted to crawl after him, but I just couldn't will myself to do it. I wanted to scream out my frustration, but I lacked the ability to do even that. I was dying.

In the end, I followed my plan and used my last available option. I raised my arm and pointed my index finger into the sky.

Chapter 10

DUDLEY

I felt that the final interview about the Battle of the Sun Bowl should be with someone other than the General. I wanted to hear what it was like to watch the fight between Jaxon and the Master, and not be able to interfere. I also wanted to know what happened to the rest of the team after they had left the church. I chose to speak with Dudley.

I wasn't disappointed.

It sucked.

"What sucked?"

Every single bit of it. From the fight at the church, all the way to the end—it just sucked.

"Tell me about it?"

Where do you want me to start?

"Start at the church, if you'd like."

The dirty bastards started throwing in zombies to set off the traps and attack us. It was a cheap move, but it worked. Before any of us knew what was happening, the battle was being fought inside the sanctuary. They had broken through our defenses and were putting a serious hurt on us.

I remember the screams.

I remember all the blood. We were fighting zombies, then vampires, and then zombies again. It was too much. We were losing. We were failing, but we never gave up. There was no reason to give up. One way or the other, we were all going to die. So we may as well go out fighting.

I still get the shakes when I think about that night. Every now and then, I would catch sight of a team member. They had that look in their eyes. You know that look? Probably not, but it's a nasty look. When you see it, you know the situation is hopeless.

Then the voice came.

Everything came to an abrupt stop. That was fortunate, but then the voice began to ask Jaxon to come outside. He didn't want to. I don't blame him for that, but when the voice promised to spare everyone's lives if he agreed to its demands…well, Jaxon had no choice at that point.

He gave me a look when he walked out. He didn't think he was coming back, but that didn't stop him. Nothing stops my uncle.

The funny thing is, I don't think the Master wanted to come inside the church. I always heard that vampires had an aversion to churches. I think there may be something to all that.

"*Didn't the other vampires enter the church easily enough?*"

I'm not sure how easily. They seemed to move pretty sluggishly. We were even able to kill the first three that tried pretty easily. Then again, maybe I'm just imagining things. We still don't know a great deal about vampires, but I did find it odd that all the survivors were sent to the Sun Bowl. My guess is that the Master wanted them away from the church to make slaughtering them easier.

"*What happened after the General came back inside?*"

He told us how the Master wanted to fight him and then we helped patch up all the wounded and gather up all the bodies. I was against Jaxon fighting the Master from the very beginning.

When we went into the office, Javie, Nick, and I tried to come up with a plan, but we were pretty much screwed from the get go. We didn't have enough cars to drive everyone from the church out of the city, and walking out of El Paso is way too dangerous with all the zombies. We also couldn't abandon them because the vampires would continue their attack with a vengeance in our absence.

As we talked, Jaxon sat alone with Merrick. When he finally spoke up, he had a plan. I hated the plan. It involved him fighting the Master. There didn't seem to be a way to avoid that, but I stopped bitching when he reminded me that the vampires still held Hardin, Miriam, and Ivana.

Shortly after Georgie came back and Jaxon began to sew his Ti-Lite inside his shorts, Jaxon revealed his next idea. It was a pretty decent idea, but I wasn't really sure we could make it work. Fortunately, Javie has some experience with plumbing.

After the plan was set, everybody got really quiet. It was almost like we couldn't really believe we were going to go through with it. To me, it felt like I was throwing my uncle to the wolves. He had to survive long enough for the plan to work.

"*Tell me about the guitar.*"

It was funny to see the smile of embarrassment on Dudley's face.

Javie found a guitar, and he and Jax started singing. That's what started everything. The rest of us just joined in because it would have been rude to let them tackle the entire song all by themselves.

"*What song was it?*"

"God's Gonna Cut You Down" by Johnny Cash. A song like that causes the adrenaline to start pumping. I merely brought out the Jack to calm everybody back down. Obviously it didn't work. We just got louder and louder, but it was nice. We were finally able to relax a bit. It reminded me of the early days back at the Safe Zone.

The survivors joined us, of course. Even Father Monarez began to unwind just a bit. Before any of us knew it, we had ourselves a pretty decent party going on. A crowd had even gathered around Jax, since he was finally behaving like an approachable human being. He was telling them some pretty humorous stories about his younger days. I swear I almost fell off my chair laughing when someone actually asked him why he was so rude all the time.

"*What did Jaxon do?*"

He was laughing right along with me. I don't remember him answering the question. I think he just laughed it off. Then we laughed even harder when Georgie asked Javie to play some Rascal Flatts. Javie stopped strumming his guitar and tried to throw Georgie out of the church.

"*What's wrong with Rascal Flatts?*"

Boy bands don't belong in country music. Georgie was lucky Nick didn't pelt him with another bottle. Anyway, the party was great. It was unexpected, but it was needed. Father Monarez even led us in some toasts for the lives that we had lost.

Then he had to screw everything up and ask Jax if he'd like to have his last rites. Jaxon, of course, had a fit. He stormed off, and when the little priest tried to go after him, I stood in his way.

"You need to let him calm down now, Father," I said.

"I'm not sure what I did that was so offensive," he said.

"You can't confront a man like Jaxon with the possibility that he might lose," I answered. "He can't think along those terms. He needs to believe he'll win. You basically just told him that you expect him to lose."

"My son," he said. "Do you expect anything different?"

I didn't answer the man. I walked away. I didn't want to think about it either. That's when I noticed the party was over. Everyone looked as if they were ashamed to be having a good time after all that had happened. Or maybe they were ashamed to be having a good time when Jaxon was about to have a battle to the death to ensure everyone's survival.

I didn't sleep that night. I'm not sure anyone slept that night. Instead, I parked myself outside the office door in case Jaxon needed anything during the night.

Shortly before sunrise, everyone was up and getting ready for the team's departure. They gave us a nasty station wagon since we would need something to carry supplies in. I couldn't believe there wasn't a truck around to spare. A truck would have suited us much better than a station wagon.

Jaxon gave us a quick pep talk, and went over all the details once more before we left. He was counting on us. If we failed, everyone would die. When he was finished up and everyone was hopping into the car, Jax pulled me aside.

He handed me his tomahawk.

That gesture almost brought me to tears. He had already loaded up his guns and backpack into the station wagon, but he made sure to hand the tomahawk to me. I looked at the weapon, and actually saw it for the very first time. It was a simple design, but in the correct hands it was an incredibly dangerous weapon. Jaxon probably bought it, played with it for about a week, and just stuck it somewhere in his house when he grew bored. He couldn't have known at the time that he would someday become famous, and that simple tool would become his primary weapon.

The blade was hair-splitting sharp. The black paint over the metal was faded and scratched heavily, but not a ding could be seen on the edge. The pale wood of the shaft was stained an odd tan color from sweat, blood, and hard use. The weapon damn near screamed in my grip when I thought about all the killing it had done in my uncle's hands.

"Don't let them die," Jaxon said. "If I fail, you need to succeed. Don't let them die."

It was hard not to get emotional.

"What about Skie?" I asked. "What do I tell her if things go bad?"

My uncle just stared at me. He tried to say something but couldn't find the right words. Instead he gave me a quick hug, and nudged me towards the station wagon. I watched him turn his attention to Merrick for a bit before he led her to the station wagon. He wanted her well away from his fight so she wouldn't be hurt.

Nick drove us away.

We had a job to do and failure wasn't an option. The plan had two parts. For the first part, we had to search the inside of the stadium. It took about three hours before we found the maintenance room we were looking for. It was a relief that the room still existed. Javie studied the controls and figured out what we would need.

It was going to require a lot of work. He wasn't even sure everything would still function, but we had to try. We had to make it happen. Lives depended on us. My uncle was depending on us.

We drove to the hardware store.

This took time as well. Before we could gather up any supplies, we had to clear the parking lot and store of all the shamblers. There were a lot of them, let me tell you. After the area was cleared, we backed up the station wagon, and loaded up.

When we got back to the stadium, Javie worked his magic with Georgie and Nick, and I got started on the second part of Jaxon's plan.

"*I'm a little bit lost.*"

You should be. I'm leaving out all the key parts, but I'll dig in deeper when the time comes, so don't worry yourself silly. Just know that we worked the entire day in an effort to set things up. That was the plan. It would have been a lot easier if the stadium still had real grass, but that kind of luck wasn't on our side.

When all was ready, we crossed our fingers and locked Javie and Merrick in the maintenance room and went outside. It was beginning to snow harder, and that was a good thing. It made finding a hiding place just a bit easier, though not very comfortable. You see, the snow was blowing down in a certain angle that kept the field from being filled with snow, but was still piling up mounds of it about midway up on the bleachers.

Georgie, Nick, and I, buried ourselves in the mounds. Each of the three of us took a side of the stadium, leaving only the entrance we were hoping Jax would walk through free. To say the least, we were freezing our asses off. I think we shivered in our respective mounds for at least two hours before the foot soldiers led the survivors into the stadium. I was glad when they finally showed up for two reasons. One, it wasn't pleasant listening to Nick bitch and moan through our ear radios while we all turned blue in the cold; the arrival of the survivors finally shut him up. Two, the survivors came through the entrance we were hoping they would be using. They were led to the immediate side of the field, situated behind a couple rows of large PVC piping that marked the out of bounds line. The foot soldiers sat on the opposite side of the field behind another couple of rows of PVC piping, as if they were supporting an opposing team.

The waiting game was almost finished.

An hour after sunset, the Master arrived. It wasn't some type of grand entrance like I had been expecting. He simply walked through the same entrance everybody else had, and strolled rather casually to the middle of the field.

My entire body was shivering uncontrollably in the cold, while the Master was barefoot and shirtless as he stood in the middle of the field waiting patiently. I was afraid my shivering would make the mound of snow above me vibrate and give away my position. Fortunately, the Master never even looked my way.

I never saw the other vampires, but I knew they were there. Jaxon warned us about that. He said they were predators and wouldn't want to be out in the open. He figured they would stay hidden until the final moments of the fight. Then, they would appear somewhere high in altitude since they seem to like being above their prey.

Time began to slow down after the Master had taken his position. I felt the adrenaline surge rampaging through my veins as I waited for Jaxon to make his appearance. Or maybe it was fear. In fact, yes, it was fear. I didn't want to see my uncle walk into the stadium. A part of me was hoping that he suddenly grew a brain and decided to run off and hide. I knew it would never happen, of course.

Jaxon was coming to fight.

When I first saw him walk out of the tunnel and step into the stadium, I almost didn't recognize him. He was stripped down to his shorts. I'm not sure how he had known that one was coming, but he had. He looked too skinny, almost emaciated, like a fighter during weigh-ins after a huge weight cut. I couldn't remember the last time I had seen him eat. The scruff on his face also looked a bit longer than usual. I had just seen him that morning and yet he looked so different.

I was worried about him more than ever before. I began to doubt the plan. I began to doubt everything. I wanted to jump out of the mound of snow and join him on the field. I wanted to grab him and drag him away, and if the Master didn't let us leave, then we'd both fight him.

Almost in unison, every single survivor began to salute him.

It was a somewhat surreal moment. It was a way for them to show respect to the man that was risking everything for their survival. Jaxon of course, didn't seem to notice. His eyes were fixed on the Master. His head was slightly lowered and his face was utterly frozen in a grim expression.

He really didn't look like the Jaxon I knew.

He began to walk to the Master. I could see his green eyes smoldering in the darkness. It was a scary sight. The stadium was quiet enough to hear a pin drop. That was the kind of tension and fear filling the air. When the voice came, it literally pierced through the nighttime sky. It was a voice of pure innocence, but it was loud and powerful at the same time.

It was a little girl. At first I thought she was shouting something and then I realized she was singing. Her voice was amazing. I can't even begin to describe it. Her mother tried to pull her back into the crowd, but she would have none of that. She really got into it. She was even jumping up and down and pounding her fists as she sang. She started things off wonderfully, but imagine my surprise when every single human being, with the exception of the foot soldiers on the opposite side of the field, began to sing along with her on the chorus as Jaxon walked by. It was amazing. It was the most incredible show of support I think I've ever seen in my life.

It's funny; my uncle isn't always a pleasant person, and he's normally somewhat awkward around strangers, but man oh man, do people support him. He may not be good at talking, but his actions speak a thousand times more than any words can convey.

I asked Mona what song she was singing when I met with her. It was "Lose Yourself" by Eminem. Apparently she sang the song almost nightly to all the survivors at the church and that is why they all knew the lyrics.

I was proud of Jaxon. I was terrified for him. Each bit of emotion began to fight, and wrestle, with the others until I was a wreck.

The snow was still falling. It drifted lazily past the stadium lights as the song ended and Jax moved closer to the Master. The vampire began to blab about something. It was hard to hear him under the snow, but Jax wasn't about to play the talking game. He hates talking smack. When things are past the point of no return and a fight is inevitable Jax won't waste any time mixing words, he just starts punching.

Or in this case, he charged and I swear to God I saw him smile when he did it.

The takedown he used on the Master was picture perfect. The vampire never saw it coming, and despite being like a thousand times stronger than Jaxon, he ended up on his back. The punches began to rain down upon the Master.

For a brief and shining second, I thought Jax was going to win right then and there. A normal human being would probably have been ready for a trip to the hospital. The Master, on the other hand, easily backhanded Jaxon away from him. I was devastated to see how easily he stopped Jaxon's attack. I was horrified to see how easily the vampire got back to his feet and turned the tables on my uncle.

Jaxon was lifted straight into the air and brought close to the vampire's face. I don't know what the monster said to him, but I'm sure it was pretty nasty. It just wasn't nasty enough. Jaxon opened up the Master's neck with a slice he never saw coming. The black blood shot straight up in the air and poured all over Jax.

The fight, to say the least, was extremely brutal. The vampire had strength on his side, to be sure. He pummeled Jaxon mercilessly. Every single strike that landed was life threatening. I could hear the sounds of his fists colliding with skin and bone, and I could hear the bones breaking from under the snow.

I thought my uncle was going to die.

I was amazed that he kept getting to his feet. He wouldn't give up, and the cuts he landed on the vampire were nothing short of lethal. My uncle knew how to fight. He knew the areas to attack. He reasoned that the vampire would become weak if it lost enough blood.

The field had been covered with a light snowfall. The blood of the vampire had painted the field black all around them. Every time he seemed to grab a hold of Jaxon, Jaxon would cut the vampire again. It wasn't very long before the blood stopped gushing, and the vampire's wounds were no longer healing so rapidly.

The Master was fighting stupidly. He should have never met my uncle in an open field. He should never have allowed my uncle to bring a knife. The vampire had underestimated him. Jaxon was a Guardian. Guardians were created to kill monsters.

Jaxon had weakened him, but the price for doing so was high. My uncle had lacerations across his face and chest. His face was battered so badly he was unrecognizable. Each blow the vampire had landed had been effective. When the Master punched his entire hand through Jaxon's back and lifted him bodily into the air by his spine, I knew the end was near.

My uncle had lost.

The question now was how badly the vampire would torture him before he put Jaxon out of his misery. I wanted it to be over. I didn't want to watch anymore. I couldn't watch anymore. It was too much. To see a family member go through so much pain, I just couldn't bear it.

"This is your champion!" the vampire shouted. "This is the man chosen to protect…"

He never finished his thought. Jaxon somehow turned and slashed at the arm imbedded into his back. The vampire dropped him instantly, but before Jaxon fell to the ground, the knife lashed out again and opened the vampire's stomach. I saw grey organs begin to slide out through the wound. Jaxon sliced his neck when the vampire bent over to hold himself together. The last of the monster's blood dumped onto the field.

The Master did the only thing he could do. He kicked the heap that was my uncle away from him. Jaxon's body rolled across the bloody field. The vampire was no longer healing. With one arm holding his organs inside his body, he stumbled towards my uncle, reached out with his free hand and crushed Jaxon's fingers before throwing the knife aside.

Jaxon was defenseless, worse than that, he was barely even moving.

"*I'm shocked that he was even alive after the vampire grabbed a hold of his spine. I can't imagine what kinds of injuries that must have caused.*"

Be assured that the injuries were indeed fatal, but Guardians are built differently. They can withstand a lot of damage and continue to function. However, Jax was dying. He could barely lift his arms in defense as the vampire began to stomp his body.

I was crying and my tears froze to my face as I watched Jaxon's body being abused. I was sure he was dead. He had to be dead. I wanted him to be dead so the suffering would end. The plan had failed. The other vampires never showed themselves, not even towards the end like we assumed they would.

My uncle was no longer moving. He was nothing more than a broken and bloody heap on the ground.

The vampire wasn't much better off. His wounds were ghastly. The organs began to slip out of his body and the loss of blood finally caught up to him. He dropped to the ground. It took the Master a long time to find his feet once again. He looked at my uncle, hesitated, and then he motioned to his foot soldiers. I saw them ignore his summons. In a rage, the Master turned his back on Jax and took a weakened step or two in their direction.

I knew he wanted their blood.

I simply couldn't believe my eyes when I saw Jaxon reach down to the cuff of his shorts and pull his backup knife. I was amazed when he reached out and sliced through the tendon above the Master's heel and dropped the vampire to the ground. I was completely astonished when Jaxon crawled after him and slashed apart the Achilles tendon of the other foot as well.

The vampire began to crawl away, but Jaxon could no longer follow. He was truly dying. What happened next was the moment I had been waiting for. I only hoped it wasn't too late. Jaxon raised one hand into the air and pointed his index finger towards the sky.

I radioed to Javie immediately and told him to turn on the water main. You see, the PVC pipes that lined both sides of one half of the field were one of the things we spent most of the day working on. Once upon a time, the Sun Bowl had an actual grass field, but some time ago the real grass was replaced with artificial grass. The maintenance room that controlled the water for the old grass field was still inside the Sun Bowl. It hadn't been used in years, but all the right pieces were in place. All we had to do was follow the old pipes they used to water the grass, find where they had been blocked off, and add our own pipes. When all was said and done—trust me it wasn't easy, because the stupid pipes kept breaking apart—we had a working sprinkler system, and a lot of water pressure.

Jaxon was right when he guessed that the vampire wouldn't know the difference. In fact, the vampire never gave our crappy watering system a second glance. He probably just thought it was an outdated sprinkler system, if he even thought anything at all.

His oversight was about to cost him dearly. Javie turned on the water. The pipes on both sides of the field grumbled under the pressure, but they held. Large jets of water sprayed out of the hundreds of holes we drilled into the pipes. The water shot high above the ground, met their cousins on the opposite side of the field in midair, and came crashing down on the field with the falling snow.

We had created rain.

While the vampire crawled towards his foot soldiers in search of the healing blood, we gave Jaxon a continuous dose of healing water. It was a beautiful thing to see. The black gore was rinsed from Jaxon's body almost immediately. He was instantly soaked, and the water would continue to spray until I radioed Javie and asked him to turn it off.

Jaxon wasn't moving.

I panicked. I broke free of my stupid snow igloo and stood straight up on the bleachers. I shouted for Jaxon to stand up. The vampire was getting closer, and closer to his foot soldiers. They didn't come to him, but they were too afraid to back away.

I saw Jaxon's arm move.

It wasn't a twitch or anything. His arm simply slid to his side, and he used it, along with his other arm, to push himself to his knees. The water was pouring over both Jaxon and the vampire. I saw Jax wipe his eyes. Then he looked over at me and smiled as he got to his feet.

The crowd of survivors began to roar and cheer.

I left my spot on the bleachers and entered the field. It was a stupid thing to do. I left my position, but I had to see the end.

When I was close enough, I saw the drenched vampire look over his shoulder. I saw his eyes go wide in fear as Jaxon slowly closed the distance. The blade of the Ti-Lite was gleaming in his hand. The crowd was still cheering. The foot soldiers were looking nervously from the Master to the General.

The vampire began to scream as he crawled. He began to plead for his life. Jaxon simply smiled. He was the monsters' monster. Does that make any sense at all?

"He's the thing that monsters fear?"

Exactly, he is the Guardian. He is the one man that can beat them at their own game, and do you know what the vampire's worst mistake was? He thought he could go toe to toe with my uncle.

When I finally reached Jaxon, I realized that he was still in pretty bad shape. He was having trouble breathing. He didn't seem able to keep his eyes open for long periods of time; he was hunched over awkwardly, and walking funny. Still, I didn't interfere. He wouldn't have wanted that. This was his fight. It was his to end. I simply handed him his tomahawk.

"You can have this back," I said. "It scares the hell out of me."

He barely even looked at me as he took the weapon. The vampire screamed in fear, but after the first swing of the tomahawk, he began to scream in pain. Four swings later, the vampire screamed no more.

The Master was dead.

The survivors were cheering and clapping. They stormed the field despite the freezing water drenching their clothes. The lot of them stood before Jaxon and gave him the salute one final time. Unlike the other times, however, Jaxon returned the salute, and then he collapsed.

"Dudley!" Nick shouted in my earpiece. "They're here!"

I cursed myself for being an idiot and scanned the tops of the bleachers. Five vampires were perched up there looking down upon us. They were on the survivor's side of the stadium.

I enacted part two of Jaxon's plan. I pulled out my detonator and set off the Semtex underneath the bleachers they were perched upon, just as they rushed towards us. In case you're wondering, my uncle got the idea from Kingsley when we first left El Paso…when Kingsley and some other guy blew up that bridge. Ever since that day, Jaxon carried Semtex in his backpack. He just never found a use for it until that day.

Jaxon predicted that the other vampires would only make an appearance at the end of the fight, and he was correct. They didn't want any survivors, and they also weren't about to pass up such a bountiful meal. He had also foreseen that the vampires would come at us from high altitudes, so when we weren't helping Javie set up his makeshift watering system, we were rigging the tops of the bleachers to blow.

We didn't have enough Semtex to take out all the top bleachers, so we made a guess and rigged up the sides, but left the ends of the stadium alone. Fortunately for us, we guessed correctly.

The explosion was loud, but it wasn't big enough to take out the entire side of the stadium. It, more or less, just took out a few of the rows. Before the dust even cleared, Nick and Georgie had burst free from their respective mounds of snow and rushed to the debris field. I pulled my machete free, and joined them at the top of the bleachers. The three of us hacked and chopped the damaged vampires.

It wasn't exactly difficult. All but one of the vampires was too dazed to put up a fight. As for the vampire that was still alert, it was missing several vital pieces by the time we found him. It wasn't much of a problem to relieve him of a few more.

The survivors cheered and cheered. Everyone was patting one another on the back. The water was still pouring down from above us. Jaxon was alert, but in obvious pain as his body knitted itself back together. Several people tried to approach him as he writhed about on the sodden fake grass, but he yelled at them to leave him be.

I came down and sat quietly by him as he healed. I didn't try and help him and I didn't say a word. When it was over, Jaxon would once again be his usual charming self. I had no problems waiting.

Father Monarez went over to the foot soldiers and began to talk with them. I could occasionally pick up bits of the conversation. They were relieved to be free of the vampires. Everything was going wonderfully. Everyone was happy and safe.

We had made a serious error: we had forgotten that the city wasn't safe.

It was Javie that alerted me.

"Dudley!" Javie shouted in my earpiece. "Are you there? Can you hear me?"

"I'm right here," I answered. "Come out and join us."

"I'm on my way," Javie said. "We need to get out of here fast."

"What?" I asked. "What are you talking about?"

"Can't you hear them?"

I found that a rather odd question. It took a brief moment or two before things clicked together and I began to understand. We had made a hell of a lot of noise. First we had cheering, then we had an explosion, and we followed all of that with a loud ass celebration.

"EVERYONE BE QUIET!" I shouted. "RIGHT NOW! STOP SCREAMING! STOP MAKING NOISE!"

It took a few moments for everyone to quiet down. I craned my neck in an effort to hear if anything was approaching. At first I heard nothing, but that was just my ears playing tricks on me. As soon as I began to relax I heard them. Unfortunately, so did everyone else.

The zombies were coming.

Everyone began to panic. The Regulators gathered around Jaxon, just as Javie, and Merrick, burst through the entrance and came running towards us. Javie was carrying a large bag of makeshift weapons. They were the same weapons the survivors had used in the church. We had taken all the ones that couldn't be concealed underneath their clothes, just in case we needed the survivors' help in fighting the vampires.

"We gotta go," Javie said. "There are a lot of them."

I looked down at Jaxon. Merrick was standing over him protectively, and he seemed to have lost consciousness. I knew that it would prove fatal if I removed him from the water. He was too fucked up, but I wasn't about to abandon him.

"Listen up everybody," I announced. "I need everyone to grab a weapon and make your way to the same exit. Stay together and be prepared to fight. The Regulators will hold them off as long as possible."

"You aren't coming with us?" someone asked.

"I can't move Jaxon. He's not healed up yet and if I take him from the water he probably won't survive, but don't worry about us. We're the Regulators. This is our job."

"Tonight we're all Regulators!" someone shouted and everybody cheered.

"I will not abandon the man who risked his life to save all of ours," Father Monarez said as he picked his chainsaw out of the bag of weapons.

In less than a second everyone was shouting different things at me.

"I won't leave the General!"

"Let's fight!"

"Protect the General!"

"I'm staying!"

"I won't leave him behind!"

In the end, I lost total control. There was a large group of survivors trapped inside the Sun Bowl, and not a single one of them would abandon my uncle. I began to pace back and forth as my adrenaline flowed into my veins. They wanted to fight. They probably wouldn't make it very far if they chose to run. They wanted to fight.

"REGULATORS!" I shouted at the tops of my lungs. "WHAT DO YOU WANT TO DO?"

"WE WANT TO FIGHT!" hundreds of voices screamed back at me.

"WHAT DO YOU WANT TO DO?" I shouted again.

"FIGHT!" they answered in unison.

"WHAT?"

"FIGHT!" they screamed.

"REGULATORS!" I screamed a final time. "KILL 'EM ALL!"

When the zombies came, they came by the hundreds. They poured through the different entrances of the Sun Bowl, and charged us on the field.

I'm proud of each and every one of those people. They formed a protective circle around Jaxon and defended him. Not a single man, woman, or child hesitated to stand in harm's way. They fought and fought and fought.

The battle was brutal. The ammo ran out all too quickly, and the team quickly resorted to blades. Not a single shambler broke through our protective circle. Not a single person abandoned the man that fought so hard to protect them. They fought with everything they had. They protected my uncle.

We lost a lot of people in the opening moments of the attack, but still we fought on. A half an hour after the battle started, I heard a voice in my ear.

"Dudley," Hardin asked. "Are you okay?"

"Not really," I answered. "We could use some helicopters with some serious fire power."

"I'm on my way," Hardin said. "Where are you?"

"Inside the Sun Bowl," I answered. "We also have about four hundred or so survivors that are ready for an extraction if you have enough of those choppers."

"Wait a minute. How did Hardin escape the vampires? Where were Miriam, Ivana, and the others who were being held?"

The vampires holding them left the area as soon as their Master was killed. I'm guessing they somehow sensed his death and decided they didn't want to stick around any longer. Anyway, Hardin is a pretty resourceful kind of guy. As soon as he realized there were no longer any vampires around, he escaped rather easily.

It took another thirty minutes for the helicopters to show up. The sight of three choppers flying over the bleachers was an extremely welcome one, but I think we enjoyed it even more when the helicopters began to open fire on all the zombies.

In no time at all, the stadium was relatively secure. More helicopters were brought in for extractions, and by that time, Jaxon was more or less himself. The Westside of El Paso had been cleared of survivors.

It was a battle that I will never forget as long as I live. In his one moment of need, it was the people that Jaxon fought so heroically to save that ended up saving him. It was a terrible battle, but the people supported one another. They stood side by side and faced the horde. In the midst of combat, I saw humanity, and let me tell ya, humanity is something worth fighting for.

In the end, eighty-four people lost their lives in the Battle of the Sun Bowl. The number was considered low, considering the odds that the people faced.

"Were the Regulators the last ones to leave the stadium?"

Yes, we were.

"Where did you go after you were extracted?"

Extracted? Sweetheart, the Regulators never left El Paso. There were still survivors waiting for help in different parts of the city. We had a job to do, and dammit we were gonna get it done. Jaxon made a promise. He told the entire world that help was coming to those in need. We weren't about to leave until we made good on that promise.

"So you planned on leaving after all the survivors in the city had been extracted?"

I wouldn't say that. Even after all the survivors were extracted, there would still be zombies in our city.

"Then you planned on completely eliminating the undead threat?"

You got that right, and if you thought vampires were pretty wild, wait until you hear that story.

Epilogue

JAXON

I had honestly thought the tale had been told. I had just sent off my collection of interviews to my publisher when I happened to catch the news. Georgie's ex-wife had been murdered in her home in Santa Fe, New Mexico.

Two weeks later, the book was well on its way to being printed when I learned about some sort of fight in Las Vegas, Nevada, involving the Regulators. I thought and thought about it, and I finally called my publisher and told her that I didn't believe the story was finished. I needed one last interview to be sure.

My publisher agreed immediately, and I began the process of arranging one final interview with Jaxon in regard to the story published in this novel.

He smiled when he walked into the room, but he definitely had a wary look in his eye.

What brings you to my door this time?

"I was wondering if you could tell me about Lucy's murder."

I had a feeling you were going to ask about that. The minute they told me you wanted another interview. Man, you move fast when you need to, don't you?

"It was a hunch that I had. I was thinking that there might be a connection between Lucy's murder and what happened in Vegas."

There is, and I can tell you about it because I went ahead and asked permission from Georgie. I felt that that was only right, considering it was his ex that was murdered. Anyway, he gave me permission. He thought it might be a good idea to let everyone know what happens when someone messes with our families.

It was Hardin that called me. I was on a different assignment when I got the call. He said that Lucy had been murdered the previous evening, and her body had just been discovered. How he found out so quickly, I have no idea. Hardin just seems to be a wealth of information, but I bet he probably keeps tabs on everyone's family just in case.

The team was in Santa Fe in less than three hours. We even landed the helicopter right on the street outside Lucy's house. The police were everywhere, but I used my badge to get by everyone. Georgie wanted to come, but I wouldn't allow him to leave the helicopter. He was taking things pretty badly, and I can't say I blamed him. Fortunately, his daughter wasn't with Lucy at the time. She had been visiting with Georgie's parents.

As soon as I walked into the overly-clean house, I smelled the scent of blood and something else. I went past all the cops and all the crime scene investigators straight up to the upstairs bedroom.

Some rookie cop tried to stand in my way, and I sent him tumbling down the stairs. After that, everyone kept his distance. The room was a mess. The nightstand had been overturned. A lamp had been broken. The sheets on the bed had been ripped to shreds. The thin metal shutters over one window had been bent and torn. The carpets and walls were smeared with blood.

At some point she must have tried to make a run for it. There were bloody footprints leading from the bed to the master bathroom. I followed the footprints and there I found Lucy's body. She was partially in the bathtub, but most of her was dangling over the edge of the tub onto the cold tile floor.

The body had been savaged. Worse than that, he took his time with her. He gave her little tastes of pain as he built up for the final strike. There probably wasn't much blood left in her body when he drank her dry.

Immediately I radioed in to Hardin.

"Is this as bad as I think it is?" Hardin asked.

"Probably worse," I answered. "Where's my wife?"

"She's still in Ruidoso doing some shopping. I can have her picked up immediately and moved to a safe location."

"No, I'll pick her up myself."

I clicked off with Hardin and dashed down the stairs just in time to grab a hold of Georgie as he tried to force his way into the house. There was no way I was going to let him see the body. He'd never get that image out of his head.

I told him I was sorry. I told him that he couldn't go inside. He didn't take it very well. He even put up a pretty decent fight, but in the end I passed him off to Nick. He sort of looks up to Nick in a weird "don't beat me up" kind of way.

The helicopter took off, and we left a bunch of cops scratching their heads. We even managed to get out of there before the reporters showed up.

The helicopter landed at the airport outside of Ruidoso. I wasn't in a particular hurry. It was only mid-afternoon. I found Skie in one of the shops located on Ruidoso's main strip. She gave me her big smile and jumped into my arms.

"What's going on?" she asked. "Why are you back so soon, and why are you still in your uniform?"

I kissed her twice, just because she was safe and sound. Then I gathered up my parents and her kids, and off we all went to Vegas. Of course she was terrified when I told her what had happened, but she put on her brave face almost immediately.

"Would he really hurt me?" she asked. "I've never done anything to him. I've always treated him like family."

"Well, Lucy never did anything to him either, and look what he did to her," said Javie from across the helicopter.

"Are you positive it was him though?" she asked.

"I saw black drool marks on the floor," I answered. "There was a bite wound on her neck. It had to be him. That's why you're going to our predetermined safe location."

The entire team has safe locations all over the country, just in case some big nasty wants to get revenge and take out a family member. My safe location area happens to be in Vegas. I chose Vegas because both my parents and Skie love going to Vegas. They have two penthouses reserved at the Luxor.

"But doesn't Kingsley know where everybody's safe location is at?" Skie asked.

"He does," I answered.

"Then why are you taking me to a safe location that isn't safe?"

"Because you won't be staying in the Luxor," I answered. "Hardin has arranged two suites at MGM Grand. I want to be able to get to you fast just in case things go bad."

"So you expect him to go after me at the Luxor?"

"He was angry enough to track down Lucy and murder her," I answered. "I'm thinking she was just convenient and close. He would much rather have gone after you. It's his way of getting even. He has a sick mind. He thinks all of us wronged him in some way. Yet, he's terrified of us, so he's going after our women instead. At least I'm hoping he's going after our women. If he doesn't come for you in Vegas, I'm going to waste a lot of time chasing him down."

"He did come for her in Vegas, didn't he? The news reports weren't very clear on what had happened, but your team did have an altercation in the Luxor."

It took him two weeks to make his way there. I spent every single evening in one of the security rooms monitoring the cameras and waiting for him to show up. I was just about to give up, and start thinking about how I could track him down, when he finally came for my wife.

I watched him on the security cameras as he made his way down the hallway to her room. I watched as he put his ear to the door and listened to see if she was still awake. I kept remembering what Kingsley said to me that last time we had spoken. He told me that when everything was all over, I wouldn't be anything more than a footnote in history. He told me that nobody would even remember my name.

He quietly broke the lock on the door and entered the room. Nick was waiting just beyond the doorway. He opened up with a fully automatic blast from his MP7. Kingsley screamed a high-pitched wail and bolted out of the room.

He ran blindly down the hallway right into Georgie. Georgie nailed him with a full auto blast of machine gun fire, just as badly as Nick did. Kingsley retreated once again. This time he was headed towards the hallway that led to the elevators.

I watched through the monitors as he punched the elevator buttons frantically, all the while looking over his shoulder, just in case he was being followed. He wasn't being followed. Javie, and Dudley, were waiting for him in the elevator. When the doors slid open, they each tore into him with their MP7s.

I watched as Kingsley screamed again and ran towards the emergency stairs. He made the frightened sounds of a terrified child as he pushed through the metal doors and entered the stairwell. He travelled all the way to the bottom floor only to discover that the metal door wouldn't open.

I watched him try every single door between the first floor and Skie's floor. I saw the terror in his eyes when he realized none of them would open. I watched him cry as he tried to break through them only to realize they had all been reinforced, and he was trapped inside the stairwell.

I finally left the security control room when he began to pound his head against the cement walls in frustration. I took my time as I walked to the stairwell. I wasn't in any hurry. Kingsley wasn't going anywhere.

I let the metal door slam shut behind me. I wanted him to know I was coming. I wanted him to be afraid. I wanted him to suffer. After all, he turned against me. He joined the other side. He wanted to murder my wife.

I walked slowly down the steps. I took my time. I let my boots echo throughout the stairwell. When I saw him up close and personal, he was huddled in a corner between floors. He was afraid to look at me.

He looked horrible. His clothes were ragged and filthy. He hadn't bathed in days, possibly even weeks. He smelled terrible.

"What brings you to Vegas, Kingsley?" I asked.

"I just wanted to see you, Jaxon," he answered after finally meeting my gaze. The black drool was running down his chin.

"What did you want to see me for?" I asked.

"I was hoping...I was hoping you could help me. I screwed up. I have nobody. I need your help."

"Did you want my help before or after you murdered my wife?" I demanded.

"I'm sorry, Jax," he pleaded. "Why did you guys leave me? What did you expect me to do?"

I pulled my tomahawk from the back of my belt. I did it slowly. I wanted him to know what was coming. I wanted him to attack, but he never did. He was too afraid. I had expected a decent fight, but it honestly didn't last very long at all. I think he was just too terrified to defend himself, and when it was all over, I realized he wasn't even enough of a threat to merit a footnote. I left the stairwell wondering how long it would take before people began to forget his name.

The team was waiting for me when I came out. Georgie nodded his head in approval. That night, we went out and celebrated. We drank hard and played merrily. At one point in the evening, we were all sitting around a big table and drinking shots of Jack. I don't remember where we were, but I remember looking around the table at my team, my dog, and my family, thinking life was pretty damn good.

BROKEN

BOOK 3 OF THE GUARDIAN INTERVIEWS

BY MICHAEL CLARY

Chapter 1

JAXON

My goal was to take a well-deserved break. The story of how the Regulators battled vampires in the Sun Bowl had just hit the bookstores and it was moving like a runaway freight train. I had already done the press junkets and the signings. I was tired. Yes, I knew the story wasn't finished. There were still zombies in El Paso, and let's not forget Dudley's tease during his last interview. He warned me that if I thought vampires were wild, I needed to wait and hear about how they finally cleared the city.

I believed Dudley.

Please don't think otherwise. I just wanted a vacation or three before I went after that story. Interviewing the Regulators is a lot of work. A person learns things they often wish they hadn't.

I received a phone call in the middle of the night: a man begging for my help. He told me a tale I just couldn't wait to investigate. I did some digging based on what the man had told me, and compared his tale to three separate events that gave him credibility. The first of these events was an assassination attempt on the President of the United States. The second was the General's famous stay at a hospital in Ruidoso, New Mexico. The third was a much-televised public threat that frightened the world and led to the closing of the borders.

Now, these events alone were nothing new. All of them had been exhaustively televised, and I wasn't much interested in what others had reported. No, I was only interested in what the midnight caller told me. I was interested in what went on behind the scenes and I just had to know if what the man said was true.

My vacation was put on hold. Phone calls were made. Interviews were set up and I was on my way to a small compound near, but separate from, Fort Bliss Army Base in El Paso, Texas.

As I waited for the General to appear, I realized for the first time I wasn't nervous. I had seen too much of the man. I was beginning to see him as a friend. In fact, I was beginning to enjoy the company of all the team members, with the possible exception of Nick.

When he walked into the conference room in full gear and dropped his machine gun onto the wooden table between us, I damn near fell out of my seat. He noticed my reaction and the blush of embarrassment spreading over my cheeks. The General was about to say something (probably at my expense) when I was saved by the large, black pit bull that bounded into the room after him before dropping the entire upper half of her body onto my lap.

"It's nice to see you, Merrick."

She must have missed you.

I couldn't help smiling as I scratched the dog behind the ears. The look of joy on her face was contagious. It was hard to believe she was capable of all the things I'd heard.

"I've missed her as well and I never thought I'd say that about a pit bull."

That's how it goes for a lot of people. It's easy to fear what you don't know. It's a shame, really. They make the best pets in the world.

As hard as it might be for me to believe Merrick was capable of violent actions, it was rather easy to believe it of the General. At just a shade under six feet, the man was wide, with large arms, big shoulders, and a thick neck. The tactical vest over his broad chest made him seem even larger, if that was possible. He looked imposing as hell, and the skull and crossed pistols boldly emblazoned on his tactical vest let everyone know he was serious.

His light brown hair was as short as it always is, and his ever-present backwards Harley Davidson ball cap was beginning to look a little rough around the edges. The green eyes were the real draw of the show however. I couldn't even begin to imagine the horrors they'd witnessed.

"How old is that hat?"

What are you getting at? It's just starting to feel comfy.

There was the briefest moment of awkwardness as I pondered how to ask what I wanted to ask. The General beat me to the punch.

Dudley tells me you're probably here to find out about what happened after all the survivors were cleared from the city. I guess he let slip some hints that we had ourselves some crazy times.

"That is exactly why I'm here. Will you tell me what happened?"

Sure. I warn you though; it's not always a very pleasant tale. Some of the boys may be a little reluctant to relive some of what happened.

"Is it that bad?"

Some of it was par for the course. There are things that definitely shouldn't have happened, but I guess we'll get to that. Where do you want to start?

"If you don't mind, can you take me back to what happened after the last of the survivors was evacuated from the city? I'm not sure you are aware of this, but people really began to panic after the last group was evacuated. They feared that, without a food source, the zombies would eventually begin to drift towards the borders of the city.

That was a worry we had as well. If any zombies got out of the city, they could spread throughout the country in an unstoppable wave. It wouldn't take very long either, not with the zombies we were dealing with. Maybe you know this, maybe you don't, but there are different types of zombies. There are slow zombies, magically controlled zombies, and there are zombies created by idiot scientists. There are a bunch of different types. The ones that took over El Paso, as you may remember, were created by a nasty and powerful curse. They also happen to be the worst of the bunch.

"Why are they the worst of the bunch?"

They move fast and they maintain their speed despite how rotted out they become. Slow zombies are the easiest to deal with, especially if they decay at a normal rate. I'll take slow, rotted out zombies any day of the week over the ones we were dealing with in El Paso.

"So the public had a legitimate concern?"

Definitely. I mean, the military had done a fine job guarding the borders of the city, not a single zombie got by them. They were dealing with limited numbers of the undead, though. A great horde never made an attempt to leave the city. They didn't have to; there were food sources that were much closer to anything outside the borders.

"So, what was the plan to keep this from happening?"

Well, we tripled the amount of soldiers guarding the borders. We also dropped speakers all around the city and started blasting the sounds of people screaming to keep them interested in the area. This was a pretty neat idea. The screams would play out on a bunch of speakers for about five minutes and then shut off, while more screams played out on a bunch of different speakers at another location. It worked pretty well, but we weren't going depend on it lasting forever. We didn't know if the undead would grow immune to the sounds.

There was a fallback plan in place. It wasn't a good one. In fact, we really wanted to avoid it. If all else failed and the zombies moved towards the borders en masse, certain people wanted to level the entire city.

"That's exactly what you had been trying to avoid from the beginning. Would the plan have worked?"

Probably not—mind you, that's just my opinion—but I don't see any sort of bomb or explosion as an end to the problem. I'm sure it would have taken out some of the undead, but what are the odds that it would destroy all of them?

"What if they used something bigger?"

Like nuclear?

"Yes. What about nuclear?"

We have no clue how that would affect the zombies. It may not even hurt them at all, unless they actually got caught in the blast. Hardin was violently opposed to that idea, by the way. He didn't want to take the chance of having irradiated zombies running around.

"That sounds pretty scary."

Exactly, and I'm no expert on nuclear bombs, but I don't even want to imagine the damage it would cause the surrounding areas.

"So, you've told me what other people wanted to do. Now tell me what you wanted to do."

I wanted to thin the herd. The more zombies we could destroy before they lost interest and tried to leave, the better. Mind you, we didn't have any great plans for this. Other teams tried different ideas, such as waiting by the speakers and shooting the zombies when they appeared. However, we favored a more direct approach.

"It sounds as if we are nearing the start of the story."

Sounds that way to me.

"Before you begin, tell me about the weapons you used."

Jaxon laughed about it; as if he was he was wondering when I was going to bring it up. I hate to be repetitive, but people seem to have a lot of interest in the tools he uses. That makes it important.

Well, the only thing that changed since the last time we spoke was my knife. The folder I was using was starting to look pretty nasty after all the use it received, so I decided to retire it with honors. I began carrying a Cold Steel Natchez Bowie as its replacement. This thing is a beast of a knife, with an eleven and three-quarter inch blade that's sharp enough to shave with. I'd wanted to try one out after seeing Georgie's Bowie.

"Did it meet your expectations?"

And then some. Other than that, I was still using the Sig Sauer P226 with a silencer, the MP7 rifle (also with a silencer), my Cold Steel Ti-Lite as a backup knife, and of course my tomahawk.

"Your trademark weapon?"

I guess so.

"Do you have it on you right now?"

I do.

"Can I see it?"

Jaxon smiled and reached behind his back. The tomahawk was nestled in a sideways holster on the back of his utility belt. It made a raspy sound as be pulled it free. He casually gave it a brief twirl in his hand before holding it out for me to grasp.

The edge of the blade looked frighteningly sharp. The bluing over the metal had faded to a dull grey from excessive use. The wooden handle was scarred and stained. My hand froze about an inch away. I couldn't will myself to grab a hold of it.

Jaxon noticed my reluctance.

Don't worry about it. It has that effect on a lot of people.

Another quick twirl and the tomahawk vanished out of sight, back on the utility belt.

"Sorry about that."

Not a problem.

"Were you still using the bite suits and tactical vests?"

Yeah. Those are pretty much required uniforms when dealing with monsters.

"How soon after the last of the survivors were evacuated did you begin eliminating the zombies?"

The very next day.

"Okay, tell me how you did it"

Like I said before, we favored a more direct approach. Instead of just staying in a safe place near the speakers, we only started things out that way. We let the speakers call in the zombies, and then one of us would run through the area and get the zombies to chase after him.

When zombies see prey, they shriek out those ugly screams they're so fond of, and that attracts more zombies to the scene. So, we would run around for a while gathering up more and more zombies. When the group was big enough, we would lead them to a predetermined area, and make for safety, while the rest of the team unloaded on them with .50 caliber machine guns.

We had been doing this for a few days. Everything was getting relatively routine, and somewhat boring. The temperature was beginning to warm up, but the nights were still pretty cold. I was on top of a single-story roof in the early morning hours. I was waiting rather impatiently for the speakers to go off, and gather me up some playmates.

I had a new wristwatch. It was a Protrek 2500 from Casio; you can add that to the list of my gear. I was playing around with it, just passing time, when the screams started bellowing out of speakers hidden beneath a park bench across the street. It scared the hell out of me and I almost fell off the roof in a panic.

"Give me a warning next time," I barked into my earpiece after giving it a tap.

The only response I received was laughter from the control room in New Mexico. Hardin isn't very big on practical jokes, but he seldom misses an opportunity to laugh at my misfortune.

Anyway, the screams were loud. It wasn't long before a small group of shamblers showed up and began to look around for the source of the screams. Unfortunately, there weren't enough of them. I happened to have a bet going on with Javie and only thirty or so shamblers weren't going to be enough for me to win.

I waited a while. I even started to argue with Dudley over our ear radios while I waited. I can't remember what started the argument, but we were arguing about whether or not Sasquatch actually existed. My reasoning was that if zombies and vampires could exist along with an untold number of other monsters, why couldn't Bigfoot? Dudley, on the other hand, kept asking for a body.

"Perhaps Bigfoot dissolves in the sunlight like vampires do," I said.

"Why would Bigfoot dissolve in the sunlight?"

"Because fuck you, that's why," I replied.

"How many showed up?" Dudley asked.

Abrupt subject changes are relatively common when speaking with Dudley.

"Looks to be about thirty," I answered. "I'm about to go for my run."

"Are you sure you want to get started with only thirty? Javie is gonna beat you easy if you don't pick up a lot more on the run."

I was honestly getting a bit nervous about losing the bet, but I'm very impatient, and I wasn't seeing any new arrivals. I just wasn't going to admit my fear.

"Yeah, I'm getting pretty bored waiting around. I'll make extra noise to make up for it."

"Wait a minute; shouldn't you know if Bigfoot truly exists or not?"

You would think so, but I have no idea.

"But you hunt monsters."

Bigfoot isn't really a monster. He's a primate. Or at least that's what people believe.

"What about Miriam? She's the expert on monsters. What does she say?"

She won't tell us. She thinks it's pretty funny that everyone keeps arguing about it. I'm thinking the only way I will ever know for sure is if one of them steps out of the forest and takes a bite out of some camper. Then I'll get sent out to shoot it.

"Good point. Now, what was this about a bet?"

We had a bet over which one of us could lead more zombies to the machine guns.

"And the loser had to what? Shave his head?"

No, they had to shave only the left side of their face for one month.

I couldn't help but laugh out loud.

"Are you serious?"

Oh yeah.

"So did you go for your run or did you wait a bit longer?"

I went for my run. Like I said, I'm impatient, and the screams were starting to get on my nerves. I jumped off the roof and landed on the sidewalk as loudly as I could. A few of the zombies noticed me immediately, and rushed over to my position.

I used my Sig Sauer pistol without the silencer to bring them all down. I hated wasting a perfectly good zombie. I had a bet to win, and shooting all my playmates before I reached my destination wasn't going to help me any, but I was hoping the loud gunshots would attract more company.

I was correct in that assumption.

Not only did the gunshots gather the attention of all the shamblers present, it also excited a group of shamblers that happened to be around the corner and out of my line of vision. Someday, I'm gonna pay for my impatience. I realized they were there only after the speakers shut off, and I heard all the commotion they were making. They were probably attracted to the speakers, but the sound of my pistol really lit a fire under their asses. I could hear the thuds of their pounding feet hitting the asphalt. I could hear the echoes of their moans and screams. It was a large mob, and they came around the corner at full speed just as the previous thirty or so zombies by the speakers sprinted towards me.

Things never go according to plan when you're dealing with monsters. My escape route was rendered temporarily useless, since the direction I wanted to go had a street full of zombies in the way. I could have tried charging through them, but the odds weren't really in my favor.

Instead, after doing a pee-pee dance of indecision, I headed in the opposite direction.

Both groups merged together. I led them down one street and up another before making some right turns and leading them all back to the place we started. It was a good workout. Not the greatest mind you, I couldn't run full out. If I did, I would have lost my pursuers.

Keeping the ever-growing gang of zombies twenty feet behind me, I finally headed towards my escape route. That was a big relief, by the way. Being chased by zombies is nerve wracking no matter how tough I tend to act.

I led the growing pod of shamblers down a long, dead end alley-way that was barely wide enough to fit one car. I turned on the speed when I hit the opening of the alley, and I mean I really turned on the speed. I left the shamblers in my dust, and damn near slammed into the brick wall of the dead end.

I grabbed the black rope hanging off the roof, and as soon as I shouted out that I was secure, Nick began to pull me up the side of the building. I was climbing over the edge when the first bunch of zombies arrived at the dead end.

"Looks like I won," Javie said.

"What are you talking about?" I asked. "I have a ton of them."

"You might want to check your math again boss," Javie said.

I looked down the side of the building, and sure enough Javie was correct. Somewhere along the way I had lost about half of my pursuers. I was crestfallen. I lost the bet. I could already hear Nick laughing heartily as he positioned himself behind one of the two tripod mounted machine guns that covered the alley.

And then the rest of my pursuers rounded the corner and showed up to the party.

There were a lot of them, many more than I intended on attracting. All I really needed was to bring in about seventy or so to win. Javie only brought in around sixty when he ran. Somehow I had a couple hundred zombies jamming themselves into the alley.

"How'd you do that?" Javie asked.

"Beats me," I answered. "I guess I'm just popular like that."

"Or maybe there's a small horde nearby that you didn't see," Dudley added.

"Nah," I said. "I'm just popular."

Nick and Georgie started spraying out a virtual wall of belt-fed lead into the zombies below as we were talking. Even with silencers, the big machine guns were still sorta loud, so Dudley, Javie, and I moved over to the opposite side of the building.

"Time to pay up," I announced.

I was already laughing as I searched through Dudley's backpack and retrieved the battery-powered razor.

"*You really made him do this?*"

You sound like Dudley, but a bet's a bet, and Javie wouldn't have shown me any mercy if the roles were reversed.

"*How do you know?*"

Because Dudley didn't want him to go through with it, so I finally asked Javie if he would have let me out of the bet if he had won instead.

"Hell no," Javie answered.

Even Dudley was laughing when the hair started falling off. I'm sure you've seen Javie. He's a pretty hairy fellow. I think it takes him about three days to grow out a full beard, so as a result he normally walks around with fuzz in order to save time from shaving every day.

"Oh shit!" Nick shouted. "He's freakin' doing it. Check it out, Georgie."

Georgie laughed the hardest. I tried making the bet with him in the beginning, but he adamantly refused to take me up on it. Still, he had no problems laughing at someone else's expense.

"Watch your corner down there, asshole," Nick shouted to Georgie. "They're beginning to pile up under that window.

I went to go see what Nick was getting all panty-wadded about. The building we were standing on was four stories tall and made out of brick. There was one boarded up window slightly above street level that happened to be on the same side Georgie was covering.

Nick was covering the other half of the alley and his side seemed pretty good. He was able to cut into most of the zombies before they even reached the brick wall of our building. Georgie, however, was having difficulties.

He probably shouldn't have taken his eyes off the alleyway. By doing that, he gave the zombies enough time to gather around the dead end and push up against the brick. Georgie corrected his mistake immediately, and directed his fire towards the base of the building in an attempt to cut down the shamblers below him.

The bullets shredded the bodies instantly, and then cut through the bodies of the next bunch of corpses that pushed forward in an attempt to take their place. This went on for some time. The pile of bodies was growing higher and higher.

Georgie's gun went dry.

He looked at me with a panicked expression as his fingers fumbled through the reloading process. Dudley rushed forward to help him. Javie stood by Nick and prepared to aid him in reloading when the time came.

As Georgie panicked, the zombies in the alley climbed over the shredded remains of Georgie's targets and reached up for us. They were hungry. They hadn't eaten in a long time. Then again, zombies are always hungry.

I pulled my MP7 around and placed the red dot inside the holographic sight onto the forehead of a very rotten looking individual in a plaid shirt. I squeezed the trigger smoothly and watched as his head jerked backwards, and a red spray splashed out onto the five zombies that replaced him.

"Now would be a good time to start shooting, Georgie," I shouted.

"I'm trying," Georgie replied, "but there's a jam."

The zombies were getting closer and closer to the boarded up window. I shot any of them that could reach out and touch it, but it was getting more and more difficult as their numbers increased.

I chanced a brief glimpse down the alley. It was filled with the dead, and more of them were coming. They pushed and shoved against each other as they fought to reach us. The smell was nasty, but fortunately the wind was picking up, and making a valiant effort to carry the smell away from us.

"It's looking pretty bad, Jax," Nick shouted. "I'm almost out."

"Javie is backing you up. He'll shoot his MP7 while you reload. Just stay calm and stay focused."

It looked as if Dudley had been correct. I had attracted a small horde to our location. Unfortunately, it didn't end with that pack. The screams and the assorted gunfire were attracting even greater numbers.

We had never attracted a mass this size before. We weren't expecting it. In retrospect, I'm guessing, with the lack of people to eat, the zombies were becoming more and more ravenous. As a result, it was becoming increasingly easy to attract lots of unwanted attention.

We were quickly sinking in over our heads. Dudley and Georgie were taking too long to clear the gun, and even on full auto, my MP7 wasn't bringing enough of them down. It didn't take the zombies long at all to reach the boarded up window.

"Here we go," I muttered. "Never gets easy."

"It's worse than that," Dudley shouted. "I think the machine gun is damaged."

"Are you sure?"

"It's busted," Georgie agreed.

"Then forget about it and use your rifles," I ordered.

We had lost that battle. I quickly left that edge of the roof and went around checking the other sides of the building. I was looking for an escape route. Unfortunately for all of us, our egos had gotten too big, and we never imagined we might need to make a run for it. Then again, why run when we could fly.

"Hardin," I called out after tapping my earpiece.

"I'm here, Jax. What do you need?"

"I need a lift off of this roof," I answered.

"I can see that," Hardin said. "All the choppers are on the other side of the city assisting one of the other teams. It will take a little bit of time for them to reach you."

"They're in the building," Georgie shouted out from the opposite side of the roof.

"I'm running low on ammo," Dudley announced.

"How long?" I asked Hardin.

"Under ten minutes."

"Do what you can," I replied.

I ran back to the team. Zombies were now flooding into the building as they climbed up the ladder of corpses brought down by machine gun fire. I looked at the flimsy wooden door that marked the entrance to the roof we were all standing on. The shamblers would go through it in seconds.

I ran to the other three edges once again. The distance to the rooftops of nearby buildings was too great a distance to jump. I thought about throwing a grappling hook, but there didn't seem to be any place for it to grab onto on any of the other rooftops.

I walked back to the team once again. They were still firing away at the zombies in the alleyway.

"I'm going inside," I said. "I'll try to bottleneck them at the window until the chopper gets here to pick us up."

"I'll go with you," Dudley said.

"Take a few mags from Nick," I told him.

"They're in the back pouches of my belt," Nick said as Dudley approached him. He was too busy with firing the big machine gun to get them so Dudley had to tug them free himself.

Together we crossed the roof and headed for the door that led down into the building.

"You ready for this?" I asked.

"Why wouldn't I be?" Dudley replied as he slapped a new magazine into his rifle.

"Because you're a pussy," I answered him flatly.

"I really don't think I'm a pussy. I certainly don't feel like a pussy. I fact, I've been feeling pretty heroic ever since I defeated that Master Vampire."

He caught me by surprise.

"That's pretty funny," I said. "I didn't know you were such a funny guy. I don't remember you fighting the Master Vampire. In fact, as I recall, you were hiding under a pile of snow while I took care of the situation."

"Too bad for you there are not many people privy to that information. If I start the rumors now, I'm pretty sure I can take all the credit."

"You're welcome to it. If that Master had any vampire buddies that are gonna show up one day looking for revenge, they'll knock on your door instead of mine."

"Would Dudley really do something like that?"

No, but it's funny for him to say that to me. Not as funny as the look on his face when I told him about vampire buddies looking for revenge, but it was still pretty funny.

I kicked in the door and our world got serious.

We could hear the shamblers down on the first floor. They were pretty riled up and making a lot of noise. With our rifles held at the ready, we charged in.

"I've got some bad news for you," Dudley announced.

"What?"

"We didn't clear this building."

"Why didn't you clear the building?" I asked.

"When we got inside, we didn't hear anything and most of the doors were closed. We just figured it would be easier to quietly make our way to the roof."

"Well, I guess you figured wrong," I said.

"What do you want to do?"

"We don't have time to clear the building now. There are like ten doors down every hall. We need to get our asses down to that window and stop the flow of zombies that are getting inside. Let's just hope the building's empty and we don't get surrounded."

As soon as I said that, the pounding started.

At first it was a casual knocking on a door we happened to pass. Then it got louder. Then it sounded as if other hands were joining in and before we knew it, other doors started sounding off as well.

"Maybe the doors will hold them," Dudley said.

"Maybe," I replied.

I took off down the hall at a sprint. As I reached a T-intersection, Dudley told me to hang a left. When I rounded the corner, I had to duck out of the way of a zombie.

My moving out of his way didn't seem to faze him in the slightest. Instead of pursuing me, he made a beeline right for Dudley, who was just a few feet behind me. So, after ducking his outstretched arms, I turned around, grabbed him by the back of his collar, and slammed him into the opposite wall.

The zombie wasn't bothered by the slam either. He spun around on me immediately, but it was too late for him. The way was clear and I could take a shot without hitting Dudley. I aimed above his shattered nose, and blew out his brains.

I didn't have time to rub it in to Dudley that I had just saved his ass. The muffled sounds of his silenced MP7 began before I even turned around. Behind me was the stairwell, and shamblers were rushing up it.

At this point, our enemy was beginning to look pretty gross. Their clothes were all nasty and stained with dark fluids. Their scalps were missing clumps of hair and their faces were beginning to show an advanced stage of rot. Their skin was a dark sort of gray mixed with a sickly yellow, and their fingernails seemed to have continued growing long after they died. What I'm getting at is how very unpleasant it was to turn around, and see a bunch of those rotted monsters charging my way.

"How many were there?"

I'm thinking around ten, at least in the first wave. It's really hard to say, because I began firing immediately. We found a target, brought it down and searched for another, all the while continuing to advance forward.

It wouldn't do us any good in the long run if we simply held our position. At least, I didn't think so. I was still hoping to bottleneck them at the window, and make my life a bit easier.

When we reached the stairs, the first wave was down and we managed to reach the third floor. After that, the attacks became sporadic. A wave of zombies would rush us, and we'd begin firing. When the wave was down, we'd make some progress only to have another wave of zombies rush up the stairs towards us.

At one point, things got pretty hairy, and a wave of zombies came at us from behind while we were busy engaging in a frontal assault. I'm not sure if they had been there all along and just got excited from the noise, or if they came from the window and somehow found a way to sneak up on us. For a moment though, we were pinned in the stairwell.

Dudley continued shooting down the attackers in front of us, and I spun around and started taking out the ones coming from behind. Like I said, it was a pretty hairy situation. The stairwell itself often made finding targets pretty difficult. We had to wait until they were right up in our faces before we had a decent angle to shoot them.

As soon as I had taken out our followers, I joined Dudley, and the two of us cleared out all the immediate threats before continuing down the stairwell.

"Jax!" Georgie shouted into my earpiece. "There are a bunch of them getting in now. We can't keep up. You guys need to get out of there."

"Let me know when you see the helicopter, Georgie," I replied. "That's when we will retreat."

Like I said before, a bottleneck at the window was our easiest bet. I didn't want to use the stairwell, or a hallway, because the window was a smaller area that the shamblers had to squeeze through. They would be struggling against each other in an effort to get inside before I even started shooting them.

Also, Georgie tends to get nervous around one zombie. I don't really start to get excited until about twenty or so show up. Despite what I had seen from the roof, I was hoping Georgie was exaggerating.

Turns out he wasn't.

The biggest wave yet came up at us just as we reached the second floor. It was bad. It was real bad. Fortunately, the confined space and the corners of the stairwell finally worked in our favor. Despite their numbers, the stairwell was too thin to allow more than a few to reach us at a time, and the corners slowed them down even more.

Our ducks were in a row. We fired and fired until our trigger fingers went numb, and then we fired some more. The stairwell was pretty disgusting when we were finished. The gore and blood painted the concrete walls. Bodies were everywhere.

We picked our way gently through the mess, and continued our journey to the first floor. I gave another magazine of ammo to Dudley and told him to pull on his big boy pants and carry more spare ammo in the future.

Despite taking out that big wave of zombies, things didn't slow down too much. We were still being rushed every few seconds or so. It was just two or three shamblers instead of a whole mess of them.

In retrospect, the bigger groups were a bit easier to deal with since they slowed each other down and tripped each other up. Alone, a zombie is pretty fast. A fast attack is much more dangerous than a slow and ponderous one, at least as far as a stairwell goes.

Finally, we made it to the first floor. The stairwell continued downward, but we weren't interested in going any farther. We could already hear the sounds of multiple zombies coming from beyond the metal door at the bottom of the stairwell.

I slammed the door open expecting trouble, and trouble was what we got. There were about ten shamblers in the hallway. We brought them all down and continued to push our way forward, only to have another bunch spring up at us around the first corner.

This new attack was way too close for comfort.

Before I knew it, a large zombie wearing a black hoodie, blue jeans, and hiking boots, was up in my face, reaching out for me. His nose had rotted away and little crispy flaps of skin still hung over the vacant hole. His hands were dry and cracking as they sought out something on my body they could grab a hold of. I reacted out of instinct and belted out a front kick that caught him under the chin and jerked his head back. His hair was so dirty it didn't even move with his head.

I followed up the front kick with another kick. This time, however, instead of striking, I placed my boot on his chest and pushed him away from me. The shambler fell to the floor but was instantly replaced.

That was fine by me. I only needed enough room to bring my MP7 into play. I rapidly lined up shots, and set about clearing the hallway. In the midst of all the shooting, I saw the once boarded up window the zombies were using to enter the building.

"Dudley," I shouted to be heard over all the zombie screams. "I'll handle the ones inside, you secure the window."

I didn't wait for a reply. Instead, I continued picking my targets. Usually, it was the zombie closest to me. Dudley was trying to secure the window, but every time he took out a zombie clawing its way inside, another one rose up to take its place.

As soon as I finished clearing out the hallway, I joined him at the window. Even with both of us firing we were barely able to hold back the tide, but that wasn't too big of a deal. The goal wasn't to wipe all of them out. Dudley and I were merely trying to buy us some time for the chopper to pick us up.

"I don't have the ammo for this," Dudley said as he dropped his MP7 on its sling and reached for his 1911 Kimber.

"Fall behind me and shoot over my head," I said. "I have a few new tricks I want to try out."

Dudley did as I asked. I dropped to my knees and took off my backpack. To be honest, it was a little nerve wracking to have Dudley shooting right over my head. But seeing as we didn't have a lot of choices, I did my best to focus on the task at hand.

I removed multiple sets of black disks from my backpack and crawled to the side of the window. After removing the thin sheet of plastic over the adhesive strip, I placed one of the disks on the wall at about knee height. I crawled to the opposite wall and repeated the procedure. I made sure the new disk was exactly opposite the first disk I put up. I knew I was on the money when I heard a soft beep. I pressed the power button and saw a thin red laser stretch across the hall to the other disk.

I used ten sets of disks placing them all at different heights along the walls. When I was finished and once again standing next to Dudley, I had about ten feet of hallway covered with lasers.

"Were they really lasers?"

Oh yeah, they were lasers. They would cut through just about anything that passed in front of the beam. Being a Regulator has its perks. We get to be the first to play with all the new gadgets that come down the pipeline.

The disks were a great booby trap, but they did have some serious limitations. The battery life was only about forty-five minutes. The disks were only good for about ten or fifteen cuts before they burned out. Also, absent direct sunlight, the lasers themselves were very visible. An enemy would be able to spot the trap easily from a pretty big distance.

"The zombies wouldn't spot them though, would they?"

Well, I'm sure the zombies saw the lasers. They're just too stupid to try and avoid them. Regardless, the disk lasers would slow them down when it came time to make a run for it.

"Jax," Nick said over my earpiece. "I can see the helicopter. Get your ass up here."

I looked over at Dudley, who gave me a nod and stopped firing. We should have taken off immediately, but both of us were a little too curious to see how well the disks would work.

The first zombie crawled through the window, followed by another and another one after that. She locked eyes with us for a brief moment, screamed and charged us. The laser took both her legs off at the knee. She then took to crawling after us and screamed out in rage, and frustration, only to run headfirst into the next laser and drop lifelessly to the ground in a heap; the top part of her skull had been sliced off in a perfectly straight line.

"I'm glad I invented those," Dudley whispered.

I gave a brief laugh and watched as the other zombies charged towards, us only to fall to pieces when they met the lasers.

"Let's go," I said.

We ran back the way we had come, but as soon as we had entered the stairwell, we heard a cacophony of screams coming from above us. I silently planned on having words with my team about clearing buildings, if I survived long enough to do so.

"How many?" Dudley asked.

"Too many and not enough ammo," I answered.

"We're about to get boxed in."

"No shit," I answered.

I popped my head out of the stairwell, and looked around frantically. The hallways on the first floor were filled with those flimsy fake-wood doors. If the zombies saw us enter them, or managed to locate us later, those things would shatter in a heartbeat.

The screams above us were becoming louder and louder. I was also beginning to hear the sounds of many, many, different pairs of feet scrape against the concrete steps. I reached into one of the pouches on my utility belt, and brought out a handful of marble-sized steel balls. I quickly placed the balls all over the first flight of the stairs.

"Looks like down is our only option," I said.

I led the way. After two flights of stairs, we arrived at another metal door. The door was unlocked, and we entered the darkness inside just as we heard the loud pops of the steel balls I had placed on the stairs.

"They were another booby trap?"

Yeah, they were pretty nasty. Essentially, they made a small explosion whenever they were squished. However, the explosion was small enough that it wasn't fatal to whoever was unlucky enough to step on one. Still, the little explosion is enough to break the person's leg or ankle, and I'm talking about a real break; one you can't walk away from.

Just for goofs once, Dudley and I bought a bag of marbles, spray painted them silver and scattered them all around Georgie's bed while he was asleep. You should have heard him scream when he woke up and started stepping on them. Ever since then, we started calling them "Georgie's boom balls."

Anyway, the room we entered was pitch black. I took a step forward and went tumbling down a bunch of stairs before I managed to grab a hold of the railing. A soft growl answered the noise I made.

My MP7 had gotten twisted around behind me on its sling, so I frantically yanked out the Sig Sauer from my side holster only to realize that I couldn't see a damn thing. I was pulling off my backpack in order to retrieve my flashlight, when the large room flooded with a dim light.

Dudley was still at the top of the stairs. He had somehow managed to find the light switch.

"Are you okay?" he asked.

"All except my ego," I replied. "Lock the door behind you."

I looked around the room as soon as I heard the click of the lock. We were in a flooded basement. I couldn't tell how deep the water was, but it seemed to be pretty deep, and the waterline reached up to just a few steps below me. There was an earthy, moldy smell in the air, and that was joined together with the all too familiar smell of rot and decay.

The basement was rather large. It easily spanned the length and width of the building, without all the doors and hallways to make it appear smaller. It was just one big open area. Floating on the water were pieces of wood and soaked papers. I also saw the upper halves of filing cabinets and boilers. Apparently, the space had been used for storage.

None of that really concerned me, though.

Something had growled at me and it didn't sound like a zombie. I wasn't sure what it was, but I wanted to find out before it swam up and took a bite out of me.

"What are you looking for?" asked Dudley.

"Something growled before you hit the lights."

"What was it?" asked Dudley.

"If I knew that I would have told you," I answered.

"Over there!" Dudley shouted with a point of his finger.

I trained my eyes over to the darkened corner he was pointing at. Whatever he saw was no longer there, but the water was still rippling in that area.

"What did you see?" I asked.

"I'm not sure what it was, but I'm pretty sure it was humanoid. It had a really weird color, sort of pinkish. It went into the water."

The area we were looking at was the darkest place in the entire room. I used my flashlight to get a better view, and I really didn't like what I saw.

The ground was built up in that area with mud. It created a small island above the water line. Above the muddy island were five corpses hanging upside down from the ceiling. We had stumbled upon something's lair.

"Jaxon," Georgie said through my earpiece. "Where are you? The helicopter is here."

"We're trapped in the basement," I answered. "You assholes didn't clear the building and we got surrounded."

"Should we come and get you?"

"No. Use the machine guns on the chopper to take out the shamblers still outside the building. After that, replenish what supplies you need and head over to the next building we picked out and continue the job. Just make sure you clear the new building before you start attracting any zombies to your area."

"You want us to leave you guys there?" Georgie asked.

"Yeah," I answered. "We'll figure a way out."

"Jax," Georgie said. "There are thousands of zombies trying to get inside the building right now. Are you sure you want us to leave you?"

"There isn't much you can do right now anyway," I answered. "We may have to hide out until they get bored and leave. I'll radio you if we run into anything we can't handle."

"All right," Georgie said before signing off.

We sat quietly for about five minutes listening to the ruckus coming from above us. Things had certainly picked up while we were inside the building.

"I can't believe there are thousands of zombies above us," Dudley said dejectedly.

"I can't believe none of them tracked us down here," I replied.

I really wasn't too worried about the zombies at the moment. I was much more concerned about what was swimming around in the dark water below me. Every now and then I would see a ripple of movement across the still surface.

"Do you think it was a zombie?" I asked.

"Zombies don't normally hang their victims upside down," Dudley answered. "So no, I don't think it was a zombie that I saw."

"You think it was a vampire?" I asked.

"I fucking hope not," Dudley answered. "I've had enough of those bastards."

"I don't think it was a vampire," I said. "Vampires like fresh blood. They keep their victims alive and in pits, like that one you found."

"Just shut up about vampires," Dudley grumbled. "I don't want to talk about vampires. You're freaking me out."

"How am I freaking you out?" I asked.

"Dude, we're in a dark cellar that's filled with water. There is a rotting food source in the darkest corner, and something is swimming around underneath us. I want to get the hell out of here."

"I want you to know that I listened to everything you said," I answered. "However, you failed to explain to me what I did to freak you out."

"Now you're just fucking with me."

"I'm not," I answered. "I'm just wondering why you want to blame me for freaking you out, when, in fact, you are to blame for our current predicament."

"How am I to blame?" Dudley demanded.

"Because you morons didn't clear the building," I answered.

"We probably should have cleared the building," Dudley agreed.

I was trying hard not to laugh, and I just couldn't resist one more jab.

"So what do you think is in that water?" I asked.

"Would you shut the hell up?" Dudley snapped.

"Fine," I answered. "I really don't feel like talking to you anymore anyway."

"Good," Dudley said. "Let's just sit here quietly until enough of the shamblers leave, and then we'll make a break for it."

I couldn't pick on him anymore. Dudley was obviously freaked out. I mean, I knew he was a little edgy, but I had no idea he was as worried as he was. He's normally a pretty steady guy.

What do you think was causing him to be so unnerved?

I can only guess. It's not like he'd ever tell me, but I'm guessing the thousands of zombies thundering around and screaming their heads off above us, combined with the new and unknown threat below us, was the cause. Also, the new threat was intelligent. It's never good to have something intelligent trying to eat you.

"*How do you know it was intelligent?*"

Because it tied its victims to the ceiling: tying something up takes intelligence. That meant there was a pinkish-hued creature with an unknown degree of intelligence swimming below us, and it had an appetite for human flesh.

"*Why were you so calm?*"

Who said I was calm? I wasn't anywhere near calm. I was just channeling my energy into picking on Dudley, so I wouldn't freak out with him. Anyway, back to the basement.

I tapped my earpiece.

"I'm here," Hardin asked.

"What do you think we're dealing with?" I asked.

"No idea," Hardin replied. "The video I'm looking at isn't very clear. I sent it over to Miriam, and she isn't sure either. Maybe you could work your way closer to the den so I could have a better look."

I looked over at Dudley and he was mouthing the words, 'Hell no,' at me.

"I'll see what I can do," I answered before signing off.

I really didn't want to sit around and wait for whatever it was to attack me. That's certainly not my idea of a good time. I would much rather have the deck stacked in my favor and go on the offensive. So, I pulled the grappling hook and rope out of my backpack.

My target was a very large filing cabinet about eight feet away. Now the movies always make it look rather easy, but I can assure you that trying to cast a grappling hook over to another object, and actually make it stick, is a very difficult thing to do. I missed my first try, and didn't fail to notice the smirk on Dudley's face.

Around thirty attempts later, my grappling hook finally found a purchase. I took my end of the line and tied it tightly to the railing of the staircase.

"Are you seriously going to do this?" Dudley asked.

I didn't answer him at first, because I felt the answer was rather obvious. Also, the entire time I was attempting to make my grappling hook stick on to the filing cabinet he hadn't said a word. Aside from his smirk, he had no reaction at all. He probably never thought I'd get the grappling hook to stick. Plus, I was little shocked that he was actually speaking to me again.

"Yeah," I finally answered, after he began cursing under his breath.

"Whatever's in that water is going to wait until you're halfway across, and then it's going to jump out at you."

"That only happens in horror films numb-nuts."

"You wait," Dudley replied.

There was no chance in hell I was going to be able to use the line as a tightrope. I don't have that kind of balance. Instead, I hung from the rope with my hands and feet, and pulled myself towards the filing cabinet.

When I reached the halfway mark, I must admit I got a little nervous. I started looking over my shoulder towards the water beneath me. I was half expecting a giant shark-thing to burst from the water.

"Any second now," Dudley announced as he lifted up his pistol and pointed it towards the water.

"I never really liked you," I told him.

Finally, I reached the filing cabinet and pulled myself on top of it. The top of the metal was wet and slippery. When the pounding on the basement door began, I jumped so high I almost lost my balance and fell into the water.

The zombies had located our hiding spot.

"This could be a problem, Jax," Dudley said.

"Yeah," I answered.

I was doing my best to ignore the pounding on the door. My attention was focused on the task at hand, and I didn't welcome the interruption. Besides, the door looked to be extremely sturdy. I had a bit of time.

From the filing cabinet, I jumped close to six feet and landed on a slightly smaller cabinet. This cabinet was just as slippery as the last one, and I slid right to the side with the bottom half of my body hanging over the edge. I rapidly pulled myself up while visions of a shark-man filled my mind. Once I was on top of the cabinet, I looked down below me at the water and noticed it was rippling.

"Did you see anything," I asked Dudley.

"Why? What's happened?"

I didn't bother to answer him. All he was really concerned about were the zombies piling up outside the door to the basement.

From the second filing cabinet, I hopped to the side of a boiler. I shimmied my way to the opposite side of the bulbous hunk of machinery, and launched myself towards a third filing cabinet. I had another game of slip and slide there before I was able to get myself secure.

The pounding on the basement door was becoming louder.

"How's it going over there?" I asked.

"The door is holding but I'm not sure for how long."

"How many are out there?" I asked.

"What do you want me to do?" Dudley snarled back at me, "Open the door and count them?"

"Testy little girl, aren't you?" I retorted.

From the final filing cabinet I was able to jump towards the ceiling and grab an exposed pipe. From there I went hand-over-hand until I reached the muddy island. I let go of the pipe and landed on the gooey surface. I briefly wondered where the mud came from, but as it wasn't immediately important, I let the thought drop.

On one corner of the small island, I saw what must have been a nest. It was a mass of shredded foam, and fabric, piled up on the sides and flattened in the middle. I took out my flashlight and started searching for clues. There weren't any to be found in the nest. So, I shone the light towards the mud and found footprints. Judging by the size and shape of them, they were all created by the same creature.

The moment I had seen the hanging bodies, I was certain we weren't dealing with zombies. When I saw the footprints, I knew we weren't dealing with a vampire either. I still had had doubts up until I saw the footprints, but upon seeing them I was positive it wasn't a vampire. The creature responsible only had three toes, and each toe had a ridiculously long claw.

The pounding on the door increased to the point where the door was shaking on its hinges. Dudley had repositioned himself farther down the stairs with his pistol trained on the wobbling door.

I went over to the hanging bodies. I found a bite mark on the first one I looked at. It was pretty difficult to miss; a huge chunk was missing from the side of its neck. It didn't take long to find the bite mark on the second corpse either. It was located on its dangling arm, and by the looks of it, it was rather severe.

"Are you seeing this?" I asked Hardin after tapping my earpiece.

"Those are zombie bites. It looks like all the victims were infected," Hardin answered.

"Any ideas?" I asked.

"Miriam thinks it could be a few things, but she isn't positive on any of them. Get a closer look at the body in the far back if you can."

I grumbled some sort of response and went to the corpse farthest from my position. This body was missing pieces. In fact, it was missing a lot of pieces. Something had been eating it and the wounds looked rather fresh.

Then I noticed the most shocking thing of all.

The body was riddled with bullet holes. Closer inspection of the other bodies showed me that all of the corpses had bullet wounds. In three of them alone, the only wound aside from the zombie bite was a single bullet hole in the forehead.

I heard gurgling in the water just a few feet from the bank of the small island I was standing on.

"Hardin," I said after tapping my earpiece. "Whatever this thing is, it's feeding on dead zombies."

"Well, a dead zombie is just a corpse," Hardin replied. "These zombies were caused by a curse. I believe that once the brain is destroyed, the zombie becomes just a regular dead body."

"So what is it, then?" I asked.

"No clue."

A loud, hair-raising growl sounded out from the darkness of the water. I immediately drew my pistol and fired off a shot in the direction it came from. I'm positive I missed, but the water began to churn.

"Jaxon," Hardin said. "I'm thinking that whatever it is you're dealing with isn't too happy about you being so close to its food source. Perhaps you should move away."

"No arguments here," I answered.

Dudley was screaming something at me. I think he wanted to know what was going on. I didn't have time to answer him. Instead, I jumped into the air and once again grabbed a hold of the exposed pipe.

I went hand-over-hand towards the nearest filing cabinet. I swung my body, and released my hold. My aim was good. I slid when I hit the wet surface, but I still managed to grasp a hold of the edge before I went over the side.

I looked over at Dudley.

Things weren't looking too great for him. The door was beginning to buckle and warp. I was shocked that the hinges were holding, but the door itself was in pretty bad shape.

"Jax!" Shouted Dudley. "What do you want me to do here?"

The corner of the door began to bend inward. I saw rotted hands reaching through and grasping for prey. I futilely looked around the basement for something he could use to reinforce the failing door but there was nothing to be seen.

Worst of all, I was too far away from him to help and something was lurking in the water between us.

The water churned and frothed once again. This time it happened right next to the filing cabinet with the grappling hook still attached to it. The cabinet wobbled in the whirling water, and then tipped over onto its side.

Needless to say, I was panicking.

I looked towards Dudley. Dudley looked towards me, and the door bent even further. I saw the upper half of a zombie shredding its own skin as it pushed itself through the too-small opening. It used to be a teenager but now he was missing an eye, along with most of the orbital bones in that area. He was wearing a t-shirt that was so dirty I could no longer read the logo. His shorts were stained with blood and other juices that had oozed from the wounds in his hip where he had been attacked.

Dudley took aim and brought him down with one shot. His brain matter sprayed through the exit wound, and the gunk landed upon the many, many shamblers desperately trying to take its place.

"Jump in the water!" I shouted.

Chapter 2

DUDLEY

Dudley walked into the meeting room wearing board shorts and one of those wife-beater t-shirts. He had his Elvis-style sunglasses pushed high up on his forehead and sandals on his feet. He looked as if he had just gotten out of the shower. Even his dark hair was messed up, which was an unusual thing for him.

I just finished up my workout, little lady. I considered coming to this all sweaty and pumped up, but I was worried you might not be able to contain yourself.

"Well, that's very thoughtful of you."

It was. Now tell me, does this interview have anything to do with the hint I gave you the last time we talked?

"It does indeed."

Crazy times; not all of it is easy to talk about. Where do you want me to start?

"Jaxon left off with the two of you being stuck in a basement. Something was in the water and zombies were coming through the door."

That's a pretty good place to kick things off…a shitty situation for me, though. The funny thing was I kept wondering why Jax was so interested in whatever was in that water. He kept trying to figure out what it was and I didn't understand why he cared so much. Let whatever the hell was in that water stay there, and start focusing on the zombies trying to find and eat us.

It wasn't until they started getting through the door that I understood what was so important about finding out what was in the water. Jaxon knew from the very beginning the zombies would eventually find us and come through the door. He knew we would eventually need to go into the water to escape them.

"And Jaxon didn't want something new attacking you when you made your escape."

Exactly. You see, shamblers can't swim. They just sink. Most of the time they won't even go anywhere near the water unless they see prey: then they'll charge right in after them. Jaxon was hoping to get both of us hidden in the water before the zombies got through the door.

The creature swimming around in there jacked up our timing. We should have been hiding in the water way before the shamblers actually got a visual on us. If we had managed that, they probably would have just avoided the water and left the room. Still, even though we had been discovered, jumping in the water and hoping for the best was my only viable option. It was either that, or be swarmed by the horde coming through the door. I unfortunately had a major problem getting into that dirty-ass water regardless of how limited my options were, and I really didn't need to hear my uncle state the obvious.

"Jump in the water!" Jaxon shouted.

"Are you fucking crazy?" I asked.

"Jump in before you run out of ammo."

The joke was on him. I had just fired my last shot. I pulled my machete free and began to hack at the zombies trying to force themselves into the room.

"I'm not jumping in that water!" I shouted.

"You don't have a choice," Jaxon answered. "I'll cover you."

"I'm not jumping in that water," I repeated. "That's poo-poo water."

"It's what?" asked Jaxon.

"It's poo-poo water," I said again.

I guess I should explain before we get any farther. Yes, I was concerned about the creature from the basement lagoon, but I was far more concerned about what also might be floating in the water. You see: I'm very particular about keeping myself clean. Jaxon, who is a clean freak as well, likes to call me a "germaphobe," and he used to take great pleasure in having people touch my hands after I had just washed them. It used to drive me crazy.

"Wait a second. You were more concerned about the dirty water than you were about whatever creature was in there and the zombies at the door?"

Hmm, maybe I am a "germaphobe."

Regardless, I was having issues.

"What do you mean poo-poo water?" Jaxon asked.

"Well, the water had to come from somewhere. I'm guessing a sewage line burst somewhere. That's poo-poo water, and I'm not getting in it."

"It's not poo-poo water, you ass hat," Jaxon said. "It doesn't smell bad."

"What are you talking about?" I asked. "The entire room smells bad."

That was no exaggeration either. The room smelled like old socks and rotten flesh. I didn't exactly put my nose to the water to have a whiff, but I couldn't imagine it would be something refreshing.

"This is moving water," Jaxon said. "It's coming from a fresh source. This isn't sewage."

"It looks pretty still to me," I shot back while hacking away at the zombies coming through the bent door.

"It looks still but it isn't. If it were still water, it would be stagnant and nasty. This water isn't stagnant."

"I'M NOT GETTING IN THE POO-POO WATER," I shouted.

As we were arguing, the zombies were making the hole in the door wider and wider. I knew in my heart I wouldn't be able to hold them off much longer. I just didn't want to jump in the gross pool.

"Get in the damn water," Jaxon growled.

"You get in the damn water," I answered.

The noise coming from the shamblers was incredibly loud. Add that to my screaming at Jaxon, and we were really bringing down the house. I've been to rock concerts that created less noise. Hang around large hordes of zombies and you kind of get used to the noise levels. Unfortunately for me, the creature in the water probably didn't hang around zombies much. It didn't seem to be a big fan of all the commotion.

"Dudley," Jax said. "Look behind you."

I didn't want to look. I really didn't. I simply didn't want to face any more bad news. I'd enough crappy news for one day, and the zombies pushing through the door was just icing on the cake. We'd already dealt with the machine gun breaking on the roof and our building getting infiltrated. It was probably time to go home and have a nap.

I looked.

A clawed hand was out of the water, and grabbing hold of the first dry step. Mind you, I've seen some clawed hands before on zombies and vampires, but none of them even compared to the back scratchers on this thing. They were four inches long, thick, black, and looked evil sharp. Almost like a mutated badger or something.

"Son of a bitch," I muttered.

The head of the beast began to rise from the dark water.

"Jump," Jaxon shouted.

The claws made it pretty easy for me. Don't get me wrong: the zombies are rough. But I guess since the team has faced them so many times, they had kind of lost their edge. I really didn't want to be anywhere near the receiving end of those claws.

I jumped into the water.

I swam as hard and as fast as I possibly could swim. I aimed my body right for the same filing cabinet that Jaxon was using. I just knew the beast was right behind me. I could just feel that clawed hand grabbing onto my leg and pulling me underwater.

It never attacked.

I reached my uncle right as the shamblers opened the hole in the door wide enough to pour into onto the stairway.

"Check it out," Jaxon whispered after he had helped me out of the water.

The zombies were massing on the stairs but their attention wasn't on us at all. Instead, they were focused on the humanoid creature that had climbed out of the water before them. It wasn't pink upon closer inspection. It had a sort of milky-white skin that was almost, but not quite, transparent. The blood pumping through its veins just gave the skin a slight tinge. You could also see the vague shapes of internal organs as well. It was pretty nasty. The head of the creature was elongated, with small ears, a big huge mouth, and a wide nose.

The creature wasn't all that large, as it stood there hunched over the stairs, facing down the zombies. I'm positive it was less than six feet tall, but it was still intimidating as hell. It wasn't just the claws either, not that I'd forgotten about those, but the mouth was just plain scary. It seemed almost overcrowded with oversized, jagged teeth. The thing looked like it could bite through a metal girder.

The zombies had one of those brief moments of indecision when they realized their intended prey had been replaced by something else, something that probably didn't smell even remotely human. The creature not only held its ground in front of them, but it bellowed a roar that should have come from a much larger creature.

Yet, it didn't attack.

The zombies charged. The creature didn't run and it didn't jump back into the water. It stood its ground, and when the first shambler approached and grabbed hold of its neck, I thought it would all be over.

Instead, the creature reacted violently.

It slammed its clawed hand down on top of the shambler's head, so hard the head caved in. After that, the zombies washed over it in a great big wave. The creature was buried beneath them in seconds.

"We need to find a way out of here," Jaxon whispered.

"Maybe after they eat that thing, they'll forget all about us."

"I don't think the zombies can hurt it," Jaxon whispered.

"How do you figure? They are currently devouring it."

"When that first zombie attacked, there was no wound. I don't think it was able to bite through the monster's skin."

As if to prove Jaxon right, the creature stood up beneath the mound of undead that had amassed on top of it. It bellowed out another roar, and advanced up the steps in order to bite and scratch at the advancing horde.

The battle wasn't going to last forever. There were way too many zombies pushing their way through the hole in the door. Eventually, their sheer numbers were going to drag the creature down. Ten zombies may not be able to puncture its hide, but one hundred or more zombies all pulling its skin in different directions was a different story entirely.

In the middle of its attack, the creature seemed to have arrived at the same conclusion. It gave a last few swats with its clawed hands and then jumped over the railing of the staircase and vanished into the dark water.

The zombies pursued it.

Some of them jumped over the railing, while others floundered down the stairs and ended up wading around the room with their hands held above their heads, as if they were afraid to get their shirtsleeves wet.

"We gotta move," Jax whispered.

"Where the hell are we gonna go?" I asked. "We're kind of trapped in here."

"No," Jaxon whispered. "There has to be a way out. I bet it's under the water."

"Oh, I really hate you right now."

"We need to move now. If the shamblers fill up the room, we'll never find the way out."

Jax didn't wait for me to reply this time. He was probably sick of hearing me complain. Instead, he quietly lowered himself into the water. I grumbled and fumed but I eventually joined him.

The water came up to our shoulders and it was cold as hell. We tried to stay hidden behind the various objects as we made our way around the room. That worked pretty well. The zombies also weren't venturing too far from the staircase. Evidently, they thought the creature was still in that area.

Jaxon led the way back to the muddy island with the upside down corpses.

"How are we going to find the way out if it's under water?" I asked.

"I'm hoping I'll feel a current. This water has to be escaping somehow."

The moaning and groaning noises coming from all the shamblers were annoyingly loud. They just didn't know how to shut up when they found something worth eating. On the plus side, it seemed as if the bulk of the horde had lost interest. There were still a lot of zombies in the water and on the stairs, but it didn't seem as if any more of them were coming into the room. At the very least, that was a relief. All we needed to do was find the exit without being seen, and we'd be home free.

The first scream made me jump.

The second scream made Jaxon curse.

The many screams that followed made us run like hell, and that wasn't very easy, being chest-deep in dark water. We had gotten lucky when the cellar-dweller climbed out of the water onto the stairs. The zombies forgot all about me and concentrated on the creature. Unfortunately, we had been discovered once again.

One of them happened to look over in the right direction at the right time, and saw us moving along the far wall. It was bound to happen. There were way too many searching eyes.

I looked towards the staircase and immediately regretted it. The stairs were once again being flooded, and more of the horde was entering the water.

"This is bad!" I shouted!

"Rarely gets worse," Jaxon answered.

He shoved his MP7 into my arms and pulled out his flashlight.

"Take out the ones closest to us," Jaxon said.

He dove under the water. It was a weird feeling when he went under. I almost felt like I was alone in the room without backup. I didn't like it; having someone next to you working toward the same goal makes things easier, especially when that someone is my uncle. With Jaxon around, it's hard to imagine yourself failing.

I know that might seem weird. We lost people. We lose them all the time, in all honesty. We're far from invincible. It's just that, for some reason, Jax gives people the belief that they can win. No matter how hard things tend to get, he never contemplates defeat.

I was missing my shots.

Tension and stress can do that to a person. The first thing to go in extreme situations is hand/eye coordination. I'm normally pretty good at controlling myself, but this was something sort of new to me. Like I said, I felt alone.

A zombie had somehow gotten to within ten feet of me. Its wet face had this doughy skin that looked as if it were about to peel right off its skull. Its screams were watery, so it must have taken water into its lungs.

I fired, and I missed.

I fired again, and hit a shoulder.

The corpse jerked with the impact but it kept on coming. For a brief moment I blamed the gun. The sights had to be off in a bad way. Then I realized my hands were shaking fiercely, and the shamblers were getting closer.

I finally nailed it, right before it could get its hands on me. The body dropped face down in the water and floated there. I didn't breathe a sigh of relief. I didn't have the opportunity. There were too many zombies willing to take its place.

I fired and fired from my position. I had no idea how many bullets I had left, and the thought of running empty was freaking me out even more. They were too close. The smell coming off them was even worse when it mixed with the water.

I found myself trying to back away from them, but I was unable to do so since my back was already against the wall. Instead, I mentally chided myself and pushed forward. It isn't easy to make yourself walk towards an advancing horde of zombies, but I did it.

All in all, the speed of the shamblers was really affected by the water. They were splashing and thrashing, trying to close the distance, but their frenzied movements only served to slow them down.

I stopped advancing. I forced myself to remain calm. I picked my shots, and brought them down. I had excellent results at first, but my success was short-lived. There were too many of them.

I began to retreat towards the wall once again. This time it wasn't a matter of nerves. I was now moving backwards to avoid being overrun.

The screams were so loud inside the basement, I neither heard nor noticed Jaxon come up from behind me and wrap his arms around my chest. I immediately freaked right the fuck out. I thought for sure one of the shamblers had gotten a hold of me.

"Relax, Dudley!" Jaxon shouted. "Hold your breath!"

I did as he ordered and down we went. The zombies were all around us, so Jaxon took us all the way down to the bottom of the cellar. We began swimming rapidly over the cement floor. The zombies could neither see nor smell us through the water. Still, it was unnerving to swim around them in a sort of undead obstacle course. It was also an effort to avoid bumping into their legs so as not to alert them to our location.

It wasn't long before I was running out of air. Jaxon had me by the arm. He was guiding me somewhere, but I wasn't going to make it. I tapped his hand and motioned that I needed air. I could barely see his face in the darkness but I'm pretty sure he shook his head.

I'm not sure how he thought I could continue with convulsing lungs, but a breath of air wasn't something I wanted, it was something I needed. I shook my arm out of his grasp and stood straight up in the water. Unfortunately, I was standing right in the middle of a loose group of shamblers.

They were pretty happy to see me.

You could almost see the enjoyment on their rotten faces. One of them grabbed me by the collar and pulled my entire body towards its jaws. Jaxon erupted behind me, and brought his tomahawk straight down on the zombie's head.

The relief I experienced when I felt its fingers release my collar was immense. Still, before I even managed to collect my thoughts and grab another breath, Jaxon was in action. There were too many of them around us. We couldn't make our escape without getting some distance first.

Jaxon was punching with his fist and slashing with his tomahawk. He was a whirlwind of destruction, hell-bent on clearing a space around us. But the dead just kept coming. That's what they do, ya know? They just keep coming. Nothing scares them. They just keep coming and coming and coming.

I fired off two shots with Jaxon's rifle, and then the gun was empty. I dropped it on its sling, and grabbed the handle of my machete. As soon as I pulled the blade free, my uncle suddenly turned on me, launched himself into the air, tackled me around the shoulders, and dragged me under the water once more.

This time I never even had a chance to take a breath. I began to fight against him as he dragged me along the bottom of the cellar. He swam towards the island. I could see the muddy mound through the cloudy water by the beam of his flashlight.

However, the island wasn't our destination. We ended up going around it entirely. I was becoming frantic for a breath of air. I knew it would be bad if I put my head out of the water, but try telling that to my convulsing lungs.

I thrashed and thrashed, but Jaxon only tightened his grip. Spots began to appear in my vision. My slaps at Jaxon's hand became weaker and weaker. I vaguely saw the flashlight shining on a dark hole in the concrete, but I no longer cared. At that point, I released the expired air I had been holding in my lungs, and went completely limp.

Before I could draw that inevitable breath of watery death, I felt myself being pushed to the surface, and when that unstoppable inhale finally came, it filled my lungs with air instead of water. I came to my senses immediately. I heard the rage-filled screams coming from all around us. I cleared my vision, saw the basement was filled with the dead, and they were all headed right for us.

Jaxon was breathing heavily in my ear.

"You ready?" He asked. "Get a good breath. I don't know how long this tunnel is, but it's better than staying here."

In other words, drowning was better than being eaten. Well, I wasn't too sure either of the two options made for a nice evening, to be honest with you. I took a deep breath of air just as my uncle's hand closed around my arm.

Under the water we went. The hole in the concrete was at our feet. I barely felt a current as we headed towards it. Maybe the water was too cold and my body had become too numb to really feel much of anything, but there must have been one. Jaxon swam like a crazy person. It was hard to see, even with the flashlight. The dirt walls and floor of the tunnel were clouding up the water.

After a bit, I began to get nervous. My air was running out. I could already feel the tightening in my chest. It was more than a mere suggestion to breathe, but I was ignoring it. I hated this. I really did. I felt completely useless. I'm not sure how Jax even managed to make any progress. I'm guessing he felt his way through the tunnel instead of relying on his flashlight too much.

Suddenly we began to rise.

It didn't take us long to reach the surface, and when we did, both of us were laughing. We crawled out of the water onto a dirt floor. I wanted to lay there for a bit and once again learn how to breathe. I'm sure Jax felt the same way I did, but he made sure to scan our surroundings with the flashlight before he even contemplated resting.

Both of us were still laughing. I'm not sure why. Maybe we were just happy to get out of that basement in one piece. All I know is Jaxon started cracking up the second we reached the surface, and I joined in along with him.

"Well, that sucked," I said.

"It looked like you were having some problems there, tough guy," Jaxon laughed.

"I thought you were going to drown me."

"I can't believe you popped your head up right in the middle of a group of zombies," Jaxon said.

"It wasn't like I wanted to," I grumbled. "I needed air."

"You want some free advice?" Jaxon asked.

"I do not," I answered.

"Why not?" Jaxon asked. "It's free."

"No thanks," I told him. "I'm okay."

"How about some friendly advice?"

"How about fuck off?" I replied.

Now, I can see you're looking at me kind of funny. That's probably because you believe Jaxon really wanted to offer me a bit of advice that may, in fact, benefit me in the future. I can assure you that he had zero intention of giving me anything beneficial. Instead, what he was trying to do was open me up so he could harass me. If I had asked him what advice he had to give me, he would have probably made fun of my lung capacity. Or perhaps he would have made fun of the faces I made after

I ran out of air, or suggested I quit the Regulators and find employment as a trumpet player since my cheeks can puff out so far.

I really don't know what form the harassment would have taken. I only knew it would last for hours, possibly even days. It wouldn't matter if I thought it was funny or not, because Jaxon found it funny, and when he finds something funny, look out.

"I'm thinking maybe later you'll probably be interested in hearing my advice," Jaxon said unperturbed.

"I can see how you would think that," I answered. "I've been giving you nothing but encouragement to continue."

"I can sense your anger, Luke," Jaxon whispered. "Anger leads to the Dark Side."

"Fear leads to anger," I added.

Jaxon was no longer paying attention. That quickly, he had lost interest in joking around. Instead, he was shining his light on the floor. I finally pulled out my own flashlight and started investigating our surroundings. We were inside a tunnel of some sorts. The walls, the floor, and the ceilings didn't look safe at all.

"What are you looking at?" I asked Jax who was staring at something on the floor.

"I found a footprint," Jaxon answered.

"Is it the creature?" I asked.

"Yeah."

"Well, it looks like we're on the right track, I guess."

"I'd say so," Jaxon said. "I also don't think the thing is normally a water creature."

"Huh?"

"None of the footprints I've seen are webbed. Its hands weren't webbed either. Did you see any gills?"

"I wasn't exactly looking for gills, man. I just wanted to get the hell away from it."

"Look at the walls of the tunnel," Jaxon said. "They're covered in claw marks. Whatever that thing is, I think it dug this tunnel out. I bet when it went too deep it busted a water line, and that's what flooded the basement."

"How could one creature dig out this huge ass tunnel? I asked.

In just our immediate area, the walls were about ten feet apart, and the ceiling was about eight feet high.

"Look farther down the tunnel," Jaxon said. "The walls get narrower."

He was correct. I didn't notice it on my first scan but farther down the tunnel the walls got pretty narrow. The two of us wouldn't be able to walk side by side.

That's when I noticed the dirt walls and ceiling were kind of shiny.

"Did you notice the shiny walls?" I asked.

Jaxon went over to the far wall, pulled out his knife, and poked the dirt. The wall stayed together. Not even a bit of dust fell from where he was picking at the wall.

"I bet it's some sort of secretion from that creature," Jaxon said.

"You don't think that it's maybe some type of chemical that someone could have coated the walls with, in order to keep the tunnel from collapsing?"

"If people dug this out," Jaxon said, "They would have added support beams and things like that to make sure it wouldn't collapse."

"Do you even need support beams when you pour a hardening chemical all over the walls?"

"I'm no miner," Jaxon said with a smile, "but I'm not sure this chemical you continue to speak of even exists, and if it does exist, I'm not sure it would be potent enough to keep this freaking tunnel from caving in on top of us."

"Perhaps you're right," I answered. "Yet, I'm sure I've read about soil coagulants in the past."

"Well, did these soil coagulants have the ability to hold back tons of dirt?"

"I really can't remember." I shrugged.

"I see," Jaxon snickered, and tapped his earpiece.

"Hardin," Jaxon asked. "You with me?"

"Right here," Hardin answered.

"What do you think we're dealing with?"

"I'm not positive," Hardin answered. "I haven't gotten a very clear image yet. Also, Miriam is indisposed right now and not answering her phone."

Miriam always takes off and goes on what she refers to as "solo adventures." It pisses Jaxon off, but she doesn't seem to care. A few months before this little adventure, she had also begun to take Ivana on her little adventures as well. I'm not going to even repeat what Jax said when he found that out.

"Jaxon seems to be rather protective of Ivana?"

She's not a fighter, and because she's not a fighter he doesn't want her anywhere near any kind of danger. He's the same way with his wife; probably even more so. Miriam normally handles exorcisms and spirit-type problems; things the Regulators would be useless at. I personally don't think it's a big deal. I bet the two of them spend most of their time drinking tea and learning to knit.

"Well," Jaxon grumbled. "That's just great isn't it?"

"Sorry, Jax," Hardin replied. "She said things were getting hairy the last time I talked to her. I'm sure she'll get back to us soon."

"By the time she does," Jaxon snarled, "I won't need her."

Without another word, Jaxon reclaimed his MP7, threw it over his shoulder, and tossed me a couple of mags for my own rifle.

"How many mags are you carrying?" I asked.

"That's the last of them," he answered.

"Won't you be needing them?"

He didn't answer. He just smiled at me and set off down the tunnel. I followed behind him. Together we followed the footprints into the darkness.

The tunnel was pretty freaky. At least, it was making me a bit nervous. The walls didn't look stable, and once we had gone a ways I was too worried about their stability to try a stab test like Jax did earlier.

It was a long walk underground. Eventually, the path we were following broke off into different directions.

"We're going to get lost down here," I said.

"Not likely," Jaxon said. "I've been tracking our direction."

"How have you been doing that?"

"My watch has a compass."

"Are you serious?" I asked. "Let me see."

We took a few minutes to geek out over all the features on his Pathfinder. I'm sure you've heard it before, but aside from the money, one of the best things about being on the Regulators is getting to play with all the cool toys.

After I vowed to pick up one of those watches, we set off once again. Both of us were keeping an eye on the creature's tracks. I mean, there were tracks all over the floor but we were only following the freshest of the bunch.

Every now and then we heard growls and shrieks in the distance. They weren't zombie growls and shrieks, though. They were something else. They made the hairs on the back of my neck stand up. It felt like we were being watched, possibly even followed.

I shone my light down one of the side tunnels as we passed by, and for a brief second I saw the reflective shine of eyes staring back at me. It was gone before I could show it to Jaxon.

"I'm not liking this," I said.

"I agree," he answered. "I can't believe these tunnels are running underneath the city, and nobody knew about them."

"I wish they did know about them," I said. "Then maybe somebody could tell us where to find the freakin' exit."

A loud growl echoed from somewhere behind us. It was followed by a series of clicks.

"Well, that's a problem," Jaxon announced.

"What is?"

"Those clicks," Jaxon answered. "They sound like radar pings. If that's the case, these things won't need to use eyesight to find us, and that puts us at a big disadvantage because we are seriously out of our element down here."

"I think we can both agree there's more than one of these creatures," I said. "How many do you think we're dealing with?"

"Impossible to say," Jaxon answered. "Let's hope we don't find out."

We went deeper and deeper into the tunnels. We had no choice. We could have found our way back to where we came in with the compass, but there wasn't much point in that. Backtracking only meant we would eventually wind up in a building overrun by zombies.

It was pretty crazy. The tunnel we followed went up and down. It angled a little to the left, and sometimes a little to the right. At one point we hit a T-intersection and had to study the footprints for a bit to figure out which direction we needed to take.

As Jaxon stood there studying the ground, the noises behind us became louder and louder. The creatures were coming for us. I aimed my light and my rifle towards the rear so we wouldn't get attacked from behind.

"I think you better pick a direction soon," I said.

"It may not matter which direction we choose," Jaxon answered.

"Why do you say that?"

"Well, we started following the tracks because we were hoping the creature would lead us to the surface. Now we know there's more than just one creature. It wouldn't surprise me if there was a community of these underground things. The one we're following might be leading us to an ambush."

"That's comforting," I said. "What do you think we should do?"

"I say we keep on following the footprints and hope for the best."

We moved as fast as we could possibly go through the tunnels. The passage got narrower, and narrower, but we didn't let that slow us down. We could tell we were being followed, and it wouldn't be long before they were upon us.

Finally, Jaxon stopped in a tunnel so narrow he could barely turn around.

"They're getting too close," Jaxon announced. "We need to set up some traps."

He began to struggle with taking off his backpack when I noticed dust drifting lazily down from the ceiling of a passage to our left. I also noticed that the footprints we had been following led down the same passage. I gave Jax a tap on the shoulder and pointed.

Jaxon moved to where I was pointing. The ground sloped upwards, and he followed it without any hesitation. The growls and clicks were coming from just beyond the range of my flashlight as I shone it behind us.

"Bingo," Jaxon said. "I found a way out."

At the top of the slope, he pushed against a lone cement block over his head. More dust drifted downwards, and the block made an extremely loud scraping sound as he moved it to the side.

Shapes were gathering at the limits of my flashlight beam a second before I gave up my vigil and climbed through the newly made hole in the ceiling. Jaxon was right behind me. I went to help him up but instead he snapped at me to check my surroundings.

We were inside a dark room with no windows.

I could sense Jaxon moving next to me. I heard the scrape and crunch when he pushed the cement block back into place.

"Where are we?" I asked when his light joined mine and the room showed its secrets.

"I bet I know," Jaxon answered without really answering anything.

Then I saw what he was looking at. Behind me and off to my right were two very old, very dusty caskets.

"Are you kidding me?" I asked.

"Welcome to Concordia Cemetery," Jaxon announced.

We had ended up inside a crypt. While I'm not extremely knowledgeable about cemeteries, Concordia is pretty famous if you happen to live in or around El Paso. It's an old burial ground from the days of the Wild West. It even has the final resting place of a gunfighter named John Wesley Hardin.

"*Any relation to Mr. Hardin?*"

I doubt it, but I wouldn't be surprised.

Jaxon went to the front door. By rights, it should have been sealed shut. It wasn't. With just a bit of force, the door opened onto the nighttime sky. It was good to breathe fresh air again. Then I had a thought that made me nervous.

"How dangerous do you think it is to be in the middle of a cemetery during a zombie invasion?"

Jaxon blew out a lung full of air before answering.

"If you would have asked me a few hours ago, I would have told you I'm not crazy enough to find out. Looking around now though, I think we're the only two people in here."

A creaking noise came from somewhere in the distance.

"Let the games begin," I muttered.

We exited the crypt and Jax drew out his pistol. We scanned our surroundings but nothing came charging out at us. I held my rifle in a ready position waiting for the barrage of violence, but it never came.

"I don't hear anything," Jaxon said after he found us some cover behind a large headstone.

"Neither do I," I replied.

Jaxon broke cover and low-crawled to the dirt road that wound its way in, and around, the various cemetery plots. I tried to cover him as best I could, but I had no idea where to look for any threats.

At the dirt road, he crouched low behind another headstone and turned on his light. I understood what he was doing; he was looking for more footprints on the dirt road. After about five minutes, he made his way back to me.

"There are tracks all over the road," Jaxon said.

"Same kinda tracks as the creature?"

"Identical," Jaxon said. "Unfortunately, the tracks are coming from more than one creature. So whatever these things are, they have been coming in and out of here for a pretty long time. I can't follow our friend from the basement anymore. Its tracks have gotten mixed up with all the others."

"What do you want to do?"

"Wait and listen," Jaxon answered.

We didn't have to wait very long either. We heard scratching noises coming from one end of the cemetery within twenty minutes. In response, we crouched low and wove our way towards the noise, using the tombstones as cover.

I had never really been to Concordia before. I'd driven past it on numerous occasions, but I can't remember ever going inside. It was a pretty large cemetery, but not huge. Some of the burial markers were made of stone, while others were made of wood, and sometimes even metal. There weren't many trees, just some desert shrub type plants and the ground itself was sand. It was an old cemetery, not at all like most people picture when they think of cemeteries.

There weren't exactly a lot of places we could use for cover either, but we stayed as low as possible and did our best. As we made our way, we heard the sounds of a zombie scream from somewhere outside the walls of the cemetery. I wondered what the zombie was screaming about. There weren't any humans left in the city except for us. I began to worry a little bit about the rest of the team.

That's when I noticed Jaxon had stopped. I couldn't see what he was looking at, but I was positive he had found our creature. I waited a few tombstones behind him until he finally motioned me forward.

I crawled to his position and he pointed towards the wall.

I saw the creature once again. It seemed to have forgotten about us entirely as it was busy digging into the ground next to an old grave. Jaxon gave out a low whistle. The creature immediately stopped its digging and turned its long head in our direction. Its eyes were black. They reminded me of a shark's eyes.

"It's completely hairless," Jaxon said. "Not very big either. In fact, it's kinda scrawny."

"It might be slim but it's covered in muscle. So if you're thinking about tackling it, don't bother.

Also, look how long its arms are. The arms hang down to its knees. No wonder it could cave in a zombie's head so easily. It's got all that momentum."

Jaxon started laughing. The creature heard him, and let out a low growl in our direction. Jax drew his pistol, and broke cover by standing up.

"Well, it's been fun," Jaxon said, "but I got shit to do."

The creature saw him immediately and crouched low. It was ready to spring as Jaxon walked closer and closer. However, before the creature felt threatened enough to attack, Jaxon halted and aimed his weapon.

The muffled sound of a silenced pistol never came.

"Jax," Hardin said in our earpieces. "Don't shoot."

"Why not?" Jaxon asked.

"I just got a call from Miriam," Hardin said. "The creature is harmless unless attacked."

"It doesn't look harmless."

"Well, it is," Hardin said, "but it's also somewhat territorial. So it's probably best if you leave the cemetery."

"What is it?" Jaxon asked.

"It's a ghoul," Hardin answered.

Chapter 3

IVANA

It had been a long time since I last spoke with Ivana. She was at the General's side when zombies invaded the city. She was also around during the vampire situation, but for the most part, she was kept well away from the city. She's considered a member of the team, but they never let her near any danger. She's not a fighter. She has no desire to ever become a fighter. Yet, through thick and thin, she stands by the team and helps out where she can.

When I contacted Ivana, she asked that we meet at a nearby bar instead of the normal conference room. It turns out she recently broke up with her latest girlfriend and thought a few beers sounded like a good idea.

She arrived at the bar twenty minutes late, but the moment she made her way inside she was full of hugs and apologies.

I'm so sorry I'm late. Jax and Dudley were telling me a story about Skie drinking too much at a wedding rehearsal. How have you been?

"*I'm excellent. How are things going for you?*"

She sighed deeply, waved down a waiter, and ordered a drink before answering.

Aside from the breakup, I'm pretty good.

"*Was it a bad breakup?*"

She ran her fingers through her short black hair and fixed me with her dark eyes before answering.

Are breakups ever good?

"*I guess not.*"

I say we skip the interview, and we drink our asses off.

I laughed at her bluntness. She seemed to have changed somewhat since the last time we spoke. It's hard to put a finger on how exactly, but she seemed to be a stronger person.

"*That would be me not doing my job if I left out the interview.*"

Have you ever considered that you might be a workaholic?

"*Once a reporter sinks their teeth into a story, it's very hard to let it go.*"

Well, Dudley loves to exaggerate, but he didn't exaggerate on this one. Some major shit went down. It's kind of hard to believe it's actually over. For a while there, I couldn't see the finish line. I was beginning to lose hope.

"I'm not sure what you're talking about?"

Ivana laughed at me.

Of course not. Excuse me, I sometimes forget most people don't have a clue about what happened with the team during the cleansing of the city. It's quite a story though. I'm sort of glad Dudley turned you on to it.

"Can you walk me through it?"

I can walk you through my part.

"Just what I wanted to hear."

Well, you may not know this, but I started hanging out with Miriam a lot. Most people probably wouldn't want to spend time with a real witch, but I really never gave it much thought. She's an awesome person, very strong, and confident. She's also very motherly. I like that. I lost my mother when the zombies came.

"You mentioned that you lost your entire family the first time I ever interviewed you."

Did I? I don't really remember. I rarely ever talk about the people I lost. Anyway, Miriam was there when I needed someone. She's really the sweetest person I've ever met, even if she does tell me I run through women too fast.

Occasionally, Miriam gets a call from someone that needs help with things the Regulators don't really deal with. The boys prefer fighting things they can hack up with their big knives. They aren't exactly cut out to deal with something you can't beat up.

"You're talking about spirits?"

Yes. I'm talking about spirits or ghosts. Sometimes she deals with possessions and demons. I started going with her on these little side jobs. I call them "little" because they aren't the type of thing that will get out of hand. They can play havoc on a family unfortunate enough to take up residence in a haunted house, but they have little effect on the world at large.

"What about possessions? I imagine those can be pretty awful."

They are. It's terrifying to see someone bend and contort while they hurl out insults in a language they shouldn't know. I damn near pissed my pants the first time I saw a kid crawl up a wall.

Miriam, however, wasn't bothered in the least. She's seen it all a million times. She's fought it all a million times. She has herbs, potions, and talismans. She uses all of these things to remove the entity.

Mind you, if it's real bad, I tend to wait outside the room. I normally try and talk to the parents, spouse, or loved ones. I try and keep them calm while Miriam does her thing.

"What does she do if it's real bad?"

I asked her that once, and she told me she calls the police. It turns out that the spirit world takes care of itself. She says there are entities that prevent other entities from interfering with the land of the living, sort of like ghost police.

Anyway, I've sort of gotten off the topic, but we were dealing with a pretty bad possession case when Jax and Dudley ran into an unknown creature in an old basement. Mr. Hardin sent her some grainy photos, and even a quick video, but despite his many phone calls, Miriam couldn't tell him what it was.

She also didn't have much time to spare figuring it out. I could tell she wanted to ask questions. She probably had a bunch. She's the resident monster expert, but the demon inside the little boy we had come to help had started twisting the child's spine so violently, she feared it might kill the body.

It took her a pretty long time to get the situation sorted out. I'm happy to say the boy lived and he is now demon-free. The parents will probably need therapy for the rest of their lives, but fortunately, the boy doesn't remember a thing.

After things had calmed down inside the boy's bedroom, Miriam was immediately on the phone with Mr. Hardin. Jaxon and Dudley had gotten more images of the creature. They had even followed it down a tunnel that went under the city in order to escape a building full of zombies.

Miriam put two and two together.

"I'm pretty sure it's a ghoul," Miriam announced over the phone. "It's actually pretty rare to see one nowadays."

"How dangerous are they?" Mr. Hardin asked over the speakerphone.

"They aren't dangerous at all unless you attack them. They have zero interest in living human flesh. A ghoul feasts upon the dead. The more rotted the better. Just make sure the boys don't attack. If they do, the ghoul will fight viciously until they kill it or it kills them."

"Shouldn't they get rid of it?" Mr. Hardin asked. "Possibly throw some explosives down in the tunnels and clear out the rest of them."

"No," Miriam answered. "Ghouls are in nearly every cemetery all over the world. They're a part of the natural order of things, and they do an excellent job of staying out of our way."

"Why do you think so many of them have taken up residence in El Paso? A basement in the Downtown area isn't exactly near any cemeteries."

"El Paso has a lot of corpses around the city lately. For all we know, they may have been migrating to the area since the beginning of the zombie invasion. An invasion of an entire city would provide an excellent food source, with all the leftover pieces of the victims that didn't reanimate."

"I'm guessing the number of destroyed zombies lying around since we began clearing out the city only encouraged more of them to show up?" Mr. Hardin asked.

"I would think so," Miriam answered. "There could literally be thousands of them under the streets. It's really not a problem, though. They will clear out when the food supply dries up. Until then, just think of them as a cleaning crew."

"Let me tell Jaxon," Mr. Hardin said. "He's been tracking one down."

Miriam sat quietly for a bit after Mr. Hardin hung up and sipped her cup of coffee.

"You're thinking about something?" I asked her.

"Yes," Miriam answered. "I'm wondering if our resident Guardian will still attack the ghoul."

"Why would he?" I asked.

"I couldn't really answer that, my dear," Miriam said. "I have a difficult time trying to understand most of the things Jaxon does."

Both of us laughed at that. Jaxon was unpredictable at best. He probably wasn't going to like hearing he shouldn't attack a monster that he'd been chasing down.

"How rare are these ghouls?" I asked.

"Ghouls aren't rare at all," Miriam answered. "Only seeing a ghoul is rare."

"Is that because they live underground?"

"Yes, they rarely venture out of their tunnels."

"And they're eating the zombie corpses?" I asked.

"Yes," Miriam answered. "A zombie corpse is still just a corpse."

"They won't get sick or turn into a ghoul-zombie?"

"No," Miriam answered. "Nothing seems to bother ghouls. Other, more intelligent, monsters even use them to dispose of corpses. I've heard about a few mad scientists using them as well."

"What kind of monster uses a ghoul?" I asked.

"Vampires use ghouls relatively often, and if you think about it, it makes sense. You see, a vampire isn't interested in a human body. They only want the blood. Once the blood is drained and the human is dead, they are left with an unwanted body to dispose of. Now, most vampires, especially the older ones, stake out a territory. They don't want a lot of bodies lying around and alerting people there's a problem next door. So, after they feed, they summon a ghoul. A missing person isn't nearly as threatening as an unwanted body. Just think of all the people that suddenly up and vanish. There must be thousands of them every year. People look for them, but very soon they are forgotten by all but their loved ones. A murdered body is a different story altogether. The police often spend years tracking down killers."

That got the wheels in my head turning big time. I had an idea. I wasn't sure if it would work or not, but there it was.

I told Miriam what I was thinking. She in turn tossed the idea about for a bit but ultimately rejected it due to the danger factor.

Still, it was there in my mind. It was no secret the zombies in El Paso were eventually going to try and venture out of the city. Time wasn't on our side, and all of us were extremely worried that the Regulators weren't going to be able to stop them from leaving.

"I've spoken to Jaxon about that. He was convinced that leveling the city was a bad idea."

Well, you should have seen Miriam. She was freaking out about it. She had no confidence whatsoever that destroying the city would work. Mind you, she didn't have a better idea, nobody did, but she was definitely against trying to explode the problems away.

"Why was she so against it?"

In order to blow shit up, all the guards on the borders would have to be removed. All it takes is the survival of one zombie. One single zombie and the problem returns again. Only when that happens, it happens outside of El Paso, and without the aid of the city's natural barriers that were so beneficial in containing the outbreak.

"Because there would be no one there to prevent the dead from escaping the city?"

Exactly, and forget about going nuclear. I've read reports about living humans surviving those explosions just by hiding inside a concrete building. I doubt that type of bomb would even slow a zombie down unless it landed on top of them.

Miriam and everyone else were hoping to end the problem in the city, well away from the borders. I however didn't see how it was going to be possible. I guess that's why I did what I did.

"What did you do?"

Well, we'll get to that, but before we do, it's probably important to tell you these events took place just a week before Jaxon's award ceremony.

"I see."

Jaxon wasn't too keen on going. He doesn't much care about rewards or recognition. Unfortunately for him, the President himself was going to be the one handing out the medals. It would have been pretty rude if Jax blew it off, and Mr. Hardin also wanted the team to take a few days off. They had been in the fight for way too long. They needed a few days without something trying to eat them.

"How did Mr. Hardin convince Jaxon to go?"

He didn't. He got Skie to do that for him. He explained to her that it was a very prestigious event, and many popular public figures would be attending. He told her the boys needed a break. It would help clear their minds, which would keep them safer when they returned to the city.

He also made plans for the event to be held in Ruidoso, which is close enough to El Paso that if anything happened, the team could get back into action very quickly. Skie talked to Jaxon immediately. It only took her ten minutes to get him to agree to come. She was excited. She loves gatherings. She loves dressing up and meeting new people. It was totally her kind of thing. I got a bit nervous when she called me up and asked me to go shopping with her. She was positive I wouldn't have anything proper to wear.

"Was she correct in that assumption?"

Yes, I'm not very big on wearing dresses or spending a lot of time on my hair.

"Did you go with her?"

I had no choice. You should see that girl when she's determined. She's no meek and mild person. She's freakin' pushy. I guess that's how she deals with Jax.

Anyway, the girl knows fashion, and she really knows how to dress somebody up. In the end, I went with a very slinky black number that was way too girly for my tastes, but I was tired of arguing against it. My mind was on that idea I had tried to discuss with Miriam.

As soon as we were finished—mind you, it took all day and well into the evening—I drove back to our New Mexico base camp and hit the computers. Of course, I couldn't find what I was looking for. I also knew I couldn't ask Miriam or Mr. Hardin for help. They would have told me I was crazy and put a stop to my plans immediately.

So, I kept looking.

As I was busy researching, the boys were still in El Paso, hard at work destroying the zombies. I was hoping to make some progress before they left the city. The awards ceremony was coming up and I knew I wouldn't get much done with them around.

The team was due to arrive the very next evening, and that's when I finally gave up my own sad attempts at research. In the end, I simply asked Mr. Hardin how they found out about monster problems that weren't on a grand scale. I never told him a word about my plan, and he was so busy he never even asked me why I wanted to know.

"We ask Momo," Mr. Hardin answered.

"What's a Momo?" I asked.

"He's the guy that keeps track of that sort of thing."

"Can I speak with him?"

"Sure, if you don't mind heading out to New York. Momo doesn't come into the field with us, and he rarely returns phone calls or emails."

I hopped a plane immediately. It was a military plane, by the way. Traveling is not only free for me, it's also hassle free. It's just a job perk that working under Mr. Hardin and Miriam, provides.

It was well after dark when the plane landed and my escort drove me to a questionable area in the city. I can't give you the location. Momo doesn't want people showing up at his work. However, I can tell you the entrance to his facility is in an alley, right off a main street, filled with restaurants and shops.

"That's not really a lot to go on."

Of course! Momo doesn't want visitors. I only told you what I told you so you would understand that his work happens right under people's noses.

Anyway, from the back alley I went down a flight of stairs and rang the bell on a metal door. A spotlight came over my head immediately. A black orb on a metal arm emerged from the door and shone a red light up and down my body. There was a loud humming noise from underneath me and I began to get nervous, but everything stopped just as suddenly as it started. The spotlight suddenly shut off, the humming noise vanished from underneath me, and the red light stopped scanning my body, then the black orb retracted back into the wall.

A cute young woman in a white lab coat opened the door.

"Hi," she said. "I'm April. Don't be alarmed by the scanners. We don't get many visitors down here. We tend to take precautions, but Mr. Hardin made sure you were cleared for entry."

"Do I look that unnerved?"

"Yes," April answered. "Not to worry though. It's a pretty normal reaction. I still get pretty nervous when I stand where you're standing."

"Why is that?" I asked after quickly moving into the building.

"That grate you were standing on can put out a shock big enough to fry a blue whale," April answered.

"What the hell do you need that for?"

April looked confused.

"What exactly did Mr. Hardin tell you about this place?"

"He didn't say much," I answered. "I just asked him how they found out about monster problems and he sent me here."

"Okay," April said as she led me down a concrete corridor. "Well, we do track down problems. We try to nip things in the bud before they become big problems. However, we do a whole lot more than just that."

"Such as?"

"Well," April answered, "in addition to providing weapons and outfitting vehicles, we also try to study monsters."

We reached the end of the dim corridor and came to an elevator. Inside the elevator, I noticed there were only two buttons, up and down. April pressed down and we were both scanned by that annoying red light.

"Why do you need to study monsters?" I asked, after I had grown bored of the silence. "I thought Miriam was pretty much an expert on them."

"She is," April said. "She's been pretty damn important to our research, but she doesn't know everything. She doesn't always know what attracts them, or how to kill them, and that's what we're really down here trying to understand. We want to know how to kill the monsters."

The elevator door came to a stop and slid open. I stepped out onto a balcony overlooking an incredibly large room. Inside the room were machines and pieces of equipment I couldn't even begin to identify. It was like the great big lab of some mad scientist. On second thought, make that *scientists*, because there were about twenty or so people running around in lab coats down there.

Along the walls were large glass cages. Some of the cages were occupied. I don't even want to tell you some of the things I saw.

"Oh, don't tease me like that. You've got to give me something."

Ivana gave a little laugh at the expression on my face and took a swig of her beer.

One cage held what seemed to be a giant spider. I couldn't see it very clearly through all the webs, but I'm pretty sure it was a big-ass spider.

"How big was it?"

About the size of a compact car.

"What else did you see?"

I saw zombies.

"You saw zombies outside of El Paso?"

I did, and let me tell you, it scared the shit out of me.

"Are you people crazy?" I asked April. "Do you know how dangerous those things are?"

"Are you talking about the zombies?" April asked innocently.

"Duh," I replied. "All it takes is for one to get loose and this entire building could become infected."

"And then what?"

"New York could be next."

"Now, how is that going to happen when the complex has only one exit and only humans with the proper clearance can use it? Don't give it another thought. Our security system is incredibly advanced. You would be amazed at how well it does its job."

"That's why you have the electrified grate out there?" I asked. "You want to make sure nothing escapes?"

"Yes, we also want to make sure nothing gets in," April answered. "We've recently had some vampires attempt to break in and pay us a visit."

"Why vampires?"

"After the Battle of the Sun Bowl, we were able to secure some vampire corpses," April answered. "We've wanted to study them for years. Now we finally can."

"I see a lot of creatures alongside the zombies. Have you ever had a breakout before?"

"This complex opened in 1965. In the early days there were some problems, but we have some really serious protocols to protect ourselves now. Also, you're seeing us on a busy day. With the Guardian being so active in El Paso with the zombie threat, other monsters have been able to rear up their ugly little heads and become a problem around the rest of the country. Once the zombie threat is neutralized, we will no longer be able to acquire as many live specimens. Guardians don't tend to leave survivors."

"How many Guardians have you worked with?" I asked.

"We don't actually work with them. We track down where the monsters are and notify Mr. Hardin. Then, we study the corpses after the Guardians are finished. But to answer your question, I've only been doing this for eight years, so the only other Guardian that's been around is Max."

"Speaking of Guardians," April said as she led the way down a flight of stairs to the room below us. "I hear you're actually friends with the General. Is that true?"

"Yes," I answered.

"What's he like?" April asked, all googly eyed.

"He's a pain in the ass, but I love him anyway," I answered.

"Is it true that he fought a master vampire with only a knife?"

A crowd of lab-coated nerds began to gather around us. The scientists were evidently pretty curious about Jaxon.

"I wasn't personally there, but yes. Jaxon took him out."

"How bloody was the fight between the General and Max?" another scientist asked.

"I wasn't there for that one either." I answered.

"Have you seen him fight?" The man continued. "I only ask because we know so little about

Guardians, and I have a theory about how the General was able to defeat an older Guardian."

"I've seen him fight," I answered.

The question brought back some difficult memories. Right before Jax risked his life to save me, I had lost my girlfriend. I do my best not to think about what happened to Jill. It's not that I don't want to remember her. It's just…painful.

"What was it like watching him fight?" someone asked, interrupting my thoughts.

"It was frightening," I answered. "The sounds of bones breaking, the noise the tomahawk made when it met flesh. It was pretty terrifying, and not just the sounds. It was also the way Jaxon moved. He was too fast. He didn't even seem human. He was just too deadly."

If I had their attention before, it was nothing compared to the way they were all staring at me now. I was a rock star.

"Have you ever held the tomahawk?" another scientist asked.

"No," I answered. "I try to stay away from weapons."

"I was wondering if what I read about a Guardian's weapon was true. I found a passage in an old text that said a Guardian's weapon will grow its own soul after it has claimed many lives."

"I can't help you with that one, buddy," I answered. "I'm not a fighter. I normally spend my days working with Miriam, or helping out the wounded."

They didn't seem to care that I wasn't often involved with the action. The questions just kept coming at me. I didn't know the answers to most of them. I'm sure they knew more about Guardians than I did, because I knew next to nothing.

Most of what they asked was based off rumors they had heard. Perhaps they read something somewhere, or heard a theory from a coworker. I don't know. I could answer questions about his personality somewhat decently. I could describe in greater detail how he fought, which I did. Yet, when it came to questions about his abilities, I was hopeless.

The questions were suddenly interrupted by a booming voice from across the room.

"Is that the muff-diver?" The voice demanded.

Everyone instantly broke away from April and me and went back to work. I was somewhat stunned by the question. It took me a moment to recover.

"Did he just call me a muff-diver?" I asked April as a bespectacled man with a shaved head emerged from an office and walked confidently towards us. April just shrugged her shoulders, and looked embarrassed.

"Did you refer to me as a muff-diver?" I asked the man when he'd gotten close enough that I wouldn't have to raise my voice to be heard.

"No," he answered while eye-fucking me to the point of ridiculousness.

"I'm Ivana," I announced. "And you can stop eye-fucking me. I'm not interested."

"I wouldn't think you would be. Bull dykes don't usually enjoy the boy parts."

"Do I look like a bull dyke to you?" I asked.

"No, but you certainly act like one."

"How does one go about acting like a bull dyke?"

"Well, you're vulgar. Inside the first sentence you ever said to me, you used a four-letter-word."

"No I didn't. It was the second sentence."

The man considered me for a moment. This time he was actually looking at my eyes instead of my body.

"I think I'm going to like you. You're okay for a lezbo."

He offered me his hand. Reluctantly, I accepted it. You see, Momo is an asshole. Yet, believe it or not, the things he says aren't really meant to offend. He just likes to get a rise out of people. It would have been nice if someone had thought to give me a warning, but whatever.

I followed Momo into his office. I expected to see pictures of monsters or paraphernalia for killing them. I was a bit shocked to see pictures of his nieces and nephews instead.

"So what can I do for you?" Momo asked, after taking a seat behind his desk.

"I hear you guys are pretty good at tracking down monsters. I happen to be looking for one."

"We're the best in the world," Momo answered. "Then again, there are only like three other places in the world that do this kind of thing. What are you looking for?"

"I want to locate a vampire."

Momo stared at me for a long moment before speaking up.

"Why do you want to locate a vampire?" he finally asked.

"It's personal," I answered.

Again the man stared at me for a long moment.

"Did you have an ex-lover get turned?"

"I didn't. I just want to locate the nearest vampire."

Again he stared at me.

"Do you understand how dangerous vampires are?"

"I do indeed. My friends had some rather violent altercations with them. Perhaps you've heard about it?"

"I have heard about that. We have some of the bodies. It was pretty impressive. However, you are not the Guardian. Normal people, even hot rug-munchers, don't go around looking for vampires. Not if they want to live."

"I have a theory I'm working on. It may help us bring an end to what's happening in El Paso."

"Do tell."

"Do you know what a ghoul is?"

"A corpse-eater?"

"Yes, a corpse-eater."

"I've heard of them. They're pretty much off our radar since they aren't a threat. So I haven't really spent a lot of time studying them."

"They are massing underneath El Paso as we speak. All the dead zombies are attracting them."

"That makes sense," Momo said. "It's like an all-you-can-eat-buffet over there."

"What if the ghouls attacked the zombies?" I asked.

"That wouldn't happen unless the ghouls are attacked, and since ghouls spend most of their time underground, it's pretty unlikely."

"I've heard that vampires can summon ghouls."

"They can. The ghouls dispose of the bodies for them." Momo said.

"Well, what if some ghouls were summoned right in front of a large horde of zombies?" I asked.

"The zombies would attack them. The ghouls would fight back. A battle would ensue."

A big smile began to spread across Momo's face.

"Do you see what I'm getting at?" I asked.

"You want to ask a vampire how to go about summoning a ghoul, so you can bring them out of the ground in front of the zombies. You want to defeat monsters with monsters."

"So what do you think?" I asked.

"I think it would work if you were able to summon enough ghouls. At least one ghoul for every twenty zombies; which is very possible if all the ghouls are indeed heading into El Paso. The real problem would be the vampire."

"What if I could offer them protection from the General in exchange for their help?" I asked.

"Who's going to protect you from them? That's what I'm concerned about." Momo answered. "Can you get Mr. Hardin to go along with this?"

"I brought it to Miriam's attention," I said. "She wasn't interested. She thought it was too dangerous. I disagree. I think we need to try it before it's too late and the zombies try to leave the city."

Momo got up from his desk and began to pace around the room. I could tell that he liked the idea. He just wasn't keen on sending me out to meet a vampire. I have to admit I wasn't very keen on meeting a vampire myself.

"I can't do it," Momo finally announced. "Miriam is right. It's too dangerous. Vampires aren't normally something that can be reasoned with. They either kill or turn humans. To the best of my limited knowledge, there really isn't a middle ground."

I expected his answer. I had powerful friends, and these friends wouldn't be happy if someone allowed me to walk into danger and I ended up getting hurt...or worse.

"What if you came with me?" I asked.

"I don't do field work," Momo answered.

"So stay in the car," I said. "If things go bad you can get us the hell out of there."

"A vampire can outrun a car," Momo said.

"Any way you look at the situation, it's dangerous," I said. "Your entire line of work is dangerous. You have zombies in a glass cage. You have a giant spider in another one. Those things are accidents waiting to happen. Park a ways down the road if you want, or drop me off, and run for the hills, but I need your help to find a vampire. It's worth the risk."

"Why don't you try and take this to Mr. Hardin?" Momo asked. "Try going around Miriam to get what you want."

"Mr. Hardin doesn't like to play around with vampires," I answered. "If I thought there was a chance he'd go for it, I wouldn't be here."

"What about the Guardian?" Momo asked. "If you're friends with him, he would hear you out at least."

"He might," I said, "or he might just call me crazy, and tell me to stay out of it. He's slightly overprotective when it comes to me."

"You want me to put you in harm's way when you have an overprotective Guardian watching over you?"

"How about this," I sighed heavily. "If you help me out, I'll let you watch me make-out with the first hot chick I find."

Momo was a horn dog; of that I had no doubt. I was also probably the first lesbian he had ever met. Men tend to be very curious about attractive lesbians, and sometimes these same men are often very willing to do crazy things in order to attract a lesbian's attention. I've seen that first hand many, many times. Judging by the way his eyes got all huge when I made my offer, I knew Momo could be bribed.

"I'll need to see a lot more than making-out to convince me to leave this office," Momo said with a smile.

"Well, watching a make-out session is what I'm offering. However, you'll have plenty of time during our trip to get me to change my mind. It's too bad we don't have a willing participant already here. You'd have an appetizer."

Momo's jaw hit the ground. I licked my lips slowly to push him a little bit further.

"APRIL," Momo shouted. "GET IN HERE!"

Anyway, that's how I convinced Momo to give me a hand. It turned out they were currently tracking the movements of five vampires, one of which happened to be right in the backyard of our headquarters.

"*Wait a second. You're not getting off that easy. What happened when April walked into the room?*"

I grabbed her and kissed her. I wanted to get the show on the road, so to speak. I didn't want to waste time trying to convince her. She freaked out a bit at first, but not enough to slap me.

"*Was that really all it took to convince him to help you out?*"

Sweetheart, you would be surprised at what a man is willing to do for a woman when the hint of sex is in the air. A woman only needs to know how to work it. With Momo I was blunt and obvious. I figured it would work on him, since he's so blunt and obvious. Another type of guy might prefer me to act coy, or maybe even domineering, but not Momo. He's willing to play the game, but he wants to know what the game is upfront.

"*Wow, I can't believe it was that easy for you.*"

I should point out that Momo is an incredible person. He comes across as gruff and rude, but once you get past that, he's really pretty cool. We've become pretty good friends, and yes, he still calls me a muff-diver.

Anyhow, after making-out with April, I grabbed him by the arm, and dragged him out of the building right to the waiting car before he could gather his senses, and change his mind. We were actually on the plane, in the air, before he started to get cold feet.

"I'm not sure I should have left like that," Momo announced after we had been in the air for a good thirty minutes.

"A little late to be worrying about that now, you pervert," I said.

"Seriously though," he said. "What if things go bad without me there to supervise?"

"You're probably not as important as you think you are," I told him.

He had relaxed somewhat by the time we reached our headquarters and landed. The second we were off the plane I had him by the arm again. I didn't want him talking to anybody. I didn't want anyone catching wind of who he was. There would be too many questions if Mr. Hardin or Miriam, found that out.

I dragged him to my truck, tossed him inside, and tore out of the base before anyone even figured out I had brought someone back with me. Plus, I drive fast, and I mean really fast. When I first started working at our makeshift base camp, I had a lot of problems with the guards at the gate because of my driving. Mr. Hardin eventually had to step in and tell them to leave me be. Ever since that day, I like to charge my truck at the gate and watch them scramble to get it open before I slam into it. It's childish, but sometimes it's fun to rub it in.

It's probably a good thing I'm such a brat. If I bothered to stop at the gate like a normal person, I would have been caught red handed with Momo. As it was, I didn't even slow down. If they even saw someone in the truck with me, I can guarantee they didn't get a very good look.

Once I was about ten minutes from base camp, I pulled over and asked Momo for directions. He pulled out a laptop and started typing away.

"You need to head west until you hit the desert," Momo said. "From there we need to find a nice place to chill out until the sun goes down."

This is the part where I really started to get nervous. Jaxon and the boys were scheduled to return sometime after sunset. I needed to get what I wanted from the vampire before anyone figured out what I was trying to do.

We found a little diner along a dusty road near our destination. The sky was a dark blue and there were only a few clouds in the sky. The morning was just beginning to warm up as we trudged from the truck to the restaurant. The only thing that could be seen, aside from the desert sand in all directions, was an old car junkyard in the distance.

"Are you sure we're in the right place?" I asked Momo after we had found a table and grabbed some menus.

"I'm positive," he answered. "The vampire is staying in an old shack about forty miles from here. I'm guessing it's a pretty young vampire, and it's probably worried about leaving the area."

"Why would it be worried about leaving the area?" I asked. "It seems to me that leaving the area would be a good idea with the Regulators right next door in El Paso."

"From the little that we've learned about vampires," Momo answered, "we believe the older ones often kill the younger ones if they don't want them in their territory. Every single vampire that was in the area, with the exception of the one we're looking for, left after the Guardian killed the local master. That tells me it's afraid to leave."

"Sounds sort of barbaric that they'd kill their own kind," I mumbled.

"Of course I could be wrong," Momo said. "It could also be waiting for a chance to strike. You know what I mean? Wait for the Guardian to relax his guard, and then pounce on him."

I was officially worried, and it must have shown on my face, because Momo started laughing.

"That doesn't sound good at all," I said glumly. "It might eat me just because I know Jaxon."

"It's possible," Momo laughed. "Maybe we should turn around and go home."

I ignored him and ordered a bite to eat.

I can't say I had a lovely time with Momo that day as we waited for the sun to set. He did his best to harass me about my sexuality. He even tried to convince me that I should have sex with him before I went out and got myself killed. I could tell he was trying to distract me from what I was about to do. I imagine that I must have looked pretty worried, and I appreciated his efforts, even if they weren't very effective.

I've never exactly been a huge sun-lover, but as the fiery orb began to set and the magic hour of twilight started covering the wide-open landscape, I began to see the sun as an old friend…a friend that I would miss terribly…a friend that kept me safe. It was a weird feeling. I've always been a night person. I like going out to clubs and partying until the wee hours of dawn. I guess I was a bit scared. Remember, I'm not a fighter. I've said it before and I'll say it again. I'm not any good at fighting. I'm an average person. I'm not truly a Regulator. I avoid the terrible things a Regulator so lovingly embraces.

I was damn near pissing in my pants.

"That's pretty understandable. I don't think I would have the guts to attempt what you were about to attempt."

I would hope not. I don't think anyone in his right mind would try it. Yet, there I was, summoning up my courage as we left the diner and walked to the truck. We spent about nine hours at the diner. Momo enjoyed three meals; I picked at barely one. I left a huge tip, but they were probably glad to see us finally leave.

My heart was pounding in my chest as I got behind the wheel. I could hear my own breathing, and it sounded incredibly loud. My hand shook as I started the engine. Finally, Momo reached across the cab and covered my hand with his own.

"Listen," Momo said. "There's no shame if you want to turn back. Nobody even has to know what we were up to."

"I can't turn back," I replied. "There's too much at stake. We need a miracle, and this might be it."

Momo nodded in response.

"If you get turned instead of killed, would you mind terribly if I performed some experiments on you?"

"Momo," I replied. "I shudder to think of the experiments you have in mind."

He laughed and we drove off towards the setting sun. A few minutes into the drive my phone began to ring. I took a look at whom the caller was. It was Miriam. I didn't have much time. Miriam was too smart. She would figure things out, and when she did, she would send someone after me. I knew all too well who that someone would be.

"Jaxon?"

Yes, and I knew it would be bad if he got involved. I'm talking scorched earth and a path of destruction kind of bad. Don't get me wrong. It's nice to know when someone cares about you, and I love him dearly for it, but if you put Jaxon in a room with something that might be threatening my safety… Well, I feel very sorry for whatever creature, or person, it may be.

The phone calls continued. Every five minutes, the phone would ring. Momo smiled. I kept looking at the caller ID. Miriam was one thing. Jaxon was another. I was really worried Miriam would tell Jaxon I was up to something. Before I knew it, we were driving past little shacks that were rotting away under the desert sun. The road we were on was partially covered with sand, and eventually we lost even that last little bit of pavement as we set out down a lonely dirt road.

The open desert gave way to rocky canyons and boulders of varying size. Magic hour slipped away and the darkness began to creep up on us. I couldn't outrun it. Every turn in the road led to more shadows. The full moon was high in the sky when a loud beeping emanated from Momo's laptop.

"Looks like we have a problem," Momo announced.

"What is it?" I asked.

"Someone is hacking into my computer."

"Can you stop them?" I asked.

"Not from here I can't."

I sighed heavily. There was always a slight chance Miriam hadn't figured out what I was up to. That slight chance had been snatched away from me by an annoying alarm. They were rapidly tracking us down.

My phone rang again.

I looked at the caller ID. It was Jaxon. He left a message but I didn't bother to listen to it. I didn't want to hear what he had to say. I kept driving.

The sun had almost completely vanished from the horizon when Momo asked me to pull over. We had entered a canyon. The dirt road ahead of us had a dramatic curve through the high walls. I couldn't see a thing beyond the curve.

"It's best that you set out on foot from here," Momo said. "If things go bad I want enough of a head start out of here."

"You really don't want to come with me?" I asked hopefully.

"Fuck no," Momo snapped. "Do I look like a stupid woman to you?"

"Yes," I answered. "You do."

Momo told me the vampire's lair was just beyond the rocky walls of the canyon. He also advised me to take my time getting there because I might be considered more of a threat if I showed up before the vampire awakes.

I jogged through the canyon. I wanted to reach my destination before I completely lost the sun. I didn't succeed. In the darkness, I almost missed the shabby little adobe shack in the middle of a large clearing, covered with scrub brush and weeds.

The shack was far from impressive. It looked as if a strong wind would send the walls crashing down. I could hear the crunch of small rocks from beneath my boots as I walked to the wooden front door. The moon was my only source of light, and even its beam seemed to stay away from the vampire's home.

I waited in front of the shack for another twenty minutes after the sun had set in an effort to be polite. Actually, that's probably not true. I kept telling myself I was being polite but the reality is probably more like me being afraid to get any closer to that front door.

Finally, I could wait no longer.

I crunched my way forward and approached the door. I could hear no movement coming from inside and I realized that I also wasn't hearing any animal noises outside either. It seemed as though even the coyotes and insects sought to avoid this frightening place.

I knocked on the door.

There was no answer. I began to wonder if the shack had been abandoned. I knocked again, and when there was still no answer, I tried the latch. It lifted easily, and the door swung inward with a loud creak straight out of a horror movie.

"Is there anyone home?" I asked with a trembling voice. "I'm not looking for trouble. I just want to talk."

The shack couldn't have been more than two or three rooms, but it was so dark I couldn't see anything past the dirt walls of the first room. With a deep breath I entered the shack and took a few steps into the blackness. I instantly felt eyes upon me. I no longer believed the lair was abandoned. I felt movement.

I was terrified.

I couldn't will myself to take another step forward. I also couldn't retreat. My legs had simply frozen up and refused to obey my commands. What my commands would have been, I couldn't truthfully answer, but I really did want to run like hell.

I suddenly remembered my small flashlight. I had placed it in my pocket earlier in the day, thinking it might come in handy. My hand slowly moved down my body towards my back pocket as if it were afraid to make a sudden move.

I fumbled getting it out, and right when I finally pulled it free, the front door gave a low creak as it slowly closed behind me. My heart skipped a beat. I gasped out loud. A spike of adrenaline rampaged through my body, causing me to become jittery and clumsy. I almost dropped my flashlight. I couldn't find the button to turn it on. I was in complete darkness.

I finally managed to remember that my flashlight didn't have a button. In order to turn it on, I had to twist the top. I could hear the sound of my lungs gasping for air. It sounded as if I had just run a marathon. My fingers fumbled for what seemed an eternity, but I managed at last to turn on the light.

I shone the light in front of me. I could see a short hallway that probably led to some back bedrooms. I shone it to the left of me; I saw a filthy, cracked window that emitted no light into the room. It was above an old writing desk that had seen better times. I turned the light towards the right. I saw a worn-out couch, a low table with a large waxy candle, and a motionless figure against the wall. I turned around and checked behind me. There was nothing but empty space and the wooden door I had just come through.

I paused, knowing something was off but unable to comprehend what.

A motionless figure against the wall.

I froze up for a moment while my brain attempted to process what should have sent me running out into the desert.

After I unstuck myself, I turned slowly back to the figure against the wall. It was a young woman with pale, possibly even grayish, skin. Her hair was very blonde, framing her face rather prettily. She wore a frilly, Mexican-styled dress but no shoes. She had no emotion on her face whatsoever. She didn't blink. She didn't move. She didn't even seem to breathe.

I was looking at a vampire.

It wasn't the unnatural way in which she composed herself that chilled me to the bone. No, it wasn't that at all. It was her lifeless eyes and black lips. The combination of those unnatural features on her pretty face made me want to scream.

You see, up close vampires really don't look human at all. They look like someone made an angry replica of a human being and filled it up with malice and razors. They even give off an aura that makes you feel dirty. It conjures up thoughts of rotting meat and vile insects slithering up your arm.

"Turn off the light," the vampire whispered.

I didn't know what to do. I sure as hell didn't want to turn off my flashlight, but I also didn't want to piss her off.

"TURN OFF THE LIGHT," the vampire roared at my hesitation.

I obeyed instantly. My fingers fumbled once again but I turned it off.

The candle on the table came to life instantly. It bathed the room in a soft glow, and I only peed myself slightly when I realized the vampire was standing right next to me.

"The artificial light hurts my eyes," she whispered as she walked around me in a tight circle.

"I...I...I need to talk to you," I stammered. "I need your help."

"You smell beautiful," she purred into my ear when she was behind me.

I was too afraid to turn around and face her. Instead, I spoke to the empty air in front of me.

"I'm not a fighter," I said. "I won't be able to defend myself. I only want you to hear me out before you do anything rash."

The vampire stopped smelling me instantly. There was a flurry of movement too fast to track, and suddenly she was in front of me. Her dead, unblinking eyes were inches from my face. A thin line of black drool oozed from the corner of her mouth.

"You know what I am?" she asked.

"Yes," I answered, "but in not here for trouble. I think I can help you."

She smiled at me sweetly, and the smile only served to make her more terrifying. From somewhere inside the folds of her dress she produced a linen handkerchief, and used it to wipe her mouth and chin.

"You know what I am and you still came?" she asked.

"What I need to discuss with you is very important," I answered.

"I'm very hungry," she said. "I could hear your footsteps all the way from outside my home. Such a pretty girl you are."

"Will you hear me out?" I asked.

"I can hear your heart beating inside your chest," she said. "Do I frighten you that much?"

"Yes," I answered. "I'm very frightened."

"Why?"

"Because I don't want to be hurt," I answered.

"Then perhaps you shouldn't have knocked on my door," she said as the smile vanished from her face.

"I work with the Regulators," I blurted out. "The Guardian is a personal friend of mine."

Her eyes grew wide as she took in my words. Then her face contorted into a mask of fury and she grabbed me by the neck. Her hand was cold and impossibly strong. I pushed on her arm with all my might. I couldn't get her to let go of me. I watched as her bottom jaw began to grow. I saw the multitudes of fang teeth burst forth from her black gums and extend past her lips.

I still had the flashlight in my hand.

I held it up to her horrid face, and twisted the power on. She shrieked when the beam hit her eyes and threw me aside before she vanished. The candle had blown out. I wasn't sure if she did it on purpose or not, but the room was too dark. Even using my flashlight, I couldn't keep the blackness from closing in on me.

I stood on shaky feet. My back was to the dirty window. The grime on the glass was so dense it probably blocked out the sun.

The vampire was screaming obscenities at me from somewhere across the room. She wanted me to know what she was going to do to me. She screamed that the Guardian had killed her sister and her father. She wanted her revenge.

"If you hurt me," I shouted while frantically casting my light about the room in an effort to locate her. "You're as good as dead. This is your only chance at life. I'm your only chance."

The screaming stopped.

"Turn out the light," she said. "Come closer to me. Let me hold you. I've been here all by myself for such a long time."

"No," I said as defiantly as I could.

"Turn off the light!" she screamed so loudly I wanted to cover my ears.

My light finally found her. She was spread out like an insect on the ceiling. I knew at that moment that I had grossly overestimated the ability of these creatures to reason. I had failed. There was no way in hell the vampire was going to help me. I needed to get away. Coming here was a mistake and I was an idiot. The vampire was clear across the room and I knew that I'd never make it to the door.

I had to try.

I moved slowly. I never ran. That would only entice her to attack. I forced myself to remain calm, even though every instinct I possessed screamed at me to run as fast as I could. I had only taken a few steps when the vampire abruptly spider-crawled across the ceiling and dropped to the floor in front of the door with a dull thud.

"Don't come any closer," I threatened weakly while back stepping away from her.

"What are you going to do to me if I do?" She asked.

"I still have the light," I said.

"Not for long," she replied while slowly advancing towards me.

My back hit the window. I could feel the chill of the night through the glass. And then it dawned on me. I had just backed up into another exit. I turned and slammed my elbow into the glass. The window shook and vibrated. It did not break.

I had only taken my eyes off the vampire for a brief second. Apparently, that was all she needed. When I turned around to face her, she was right in front of me. I raised the flashlight to her face in an effort to chase her away again. She simply grabbed my arm, took the light from my hand, and threw it to the floor.

The flashlight spun around on the dirty ground, making the room to go from light to dark, until it finally settled with the beam pointed towards the vampire's back. Her face was in shadow, but I was still able to see her extended jaw. I heard soft popping sounds as the rest of her fangs broke through her gums.

I cursed myself for being such a fool. I should have listened to Miriam—I should have listened to Momo—and I should have stayed where I was safe. I was a fool to play the part of the hero. I started crying. I remembered how Jax had run out and saved me from the zombies. He would save me now if he could. The vampire wouldn't stand a chance against him, but Jaxon wasn't here. I was all alone.

I was going to die alone.

She still had me by the arm. I couldn't break her grip. It was like being caught in a vise. I felt the bones in my arm bend, and I cried out in pain. The vampire enjoyed this. I could see a large smile spread across her distorted features.

"Fear not my brave and beautiful visitor," she whispered into my ear. "I won't hurt you needlessly. I'm much too hungry for those types of games."

She wrapped her other arm around my waist and pulled me in close. The harder I struggled, the harder she squeezed my wounded arm. I felt her lips against my shoulders and neck. I felt the sharp teeth against my skin. Slowly, she bit down. Her fangs were so sharp I barely felt any pain…and then she bit harder.

I screamed.

I screamed as loud as I could. I actually felt her sucking out my blood, but I refused to quit. I refused to die. I kept on screaming and struggling. My heart was hammering against her. It was so loud and fierce I could actually hear it.

THUMP. THUMP. THUMP.

The sound went on and on. And then I felt the glass of the window shatter behind me. Shards of it sprayed my face like a sharp rain. I opened my eyes, and I saw a muscular arm reach through the window and grab the vampire's hair. I saw her eyes go wide as she was slammed against the wall beneath the window. I heard her scream as she vanished into the night.

You look confused.

"I am confused."

That's exactly how I felt. Nothing made sense. I had no idea what had just happened. One second I was being drained by a vampire, a moment later I was lying on a dirty floor all alone.

I was bleeding, but my injuries weren't too severe. The vampire had taken her time with me. Still, there was a lot of blood and that freaked me out. I pulled off my outer shirt and wiped at my wounds. There was a trickle still flowing when I was finished. Most of the blood covering me must have fallen from the vampire's mouth when she was attacked.

There were violent noises coming from outside the shack.

I got to my feet. It wasn't easy. I was feeling pretty woozy. I used the walls for support and made my way to the front door. Only then did I realize that the inside of the shack was ablaze with light. I opened the door and stepped out into a battle zone.

Actually, that isn't really accurate. In order to have a battle, two sides need to be fighting. What I saw instead was Jaxon beating down the vampire. He still had her by the hair, and was slamming his fist into her face over and over again.

Suddenly I felt hands upon my body. I struggled. I was so dazed and confused I thought I was being attacked again.

"Take it easy, Mamacita," Dudley said. "I've got you now. It's going to be okay."

I was safe.

I laughed out loud. It felt good to be alive. No, it felt great to be alive. My protectors had arrived. I warned her, didn't I? She should have listened.

Javie was with Dudley. Before I even stopped laughing, he had cleaned out my wound, and started rubbing some sort of gel over the bite. Whatever it was stung like hell, but I wasn't paying a lot of attention. I was watching Jaxon beat the vampire under the glare of the spotlights mounted on the helicopter hovering above all of us.

It wasn't the sound of my heart beating that I had heard as the vampire drained me. It was the sound of a hovering helicopter.

"Why didn't the vampire hear it?"

I guess she was too preoccupied with feeding on me.

"So the Regulators managed to track you down. That didn't take them very long did it?"

No, it didn't take them very long at all. I really can't complain though, can I? They saved my life.

I watched as Jaxon beat the vampire. He was merciless. I mean, the vampire tried to fight back, but Jax was too tough. The fight was one sided. She must have been a very young vampire.

Jaxon was also dragging out the inevitable. He must have been very angry. He's normally rather quick when it comes to finishing things off. The vampire began to beg. She began to try and talk to him like I had tried to talk to her.

Nick and Georgie were standing at a distance on opposite sides of the vampire. Their faces looked angry. None of them were here to take prisoners. There would be only one outcome. Jaxon pulled his tomahawk free from the back of his belt. I watched as he slowly twirled it in his hands.

The vampire began to cry.

More helicopters began to approach from the distance. The battle was all but over. The new arrivals were only coming to clean up the mess. I had but seconds to act.

I bolted away from Javie and Dudley. I ran straight towards Jaxon. Georgie tried to stop me, but I somehow managed to sidestep around him and place myself between Jax and the vampire.

I didn't like the look on my friends face.

"Move!" Jaxon growled at me.

"Just wait, Jaxon," I pleaded. "Just hear me out."

"Move!" Jaxon repeated.

He wasn't listening to me. He wasn't even looking at me. His eyes were locked upon the beaten vampire. The helicopters had landed around us. There were four of them. Out of the corners of my eyes I could see soldiers piling out. They took up positions all around us, with their guns trained on the vampire.

"You can't kill her," I said. "We need her."

Finally, Jax turned his gaze upon me. If I thought the vampire was pretty damn scary, it was nothing compared to the look on my friend's face. His upper lip was twitching in rage. His eyes were burning with a cold fury I didn't even know he possessed.

Then, he moved.

He moved almost as fast as the vampire. I screamed when he grabbed a hold of my arm and dragged me away from the violence. Nick and Georgie tried to follow, but Jax waved them away.

His grip on my upper arm was frightening.

"Jaxon," I said. "Jaxon, you're hurting me."

He immediately let go of my arm. We were far enough away from the circle of soldiers surrounding the vampire that we didn't need to shout to be heard. Jax was glaring at me. I had really pissed him off.

"What the hell did you think you were doing?" Jaxon shouted so loudly that more than a few heads turned our way.

"I had an idea," I replied. "I think it might work—"

"Fuck your idea," Jaxon interrupted angrily. "You have no business out here. You should be dead right now. If we had gotten here thirty seconds later…you'd be a corpse."

"I know," I said. "I know I underestimated the situation. I made a mistake. I thought I could handle myself."

Jaxon held out the handle of his tomahawk.

"You think you can handle yourself?" He asked. "Then take it. Take it, go over there, and show me what a badass you are. You want to fight? You want to put yourself in harm's way? Then, let's get you started."

"Get that thing away from me," I said. "It makes me nervous."

"You started this," Jaxon repeated. "Consider this day one of your training. Take it."

"And do what with it?" I asked. "You want me to go fight her?"

"No," Jaxon snapped. "She'd kill you. I'll hold her down. You take the swing. Aim for the neck. You want to remove the head. Keep swinging until it comes off."

"I can't do that," I muttered.

"No shit, you can't do that," Jax growled. "Most people can't. Then again, most people don't try and fuck with a vampire."

Jaxon tapped his earpiece and called for a car to come and pick me up.

"I'm sorry," I said. "It won't happen again. I didn't realize how bad it would be."

"If it does happen again," Jaxon said, "if I even think you might be entertaining a thought of endangering yourself, I'll have you fired. I'll have you thrown out. You can't put yourself in harm's way if you don't know what's out there, or how to find it."

I started crying. I couldn't help myself. My eyes filled up with water and the tears started rolling down my cheeks. Jaxon took one look at me and walked away. I didn't follow him. I didn't want to risk having him yell at me again.

He stopped about thirty feet away, stuffed his tomahawk back into his belt, and put his hands on his hips. He sighed deeply. I couldn't hear it but I could see the movement of his big shoulders. He turned around and marched right back up to me.

I could still see the anger on his face.

I looked into his eyes. I watched his face go from angry, skirt around confused, and finally find a home with worried. He held out his arms for me, and I ran into them. Nestled in his embrace I felt safe for the first time that evening.

"I already know what's out there," I cried into his shoulder.

"Yes, you do," Jax whispered. "You most certainly do."

"I'm glad you found me," I said.

Chapter 4

SKIE

Talking with Skie is always a fun time. Her happiness is infectious. I don't meet with her at the compound. Skie doesn't like to go there. Instead, I meet with her at her home. She answered the door with a bottle of wine and a smile so big it made her eyes almost vanish.

She was wearing jeans and a white Harley Davidson t-shirt. Her boots give her an inch or two of extra height, but she's still pretty tiny. I'm guessing she's just a bit over five feet without the boots. Her dark hair has grown longer, but the face is the same. The big brown eyes, and the constant smile, make her look as if she's barely out of her teens.

"We didn't get to talk the last time I was doing a series of interviews."

Nope, I didn't have much to do with whatever went on with all the vampires.

"What do you mean, 'whatever went on with all the vampires'?"

Wow, you're good. I didn't even mean to let that slip out.

"Do you not know what happened with the vampires?"

Skie gave me a warm smile.

Are you married?

"No."

"Do you have a man in your life?"

"Not currently."

Have you ever been in love?

"Yes."

Good, you'll be able to relate because I'm very much in love with Jaxon. I love him completely. I will love him until the day I die and probably long after. Yet I hate what he does. I'm a wife: I worry. I understand why he does it. I understand what it means when he does it, but I wish it were someone else.

I've never made it a secret that I worry about my husband. I've never denied I dislike the long periods of time we spend apart and the danger he places himself in. I don't nag at him. I don't hound him to quit. I never let it affect our marriage. I understand he can't stop. I understand people will die if he turns away from his destiny. I probably love him even more knowing how much he cares about the people that need his help.

Still I have a dream that someday he'll give it all up. Maybe someone else will come along and take over for him. Maybe the world simply won't need him anymore. It's a very fond dream and it means a lot to me. I believe that someday it will come true; I believe it with all my heart.

When the day finally comes that my husband and I are finally free to live our lives in peace and happiness, I will pick up your books. I will read about the deeds of my husband and his friends. I will probably laugh a lot. They tend to crack me up. I'll probably get angry a few times. My husband is a bit more reckless than I would prefer. Most of all, I'll cry. I will cry at all the things he's gone through. I will cry over the pain he's felt, the betrayals he's received, and the sacrifices he's made.

…But not today.

I can't and won't hear those things now. I don't want to know what vicious monster is out there waiting for him. I don't want to know how dangerous his life is. I've already seen him fight. I hated it. I never want to see anything like that again. I don't even want to hear about it.

I mean, don't get me wrong. I still hear things. The boys are loud, but I try my hardest to avoid hearing too much. I do my best not to ask questions. I know too much already.

"Tell me what you know. Take me back to the night of the awards ceremony."

Is that where you want me to start?

"Actually no, can you begin when Jaxon got home? I'd like to hear a bit about what life is like for you."

Well, we were in Ruidoso, New Mexico. Jax came home a few hours late. I figured he had been held up with something zombie related so it was a shock when he started mumbling something about Ivana.

I didn't ask questions. I was just happy to have him back. I had even rented us a quiet and secluded cabin, well off the beaten path. I didn't tell anyone where we were, and I confiscated my husband's phone as soon as he walked in the door.

We had some catching up to do. I didn't want interruptions. Of course I had brought Merrick with me. Both of them would never have forgiven me if I hadn't. You see, the team had been climbing a lot of rooftops, and Jax thought things would go easier if she stayed behind.

Merrick was not too happy this.

As soon as Jax walked into the cabin, Merrick jumped right up into his arms. Jaxon laughed and held her with one arm while embracing me with the other. I think we held onto each other for a good five minutes before he stepped away and headed for the shower.

That night Jaxon and I had a few drinks before going to bed. Merrick slept in between us under the covers and refused to budge. It would normally have irritated the hell out of me but I let it go since both of them seemed so damn happy.

Around three in the morning, Jaxon had a nightmare. I felt him shudder. I heard him groan, and saw him suddenly sit straight up in the bed. He was covered in sweat and pale as a ghost. I tried to get up with him. I wanted to make sure he was okay. Instead, he rubbed my back and apologized for waking me. After that, he went into the kitchen and made himself another drink.

"I imagine nightmares are pretty commonplace with all the horrible things he's seen. If I ever had just one monster try and eat me, I don't think I'd ever sleep again."

Nightmares *are* commonplace for him. Except it's not the monsters he sees in his dreams. I wish it were that simple. Instead, he sees the faces of all the people he couldn't save. He sees the lives that were lost. Those lives haunt him at night.

"It must feel terrible to hold yourself responsible for the lives you couldn't save instead of celebrating all the ones you did."

I wish I could talk to him about it. I wish he would listen. It's a subject he touched on just once. He never mentioned it again, and he changes the conversation immediately if I try to bring it up.

The next morning, Jaxon was already cleaning up his weapons and gear by the time I got out of bed. He smiled at me and pointed to the kitchen. The coffee was in the pot, just waiting for me. Jaxon makes the best coffee, by the way.

After both of us had showered, we drove up to Jaxon's parents' cabin. His parents and my kids were waiting for us on the front porch. His mom made an incredible breakfast. Jaxon stuffed himself.

He always stuffs himself when he can. Sometimes while he's working, he won't be able to eat for a few days.

All of us spent the day together. It was a great day. I remember that very much. Jaxon was very relaxed. The kids were enjoying themselves. Zombies were never once mentioned.

Sometime in the late afternoon, I pulled Jaxon upstairs to the room we normally used and I fitted him in his tuxedo. I had picked it out for him myself. I went with Ralph Lauren. I thought it would be able to manage his gigantic shoulders quite nicely, and I wasn't wrong.

As I was working on the adjustments, Jaxon took a nap on the sofa. This time he wasn't bothered by nightmares. The entire house became very quite in an effort not to disturb him. It was near sunset when he finally woke up.

He wanted to go to the garage and work on his motorcycle but I was having none of that. The limousine would be arriving in under an hour, and we were for damn sure going to be ready for it.

"Where was the rest of the team staying?"

They all had rooms at a place called, "The Inn of The Mountain Gods." It's one of the nicer hotels in Ruidoso. I'm not sure how they felt about not staying in the same place as their leader. I mean, Jaxon considers them family, and so do I. I just wanted a slightly less rowdy time with my more immediate family before the awards ceremony.

"They are pretty rowdy when they get together, aren't they?"

It takes some getting used to. Don't get me wrong, though, I normally find them hilarious. Each of them is so inventive with the way they harass one another. Except for Nick, he's not as creative.

The argument started as soon as the rest of the team arrived at the cabin. Dudley kept telling everyone he was James Bond, and then he went around posing in James Bond style.

"Why the hell are you, James Bond?" Jaxon laughed. "I should be James Bond."

"I'm the one wearing a tuxedo by Tom Ford, dipshit," Dudley announced.

"So?" Jaxon demanded.

I cringed. I was the one that had picked out everyone's tuxedos.

"Tom Ford is the maker of James Bonds suits," Dudley said.

"Is that true?" Jaxon asked me.

"That might be true, sweetie," I reluctantly answered.

At this point in the argument, the rest of the team began gleefully joining in. It wasn't long before each of them had chosen a side and added to the chaos. Everyone was talking at the same time. The noise level was deafening. Merrick got so excited from all the commotion she began to bark loudly in a high-pitched sort of bark that was so loud it hurt my ears.

Then Ivana walked in the front door in the dress I had picked out for her. Everyone abruptly became quiet. They weren't used to her wearing a dress.

"Oh, fuck you guys," Ivana growled.

"Tell her she looks pretty, you jerks!" I shouted.

Everyone blurted out how hot the two of us looked. I beamed with pride. It's not easy to get a compliment out of that bunch, and I wasn't even asking for them to compliment me.

"Hey, Buffy," Javie said. "How are you going to slay vampires in that outfit?"

I didn't get the joke. Truth be told, I didn't really want to get the joke, but the sudden chill in the air made me think that maybe not enough time had passed for that comment to be funny. That is, until Jaxon started laughing and pointing at Ivana while he laughed.

It didn't take long before everyone began to snicker. Well, except for Ivana. She was too busy staring at Javie with an arched eyebrow.

"What?" Javie asked. "I got jokes to tell."

Ivana finally cracked up. As soon as she did, Javie crossed the room and gave her a big hug. Drinks were passed around immediately after. It was wine for me and whiskey for everyone else, including Ivana.

I thought the tuxedo drama was over until Dudley began to go around introducing himself to everyone, saying his name was "Bond, James Bond." That, of course, got my husband riled up all over again.

"Seriously, Skie," Jax demanded. "Why is he wearing a Tom Ford, and I'm not?"

"Because your big-ass gorilla shoulders won't fit in a Tom Ford," Georgie answered.

"My shoulders aren't that big," Jax said gloomily.

"Dude," Nick said. "Your shoulders are freakish. I'm not even sure my shoulders are that wide."

It was a bold statement considering how big Nick is.

"How the hell did Nick get invited to this thing?" Jaxon asked.

"Because I'm on the team, dumbass," Nick answered testily.

"You're more like a pledge," Dudley laughed. "You haven't really been with us long enough to be a member."

"Well, you're more like Q than James Bond," Nick retorted.

"SURRENDER TO MY AWESOMENESS!" Jaxon shouted at Dudley.

"I'm no Q," Dudley growled. "I'm a freakin' badass."

"Nope," Georgie said. "The badass title goes to the General."

"SURRENDER TO MY AWESOMENESS," Jaxon laughed.

"I'm not saying Jax isn't a badass," Dudley explained. "I'm merely saying he's more like blunt force trauma when he fights. I, on the other hand, am a highly-skilled ninja assassin."

"Wait," Jaxon said. "Did you just imply that I have no skill?"

"Not really," Dudley answered. "I'm saying that you have no style."

"Those are some bold words," Nick said. "I think we need to have a grudge match."

"Two may enter," Javie said in an ominous tone. "One may leave."

"All I want is far beyond the Thunderdome," Georgie sang out in a high-pitched voice.

I didn't get the movie quote. Javie throws out way too many of them for me to keep up with. Ivana and I made eye contact and just shrugged it off as one of many things we weren't going to understand.

"I'm up for a grudge match," Dudley said.

"Bring it on pretty boy," Jaxon challenged.

Everyone started hooting and hollering. A wrestling match was about to break out. Even Ivana was pounding her fist in the air. I had had enough. I hiked up my dress, climbed up on the kitchen table, and put up my tiny fists.

"The first one of you that even thinks about ruining their tuxedo is going to have me coming at them like a spider monkey," I announced to the stunned group. "I've spent way too much time and effort picking out everyone's clothes, which I also paid for with my own money. So, we are all going to this party, immediately. We are going to arrive there in one piece, and we are going to behave ourselves properly. Do not even think about ruining this night for me, and can someone please explain why Javie has only shaved one side of his face?"

Jaxon immediately scooped me off the table. I squealed and laughed as he swung me over his shoulder and made his way to the door. The giant limo was waiting for us in the driveway. All of us somehow managed to fit inside of it and we waved goodbye to the kids, Merrick, and Jaxon's parents as we drove off to the awards ceremony.

"*I take it the argument was over?*"

Oh, hell no! Not even close. Two minutes after we left, Jax and Dudley were at it again.

"How the hell can you say I have no style?" Jaxon asked.

"You're more about beating the living crap out of your opponents," Dudley answered. "You don't exactly look like a skilled ninja assassin when you do it."

"Jax has a *beat your ass* style," Georgie added. "It looks pretty impressive to me."

"I think you're probably using the wrong word," Javie told Dudley. "Style would be better used when describing fashion, and perhaps his overall look."

"What the hell is wrong with my look?" Jaxon asked.

"Boots, jeans, t-shirt, and a wallet with a chain aren't exactly the hallmarks of high fashion," Georgie added.

Dudley started laughing hysterically.

"Tight jeans and a shirt that's three sizes too small doesn't really work either," Georgie told Dudley, which shut him up immediately.

"If we're involving fashion," I said, "the only one of you truly worthy of being called 'James Bond' would be Javie."

Everyone just stared at me.

I realized my mistake immediately. I had joined in on their reindeer games, and become one of them. I had finally been corrupted.

"Damn you," I shouted. "Damn you all."

Nick pretended to wipe a tear from his eye. Georgie made a sound as if he was quietly crying. Jaxon called for silence. Georgie pursed his lips, shook his head proudly, and began *The Clap*.

"What's the clap?"

Skie laughed mischievously at my mistake.

"Is there an actual definition, or were you just messing with me?"

No, there is. That was just too funny for me not to laugh. *The Clap* is what they used to do in comedies from the eighties. It's normally reserved for when the nerd or underdog gives a big speech at the end of the movie and the entire school starts to applaud. It begins with one person. They do a slow, but loud, clap and then everyone slowly joins in.

Ivana was the last to join in. By the time she did, I was looking out the window and pretending I was alone in the car.

I think the driver was glad to be rid of us when we reached the banquet hall. I can't say I blamed him either. The drinks hadn't stopped pouring. For the most part, they were mixing whiskey with soft drinks, but every now and then they downed a few straight shots just for the heck of it. It was crazy. I try and limit myself to two glasses of wine, due to low tolerance, but even I was on my third glass. At one point I was even joining everyone in fist pumps while Jax and Dudley did a row of shots.

Secret service agents were all over the property of the banquet hall, and probably in the woods beyond as well. I had forgotten all about the important people on the guest list. The thought of being in the same room with the President of the United States had a somewhat sobering effect on me. I stopped drinking immediately. His first impression of me wasn't going to be that of an immature alcoholic.

There were a lot of eyes upon us as we made our way to the entrance. Even more turned to look in our direction when a shoving match broke out between Jaxon and a couple secret service agents.

The agents apparently didn't want the boys to enter the banquet hall with firearms.

"Jaxon, are you carrying a gun?" I asked. It was news to me.

"Possibly," he answered.

"Hand it over, please," I pleaded. "I'm sure we will be well protected while we celebrate. Look at all the agents that have shown up just to make sure everyone stays safe."

"I'm not giving up my knife," Jaxon grumbled as he pulled a snub-nosed revolver from the back of his jacket and handed it to the agent.

"Would you please check in and see if my husband and his team can keep their knives?" I politely asked the agent nearest me while simultaneously giving him my prettiest smile.

"I'm sorry, ma'am," the agent said. "The orders are firm. No weapons allowed inside the banquet hall."

I was not to be deterred.

"Dudley," I said. "Would you mind calling Mr. Hardin? Perhaps he can help us get past this roadblock"

We waited patiently. I say we, but I think Ivana and I were the only patient ones. The team was ready to pack it all up and head home. With nothing else to do, I began to take in the beautiful countryside. The forest was thick behind the banquet hall, but across the street and to the sides was all rolling grasslands. I even got to see some wild horses running in the distance.

The police arrived during our wait and began directing the traffic, which was rapidly becoming congested. I found it odd that so many people were showing up to an invitation-only event, but I assumed they only wanted to get a look at my husband or the President.

The agent blocking our entrance began talking into a microphone on his sleeve. I doubt it was Mr. Hardin who he was speaking with, but the results were the same. The boys were allowed to bring in their sharp, pointy things.

As I said before, Jaxon had already given up his gun. Nick handed over two large .357 Magnums. Dudley handed over a very battered .45 and warned the agents not to scratch it. Javie handed over a 9mm. Georgie handed over two pristine-looking .45s from his belt. Then he leaned over and pulled out two more snub nosed revolvers from his ankle holsters.

I had no idea the boys were even carrying weapons. I was pretty shocked. Ivana was laughing.

"Georgie needs a lot of guns," Dudley whispered loudly. "He tends to empty them rather quickly due to his shitty aim."

That got everyone laughing. The mood was instantly restored as we walked inside the building. On our way to the hall, we were beset by many well-wishers, and hand-shakers. Some of them were politicians. I follow politics very closely, by the way. I have since I was a teenager. Jax, on the other hand, had no idea who anybody was, so I needed to whisper the names of most of the people into his ear.

"*Does Jaxon not follow politics?*"

Not at all. He has zero interest in anything political. To him, it's just a bunch of stuffy men and women having boring conversations that put him to sleep. The man doesn't even vote.

Once inside the gigantic hall, the boys made their way straight to the bar, while a nervous hostess tried desperately to usher our group to our seats. I felt sorry for the girl as she repeated over and over that our waiter would take our drink orders.

Finally, after Jaxon liberated a bottle of Jack from the bartender, we grabbed our seats. We were at the front of the room. Before us was an empty expanse of wooden floor, beyond that was a raised podium. I was really finding it hard to believe that the President was going to speak on behalf of my husband and his friends.

The hundred or so tables behind us began to fill up slowly. By the time the boys opened their second bottle of Jack, the room was filled. Shortly after that, everyone became silent as a man walked to the podium and introduced the President. Everyone watched as he calmly walked to the podium, shook his announcer's hand, and then smiled directly at our table.

"I understand the man of the hour isn't big on speeches," the President said. "So, taking that into consideration, I will make this as short and sweet as I possibly can while still maintaining the honor I wish to bestow."

Jaxon squirmed in his seat.

"On a summer morning in the not so distant past, this great country had its entire sense of reality shattered. A nightmare crawled out from the darkest part of our imaginations. It was a nightmare that the government was powerless against. We could not render aid. We could not evacuate our citizens from danger. We had no choice but to close our doors. Too many of the people of this great nation were left out in the cold."

Jaxon squirmed some more.

"It's a sad thing to be a leader of this country and not be able to help the people that call this land home. I was powerless. We were, all of us, powerless, and our people were frightened. Our people were without hope."

I put a hand on Jaxon's leg to stop him from squirming.

"That is, until one man stood strong against the nightmare. He braved the shadows, and he brought hope to an entire country with his courage, and his deeds. Tonight we celebrate the man known to most of America as the 'General.' Tonight we celebrate the fearless men that follow him. You are all true American heroes."

The applause was deafening. I sort of expected that. I didn't expect the standing ovation. All those men and women cheering for my husband brought tears to my eyes.

Jaxon looked extremely uncomfortable at the attention, and he sort of stared at the floor in an effort to ignore what was going on. I expected that as well. Javie was pretty cool about everything; he simply smiled proudly and nodded his head. Dudley, Nick, and Georgie had the very best reaction. Each of them raised their arms in the air as if they were conquering barbarians.

A man quietly approached our table amidst the applause and escorted the boys to the podium.

The President himself shook each of their hands, and placed a golden medal on a red white and blue ribbon over their heads.

He ushered Jaxon to the podium to say a few words. It was a good thing he didn't know this was coming. He would have never shown up. I watched as he looked around shyly before clearing his throat.

"Thank you," Jaxon said. "Thank you for your support. I don't...I don't really know what to say. I guess...I guess I'm just glad I could be some sort of help. I've done what I can. I'll continue to do everything I can..."

"WE LOVE YOU, JAXON!" Ivana shouted out when his words began to falter.

Jaxon smiled.

"I'm just...I'm just not sure how much of this I deserve. I was given a responsibility. I've tried my damnedest to make a difference. I wouldn't have achieved anything without my team watching my back. Each and every day they put themselves in mortal danger. Each and every day they follow my orders."

The applause came again.

"What I'm saying is," Jaxon continued. "I make mistakes. I've lost people. I wish...I wish I could have saved more lives. I wish I could have been there for all the people that didn't make it."

The crowd became still. I was worried for my husband. I was so worried I was biting my lower lip. I knew he was having problems. I knew he had nightmares. I didn't want him to unravel in front of all these strangers. I wanted to whisk him away to somewhere safe, someplace quiet, and hold him until he felt better. No matter how long that might be.

Jaxon was just standing there with a blank look on his face. I don't know what dark corners of his memory his mind had wandered off to, but he was no longer in the here and now. I was about to go to him. I was about to lead him away. The President got there before me.

"Son," the President told him. "You've done more than any man could ever be expected to do. You have accomplished more than any man could ever be expected to accomplish. We thank you. We support you. We believe in you. Every war has its losses. I wish things were easier on you. I know what you've been through. I know the challenges you've faced. Perhaps you've thought of yourselves as alone in this. I can assure you, you are not alone."

The applause was back louder than ever, and just like that, my husband was back. He nodded his head in understanding. When he saw what must have been a very worried look on my face he even managed to give me a small smile.

"I'm not sure if you're aware of this or not," the President continued. "But you've made quite a few friends throughout your journey. Perhaps it's time for you to get reacquainted."

The lights in the ceiling dimmed, and the hall grew dark. After a brief pause, a single spotlight blazed down from the ceiling onto a little girl sitting on a stool with a large guitar in her lap. There was a microphone in front of her, and when the audience had quieted down she began to sing.

"That's Mona," Ivana whispered.

I nodded my head that I understood. I had never met the little girl before but I had certainly heard about her. I'm not sure if you know this or not, but that brave girl stood up and sang Jaxon a song before some sort of fight.

"Yes. I've heard about her. What song did she sing for him at the banquet?"

She sang "True Colors" by Cyndi Lauper, and my God, she did it justice. That little girl can belt out a tune. Her voice was just so pure, and far, far beyond her years. It reached out and caressed each and every person in the room. I struggled to hold back the tears. I really did, but then I saw Ivana. She was wiping her eyes, and her bottom lip was quivering.

I began bawling right along with her.

I looked at the stage. Jaxon's eyes were wet, but he had somehow maintained his composure. The same can't be said for the rest of the team. They were just as bad as Ivana. Nick was even worse.

There's a part in the song that talks about the world making you crazy and the singer promises that they will be there. Well, when Mona hit that part she stood up from her stool, and really kicked it in. Her voice suddenly became a thousand times more powerful, and what sounded like hundreds of other voices joined in with hers.

The doors at the back of the room opened widely and Father Monarez strode proudly through it with a candle in his hands. He was followed by many, many others…at least three hundred people. They had candles as well, and the light bathed the room in a soft glow. The crowd of people flowed between the tables until the room was full.

All of them were singing.

I saw Jaxon wipe his eye. When the song ended the people began to hum softly as Mona continued to strum her guitar.

"We weren't really expecting such a turnout," the President said into the microphone on the podium. "In the beginning, we asked just a few people to come and say a few things. Word, however, began to grow. The White House was flooded with calls. These are the people whose lives you have touched. Some of them have traveled very far to honor you. The least we could do was to make it possible."

Mona began to sing again. I can't remember if she started the song over, or repeated the second verse. I'm not sure. Everyone in the banquet hall joined in with her, and it was no longer only the people holding candles that were singing. We all stood up and sang along.

My voice was cracking, but I didn't care. I wanted to honor my husband and the team. It was the first time that I truly began to understand the scope of what he did. All of the people in the hall had been touched by him in some way, shape, or form.

If he saved the life of one little girl, well, that little girl has parents. She has grandparents, brothers, and sisters; she has cousins, aunts, and uncles. Someday she would have children and she'd tell them how the General saved her. It was a sobering experience for me.

When the song ended, Jaxon and the boys walked outside where an entire area had been prepared for the party. There were heat lamps, tables, a bar, a dance floor, and a band that was ready to play.

"Who planned all this?" I asked Ivana.

She shook her head and raised her arms to let me know she had no idea. Imagine my surprise when the First Lady gently touched my arm, and offered her hand.

"My husband planned a lot of it," she said. "He wanted to honor your husband without the usual ceremony. I hope it's okay?"

"It's more than okay," I grinned. "It's incredible."

Everyone grew quiet and began to gather around the General. He looked out over the crowd for a long while. I could tell he recognized more than a few faces. He struggled to say something, but couldn't find the words. The crowd of people saved him the effort as, one by one; they all crossed their right arms across their chests and held a fist over their heart.

It was the standard salute people gave him. Jaxon acknowledged it and returned the gesture. Then the crowd erupted into cheers.

"Let's dance!" Javie shouted with glee when the cheers had begun to die down. The band heard their cue, and began playing immediately.

"*All those people must have been a nightmare for the President's security detail.*"

I'm sure they were, but the President hung in there rather courageously. Eventually, something important came up, and his people rushed him out of the building. An hour or so before that happened, however, he managed to pull Jax aside and have a talk with him.

"I've talked to my advisors," the President said. "They want to blow El Paso off the map. At this point, I very much agree with them, but I've also talked to Mr. Hardin. He believes that's the worst possible thing that could be done. What do you think? Can the city be saved?"

"Yes," Jaxon answered calmly. "I'll clear the city."

"Do you think you can do it before those things try to escape?"

"I don't have much choice in the matter," Jaxon said.

"Okay son," the President said. "I'll take that under advisement. When do you go back?"

"The day after tomorrow," Jaxon answered.

"Be safe," the President said before returning to his wife.

Jaxon merely smiled in response.

"So Jaxon advised the President?"

I doubt my husband would see it that way. In his mind, he simply answered a question.

"There must have been a lot of pressure on Jaxon. How did he handle it?"

Actually, it didn't seem to bother him at all. He just went back to the party. Remember, the Regulators know how to party.

Shortly after the President left, the massive crowd began to thin out. They had come to honor the General, and perhaps shake the hand of the man who saved their son or daughter. Some of them just wanted to wish him well. Everyone gave him words of encouragement. All of them were very kind. After enough backs were patted and kind words shared, many of them departed.

Around one or two in the morning, the remaining partiers moved back into the hall, along with the band, which was taking requests and having as much fun as everyone else.

"How many people would you estimate were still there?"

I guess there were probably one hundred and fifty to two hundred people left. We were having a good night. I remember dancing with Jax. I was glad to be inside finally, the night had gotten a bit too chilly for the heating lamps. I was looking up at him and he was smiling at me.

It was nice.

I can't remember how much I drank but I do remember snorting wine out of my nose when the band began playing "Drops of Jupiter," and Javie launched from his seat, ran across the dance floor, and jumped on the stage. A brief struggle with the singer over the microphone and the next thing we knew, he was the band's new lead vocal. Too bad he never had singing lessons, but no one seemed to mind. In fact, we all began to sing along. Javie took that as a sign of encouragement, and proceeded to rip off his own shirt, exposing his very hairy chest.

"Redheads only," Javie announced through the microphone when all the girls began to scream for him.

Eventually, most of the team ended up on stage. Jaxon stayed with me. I was holding him tightly as we danced to Javie's horrible singing. It was the most fun I'd had in a very long time.

There was a girl next to me who was yelling and raising her arms in the air. I think she was trying to get Dudley's attention. The bullet ripped through the back of her head, exploding brain matter and a red spray all over my dress.

I looked down at the mess. I saw and felt the wet stickiness on my skin. I couldn't understand what was happening. Jaxon was barely touched by the spray. He had no idea what had happened.

I stiffened in his arms. I tried to say something. I tried to form words but I couldn't. My mouth kept making a gurgling sound, and no words would come forth. Jax pulled away from me gently. He looked down at the splatter of blood and brains on my dress. Confusion twisted his features. Then his eyes went wide, and he began to roughly check me for damage.

This all happened in the span of seconds. At least, I'm thinking it was seconds. We were all very drunk. Still, I was frightened. I mean…I've seen violence before. I was there when my husband battled the undead on the border of El Paso and New Mexico. I was there when he fought the former Guardian. It's just that, I don't know, maybe I sometimes have trouble processing the ugliness of the world. That poor girl died so horribly.

More gunshots followed.

I heard a rapid succession of cracking thumps that overpowered the music and forced everyone to scatter about the room. Jaxon was already moving before any of that though. He was holding my head down, and dragging me away from the crowd of people, back towards the heavy tables.

He flipped the very first table we came to on its side, breaking the glasses and plates still upon its surface all over the floor. I watched him pull his knife from his pocket. The blade made an audible click as he snapped it into place.

A masked gunman dressed all in black came around the corner of the table and fired his rifle at us. A burst of red came from the side of Jaxon's bicep, but he somehow crossed the distance between them, and plunged his blade into the murderer's throat.

He stabbed him in the neck several times.

The room was in complete and utter chaos. People were running and screaming. The sound of gunshots reverberated inside the room so loudly I couldn't gather my thoughts. Jaxon was calm.

"The doors are locked," he said as he looked around the room. "There are fifteen more gunmen and we're trapped in here with them."

Suddenly, Ivana was crouching down next to me and behind her was Georgie.

"What the hell is going on?" Georgie asked.

More and more bodies were falling to the ground as the killers advanced across the room.

"You protect them!" Jaxon shouted. "You keep them safe."

He gave Georgie the gun that belonged to the man he just killed. Georgie checked out the weapon. He made sure it would fire when he pulled the trigger, and he positioned himself in front of us.

Jaxon grabbed my face and made me look at him.

"I won't let them hurt you," he said. "I won't let them get anywhere near you."

I nodded that I understood and my husband went into action. Georgie fired careful bursts of bullets at the approaching gunmen. They, in turn, fired back at him.

"Skie!" Georgie shouted. "Check his body for more ammo."

I heard him. I heard him very clearly but I was unable to move. That's how frightened I was. I couldn't control my own body and I was afraid that if I did start to move, I'd start running even though I had nowhere to go.

Across the room, I saw a crowd of people trying to get out through a locked door. I couldn't understand why they didn't just break it down. I watched as a gunman approached within twenty feet of them and began to slowly shoot them down, one after another.

I moved.

I crawled to the body. I frantically searched through all his military gear until I found the ammunition Georgie needed. I scooped up five magazines and crawled back to him.

I didn't want to look back towards the crowd of people at the locked door, but I couldn't help myself. There were now two gunmen shooting at the screaming group of people. Jaxon and Nick came out of nowhere. They sort of appeared out of the chaos. Each of them came up behind a shooter and slit their throats.

Nick grabbed a rifle and vanished. Jaxon picked up the other weapon, fired two shots into an advancing shooter, and tossed the gun to Javie, who had also appeared out of thin air.

Then I understood. People were running around everywhere. They were crisscrossing the room over and over again in an attempt to avoid the gunmen. The crowd was so thick that the team easily got lost in them.

I watched Jaxon pick up a chair and hurl it across the room. I saw a shooter drop to the ground on impact, and then I saw Dudley jump upon the man's back as he attempted to rise. Dudley plunged his knife into the killer's ear over and over again.

It was horrible. We were all having so much fun. We were all enjoying a bit of what life used to be like before Jaxon became the Guardian. Somehow, the ugliness and violence of his new life had found us.

There was blood on the floor. I watched as people began to slip and slide. I saw a wounded young woman by the stage. She had a white dress that was covered in blood. She was calling for help. She was reaching out to the frantic people running all around her. Nobody would stop and help.

I wanted to go to her. I wanted to save her. I waited until I saw that Georgie was shooting again, and I got my feet under me so I could run to the stage. The young girl was dead when I looked back at her. I had only taken my eyes off of her for a brief moment, one brief moment, and she died. Half her face was lying in a pool of blood. Her eyes were staring blankly away from her, waiting for help that would never arrive.

"Why couldn't she wait for me," I cried. "Why couldn't she wait a few more seconds?"

Ivana grabbed a hold of me. Apparently, I had stood up and she was dragging me back down.

"Why did she have to die alone?" I asked.

"Sweetheart," Ivana cried out. "Get a hold of yourself. We need to stay under cover."

She was holding me down. I could feel her straining against me as I attempted to push myself up. I don't know what I was planning on doing. I don't know where I was going to go. I only wanted to help someone. I couldn't stand to see so much suffering.

"Why are they doing this?" I cried out. "They aren't even monsters. They're humans. Why are they doing this?"

Ivana was yanked away from me. Another killer dressed in black had appeared. He slammed his pistol into the side of her head, and she dropped to the floor like a rag doll. He then turned his pistol on me.

I knew I was going to die. I wasn't sure what my reaction should be. I was crying but I had been crying for a while at that point. I didn't know what to do. So, I ended up looking into the man's eyes. I saw nothing there. Maybe it was the ski mask hiding his face. I don't know, but I couldn't find any humanity.

I closed my eyes.

Three gunshots joined in on the cacophony of the room. I noticed them because they were so close to my ear. I opened my eyes and realized that I hadn't been shot. The gunman had.

Georgie had finally noticed what was going on right behind him. Not that it was his fault, mind you. He had been busy fighting multiple gunmen in the other direction. Until the very last moment he had no idea one of them had snuck up behind him.

"Thank you," I told Georgie.

"No problem," Georgie replied just before he arched his back wickedly and collapsed to the floor. He'd been shot in the back. I watched as he frantically thrashed against the floor while reaching behind his back as if he could stop the pain of the wound with his hands. It wasn't very long of a struggle, and slowly Georgie became quite still except for the involuntary twitching in his legs.

His eyes remained fixed upon his fallen rifle.

Our attackers must have realized they finally shot him. Two of the men began to move closer to us. I reacted. I dove forward, gathered up Georgie's weapon and pulled the trigger just as the two killers came around the table.

I killed two men.

Ivana was screaming behind me. She was trying to help Georgie. Poor, poor Georgie who had been so brave, now just a limp mass in a pool of blood. Ivana had her hands over his wound. She was trying to prevent the pool from growing.

She was also yelling something at me. I couldn't focus on her words. I couldn't stop staring at the two bodies in front of me. I was barely paying any attention to Ivana. Georgie was going to die. Perhaps he was dead already. Ivana kept yelling at me.

Someone punched me in the chest.

At least that's what it felt like. Everything sort of slowed down as I fell straight back onto my butt. All the noise in the room sort of became a loud throb, and I finally understood what Ivana had been yelling. She wanted me to get down. In my shock, I was standing straight up in a room full of gunfire.

I wanted to laugh. I wanted to tell her I was fine; I had only lost my breath for a moment. When I tried to turn in her direction, I lost control of the upper half of my body. She screamed as I finished my fall, and landed with my head upon Georgie's shoulder.

There was a small rosebud in the center of my chest. It was odd that a beautiful rosebud ended up right where I had been punched. My legs wouldn't move, neither would my arms. The room had grown terribly cold, and the rosebud began to blossom and spread.

The last thing I remember seeing was Ivana's face above mine. She was crying. She was screaming. I felt her hands pressing down upon my chest and then I was gone.

Chapter 5

JAXON

There was a moment after I had told Jaxon about my meeting with Skie in which I was truly afraid. It was the way in which his eyes narrowed and his lip curled. He seemed a man very capable of committing unspeakable acts against anyone foolish enough to harm his loved ones.

And then, just as quickly as the rage appeared on his face, it was gone.

Can I tell you something?

"Of course you can. That's why I'm here."

It's the intelligent ones you have to worry about. Only intelligent beings can be vindictive. The zombies are dangerous. There's no doubt about that. If but one of them escaped El Paso, the entire country…the entire world would be in danger.

But a zombie isn't capable of seeking revenge. Only intelligent creatures are truly capable of intentionally hitting you where it really hurts. Only intelligent beings are vile enough to open fire upon a group of innocent people.

My wife had been gravely injured. That was something that never should have happened. It was a mistake we never made again. Nowadays, we expect the smart ones to be vindictive.

Each and every member of the entire team's family is now protected. If something goes wrong, if for any reason we feel they might be threatened, a bubble of safety is instantly projected around them.

I can't tell you a whole lot about our methods. That's top secret, but I'm sure you remember how fast we were able to react when Kingsley killed Lucy.

"I do remember that."

I believe I told you that I thought Hardin probably kept tabs on all our families. Well, he does. I just didn't want to go into too much detail at the time. Our security measures were put in place because of what happened to Skie that evening. It isn't really something I like to talk about.

"I understand."

I'll tell you what happened, but just so you know, I'm far from proud about many things I did that night. The beginning was pretty confusing. We never expected to be attacked. El Paso was the dangerous place, and we weren't in El Paso.

The gunmen had locked us all in the banquet hall. The doors were made of metal and covered in wood. None of us had any idea we were even being locked in. We were too busy drinking and partying. Hell, we were so drunk it took us a while to even react to being shot at.

After the first girl died, I shoved Skie under the cover of a solid table I flipped on its side. Keeping her out of harm's way was the best I could do for her. At least, that's what I thought at the time. Ivana was with her. I even placed Georgie there to protect them.

"What did you do?"

I went to go kill all the assassins.

There was a slight pause as Jaxon stared at the floor before locking eyes with me once again.

Did my wife really describe her gunshot wound as a rosebud?

"Yes."

Jaxon was quiet for a moment. His eyes were once again fixed in a hard stare upon the floor. Merrick left my side and padded softly to him. She gently reached up with a paw and scratched at his leg until he relaxed and reached down to pet the top of her head.

Sorry.

"There's no need to apologize."

Okay.

It took us a little bit to regroup. It also took us a bit to get our hands on some firearms. Still, one by one, we armed up and went after them. By the time I realized Georgie was under heavy fire, I was under some pretty heavy fire myself.

Javie was next to me. He took a few rounds in his hip and went down. I couldn't do anything for him either. If I broke cover, I'd be shot. If the shooters broke cover, I'd shoot them. It was pretty much a stalemate.

Fortunately, Dudley and Nick weren't pinned down. Those two were the ones that saved most of the people. They went around the room shooting down any assassin that was firing on the partygoers. It took them some time to get to us. The killers fought back immediately when they realized Dudley and Nick were picking them off one after another instead of fighting alongside Javie and me, so they had their own nasty and bloody fight.

At some point, Nick shot at one of the large windows, then threw a chair through the cracked glass. The people now had an escape route and they were fleeing the attack.

While all that was going on, I managed to shoot down two more of the assassins, but I also took a round in my stomach. It hurt like a bitch, but I couldn't afford to fix the damage while I was under fire. As soon as Dudley found me, I ducked down to see how badly I'd been hit while he took over shooting for me.

It wasn't the worst wound I'd ever seen, and it was nothing compared to how badly Javie had been hit. He was bleeding like a stuck pig. His features were pale, and he wasn't even trying to staunch the flow of blood.

I crawled over to him, ripped off a piece of tablecloth and pressed the white material against his wound. The tablecloth turned red with blood almost immediately. I turned him slightly and noticed that one of the bullets had struck him in the lower back.

I panicked. Slapping Javie in the face brought him around. I told him to keep pressure on the wound and I crawled away to find some water.

Nick ran into me as I scurried here and there in an attempt to find a pitcher of water that hadn't been spilled or shot to hell. He grabbed my ankle to get my attention, and I almost stabbed him in the face.

I told him what had happened to Javie. I told him to look for a water source. My voice was loud, and I realized the screaming and gunfire had stopped. I crawled to my feet.

Dudley was pointing out the window.

The remaining gunman had fled the scene after killing seventy-four innocent partygoers and secret service agents.

That's when I heard Ivana crying for help.

My blood went cold. My stomach dropped, and a horrible feeling crept up my spine. My legs were jelly as I ran to her. I didn't know if it was because of my wounds or my fear.

She was kneeling over Georgie and a somewhat smaller form. My mind refused to accept what my eyes were seeing. I stood there numbly, staring down at them.

"Jaxon," Ivana cried. "I don't know what to do. I don't know what to do."

She moved away slightly, and I saw my wife's face. I was sure she was dead. She had to be dead. The damage was too great. There was too much blood. The wound was in the middle of her chest.

I don't remember grabbing Skie. I don't even remember moving, but somehow I had dropped to my knees and scooped her up in my arms. Blood from the wound in my arm was dripping down upon her dress as I squeezed her body against mine. There was a noise. I had no idea where it was coming from but it sounded like a long moan that wouldn't end. I really wanted the noise to stop, instead it grew louder and louder. Eventually it turned into a scream, and I realized that it was coming from me.

After that, I only saw red.

There was no thought except destruction. There was no meaning in the entire world except vengeance. I wanted blood. I wanted to rip apart anyone or anything that had a connection to what had just happened.

The scream became a growl.

The growl became a roar.

Dudley was in front of me. Behind him, Nick was carrying Javie. Dudley's eyes were wide with fear. He was shouting something at me; I couldn't hear him over the noises I was making. Then he was trying to take Skie away from me. I fought against him, and Ivana tried to hold me back.

Dudley pointed to the window. I finally understood. There was grass outside. Natural things will heal us. I ran through the broken window. Dudley followed with Georgie. I heard gunshots and saw flashing lights in the distance. The police had finally arrived.

I placed my wife down on the grass and waited for something to happen. She's been touched by the Guardian's power but not nearly as much as the team. She wouldn't age, but she wasn't any stronger, and she certainly didn't heal like the rest of us.

The grass didn't move.

It didn't cover her body and heal her wounds. I could already feel the tendrils creeping up my legs in an attempt to heal the damage on my body but they did nothing for Skie. Water began to pour over her chest. I looked up, and saw that Ivana had found a hose.

I pushed my wife's damp hair out of her face and made room for the spray of water. I started talking to Skie.

"Don't you leave me," I begged. "Don't go, baby. I'll get you out of this. I'll get you someplace safe. Come back to me."

I started crying. No, that's not true. I started bawling. Horrible wracking sobs that were so loud they hurt my chest as they poured out of me. My wife wasn't moving. She wasn't responding. She was limp in my arms. Her hand was cold against mine.

Dudley had his arms around me, trying to pull me away. I wouldn't budge. I kept rocking my wife's still form back and forth. I also kept screaming. A terrible rage that alternated violently with intense sadness kept pouring forth. I couldn't control it. I was a slave to its power. I never once checked her pulse. I never once laid my head against her blood soaked dress and attempted to hear a heartbeat.

The paramedics arrived and I was still holding my wife while Ivana poured water over her wound. It was a struggle for them to get her out of my arms. I'm pretty sure I hit a few of them before Dudley and Nick helped hold me down.

"I've got a pulse," a paramedic announced.

I stopped struggling.

"What?" I asked. "What did he say?"

Dudley was wiping tears out of his eyes.

"They found a pulse," Dudley said. "It's not over yet."

I remember seeing them pull Javie and Georgie out of the grass that had grown around them. I remember driving in a car towards the hospital. They wouldn't allow me in the ambulance. I was too out of control and way too dangerous for something like that.

I don't know who drove me. Nick was beside me the entire way. Ivana rode with Skie, and Dudley rode with Georgie, and Javie.

Doctors came up to me in the emergency ward. They wanted to fix the damage to my stomach and arm. I told them to leave me alone and when they didn't listen I shoved them away.

Eventually Dudley and Nick were forced to stand next to me. They did this so no one would approach me and get hurt. Through a little window on a pale door I watched as doctors and nurses attempted to save my wife's life.

You see, I don't talk about her much, but Skie is my life. She means the world to me. I adore her. Her smile brightens my day. When I've been out killing monsters and fighting for my life, her voice is the beacon I need to find my way home, to get up and fight harder so I can hold her one more time. I need her. I absolutely one hundred percent need her.

Tears began to softly fall from the General's eyes.

Excuse me.

"No need."

It was a tough time.

"I can only imagine."

Finally, a doctor came out of the room, and walked over to me.

"You're her husband?" The doctor asked.

"Yes," I answered.

"We were able to remove the bullet," the doctor said. "But she has extensive damage to her heart and one lung. Somehow, some of that damage seems to have healed, which is probably why she's still alive, but in all honesty, I don't think she'll make it through the night."

The words hit me like a runaway freight train. Dudley began to ask questions. Ivana began to ask questions. I stood there as still as a statue. My heart was running wild in my chest. I wanted to scream. I closed my eyes in an attempt to calm myself down. My hands began to shake.

I could hear the doctor telling everyone that the wound was fatal. I could hear him spelling it out for Ivana so that she wouldn't cling to any false hopes. My wife was going to die. I had failed her. I had saved so many people, but I couldn't save my own wife. It wasn't fair. It wasn't acceptable.

My eyes opened.

I saw the doctor backing away. He'd given his best effort towards my wife, and he was now allowing nature to take its course. I was on him in an instant. My friends were too shocked to react as I grabbed the man by the back of the neck and marched him into the room in which they had been working on my wife.

I dragged him to her dying body and I forced him to look at her.

"Do you know who I am?" I asked.

"Yes," the doctor answered.

"This is my wife," I growled.

There were nurses in the room. They ran out almost immediately. Security rushed forward to replace them. I heard them coming down the hall. I saw Nick and Dudley stop them at the door. They were buying me time.

"I understand she's your wife, sir," the doctor said. "I've done my best for her—"

"Your best isn't good enough," I snarled and shoved the doctor against the nearest wall. He bounced off and would have hit the floor, but I caught him with my arm. Fingers that were barely under control wrapped around his throat and I lifted him in the air. His feet and hands scrambled against the wall behind him.

"If she dies," I whispered in his ear after he had stopped struggling. "I'll kill you. I will find you and I will kill you. If you have a family, I'll kill them as well. Your wife and your children will feel my pain..."

"Jaxon, please," Ivana cried out from behind me. I squeezed harder on the doctors neck. I felt a soft hand touch my arm. I turned and looked into Ivana's face. She looked so sad I melted. I dropped the doctor and left the room.

Nick and Dudley immediately followed me. They kept the security away. I honestly don't know where I was headed. I only knew I had to move away before someone got hurt.

Miriam appeared before me.

I don't know where she came from; she was just suddenly right in front of me, and grabbing my arms.

"Hope is not yet lost," Miriam announced.

I think I sagged just a bit. That's all I could really do. I mean, I probably would have dropped to the floor, but the woman is pretty damn strong.

"Do you hear me, Jaxon?" Miriam demanded. "Hope is not yet lost."

Her words gave me no comfort. I knew she spoke with the best of intentions but she hadn't seen Skie. She didn't hold her still form and feel the warmth leave her body. My wife was gone. Nothing would bring her back, and Miriam was no doctor.

Dudley's phone rang.

"Answer it," Miriam ordered.

Dudley did as she asked. He spoke for a few moments with whoever was on the other line, and when he hung up he seemed angry.

"That was Hardin," Dudley announced. "He said that five of the shooters have been apprehended. High winds at the local airport are keeping the President's plane from taking off, so the shooters are being re-routed to Roswell in order to keep both parties away from each other. He wasn't sure where they're flying to after they drive to Roswell, but right now they are being held at the police station while they await transport."

"So what?" Nick questioned.

"He said some of his government contacts are warning him that something's in the wind, whatever that means. He wants us to find out who's behind the shooting, ASAP. He sounds a bit worried, but he wouldn't elaborate on anything."

"Then let's go to the police headquarters and talk to the shooters," Nick said.

We borrowed Miriam's car and hauled ass to the station. Everyone looked at me sort of funny when I announced I was going as well. It wasn't because I didn't care about my wife; I simply needed to do something. The rage was burning a hole in my chest. I was having a difficult time keeping myself under control.

Maybe I was also a coward.

"*Why would you say that?*"

I think a part of me just refused to say goodbye. A part of me wanted to run away from the pain. I couldn't stand the thought of spending another minute in that hospital. I couldn't stand the way everyone stared at me.

The police force in Ruidoso is pretty small. There were only a couple cops in the entire station when we showed up. Most of the force was probably at the banquet hall, doing whatever it is that police do when a mass shooting takes place.

The two cops were shocked to see us walk into the reception area, wearing our bloody clothes. I held my badge up to the nearest of them and demanded to see the shooters.

"Just a minute," the cop said before vanishing down the hall.

I didn't like the way the remaining cop sized us up as if we were something stuck to the bottom of his shoe.

"You got something to say?" I asked him.

Before the man could reply, his buddy came back with four other men. They weren't cops. Their cheap black suits reeked of government, but they didn't give me a secret service vibe. They seemed a bit more on the sinister side.

"I'm the one that has something to say," the leader of the group announced.

I didn't like the situation, and I didn't like the man's face either. He seemed as if he were trying to take charge of things.

"You know who I am?" I asked.

His men flanked out around the room.

"I do indeed," the man smiled. "I have some questions for you boys. Why don't we go on back to the sheriff's office and have ourselves a nice chat?"

He made the mistake of grabbing me by the arm. I was apparently wrong. The man wasn't trying to take control of the situation. He thought he already had control.

I jerked my arm away from his grasp, and punched him in the sternum. It wasn't my hardest punch but it was enough to put him on the floor. The three other men responded immediately. Each of them reached into their jackets for their pistols.

Unfortunately, they never faced off against anyone like us before. Not a single weapon cleared leather before all of the men were down and out.

The two cops never moved.

"What the fuck is going on?" I asked the one with the attitude.

"Not sure," Mr. Attitude replied. "Those government assholes came in about twenty minutes ago, and took charge of the entire station. They sent the surviving secret service agents out of town, and put the police department on traffic control around the banquet hall. A more impolite bunch of people I never did meet. The chief tried to make some calls and find out who they are, but whoever he called wouldn't tell him anything other than to give them whatever they wanted. The chief was so pissed, he up and went home for the night."

"Where are the shooters?" I asked.

"They were shipped out a few minutes before you got here. They're in a black SUV, guarded by four more of those agent fellows you just beat the snot out of. I think I heard something about Roswell."

"We need to move," I growled.

"I'm not sure you do," the policeman added. "The main road to Roswell is out right now due to a rock slide. Unfortunately, nobody told the agents that. My guess is they'll go all the way up to Lincoln, before they realize they need to turn around, and take a detour through Devil's Canyon. Maybe next time they come into our town they'll mind their manners a bit more."

"All right," I growled. "That gives us more than enough time to stop at the cabin and suit up. If these fuckers want a problem, let's give them one."

"Correct me if I'm wrong," the policeman interrupted, "but you're the fellah that's been running around and fighting them zombies, ain't ya?"

"Yeah, that's me."

"My sister was in El Paso," the policeman said. "Your team saved her life."

With that, the man offered me his hand, which I accepted. Maybe he didn't have such a bad attitude after all.

No one said a word as we drove to my parents' cabin. My parents were, of course, worried sick. They had about a thousand questions, but I really wasn't able to answer any of them. I left all of that up to Dudley and Nick. Fortunately the kids, Otis and Amy, were asleep. I don't think I would have been able to tell them about their mother.

As soon as we could, we made our way to the backyard.

"*What was in the backyard?*"

My own personal Batcave…Or, more accurately, an underground bunker, marked only by a hinged metal door in the ground that opens up to a ladder, and descends ten feet under the earth. At the bottom of the ladder is a metal door that opens up by keypad. Beyond the door are four buried storage containers that have been outfitted into a modified living space.

It's also where I keep a lot of spare weapons.

To be honest, I wasn't sure why I even had the place. Nobody ever used it. I guess I thought it might be a good idea to have it if anyone staying at the cabin needed a decent place to seek shelter, in case the shit ever hit the fan.

Dudley and Nick followed me down. The three of us suited up in our bite suits and grabbed our weapons. I had a sudden stab of sorrow as I grabbed my tactical vest. I'm not sure if I ever told you this before or not, but it was Skie that designed the bandana-wearing skull and crossed pistols I wear on the chest of my vest.

"*I don't believe you mentioned that to me.*"

Well, we took the name Regulators from a gang Billy the Kid was in. It's kind of homage to the West. Skie always thought I needed something on my chest that people could recognize. That's why she made me a design that paid tribute to the name of our group.

"*Is the bandana over the skull's mouth a reference to outlaws?*"

It is, but she goofed on the musket pistols. In the days of Billy the Kid, single action Colt revolvers ruled most of the land. Skie didn't know that. She's not really all that interested in gunfighter history. I think I loved the design even more with the little mistake.

"*I've noticed that the team members have started wearing the design as well.*"

Yeah. They all have a patch on the left arm of their bite suits. Georgie and Dudley even went so far as to have it printed on t-shirts. It helps them pick up girls when they go out.

"*Did the others notice you were having difficulties?*"

Not at that moment. They were more concerned about catching the shooters.

"So what's the plan?" Nick asked abruptly.

"We get to Devil's Canyon ahead of them and take the prisoners."

"An ambush?" Dudley asked.

"Pretty much," I answered.

"What I don't get," Nick said, "is why we need to do any ambushing in the first place? Why were those government pricks trying to get us into the back of the station? Because to me, it looked like they were going to arrest us. I know what being arrested feels like, and trust me, it feels a lot like that."

"It felt like it was heading that way," I agreed.

"Hardin said something was in the wind," Dudley said. "But what the fuck did we do wrong? How many people at that award ceremony are alive right now because of us? We're freakin' heroes as far as I'm concerned."

An image of Skie forced its way into my head. I wasn't a hero. In my mind, my wife was covered in blood, and she wasn't moving. I had to grip the edge of a nearby table to keep myself from falling. My wife was dying. I was powerless to save her. It suddenly became very hard to breathe. I felt beads of sweat forming on my brow.

Dudley put a hand on my shoulder. He noticed that time.

"It's okay, Jax," Dudley said. "You can sit this one out if you want. We can go get these guys and get whatever answers we need."

Without another word, I left my underground bunker.

As soon as I got above ground, I could hear sirens coming from the banquet hall in the distance. The sound made me wonder if any of those odd government morons we'd met at the police station were headed our way. Dealing with government agents didn't really worry me, but I found it irritating. All that mattered at the time was getting my hands on the shooters. I wanted to hurt them. I wanted to teach them all about regret. Nothing was going to stop me.

"All right," I said. "Let's get a few things straight. Obviously, there is some group of government-type agents against us. These agents have assumed control over the police force, and they don't seem to give a shit about my pretty little badge. I don't know what they want, and I don't know who they're working for, but it's probably very safe to assume they aren't on our side. Fuck that! I'm going after the men that shot my wife and friends. I'm going after the people responsible for the massacre at the banquet hall. My plan is simple. I'm going to kill them all. If anyone stands in my way, I'll go through him. Are you two certain you want to come?"

Dudley crossed his right arm over his chest, and made a fist over his heart.

"I'm a Regulator," Dudley said. "Until the bitter end."

"Fuck yeah," Nick smiled.

"Then leave Miriam's car," I said. "We're taking the Harleys."

Merrick came running up to me in the garage. She didn't want me to leave her behind. I stopped, scratched her behind the ears, and then walked her back to my mom and dad who were watching us from the front porch.

"You be careful out there," my mom said as she hugged me.

Nick and Dudley weren't exactly experts when it came to riding motorcycles, but I figured if anyone was after us, they probably knew we had Miriam's car. Anyway, the Harleys were fast. We knew the area, we had a gigantic head start, and if by some chance we did get spotted and pursued, we'd also have an easier time losing them on the bikes.

"How many Harleys were at the cabin?"

I think, at that time, we had five in the garage. Two of them were mine, and three of them belonged to Georgie.

I grabbed my Sportster 72. I wanted a light bike that would be easy to maneuver. Dudley chose Georgie's Street Bob, and complained loudly when Nick climbed on the back. I guess Nick didn't really feel comfortable enough on a bike to ride his own. When I think back on it now, the two of them sharing a Harley is pretty damn funny. At the time, however, not much was breaking through to me.

We set out immediately. My parents waved, despite being unhappy about us leaving. I think among other things, they were also worried about my mental state. Maybe it was coming out in the few words I spoke; perhaps it the look on my face. I'm not sure, but I think I was making people nervous.

The wind was cold. Even I could feel it on my fingers. Fingerless gloves aren't all they're cracked up to be when riding a motorcycle. I hit the barely paved road leading to Devil's Canyon doing about sixty. I slowed down and corrected my speed to allow Dudley an opportunity to catch up. The twists and turns of the single lane road could be perilous. I didn't want him to endanger himself trying to keep up with me.

It wasn't long before we found the perfect spot for our ambush. It was at the bottom of a hill, which meant the government agents would be right on top of us before they even knew we were there.

I parked my bike in the middle of the road. We pushed the other Harley into the woods, and Nick and Dudley took up their positions.

I put my earpiece in my ear and tried to radio in to Hardin. There was no answer. I tried again and again. Still, there was no answer. I kept trying. It was a good way to pass the time. One time I thought I actually heard someone answer, but the voice was muffled and gone before I could be sure.

Three hours after we took our positions, my attempts at contact were interrupted.

"I see lights in the distance," Dudley said through his own earpiece.

"Be ready," I answered.

I leaned against my Harley and waited for the SUV to make its way down the small hill. A moment after the headlights announced the descent of the vehicle, I blared the high beams of my Harley. The SUV slammed its breaks to avoid hitting me, went sideways for a moment, but eventually righted itself on the road.

I didn't move. Instead, I let them see me. I let the headlights wash over the skull on my chest. I wanted them to know it was me. I wanted to give them a chance to turn over their prisoners.

The driver stepped out of the vehicle.

He was wearing another one of those cheap black suits. I couldn't make out his face over the headlights, but I made sure that I could see his hands.

"What's your plan, General?" the man asked.

"That depends on you," I answered, "but I'm taking your prisoners."

"I think perhaps your boss, Mr. Hardin, might have led you a bit astray," the man countered. "Things are changing up a bit. I think the best thing you can do is wait right here while I call some of my associates to pick you up."

"If you move," I said, "I'll kill you. If you reach for the gun on your hip or reach for the phone in your pocket, I'll shoot you dead."

The agent smiled.

"Are you sure this is the route you want to take?" He asked.

"Try me and find out."

He did.

He actually went for his gun. His fingers almost managed to rub against the grip when I pulled my Sig and put a nine-millimeter round through the center of his forehead.

After that, the SUV erupted with movement. The rest of the agents came spilling out of the doors immediately. Dudley and Nick jumped out of the woods on either side of the vehicle. Everyone began firing. It was a quick fight.

Echoes of gunfire rolled out over the hills and valleys. The air smelled of gunpowder. Four government agents were dead on the roughly paved road.

"We're in it now," Nick said.

"Let them come," I replied.

On the horizon, the sun was just beginning to peek out over the mountains in the distance. We needed to move.

Nick took the large SUV. Dudley and I fired up the bikes and away we went. Sooner or later, the area was going to be hot with more agents, and possibly even the police. We needed some distance and a good place to hide.

Dudley had that covered. He occasionally knocked boots with a girl whose parents owned a cabin closer to town. According to him, the girl's parents didn't actually live at the cabin; they just used it for vacationing. Most of the year the place was empty, so it sounded like an excellent hideout for us to use during the day.

As we pulled out, we heard cars tearing up the unpaved road in the distance. The agents must have radioed their predicament in before they got out of the car. It wasn't a big deal, however, I knew all the twist and turns, so avoiding them was relatively easy.

The cabin was alone on the top of a small mountain. The road leading up to it revealed no other driveways, so we didn't have to worry about any nosy neighbors. We stashed the vehicles in the garage. I watched from a distance as Nick led the prisoners out of the vehicle. Each of them was handcuffed and wore a black bag over their head.

I grabbed my binoculars and scanned the landscape. We weren't being followed so the vehicle evidently wasn't bugged. Regardless, I stayed outside in the morning air and planned my next move.

My tomahawk was on the back of my belt, as always. My hand twitched with the longing to pull it free. I told my hand to be patient. We had time to kill, and the prisoners weren't going anywhere.

When I finally made my way into the house, I noticed Dudley and Nick had cleared out all the furniture from the living room. In place of the furniture, five chairs had been brought out for the five prisoners. They were still wearing the bags over their heads.

"Remove the bags," I said.

Nick complied immediately. One man looked defiant. He openly glared at me with hatred in his eyes. Three of the others avoided looking at me altogether, and the final man looked frightened.

I stared at them for a moment.

Then I withdrew my tomahawk slowly from the back of my belt. Four of the men tensed up; the defiant man did not. I calmly centered my gaze upon him, and he glared back at me in defiance. With a snarl, I launched myself towards him. My first swing buried the tomahawk into the center of his face, ending his life instantly.

The man's chair toppled over from the impact. His buddies screamed out in fear. I paid them zero attention. I ripped my weapon free of the man's face and brought it down again and again. I think I was growling, maybe I was snarling, probably I was screaming.

I ended the assault, composed myself, and stepped in front of the four remaining prisoners.

"I want you each to know that I'm going to kill you," I said in a calm voice. "Nothing on the face of this earth can prevent your death. I'm going to make you pay for what you did. I'm going to make three of you suffer horribly, but only three. The remaining man will go painlessly because that will be the man that answers my questions."

I walked away. Dudley and Nick followed.

"You think they'll talk?" Nick asked.

"They have no choice," I answered.

"Are you going to be able to do this?" Dudley asked.

"Do I look squeamish to you?" I asked in return.

"That's not what I meant," Dudley answered. "I only meant that torture isn't really your kind of thing."

"Ssshhh," Nick interrupted. "They're talking in there. I can hear them.

All of us got quiet. We could hear them whispering in a foreign language, so we couldn't understand what they were saying. Suddenly the whispering began to sound more like gagging and retching.

"What the fuck kind of language is that?" Nick asked.

Confusion turned to realization in the span of a heartbeat, and I ran back into the living room. Three of the four men were dead but still twitching. The only one left alive happened to be the frightened man. He was frantically snapping his jaws open and shut while his tongue worked against something in the back of his mouth.

I swung my fist in a downward motion. The blow broke his bottom jaw, and snapped it out of place. My punch was a bit on the side of overkill but it worked regardless.

I reached into the man's mouth, and searched until I found what I was looking for. He had a fake tooth containing poison. The pricks were killing themselves.

In retrospect, I'm glad things went down the way they did. I was fully prepared to torture and kill each of them. They shot my wife. I wanted them dead. However, while I have no problems killing someone that's trying to kill me, I worry about the damage to my soul should I ever follow the path of a torturer.

"Now what?" Dudley asked.

"Same as before," I answered. "I just concentrate everything on this guy."

The man started crying.

I pulled out my Bowie knife. I ran the tip down the man's shin. He began to mumble.

"They were supposed to let us go," the man mumbled. "They were supposed to let us go after we left the city."

"Who was supposed to let you go?" I asked.

"The men driving us," he answered. "The men in black."

"Were they going to take you somewhere?" I asked.

"We were to regroup in El Paso."

That one floored me. Why would anyone want to go to El Paso?

"What's in El Paso?" I asked.

"Our leader is there," the man mumbled in answer. "My fellow soldiers are there."

Things weren't making a lot of sense.

"Who was your target at the banquet hall?" I asked. "If you were after the President, you were a little late to the party. Maybe you were after me?"

The man looked confused.

"We…we…we were told to kill the woman," he finally stammered.

"What woman?" I shouted.

"Your wife," He answered through his broken jaw. "We were ordered to kill the wife of the General."

It was a struggle to maintain control over myself. It was a struggle to keep my hands from closing around the man's neck and squeezing the life from him.

"Why go after my wife?" I asked. "Why not just come after me?"

"Because our leader hates you so very much, he wants you to suffer. He wants you to come to him, so he can kill you himself."

I stepped away from our prisoner. I walked to the other side of the room and opened a window. The cool air felt good on my face. I needed it. I was having problems focusing. I noticed that the wounds I received during the attack had begun bleeding again.

"Who the hell are you assholes?" Dudley demanded. "Where the hell did you come from?"

"I am Albanian Mafia," the man mumbled. "All of us are Albanian Mafia."

"This makes no fucking sense," Nick grumbled loudly.

"Who's your leader?" Dudley asked the prisoner.

"I do not know his name. We simply call him the Monster."

"Why are you working for him?" Dudley asked.

"My brothers and I were in the worst prison this world has to offer. All of us had death sentences, but on the day of our executions we instead met with our Bajrak in a room deep underground. They informed us of an alliance they had made with a military man from your country. In exchange for our lives, we were to serve as his army."

"So their leader is someone from the United States military." Dudley mused aloud.

"No, we never met the military man. The Monster is someone else, someone who works for the military man."

I had heard enough. I really didn't care who did what. I planned on killing all of them, and the so-called leader of their little group was the best place to start. I walked over and stood once more in front of our prisoner.

"How many of you are there?" I asked.

"Forty of us came to your country," the man mumbled and coughed. "Many fell to the Monster's rages. Some of us were sent to kill the woman. Twenty remain in El Paso."

"How do I find the Monster?"

"You go to El Paso and he will find you."

"Fair enough," I answered.

I went behind the prisoner, and after a swift cut with the knife, he was free. The man reluctantly got to his feet. I then went to Dudley and held out my hand. It took a moment for him to register what I wanted but eventually he handed me his battered .45. It was a bit of a shock to see the weapon. To this day, I'm still not sure how he got it back after he surrendered it at the banquet hall.

Anyway, I tossed the pistol at our former prisoner. He was clumsy about it but he caught it. I squared off against him. Dudley and Nick backed out of the way. The former prisoner looked at the weapon in his hands. The pistol was cocked and loaded. All he needed to do was bring it up and pull the trigger.

His eyes met mine.

I smiled, and drew my Sig.

He wasn't very quick. I could have put at least three more bullets in him in the time it took him to raise the gun. I settled on only the one.

The three of us watched his body crumple to the floor in a heap. I picked up Dudley's gun and handed it back to him.

"I wish you would quit doing that," Dudley said.

"So do they," I answered.

"We've got problems, you guys," Nick interrupted. "Mr. Hardin was right. There is something in the wind. I bet those agents are working for the bad guys, which means everything's a big cluster-fuck full of Albanians, black-suited government agents, some military dude, some asshole called the 'Monster,' and all of them want to arrest us or kill us."

"He's right," Dudley agreed. "For whatever reason, the government has turned against us."

"We don't know how bad it is," I said. "This could only be a small group. Hardin still has our backs. I'm sure he's working on it."

"Mr. Hardin is MIA," Dudley said. "We haven't been able to reach him."

"He's probably pretty busy trying to figure out who's coming after us," I said. "He'll make contact after he gets somewhere. In the meantime, we continue as we were. We're going to El Paso, and we're going to bring down the man responsible for the death of my wife."

"Jax," Dudley whispered. "She's not…you don't…"

"Just let it go," I said. "I'm grabbing some shut-eye. You guys should do the same. We're heading out at sunset."

I walked away. I had nothing more to say. I didn't want to talk about my feelings. I didn't want my friends to try and console me. I wanted the anger. I wanted the rage.

I spent the day in a sort of trance, deadening my sorrow. If I let what happened to Skie consume my mind, I would fall apart. I would collapse on the floor and never rise. She was my "everything," and she was dying. For all I knew, she was already gone.

A part of me wanted to call the hospital and find out if she was still alive, but I was terrified of the answer. I couldn't stand the thought of somebody telling me she had died during the night. So, I put my feelings away. I locked them deep down inside me. When all was said and done, when the people that hurt her were all rotting in the ground, I would go back to my wife, but not before. The uncertainty was better than the impending sorrow.

After seeing the damage they did to her…Well, it was an almost mortal wound that rocked most of my sanity right out of me.

What was left was frightening. I was little more than a beast. A raging sea thrashed and churned inside me. I couldn't wait to let it out. I couldn't wait to destroy the Monster.

Anyway, that's how I spent the time. I didn't sleep; I sat by the window and looked out at the forest. I wasn't aware of the passage of time. I wasn't even aware that the sky was darkening until Dudley knocked gently, and came in the room. He had to call my name a few times before he got my attention.

"What is it?" I mumbled.

"The sun is setting," Dudley answered.

"Then let's go," I said.

We took the SUV and left the motorcycles behind. I didn't plan on running from anyone. If someone stood in my way, I was going to take him down hard, and he wasn't going to get back up. Still, we took the secret roads out of town, and never met any resistance.

The drive from Ruidoso to El Paso normally takes around three hours. We made the drive in about two hours and it only took that long because we switched vehicles three times. Curiously, it was Dudley that hotwired our borrowed vehicles.

You stole three cars?

I prefer the term "borrow" and, yes, we "borrowed" three cars. Those damn agents had the highway covered in check points. The hunt was on, and we could no longer use the road. Instead, we "borrowed" four-wheel drives and went straight through the desert.

It wasn't too difficult for us, even though we almost got spotted by a helicopter with a searchlight once or twice.

As easy as the journey was, entrance to our destination proved to be much more difficult. El Paso had been encircled by a gigantic fence…and I'm not talking about some sort of average chain link. No, this fence was close to fifteen feet high, covered with barbed wire, and went on as far as I could see. It suddenly occurred to me that I hadn't been on this side of El Paso since the outbreak. I had no idea a fence like that even existed.

We could have ditched the vehicle and climbed over but walking through zombie infested territory really wasn't a good idea. Instead, we followed the fence back to the highway. After climbing a few hills, we saw gigantic watchtowers with blazing lights in the distance.

We also saw fires.

Of course we knew what had happened from following the fence. There were no guards. There was a walkway on top of the fence for patrols, but it was vacant. The walkway had been deserted.

When we reached the highway and stood before the towering gates, our worries were confirmed. The fence had been attacked.

We searched for survivors and found none. Vehicles were overturned and burning. The road was torn up. Military structures were reduced to rubble. The fallen lay sprawled across the landscape where they died. Most of the bodies were riddled with bullet holes. Some of them were beaten to death, as if someone had battered their bodies until the bones shattered and the skulls caved in.

An entire battalion of soldiers had met their end here, attacked by a force they never anticipated. A force they were unprepared for. Those brave men kept the zombies from escaping. They died so that something even worse than the dead could enter the city.

Eventually, I was able to pull my eyes away from the ground. I looked over, and I saw that the gates were wide open and hanging from their hinges. Now, these gates were huge. They were also very solid; they had to be. In case of an emergency, these gates needed to be strong enough to hold back the zombies.

"Who the hell could have done this to so many soldiers?" Dudley asked.

"I'm not sure," I answered, "but I mean to find out."

"It looks like every soldier on this side of the mountain came to help," Nick said.

"I'm guessing about a hundred and fifty to two hundred dead," Dudley said. "Why didn't they radio in for some real backup?"

I picked up a fallen radio from a pile of rocks and cement. The casing had been shattered, and the wires and other components inside were falling out the cracks.

"Who said they didn't call for help?" I whispered.

"You think they were abandoned?" Nick asked.

"Oh shit," Dudley said. "How many times have we tried to get into contact with Mr. Hardin? We haven't made contact with him, or anyone else, since he called me at the hospital."

"You think the headquarters was attacked?" Nick asked.

"Why else would nobody be communicating with us?" I asked.

"Dude," Nick grumbled. "It's not possible. There're only twenty of these Albanian fuckers. Twenty guys couldn't tear through our headquarters and then do all this damage. At our headquarters alone, there are a couple hundred soldiers, and that's not counting the elite groups that help clean out the city."

"Maybe," I admitted. "But something kept the big guns from arriving."

"You don't think any zombies got out do you?" Dudley asked.

I looked at the damaged gate once again. Then I cast my eyes down the road in the opposite direction.

"I don't think so," I answered. "Most of the soldiers were armed with sniper rifles. They probably kept the area pretty clean. Still, with the noise of battle and the smell of blood in the air, it won't be long before this place is a hot zone."

"I bet I can fix those gates," Nick said. "It won't be extremely secure but it should hold until someone with some know-how gets here."

I thought about it for a bit. I didn't want to waste time fixing stupid fences. I wanted to chase after the man that ordered the attack on my wife. Still, I couldn't leave the gate open. I couldn't risk the outbreak spreading outside the city.

"All right, Nick," I said. "See what you can do about the gate. Dudley, you scout around and see if you can find anything that might be interesting."

While Nick and Dudley went to work, I climbed to the top of the fence underneath the spotlights. The walkway was damaged. I could see hundreds of bullet holes. I also saw some heavy scarring that probably came from an explosion of some kind.

My guess was that the men at the gate were attacked suddenly and violently. They called for backup, and the only help they received came from soldiers farther down the fence. The only thing the enemy had to do was open fire whenever someone new arrived on the scene.

Still, something wasn't right. The soldiers were combat trained. A piece of the puzzle was missing. Nick was correct; twenty men couldn't take out so many soldiers. Unfortunately, I wasn't exactly in a good state of mind. I wasn't spending enough time trying to puzzle out what was happening all around me.

"Your thoughts were on your wife?"

The question came out bluntly and without tact. The General was so shocked by the question; it took him a few moments to reply.

My thoughts were random and chaotic. There was still a great need to know if she was alive, and that need was growing in intensity with each passing moment. I wanted her to be alive. I needed her to be alive. Realistically, I didn't have much hope. Not after speaking with the doctor, and I knew I wouldn't be able to bear the news. That was the important part, that's why I didn't make the call. I knew I wouldn't be able to bear it if she was gone. I wasn't strong enough. So I continued to tell myself to wait. I continued to push it off until the right time. Deal only with what I could handle. Punish the men responsible.

Mind you, these thoughts were all locked deep inside the cellar of my mind, but that didn't mean they weren't still there. They clawed at the doors that barred their way. They scratched at the walls, and echoes of their need crept into my mind. Is she still alive? Is she still alive?

I would immediately shove away the slightest glimmer that managed to escape, and then I would refocus on what was before me. Still, I wasn't all there. I should have been watching out for Nick. I should have been keeping an eye open for shamblers.

I heard movement farther up the road. It was a dull sort of slapping sound that pulled me away from my internal struggle. I looked below me. Nick was wedged into the gate. His position was so awkward; he couldn't reach for his pistol in the holster at his side and his rifle was nowhere to be found. I watched as he struggled frantically against the gate but he appeared to be stuck somehow.

I couldn't find Dudley. He was lost somewhere in the carnage of burning cars and broken buildings. It was up to me. I raised my rifle. I put the red dot on the first zombie that came before me. I fired. I missed, cursed, and fired again. I missed a second time.

The third shot was a hit. The shambler's legs turned to jelly and he collapsed mid-run. His friends were close behind him. They tripped over his body and skidded down the street.

I fired on the first one to his feet. I took him out instantly. I fired on the second zombie, and I missed the headshot. Instead I plugged a hole into her shoulder, and spun her around. My second shot went into her ear. She dropped on top of the other two.

I sighed deeply and realized I was covered in a cold sweat. It worried me that I missed so many times. That wasn't like me at all.

There were more zombies in the distance.

I could hear their moans. I could see their faint outlines becoming clearer and clearer. Eventually I heard their screams. Dudley had finally appeared. He immediately began helping Nick free himself from the gate.

I tossed my rifle over my shoulder, and jumped off the fence into El Paso. I didn't roll when I landed. I just absorbed the shock with bent legs and then walked over towards Dudley and Nick.

"What's wrong?" I asked.

"His leg is pinned," Dudley answered.

"I didn't expect the gate to weigh so much," Nick said. "When I popped it back into the hinge it slammed into me and got my leg."

"Can you get him free?" I asked Dudley.

"Almost there," Dudley replied. "Just a few more seconds."

"Okay," I said. "I'll buy you some time."

In the center of the road, I took a knee, and aimed my weapon. That's when I noticed my hands were shaking. I watched them for just a brief moment, took aim, and fired off a shot.

I hit the zombie on the chin and removed most of its lower jaw. My second shot hit its shoulder. My third shot left a puckered red hole in the center of its chest. My mind flashed to Skie. She had a hole in her chest.

I started hyperventilating. My vision blurred; I couldn't aim. I became so dizzy I fell to my side. I could hear Dudley screaming for me. I felt something wet against my waist. I reached my hand under my shirt, and it came away wet with blood.

I had forgotten about my bullet wounds. I never healed them up properly. During the day I had managed to splash just enough water on them to stop the bleeding, but I still had a hole in my stomach.

It trickled blood occasionally during our drive. I knew this because the trickle felt like a bug crawling down the inside of my bite suit and annoyed the shit out of me. The jump off the fence must have royally screwed up the injury. The trickle had increased to a flow.

I tried to find my feet but the asphalt of the highway was too inviting. I was tired. I hadn't slept. Dudley kept shouting at me. I wanted to see what he was getting so upset about, but turning around to look at him seemed to require too much effort on my part.

Something landed on top of me. I felt the weight of it slam into my body. There was a tugging sensation against my bite collar. It was irritating, so I tried to smack it away. A horrible pinching sensation ignited my arm on fire. I think it was the sudden pain in my arm that snapped me out of my stupor.

A shambler was latched onto my arm. She was biting down on the bite suit, so it wasn't puncturing flesh, but she had a hold of the skin under the sleeve as well, and it hurt like hell. I freaked out, and began beating my fist against the top of her head.

She barely seemed to notice.

I felt another slam. The zombie hit my legs and again came that horrible pinching feeling, this time it was in my thigh. The bite suit did its job—it did its job very well—but that didn't mean I couldn't feel the pain.

I screamed out.

I didn't have the strength to get them off of me, and I was getting pissed. Obviously, I still wasn't in my right mind. I'm not sure if that was because of the blood loss due to my stomach wound or my emotional state, but it never once occurred to me to grab my weapon and shoot them.

The zombies were jerking me all over the road as they gnawed their teeth against my bite suit. At some point, I got a good look down the road. There was an even larger group of zombies headed right for me.

I panicked and struck my attackers even harder. In response to my clumsy attack they doubled their efforts to find the flesh and blood underneath the suit.

At that point, I really thought the end was rapidly approaching. I didn't stop struggling, because giving up isn't in my nature, but I really thought they were going to get me.

A blade whistled through the air, the sound ending abruptly with a moist crunch. The female that had me by the arm flopped on top of me. There was another whistle of air and the zombie that had me by the leg dropped to my side.

Dudley pushed the female shambler off of my chest. His machete was barely dripping any blood; his strikes were that deadly. I felt rather proud of him.

He dropped to a knee, put a hand on my chest to keep me down, and he began firing at the charging zombies. Beyond him, Nick had taken the same position and was firing his weapon.

The fight was over inside of five minutes.

"What the hell happened to you?" Dudley asked.

"Stomach opened up," I answered.

He unzipped my utility vest, lifted my shirt, and took a look at the wound.

"Son of a bitch, Jaxon," He growled. "Why didn't you heal that before we left?"

"Because I'm an idiot," I answered.

Apparently, all three of us were idiots, because not a single one of us had a drop of water. Sure, we grabbed some backpacks but unfortunately they were all devoid of water. We did, however, have an experimental blood-clotting agent. It burned like hell when Dudley dumped it on the bullet hole but it did stop the bleeding.

I took a few minutes, then got to my feet. Dudley had found something and he wanted to show it to us. So we walked back to the now working gate, exited El Paso, and stepped back into the path of destruction and fallen soldiers.

We didn't need our flashlights. The still burning fires gave off enough illumination for us to pick our way through the debris.

"You're not going to believe this shit," Dudley said after we had followed him behind a broken building.

With a flourish, he pulled an old tarp from one of our armored Jeeps. The vehicle was undamaged. Nick ran his hand down the black matte paint and approached the driver's side door.

"Looks like the Monster wants you to drive safely," Nick announced.

"What do you mean?" I asked.

"He left you a note on the steering wheel," Nick said.

He handed me the note.

"Welcome home, Guardian," I read aloud.

"The word 'home' is underlined three times," Dudley said. "You think that's an invitation?"

"We're about to find out," I answered.

"It's bound to be a trap," Nick said.

"Of course it is," I replied, "but we know the area. We can get in there, check things out, and bring their little trap down upon their heads."

We spent about thirty minutes investigating the Jeep. We didn't want the damn thing blowing up on us when we turned the key. Regardless, I think we were all a bit nervous when the engine hesitated a bit before turning over.

We drove through the rubble carefully. We didn't want to run over any of the soldiers. Nick jumped out at the gate and let us through before closing it up tight behind him.

There were more zombies in the area. This wasn't a problem for us. If one of them got too close for comfort, Dudley shot him down from the backseat.

We entered through the Northeast side of town. I'll be the first to admit I am relatively unfamiliar with that side of El Paso. I spent most of my time in the Westside and Upper Valley. Nick, however, had spent a lot of time over there so he was able to show us the easiest route to Trans Mountain Road.

"Can you tell me what Trans Mountain Road is?"

Between the Northeast and the Westside of El Paso is a mountain range called the Franklin Mountains. This mountain range has a long winding road—called the Trans Mountain Road—that cuts right through it. It saves people a lot of time, because without that road they would need to use the freeway and drive all the way around the range. We already knew the freeways on the Northeast were impassable due to abandoned cars. So we headed for the mountain.

"How did that go?"

It went pretty badly right from the beginning. Before we even got there, we encountered numerous roadblocks, and had to find alternate routes that ate up both my time, and patience. We had a really nifty GPS in the Jeep. It didn't just show us directions; it had a feature that was able to show us the width of the road and where we were on it. That thing came in handy once Dudley explained to Nick how to use it.

Eventually, we found our way to the stretch of road that marked the first leg of ascension. Things looked pretty easy going at that point. The road was clear of the abandoned and wrecked vehicles that normally slowed us down.

The part of Trans Mountain Road we were traveling is right before the actual mountain, and therefore a miniature desert of flat land lies on either side. The night was dark. We had left the lights of civilization behind, so we had no idea that the living dead littered the desert around us.

At first, only a few of them came running up behind the jeep. Dudley took care of them pretty easily. A sharp zombie scream would pierce the quiet night. We would scan our surroundings for the culprit, and Dudley would take aim at the shadowy figures running madly towards us, once we found them.

That's how things began. That's what the first few minutes looked like. We weren't worried. An occasional group of four or five zombies could be expected. Halfway up that first stretch of road, things took a turn for the worse.

The groups of zombies became larger, and they appeared more frequently. Dudley eventually stopped shooting at them. He didn't want to run out of ammo like he did when we were stuck in that building downtown. By the time we hit the first curve of the road, we had a pretty decent horde running behind us.

We were a little nervous about that, but things weren't all bad. All I had to do was drive fast enough to keep them from grabbing onto the Jeep. That wasn't a problem; let me tell you. Nothing motivates you to step on the accelerator more than a horde of screaming zombies so thick they fill up the entire street.

I was driving pretty fast. I wanted to create a big enough gap between us, and the horde, for when I had to slow down on the turns. You really don't want to haul ass in a Jeep and then hit a sharp turn. The last thing we needed was to flip our wheels with all those ravenous corpses hell-bent on catching up to us.

The very next turn was a descent into madness.

The zombies were waiting for us. No, that's not right. They weren't actually waiting for us with wide-open arms or anything, but they were there. Groups of them were spread out across the road.

Their numbers were nowhere near as impressive as the horde chasing after us, but there were enough of them to force me to slow down considerably. Still, we fought our way through. Dudley began firing his weapon once again, and Nick even joined in to lend him a hand.

I ran over any shambler that was brave enough to step out in front of the Jeep, but I wasn't dumb enough to hit them too hard. I didn't want to damage our wheels. Even with the large, reinforced front bumper, a vehicle can only take so much.

The next turn was a descent into Hell.

We had driven right into another horde and were trapped. The mountain rose up on each side of the road at this point. The zombies were so thick on the ground; we could see nothing beyond their headlight-illuminated forms. They rushed immediately. They must have heard us coming from a long way away with all those zombie screams following us up the mountain. It looked as if they were on edge, and actively looking for the reason for those screams, well before we rounded the bend.

I slammed the Jeep in reverse and hit the gas.

One of them managed to jump onto our hood, despite my frantic retreat. Nick had to reach for it over the windshield and push it off the side. Then, we almost lost Nick. He slammed into the windshield when I smashed the rear bumper into the shins of the fastest zombies from the trailing horde and slammed the brakes.

He gasped for air as the breath was knocked from his body.

I didn't ask him if he was okay. I didn't have the time. We were surrounded, and had only a few seconds to spare before the rotting faces with their gnashing teeth filled the vehicle. Instead, I grabbed Nick's arm and yanked him back into his seat. I yelled for Dudley to get down and hit the lever next to the four-wheel drive stick.

The armored top shot up and out, instantly wrapping the three of us in its protective cocoon. Dudley began to laugh from the backseat. It wasn't a real laugh, mind you. It was only his way of getting rid of all the tension.

Clawed hands scratched at the windows. Rotting bodies crawled onto the hood. I could see ruined faces peering at me through the safety glass. I could hear their teeth grinding against the armor.

"Now what?" Nick asked.

"We need to keep moving forward," I answered. "There're too many of them. They can flip the Jeep if we stay still too long."

I pressed my foot on the accelerator; the Jeep inched forward. The shamblers pushed back. The tires began to squeal against the asphalt. The rear left corner began to lift into the air, then something gave, and we moved forward into the mass of undead.

Corpses banged and thumped against the front of the vehicle. Dead flesh slapped against an unyielding bumper, straight out of a Mad Max movie. Legs were broken; skulls were crunched under the tires. The dead did their very best to hold us back, but the big ass, souped-up engine, on our Jeep would not be denied.

"You need to move faster," Nick shouted in my ear. "You really, really need to move faster."

"I can't," I replied.

"Why the fuck not?" Nick asked.

"I can't see where I'm going," I answered.

The dead were too tightly packed and the stretch of road was too narrow. We were fish attempting to swim upstream with bears trying to grab us.

"I can't even see the damn mountainside," Dudley shouted in agreement.

The Jeep began to rock back and forth as the zombies pressed and shoved against it. I saw the face of a young woman pressed up against my window. She'd probably been an attractive girl when she was alive. Now, her features were distorted with rot, and hunger. Her neck had been savagely torn open. The grayish skin on her face was blistered and cracked. She couldn't be reasoned with. She couldn't be satisfied. Only a thin piece of armored glass kept her snapping jaws away from me.

We were moving forward but slowly, way too slowly. We were blind, and I was afraid to drive off the road, or crash into the rock of the mountainside.

Then a glow from the dash caught my eye.

"Nick!" I shouted. "Use the GPS."

"Do what?" Nick asked.

"Use the GPS to see our position," I shouted.

Nick immediately began to play with the GPS. I could tell he was having problems concentrating with all the noise. There were zombies banging against his windows. The screams threatened to split all of our skulls, and I'm not even gonna tell you how bad the shamblers smelled.

"Keep going straight," Nick said.

I did as he asked, and picked up the speed.

"Turn to the left a little bit," Nick said. "You're getting too close to the rocks."

I obeyed his directions.

I wasn't able to drive very fast but our pace had definitely improved. As a result, the Jeep was no longer in danger of being tipped to its side.

Eventually, the left side of the mountain dropped off and faded away. The road ahead opened up; the zombies were more spread out. I picked up a lot more speed at that point. I wasn't about to win any races, but I was able to maneuver in and around the charging corpses and make up a bit of time.

Unfortunately, all too soon, the mountain rose up again and we headed into another canyon of rock. For whatever reason, this canyon was even more packed with zombies than the last one. Even from inside the vehicle we could feel the pressure against the front bumper as the Jeep pushed against them. The resistance was immense but I pressed down even harder on the gas pedal and inch-by-inch, we found our momentum.

"This is fucking ridiculous," Dudley grumbled from the back seat.

I looked at his reflection in the rearview mirror. He was hunched over in the middle of the backseat. His eyes were focused gloomily on the front windshield, and the corpses were banging against the windows all around him.

With Nick giving me directions we parted the sea of dead. It wasn't an ideal position for us to be in, but I was confident we were going to make it out in one piece. Eventually, the canyon of rock would open up and we'd have enough space to pick up some speed. When that happened, my plan was to push the pace. I wanted to leave them far behind as we made our way down the other side of the mountain. As things were, the zombies were ruining my plans. I didn't want to fight them. I didn't give a shit about zombies at that particular moment. I wanted to fight the Monster.

"Turn a bit to the right," Nick said. "Too much; back off a bit. There ya go."

CRUNCH!

The front of the Jeep slammed into something immovable, but we couldn't see what it was for a few moments due to all the hungry dead on the hood of the vehicle.

"What did we hit?" I asked.

"No idea," Nick answered.

"Did you run us into the fuckin' mountain, you asshole?" Dudley demanded.

"No," Nick answered. "The little arrow on the GPS says we're in the middle of the road."

A number of zombies moved in just the right way and I was able to see that we had run into the rear end of a semi-truck trailer.

"We hit a semi-trailer," I announced. "I'll back up, and we'll go around it."

Secretly, I was having flashbacks about the time that vampire chick was chasing me down, and I got my front bumper stuck on another car after I ran into it.

The Jeep tipped obscenely to the left as I was having that thought. The dead had finally gotten a good grip on us. Dudley screamed out from the backseat and slid into the side window. Fortunately, Nick was buckled into his seat or I would have been smooshed beneath his bulk.

I slammed the shifter into reverse and floored the gas pedal. Tires met flesh and zombies were thrown away from the wheels. It was the moment I needed. Not all of the shamblers had been thrashed by the tires, but the ruckus weakened them enough that we reversed out of their grasp.

We didn't go far, mind you. Almost immediately we crunched and shattered the shinbones of the dead behind us. I kept going, though. I backed into them relentlessly. I probably gave myself about ten feet of distance from the semi-trailer, and then I punched forward once again.

I'm not sure what happened. Maybe it was the sudden lurch in speed, but most of the zombies weren't being smacked out of the way. Instead, they were being sucked under the tires. The ground beneath us suddenly became squishy and soft.

I wanted to go wide around the semi-trailer, but I didn't have enough control with the bumpy, loose corpses, underneath the tires. The side of the Jeep ground against the metal of the trailer, and we sparked our way down its side.

Nick was screaming.

He was worried that his window was going to break away. The screeching sound was horrendous. It was louder than the zombie screams. It was louder than Nicks screams. Under better circumstances, I would probably have been laughing at him.

Then we were free of the trailer. We were over the mass of corpses. The tires met road with a satisfying forward jerk of traction, and we were once again on our way.

I was going a bit slower than before. I didn't want to meet up with another abandoned vehicle. I was too worried about getting stuck and giving the zombies enough time to flip us.

"How much more of this shit do we need to go through?" Dudley asked.

I didn't answer. I was more familiar with Trans Mountain Road than he was. I didn't want to tell him the bad news. Instead, I kept driving. I kept moving forward. Never stopping—stopping was bad. Stopping would get us killed.

We pushed and pushed. The zombies in our windows became a blur of forgotten faces. In our minds for a brief moment, and replaced by a hundred more the next. All in all, the drive took about three hours. We scraped some more cars along the way, but we never hit them hard enough to require any backtracking.

The drive was scary. It would make an incredible ride at an amusement park. Drive through zombies in an armored vehicle, ten dollars a ticket. See if you can make it across the mountain.

The horde began to thin out on the final downward slope.

We picked up speed immediately. I could finally see the road ahead of us. Nothing was going to hold us back. There were only a few cars in the road ahead, and going around them gave us no problems.

I kept peeking at my rearview mirror in order to watch all the rotten faces become smaller and smaller. They did their best to keep up with us. I've gotta give them that, but it was pretty easy to leave them behind.

"They're still chasing after us," Dudley said as we pulled farther and farther away.

"Let them," Nick replied. "Not like they're gonna catch us now."

"Well," Dudley continued. "We just led thousands upon thousands of zombies to the Westside. We need to be on the Westside. Am I the only one thinking there might be a problem?"

Dudley was, in fact, the only one thinking that. All those zombies would be pouring into the same side of town we needed to be on. To make matters worse, my old house was located in the Upper Valley, and the Upper Valley wasn't really all that far from Trans Mountain Road.

Not good. I wasn't thinking ahead. I was charging blindly into danger. I needed to start using my brain before one of us got hurt.

I slowed down immediately. I couldn't take the chance of them infiltrating my old neighborhood. I needed to lead them in the opposite direction. So, I took the first left turn we came upon.

"I'll lead them to the desert past our old Safe Zone," I said. "Then we'll take Redd Road back to my house."

Getting zombies to follow after you is a really easy thing to do. All you have to do is let them see you. Dudley and I were pretty used to it, but it always had some sort of weird effect on us. It probably always will. I'm not sure how to describe it, except to say that it's chilling.

I led the horde away from the Upper Valley. In fact, I led them back in the same general direction we had all come from; I was just using a different road. This time, however, I also had the option of using intersecting side streets if I needed to change course on our long journey to the desert. I waited until I had a massive group following in the right direction, and then I hit the gas.

I left them far behind as we headed towards our destination. When I was finally out of their line of sight, I honked the horn so they would be able to hear that we were still ahead of them, and would head towards the sound. I had to take a few turns, but I eventually got to a place where the roads ended and the desert began.

We made a lot of noise once we got there. We honked the horn, and we screamed out the windows. Then, we listened. The night was quiet, so we began making noise again.

We had to do this about five times. It wasn't much really. Zombies don't need all that much. On the fifth time we were making noise, we finally heard them. They were far away, but they were coming. We sat there listening to them for a few minutes. We needed to make sure they didn't get distracted.

Their moans kept getting louder and louder. The rumbling sound of those many, many bodies moving towards us became more and more distinct.

We left.

I gunned the Jeep down the road. I made sure to keep at least a few streets between us and the road that the horde was using, but we still heard them as we passed by. The plan had worked. The shamblers had lost our trail. Hell, for all we knew, once they ran out of road they might forget about us entirely, and just wander back to Trans Mountain.

The way to my old house was now clear. Very soon I would have my vengeance. I was shivering with anticipation.

"You okay?" Nick asked after noticing.

"I'm fine," I answered.

"Then why are you shaking so much?" Nick asked.

The shaking was getting pretty bad. Or at least bad enough that I could no longer chalk it up as anticipation, even though I had no other explanation. Then it hit me.

I was cold.

I turned on the Jeep's heater and warmed up the car.

"You normally don't get very cold, Jax," Dudley said. "Are you sure you're okay?"

"I'm pretty fucking fine, considering how much blood I lost from that hole in my stomach," I snapped. "Now stop worrying about me. Get your head in the game. I want a plan in place before we reach Doniphan."

Doniphan was a street that cut right through Redd Road. Once we hit that street, we were only a few minutes from my old house.

"I think we should leave the Jeep on Doniphan and head out on foot," Nick said. "We can move all stealthily and shit like that. Get a good look at things without anyone hearing or seeing us."

A few zombies came running out from between two houses. I hit the lever by the shifter and collapsed the armored top. Dudley took aim with his MP7 and brought the zombies down quickly. One of them still managed a scream but it wasn't extremely loud.

"What the hell were so many zombies doing on Trans Mountain?" Nick asked. "That doesn't make a lot of sense."

"I'm thinking a bunch of them on the Westside heard the battle sounds when the Monster broke into the city. They probably all started wandering up the mountain together looking for a meal."

"I guess so," Nick said. "I was just hoping it wasn't a trap or something. I've never heard anyone say anything about hordes of zombies on the mountain."

"Nah," Dudley said. "I don't think it was a trap. If the Monster wanted to trap us, he would have found a way to disable our vehicle in the middle of all that shit. That would have been a death sentence for sure."

"Instead, the Monster probably assumed there would be some heavy zombie activity after the battle," Nick said, "so he left us an undamaged Jeep in order to travel safely. Does that sound right to you?"

"It does to me," I interrupted. "He wants to fight me. He went after my wife to bring me here, and now he wants to make sure I show up."

"This asshole is going to get a lot more than he bargained for," Nick said.

"You got that right," I agreed.

Once we reached the intersection of Doniphan and Redd Road, we killed the engine and sat in the Jeep for a bit. I had parked between some abandoned vehicles so we had plenty of cover. Anyone passing by might even mistake our ride for just another derelict automobile polluting the street.

None of us could hear or see anything out of the ordinary, so we quietly set out on foot. In order to stay unseen, we ran through an apartment complex. The place looked a mess. Doors were shattered, and human remains littered the ground.

It wasn't pleasant at all. We could still see dried blood on the walls of some of the buildings. It's sometimes rather hard to remember all the good we were able to do. Especially when we see how much we lost. Who were these people? They lived so close to me, and I never knew them. How many died here? Would we ever find out?

Dudley tapped me on the shoulder. He pointed back towards the mountain. Even from where we were on the ground we could see the muzzle flashes of weapons being fired.

"Somebody followed us," I said.

"Why would anyone wanna go and do that?" Dudley asked.

"Beats me," I answered. "They must be dumber than we are."

"How many shamblers do you think followed us off the mountain?" Nick asked.

"A good bunch," I replied. "They're moving faster than we did."

"You think they're looking for trouble?" Dudley asked. "I doubt those government boys would follow us into El Paso. There are easier ways to get yourself killed."

"Let's expect trouble," I said.

Then I began moving through the alleys of the apartment complex. There were moans coming from behind a few of the closed doors. We also heard the scratches of broken nails sliding across glass windows.

"None of them are screaming yet," Nick whispered.

"That's because they haven't seen us," I said. "I think they just smell food."

"How bad do you think it'll be if one of them screams out?" Dudley asked.

"Not as bad as the mountain," I answered.

We continued on. We took cover where we found it, and stayed out of the open. Bushes and shrubs were our friends. Dark passageways became our allies.

At the opposite end of the apartment complex was a rock wall. We scaled it quietly. At the top we looked for danger. A sea of overgrown backyards ran from left to right, as apartments gave way to houses. The yard before us had a swimming pool. In the pool was a zombie. It had seen us through the water and was frantically trying to make its way to the shallow end in order to climb out and attack us.

"Looks like this is as good a place as any," Dudley said.

The three of us jumped. The landing hurt my stomach. It was a sharp pain that made me grit my teeth. I was getting cold again.

I met the zombie as its upper body breached the surface of the pool. It made watery moans, but it couldn't scream. The greenish flesh on its face looked doughy and ready to fall off. The tomahawk was in my hand. I didn't remember grabbing it but I used it anyway.

The corpse slid back into the water with barely a sound.

We went around the house. There was no reason to go through it. That would have only added more danger, and we'd had our fill of zombie fun for the evening.

At the edge of the front yard, the three of us crouched behind a bush (in dire need of a trim), and surveyed the street before us. A few of the porch lights burned in the surrounding houses, but other than that, darkness reigned.

We bolted across the street, ran through the front of another yard, moved around the side of that house, scaled a low wall, and entered a backyard. This yard had four zombies, one of which was a child.

I took out the kid first. Let the image of that kill find a final resting place in my head. It could fight to be remembered along with all the other crappy things I wish I never had to see. Dudley and Nick didn't need to have that on their consciences.

The other three zombies were easy enough to bring down. We were moving quickly and efficiently. None of them were even able to scream out. We were on them too quickly for that.

"AAAAWWWWWOOOOAAAA!"

That's the best way I can describe the sound. It was like hearing the demented combination of a human being and a foghorn. One minute everything was quiet and the next that sound was reaching out across the night sky, echoing across the flat land surrounding the area. Each of us looked at the other, first in confusion, and then in worry, due to how loud the sound was.

"What the shit was that?" Nick asked.

"That's no zombie," Dudley said. "That's something new."

"It wasn't human," Nick whispered. "There was no way that could be human. It had to be a machine. Maybe it's some sort of alarm at that milk factory at the end of the road."

"No," Dudley said. "The milk factory doesn't have an alarm."

I was ignoring them. I wasn't ready to be concerned about the source of the sound. I was still stuck on what effect the sound would have. I listened as hard as I could.

I didn't take long.

The neighborhood was coming to life around us. Well, I guess you can't really say that. There wasn't anything living nearby. No, I think it would be better to say that the sound was loud enough to wake the dead.

I heard the sounds of shuffling from inside the nearby homes. I heard fists pound against doors. I heard the moans behind the walls. There were a lot of zombies in the area.

After Nick and Dudley quieted down for a moment, they began to hear them as well. Nick's face darted around as he picked up different sounds from different directions. He was looking nervous.

The sound of splintering wood could be heard from several different directions. The zombies were leaving their resting places.

"Time to move," I said.

We kept low, communicated through hand gestures, and remained undetected. Around us, we could hear the shamblers take to the streets. They were searching for prey. It wasn't long before we saw a few small groups of them wandering aimlessly farther down the road.

We stayed clear of them, and continued on our way until we came to the canal at the very end of Redd Road. It wasn't much too see: two small hills divided by a flowing body of water. The top of each hill was wide enough to fit a car. In fact, Dudley and I took the canal trail on the first day of the outbreak. The roads had been packed with cars. The dead were following us. The only choice we had was to take the canal all the way to the Rio Grande.

One side of the canal bordered on a street called Montoya. The other side ran along the backs of rock walls. Between the walls and the canals was a long, low, ditch. We stayed away from the street. The street had too much movement.

We did our best to move quietly, but it was difficult with all the ground litter in the muddy ditch. Thin branches and dead leaves were our enemies. We moved slower to cut down the noise. We stayed in the shadows.

"Maybe we should make a bunch of noise," Nick said. "Get all the zombies in the area to follow us. Then lead them to your old house and let them deal with this Monster fucker."

"No," I said. "I'm going to deal with the Monster. Keep it quiet. If you get spotted, attack quickly before they can scream."

After moving down the ditch for a while, I crawled up the small hill, and peered over the top of the canal. We were right where we needed to be. Looking out over Montoya, I could see my old street. The lights of my old house were the only lights on in the neighborhood.

Other than that, I saw nothing.

"No movement on the street," I announced. "The lights are on though. I'm going to make a run for it."

"I have a better idea," Dudley said. "Let's stay out of the open. We can move farther down the canal, cut down the next street over, and move through the open field behind your house. I bet the grass has grown pretty long. It'll be great cover."

Dudley was right, and from the field we would be able to use our binoculars to get a better look at the situation. I still wasn't using my head. I was rushing things in my desire to get my hands on the Monster. I was being an idiot.

We moved a street over. On our way there, we ran into another zombie. This one was missing half its body. It gurgled and moaned when it saw us. I would have shot it, but we could hear a sizable group of shamblers on the road on the other side of the canal. A muffled weapon still makes a sound, and we couldn't afford any attention.

So, I jumped on the bastard.

I also shoved his filthy head into the mud he was crawling through. I was fast enough to prevent him from screaming out but his thrashing arms were still making too much noise. I fumbled around my utility belt a bit before I managed to find the handle of my Bowie knife. It made a soft sound as I pulled it from its leather sheath.

I buried the blade into the base of the zombie's skull. The creature went still beneath me. I looked up at Dudley and Nick. Their eyes were wide. I motioned for one of them to look over the top of the canal and see if the other shamblers heard any noise.

Dudley crawled to the top. He surveyed the street for a few minutes; then he slid back down and shook his head.

"How bad is it on the street?" I asked.

"There are about five big groups of ten or more, and a bunch of lone wanderers," Dudley answered.

"Can we make it across Montoya?" I asked.

"I think so," Dudley answered. "No guarantees though."

The three of us crawled to the top of the canal. Once we reached the top, we'd stay as low as possible. Fortunately for us, the top of the canal was overgrown. We were camouflaged by the weeds and grass. The growing things kept trying to heal my wounds as we moved.

Since we were all crawling, it took some time for us to reach the little metal bridge that provided the easiest way to cross the canal. I went first. I moved at a crouch. I also moved slowly, so my footsteps wouldn't echo on the metal.

Once across, I lay flat in the weeds, and again felt them slowly crawl across my body. I didn't like the looks of the street. There were too many zombies, and attempting to clear them out would only attract more. We were in a situation. Nick came across next and took a position right next to me.

Peering through the weeds, he grimaced and frowned at all the zombies.

"This sucks," he said.

"I agree," I said.

Dudley made his way across and took his position next to Nick.

"Let's wait them out," Dudley said.

"How long is that going to take?" Nick asked.

"Well," Dudley answered. "They all seem to be moving away from this location. So hopefully, it won't take too damn long."

The wait was longer than I would have liked. According to the Protrek on my wrist, it took thirty-two minutes. During that time we moved as little as possible. Once, one of shamblers wandered uncomfortably close to our position. None of us moved, but the zombie still managed to catch our scent. Using its hands and feet to dig into the mud, the shambler began to climb up the muddy hill. When he reached the top, he was face to face with Dudley. The zombie's eyes grew big when he saw the waiting meal only inches away. Dudley had his complete attention. The corpse never noticed Nick's small pocketknife moving towards its head until it was embedded hilt-deep into its temple.

Dudley moved quickly as soon as the body went limp. He didn't want to risk any noise by having the body tumble down the side of the canal, so he grabbed it under the arms, and with Nick's help, pulled it on top of him.

The dead zombie was a life saver. The smell masked our human scents. It kept others of its kind from investigating our area.

Finally, it became a bit safer to make our way across the street. I was the first to move. I slid down the hill of the canal face first and crouched at the bottom. I surveyed the area, and then bolted across the street.

Dudley rolled out from under the corpse and followed behind me. Nick came immediately after him. We got our bearings while hiding next to a large, droopy tree. Then we moved down the road.

We quietly passed house after house until we came upon the open field we were looking for. The field was enclosed with a rusty chain-link fence. We scaled it easily. Dudley was right about the grass in the field, it was, at least, four feet high. It wasn't exactly healthy grass, perhaps it wasn't even grass at all. The color suggested a dire need of water. But that didn't stop the wispy tendrils of life from clinging to my body in an effort to heal the damage on my arm and stomach.

I investigated my wounds. My arm seemed pretty good. There was very little blood, but it emitted a dull ache whenever I moved it. The hole in my stomach was oozing slowly. All the movement must have aggravated it again.

"You okay?" Dudley asked.

"I think so," I answered.

"Well, you better be sure," Dudley said. "We have no idea what we're about to face."

"I'll be fine," I grumbled.

"Is he bleeding again?" Nick asked from a short distance away.

"I think so," Dudley answered.

"Fucking Jax," Nick growled. "Get yourself fixed up before you bleed to death, dumbass."

A moan came from somewhere to our left.

The three of us dropped to our stomachs in response. We weren't alone in this field, and Nick's shitty volume control let them know they had company.

We waited silently.

Finally, a zombie rose up from the tall grass. It was followed by another, and another, and another. There were about twenty zombies in the field with us. I can't tell you what they were doing there lying down in the grass. I can't even tell you how long they had been there. Zombies do some weird shit when nobody's looking. Some of the monster geeks think that when there isn't a food source around, the zombies can occasionally fall into a sort of slumber. I'll take their word for it. Most of the zombies I've seen were trying to eat me.

The hunt was on.

The zombies were searching for us in the grass. We were hunting them. Our goal was to bring all of them down, before they could scream and give away our position. Their goal was to eat us, and they were probably pretty damn hungry.

The zombies moved, and we moved. They made their way to our position by the fence, and we circled around them.

Our attack was from the rear. We avoided being seen, in an effort to avoid any screams. We moved through the grass like lions. When we got behind a zombie, we launched ourselves up, and brought them down as violently as possible.

The three of us split up. We began to attack from different angles as the zombies spread out all over as they searched for us. In the first attack alone, all of us were successful. Three zombies went down silently.

The shamblers never even realized the prey had become the hunter. Not that it would have mattered if they had. They would have simply kept coming for us; that's what zombies do.

I guess I had about five kills when I caught a glimpse of Nick bringing down a zombie out of the corner of my eye. Unfortunately, there was another zombie a mere five feet away that Nick never saw. Well, that zombie sure as hell saw Nick jump up and drag down its undead buddy.

It crouched forward and began its undead stalk through the grass. I'm not sure why it didn't scream out. Perhaps it only caught a glimpse of Nick's movement. Not enough to be positive it saw food, but enough to make it curious. That's only a guess, though. Its posture, however, made it painfully obvious that it wasn't taking any chances. It even clawed its hands up like a Velociraptor.

I moved to help Nick.

Staying low, I made a beeline straight for him. When I stopped to look again, the zombie pursuing him had vanished. I moved faster and, in doing so, made more noise. I heard him from a few feet away. I couldn't see him through the grass, but I could hear him grunting, and cursing.

I parted the grass in front of me. Nick had managed to kill his first zombie, but the second one—the zombie that spotted him—was in full attack mode, and poor Nick was pinned to the ground by its immense bulk.

Now, I had seen the shambler coming for him from a distance. It looked to be pretty fat, but that was nothing compared to seeing it up close. The zombie was probably over four hundred pounds.

Nick could barely breathe, and I had no idea how he even managed to turn around so they were chest-to-chest after the zombie jumped on him. However, he managed to do just that, and the only reason the fat zombie hadn't screamed was because Nick had jammed the handle of his fire axe into its snapping jaws.

I swung my tomahawk.

The back of the shambler's head went flying off into the grass. The body dropped limply on top of Nick. Nick grunted, and then gagged as black juices from the open skull poured onto his face and hair.

"Get this thing off of me," Nick shrieked.

"Be quiet," I whispered.

I grabbed the corpse by the arm. I pulled, and Nick pushed. Together we rolled the beast off of him. Nick got to his knees immediately, and began to frantically rub away the vile juices with his sleeve.

"Oh man," Nick said. "Oh man, I got some in my nose."

"Be quiet," I said.

It was too late for my warnings. We had already drawn attention. Four of them came at us through the grass, one after another. The first one was a woman. She made a weird sigh when she saw us. She wore a filthy t-shirt and torn jeans that showed the putrid flesh of her thighs.

I threw my tomahawk the second I saw her. The blade punched through her face, and stuck. I heard a crunch behind me and spun around with my Bowie knife. Before the shambler's hands could get a hold of me, I brought the knife down in a chopping motion, and cleaved its skull all the way to the nose.

The corpse of an old man without a shirt tackled me from the side. I spun before I hit the ground, and buried my knife into the roof of its mouth, deep enough to penetrate the brain.

The final zombie came at Nick.

It was a skinny girl: probably a teenager judging by her skirt and tiny shirt. Nick swatted her to the ground with one hand. Pushing himself up with the other, he buried his fireman's axe in her skull before she got back to her feet.

My stomach was bleeding again.

I could feel the slight trickle of blood oozing down around my stomach. I hated the feeling. I hated myself for not healing the wound properly, and I silently vowed to not allow it to weaken me.

I clamped a hand over the wound. I couldn't really put too much pressure on the damage due to the bite suit and vest, but it seemed to work sufficiently.

Dudley came up to us as I was retrieving my tomahawk.

"What the hell have you guys been doing?" Dudley asked.

"What do you think, asshole?" Nick replied testily.

"Well, I took out the rest of them," Dudley said, ignoring Nick's question entirely.

"Are you sure?" I asked.

By way of reply, Dudley stood up in the grass. Nothing charged him, and no screams shattered the quiet night.

"How did you guys keep all those fuckers from screaming?" Dudley asked after surveying the bloody scene a second time.

"We nailed them as soon as they saw us," I answered.

"Damn," Dudley said. "That's some good work."

"I did most of it," Nick grumbled while he continued to wipe at his face.

"You look like you tried to wear one of them for a hat," Dudley said to him.

"Well, let's see what you look like after having the weight of some fat ass drop on top of you," Nick replied.

"How much noise did we make?" I interrupted.

"Not much," Dudley answered. "I thought I heard Nick saying something. I might have heard the weapons hitting the zombies, but you guys were pretty quiet."

"All right," I said. "Let's get to the house."

I led the way. Dudley and Nick fanned out behind me. After the grass came a thin stretch of old trees, and beyond that was my backyard's rock wall. We climbed over the wall and landed in the landscaping of my backyard. We crunched past the rocky part of the landscaping to the grass area, and made our way onto the rear patio.

Light from the windows blazed down upon us. I didn't appreciate stepping out of the darkness, but at least nothing would be able to creep out at us through the shadows.

The three of us went to the side entrance, where ages ago a trio of dead had slammed against the sliding glass door, and chased us from my home. I don't know what I expected to see but things were just as we had left them.

The glass door was still broken. Only the frame and a few jagged shards were left to keep out the dirt and weather. The carpet inside was ruined. No amount of cleaning would ever make it right again.

The zombies chasing after us stepped on the fallen glass. Bloody footprints ran from the side entrance all the way to the remains of the flimsy wooden door that led to the garage.

"Wow," Dudley whispered. "It feels weird to be back here."

"Do you remember leaving any lights on?" I asked.

"I don't," Dudley answered.

"Then you guys had company," Nick said. "Because someone came in here and turned on all your lights."

"Captain Obvious," Dudley said.

"I saw the place from the street," I said, "so I knew the lights were on, but I only took a quick glance, so I figured it was only the outside lights. Why would someone come in here and turn on every single light?"

"It doesn't make much sense," Dudley said.

"You guys check out the downstairs," I said. "I'll go up and check out my bedroom."

I didn't wait to receive a response. I wanted to see my old room too badly for that. I wanted to face the dread creeping into my heart. Of course, I had no idea what I was dreading. Maybe it was the thought of someone disturbing the bedroom.

Bedrooms are normally a private place. They aren't something visitors often spend a lot of time in. It was also the only room on the second floor. So intruders from parties, or whatever, weren't normally inclined to wander so far away from the usual groups of people in the kitchen and backyard.

Then again, maybe it was none of that. This was Skie's room as much as mine. Perhaps under the circumstances, I couldn't bear the thought of anyone entering a place that held so many memories dear to my heart.

I saw footprints on the dusty stairs. My guard was up. Something wasn't right about the house. The lights had been turned on for a reason. We had taken the bait, and stepped into the trap. When was the damn mystery going to reveal itself?

I entered my old bedroom slowly and cautiously. Nothing was out of place. I checked the closets. I checked the bathroom. Finally, I stopped before the bed.

I'm sure it was my imagination. It had to have been my imagination, but I caught the faint scent of Skie's perfume. It was coming from somewhere in the sheets. I moved closer to the bed. The scent was coming from her favorite pillow.

I picked up the pillow, shaking the dust off it. I smelled it again. Nothing. I pushed my face into it. The softness…the gentle touch of the fabric of the pillowcase against my skin took me to a different place. It brought up memories I didn't know I still had.

I never found the scent again.

However, I had something else. I had memories of better times, a past that had never known the evil of the present. I'm not sure how long I stood there with my face pressed into that pillow. I lost track of time. My world was falling down around me, but alone in that room, I was with my wife.

I sat down on the bed. A sudden wave of grief crashed against the rocky shore of my soul. For a brief moment, I let it flow all around me. I let it consume me. With a groan, I began to push it away.

A loud crack echoed through the quiet night. Glass broke from somewhere downstairs, a soft crunch and a tinkle of sound, followed by two dropping bodies. Nick cursed loudly.

"This is it!" he shouted out when he finished with his litany of four letter words.

A brief moment later, the windows downstairs began exploding inward as bullets peppered the house. The sound was deafening. We were facing some serious firepower.

The bedroom, however, was not under fire. I gently placed the pillow back on the bed and tapped my earpiece.

"Dudley," I said. "Kill the lights."

"On it," Dudley replied.

Peeking my head out the door, I watched as one by one, the lights downstairs began to extinguish. Some of them were simply turned off, others had their cords yanked out of the sockets and others, too far away to reach, were shot out. I quickly turned off the bedroom and bathroom lights then had to brave the hail of gunfire to extinguish the hallway light outside the bedroom. For that, I almost took a bullet in the hand.

"Can you make it upstairs?" I asked.

"Not unless we wanna get shot," Dudley answered. "Can you make it downstairs?"

"No," I answered. "Return fire and distract them. I'm going to the roof."

I went to the sliding glass door that led out to the balcony. I checked around, and saw plenty of places that would be great for a sniper wanting to take a shot at me. However, none of them were very secure, and with all the noise the dead were headed towards us. I could see them climbing the fences of the field we had used to reach the house. I could hear them moaning and screaming from the street in the front of the house.

No sniper would find a safe place in the midst of the moving dead. I was pretty sure I wasn't going to get shot at, so I went out on the balcony, and quietly climbed up to the roof. Now, the roof has many angles, and different levels. Therefore, it wasn't too difficult for me to remain unseen by the bad guys as I made my way to the front of the house.

I could see the muzzle flashes easily. The attack was coming from the house next door. I moved to a different location to get a better look. The doors and windows of the house were all reinforced.

The house had been prepared for war.

The trap became very clear. Our enemy used a human foghorn to wake up the zombies in the neighborhood. Then they opened fire on us as soon as we had trapped ourselves in a home with all the lights on. All the while, they remained safe in a house with boarded up windows. After that, it was a toss-up as to who would get us first: the shooters, or the shamblers responding to all the noise?

We were in a bad spot.

Yet that didn't worry me. I had expected a trap. We endangered ourselves, and allowed them to make the first move so we could find them. I was even a bit shocked that the morons hadn't managed to wound at least one of us.

I had explosives. My plan was to sneak down and blow the front of their house open. I wanted to see how brave they would be if the zombies had access to their sanctuary. I tapped my earpiece.

"Stay low," I told Dudley. "I'm going to open up their sardine can."

"Not a problem," Dudley answered. "Take your time."

I made my way down the opposite side of the house. My boots crunched on the rock landscaping. I shot down three zombies making a run for me, and began to worry about how much time I would have to set the explosives.

I ran to the front of the house. The dead were everywhere. I looked to the house next door where the shooters had taken up residence. The front yard on that house was getting pretty crowded with the dearly departed.

I wasn't going to be able to use the explosives. At least not the way I had intended. I had a moment of indecision, a brief loss of situational awareness. A cold arm wrapped around my neck and tried to yank me to the ground.

I heard the sound of teeth scraping against my bite collar, and I shoved the shambler away in a fury. I looked around. The dead were surrounding me. I sized up my chances. It didn't look good.

There were too many.

I spun around. I needed an exit through the crowd. My plan had gone to hell and I couldn't think of a backup. I needed a moment to collect my thoughts, and that wasn't going to happen while I was being attacked.

I saw the gap I was looking for, and something completely unexpected. The house directly across the street from mine had an upstairs light on. I could see the glow through the large window. Even more important, was the solitary figure standing there with his arms crossed as he watched the scene below him unfold.

I had found the Monster.

I charged through the gap. Dead hands reached out for me. Jaws snapped when I got too close. I ducked, dived, and wove in and out, making my escape. I didn't run directly to the Monster. Hell, I'm not that stupid. Instead, I ran down the road.

My new plan was to lead the gathering horde away. This would improve the odds for Nick, and Dudley, and I also didn't want a bunch of hungry zombies following me into the Monster's house.

With my stomach injury, I wasn't moving as fast as I usually can. In order to compensate for the lack of distance I would normally be able to create with a sprint, I cut off down the road and jumped a rock wall.

I screamed out in pain as I hurled myself on the other side. The tearing sensation in my stomach was bad. I didn't even land cleanly. Instead I slapped cement with my tailbone and elbows. The hard plastic guards protected my elbows worked pretty well, but my ass took a beating.

The dead were right behind me.

I didn't have time to cry about things. I got up and limped to the next wall. I was slower going over this wall but that didn't mean it hurt any less. Immediately I scanned the new yard. The house had a clawed up wooden door, and it was hanging open.

I ran for the door. The zombies were starting to climb over the rock wall. I could see their disgusting hands reaching up for a grip. I closed the door quietly behind me. I heard a quiet moan emanating out from the shadows surrounding me.

I wasn't alone.

Through a small window, I saw the majority of the horde run out of the backyard as they searched for me. Unfortunately, some of them decided to hang around and investigate. Eventually, the hang-arounds were gonna sniff me out.

I set off away from the backyard door and made my way deeper into the dangerous shadows. I used my flashlight, keeping my fingers over the beam so it wouldn't be too bright. In the living room, I found the half-eaten remains of four bodies.

I heard banging on the back door.

I sped up. I listened for the quiet moan, and when I heard it again, I zeroed in on its location. The house I was in was only one-story but it was a big one. So, the dead were already through the wooden door, and searching for me, before I managed to locate the former owner.

I found her in one of the back bedrooms. She seemed to be an elderly woman, though age can often be difficult to determine due to a zombie's decay. Her grey hair was more than enough evidence for me. She'd been tied at the wrists to the frame of a hospital bed, and a wall of medical equipment, long turned off, was next to the bed.

My best guess is that she had been someone's sick grandmother. The former occupants of the house probably attempted to take care of her after she was bitten, but eventually the zombies broke in and got them all. At least that would explain all the scratches on the back door and the corpses in the living room. I'm not sure what the medical equipment was for. I suppose the woman had health problems before she was bitten.

Regardless, grandma was excited to see me. She moaned and groaned happily while she strained against her bonds. She even tried some sort of scream but for whatever reason, it wasn't very loud.

The stink in the room was horrible, but I didn't let that bother me. I grabbed the sheets right off of her and crawled under her bed.

The dead were close behind me. Then again, when are they not?

They rushed into the room. They knocked over the medical equipment. I stayed perfectly still under the sheets. Grandma was jabbering about a mile a minute, but the zombies couldn't understand why she was so excited.

In no time at all, they moved out of the room and began to search the rest of the house. I think I had to stay there about thirty minutes before it was safe to leave.

During my wait, I tapped my earpiece.

"I couldn't blow the front of their house," I told Dudley. "There were too many shamblers out there. How are you guys doing?"

"We finally made it to the upstairs bedroom," Dudley answered. "But we're still trapped."

"I found the Monster," I said. "Let me take him out, and then we'll see what happens."

"Make it quick," Dudley said. "The freakin' shamblers are starting to get inside the house."

That wasn't the best of news. Obviously, more zombies had arrived, because I had led the bunch in front of the house away. I sighed heavily, and sat back to wait things out.

When I could finally leave the safety of my hiding place, I stood up and took stock of my injuries. The wound in my stomach was bleeding again. My arm hurt like a bitch. None of it bothered me very much though. I would soon have my revenge.

I paused at the door.

Grandma reached out for me. If it hadn't been for her stinky room, I would have been devoured. In a sense, she saved my life. I went back and put her out of her misery.

After that, I put down a few more zombies as I made my way to the front door. I used my tomahawk. I wanted to feel the weapon in my hands. I wanted to hear the blade sing through the air. The road outside appeared to be clear. Regardless, there was no sense in taking a chance. I hugged the rock walls and bits of shrubbery as I made my way back towards the Monster's house.

It took a bit of skill in order to remain undetected. It also took a bit of time. However, the time was well spent. The streets were full of the dead. I couldn't risk being spotted. Otherwise, I'd be spending my time trying to lose my pursuers instead of breaking the Monster.

I hated the man. I wanted to punish him. I wanted him to suffer. I wanted to bring him pain. I had just the briefest glimpse of his silhouette in the window, so I really couldn't picture him in my mind, but I was still able to break that shadowy image. I was still able to crush his ribs and cleave into his skull, if only in my imagination…for the moment, anyway.

I was almost discovered by the horde in the street numerous times, due to my daydreaming, as I made my way to the correct house.

Once there, I spared a brief moment to look across the street in order to see how the remnants of my team were doing. Things weren't horrible. The zombies were concentrating on the house next door, instead of my old house. That made sense. All the gunfire and noise were from next door. Yet, there were still twenty or thirty curious zombies just loitering around my front yard. They would eventually find their way in like the others had. I was hoping Dudley and Nick had enough ammo to hold them back.

After I took out the Monster, I planned on healing myself and making a run for the Jeep. Then, I would head back and pick up Dudley and Nick after they blazed their way to the vehicle.

I went to the front door of the Monster's lair. The knob turned in my hand, and I entered. I waited the briefest of moments in order to allow my eyes time to adjust to the darkness. Then I set out, searching for the stairway.

I found it right outside the main hallway. The stairs were carpeted. My footsteps were muffled. I dropped my rifle and let it dangle by the strap. I didn't plan on shooting the Monster. I planned on ripping him apart with my hands.

My fists clenched and released. For the first time, I realized how cold my fingers had become. I wasn't sure if that was due to the temperature or the blood loss, but I could feel their coldness through the leather of my half-fingered gloves.

Like my old house, there was only one room upstairs. The door was wide open. I could see a large section of the room. The light was still blazing, but the Monster was no longer in front of the window.

I looked behind me. I was afraid he'd outsmarted me and was sneaking up to stab me in the back.

He wasn't. There was nothing behind me but a small table in the short hallway. I waited for him to stand before the window once again. I waited patiently. The end was near. There was no reason to rush anything and make a mistake.

Eventually, he entered my field of vision. He wasn't a large man. He was smaller than me. He was also unarmed.

I stood up from the shadows and silently approached him.

I crept forward slowly. He had no idea I was behind him. His attention was fully on the scene that was taking place below him on the street.

From five feet away I lunged. My hand found the back of his skull, and I slammed his head on the window so hard, the glass cracked. Then I spun him around. His forehead was bleeding but the man was wide-awake. His eyes were wide with fear.

He put a hand upon my chest as if he could push me away. I reached up and broke four of his fingers. He screamed out, but I clamped my other hand over his mouth as I forced him to his knees.

"This won't be over quickly," I whispered into his ear. "I'm going to spend days taking you apart. Welcome to Hell."

His eyes began to fill with tears. I struck him in the face but I knew. I knew it but I didn't want to admit it. He tried to speak and I hit him again. He began sobbing after that. I released him from my grasp and he dropped to the floor.

I paced the room in a fury.

"If you have something to say," I growled. "You better spit it out."

"I…I…I am not the man you are looking for," the coward stammered.

No shit. No man who earned the name the Monster among a foreign mafia would start crying like a baby the second he got hurt.

"Tell me where he is," I growled.

"I…I will take you to him," the coward said. "That…that is my job."

Everything clicked.

I was wrong about the trap. The trap was only to separate me from the rest of my team. The bad guys didn't fire a single shot into the upstairs bedroom. Nick and Dudley were pinned down but I was able to leave easily. I saw the man in the window when I was outside in the front yard. I went after him, and left my team behind.

I was an idiot.

I was outsmarted.

There was only one thing left to do; play the game.

"Let's go," I said.

I lifted the man by his collar and shoved him in front of me. We went down the stairs, and as I was about to leave through the front door, he motioned me to the garage. Inside was another one of our Jeeps.

"Upon entering the city," the coward said, "we stole many weapons and a few vehicles."

"You also killed many people," I replied.

"The Monster has declared war," the coward said. "In war, there are casualties, but the war shall soon end."

"It's going to end?" I asked.

"Yes," the coward answered. "The Monster will soon kill you."

"Get used to disappointment," I said.

"Yes," said the coward. "I understand. You think you can beat him. You cannot. No one can defeat the Monster."

I didn't have much to say after that. I kept my weapon aimed at the man and I let him drive us out of the neighborhood. The zombies were everywhere. They rushed at the Jeep and bounced off the armor. The man didn't drive very fast, but he drove fast enough to not get surrounded by any large groups.

From a few streets over, I heard the sound of squealing brakes, and the muffled thumps of silenced gunfire. Somebody was coming late to the party, and that didn't bode well for Nick and Dudley.

"More of your people?" I asked.

"No," answered the coward.

I didn't believe him. I wanted to go back to my team. I tapped my earpiece.

"You have company headed your way," I told Dudley.

"Good guys or bad guys?"

"Undetermined," I said.

"Fuck it then," Dudley said. "We made our way to the roof. So, we're sitting nice and pretty for the time being. You kill that bastard yet?"

"On my way now," I said.

"I'll see you when you're done."

We eventually made our way to Redd Road. He wove the vehicle in and out of abandoned cars. He even used the large front bumper to push cars out of his way when he couldn't find an alternate route.

We crossed Doniphan and continued up Redd. We were headed in the same direction as our old Safe Zone.

However, instead of continuing up the road, the coward turned into the large parking lot of the supermarket near Georgie's house and parked the Jeep. I've told you about this supermarket before. I'm not sure if you remember, though.

"Is this the place you tried to go to shortly after the outbreak happened?"

Yes. Then a bunch of shamblers rushed us. I ended up falling out of the Jeep.

"I remember you telling me about that quite well."

It looked different this time, let me tell you. There were zombies all over the place but they weren't exactly moving. Someone had gone ape-shit and killed every single one of them. There were mounds of burning corpses piled four feet high in some places.

I could smell the stink from inside the Jeep. It was horrible. I looked to the supermarket. There were lights on inside but not all of them. The interior was shadowy.

"The Monster cleared the way for you," the coward said. "He does not wish to be interrupted while he kills you."

"He's inside the supermarket?" I asked.

"Yes," the coward answered.

"Thanks," I said before jamming the blade of my Ti-Lite into his neck and killing him.

After his body stopped thrashing around, I got out of the vehicle, and walked around to the driver's side. I pulled the corpse from behind the wheel, and I pocketed the keys.

I felt good. The pain in my stomach had calmed down somewhat. The oozing blood seemed to have stopped. The pain in my arm was still there but I had full mobility. I was ready.

I moved towards the open glass doors. I could see inside but didn't see anything important. I looked behind me towards the parking lot at the many mounds of burning corpses. The man who did that would be one hell of fighter. That was good. I wanted him to be a fighter.

I went inside the supermarket.

Most of the overhead lights had been shot out. The ones left intact created a dim and moody atmosphere.

The design of the place was simplistic, an immense rectangular room. Except for the odd piece of trash littering the concrete floor, the place was completely empty, broken up only by large support columns that ran from ceiling to floor. The racks, which created the many aisles and shelves of a typical supermarket, had been pushed off to one side, creating a mountain of debris. There were no lights above the mountain, and as a result, I couldn't make out much detail in that area.

My eyes scanned from left to right. I saw nothing. I threw my rifle to the floor. I could always grab my pistol if I took any fire, but I didn't believe the Monster would shoot at me. He wanted to kill me with his bare hands. For some reason, this man hated me. I didn't really care why he hated me. I rarely care why anyone hates me. What I cared about were the places his hatred led him.

The stale air of the supermarket was a big improvement from the parking lot. I strained my ears in an attempt to locate the Monster.

Nothing.

Not a sound.

I walked to the center of the vast room and I pulled out my tomahawk. If the asshole wanted to play hide 'n' seek, he was going to play it alone. I was here for a fight.

I heard singing. The open space echoed, so I couldn't pin down where it was coming from. The voice simply reverberated off the walls, and to be honest, it made me nervous. The Monster wasn't afraid of me. His voice sounded entirely too calm.

The voice was also off somehow. I'm not sure how to describe it. It sounded metallic. If you've ever heard rain pouring down on a tin roof, well it sounded sort of like that, but in a voice. Then the singing was abruptly cut off.

"Welcome to El Paso," said the tin-sounding voice.

A dark shadow rose up and detached itself from the debris on the far end of the room. I had seen that particular mass of shadow when I entered but I assumed it was part of a shelf. I was wrong. It was a large man.

At first glance, the man was larger than Nick, and that's not an easy thing to accomplish unless you're a basketball player. I'd estimate his height at least around six-foot-five. He was also very wide. People like to say that my shoulders are huge; I had nothing on this guy. He was about two of me put together.

"The Guardian arrives," said the Monster.

"I'm going to kill you," I said. "Then I'm going to go back and kill all your friends."

"Is your wife dead?" The Monster asked.

I didn't answer.

"I knew if I went after your wife it would have an effect on you. It would bring out the anger. I want your anger. I want your hatred. It's best not to give a smart one like you time to think and plan. That's how you beat me the first time we met. I underestimated your intelligence. You outsmarted me. This time, I believe the shoe is on the other foot."

The voice was vaguely familiar.

The large man stepped into the dim light.

I didn't recognize him at first. His face was covered in scars. He wore combat books and camouflage pants. On his chest he wore a black tank top underneath a denim jacket. He slowly removed the jacket, and I saw that the scars also crossed his arms. A glowing disk was attached to his chest directly over his heart.

He stepped a bit closer.

His long black hair gave him away instantly, but the open wound on his left check was no longer quite the same. It had been covered up with a piece of metal that somehow fit flush with the rest of the skin on his face. I was looking at Max.

"Wait a second. You were looking at Max, the former Guardian?"

Yeah.

"But you killed him."

I did.

"I don't understand."

Neither did I.

"Do you remember me, Guardian?" Max asked.

I was at a loss for words. Max wasn't nearly this large of a person. He used to be skinny and not extremely tall. It looked as if someone had glued his head on top of some behemoth's body.

Max stepped closer.

His skin had a pale bluish hue. It looked waxy. Not quite human. I took an involuntary step back.

"How?" I asked.

"I have Major Crass to thank for my present condition," Max answered. "It turns out he hates you far more than me. I am to handle you, and he is to handle Mr. Hardin. Tell me, have you talked to Mr. Hardin lately? I'm curious to see how he's holding up against Crass."

"Major Crass is the man who was running things after Mr. Hardin retired, correct?"

Yeah.

"What happened to him after Mr. Hardin came out of retirement?"

No idea. I never saw him again. Hardin had him out of there long before I ever came back. With all the shit he pulled, I always assumed they put him in prison.

"I killed you," I said.

"You did indeed," Max laughed. "I was the better fighter but my powers were waning while yours were growing. I thought you would be easy prey. I was wrong. It's a mistake I won't be making again."

"Crass wasted his time," I said.

"How so?" Max asked.

"I'm just going to kill you again."

I closed the distance between us and swung my tomahawk. Max dodged out of the way. He moved impossibly fast for someone so large. The force of my swing spun me around, and I kicked out with my left leg. My foot connected with his lower stomach, and I heard a great gush of air leave his body.

"A fine hit," Max said. "I think you have become stronger than I was when I held the mantle of Guardian."

He swung a meaty fist towards me, and I barely ducked out of the way. We circled each other. Each of us was looking for an opening; each of us was searching for a drop in the other's guard.

I got tired of waiting.

I faked low and struck high with my tomahawk. Max fell for it. He blocked low, and I buried my tomahawk in his shoulder. He growled in pain, and jerked away, ripping the handle of the weapon out of my grip.

"Tricky bastard," Max snarled as he pulled my tomahawk out of his shoulder and casually cast it away. His blood was clear and thick with a pink tinge. It didn't gush or even flow out of the wound. It seemed to have the consistency of Jell-O.

I came at him again.

I wanted to strike while he was injured. I had no idea if he could heal or not. I dove in low for the take down. Ground fighting wasn't exactly his thing last time we met. I was hoping it still wasn't.

I slammed my head into his groin and gripped the backs of his tree trunk-sized legs. I pushed forward with all my might but I couldn't bring him down. He drove an elbow into my spine that made my legs go weak.

I backed off.

Then I came at him again.

I tried to grab him around the waist. I wanted to lift him into the air and slam him on the ground. He was so wide: my fingers could barely touch. I tried to lift him anyway. He slammed a knee into my groin.

I lost air, and even worse, my wound began to bleed once again.

"What's this?" Max asked noticing the blood dripping to the floor from under my shirt and vest. "You came to me injured? Are you that stupid?"

"Go fuck yourself," I answered as I pulled free my large Bowie knife.

Max began to laugh.

"Of course you are that stupid," Max announced. "Don't you see how well I played you? I attacked your wife. Because of that, you have lost all reason. You're a dangerous opponent because you're so smart, but fill you up with rage, and you become a mere plaything. You've lost this fight before it ever began, little Guardian."

I sliced at his stomach. I wanted to spill his guts on the floor. I figured that would slow him down. Most of all, I wanted him to shut his mouth. His mocking voice was driving me insane. My blade sank but the flesh was tough. The cut took effort. It felt like I was using a dull blade. I left my mark but his guts didn't drop to the floor, instead more of that pink tinged gelatinous fluid oozed slowly from the wound.

Luckily, the cut had a decent effect. He grunted and folded over. I really went to work on him then. I jumped onto his back and began hammering my knife into his shoulder blades. He screamed in agony, grabbed a hold of my legs, and ran full speed in reverse until my back collided with the nearest support column.

The impact stunned me.

I fell to the floor while Max slowly walked away. He then turned and stared back at me with the slightest bit of respect. He thought he could beat me. I could see it in his eyes. He really thought he could beat me. He simply needed to be a bit more careful

I charged him.

I moved fast. I have to hand it to myself. From a position of injury, I was on my feet, and back in the fight in a frightening instant. It didn't much matter though. Max dodged me like a bullfighter, and then grabbed me by my bite collar and utility belt. My knife fell from my hand as he spun my body around and hurled me across the room.

After gravity took over and I hit the ground, I slid for another ten or fifteen feet right past my discarded tomahawk. My hand snaked out and grabbed it up. When the ride finally came to an end, I was on my feet again.

I stared at Max. Max stared at me and smiled. I screamed out my frustration. He smiled harder. Both of us walked back towards the center of the room.

Once there, we began circling each other again.

"I can see your hatred," Max said. "It makes you sloppy. It robs you of thought. I have your wife to thank for that. Her sacrifice has granted me victory."

His words bit deep. In a rage, I made my move. I swung my tomahawk. He snatched my hand out of the air and wrenched my wrist. A bone snapped, and when we broke apart, he had my weapon.

"A worthless tool," Max said as he studied the blade. "You shouldn't rely on it."

He snapped my tomahawk in half over his knee and threw the pieces to the ground. Breaking my weapon had an effect on me. It felt as if I'd been struck.

We flew at each other. Despite the broken wrist, I was still punching him. Unfortunately, he was also punching me. For every hit I managed to land, he was able to connect with four, and he hit a lot harder than me. I could feel the damage. I didn't need a mirror in order to figure things out. My face was being battered. His face, however, didn't have a mark on it.

The brute was tough. I couldn't allow him to continue punishing me. I started trying to avoid his blows. Whenever he'd miss, I'd throw out a power punch with enough force to cripple a mule. If I managed to connect, I'd hear the impact, but I never felt any of his bones break. I never managed to slow him down.

"Can you feel what's happening?" Max asked. "Is your arrogance so great that you fail to realize what's right in front of your face? You're losing, Guardian. You're becoming weaker. I am beating you."

We broke apart from one another. There wasn't a sound in the room except for my breathing, my loud, obnoxious breathing. I was sucking serious air. I was hurt. I was dizzy. I was tired. Max was correct. I was losing.

I pulled out my pistol and started shooting him. I watched his body jerk and fall backwards to the floor. Once he was down, I emptied the weapon on him.

It was cheating—I realize that—but there was no way I was going to let him win after what he'd done to Skie. Victory was mine. At the end of the day, I managed to outsmart the dumbass. He showed up to a gunfight with nothing but his fists. There was a weird rattle in my lungs from the punches to my body but that didn't really concern me. I'd survived worse after fighting the Master Vampire.

I stared down at Max's body. I even snickered that despite how fierce he had become, I still whooped his ass. Hell, it was easy once I pulled my pistol out. I wondered briefly about what Crass had done to bring him back. I also wondered why two people that hated each other started working together. Then I decided I didn't give a shit.

The drama was over. True, I wanted the Monster to suffer. I wanted to tear him apart with my bare hands but things seldom turn out the way we want them to. I was lucky enough to come away with my life.

I kicked Max in the head as I walked away.

My friends needed my help. I fully intended to be there for them. On the way towards the entrance,

I stopped and picked up the pieces of my tomahawk, stuffing them in my backpack. As I searched for my rifle, I heard something metallic clatter to the floor behind me.

I spun around as quickly as my bruised body would allow. Max was no longer on the floor. He was nowhere to be seen. I suddenly felt very tired. My body was finished. I went looking for him anyway.

There were smears of his gelatinous blood on the concrete floor where I had shot him. Other than that, not a sign of him remained. I looked to the side of the room where the debris had been piled up.

I searched for movement.

Nothing moved.

I looked around the room. It was empty. He had to be in the mountain of debris. I slowly walked over there. It was a tangled mess of twisted steel and broken plastic. I'm guessing it was about eight feet deep, and it ran the entire length of the wall.

I stayed a few feet away for the debris. I couldn't make out any details in the darkness. I reloaded my pistol then shone my flashlight over everything. I walked from one side to the other in front of the tangled mess in an effort to locate my enemy.

I heard the sound of a vehicle outside the supermarket.

I turned my head for the briefest moment, and I felt a warm hand reach out and snatch my pistol away.

I jumped back in an effort to gain some space and fell on my ass. I was too slow. Max stood up in the mass of trash. Metal bent, and clattered to the floor around him as he shoved his way out of the debris, and rushed towards me.

"You gave it a good try," Max sneered. "You really did. I'm almost shocked you lasted so long. But you're out of your depth. The last time we met you won. This time it'll be me. This is how it should have been all along."

"Go fuck yourself," I responded.

Max reached down for me slowly, his impossibly big hand getting closer and closer as if he had all the time in the world. I reached into my pocket and placed my hand on my Ti-Lite folding knife.

The muffled sounds of automatic gunfire peppered against Max's big chest. I spun around and saw Nick and Dudley, but they had some friends with them as well, who were firing from a position of cover, whereas Nick and Dudley strode boldly into the open.

Max screamed out more in rage than pain as his body jerked underneath the onslaught of bullets. I scurried out of the way as quickly as possible. By the time Max dropped, I was standing next to Dudley.

"You look like shit," Dudley said.

I didn't answer him.

"We need to move," a voice called out. "How bad is he?"

"He took a beating," Dudley answered. "But he'll live."

"Can he fight?" The voice asked.

"We need to get him healed up," Dudley answered.

"Then let's go."

Dudley made a move to help me walk but I shrugged him away. I think it was the sting of my wounded pride. I had been beaten. Shooting the bastard didn't win the fight for me. My friends had to come to my aide. My Ti-Lite wasn't going to save me, and I wasn't used to losing. I didn't like it one bit, but I sure as hell deserved it.

I had charged into that fight without a plan. I had no idea who or what I was fighting, and I never took a second to find out. I was blinded with rage. My head wasn't in the game, and I almost got killed for it.

Failing isn't something I'm used to doing. I didn't much like the feeling. I walked to the entrance without a backwards glance. I wanted to leave. I wanted to go to my wife. My vengeance wasn't entirely satisfied, but it was the best I was going to get.

I passed our friends as I made my way out the building. Snake Charmer and Scalp Hunter stood up, and followed behind Dudley as we left.

"Where did they come from?" I asked Nick who was in front of me.

"They bailed us out of your house," Nick answered. "They've been following us ever since we entered the city, but they got a bit delayed on the mountain, dumbasses."

"We've been in the city for a few weeks now," Snake Charmer added. "We were finally sent back to help with the elimination of the undead population. Everything was as normal as it gets around here, until the Northeast entrance was attacked. Communications went down shortly after that. We made our way over there anyway. Obviously, we were too late to do anything, but we saw your Jeep's lights headed up the mountain, and we figured we might as well follow."

"I saw them coming down the road while we were on the roof," Dudley added. "I figured, I'd try and radio them, just in case they were the good guys."

"We heard you radioing in for Mr. Hardin plenty of times," Snake Charmer said. "We weren't sure if it was a trap or not. Good thing I recognized Nick; we weren't sure who we should attack."

"They pulled up in front of the bad guy's house, and let loose with some serious firepower," Nick said. The bad guys stopped shooting at us—the zombies got distracted by the new arrivals—so we made our way off the roof and hauled ass down the street. As soon as we were in the clear, they picked us up."

"Don't you boys normally travel in bigger teams?" I asked.

"We were reinforcements for another team that suffered some casualties," Scalp Hunter answered. "Unfortunately we…"

I turned around immediately. Everyone turned around immediately.

Max was standing behind us. He was holding Scalp Hunter's severed head in his hand.

"You think it's going to be that easy?" Max asked before throwing the head at me.

Then, he puffed up his chest, and arched his back before letting out the very same human-foghorn bellow we had heard before. The dead would soon be coming.

Snake Charmer screamed out for his fallen friend. Dudley and Nick began shooting at Max. Max began forcing his way towards us, despite the bullets peppering his body.

From across the street, I heard squealing tires followed by the cracking sounds of many machine guns. Max's Albanian Mafia friends had arrived in two stolen Jeeps.

I grabbed hold of Snake Charmer and I pulled him towards the Jeep I had used to get to the supermarket. Fortunately, it was parked between us and the Albanian Mafia trying to shoot us. I dove in with Snake Charmer. Nick grabbed onto Dudley, and both of them jumped in the seat. Somehow, despite their tangled bodies, Nick was still able to close the door behind him.

Max approached the window.

He was smiling.

His face and body were smeared with that weird gelatinous blood of his, but he didn't seem in pain.

Then the smile faded as I handed Nick the keys and he started the Jeep. Max tried the door. Nick had locked it. Max began to pound on the window. The Jeep rocked from the impact of his fists.

"Holy shit!" Nick exclaimed. "Who the fuck is this guy?"

"He's the former Guardian," I answered.

Nick tore off right as a mass of zombies flooded into the parking lot. I then understood why Snake Charmer wanted to leave so quickly; shamblers had followed them.

"Slow down," I ordered from the backseat. "I wanna see this asshole get eaten."

I was hoping to see the horde of shamblers tear Max to pieces. I wanted to see them tear him to pieces. I wasn't able to beat him but that didn't mean I wanted him to have a free pass. Dead was dead, and I wanted to see him die.

The zombies rushed towards him.

Max didn't move.

I think he was still smiling.

They approached him, and slowed down. They surrounded him. They sniffed at him. Then they lost interest, and started chasing after the Albanians who immediately stopped shooting at us, and fled the scene in their stolen vehicles.

"What the fuck?" Nick asked.

"I have no idea," I said.

Nick sped off. I'm not sure where he was headed. That wasn't really important at the moment. The only important thing was that we put some distance between Max, the horde of shamblers, and us.

We drove in silence for a while. Nick was driving, so we were all occasionally thrown around the vehicle as he went over curbs and bumped into abandoned cars. I was worried about Snake Charmer. The man had been close to Scalp Hunter. That was obvious from the first time I met them.

Still, he was a professional.

"Head Downtown," Snake Charmer advised. "The city has the highest concentration of the undead. They may not go after the former Guardian, but they'll go after his men. I doubt they'll follow us down there."

"Maybe not," Nick said, "but the shamblers will definitely come after us, along with Max's men."

"Do what he says," I added. "We have experience on our side."

The ride was uneventful, even with the occasional small group of zombies chasing after us. None of them warranted a bullet, not with Nick behind the wheel.

A block away from the city, a voice appeared in our ears.

"Headquarters contacting the General," the voice said. "Headquarters contacting the General. Come in Jaxon."

I tapped my earpiece.

"This is Jaxon," I answered. "Who's this?"

"Are you alive and well?" The voice asked.

"We're fine," I answered. "Now who is this? Where's Hardin?"

"Hardin has been injured," the voice answered. "There was an attack. I'm here to arrange your extraction."

"How many times do we need to attempt contact with you morons before you answer us?" Nick interrupted.

"I'm sorry, sir," the voice answered. "There was an attack. We established communication as soon as we could."

"Well, fuck you anyway!" Nick yelled.

"We'll be on the roof of the Abraham Chavez Theater," I said. "Pick us up there."

I'm not sure if you remember this or not, but the Abraham Chavez Theater is where I killed Max. I wanted to see if his body was still there. I was having a hard time believing he was somehow resurrected from the dead.

"*Wouldn't the zombies have picked his corpse clean?*"

That was certainly a possibility, but even if they had, I was still hoping to see some bones. Zombies don't normally eat bones. They seem much more interested in the red and bleeding parts.

We used the parking garage entrance. I borrowed a pistol from Snake Charmer. It was a Remington .45, a 1911 that had been customized for a silencer. Not a bad weapon at all, but a little bit much for plugging a zombie in the head.

He also didn't have a lot of ammo for it.

We didn't run into much opposition. A few zombies rushed out at us from between the cars but they were put down immediately. Snake Charmer's shooting was impressive. He hit the forehead on every shot. I had developed a bad case of double vision, so I didn't even bother trying to shoot. I left it to the others and conserved my ammo. Besides, I hadn't been shooting very well since I entered El Paso.

Silently, we walked into the theater.

The last time we were here, we left the place crawling with shamblers. There were certain to be a few around. A part of me wondered about Snake Charmer. The man was only human, but he was with us one hundred percent. A bite would be fatal to him, but he never seemed too concerned about that. The man followed us into danger like a consummate professional. He impressed me. If Georgie or Javie died from their wounds, we probably already had our next team member.

The thought of losing Georgie or Javie tore me up inside. They were my friends, my family. They had to be okay. Whatever power worked inside of me, also worked inside of them. They were stronger than Skie. They healed fast. Not as fast as me, but they still healed pretty fast. They had to be okay.

Skie.

I had one chance to avenge her, and I had failed. I had charged in like an idiotic ape, and I had lost. The Monster tore me apart like I was an amateur. He would have killed me if the team hadn't arrived when they did. I couldn't stop thinking about that. I couldn't believe that someone had beaten me so easily. It was all I thought about on our journey downtown. It kept circling around in my mind. The Monster had beaten me.

NO.

I couldn't think like that. I could beat him. I would have beaten him. My Ti-Lite was in my hand. It had worked for me before. I was ready to make my move. The opportunity never came, because reinforcements arrived. Forget my earlier thoughts. Forget how tired I was. Forget about the injuries I suffered. I could beat him. I could kill him. I needed another chance.

I wanted another chance.

Someone turned on a light in the hallway. I panicked at first, but nobody else did. It was one of us that had found the switch. Everyone was looking at me. I wasn't paying attention. I was lost in my own head with my stupid pride.

We made our way to the theater where Max and I had our battle.

The place hadn't been touched. It looked exactly the same: the little walkways made in the seating area and the chains hanging from the ceiling.

"Don't touch the chains," I warned.

I moved to where Max had fallen. I remembered it quite well. The carpet was heavily stained with his blood. There was no body. There were no bones. There were no remains at all. I sighed heavily. My head was pounding. I probably had a concussion from too many shots to the head.

"Well, that settles it," Dudley said. "Let's make our way to the roof now. We'll figure out how to beat this fucker later. We'll come back with the rest of the team. We'll take him out big time. "

"Yeah," I mumbled.

We left the theater area without a backwards glance. Somehow, Max was still alive. Somehow, he was different. He was bigger. He was stronger. Injuries had no lasting effects on him. I had made a grave mistake bringing everyone here. We were lucky to be alive. Scalp Hunter paid for my error with his life.

I should have planned. I should have known my enemy. I shouldn't have come when I wasn't in the right frame of mind.

I didn't want to leave. There was still some fight in me. Another round with the Monster was what I felt like doing. I had so much anger, and I was ready for another fight.

He went after my wife.

Out of all the cowardly things a person could do, I think that one tops the list. Skie was innocent. She wasn't a fighter. He went after my wife.

I could feel my busted lip pulling away from my teeth in a snarl. What the hell did I do wrong? A mistake was made somehow. I should have beaten him easily. Too many punches to the head, that's what messed me up. A little more blocking, a little more dodging, that's what I needed.

If I could get behind him, I'd be able to choke him out. Maybe even break his neck. Let's see the bastard walk around with a broken neck. My hands were swollen from punching him. I clenched them into fists anyway.

"Jax," Dudley asked. "You okay?"

"Yeah," I answered.

"Seems like you drifted off for a minute there," Dudley continued.

"I'm fine," I said. "Keep walking."

I had no idea where we were even going. I was only following the group. I know Nick mentioned something about banging a girl that used to work in the theater. Since he was leading the way, I assumed he knew a way to the roof without having to use the air ducts.

The hallway we had entered seemed a bit unfinished. The walls were white and rather flimsy looking. They weren't painted, and you could see the different sections of dry wall that had been tacked up. It was a long hallway but the lights were working when Dudley hit the switch. We could see a single wooden door at the far end.

"Obviously they've done some remodeling since I've been here," Nick said. "But I bet this hallway still leads to—"

"AAAAWWWWOOOOAAAA!"

We all froze, and looked back and forth at one another. Max had arrived. He was in the theater.

"We need to move," Snake Charmer said. "That guy will mow through all of us in this enclosed space."

"Speak for yourself," Nick grumbled. "I haven't taken him on yet."

"He's just attracted an army of the dead to back him up," Snake Charmer added. "You like those odds?"

"Not really," Nick said.

We picked up the pace. From outside the building we could hear the screams of the dead. From the inside of the building we could hear moans, screams, and bodies scraping against the walls.

"I can smell them," Dudley said. "There's got to be a bunch."

I never noticed it before, but the hallway didn't have the smell of rot. The air was stale but it was clean. That was all changing rapidly. I didn't even want to think about how many shamblers had entered the building.

When we drove up, we avoided streets that would put us out in the open. We stayed in alleys, kept our lights off, and didn't see any of the large hordes that populated the Downtown area. That didn't mean they weren't there. It only meant we were successful in our sneakiness.

The Monster didn't bother hiding himself. He had no need to fear the dead. Max had probably been doing his best to attract them since he entered the area. Judging by the current noise level and smell, he had been successful. Hordes of them must have been right around the block from where we entered the parking garage.

We needed to be long gone before they found their way to the roof.

Something seemed off when we reached the lone door.

"Wait," I said.

Nick pulled his hand away from the knob immediately.

Everyone was looking at me.

"What's beyond that door?" I asked.

"A concrete stairwell to the roof," Nick answered.

"I dunno," I said. "Something feels off."

"Maybe it's the beating you took," Nick said.

"Show some respect," Dudley snapped.

"Well, look at him," Nick said. "His face is all fucked up. He took some lumps. He might not be thinking clearly."

"Disrespect him one more time," Dudley shouted. "And I'll leave you here."

"I'm not disrespecting him," Nick said. "It's the truth. Jax is injured."

Dudley was about to argue.

"It's fine," I interrupted. "I am injured. I know I'm having problems focusing. Let's just go."

Nick opened the door.

It must have been a pretty solid-ass door. Because, for some reason, we were unable to hear the horde of shamblers rushing up the stairwell right beyond it. Or, perhaps, we were unable to hear them due to the noise level in general. I'm sure I've said it about a thousand times, but zombies are freakin' loud when they're chasing down their supper.

A zombie immediately attached itself to Nick. In response, Nick stumbled backwards in an attempt to throw it off. He ran straight into me, knocking me off my already unstable feet.

From the ground, I watched as Dudley and Snake Charmer attempted to close the door. It was too late for that, however; shamblers were already trying to push their way into the hallway.

Snake Charmer pulled a grenade from his vest. He lobbed it beyond the door. Dudley fell away as the explosion rocked the building. Snake Charmer was somehow unaffected by the blast. He was attempting to close the door.

I'm not sure if it was an arm or a leg, but something was jammed. Dudley tried to help him clear the jam but they weren't in synch. The door remained open.

I shot the shambler on top of Nick. Its brains splattered against the white dry wall. Damn, the .45 was overkill when it came to zombies.

"It almost bit me," Nick screamed. "Damn that was close. I could feel its fucking teeth through my sleeve."

"Relax," I said. "We're almost out of here."

The dead kept pushing against the door.

Eventually, Dudley and Snake Charmer abandoned their efforts. Instead, they backed away, and shot at the rushing horde. In the first moments of action, they were able to drop every single one of them at the doorway, but the horde was relentless. They climbed over the fallen bodies and shoved against each other. They kept pushing through the doorway until a wave of corpses finally flooded into the hallway.

Dudley and Snake Charmer remained calm. They kept up a backwards retreat, and continued firing. I yanked Nick to his feet.

"We need another way out of here," I shouted.

"I don't know another way to the roof," Nick said.

"All right," I said. "We'll take the air duct like we did last time. Help Dudley and Snake Charmer. I'll make sure the way behind us is clear."

Nick jumped into action. He lined up next to Dudley immediately and the three of them kept the approaching horde from overtaking us. Since I had only the pistol, and limited ammunition, I covered their backs.

The hallway was filling with smoke but I somehow managed to see the door we were headed towards. I saw it fly right off its hinges as if it had exploded. I also saw the large man standing beyond the doorway.

Max had arrived.

I looked back towards my friends. They were in retreat and preventing the mass of dead from overtaking us.

"Hold your position," I shouted. "I'll clear the way."

Everyone did as I asked. They stood their ground and they spent their ammo. I faced Max. Both of us walked down the long hallway towards each other. He had abandoned his shirt. His body was riddled with holes, and all the holes were seeping that thick, gelatinous blood of his.

I rolled my head on my shoulders in an effort to prepare myself. I had been given a second chance at revenge. I wasn't about to fail.

My eyes focused on the glowing disk above his heart. It was pulsing out a black light. It would be my target. He had to have a weakness. I should have gone after the disk before.

I unloaded the 1911 on him. Only one of my shots hit the disk. Max began to laugh as the disk shorted out. Then he ripped the damn thing out of his chest.

"If that was a weakness," Max said, "don't you think I would have covered it up?"

I rushed him.

At the last second, I dove at his waist in another attempt to take him down. I failed just as I had failed before. He merely sprawled backwards slightly, and elbowed my spine once again.

I dropped to my knees and came up with a beautiful uppercut. Max absorbed the punch and smiled at me. Then, he picked me straight up by my vest.

I felt helpless.

I never feel helpless.

I struck out with both hands and clapped his ears. He dropped me instantly. I landed on my feet and began to punch him.

I punched him, and punched him, and punched him. I battered his head until he dropped to his knees. I stomped his face. I punched his neck. The skin underneath my gloves began to split around the knuckles due to the amount of strikes I had given him.

I was gasping for air.

I began to scream out my rage as I beat the man to death.

Max began to laugh.

He was playing with me.

I hadn't left a mark on him.

He easily got to his feet. I backed a step or two out of his way. I wasn't finished. I wasn't discouraged. I attacked him again as soon as we locked eyes. He blocked my punches. He absorbed my kicks.

Then he fought back.

His first punch was to the side of my head. The impact wobbled me. His second attack came at my left knee. I felt something pop, and I dropped to the floor.

"I have you now, Guardian," Max said. "Your team can't hold back the tide forever. Soon they will be overcome, but not before I break you. Not before I beat you down. Not before I snatch the life out of you."

With those words, the beating began. I tried my best. I tried to fight back. I tried to hurt him but he rained his fists upon me. He battered my head and body. Each of his punches took years off my life. He hit that hard.

I found myself on the ground, pinned between the unfinished wall and his flying fists. I was trapped. The punches kept coming. I tried to put my arms over my head in order to protect myself but it was too late. The damage was already done. Also, with both of my arms occupied, I couldn't get off the floor.

Blood was flowing freely from my shattered nose due to one of the many punches that got past my feeble defense. I could feel it running past my mouth. I saw large drops splatter on the floor as I sank lower and lower. It was hard to see. My eyes were almost swollen shut. My left leg didn't seem to be functioning below the knee. It was hanging awkwardly to the side.

I needed just a brief moment. I waited. I took the punishment.

Finally, Max stood back to gloat.

"Are you still alive?" Max asked.

I sprang at him using only my right leg to push off with. In my hand was my Ti-Lite. I drove the blade straight towards his heart with one hand. The other hand curled around the back of his head so I could stare into his eyes as I turned the tide of the fight.

My knife sunk less than an inch before it met resistance. I pulled it out and stabbed him again. The blade bent in my hands. It didn't puncture. There was something under his skin that protected his vital organs.

He swatted me to the floor.

The useless knife fell from my hand. I felt his heavy boot step down on my fingers. I felt the bones snap and pop. I screamed out when he began to grind his heel. Through the pain, I found focus. I reached into my utility belt.

Max seized me by the vest once more, and when he lifted me up I slammed a handful of Georgie's boom balls into his face. The small explosions destroyed my good hand. I wasn't missing any fingers but the end result was horrible to look at. My fingers were splayed in a variety of directions, and none of them wanted to work.

Max dropped me, took a step back and rubbed his face. I wanted to move. I wanted to press the attack, but my leg was shot. My hands were shattered and I could barely see. I tried anyway. I forced myself to roll onto my knees. I put my arm against the wall and tried to lever myself to my feet.

I was about halfway up when Max shattered my hip with a kick. I dropped back to the floor limply. For the first time I noticed the hallway. There were blood smears all over the walls, and none of them were from Max. I had a sudden realization that I wasn't going to survive.

"I respect you, Guardian," Max said. "I need you to know that. Never before have I fought a man or monster with more determination than you. Your body has been defeated but your spirit still rages against me."

"Fuck you," I gurgled through a mouth full of blood. In my delirium I found the gurgle just a bit funny, and I snorted out a laugh. That was a big mistake. Blood gushed out of my nose, and my eyes instantly swelled shut. The last image I had was of Max's nose. Georgie's boom balls had really fucked it up.

I felt myself lifted into the air. I felt myself slammed onto the floor. I felt the movement but I was powerless to do anything. My body was a ragdoll being tossed around by a giant. I tried to lift my head. I didn't want to quit. I didn't want to give up. I wanted to fight. I wanted to live just long enough to kill the bastard.

There was a final impact on the back of my head. After that, I don't remember anything.

Chapter 6

IVANA

My second meeting with Ivana is at the same bar as our last meeting. She showed up late again and seemed to have been drinking prior to our meeting. Still, she greeted me with a warm hug, and then navigated to the cushioned bench opposite mine.

"I'm curious as to why you're late?"

I had to get my drink on.

"You had to get your drink on before meeting with me?"

What can I say? I'm shy. Plus, I had to get permission to talk about the things we're gonna talk about.

"I thought everyone already had permission to speak with me?"

We do. I just wanted to make sure Miriam was okay with it.

"Miriam?"

Yes. This is sort of her part of the story. I wanted to make sure she was okay with me talking about it.

"Was she?"

Yes.

"Okay then. So Jaxon, Dudley, and Nick left you after the phone call from Mr. Hardin. Is that correct?"

Yes, that's correct.

"Did you have any knowledge of their activities after they left?"

I found out everything later.

"Can you tell me what happened after they left?"

Miriam did her thing.

"Can you elaborate?"

Miriam was concerned about Skie. She wanted to see her. The staff wouldn't let her. Miriam was very upset.

"I need to get past these idiots," Miriam said. "I'm running out of time and so is Skie."

She kept repeating this over and over.

By the time we were finally allowed to see her, she'd been given her own private room on the fifth floor of the hospital. There were nurses in the room when we entered. They were checking Skie's vital signs and attaching various wires and tubes.

Poor Skie was so pale.

Miriam told the nurses to leave. As the last one passed me, she whispered in my ear.

"She's not suffering," The nurse said.

I started crying. I stood in the doorway and sobbed. Skie was my friend. She was the sweetest person I knew. She didn't deserve to die.

Miriam went straight to her side the second the nurses were out of the room. She pulled these strange little instruments out of her purse and began looking into Skie's ear. She felt her pulse. She used another sort of strange funnel thing to listen to her heart.

"Her soul is preparing to depart," Miriam announced. "I need to work fast."

In my mind, it was over. We had lost a member of our family that was never supposed to be in danger. I didn't believe any of us would ever recover. I knew Jaxon wouldn't. I worried about him terribly.

Miriam spent hours arranging candles around the room. She drew strange symbols on the two windows. She poured an ugly smelling powder by the doorway. She also began to draw more strange symbols on Skie's body.

I kept staring at the red stained bandage above her heart.

When Miriam was done with her symbols and candles, she pulled a small bowl out of her purse. She put many different ingredients into the bowl. I couldn't tell you what a single one of them was, but I do believe I saw a human finger. She eventually set the ingredients on fire. A harsh green smoke filled the room.

Miriam began to chant as the sun came up. She stood before Skie and mumbled the same strange words over and over. For some reason, the nurses never returned.

I guess it was right before dusk when Miriam finally came up for a breath. She looked tired, but she was still buzzing around the room with all the energy of a child.

She pulled out her strange instruments once again and checked on Skie's vitals. Finally, she found a seat, and sat back with a small smile.

"I did it," Miriam said. "I bound her soul to this room. For a few moments there I almost lost her. I was lucky."

"What are you saying?" I asked.

"As long as her body remains in this room," Miriam answered. "Her soul will not be allowed to cross over."

"What good does that do us?" I asked. "Will she wake up?"

"Only if her husband comes for her," Miriam said. "It needs to be something huge in order for her soul to force its way back into her body. She needs Jaxon to walk through that door for her."

"Is her body dead?" I asked.

"Not really," Miriam answered, "but it's not alive either. It's sort of frozen in-between. Not really a big deal, especially with all those machines she's attached to. We keep her body in this state and we make sure she doesn't leave this room. When Jaxon returns, all will be well."

Obviously, I had my doubts. I wanted to believe things would turn out all right. Miriam had never been wrong before. It all just sounded a bit weird to me.

"I'm going to go and check on Georgie and Javie," I told Miriam.

In response, Miriam reached back into her purse and pulled out a waxy looking blob. She grabbed my arm and drew a few symbols onto my skin.

"What's that for?" I asked.

"That's so you can find your way back," Miriam answered.

I left the room and made my way to the nurse's desk. I asked about my friends. They gave me directions to their room. It was one floor up. The clean air of the hospital was a relief after the strange smells coming from Miriam's bowl.

I rode the elevator alone. I heard Javie and Georgie arguing the second the doors opened. I didn't need to ask for further directions. I followed the sounds of bickering.

"What are you doing out of bed?" A nurse was asking Javie, who stood before her completely healed, and wearing only a towel.

"I've already told you like five times," Javie answered. "For whatever reason, you seem to have a problem hearing me."

"Get me to the shower," Georgie interrupted.

"No," the nurse answered. "You need to stay in bed. You've both been seriously injured—"

"I'm in pain, you daffy bitch!" Georgie screamed. "Get out of the way."

I jumped in immediately.

"The water will heal them," I said. "You need to let him go to the shower."

"That's ridiculous," the nurse said.

"I know what it sounds like, but there are forces that can't always be explained," I continued. "Take a look at Javie. How bad was he when he arrived?"

"He could die if he leaves the bed," the nurse said.

"He won't," I said. "He'll start to heal as soon as he gets into the water."

"I'm going to call security," the nurse said when Javie and I went to Georgie and began to lift him from the bed.

"I'm a Regulator," Javie said angrily. "Your security team will be the least impressive thing I ever beat the shit out of."

"Relax, Javie," I said. "She doesn't understand. She's only trying to protect him."

"Well, he could die with all this protection," Javie said. "Those sons-a-bitches operated on us, did you know that? Why didn't they just leave us in the grass?"

"It was a cluster fuck," I answered. "Everything went bad."

We pulled Georgie from his bed to the shower stall. We positioned him so the water would pour directly upon his stitched-up wound.

"How is Skie?" Georgie asked.

My heart went out to him. He was barely conscious but I could see the worry in his face.

"We'll talk later," I answered.

"Answer me now!" Georgie shouted with a strength that shocked me.

I hesitated.

"How is she?" Javie asked.

"Not good," I cried. "I think we lost her."

"Aww no," Georgie groaned. "No. No. No. No. No. I had one job. One fucking job and I screwed it up. No. No. No. No. No. It's my fault. It's all my fault. I should have protected her."

He began to cry. His sobs shook his entire body. I knew it caused him pain. I saw it in his face. Still, he sobbed harder and harder. Javie, confronted with his own grief, backed away from the shower and dropped on top of the toilet with his face in his hands.

Georgie began to thrash in the stall. His stitches popped and his wound opened up. The blood began to flow once again. I tried to talk to him. I tried to calm him down. I turned on the water in an effort to heal up the damage he was causing himself. It didn't work.

In order to calm him down, I ended up jumping on top of Georgie. The water poured onto my clothes as I held him close.

"You did your best," I said. "It's not your fault. Georgie. It's not your fault. No one blames you."

"I blame me," Georgie said. "I blame me. Poor Skie, what are we going to do? What are we going to do?"

"I don't know," I answered. "I wish I knew, but I don't. I wish I could do something but I can't. I lost my friend, and I don't know what to do!"

"Where is he?" Georgie asked in abrupt subject change.

"Out there, somewhere," I answered. "He's looking for the people responsible."

"Dear God," Georgie whispered before he passed out. "He'll scorch the entire planet to find them."

I agreed with him. I wouldn't want to be on the receiving end of Jaxon's anger. I pitied anyone that got in his way. There was something scary in my friend's eyes when he left the hospital. Many people were going to die before the rage in his heart would subside—if it ever subsided.

I left Georgie in Javie's care. I wanted to see what Miriam was up to. I wanted to see something that would make me feel the world hadn't stopped spinning. On the way back to the room, my cell phone rang. I answered it immediately in the hopes that it was Jaxon.

It wasn't. It was Mr. Hardin. Apparently Miriam wasn't answering her phone, so Mr. Hardin gave me a message. He said two words. I had no idea what they meant, but I was supposed to repeat them to Miriam.

Getting back to the room proved rather difficult for me. My vision began to blur the moment I entered the correct hallway and I couldn't quite find the right door. My memory also began to fail me, and for a brief moment, I actually forgot why I was in the hospital in the first place.

Finally, my hand found the latch to the door and I entered the room. Miriam was quietly sleeping in a chair next to Skie's bed. I touched her arm gently and her eyes snapped open.

"Mr. Hardin just called me," I said.

"He's probably worried about Skie," Miriam answered. "I bet the magic drained my phone battery. Did you tell him all would be well when Jaxon returns?"

"He didn't ask about Skie," I said. "He told me to tell you 'Black Dawn.' What does that mean?"

Miriam was suddenly on her feet.

"Oh dear," Miriam said. "Has it gotten so bad so soon?"

"I don't know what's going on," I said.

I was becoming frightened.

"The government has turned against us," Miriam said. "Mr. Hardin has had to abandon his post, and he's advising us to vanish."

"What the hell?" I asked. "Why would we need to go into hiding?"

"Because our lives are in danger," Miriam said. "Go to the window and keep an eye out. I need to think. I need to make sure they don't remove Skie's body. If they take her away, it will all be lost."

I was panicking. There's no other way to say it. I took a post at the window, and I kept a look out while Miriam paced up and down the small room.

An hour later, the black SUVs pulled up in front of the hospital. There were four of them, and they were filled with men in black suits. I didn't recognize any of them until the final man put his feet upon the pavement.

"Oh my God," I said. "Miriam, I think they're here."

Miriam stopped dead in her tracks.

"What did you see?" She asked.

"Four black SUVs pulled into the parking lot," I said.

"Did you see a bunch of men in black suits?" Miriam asked.

"Yes," I answered.

"Those are the Men in Black," Miriam said.

"Like the movie?" I asked.

"Hardly," Miriam answered. "The Men in Black are assassins. Their job is to eliminate anyone that might reveal certain secrets the government would rather keep quiet. Mr. Hardin never uses them. He doesn't approve of their methods."

"Major Cross was with them," I blurted out.

"We have very little time," Miriam said. "Listen to me very carefully. I can keep you safe. I can get us both out of this, but I need you to follow my every command. Can you do that?"

I shook my head up and down.

Miriam jumped into action. She reached into her purse and came out with a thick piece of chalk.

"No matter what happens," Miriam said as she began to draw a circle around me. "Do not leave this circle until I tell you it's safe."

"Okay," I said.

"We need to flee," Miriam continued. "We need to vanish until Mr. Hardin can sort things out, but before we do so, I need to make sure Skie will remain safe in my absence. In order to provide her with that sort of protection, I must summon something powerful enough to protect her."

Miriam then threw the contents of her bowl onto the floor and began adding new ingredients.

When she was finished, she drew a silver dagger from her purse and opened up her wrist. She allowed her blood to flow into the bowl.

"Miriam!" I shouted when I saw the amount of blood she was losing.

I was about to leave the circle. I was that worried about her.

"KEEP YOUR WORD," Miriam shouted in a voice that wasn't quite normal.

"Your wrist," I said.

"Dark magic requires an offering," Miriam said. "The one I call requires even more."

"Okay," I said. "I won't leave the circle."

Miriam nodded in my direction.

"Paper dolls with jagged edges," Miriam shouted in the air. "Screaming girls and bleeding boys. I call you forth, Sally. I call you from the darkness. I call you from the mist of your land. Paper dolls with jagged edges. Screaming girls and bleeding boys. Send forth the one that cuts. Send forth the lover of blood and pain. I am Miriam. I am worthy of your attention."

The room grew instantly cold. Dampness filled the air and it chilled me to the bone. Miriam's voice grew louder and louder.

"Paper dolls with jagged edges," Miriam said. "Screaming girls and bleeding boys. A cut a slash, it's all the same. I call you forth. I call by name. Sally Scissorcut, heed my call. I need you now. I am Miriam. I am worthy of your attention."

I heard pounding but I couldn't tell you from where it was coming. I even heard scratching from inside the walls. Both of these sounds became louder and louder. Miriam's bowl erupted in a black flame. I jumped. Goosebumps spread across my arms and I broke out in a cold sweat.

The noises got louder and louder. I then began to hear moaning and screaming as well. The sounds were horrible and they were coming from all around me. I put my hands over my ears in an attempt to keep them out of my head. It proved to be a futile attempt, and I collapsed upon my knees.

The horrible sounds stopped abruptly.

"Prepare yourself," Miriam said.

The room was deathly quiet. I couldn't even hear the normal sounds of a busy hospital in the background. The cold, however, remained.

Minutes ticked upon the clock. Still, I heard nothing. It was as if the world beyond the hospital room ceased to exist.

Finally, I heard the clicking sound of heels upon a tile floor.

It was coming from somewhere beyond the door to Skie's room and it was getting closer and closer.

"She's coming," Miriam whispered. "Do not leave the circle; she'll kill you if you do."

No problem there. I had no intentions of leaving the damn circle.

The clicking heels came to a sudden stop outside the room. I can't tell you how frightened I was when I heard a knock upon our door.

"Don't answer it," I said.

Miriam ignored me and went to the door. She gently placed her hand upon the handle, and she slowly opened the door. The hallway was empty.

I breathed a heavy sigh of relief. Then I noticed we were no longer alone in the room.

"Hello, Miriam," a young woman said.

"Hello, Sally," Miriam replied. "I need your help."

Sally was drop dead gorgeous. I have no other words to describe her. She was that freakin' hot. Her chestnut brown hair was long with a slight curl, and it fell out of her red leather bandanna past her shoulders. He eyes were a sultry dark color I couldn't place. Her skin had a slight tan. She dressed in red leather heels, and slashed up red leather pants. Her red top revealed her soft arms, and the tops of her perfect breasts.

I was in love, but I wasn't stupid enough to leave the circle. There was something cold about her, something dangerous. She radiated sexuality, but she also radiated something else, something dark.

"Do you now?" Sally asked. "The last time you asked for my help, you cursed me afterwards. I'm very angry with you, Miriam. I thought we were friends."

"I have done wrong by you," Miriam said. "I come to make amends. What would you have from me?"

Sally ignored her. Instead, she cast her gaze upon me.

"You have a friend with you," Sally said as she walked towards me.

"Yes," Miriam said. "She's under my protection."

"That doesn't impress me, Miriam," Sally said. "Come out of the circle, pretty girl. Let's show Miriam a few new tricks."

"Miriam," I said. "What do I do?"

"Stay where you are," Miriam answered. "She can't hurt you."

"Oh, but I could," Sally said. "I could scratch right through that circle given enough time. Don't you worry about that."

"This isn't what I want," Miriam said. "I need your help."

Sally finally turned and looked at her.

"Really?" Sally asked. "You come to me for help once again?"

"It isn't for me," Miriam said. "The girl on the bed needs your protection."

Sally cast her hungry gaze towards Skie, as if she was just now noticing her for the first time.

"A sleeping beauty," Sally said, and walked towards her.

I took a slight protective step forward inside the circle.

Sally's head snapped immediately towards me.

"Do it," Sally said. "Cross the circle."

"Ivana!" Miriam shouted. "Control yourself."

"You're no fun, Miriam," Sally pouted.

"I ask you to not harm the three of us," Miriam said. "I beg for your protection."

Sally approached the bed, and examined Skie.

"This one is dead," Sally said. "Wait a minute. Did you anchor her soul to this room?"

"I did," Miriam said. "I beg you to protect her body. Let no one take it away. Force them to care for her in my absence. Forbid them from ending her life."

"You cast a very powerful spell," Sally said. "I can sense it working all around me. What happened to her?"

"She was shot," I answered.

"Was she?" Sally asked. "Let me see."

She ran her hand down Skie's face. She gently touched the tube going down her throat, and she slowly pulled the covers away from the bandage over her heart.

"Miriam," I said. "Do something."

"Quiet," Miriam said.

Sally looked at me, and smiled sensually. Then she ripped the bandage away from Skie's wound.

"Oh," Sally said, "how ugly: a blemish on the skin of a sleeping beauty. Can I have her Miriam?"

"You may not," Miriam said. "You can help her, though."

"I don't like the wound," Sally said. "It's way too ugly. A beautiful girl should be free of such ugliness."

Suddenly, Sally dug her hands into Skie's skin around the bullet wound and ripped free a chunk of wet and bleeding flesh. She then threw the wet mess upon the floor, where it bubbled and steamed, and eventually turned to ash.

I screamed but both Miriam and Sally ignored me.

"That's so much better," Sally said as she looked at the flawless skin where the injury used to be.

"Will you help me?" Miriam asked.

"The cost will be high," Sally purred as she stroked Skie's hair.

"You can't have the girl in the circle," Miriam said.

"I don't really want her," Sally said. "She's been had by too many."

I wanted to argue. I really did. I mean, this creature was essentially calling me a whore, but on the flip side, her lack of interest was probably a good thing.

"Name your price then," Miriam said.

"Two sacrifices a month," Sally said. "For as long as my protection lasts."

"Every full moon?" Miriam asked.

"I like the sound of that," Sally said. "If you fail, I'll leave her."

"I understand," Miriam said. "Ivana, you can now leave the circle."

"Are you sure?" I asked.

Sally looked at me and smiled.

"I'm sure," Miriam said. "Our deal has been struck. Sally wants her offerings."

I stepped away from the circle. Sally's smile became a sneer. I was terrified of her. I knew what she could do to me. Don't ask me how, but I knew she could rip me apart with very little effort. Sally knew what I was thinking. She enjoyed my fear.

"What are we going to do now?" I asked.

Sally evidently found our conversation boring. She turned her back to us and began softly stroking Skie's hair.

"We need to leave," Miriam answered. "Major Crass and the Men in Black are coming for us."

"Are you sure?" I asked, motioning with my eyes towards Skie and Sally.

"She's safe," Miriam said. "Sally will protect her as long as I feed her sacrifices every month."

"Oh, Miriam," Sally interrupted. "Make sure those sacrifices are human."

"I understand," Miriam said.

"We'll see," Sally said with a wink in my direction.

There was a commotion coming from down the hallway. I heard a nurse scream out, and then I heard the sounds of rustling bodies.

"I'm going to pay in advance," Miriam told a grinning Sally. "Ivana, you are under my protection. Despite what you see, you'll have nothing to fear from me."

"What's going on?" I asked. "Why are they coming for us?"

I was worried about Georgie and Javie. I never expected I would be in danger.

"They are tying up all the loose ends," Miriam said. "Now be strong and brave."

Miriam stepped into the hallway.

I was alone with Sally.

I looked back towards her. I was hoping she'd offer some sort of help but she was gone. I was alone in the room with Skie's body.

I went to the door. At the end of the hallway were four of the Men in Black. Miriam walked right towards them.

"This hallway is off limits to the likes of you," Miriam said when she was about four feet away. "Turn back now and keep your lives."

One of the men pulled a silenced pistol and shot her four times in the chest. Steam poured out of the wounds, and Miriam crumpled to the ground.

I screamed.

The men all looked in my direction.

"How could you?" I shouted. "She's a harmless old lady!"

They didn't seem to care. The four of them stepped over her corpse and made their way towards me. I was alone. I had lost another friend. I wasn't a fighter. I wasn't a warrior. I wasn't much of anything. Yet, I was going to fight. I was going to protect Skie's body.

I was going to die.

I stepped out into the hallway.

I scowled at the Men in Black. Miriam rose to her feet behind them. Well, it wasn't quite Miriam, but it used to be Miriam. The figure that rose from the ground was different. The softness had left her. The warmth had vanished. The plumpness of her body was gone. She was dangerously thin. Her face had sharpened. Her nose had grown. Her grey hair had turned as black as coal, and more importantly, her skin had taken on a greenish hue.

She cackled out loud as she dusted herself off.

The Men in Black turned to face her.

Miriam stood before them, cackling.

Her shoulders were hunched and her head hung low. Her clothes were loose on her body as if they were rags, but her eyes were alive with a fury I'd never seen before.

"Did you think it would be so easy?" Miriam asked in an unholy voice. "Did you think you could kill one of the twelve so easily?"

The Men in Black did not reply. Their faces remained impassive. Yet all of them had drawn their weapons. All of them began to fire on the witch. Yes, that is what she was. My sweet loving Miriam, had transformed herself into something different, and even though she frightened me, I screamed out when they tried to harm her.

I was wasting my worry meter.

The witch simply froze the bullets in the air with a wave of her hand. Then she took a mighty breath before doubling over forward. I heard a loud cracking sound come from her body, but she proved herself unharmed when she stood back up. Her throat inflated like a bullfrog's. Except, unlike a natural creature, there was something moving and wriggling under her skin, I thought I was losing my mind. I backed up against the nearest wall and slid to my butt.

Then Miriam roared.

A million locusts flew out of her mouth. They swarmed the room. I could barely see through their tiny bodies, but I heard the screams. I knew what was happening. The bugs were devouring the Men in Black.

I fell to my side. I covered my face and head, but the locusts had no interest in me. Their attention was only upon the Men in Black.

A figure approached me through the cloud of bugs. A cold hand with fingers like tree branches grabbed me by the arm, and yanked me to my feet.

"Time to go," the witch laughed as she pulled me behind her.

"Where are we going?" I asked.

"Down," the witch answered. "Down, down, and down. I seek the place where the cold ones sleep their eternal slumber. An army against an army; so shall it be."

I had no idea what she was talking about, but I knew the four Men in Black were not alone. I had seen the amount of people that exited the SUVs. I had a pretty good idea where one army was coming from. I just didn't know how Miriam was planning to raise up an army in our defense.

We were in an elevator when I finally managed to face my friend and look her in the eyes.

"Miriam," I said. "I'm scared. What are we doing?"

The witch laughed.

"We're killing them all," she answered. "Every single one of them. We accept no traitors in this business. We bury our dead. We fight the fight. We continue the war, but we will never suffer a traitor. I mean to set an example."

"What about Javie and Georgie," I asked. "They are in danger. They need us."

"They are touched by the Guardian's power," Miriam said. "Mere mortals cannot hope to survive an encounter with those that are touched by the Guardian's power. They will be fine. Your friends have no idea what they are truly capable of doing. It's about time they found out. Meanwhile, we will see about earning the respect of our enemies."

"You're scaring me," I said. "Miriam, you're really scaring me."

Finally, I saw a flicker of humanity in her green-hued face.

"Forgive me, my dear," Miriam said. "I used the darkest of magic, and have merely revealed my true nature. As frightening as my appearance may have become, I am old and out of practice. Saving Skie took too much out of me. I'm tired. I need help. Just pray that I am strong enough to control what I unleash."

I was quiet after her explanation. I had nothing left to say. I was along for the ride. In truth, I was merely a human girl, surrounded by terrifying things I really didn't understand.

The elevator stopped.

We were in the basement. Miriam dragged me down yet another hallway. I noticed for the first time that her fingernails had turned black. Her head, with its shaggy mane of black hair darted left and right as she searched for what she was looking for.

Finally, she found it.

"Ah," Miriam said. "Here we are."

She dragged me into the morgue. The fluorescent lights began to flicker as soon as she entered. The walls were covered in sickly green tiles. The floor was a grey concrete with drain holes spaced every ten feet or so. I could see the stainless steel doors of a walk-in freezer at the far end, but I paid it no attention. No, my attention was focused on what filled the large, cold room. Tables upon tables upon tables, and on top of each rectangular slab, rested a body from the awards banquet. I wished they had been covered with sheets like the movies always depicted, but they weren't. I recognized many of the faces.

"Did we lose so many?" I asked.

"Save your tears, Ivana," Miriam said. "The dead are at rest. The shells are empty."

"What about Skie?" I asked. "We left her."

"Skie is the safest person in the world right now," Miriam cackled. "Your fears are misplaced."

"Who was that girl you summoned?" I demanded. "Was she a...demon?"

"Sally Scissorcut is close enough to a demon but not quite," Miriam answered. "She has the power of a demon. Yet, she isn't necessarily evil."

"Could have fooled me," I said.

"That wasn't evil, child," Miriam said. "That was simply Sally being angry with me."

"Why is she angry with you?" I asked.

Miriam stopped looking at all the many bodies in the room and stared at me.

"You ask difficult questions," Miriam said. "You'll hate me if I answer."

"Do it anyway," I said bravely.

"I was a young girl once," Miriam said. "If you can believe it. My abilities were just beginning to develop. In a moment of great despair after my grandmother died, I accidentally called upon an entity; a very powerful entity. Instead of killing me outright, this entity took pity on me. She became my friend. She taught me how to use my abilities."

"How did you get your abilities?" I asked.

"I am descended from a long line of powerful witches," Miriam said. "Gypsies are full of witches but none of them were nearly as powerful as I was. None of them had been taught by Sally. I quickly surpassed my mother and grandmother. I brought down fortune on my entire family. I was loved. I was admired. I had Sally to thank for all of it."

"Okay," I said.

"She was my friend," Miriam said. "I confided in her. I loved her. As I grew into a young woman, she was there for me. On my wedding day, I felt her watching over me. When my first child was born, I named her Sally. I was happy. I was truly happy. I loved my daughter. She was beautiful. She was vibrant. She was the sweetest little girl; she never had a bad thing to say about anyone."

"Did Sally hurt your daughter?" I asked.

"Of course not," Miriam answered. "But youth doesn't last forever. My daughter eventually grew into a young woman. She was very beautiful. You remind me of her a little bit. So does Skie. Skie has her beauty. You have her attitude."

"What happened to her?" I asked.

"A traveling caravan came to visit our village one summer," Miriam said. "They weren't familiar to my clan, but people of Gypsy ancestry tend to welcome others of their kind. My daughter was old enough to venture out on her own. One night she met a boy from this traveling caravan. I thought nothing of it. She was a good girl. I didn't have to worry about her. She wanted to go to the lake with him, and I granted her request immediately. Sally appeared before me the moment she left. Sally was angry. She didn't trust the boy. There was a foul air about him in her opinion."

Things were beginning to fall into place. I didn't like what I was hearing, but regardless of that, I needed to hear it.

"What happened when she went to the lake with the boy?" I asked.

"He raped her," Miriam answered. "After that, he slit her throat. When my daughter never came home, I searched for her. When I couldn't find her, I called upon Sally. Sally found her immediately.

She brought my daughter's lifeless body to me. I flew into a rage. The plates and glasses in my cottage flew from the shelves and shattered against the floor in my anger."

"You had a right to be angry," I said.

"It wasn't only anger," Miriam said. "I wanted revenge. Sally stood before me as I made my way to the door. She asked what I planned on doing. I told her that I planned on killing the one responsible. Sally had another idea. Instead of taking my revenge out upon the one responsible, she advised me to take my revenge out upon the entire family. Let all of them suffer. Sally could show me how to do it."

I couldn't believe what I was hearing.

"What did you do Miriam?" I asked.

"I cursed the family," Miriam said. "I cursed them with the most powerful curse Sally could teach me. It was a curse so horrible, it has claimed thousands upon thousands of lives. It was a curse that I have regretted ever since. Once it started…once the first zombie rose up and spread its vileness, I tried to stop it. Yet, this type of curse cannot be stopped. I begged Sally to put an end to it but she refused. She wanted the boy's entire family to suffer. She loved my daughter. She loved her so much that even when I cursed her name, even when I cast her away from me, she would not reverse the curse."

"You were the one that started everything weren't you?" I asked. "You created the curse that took over El Paso."

"Clara," Miriam said. "That's her name. She is a descendant of the family I cursed. Her pain is because of me. The people of El Paso have suffered because I cast a curse I couldn't control. In the end, it was a Guardian that came and put an end to things. It was a Guardian that righted my wrongs. Ever since then, I have aided the Guardians."

"How sad," I said as I watched the tears fall from Miriam's eyes.

"I lost my husband," Miriam said. "I lost everyone I loved in that initial outbreak. I never spoke to Sally again until today."

"I'm sorry," I said stupidly. "I can't imagine what you're going through, but what the hell are we doing here?"

"My dear," Miriam said as she stroked my chin with her black nails. "I'm about to make the very same mistake once again. Let's just hope I've learned a few things."

Miriam began to cackle.

I backed away from her as fast as I could. I was afraid. I have no shame in admitting my fear. I never try to be tough. If something scares the crap out of me, I have no problems admitting it, and Miriam was scaring the crap out of me.

She started chanting. She started waving her arms around. Her voice was shrill, and horrible to hear. From pockets in her clothes she drew powders that she flung on the many victims from Jaxon's banquet party. She slashed her wrist again. A drop of blood was placed upon the foreheads of seven corpses.

Then Miriam looked at me.

"Hold my hand," she said. "If you let go, they will eat you."

Despite my fear, I ran forward and grasped her cold hand. The seven corpses began to shake on their slabs. They began to twist and moan.

I started to cry.

"Miriam," I said. "What have you done?"

"Fear not, child," Miriam laughed. "I have better control now."

The zombies rose off their cold metal slabs. Their steps were shaky at first but they soon grew accustomed to their new condition. Immediately, they focused on Miriam and me. I panicked. I tried to run but Miriam held me fast.

"Heed my words, girl," Miriam shouted. "Heed my commands."

I stayed where I was. The zombies approached. They looked us over. They smelled us from toe to head but Miriam didn't move an inch. I cried when the zombie closest to me began to smell my neck. I cringed but Miriam held onto me.

"I called you forth for a reason," Miriam shouted. "I called you forth to strike down my enemies.

Go now and do your duty."

The dead obeyed.

They ran out of the room. Miriam and I followed them. The elevator doors opened at the end of the hallway. Six of the Men in Black stepped forth, and the shamblers fell upon them instantly.

Miriam watched as the dead devoured the living. She smiled when they were finished.

"Let's go collect Georgie and Javie," Miriam said.

She then led me to the elevator. The zombies came with us. I can't even begin to tell how it felt to be trapped in an elevator with seven naked living corpses. I was terrified. If it wasn't for the steel-like grasp of Miriam's black nailed hand, I'm sure I would have freaked out and been devoured.

I could feel their eyes upon me. I could feel their hunger. Miriam's control over them was tenuous at best. I could see the beads of sweat on her brow from the strain.

"Are you okay?" I asked her.

"You will most certainly know if I'm not," the witch smiled.

The ride seemed to last an eternity. When the elevator doors finally opened, my salvation wasn't waiting beyond. The hallway had turned into a warzone. I immediately saw the bodies of several nurses, and many Men in Black.

I made an effort to run to my friends. Miriam nearly yanked my arm out of the socket.

"What did I tell you?" Miriam asked.

"But Javie and Georgie…" I started.

"They are Regulators," Miriam said. "Perhaps you are incapable of understanding what that means."

The smell of blood excited the zombies. They charged out of the elevators. They ran down the hallway and rounded the corner. I heard the shrieks of the Men in Black, but that didn't stop me from pulling Miriam behind me as I ran to Javie and Georgie's room.

When I came to the doorway, I had to step over corpses.

"Javie," I called out. "Don't shoot. It's Ivana and Miriam."

"Get in," Georgie said. "Get in and get down. These fuckers are trying to kill us."

"They're the Men in Black," I said.

"Like in the movie?" Georgie asked.

"Do I need to answer that?" I asked.

"Why are they trying to kill us?" Javie interrupted.

By this time, I had stepped into the room. I saw seven bodies. The boys had been busy. They were using firearms stolen from the corpses at their feet. This, by the way, is one of the many mental images I'll never get out of my head. In a million years, I could never picture Javie and Georgie capable of such violence. It was a shock to see what they could unleash. It was a shock to see the blood on their hands.

The world around me had certainly changed. Out of the entire group, those two were the least likely to ever hurt anyone. The Guardian power had made them all killers.

"It's a long story," I answered. "Miriam will explain everything later. Right now, we need to get out of here."

The moans of the dead began to echo up and down the hallway outside the room.

"Oh fuck me," Georgie said. "Are those zombies? Has there been an outbreak here?"

"Get behind us," Javie ordered. "Where's Miriam?"

"This is Miriam," I said.

Javie did a double take. I saw his mouth working as he attempted to figure out why her appearance had so drastically changed.

"We won't be cowering in a corner, boy," Miriam laughed. "Now is the time to flee. Our allies will soon become our enemies."

"You need to trust us," I added. "Don't let go of my hand. No matter what, don't let go of my hand."

It took it took a bit more convincing than that, but eventually Javie grabbed my hand and Georgie grabbed his. We left the room. As soon as we entered the hallway, three zombies rushed us.

Georgie raised his gun. Miriam told him to be still. The zombies smelled all of us but Miriam. Then they passed us by. We slowly continued on our way. Several corpses began following us. Georgie kept his weapon in a ready position. I gripped Javie's hand tighter.

"Don't let go," I said. "If you do they'll kill you."

Javie nodded that he understood. Yet, I could tell he'd rather rely on a weapon than holding my hand. At the elevator, the dead crowded around us. Miriam allowed five of them to enter.

"How are you doing this?" Georgie asked.

"Magic," Miriam answered.

"What about all the innocent people that get in their way?" Georgie asked.

"They will be fine if I can retain control," Miriam answered. "They are currently only attracted to those near me, and those threatening me."

"What happens if you lose control?" Javie asked. "How bad will it be?"

"How bad was El Paso?" Miriam countered.

As we rode the elevator to the first floor, Miriam began to sweat profusely. Her chest also began to bulge and shudder. A large lump began growing underneath her ribcage. It looked as if she were about to explode. I could hear her bones pop in an effort to make room for it.

I tried to talk to her. I tried to ask her if she was okay, but she ignored my questions and began to chant quietly under her breath.

The elevator doors opened once again.

The world erupted around us. Gunshots blazed from all corners of the room. Georgie returned fire. The zombies ran out to devour our attackers.

Miriam strode forward without a care in the world. A bullet hit my wrist. My hand was knocked away from Miriam's grasp. I had lost her protection but I still had the Regulators.

I cried out, and clutched my bleeding wrist. Javie took a position over me. He returned fire on the Men in Black, but they were everywhere, and they had been waiting for us. The only reason we weren't already dead were the zombies. Our attackers weren't expecting to be charged by the living dead.

"Zombie," Georgie shouted to Javie.

Javie immediately spun around and put a bullet hole in the head of the shambler headed our way.

"Looks like we're back on the menu," Javie announced.

After long moments of scrambling for cover, I noticed the zombies were multiplying. In addition to attacking us. I also saw several groups of newly risen, half-eaten corpses bearing down on our attackers.

Javie and Georgie eventually dragged me behind a heavy, overturned table. I could see the exit to the building. It was so close, but it might as well have been miles away with all the bullets flying towards us.

I realized we were in the lobby. I could see the corpses of the dead security team. I could also see that they weren't re-animating. The reception desk was covered in blood. I knew almost nothing about the Men in Black, but I knew I hated them. They killed innocent people.

I looked for Miriam. She was standing in the middle of the room. The bulge in her chest had gotten even bigger. It had also begun to press against the bottom of her throat. I was hoping she was building up another swarm of locusts, but something told me I was wrong.

A bullet hit her shoulder. She was twisted violently to the left from the impact. Another hit her in the stomach. She bent over, and then she leapt to the ceiling. With her back pressed against the tiled panels, she began to rapidly crawl towards the men shooting her.

Once she was above them, she dropped from the ceiling and landed in the middle of their group. I saw her flashing claws. I saw streaks of blood fly into the air. The group was dead before they could even scream.

Miriam leapt to the ceiling once again. She began her disjointed crawl to the next group of men barring our way to the exit. I didn't want to watch but I couldn't help myself.

I felt something pulling on my leg.

A zombie had grabbed a hold of my ankle. He was attempting to pull me closer so he could bite into my calf. I screamed out and began to kick my legs. I couldn't break free. Javie and Georgie had no idea I was being attacked. They were concentrating on shooting down our enemies, both living and dead.

"Georgie!" I screamed. "Georgie!"

Suddenly, a bare foot connected with the zombie's head, and it released its grip. Georgie then proceeded to stomp down on its head until the skull was mush beneath his feet.

"*I'm sorry. I need to ask a question.*"

Feel free.

"*Why wasn't Georgie wearing any shoes?*"

Oh, I'm sorry. I should have told you. Both Georgie and Javie were wearing their hospital gowns. Their clothes had been cut off of them when they first got to the hospital. Their butts were bare to the entire world.

"You stay next to me," Georgie said as he killed another shambler that had gotten too close.

I had lost track of Miriam, but I could hear screams coming from the other side of the room. My world was on fire. I had flashbacks of the banquet hall. I had already lost Skie. Who was I going to lose next?

Suddenly, everything became quiet.

I could hear Miriam cackling, but I couldn't see her. Through the large wall of front windows, I saw a running form. For a moment, I worried that it was a zombie, but it was Major Crass. He had survived.

I crawled to the window and I watched as he ran across the parking lot. More SUVs were pouring in to greet him.

"We need to go!" I shouted. "Reinforcements are arriving now!"

"Alive or dead?" Javie asked.

"Alive," I said.

I turned around. Miriam was standing behind me. The look in her eyes was frightening. She had killed many human beings and she seemed to be enjoying herself. She offered me her bloody hand. For a moment I hesitated. Then I took it, and she pulled me up.

I could see corpses attempting to rise to their feet through all the gunfire smoke and clutter of broken chairs and tables. It looked as if the newly fallen had begun to turn.

Miriam held a hand up to us as she watched the dead find their feet. She went to them with open arms, as the three of us stared on in shock.

"Come to me, my children," Miriam said. "Don't be shy. Open your eyes, and gather around. I shall lead you to food. I shall stop the hunger in your bellies."

Behind us, a small army of men gathered outside the windows and door. They were getting ready to storm the lobby. I even saw the smug look on Major Crass's face as he shouted out orders.

"Fuck me," Georgie said. "This is bad."

"Man," Javie said. "I wish Jaxon was here."

Inside the lobby, the dead continued to rise. They massed behind Miriam in an army of their own. I heard Major Crass shout out the order to enter the lobby.

Miriam spun around and smiled at him through the glass. Then she clapped her hands together, and the glass windows exploded in a storm of cutting pain for the rushing Men in Black.

Immediately behind the flying glass were the dead. A rushing, hungry, gang of them, and Major Crass once again found himself in danger.

"Let's move," Georgie shouted.

All of us, Miriam included, ran for our lives into the parking lot. Once we hit pavement, we veered to the right, in the direction of the emergency entrance. An ambulance was waiting there. We got inside; the keys were in the ignition. Georgie got behind the wheel, and peeled out of the parking lot as Javie bandaged up my wrist.

A block away from the hospital, Miriam began to convulse.

"Miriam!" I shouted. "Miriam!"

I tried to hold her down. I tried to prevent her from hurting herself. Her convulsions were so violent, I found myself thrown away from her. Javie helped me lay her down on the floor of the ambulance, but it didn't seem to help. Neither of us could hold her down.

"What do we do?" I asked.

"No clue," Javie said.

Miriam went still. I was worried that we had lost her. Perhaps she had pushed herself too far, used too much magic.

Georgie drove on through the woods. I could tell we were gaining altitude, but I had no idea where we were. I held her close as Georgie drove us away from danger.

Javie tried to check her pulse.

Miriam sat upright.

The lump in her chest had grown horribly and pushed against her throat.

"Stop the car," Miriam choked out.

Georgie immediately pulled over to the side of the winding road. Miriam got out of the rear of the vehicle and walked across the street. There was a clearing on the hillside. From the clearing we could see the front of the hospital. Gunshots and screams echoed towards us across the night sky.

Miriam watched the chaos unfold calmly.

"Have we started another outbreak?" I asked.

"No," Miriam answered. "It will all be over soon."

Then she doubled over in pain. I heard the sound of retching coming from deep inside her. It was an ugly sound, a gagging, choking, cough that wouldn't end. Each retch was louder. It was inhuman. I covered my ears but couldn't block out those horrible noises.

"Stop," I cried out. "Miriam, please. Stop!"

Eventually, she did. She stopped making her horrible noises. She stood up straight once again. For a brief moment, the two of us locked eyes, and then she turned back towards the hospital, and roared.

If I thought the gagging and choking noises were loud, they had nothing on her roar. The roar was horrible. It sounded like some gigantic beast of war was bellowing over its territory.

I once again had no idea what was going on.

Black smoke violently burst from her mouth. It expelled itself into the sky and formed an ugly cloud of sharp edges and frightening shapes I had never seen before. The smoke poured from her mouth until the lump in Miriam's throat shrank away.

By that time, the cloud was immense. I watched as it moved away from us toward the hospital.

"What did you do?" I asked.

"I'm ending it," Miriam answered.

"That cloud?" I asked. "It will stop the zombies?"

"Indeed it will," Miriam said. "I'm very sorry to have frightened you, my dear. I used the darkest magic to save our lives. It seldom looks pretty. Please forgive me. I had no choice."

"Why can't you do the same thing to El Paso?" I asked.

"I've tried many times," Miriam answered. "Over the years, that particular curse has grown in strength. There is no stopping it, and there is no cure for the ones that are cursed."

We saw a car approaching the hospital. It was easy to spot. It was the only thing headed in that direction. The vehicle halted right before the parking lot.

"We need to warn people," I said. "They could get killed."

The cloud meanwhile had settled itself over the hospital. Black drops of tar-like rain began to fall, and when the drops hit the ground they instantly turned into a dark vapor.

"No need," Miriam said. "It's already over."

Indeed, I could no longer see the vague outlines of violence in the distance. I could no longer hear the screams of the dead and suffering.

The driver of the lone car finally got out. Georgie recognized him instantly.

"That's Father Monarez," Georgie said. "What's he doing there?"

"He's probably worried about everyone," I said.

"I don't think so," Georgie said. "He's carrying his chainsaw. I'm going to call him."

I didn't argue. I just handed him my cell phone. Georgie had excellent eyesight. All I saw was a small blob. There was no reason for Father Monarez to endanger himself. Miriam had the situation under control; despite the fact that she was scaring the shit out of me, I still had faith in her. Georgie would be able to send the father home, and keep him from getting involved in our mess.

Father Monarez didn't seem very cooperative when he picked up the phone. From what I could follow of the conversation, he was asking about our location so he could meet up with us.

Georgie gave him directions. To be honest, I really didn't know the man that well. I know he had fought alongside the Regulators. Then again, so have a lot of people. Anyway, the boys trusted him. They saw him as a warrior; a bit nerdy, but still a warrior.

We dozed around the ambulance after that. Each of us was tired. The evening had certainly taken its toll, but we woke up instantly as we saw the approaching headlights. Father Monarez pulled his car up behind our ambulance. He was out the door and running towards us almost before the vehicle came to a stop.

"I spoke with Mr. Hardin," Father Monarez said. "I'm aware of the situation. I'm supposed to get the lot of you into hiding."

"You realize the Government is trying to kill us?" I asked.

"The Government may have turned on you my dear," Father Monarez smiled, "but the church has not. We will protect you. We will keep you safe until everything gets sorted out. First however, we must go to the local airport. The rest of your team is in danger."

Chapter 7

NICK

I met with Nick in the standard meeting room. I knew better than to meet him anywhere else. He arrived on time, and in full gear. His boyish face looked as young as ever but his large frame had slimmed down a bit. It seemed as if the man had been exercising.

He smiled as soon as he saw me. I smiled back and we shook hands.

You're looking good, girl.

"Thank you."

When are we going to go out on a date? I'll take you anywhere you wanna go. What do you think?

"I heard you had a girlfriend?"

Who told you that?

"Uh-huh, let's just stick with the interview, how about that?"

Let's just make out one time and see what happens. I bet you'll like it.

"Nah, let's just do the interview."

Nick sighed heavily, and motioned me to begin with the questions. I had to laugh at his attempt. He obviously expected me to turn him down, nevertheless he felt obligated to try.

"You've been informed about the new subject matter, correct?"

Yup, shitty times.

"When I spoke with Jaxon, he took me all the way to the Abraham Chavez Theater. I believe it was you, Dudley, Snake Charmer, and Jaxon. The four of you were headed toward the stairwell in order to gain access to the roof when you were pinned between a mass of zombies and the Monster."

Sounds accurate.

"Can you take things from there?"

Sure. We were in a bad, bad position. The shamblers had invaded the freakin' stairwell before we'd gotten to it. Dudley, Snake Charmer, and I, kept them from advancing upon us as we retreated. That's when the Monster entered the hallway behind us.

"Why didn't any of the three of you engage the Monster along with Jaxon?"

We couldn't. I mean, Dudley tried several times, but each time he tried to break away we started getting overwhelmed. Like I said, shitty times. Jaxon was in no shape to go and fight that guy. He'd taken too much damage the first time they mixed things up.

"Then why'd he do it?"

Because he's the General, that's what he does. By rights, someone else should have disengaged from the group and tried to deal with the Monster, but try telling that to Jaxon. I personally think he wanted to be the one to kill the fucker. He wasn't exactly thinking straight at the time. I can't blame him for that. I don't want to even begin to imagine what he was going through. I've been married a couple times. If one of my wives had been shot, well, there'd be hell to pay.

"Were you able to see the fight?"

I caught glimpses of it. It was a slaughter. Dudley was the one that really watched it, though, he kept getting distracted. Snake and I had to save his ass more than a few times. The zombies would grab a hold of him, and we'd have to yank them off.

I can't blame him either. His uncle was being beaten to death right behind us. We needed to do something. Unfortunately, Jaxon was limp by the time an opening presented itself. Snake threw the last two of his grenades into the stairwell and suddenly the tide of dead stopped flowing.

"I'll buy us some time," Snake Charmer said, as he took out the remainder of the shamblers still in the hallway with us.

Dudley was already rushing towards the Monster. He fired on that freak at point blank range. The Monster merely reached out and slapped the barrel of the weapon to the side. Then he swatted Dudley away like he was an annoying bug.

He was back to stomping on Jaxon's body when I tried to tackle him. Putting all of my weight behind me barely made him move an inch backwards. The next thing I knew, he had me by the collar of my utility vest, and was lifting me into the air. The dude was so big: he made me look small.

That's when Snake entered the picture.

He opened up on the Monster from the side. I was dropped roughly, as the Monster made an attempt to grab a hold of Snake. I struck out with my fire axe the second he let me go. The fire axe cleaved only a little bit into his back before getting stuck.

I didn't realize Snake was just a distraction until glass was breaking and flames were spreading. Dudley had thrown a Molotov cocktail, and he nailed the Monster right in the face. The bastard screamed as the flames spread all over his body.

It was the first time he'd been hurt.

Dudley immediately ran to Jaxon as the former Guardian thrashed and screamed away from us down the hallway. I picked up my fire axe from the ground and started running after him when Snake grabbed me by the arm.

"There's no time for that," Snake Charmer shouted. "We need to boogie."

I ran to Dudley and threw Jaxon's limp form over my shoulder. The three of us then ran to the stairwell. We had problems. We had big, big problems.

Snake Charmer's grenades didn't finish off the mass of zombies in the stairwell. It only knocked them back a bit. After Snake had dealt with the shamblers in the hallway, he must have gone into the stairwell and set up a bunch of those black disks with the lasers.

There were piles of human shaped pieces below us, obviously the remains of the dead after charging through the lasers. The mass of zombies however, kept surging upwards. Eventually the lasers would burn out. We needed to move fast.

"How many of the disk lasers did Snake Charmer activate?"

Fifteen or twenty; he must have run a bit down the stairs and started slapping them on the walls before the zombies recovered from the grenade explosion. That was a gutsy move on his part. He could have easily gotten eaten, but it was help we desperately needed. Without him doing that, we would have been overrun.

"Why didn't everyone use the air ducts to gain access to the roof, like they did the last time they were at the Abraham Chavez Theater?"

My way should have been easier and quicker. Besides, have you seen the size of me? I'm not sure I would even fit through an air duct.

So anyway, we hauled ass up the stairs. Jaxon isn't exactly a small guy, so I was beginning to have problems catching my breath by the time we got to the last flight of stairs.

"How many flights of stairs were there?"

Three or four, I forget.

I had to stifle a laugh at that point.

Oh, I see how you are. Well, trust me. Jaxon was out. I wasn't even positive he was alive. So, I was carrying a big, heavy sack of potatoes up the stairs. I wasn't falling behind, and I still managed to hit the door to the roof with enough force to knock it off its hinges.

Of course, I had no choice but to keep moving. Right after we made it up one flight of stairs, the zombies broke through the disks.

"Nice job," Dudley cried out as he tried to fit the door back on the frame.

I wasn't listening to him. I was headed to the waiting helicopter. I ducked low and approached. There were four soldiers inside the chopper in addition to a pilot and co-pilot. The soldiers took Jaxon away from me, and I immediately spun back around to fire on the zombies that had already made it to the roof.

Dudley was down. The door was on top of him. Three zombies were on top of the door. Snake Charmer was firing into the doorway in an attempt to keep any more zombies from getting to the roof.

"I'll grab Dudley," I shouted.

Snake gave me a slight nod and continued firing.

I smacked the dead off Dudley and helped him to his feet. He was dazed. When the shamblers charged the door, he must have taken a hit on the head. He put his arm around me and we made our way to the helicopter. As I passed Snake, I tapped him on the shoulder and he retreated with us, never once taking his eyes off the doorway.

As soon as we were in the helicopter, we took to the air. I watched as the dead swarmed the roof. Some of them even fell off in their eagerness to jump up and grab the rising chopper.

After one last look at the Hell we had so narrowly avoided, I turned my attention back to Jaxon. One of the soldiers was working on his gunshot wound, and administering basic first aid. The other three soldiers were pointing their guns at Snake, Dudley, and me.

"What the fuck?" I asked.

"You assholes have a good time shooting our friends?" A soldier asked.

I didn't recognize any of them. They weren't our usual pilots.

"I take it you jack wagons are more of those government agents?" Dudley asked. "Shouldn't you be wearing black suits?"

"Who we are isn't important," the soldier replied. "Just know that you're expendable, and if you make any sudden moves, we'll kill you."

We were disarmed. They moved efficiently for such big guys. I waited for an opportunity to attack but they gave me none.

"So you fuckers attacked Mr. Hardin," Dudley said. "You took over his base, and then you went after us."

The men didn't answer.

"I bet you had something to do with the shooting at the awards ceremony," Dudley continued.

"Nope," the most talkative of the soldiers answered. "We're just the cleanup crew."

The other soldiers laughed. I fumed. I was stuck, and I didn't like it. On the floor of the chopper, Jax began to moan. I was relieved he was alive but he was too messed up to be of any use in our present situation.

"I don't get how this guy is still alive," the medic soldier said.

"He's the Guardian," the talkative soldier laughed. "Don't you know anything?"

All of the soldiers began to laugh at that point. It pissed me off. I hate being laughed at. I hated for Jaxon to be laughed at. I began to shake, I was so angry. Snake Charmer put a hand on my arm to calm me down.

"He needs water to heal," Dudley said.

"We don't want him to heal," the talkative soldier said. "We just want him to survive."

After that, nobody said a word.

The second we left the airspace above El Paso, it was obvious where we were headed. It made sense; the rest of their unit was probably still in the area.

"I hope you assholes put some men on those fences," I said. "When the real bad guys got in they killed everyone guarding the gates."

"I think we have things under control, big guy," the talkative soldier said. "Thanks for the advice, though."

The fuckers began to laugh again.

Eventually we landed in Ruidoso. The airport was empty of everyone except those black-suited government jerks. There was a small army of them around the helicopter the minute we touched the ground.

All of us left the helicopter at gunpoint.

Jaxon was taken away in a black van. Dudley took a small step towards him when they started carrying him off, and they shot him in the leg. Snake and I couldn't go to his aid for fear of being shot as well.

"How the hell did all of them survive?" A middle aged, geeky-looking man asked as he shoved his way through the black suits.

"No clue," the talkative soldier replied. "Your man must have failed his objective."

"Is my man still alive?" The geek asked with a pissed off expression.

"No clue, sir," the talkative soldier answered. "We never saw him."

"Major Crass," Dudley said as he tried to rise to his feet. "You motherfucker."

Major Crass looked him up and down.

"Well," Major Crass said, "things aren't a total bust. We have the Guardian, and we have two of his men. It won't be long before we get the other two."

"What do you want to do with them, sir," the talkative soldier asked.

"Kill them," Major Crass answered. "All we need is the Guardian, and when you find the other two, kill them as well. In fact, put out a kill order on anyone connected to the Regulators. That includes Hardin, Miriam, and that lesbian girl."

"What the fuck?" I asked to nobody in particular.

Snake Charmer was stoic. Dudley was still rolling around on the ground and clutching his leg. I, on the other hand, had made up my mind. I was a Regulator. I was a warrior. I wasn't going down without a fight.

I grabbed the closest man and wrapped my arm around his neck. The circle around us instantly raised their weapons. I was about to take a bullet in the back, but suddenly I felt Snake's back pressing against mine. He had managed to grab a man as well.

After that we were sort of stuck.

"What are you waiting for?" Major Crass asked his men.

"I'll break his neck!" I shouted.

They didn't seem to care. Fortunately for us, right before the bullets started to fly, a bunch of the black-suited men burst into flames. The circle around us broke apart. Snake dropped his captive and went immediately to Dudley, helping him up.

Gunfire came out of the darkness. Our enemies were forced to retreat. Snake, Dudley, and I, grabbed our confiscated weapons and ran in the direction of the gunfire. I had no idea who was firing, but they weren't trying to kill us, so I thought it was a safe bet to head that way.

Dudley caught another round before we cleared the lights of the airstrip. I heard him cry out. Snake Charmer dropped to the ground next to him, and placed his own body over Dudley's.

"We have a man down," I shouted into the darkness.

Shapes appeared. I saw Georgie step out of the dark woods. I saw him shooting down the men that were trying to kill us. Javie came next. They flanked us and provided an opportunity to retreat.

As soon as we stepped away from the lights and entered the woods, Ivana ran towards Dudley. She had bottles of water and began pouring them on his wounds. Miriam didn't look right. She scared the crap out of me. There was something evil in her distorted features. Also, her damn hands were on fire.

"What the fuck is going on?" I asked.

No one paid me any attention. I watched as scary Miriam walked out of the woods. She went to the edges of the lights and began motioning with her hands. I looked back towards the airstrip; I saw a great ball of fire that seemed to be following her commands.

"Wow," I said. "Didn't know you had it in you."

I had always heard that Miriam was a witch. That was nothing new to me. However, I had never seen her do anything even remotely witch-like. Seeing her there with her features all distorted and her pale green skin, it was nice to know she was on our side.

The government assholes eventually had enough. Every time they tried to return fire, Miriam would nail them with that great big ball of fire, and if it wasn't Miriam, it was Georgie or Javie shooting them.

They finally fled back towards the airport.

"Jaxon," Dudley said. "They took Jaxon."

All of us stood in silence and watched our enemy retreat. I wish we could have done something. I wish we could have chased after Jaxon to rescue him but we had no idea where they had taken him.

"We need to get out of here," Georgie said.

Dudley tried to argue. He wanted to go after Jaxon. I didn't blame him. Each and every one of us would have gone after our leader if only we had known where to go. Instead, we dragged Dudley behind us and made our way into the woods.

After a short hike, we came to a dirt road. We followed the road for about a mile until we got to a waiting car. Father Monarez was behind the wheel.

"Where's the General?" he asked.

"They got him," I answered.

No one said a word as we drove away.

We left Ruidoso. There were no longer any roadblocks. In fact, nobody even seemed to be looking for us. Miriam had fallen asleep next to me. Her features seemed to be relaxing as she slept. She was beginning to resemble the old lady everybody knew and loved.

Some hours later, in some old and forgotten town that had just a few stores and a single gas station, we pulled off onto yet another dirt road. We followed this road for about two hours, and eventually came to an old, rundown church in the middle of the desert.

Mr. Hardin was waiting for us by the front door. Behind him were a few priests, and about ten soldiers.

"You better start talking!" I shouted, as I got out of the car. "We tried to radio you about a thousand times. If you have a problem picking up on your end, how about I surgically attach the radio to your face?"

"I was attacked," Mr. Hardin said. "Most of the people in our base were killed. I never got your radio transmissions because I was on the run."

"Well," I said. "That sucks."

"Dudley needs to finish healing," Ivana interrupted.

"We have tubs of water waiting, just in case," Mr. Hardin said.

The priests came forward and helped Dudley into the church.

"Is anyone else injured?" Mr. Hardin asked.

"They took Jaxon," I said. "What's going on?"

"We'll talk soon," Mr. Hardin said. "After Dudley has recovered."

It took Dudley a long time to heal. While he was healing up, everyone traded information so that we'd all be on the same page when the meeting began. The sun was coming up when Dudley finally joined us. Everything looks different in the light of day. In this case, anger gave way to hopelessness. Every one of us looked defeated.

"We need to find my uncle," Dudley said.

"Yes," Mr. Hardin answered. "We do."

Mr. Hardin led us behind the church to what appeared to be a couple of old wooden doors that looked like they would lead to a dirty cellar. He placed his hand upon a flat rock five feet away from them, and the doors slid open with the hiss of technology.

We went down the metal stairs to a state of the art control room. Beyond the control room were bedrooms, showers, and a living space.

"Get used to this place," Mr. Hardin announced. "This will be your home for the next few weeks, because all of us are in danger. The worst has happened. Our very own government has turned against us."

"Why have they done that?" Dudley asked.

"We've been framed," Mr. Hardin answered. "Before I was forced to flee, I was able to discover some of the truth. Major Cross has framed us for an attempt on the President's life."

"How the shit did he do that?" I asked. "They weren't even after the President. Skie was their target. The President wasn't even there when the attack on the awards ceremony began."

"He wasn't there because Major Cross called him away," Mr. Hardin answered. "My sources tell me that he planted evidence against us. Evidence showing that we snuck a large group of criminal Albanians into the country for the purpose of assassinating the President."

"How is that even believable?" Ivana asked with a quiver in her voice.

"It's believable because Major Cross has fabricated a significant amount of evidence that points to its authenticity," Mr. Hardin answered. "Major Cross was very clever. They went after Skie, and gave us a formidable enemy in the President."

"Why would we want to kill the President?" I asked.

"I have been arguing rather aggressively with the President against the use of nuclear weapons on El Paso," Mr. Hardin said. "I believe we've all been painted as extremists, willing to kill certain officials that do not agree with our opinions."

"Have there been any other attacks aside from the banquet hall?" Dudley asked.

"Apparently, a number of officials and military advisors that share the President's views have been eliminated within the past forty-eight hours," Mr. Hardin said with a sigh. "Things look very bad for us right now, gentlemen."

"Why have the Men in Black gotten involved?" Miriam asked.

"I can only speculate," Mr. Hardin answered. "The Regulators represent the hope of the nation. In the eyes of the public, they are the force that keeps the outbreak from spreading outside of El Paso. If Major Cross kills the Regulators off quietly, he can keep their deaths a secret. As far as the world would know, the Regulators are hard at work fighting zombies, and the citizens of this country continue to feel safe."

"That's why the checkpoints have all been taken down," I said. "That's why our faces and names haven't been posted all over the news. Major Cross wants to kill us off quietly. He wants everyone to think we're still doing our thing. Eventually, if he ever figures out a way to end the zombie outbreak, he'll probably release some story about how the entire team died in the line of duty."

"I agree," Georgie said. "Major Cross looks like a hero because he uncovered us traitors, and saved the President's life. Meanwhile, we all get killed off quietly so that the world thinks we're still out there protecting them. This is some fucked up shit."

"Major Cross brought Max back to life somehow," Dudley added. "He had him waiting for us in El Paso. Headquarters was attacked in an effort to kill off Mr. Hardin, and these so called Men in Black fuckers were sent to the hospital to take out everyone else. Wow, he really wanted all of us dead."

"Let me interrupt, and see if I understand this correctly."

Go ahead.

"Major Cross wants his revenge. So, he teams up with a resurrected former Guardian. He plots an assassination attempt on the General's wife. He then masks that assassination attempt on Skie's life as an attack upon the President, planned by Mr. Hardin and the Regulators?"

You got it.

"What about witnesses? People saw you fighting the Albanians. They saw you defending them?"

There weren't many witnesses. A lot of people were killed at that banquet hall. It was, by all accounts, a massacre and the ones that survived weren't exactly paying attention to who was shooting whom. They were just trying to survive. In the end, it looked just like a botched assassination attempt. Hell, they even thought we turned on the Albanians, like that was all a part of our plan. Let them come in and do the dirty work, and then take them out so we look like heroes that failed to save the

President, but still managed to rescue everyone else.

"But Major Cross never intended to kill the President?"

Nope. He wanted the President on his side. So, he comes in, and has the President removed from the banquet hall, like some kind of hero. Immediately after he pulls him out of there, and shows him a bunch of bogus evidence about us, the attack on the banquet hall happens. Pretty convincing if you ask me. After that, Major Cross immediately goes after Mr. Hardin and attacks his base, because he needs to make sure Mr. Hardin never gets a chance to talk.

"Major Cross also knew that Jaxon would track down the person responsible for shooting his wife and go after them."

Exactly, and Jax, Dudley, and I, were supposed to die in El Paso, and the second the Monster failed to kill Jaxon, in came the backup plan with the fake soldiers sent to rescue us.

"His plan sounds perfect."

It does, doesn't it?

"Then what went wrong? He failed on all sides. All the Regulators survived; Mr. Hardin survived. The plan went to hell."

Did the plan go to hell? I'm not sure it did. The asshole had Jaxon and the rest of us secretly branded as traitors. If we poked our heads out of the burrow, we were going to get a bullet in the brainpan courtesy of the Men in Black.

"But everyone survived. All of you were supposed to be dead. How did all of you survive?"

Luck. I don't know what else to say. Mr. Hardin somehow got a warning that bad things were about to go down. He was ready when Major Cross's people came for him. Dudley, Jax, and I, survived El Paso, but we might not have if Snake Charmer hadn't turned up. The Men in Black attacked the hospital. They should have been successful, but no one expected Miriam to be such a badass. Maybe they underestimated us. Maybe it was just luck. Who can say?

"The Men in Black were the only people trying to kill you? Are they really deadly enough to be the only ones assigned to that task?"

I wondered the exact same thing. I mean, how many had we already mowed over? They didn't impress me much at all. Eventually, I found out they were secret keepers, which was a nice way of saying they killed anyone that attempted to release information they didn't want released.

It was Dudley who finally asked the question, though.

"Before you became a part of the Regulators," Mr. Hardin answered, "did you ever hear about zombies, or vampires, or anything else that shouldn't exist? They make a habit out of killing journalists and threatening family members."

"That sounds pretty dangerous," I said. "There go any attempts on our part to take things public."

"That might be a good thing," Georgie said. "We don't have every law enforcement agency in the country hunting us down. We'll be able to operate without a lot of interference and clear our name."

"I think you're underestimating the situation, Georgie," Mr. Hardin said. "The Men in Black have been issued orders to kill all of us on sight. As we speak, they are tracking your relatives, your friends, and any other known sources you might turn to."

"You think they could beat us?" I asked.

"You'll never even see them coming," Mr. Hardin answered. "There's only one way to play this out. All of you need to stay in hiding while I go to Albania. I have connections there. Perhaps I can find a way to clear our names."

"Why don't we go with you?" I asked.

"Your faces are too famous," Mr. Hardin answered. "I'd never be able to operate the way I need to operate with you boys with me."

"What about Jaxon?" Dudley asked.

"I don't know, Dudley," Mr. Hardin answered. "I'm not sure why Major Cross took him alive. It certainly wasn't a part of his original plan. I don't even want to hazard a guess about his current intentions, but I think we can all be sure those intentions aren't going to be anything good."

Dudley said nothing. Then again, what could he say? We were screwed. We couldn't move left, and we couldn't move right. Major Cross had assumed Mr. Hardin's job. If we went after him directly we'd have to fight our way through the military, and killing soldiers wouldn't make a great case for our innocence. We had zero options left to us. Mr. Hardin going to Albania in an attempt to clear our names seemed like a long shot as well, but it was all we had left.

"What types of evidence did Major Crass have against you?"

We had no idea at the time, but we eventually found out that he had everything from cell phone recordings all the way to photographs and videos. All things that could be faked with the right equipment, but under those circumstances, nobody was questioning anything.

"Do you think Major Crass told anyone about Max?"

Hell no. Max was connected straight to the Albanians. Major Crass couldn't be a part of that mess. The three of us running to El Paso for revenge probably looked like we were trying to regroup with our Albanian buddies and plan out our next steps.

"So what did you do after Mr. Hardin left?"

We waited.

I think we stayed in that location for about a month. After that, Father Monarez took us to Detroit. The church had places set up for us all over the country. We had to move every few months because the Men in Black were always right behind us.

I don't know how they managed to track us down, but they just kept coming. It was frustrating. In the first six months alone, we had about five gunfights with them.

"Wait a minute. In the first six months alone? How long were you on the run?"

We were in hiding for a year and a half.

"Oh my God, I had no idea."

That's kind of the point, isn't it? Everyone thought we were all in El Paso doing our thing, but nope; we were hiding the entire time. Georgie flirted with a girl at a gas station once during a transfer to another safe location. The next day she turned up dead. The Men in Black were probably worried he was passing information to her somehow. I still don't know how they even knew he talked to her. I guess they probably saw his mug on a security camera or something.

"A year and six months after the attack on the awards ceremony is about the same time Jaxon was taken to a hospital in Ruidoso. Supposedly he was injured in El Paso. I always thought it was odd that they sent him to Ruidoso for medical attention but very little information was ever released about the incident."

You're jumping ahead.

"Am I?"

Yes. Jaxon was indeed taken to the hospital in Ruidoso. He was indeed very injured but he didn't receive his injuries in El Paso.

"Where did he receive his injuries?"

I'll get to that, but first, let me tell you what it was like to be in hiding for a year and a half. I'll skip through the boring day-to-day repetitiveness. I know that's not what you want to hear, but there are other things you need to know. Things that will maybe give you a better idea of what we were dealing with when things finally came to a close.

"I'm listening."

It was rough. It was really rough. Mind you, Father Monarez took us to some pretty nice places. We weren't roughing it by any means, but we had no contact with our family members. We couldn't risk them being killed. We rarely received news from Mr. Hardin, and when we did, it wasn't anything good. Life for us became very tedious, sprinkled with occasional bits of paranoia over being discovered.

Week after week went by at a snail's pace. All of us were ready to fight. We were eager to get back into the game, but the game was over. Our lives were an endless road of boredom. We hoped for the best, but the light at the end of the tunnel grew dimmer with each long day.

At some point, the Men in Black realized Mr. Hardin wasn't with us. So, Snake Charmer left to go meet up with him and his small group of soldiers in order to provide protection. Father Monarez, Miriam, Dudley, Ivana, Georgie, Javie, and I were the only ones left.

Father Monarez was the one that held everything together. He's the one that kept us going. That man never gives up. He never gets defeated. He's a very strong man. The church believed in destroying monsters. Father Monarez believed in us. Therefore, we continued to receive the aid of the church.

I think all of us were pretty worried the church would eventually get tired of hiding us, but Father Monarez is pretty well connected. Their support never wavered.

I think we were in Florida when things turned ugly. It was probably about six months after we went on the run. It was a nice place, if I remember correctly. At least it was on the inside. On the outside, it was just a rusted metal door in the middle of a swamp. I got out of bed sometime in the afternoon. My back was killing me and I was trying to stretch it out.

Dudley started screaming.

Everyone came running. He was in the bathroom. We all got to the door at the same time. Apparently Dudley was shaving, and had somehow nicked his face. It was a pretty decent cut but nothing to get concerned about.

"It's just a cut," Georgie said. "It's not that bad."

Dudley ignored him, and started to rub water on the wound.

"Dudley," Georgie said. "You need to calm down buddy. It'll go away, just pour water on it."

That got Dudley's attention.

"I've been pouring water on it!" Dudley shouted. "I keep washing it out. It's still bleeding. It won't stop bleeding."

I couldn't figure out what his problem was. I was more concerned with my aching back. I was in the middle of another stretch when everything clicked into place. I don't get aches and pains. At least, I haven't gotten them since I became a member of the Regulators. Something was wrong.

"How long have you been bleeding?" I asked.

"About five minutes," Dudley answered.

"What's going on?" Georgie asked.

I shoved everyone out of my way. I grabbed Dudley's razor, and I slashed a slight cut into my hand. As soon as the blood started to flow, I put my hand under the water faucet. Despite the water, the wound continued to bleed.

"Oh shit," I muttered. "What does this mean?"

Miriam's hand went to her mouth.

"Miriam!" I shouted. "You need to answer me. What does this mean?"

Tears began to fall from her eyes.

"You stop that!" Dudley shouted. "You stop that right now. He can't be dead. He can't be dead. He's my uncle. This is bullshit. We're gonna find him. Mr. Hardin is gonna clear our names, and we're gonna rescue my uncle."

Everyone figured things out at about the same time.

Javie put his arm against the wall and buried his face. Georgie walked away. Ivana fell to the ground, and started sobbing. Miriam hadn't moved an inch. I walked back to my room. I needed some privacy.

"The Guardian has fallen," Miriam said as I slammed the door shut.

Father Monarez was out picking up supplies when all of this happened. He returned to a rather gloomy house. In the six months we spent together, all of us had gotten pretty tight. I mean, we were close before, but now, I don't know. We needed each other. We relied on each other. We had to, how else could we get through all the bad shit?

There were a lot of tears, and there were a lot of hugs as we explained to Father Monarez that Jaxon had died. Later on that evening we all traded stories about him. Everyone but Miriam and Father Monarez had known Jax for a pretty long time. Jaxon was, without a doubt, a funny individual. I mean, the shit that boy got into.

It was a fun time. It was a sad time as well. One of us would be in the middle of a story, and just lose it. The person next to them would hug them tightly, until they regained their composure. Dudley never said a word. He sat in a chair the entire time with his legs folded up under his chin.

The next day we had a funeral.

Father Monarez led the services. We had no body, but that didn't matter to us. We wanted to pay our respects to our leader. We wanted to honor our friend. Jaxon was an incredible human being. He was one of a kind.

Dudley went before everyone to say a few words.

"You all know my uncle," Dudley said with tears in his eyes, and a tremble in his voice. "He was the best of all of us. He threw himself into harm's way more times than I can count. He was a hero. He didn't deserve…he didn't deserve…I'm going to kill them. I'm going to kill every single one of them. The man was a hero. He saved everyone. He risked his life so many times. I used to get so worried about him. When he fought that stupid vampire, I thought we were going to lose him but we didn't. He actually won that fight. I couldn't believe it. After that, I thought he was invincible. He should have been invincible. All of those fuckers are going to die. Everyone that did this to him is going to die. I don't care how long it takes. I won't give up. They'll have to kill me."

After that, Georgie led him away. There was no way we were going to be able to avenge Jaxon's death. We had all lost our power. We were normal human beings. We were no longer durable, we no longer healed, and we weren't super strong anymore. We were just regular human beings and we could die just as easily as everyone else.

For the next month or so, we all moped around. At that point Father Monarez began to talk to us about leaving the country. There were places in the world that were protected by the church. We would no longer need to run. The Men in Black would never dare chase us to the places Father Monarez had in mind.

None of us took him up on his offer.

We wanted our revenge. We began to ignore the fact that we were no longer empowered by the Guardian. We refused to accept our defeat. Six long months on the run with all of us desperately clinging to a failing shred of hope, only to discover that our friend and leader had been killed. No, scratch that, I misspoke. We were more than friends. We were family: we were bound by blood we had shed in defense of others. It was a brother we had lost.

Due to treachery and deceit, my brother had fallen. We began to plan. We had long discussions about how we could take down Major Crass and the Monster. Unfortunately, the obstacles against us were too damn insurmountable. Attacking him outright wasn't going to work. Without our powers, we would've been killed instantly. Our ideas were more like suicide missions, and we were okay with that.

Ivana tried to talk us down. She didn't want us to die.

"We've lost so much," Ivana cried. "I can't stand to lose anymore. Let's go away. Let's go somewhere safe. Please, I'm begging you. I don't want to lose anyone else."

She broke my heart, but I never gave in to her pleas. Neither did Dudley, nor Georgie, nor Javie. The latter two were quieter in their thoughts, but you could see the hatred boiling right beneath the surface of their calm expressions.

A few months later, Dudley began to behave erratically.

Something wasn't right with him. He began talking to himself at night. He began drinking profusely. We were all worried. He kept his pistol with him at all times, and he began cleaning it every four hours.

One night, after he had downed an entire bottle of whiskey, he snuck out and assaulted a police officer. By the time we tracked him down, he had the cop on the ground. He had his pistol in the back of the man's head and was demanding to know where the vampires were hidden.

It took both Miriam and Ivana to calm him down.

It was Father Monarez that explained he was exhibiting the symptoms of Post-Traumatic Stress Disorder.

Miriam eventually explained that the Guardian power protected us from such things. Well, we were no longer protected. We moved to the next location a day later.

Georgie was the next to have problems.

He was no longer able to sleep at night. Instead, he would pace back and forth in front of his bed. He would also slap himself on the forehead and curse himself for whatever mistakes he blamed himself for making.

I started getting nightmares. They were horrible dreams. All the people I lost. All the people I saw die. It was rough. After that, I dreamed about zombies. They were chasing me. They were cornering me. Every night in my dreams I would be ripped apart and devoured. I started taking pills in order to stay awake. I started hallucinating from lack of sleep but that was preferable to the nightmares.

Georgie tried to kill himself.

We should have seen it coming but we were all too busy dealing with our own private Hells. The things we'd seen were just too much. All the violence we'd committed was coming back to haunt us.

It was Ivana that stopped poor Georgie.

She bandaged up his wrist. She stopped the bleeding. He cried for an entire day, and she held him tightly the entire time.

"Don't you leave me, Georgie," Ivana cried. "Don't you dare leave me."

I started bawling when that happened, because honestly, I'd been giving some serious thought about doing the same thing. That's not easy for me to admit, mind you, but it's true. I was in bad shape. There was no joy in my life, and all the things I'd been through were haunting me.

Dudley was the worst.

He began to seclude himself from the rest of us. Where Georgie sought our help, Dudley kept his pain to himself. His mental health began to deteriorate rapidly. He no longer bathed. He no longer spoke to the rest of us. He just sat in his room cleaning his pistol every four hours.

I tried to talk to him.

"Dudley," I said. "We're getting worried about you. All of us are going through the same thing. You need to talk to somebody. Will you come out of your room?"

He ignored me.

Soon after that, Father Monarez moved us to another location.

I'm not sure where we moved that time either; for some reason I'm thinking it was California. There were so many places. I do remember it was in the woods. We were staying in yet another underground hideout. This one happened to be near a cliff overlooking the ocean.

Father Monarez once again tried to talk us into moving out of the country. He wanted us to be safe. He could see that we needed help. Javie began to agree with him. Javie, out of all of us, seemed the least affected by PTSD.

"At that point, how long had you been on the run?"

We had been on the run about a year and a half. I missed my kids. I would never have let them see me in the state I was in, but I missed them terribly. Father Monarez, Miriam, and Ivana, did their very best to hold us together, but it was tough. They had three mental cases on their hands, and we weren't getting any better.

Dudley began to scream out bloodcurdling screams in the middle of the night. He yelled about taking revenge, but the rest of us no longer shared his thoughts. We knew we were broken. We were but mere shadows of what we used to be.

I was in the deepest wave of depression yet, when Father Monarez came to me a final time.

"We need to leave this place," Father Monarez said. "You need help. I can get that for you. I can protect you. I can give you back your life. All you have to do is come with me."

The thought of suicide sounded pretty good at that point. Still, I heard his words. I began to wonder if there was a way out. I wanted a way out. I wanted the depression to end. I wanted the nightmares to stop.

I agreed.

Georgie was probably worse off than I was, and it took a while to convince him to leave. He felt that by agreeing to move away, he was turning his back on Jaxon. But Jaxon was gone, and the rest of us were wasting away.

Ivana was the one that talked him into it in the end. She was the one with the patience needed to get through to him.

Dudley was next. He punched me in the face the first time I tried to talk to him. He called me a traitor. He swore he'd kill me along with everyone else on his hit list if I ever brought it up again. He wanted to wait. Something would happen. Our time was not over.

Miriam and Ivana talked to him. Jaxon wasn't coming back. Never again would any of us be touched by the power of the Guardian. Jaxon wouldn't want the rest of us to waste away and die. He'd want us to grab our chance at a new life and take it.

"What about Skie?" Dudley asked with tears in his eyes. "Who's going to rescue her? I feel like such a fuck up. I feel like I should be doing something other than hiding."

The guilt was killing him. He was blaming himself for Jaxon's death. I searched for something to say to him. I came up empty.

"Come with us," Ivana said. "We need you. We need your protection. We need you to get back on your feet. Without you, all of us will die."

Those were the words that needed to be spoken. Despite all his pain, despite all the suffering Dudley was going through, he would never allow Ivana to come to harm. He would protect her with his dying breath.

It was decided. We were leaving the country. We were headed for greener pastures under the protection of the church. We would all get the help we needed. We would be safe for the rest of our lives.

The Men in Black had other ideas.

Javie and I were packing up the car with our meager belongings when the bullets started flying. I immediately ducked behind our vehicle after getting nicked in the shoulder. Javie began shooting back at them. It had been a long time since they had last found us. I guess we had gotten a little too comfortable, or maybe we simply didn't care as much anymore. Regardless, we were in it big time.

It figures that things would come down on our heads like that. We had fought them off easily in the past. I mean, there were a few scary moments, but we always got away. Now, on the eve of our journey to a better life, they found us again.

Dudley came out of the underground bunker.

He wasn't using cover. He wasn't trying to keep himself safe. He stood there lining up his shots and shooting our attackers. His shots were perfect. Every time he squeezed his trigger, a man died.

I began to yell at him to get down. Eventually, a bullet was going to find him. Eventually, he was going to get killed. It was a matter of time.

Georgie came out as well. He tried to grab hold of Dudley, but Dudley wouldn't go with him. Georgie ended up sliding through the dirt and taking up a position next to me.

The shootout was in full rage by the time the helicopters started circling overhead. We were doing pretty well in my opinion. Dudley hadn't gotten himself killed yet. We had brought down at least ten of our enemies. Of course, we had no idea how many were lurking in the woods. It seemed like an entire battalion from where I was standing.

One of the helicopters had a large machine gun.

I had long since made peace with death. The end was upon us. We were trapped, and we weren't getting out. I stood up and joined Dudley. Javie was right behind me.

Georgie began screaming at us. We ignored him and fought on. We were Regulators. We were going to die with weapon in our hands. We were going to die fighting.

Georgie joined us.

The helicopter finally found the right position in the sky. I lifted up my pistol and began shooting at it. In a few seconds all of it would be over. I had a hell of a good run. I can't even tell you how many women fell victim to my charms, or how many zombies I managed to destroy. I was smiling as I pulled the trigger.

The strangest thing happened. The helicopter fired upon the Men in Black instead of us.

The machine gun lit up the woods. It rained down so much hell that trees actually began to fall over. I immediately stopped shooting at the helicopter. I looked towards my teammates. They were as dumbfounded as I was.

Finally, the shooting stopped, and the helicopters began to land in the clearing around our bunker. Snake Charmer stepped out of the helicopter and ran towards us. He wasn't alone. He had four other men with him that radiated combat experience the same way he did.

Mr. Hardin stepped out of the helicopter behind them. He was wearing a grey suit, and he was smiling from ear to ear.

"Gentlemen," Mr. Hardin said when he was close enough. "What do you say we go back down in that bunker and catch up a bit?"

Inside the bunker, we all sat around a metal table. Dudley kept his distance, choosing a spot far away from Mr. Hardin.

"We're all in the clear," Mr. Hardin said.

"What are you saying?" Javie asked.

"Major Crass came forward and confessed everything," Mr. Hardin said. "He confessed to aiding in the orchestration of an assassination attempt upon the General's wife. He admitted to disguising that same attempt on her life as a hit on the President. He admitted to resurrecting the former Guardian. He even admitted to smuggling a number of criminal Albanians into the country. Our names have all been cleared."

Everyone at the table cheered.

"Why would he do that?" Dudley asked. "And where the fuck have you been? We haven't heard from you in months."

"I apologize for that Dudley," Mr. Hardin said. "It couldn't be helped. The Men in Black were closing in on me. I was in Albania and was getting close to capturing a high-ranking member of the Albanian Mafia that knew the truth about Major Crass. If I had made an attempt to contact you boys, the Men in Black would've been on me in a heartbeat. I couldn't risk it."

"You didn't answer all of my questions," Dudley said.

"I was not able to catch the man I was after," Mr. Hardin said. "That particular fellow died as we attempted to apprehend him. Things were looking bleak. Our numbers were small, and we simply didn't have the manpower to bring down an entire Mafia; which is what it would have taken in order to get to the truth. My plan had failed miserably. The Albanians were on to us."

"I'm sure you did your best," Georgie said.

"I did indeed," Mr. Hardin said. "Yet, my best wasn't good enough. All the time spent tracking him down, and I let him get killed. I contacted some of my associates in the government after that. I wanted to arrange my surrender, and see if I could somehow offer something up in exchange for the freedom of the Regulators. I didn't have high hopes, but it was worth a try. Imagine my surprise when I was told that Major Crass wanted to meet with me."

"What?" I asked.

"He needed my help," Mr. Hardin laughed. "I flew back to the States immediately. We were all arrested the second we exited the plane. For a moment there, I thought I'd been played. I thought my associates had been turned against me. Instead, I was flown to New Mexico, to our old base of operations. Major Crass was there, waiting for me."

"You've got to be kidding me," Georgie said.

"I'm glad I'm not kidding you," Mr. Hardin chuckled. "It seems that Major Crass resurrected Max, not only to kill off Jaxon, but to pick up where Jaxon left off. You see: Major Crass wanted to finish up what all of us had started. He wanted to be the man responsible for cleaning up El Paso. Unfortunately for him, Max had other ideas. Their relationship began to deteriorate immediately after Jaxon escaped the city. Max has his own agenda. We just aren't sure what that agenda is at the moment."

"I doubt it's anything beneficial," I said.

"You're right about that," Mr. Hardin said. "At the moment he seems content to merely inhabit El Paso, but he doesn't allow any intruders. Whenever Major Crass sent forces into the city in order to cut down the zombie population, Max would attack them and kill them off."

"So Max is the ruler of a city of corpses," I said.

"He is indeed," Mr. Hardin said. "Major Crass has lost all control over the situation. Max is running wild. The last time he ran wild, he created the outbreak in El Paso. Major Crass fears his new scheme is to release the zombies from the city."

"Wait a second," I said. "What do you mean release the zombies from the city?"

"That's what Major Crass believes," Mr. Hardin said. "I've had no contact with Max, so at this point it's all just speculation."

"Holy shit," Javie said.

"Holy shit is right," Mr. Hardin agreed. "Major Cross had no other choice. The zombie outbreak is an extinction-level emergency. Major Cross wanted his revenge on us, and he certainly wanted my job, but he never wanted to end the world. The man has four children he loves greatly. He doesn't want them living in a world full of zombies. He was forced to do the right thing. He confessed everything, and begged me to clean up his mess so his children wouldn't have to face a world of shit."

"So we're free?" Ivana asked.

"We are much more than free, darling," Mr. Hardin laughed. "The Regulators are back in business."

We all just stared at him.

Mr. Hardin stared back at us.

"This isn't exactly the reaction I was expecting," Mr. Hardin said.

"There are some things you should know," Father Monarez said. "The team has lost—"

"My uncle is dead," Dudley interrupted. "My uncle is dead, and we lost our powers. Go tell Cross he's too late. Go tell him that his kids are fucked because he killed off the one man who could have saved the day."

Mr. Hardin looked at Dudley. Then, he looked at the rest of us. Finally, he could see it. He could tell by our appearances that we were broken.

"You boys have had a rough time," Mr. Hardin said. "That's horrible, and I'm truly sorry for all that you have suffered. I can't even imagine what things were like for you. However, it's time to pick up the pieces. We have a world to save."

"Are you not listening to me?" Dudley asked. "Jaxon is dead. We can't help you."

"I'm not sure where you came by that information, son," Mr. Hardin said. "But Jaxon is very much alive, according to Major Cross. In fact, I think it's about time we went and freed him."

Dudley stood up from the table.

Everyone except Mr. Hardin tensed up. We weren't sure what Dudley was going to do. We weren't sure of what he was capable of doing.

"Where is he?" Dudley asked.

"He's in prison," Mr. Hardin answered. "Would you like to come with me to bust him out?"

The entire fucking table stood up.

Chapter 8

WARDEN SMILES

At this point, we now begin with what must be my strangest interview ever. It was conducted over the phone. I never met the man I was talking to in person. This is the phone call that woke me up in the middle of the night.

The caller said his name was Warden Smiles. He wanted my help. This is his story.

"I don't know anyone by the name of Warden Smiles."

I understand that madam, but I know who you are. You're the reporter that keeps interviewing the Regulators.

"Even so, I don't normally take calls in the middle of the night. If you have something important to say, you should call my agent. He'll take down all your information. If I can use it in my next book, I'll give you a call and set up an interview."

Excuse me if I skip that step. My life is in danger. You're the only one I can talk to. I need to get my story out. If they hear my story—if they see my confession—maybe they'll stop chasing me.

"If someone is chasing you, you should go to the authorities."

I can't do that. They'd get me for sure if I did that.

"Who is after you?"

The Regulators.

I was speechless for a moment.

"You should start from the beginning."

That's the thing. I don't know the beginning. I don't know what went down before he was brought to me. All I know is what happened after they brought him in.

"Whom did they bring in to you?"

I didn't know who he was. His face was demolished. His body was ruined. I had no idea who he was.

"Whom did they bring in to you?"

Prisoner 187.

"I don't know who that is. I'm going to need you to be clearer on who you're talking about."

Okay, just listen. Not so long ago, I was the warden at a prison in Louisiana called Felltrop Prison. It wasn't the greatest facility. It was in dire need of repairs, manpower, and upgrades. The swamp has a way of wearing things down, and unfortunately, Felltrop was placed in the middle of some swampland, and mostly forgotten. I'd been the warden there for about fifteen years when everything happened. I did my best, of course, but without the right funding, I was fighting a losing battle.

"Tell me what happened, Warden Smiles."

A man named Major Crass came to see me.

Warden Smiles finally got my attention.

"I know who that is, please continue."

Most of the world doesn't know this. This is some seriously top secret shit but wardens often play a very important role in the nation's security. Sometimes, when special agencies working within our government capture individuals that aren't supposed to exist, or individuals whose capture must remain unknown, they hide them in certain prisons. These criminals are mostly a threat to the nation. Oftentimes the rules are bent and they remain behind bars for extreme periods of time without trial. The goal is to keep them anonymous. The public doesn't need to hear about all the dangerous threats that are thwarted on an almost daily basis.

Such an enterprise had never come my way until Major Crass paid me a visit. I'd heard about them, but I'd never in all my fifteen years been approached. The meeting took place in my office.

"I had many irons in the fire," Major Crass said. "They didn't pan out the way I wanted them to, but in the end things turned out pretty well indeed. However, I am left with a small inconvenience. I need a man in my custody to disappear. If the public found out about him it would be very bad. A panic could break out."

"Who is this man?" I asked.

"That's not important," Major Crass said. "Just know that the man is very dangerous. Perhaps more dangerous than what you are accustomed to dealing with in these parts."

"My facility can handle anything you have in mind," I said defensively. "I also see that you have all the correct paperwork to deliver your man into my custody. The only thing left in this transfer is my approval."

"You're absolutely correct," Major Crass said. "I do need your approval, and this prison needs the proper funding. Your office looks like a crack whore's living room, and excuse me if I pass on a tour, but I'm rather afraid I might be shanked with a homemade knife."

"If you have a point," I said. "You should get to it."

"My point is," Major Crass said. "Take my prisoner, and I'll give you the funding to fix this place up. You're running a shithouse in the middle of a swamp. I can change that. I can make you the warden of the finest institution in this country."

"All you want me to do in return is take possession of your prisoner?" I asked.

"That's all I want," Major Crass said. "Like I said before, the man is dangerous. You'll be earning your keep."

"How long will I be holding your prisoner for you?" I asked.

"As long as it takes," Major Crass said with a smile. "And don't ask me how long what takes. Just know that I'll retrieve him as soon as I can. After all, I have very important plans for him."

The deal was struck.

We took possession of the prisoner a month later. Construction had long since begun, so Major Crass was a man of his word, and I was eager to hold up my end of the bargain.

"You didn't know who the prisoner was once you got a look at him?"

I didn't have a clue. Like I said, his face was demolished, and his body was ruined. They delivered him by helicopter. The man was strapped down and restrained to a bloodstained gurney. He didn't even look alive. I was shocked when I saw his arm move.

"This man needs medical attention," I said. "He's not going to last very long in that condition."

"Believe it or not," Major Crass said. "He's already received all the medical attention he requires. Now, let's go over some very simple rules that need to be followed."

The rules were confusing. The prisoner was never allowed to bathe. He wasn't allowed more than a few sips of water at regular intervals. He wasn't allowed to leave his cell. No plants of any kind were allowed anywhere near him. We were also told to treat him as a violent criminal at all times, and we were warned that no less than five guards should be present whenever we entered his cell.

Major Crass then pulled me aside as my men took the prisoner away.

"I will be doing some upgrades on your office as well," Major Crass said. "I'm building you a secret exit behind the bookcase. If anyone besides me should ever show up to collect the man I turned over to you, take the exit. Hit the red button on the podium, and run like hell."

"What does the red button do?" I asked.

"Never mind that," Major Crass said. "I doubt you'll ever need to use it. It's simply an available option if you do."

Major Crass left after that, and my nightmare immediately began.

We called the man Prisoner 187. All our prisoners were given numbers instead of names. So, it really wasn't a problem not knowing the man's true identity.

I gave him the rules as my men wheeled him inside Felltrop. It didn't appear to me that he was paying attention. I wasn't sure if that was due to his injuries, or if he was just being a pain in the ass.

I came to a stop.

My men stopped as well.

"I don't care who you are," I said. "I don't care what you did. You old life is over. I now own you. Step out of line and I'll deal with you. Do you understand me?"

He didn't even look at me. So, one of my men smacked him upside the head to gain his attention. It worked. The man turned and looked me right in the eye. I didn't like the look on his battered face. The rage behind his eyes made me wonder if he was insane.

"What happened to my wife?" Prisoner 187 asked.

"You no longer have a wife," I said. "Were you not listening to me?"

Apparently, it was the wrong thing to say. The man's hand savagely ripped free of his restraints, and wrapped around my throat. Yet, with all the damage done to his hands, he couldn't keep his grip on me, and I was able to pull away from him before he could clamp down tightly.

It was a stupid thing for him to do. I had ten guards with me. They were on him immediately. Somehow, as they beat him, he broke free of the rest of his restraints and fell from the gurney.

His leg was so badly mangled that he could barely stand. My men had to help him to his feet. Again he locked his eyes upon me as I stood before him.

"I asked you about my wife," Prisoner 187 demanded.

"You have no wife!" I roared at the swollen and scabbed face before me.

He head butted me so hard my nose broke, and I fell to the ground. One of the guards, his name was Pete, punched the prisoner in the kidneys. The prisoner went after him next. He struck Pete on the bridge of the nose. The strike pushed bone fragments into Pete's brain and killed him.

The rest of my men reacted instantly. All of them were highly trained guards, but Major Crass wasn't exaggerating. Prisoner 187 was a dangerous man. It took five, high-voltage stun guns to finally bring him down. One of the guards received a broken leg in the scuffle, another two received broken arms, and a final guard took a blow to his head that put him in intensive care for a week.

Prisoner 187 wasn't treated very well after that.

We put him in the worst cell in the entire prison, designed by Major Crass especially for the prisoner. It was built on the lowest level of the prison. It had only one access point, and that was by elevator. From the elevator, a guard would need to scan a handprint on the security door, and after the security door, they came upon a brick-lined hallway.

Prisoner 187's cell was at the end of the short brick-lined hallway. The entire level was kept dark. I didn't feel the prisoner deserved even artificial light after what he had done to my guards. His cell was small. The bars were black.

Beyond the security door, it was hot and humid. There were puddles on the floor of the hallway from leaky pipes. The brick would sweat in the summer, but it was never enough water to satisfy the man. It was only enough to torture him. It was a dark and dank Hell, and that is where the prisoner remained. His body eventually healed, at least the swelling and bruising went away. His jaw hung at an odd angle. His damaged leg made it difficult for him to get around, he was stooped over from what I guessed was an untreated spinal injury, but worst of all were his hands. They were difficult to look at.

"Did you recognize him when he had healed?"

I did not. His beard had grown, his hair had grown, the dim lighting of his environment: all of those elements kept us from identifying him. The younger guards occasionally made guesses about his identity. The most popular belief was that he was a terrorist of some kind.

"Did the prisoner ever say anything?"

He demanded to know about his wife. That's all he ever asked for. He wanted information about his wife. He would become quite agitated about it. I remember him pounding away on the bars and screaming out to the camera in the hallway. It was a nightly ritual. His hands were getting worse every day from the pounding. I remember him banging his head as well. He split his forehead open once. The guards came in to help him that time. The cut was quite severe.

Three were killed.

The guards tried to get their revenge after that. It's the way of the prison. When an inmate attacks a guard, there is always some sort of retaliation. As warden, I look the other way. If I didn't, the men wouldn't work for me.

Prisoner 187 was tortured terribly, but he still somehow managed to kill another one of my guards. After that, I alone possessed the key to his cell. I needed to keep my men away from him. I needed to keep him away from my men.

Almost six months after Felltrop took possession of Prisoner 187, the prisoner escaped his cell.

"How did he do that?"

He wedged the frame of his bed between the bars of his cell and bent them apart. It took him that long to unscrew the bed frame. His mangled hands weren't very useful, but still, it must have required tremendous strength to unscrew those bolts from the wall.

He killed another three guards. They saw him squeeze through the bars on the security monitors. In a panic, they came through the security doors without adequate back up. It wasn't until the prisoner entered the elevator that we were able to regain control of the situation.

Major Cross had a tank filled with some sort of knockout gas built into the elevator as an extra security measure. Prisoner 187 went down after five minutes of choking. Still, the guards were rattled. New guards had to be trained to replace the ones we had lost. I had a lot of explaining to do. I was forced to lie quite a bit.

Lying made me nervous. I wasn't a liar. I wouldn't normally mind holding an extra prisoner in exchange for the offer Major Cross had made, but Prisoner 187 had succeeded in making me regret ever laying eyes upon Major Cross.

The breakout was the last straw. Something needed to be done. The guards were afraid to even move past the security doors.

I contacted Major Cross. I explained all that had happened. To my surprise, the man didn't seem shocked. He paid Prisoner 187 a visit two days later.

Say what you will about Major Cross, the man had balls. He walked past that security door and straight down the hallway all by himself. He spoke to Prisoner 187. I'm not sure all that he said. I could only pick up a few whispered words every now and then through the speaker system of the security monitor. I saw the prisoner collapse to floor in his cell. I saw Major Cross walk back towards the elevator with a smile on his face.

Prisoner 187 was finally defeated.

"What did Major Cross say to him?"

From what little I could hear, it sounded like he told him his wife had died.

After that, Prisoner 187 never assaulted another guard. He also didn't move from the floor of his cell for three days after Major Cross paid him a visit. It looked as if he was dead, and that worried me, so I went in with ten of my men.

We checked his pulse. Prisoner 187 was alive, but he was broken. He didn't even try to attack us. At that point, I ordered my men to get revenge for our fallen friends. They beat the shit out of him. He didn't scream. He didn't react. The man was a hollow shell, and a few words from Major Cross were all it took.

I, on the other hand, was a happy man. Things in the prison immediately got back to normal. The guards were no longer afraid to enter that damn hallway. Things were going great. Occasionally, I would hear some rather odd noises coming from beyond my bookcase but that didn't bother me much. I had no interest in investigating. My career was finally taking a massive upswing. I even won some prestigious awards.

Then, Prisoner 187 stopped eating.

That didn't concern me at first. I didn't even bother to look at him through the monitors when his situation was reported to me until he stopped drinking his small allotment of water that ran through a pipe in his cell. A puddle of water forming on the floor is what tipped us off.

I contacted Major Cross once again.

"What do you mean there's a puddle of water in his cell?" Major Cross demanded.

"The hell with the puddle," I said. "Your prisoner won't survive very long if he's not drinking."

"You idiot," Major Cross screamed. "You have no idea what'll happen if he comes into contact with water."

"Not a damn thing," I countered. "He's been lying in it for a few days now."

Major Cross arrived that evening.

He turned the lights up to full power in the cell, and in the hallway. I went with him as he visited Prisoner 187.

The prisoner looked horrible. The amount of weight he had lost was staggering. His breaths were ragged. His body was limp. He had a chill due to the wetness in his cell.

"He's sick," Major Cross said. "He's lying in a puddle of water. He hasn't healed from his wounds, and he's sick. I don't understand this at all."

"He's very sick," I said. "If he doesn't receive medical attention soon, he's going to die. What do you want me to do? We have a doctor on the premises."

Major Cross continued looking at the prisoner. It was as if he couldn't quite believe what he was seeing.

"He looks so old now," Major Cross said. "Look at all the grey in his hair."

"Do you want to let him die?" I asked.

"What?" Major Cross asked. "No, keep him alive. I still have plans for him."

I never saw Major Cross again.

I had tried to contact him several times but he never returned any of my messages. The prisoner continued to deteriorate. The prison doctor did what he could. Eventually they resorted to a feeding tube and IVs, which the prisoner would immediately remove the moment he was left alone.

We strapped him down to a hospital bed in order to keep him alive but eventually that became unnecessary. The prisoner became too weak to remove the tubes. I wasn't sure what plans Major Cross had for the man, but I knew he was running out of time. The prisoner was dying. The damage done to his body and then the hunger strike had taken too much of a toll.

It was a cruel fate, but one I felt he deserved, and he seemed to want. Unfortunately for him, it was my job to keep him alive. He got around the clock care. I even brought in a small staff to see to his needs. They were appalled by the look and smell of him of course, but I had plenty of funds to keep them quiet. With their help, I would be able to force the man to stay alive for months, maybe even a year if I got lucky.

Prisoner 187 contracted pneumonia.

The staff was convinced they were going to lose him. Actually, they were surprised he had even managed to live as long as he had. The man was completely unresponsive to any stimuli. I tried to contact Major Cross for the final time. I received no response. I paid off the medical staff, and I had them remove all the tubes and IVs. After that, I placed Prisoner 187 back in his cell, and I waited for him to die.

I won't lie to you. I wanted the man to die. I planned on throwing a party for myself when we put him in the ground. I hated him that much. Those wild eyes of his haunted my damn dreams. His freakish strength had frightened my men, and guards at a prison can't afford to be frightened. He was like one of those stupid axe-wielding killers in a movie. No matter how many times we knocked him down, he kept getting back up for more. And he always gave better than he got.

He was the worst kind of prisoner. He was dangerous and we couldn't deal with him. It took Major Crass to finally break him, but Major Crass had done his job too well. The ruin he left behind needed expensive care. Well, I was done with all that. A major thorn was about to be removed from my side. If Major Crass had a problem with any of my actions, he should have picked up the phone when I attempted to contact him. As far as I was concerned, my life had just gotten easier.

Then the Regulators came to Felltrop.

My world turned to shit.

They came in fully suited up and armed to the teeth. With them, they had an older gentleman, with flecks of grey in his dark hair. The man was wearing an expensive suit. He introduced himself as Mr. Hardin.

They also had a small battalion of soldiers with them, but they left these soldiers outside the prison. The group that entered didn't look military. Instead, they looked like a band of marauders. There was a menace that seeped out of their narrowed eyes and scowling faces. Each of them wore a large patch on his arm depicting a bandana-wearing skull with two musket pistols.

I wish I could have prevented them from entering, but the Regulators aren't bound by law. I made calls. Nobody wanted to step on their toes. Before I knew it, they were all standing in my office.

One man wasn't wearing that patch. He seemed a bit more military-like than the others, but the bushy beard on his face told me he wasn't an average soldier.

"How much did you know about the Regulators at that point?"

Just what the news had shown. Obviously, I knew about the zombie outbreak in El Paso, Texas. I also knew there was a team of men assigned to deal with it. That wasn't anything new by a long shot, and I had seen the footage where one guy is fighting off a horde of the dead. It looked rather faked to me. Regardless, whatever was going on down in Texas wasn't happening in my neck of the woods. I gave it very little attention.

"What about your guards?"

The younger guards knew all about the Regulators. They even grouped around them, looking for autographs and pictures. The older guards were as ignorant as I was.

"So what can I do for you, gentlemen?" I asked.

"We are here to retrieve the General," Mr. Hardin stated.

"I'm not sure who that is," I said.

"I think you do," Mr. Hardin said calmly. "He's easy enough to recognize, if not by his appearance, then by his actions."

I immediately knew whom they were talking about. There was only one prisoner in Felltrop who matched that description. The sinking feeling in my gut must have registered on my face.

"Who is this man to you?" I asked.

"He's the leader of the Regulators," Mr. Hardin said.

I began sweating profusely. I didn't know much about these men, but I knew enough to be worried. I was in trouble. I hated Major Crass at that moment. I hated him for bringing this trouble to my front door.

"I'm not sure I have the man you're looking for," I lied. "Perhaps you would like to look at our roster? Maybe you can point out his picture."

"I doubt he's on your regular roster of inmates," Mr. Hardin smiled. "Major Crass would have told you to keep him a secret."

"Things are about to go very badly for you," the youngest of the group said from the back of the room. "Give up my uncle, NOW!"

I didn't like the look of that one. He was younger, rasher, and there was a hint of violence lurking just behind his imposing stance. His fingers were even twitching at the 1911 holstered on his right hip.

The largest of the bunch, a virtual giant of a man, exhaled loudly. It sounded like a bear waking up from hibernation. These men were about to hurt me.

"Let me make a call," I said. "I may know a prisoner that fits that description."

I called the control room for Prisoner 187's cell. I told them to bring the man up to the infirmary.

Then I called in four guards to escort the Regulators to their leader. I couldn't warn my men outright but I managed to slip in a code word that meant they should arm themselves.

Mr. Hardin insisted that I accompany them to the infirmary.

"You're not looking very well, Warden Smiles," Mr. Hardin said. "Is something troubling you?"

"I don't like a group of armed men entering my prison," I replied. "I don't like the air of you people. It's as if you're looking for trouble."

"Is that why your men are armed?" Mr. Hardin asked.

"They always carry weapons," I said.

"I doubt that," Mr. Hardin said. "But don't doubt this. I have very little control over this team. Their leader better be one hundred percent healthy, or there'll be hell to pay."

"I was brought a prisoner to watch over by Major Crass," I said. "He is well aware of everything that has happened. If you have any problems, you can speak with him."

"I've already arrested him," Mr. Hardin said.

We waited in the infirmary for about twenty minutes. The young one was pacing up and down. He was cursing under his breath. My guards kept their hands on their belts near their pistols.

Finally, two more of my men wheeled prisoner 187 into the infirmary. They parked his gurney against the nearest wall and stood back.

The team didn't recognize him.

Instead, they were looking to me expectantly.

"I believe this is the man you're looking for," I said with an arrogance I certainly did not feel.

"What the fuck are you talking about," the young man said. "I'm sick of playing games with this asshole, Nick."

The big man stepped up behind me. I'm sure he was going to hurt me but another team member interrupted.

"Wait a second," the only man wearing a helmet said as he studied prisoner 187. "Oh my God, I think this is him. I think this is Jaxon."

The young man went over and took a closer look at prisoner 187. He then began to tremble. Perhaps I could have calmed things down. I'm not sure. I never got the chance; one of the guards that wheeled the prisoner in chose that very moment to open his mouth.

"Serves the bastard right," the guard joked. "Shitty way to go, but he sure as fuck deserves it."

The young one raised his head up slowly, and looked at the guard. Then he calmly walked over to him, drew his pistol, and shot my man in the face. Brain matter exploded all over the white wall.

"Damn it, Dudley!" Mr. Hardin shouted. "Control yourself. How am I going to explain that?"

"About as well as you explain this," the big man said as he raised the machine gun strapped to his chest.

My guards didn't react fast enough. They should have drawn and fired as soon as the young man drew his pistol. However, when the big man raised his weapon, my guards finally went into action.

A firefight exploded, right in my infirmary. I ducked down, and ran out of the room. I went down the long hallway and up a short flight of stairs.

"You think you're getting away?" The young man screamed behind me. "You're a fucking dead man!"

I was being pursued. The young man was going to kill me. I yelled for my secretary to sound the alarm as I ran into my office and locked the door.

I heard the bells echo throughout the prison as I made my way into the secret bookshelf exit. It was my first time using it. I had never seen the inside of the long hallway of the secret exit. I was shocked as I stepped out on a metal platform, and overhead lights began to turn on, one after another. Below me was a short flight of steps. Directly in front of the steps was a large podium with a single red button.

I ran to the red button. I poised my hand above it and I began to have second thoughts. I didn't know what would happen if I pressed it. I looked down the concrete hallway. The lights were still turning on. I could see metal doors recessed into both sides of the concrete.

There was a car parked at the opposite end. A door slid open to the outside world just beyond the car. I had a way out but I still had doubts about pressing the button. I heard gunfire coming from the open door of my office behind me and I made up my mind.

I pressed the button.

A loud alarm began to blare. It overpowered the alarm of the prison. A voice came over an intercom. The voice told me to run to the vehicle and exit the building. I hesitated. I worried about what I had unleashed upon my employees still inside the prison.

The metal doors along the walls began to slide open slowly. A horrible smell permeated the hallway. I heard moans; terrible, dark moans that spoke of a hunger never to be satisfied. A metal grate began to descend from the ceiling just in front of the car.

I ran for my life.

I had to get beyond the metal grate before I was trapped inside the hallway. I'm not exactly in shape. The hallway was long. Dark shapes began to emerge from the walls. I heard screams. I felt hands reaching out for me.

The gate was halfway down.

I didn't look behind me. I refused to look. Still, I could feel their presence. I could sense their hunger. The young man finally came through the bookshelf. I heard him curse. I heard him shoot his weapon.

I slid under the gate.

I finally took a brief moment to look behind me. The hallway was filled with zombies. There must have been close to a hundred of them, but maybe that's only my mind exaggerating things. At the opposite end, the young man was firing his pistol into the heart of them.

I got into the car. The keys were waiting for me in the ignition. Thankfully, the vehicle started. I drove out, and as I peeled away, I took one final look back at Felltrop. Metal bars and doors had descended from hidden slots in the building I had just vacated.

Everyone inside was now trapped with a whole mess of zombies. I had done that. I knew not to press that button, but I did it anyway I had doomed my employees.

"How many people do you think were in there?"

There were guards rushing in before I hit the button. There was also the regular staff. Fortunately, the section that housed my office didn't have any prisoners, but I'm still guessing that around thirty people were trapped, not including the Regulators.

"What did you do after that?"

I didn't stop driving until I was out of the state. I left my wife, and my children. I ran. At the first gas station I came upon, I opened the trunk. Major Crass had provided the documents and funds I needed to begin a new life.

That's my story.

I'm not sure what happened after I left the prison. I do know that whatever happened never made the papers. I missed my family, but I knew I could never return to them. Instead, I travelled. Why not? I had the money.

Almost a year passed without incident. Then, at a truck stop in Baltimore, I saw a man in a black suit write down the license plate number of my car. Later that night, a group of black suited men entered my motel room. I barely made it out the bathroom window alive.

People are after me.

I know it's connected with the Regulators. I know they want me to pay for what I did to that man. I just want them to know that I didn't know who he was. I would never have let things happen that way if I had I known.

I need your help.

I need you to tell them that I'm sorry. I want to return to my wife. I want to see my kids. I don't want to die. I didn't know who he was.

Just tell them, please. Tell them it was an accident.

The phone line went dead.

I never heard from Warden Smiles again. His body was found three months later in a ditch outside Pennsylvania. He had been stabbed twenty three times.

It should be noted that the voice I recorded was authenticated by surviving members of Warden Smiles' family.

Chapter 9

GEORGIE

Meeting with Georgie is always fun. I'm not sure why that is, but he always seems to make me laugh. This time, things were different. We were in the usual meeting room. Georgie was wearing a button down shirt and some slightly baggy jeans.

I hate talking about that period in my life.

"I see Nick told you about our last interview."

Yes, it's a time that we don't much talk about. I did some things that embarrass me now. I guess everyone did, well, everyone but Javie.

"Why do you think Javie didn't suffer from Post-Traumatic Stress Disorder?"

Javie's a weirdo. I'm really not sure. I asked him about it once. He sort of shrugged, and said something about doing what he had to do and not feeling bad about it.

"That doesn't really cover the entire spectrum of PTSD."

No, it doesn't but that's all I got out of him. He's just not a guy that gets bothered by things.

I could tell Georgie was very uncomfortable. I could also tell he was getting ready to leave the room. He was only looking for an excuse. If I didn't give him one, he would probably make one up.

"Listen, I've got things pretty much covered from the time everyone went on the run till the end. So we don't need to talk about any of that. How about we talk about something different?"

Georgie perked up immediately.

Like what?

"Tell me about going to Felltrop."

Okay. What would you like to know?

"Take it from the beginning."

We hauled ass to get there. We jumped into our gear, said goodbye to Father Monarez, Ivana, and Miriam and took off. The helicopters took us to the airport. We hopped a private plane to Louisiana. After landing there, we jumped on another helicopter.

"Where did Father Monarez, Ivana, and Miriam go?"

I don't know where Father Monarez went; he had to report everything that happened to someone. He kept a lot of things secret. We never saw any of his allies, but he would meet with them on occasion. Miriam and Ivana went to Ruidoso. They were going to Skie.

"It must have been a bit of a relief to have everything coming to a close."

To be honest with you, I wasn't doing very well, mentally. I'm sure Nick filled you in on everything, but I wasn't in good shape. I was still excited to find out that Jax was alive. That bit of information made all of us pretty damn happy.

Once we hit the ground, Mr. Hardin ordered the small battalion of soldiers with us to stand by the helicopters. The team, Mr. Hardin and Snake Charmer went in. Most of the staff was friendly. I'm not sure we were very friendly in return.

"Why is that?"

They had Jaxon. We weren't too happy about finding out that our boss had been in a prison all this time. I was truly dreading what he was going to do when they finally freed him and restored his position in the Regulators. Beating the crap out of his captors would be very Jaxon-like.

All of us got a sort of weird feeling when we met the warden. That fucker looked guilty of something. I don't know why, but he made me very ill at ease. Mr. Hardin started talking to him, and he started acting guilty as well. He was acting like he had something to hide.

Dudley got very agitated.

Mr. Hardin did his best to calm the situation down. Fortunately for the warden, he began to realize we weren't there to play games. He had Jaxon sent to the infirmary. At that point, I knew without a doubt that something was rotten. Why the infirmary?

We waited.

Dudley became more and more agitated, and that was very worrisome. You have to understand; Dudley wasn't all there. He was pretty messed up. I'm not sure any of us should have been placed in a tense situation. Mr. Hardin didn't understand how bad off we were.

The scene started to unravel when some guards brought in some hobo on a gurney. Dudley was tired of the warden's games. Nick was happy to help him out. I was barely paying attention to them. I couldn't stop staring at the hobo.

The man had long hair polluted with a ton of grey. He also had a long beard filled with grey as well. He reeked horribly, and his body was ridiculously thin. The man had been starved. I'm not sure what was worse, the horrible condition of his body or his ruined hands.

Something about him looked familiar.

It was Jaxon. He looked as if he had aged twenty years. I said something. Everyone looked at Jaxon. Realization began to set in. Dudley went completely off his rocker. He was literally vibrating right in front of everyone.

One of the guards made a wise-ass remark about Jaxon's condition. Dudley shot the man instantly. The boom from the gun was deafening in the small room. I know I flinched like a bitch. I know I did that but I didn't do much else.

There was yelling. Then everyone began shooting. The warden slammed right into me as he ran out of the room. Dudley eventually ran after him. The gunfight didn't take too long, not with everyone standing within ten feet of each other.

Nick and Javie eventually ran after Dudley in case he needed backup. We were only regular people at that point. We didn't have special abilities to help us stay alive. We could die just as easily as anyone else.

Mr. Hardin and Snake Charmer stayed behind with Jaxon and me. Mr. Hardin immediately grabbed a doctor and put the man to work on Jaxon. That's when I found out he had pneumonia.

Mr. Hardin was pissed. I'm not sure I ever saw him get angry before, but he was really pissed then. He told the prison doctor to stabilize Jaxon for transport. I watched as he plugged IVs and monitors to my friend.

I suddenly found myself growing angry as well.

I hadn't been angry in a long time. I normally just felt lost and empty. Anger was something I wasn't used to anymore. Yet there it was. I was angry that these people hurt my friend. I was so angry, I couldn't move. I couldn't stop staring at the damage they had done to Jaxon.

"What did you do to him?" I asked.

The doctor ignored me and called a male nurse to come and aid him.

"What did you do to him?" I demanded.

They looked at me but continued to work.

I began moaning. It was a strange sound that came from the depths of my soul. I couldn't control it. I was making an idiot out of myself, but I had no control. The sound became louder and louder.

Snake Charmer came and put his arm around me.

"I need you to relax," he said. "Get control over yourself. These people need to work."

"What did they do to him?" I asked. "Look at him. There are burn marks on his arms. They tortured him. They hurt him."

"I know they did," Snake Charmer agreed. "We'll come back here. We'll all come back here and tear this place to pieces; but right now they need to work. They need to keep him alive and get him stable enough to get him out of here."

"I'm going to kill them," I said. "I'm going to kill them all."

Snake Charmer spun me around. He faced me towards the window so I wouldn't be looking at Jaxon. I looked past the bars. It was a sunny day. Snake Charmer talked me down. He helped me gain control over my breathing.

In the distance, I could hear alarms blaring. I'm not sure when they began, but I could sure as hell hear them then. I also heard gunshots in the hallway outside the infirmary.

Eventually, I heard screams.

They were the screams that haunted my nightmares. They were screams that came from something that was no longer human. I heard people yelling, pounding feet, and more gunshots.

Snake Charmer ran from my side. He was at the door with his weapon. He was shooting at something. I heard loud clanging sounds. I didn't know it at the time, but we were being shut inside the building. The clanging sounds were security doors coming down from the ceilings and locking into place on the floor.

There was more screaming.

I heard Dudley and Nick calling for help.

Snake Charmer left the room.

Mr. Hardin looked over at me.

"Georgie," Mr. Hardin said. "I need you to protect Jaxon. Can you do that?"

I nodded that I could.

"Don't let anything happen to him," Mr. Hardin said. "All is lost if the General falls."

I slapped myself in the face. I needed the focus, and focusing wasn't something I was particularly good at in those days.

Mr. Hardin pulled a pistol from a pocket in his suit jacket, and calmly walked out into the hall. I was alone with Jaxon, a doctor, and a male nurse. I hadn't moved from the window. I knew I should go out and close the door, but I couldn't move. I kept hearing the screams of the dead.

The male nurse began to freak out. The doctor tried to calm him down but he couldn't. The male nurse fled the room. Still, I couldn't move.

"What's going on out there?" The doctor asked.

"They're here," I answered. "No matter where we go, they're always there. There's nowhere to turn."

"Who's out there?" The doctor asked. "What's out there? Why's everyone screaming?"

"The dead have come to this prison, Doctor," I said. "Stay with the General. He'll protect you. He protects everyone."

I wasn't making much sense. Obviously the doctor realized that. He ran for the door. He didn't make it through the doorway. Instead, he came face to face with a zombie. A grey-colored, dried up corpse in a flannel shirt. I watched as the doctor's eyes grew wide in fear. The zombie bit him in the neck.

Blood flew out in an arterial spray. It splashed over the white blanket covering Jaxon's legs. The doctor screamed an awful cry. He did his best to fight off the zombie. His fists pounded and pounded against the beast's shoulders, but the zombie refused to let him go.

By the time another shambler came through the door, the doctor's strikes had gotten very feeble.

The second zombie latched on to his leg. There wasn't a lot of blood. I stood there listening to the sounds of their chewing. I couldn't move.

I heard an explosion from another part of the building. It shook the entire room. Three more zombies entered. One of them joined the previous two zombies, and latched onto the doctor. I closed my eyes in the hope that they would go away. They didn't.

The zombies that didn't attack the doctor looked from Jaxon to me, and back again.

If they had come for me, I probably wouldn't be here right now. I don't think I would have reacted. I would have let them tear me apart. Instead, they went for Jaxon.

Something inside of me snapped.

I roared out my anger.

It was a barbaric sound. It was filled with everything that had darkened my soul. It was a war cry.

"You can't have him!" I shouted. "You can't have him!"

I came to life instantly. My hands went for a weapon, and what they found surprises me to this day. I'm a gun guy. I like the feel of a pistol or a rifle in my hands. I like the distance those weapons keep me from my enemy.

I pulled out my Bowie knife.

I charged the zombies right as they reached their skeletal hands towards Jaxon. I hacked the first one right on top of the head killing it instantly. The second one turned on me as I attempted to un-wedge my knife from the skull.

I put up my arm in an attempt to fend off the second shambler. It bit into my bite suit. It hurt like the blazes, and I screamed out. My knife came free, and I pushed the point of the blade deep into its eye socket. I pushed with all my might. I drove the zombie backwards into the wall. I kept on pushing until my blade burst through its skull and embedded into the plaster.

I was tackled from behind.

I twisted as I fell. My helmet banged on Jaxon's gurney. The next thing I knew, there were three of them on top of me. I never even saw them enter the room. I flailed as I felt their teeth clamp down. I screamed as I felt their strong hands pulling at the fabric of my bite suit.

My Bowie knife fell from my hands.

As this was happening, some dim part of my brain realized I was only human. A bite would be lethal. I realized I would probably die and it scared the hell out of me.

Their hands were rough. They pulled and bit, pulled and bit. My bite suit held up but the protection wouldn't last forever. Eventually they would find the flesh they sought. I pounded on their heads. I struck them as hard as I could. I tried everything. I couldn't get them off of me.

Then I felt it.

A bony hand had made its way up under my shirt and utility vest. It clawed at my vulnerable skin underneath. I grabbed the arm and tried to pull it out. The owner of the arm bit down on my wrist. I felt its teeth grind and crunch against my wrist bone.

I heard another explosion.

It sounded closer. I turned my head to the door in the hopes that help was coming. All I saw was more shamblers entering the room but they weren't interested in me. They were headed for Jaxon.

I screamed once again.

I scanned the floor and found my knife. I began to furiously slash and stab. I wasn't just aiming for their heads. I was aiming for anything I could hit. The blade cut deep each and every time. It cut through tendons, and cleaved into bone. Arms became useless and I frantically got to my feet.

"You can't have him!" I shouted.

I meant it. I lost Skie. I was supposed to protect her. Jaxon gave me a job and I failed. He trusted me and I let Skie come to harm. I should have been better. I should have been tougher. I failed. What happened was my fault. If I had managed to protect Jaxon's wife, he never would have...he never would have...

Georgie began to cry. It wasn't loud, but before he turned his head away from me, I saw the soft tears fall from his eyes.

"Georgie, it's not your fault."

His shoulders began to shake. I said no more. I merely waited patiently for him to regain his composure and continue his story.

Where was I?

"You had just climbed to your feet."

Yeah, that wasn't easy. In fact, everything was a lot more difficult since we had lost our powers. Even getting out of bed was a pain in the ass. I was in my late thirties at that point, but I had stopped aging before things began to creep up on me. The amount of aches and pains a body accumulates in just a few years is staggering. Especially when you wake up powerless one day and everything hits you all at once.

Anyway, my rage continued when I got to my feet.

"You can't have him!" I screamed. "You can't have him!"

I rushed forward. I stood between the dead and my fallen leader. I was ready to die in his defense.

"I am a Regulator!" I screamed out to the world. "I am a warrior! I am a hero! I will not fail!"

I charged into them.

I hacked and I slashed. I think there were about six of them. I can't even remember. Everything was in a fog. I just kept swinging. I had an MP7 on a strap and a pistol on my hip, but I only used the big Bowie knife. Jaxon would have been proud. Cold Steel lived up to its reputation. I felt like I was wielding a damn light-saber.

They grabbed at me but I twisted. I hacked at their fingers and hands. I punched them with my free hand. The blade carved bone and bodies began to drop. It was easier when I took out their hands. All they could do was swing at me. I didn't mind the punches and slaps. Those didn't slow me down in the slightest.

Things got easier and easier. Still, I was tired. My body was slowing down. The sounds of my breathing became louder than the growls and moans of the dead. I fought on. I never gave up. I won.

The room was a mess. One last corpse crawled to Jaxon's gurney. I must have taken out its legs at some point. I watched as it pulled itself up. I came up behind it silently and rammed my knife downwards through the top of its head.

It was destroyed, but I kept on stabbing it. Over and over I stabbed at its face and body.

"I will not fail!" I screamed. "Never again! I will not fail!"

I stabbed so hard my knife pierced the body and took chunks out of the floor. I kept on stabbing.

"Georgie," Dudley said. "Georgie, c'mon back buddy."

I heard his voice somewhere in the back of my mind, but I ignored it. I was in combat mode. All I needed was another victim.

"You did it, Georgie," Dudley said. "Jax is safe. You saved him."

I kept on stabbing.

I felt strong arms come around my back. I fought against them, but they continued to hold on to me. My arms were pinned to my sides. I struggled even harder.

"I gotcha, Georgie," Nick whispered in my ear. "It's okay. I got you."

I looked over my shoulder. I saw his worried face.

"I gotta protect Jax," I said.

"You already did," Nick said.

He sat back and pulled me with him, but he kept his arms wrapped around me. He was rocking me back and forth.

"I'm sorry," I cried. "I tried to save her. I tried."

"It's okay," Nick said. "Everything is going to be okay."

"There are more coming," I cried. "They're always coming."

"We took care of them," Nick said. "It's over now. Jaxon is safe. You kept him safe."

"Did I?" I asked.

"You did," Nick said. "You took out like ten zombies all by yourself. We won."

I took that in for a moment.

"Fuckin-A-right I did," I said.

I heard Javie laugh from across the room, and I finally turned to see everyone standing there. They looked worried. All of them were splattered with gore, but they were worried about me.

I patted Nick's arm, and he let me go.

"I'm fine," I said as I got to my feet. "I did my job. I did my fucking job."

Dudley came and put his arm around me.

"You're the man," Dudley said. "You're the hero."

Sometimes, my team amazes me. I see the things they do. I see them charge into situations that would make a normal person piss their pants and run screaming into the night. I see them get hurt, and I see them pick themselves up, dust off, and go at it again. Yet, despite all that has happened, despite all that they so recently went through, they were there for me. They talked me down.

I truly walk among giants.

Chapter 10

DUDLEY

Dudley was all smiles when he walked into the room. He gave me a high-five instead of a handshake. Then he pulled me out of my chair and spun me around in a strange dance move despite the lack of music.

"What puts you in such a good mood?"

I'm just thinking that I'm the one that gave you the teaser for this story. I told you it was pretty wild.

"Yes you did."

Now I'm guessing you want me to come in here and wrap things up. Make it nice and pretty like a little present.

"I'm not sure if I'm ready for the wrap up. I imagine there's a bit more to tell."

Wait a minute. How far did Georgie take you?

"He took me up to his meltdown at the prison. Can you take it from there?"

Well, shit.

"Come again?"

That punk ass lied to me. He didn't want to cover this next part, so he told me he took you all the way to the wrap up.

"Sorry about that."

Yeah. Me too.

"Can you start from after Georgie's episode?"

Might as well, I guess. Let's see, it took about twenty minutes to cut through all the bars and security gates that came down when the zombies were released.

"Actually, can you tell me how you defeated so many zombies so quickly?"

We didn't. Snake Charmer brought explosives, and we just blew enough shit up to barricade them behind some rubble. Hell, none of us wanted to tangle with that many shamblers without having our powers. We would have gotten eaten or turned.

"Then, was it safe to cut through the security doors that came down?"

Probably not, but we weren't going to stay there forever. We needed to get my uncle to the hospital. He was in some seriously bad shape.

Don't you worry though; there isn't a prison down in Louisiana that's filled with zombies. As soon as we got out, we burned that section to the ground. After the walls came down, Mr. Hardin's men spent four days clearing out the debris, and making sure there weren't any zombies still alive and kicking.

"Where was the team when all that was happening?"

Snake Charmer stayed behind, but the rest of us flew immediately to Ruidoso. We needed to get Jaxon to the hospital.

"Weren't there hospitals in Louisiana?"

He needed to be near his wife. Trust me, it was debated pretty heavily, but in the end, we went for it. We took the risk, and brought our leader to his family. Mind you, a medic was with him the entire time. We did our best to make sure Jaxon remained in a stable enough condition. If there had been any problems with his health, we would have abandoned Ruidoso in a heartbeat and taken him to the nearest hospital.

Throughout the different helicopters and airplanes, the team never left my uncle's side. We refused to leave him. People tried; there were military dudes and guys in suits that wanted to talk to us at the first airport we landed in. We pushed through them and stayed by my uncle.

I couldn't get used to how skinny he looked. The ragged orange prison uniform he was wearing hung off of him. I couldn't see any muscle mass whatsoever. There was only skin hanging off bone. There were also scars, horrible marks, all over his exposed flesh.

I lifted up his shirt. There was a nasty scar where he had been shot. My uncle had never been given a chance to heal from the injuries he received in El Paso. I was pissed. Major Crass had put him through the ringer. When all was said and done, I promised myself that he'd pay for what he did to Jaxon.

Eventually, we landed on the hospital roof. An emergency staff of doctors and nurses were there, waiting for us. They took him immediately and wheeled him inside. The team followed. The doctors and nurses tried to shoo us away. We gave them space, but we kept our eyes on them. We kept our eyes on everyone.

I'm sure Nick and Georgie told you about how we were all kinds of mental. Well, they weren't exaggerating. We were pretty dangerous at that point. The slightest thing would have set us off. We trusted in no one.

Miriam came down to see us. She's a hard lady, but even she got all teary-eyed when she got a look at Jaxon.

"How is Skie?" I asked.

"Just as we'd left her," Miriam answered. "All will be well when he walks into her room."

"Miriam," I said. "I'm not sure he's ever going to walk again. Did you see what they did to him?"

"I'm not blind, dear," Miriam said.

Eventually, the doctor came out. He was the same dude that worked on Skie back when everything started.

"How is he?" I asked.

"He's in bad shape," the doctor replied. "His body is a mess. Starvation and dehydration are just the beginning. Those we can fix. It's the other problems that have me concerned the most. He has multiple broken bones that were never set properly. They've healed wrong. We can't do anything about that now, not in his current condition. One of his knees is severely damaged. He'll never walk normally again. He has infected burns over forty percent of his body, and that makes me think he was tortured. His hands are the worst. They have been mutilated. I'm not sure what can be done about those. On top of that, he has pneumonia."

"Will he make it?"

"I think so," the doctor answered. "He's a tough man. If you'd waited another day to bring him in, I'd have said no. As long as we can control the pneumonia, clear up his lungs, and handle the infection on his burns, I think he will recover. It's going to take time though. It's likely he's going to have pain for the rest of his life."

They moved Jaxon after that. They gave him his own room, and they closely monitored his condition. We stayed with him. There was always at least one of us in his room. The normal rules of the hospital didn't apply to us, and nobody there wanted to push the issue.

Eventually, I went upstairs to see Skie.

The floor she was on looked very different from the rest of the hospital. It was dusty and had an overall look of neglect about it.

"What's up with this place?" I asked the nearest nurse.

"This floor is haunted," she answered. "Only a couple of the nurses are allowed up here. We've had to move the other patients in order to keep them safe."

"Safe from what?" I asked.

"I don't know what it is," the nurse answered, "but it's attached to the General's wife. If anyone tries to move her, they get attacked. Some men in suits came in one day. They were all killed."

"Are you for real?" I asked.

"It's been horrible," the nurse said.

I knew Miriam had worked some of her mojo in order to keep Skie safe, but I had no idea how powerful it could be. It wasn't something I ever asked her about.

"So if something ghost-like is on this floor, why is there like an entire staff here now?" I asked.

"The elderly woman with you folks said it was safe now," the nurse answered. "We're going to clean it up. I'm not sure what she did, but it certainly doesn't feel anywhere near as menacing as it used to on this floor."

I left the nurse and walked into Skie's room.

Miriam was sitting quietly by her bed. Ivana came up and hugged me. She had tears in her eyes.

"How bad is he?" She asked.

"He's pretty bad," I answered. "The doc thinks he'll pull through but it's going to be a long road, and he'll never be the same again."

"I need to go see him," Ivana said. "Is he awake?"

"No," I answered. "He's been completely unresponsive since we found him."

Ivana left the room and I was alone with Skie and Miriam. I went to Skie's side. She hadn't aged a day, or changed even in the slightest. She certainly didn't look as if she'd been in a coma since she was shot.

"Is it a spell that's keeping her looking so good?" I asked.

"It is," Miriam said.

Skie looked like a sleeping angel. My heart went out for her. She should never have been touched by the evil the rest of us face. It wasn't the way things were supposed to end up.

"Do you really believe that if Jax walks in here, everything will be okay?" I asked.

"I do," Miriam answered.

"Why did we lose our powers?" I asked. "Jax is still alive. It doesn't make any sense."

"I have no answer for that," Miriam said. "I wish I knew but I don't understand it any more than you do. The situation is unprecedented."

Ivana came in, bawling, about thirty minutes later. I put my arm around her but I didn't have any words of comfort to offer.

"What did they do to him?" Ivana asked. "Dudley, they hurt him so bad. Why would someone do that?"

I pulled her in tightly at that point. She hugged me back. She even shocked me a bit with how tightly she embraced me. My shoulder became drenched with her tears.

What about Jaxon's parents and Skie's children?

They all came. I only waited for them to stabilize Jaxon before I called. Skie's kids had been staying with my grandparents during our absence. They'd also been visiting her every single day. Whatever presence Miriam had summoned had no problems with their visits.

Everyone exchanged hugs and tears when they arrived. I did my best to keep my grandparents from seeing Jaxon. I didn't want them to see him that way. My best efforts were futile. My grandpa wasn't having any of it. He wanted to see his son, and by God he was going to do just that.

My grandma cried. My grandpa went over to Jaxon's side. He sat in a chair next to his son and held his arm. Then he started talking to him, just whispering things into his ear. They stayed with him for hours. Neither of them wanted to leave his side.

"*What did his father say to him?*"

It was a private conversation.

"*I understand.*"

Anyway, it took four days for Jaxon to open his eyes.

"*That must have made everyone happy?*"

Yes and no. My uncle was awake, but he wasn't responsive. He wouldn't speak to anyone. He wouldn't look at anyone. No one could reach him, and boy did we try. This went on for another week.

Meanwhile, Mr. Hardin brought in a specialist to talk to all of us. I'm not sure talking about things with the shrink made me feel any better, but he prescribed some decent enough drugs. Those took the edge off. The man had zero results with Jaxon.

The doctors had a feeding tube in him. They tried taking it out at one point, but my uncle refused the food they offered and they were forced to put it back in.

"I don't understand," the doctor said. "He's just not improving. In fact, he's slowly deteriorating. It's almost as if he's lost his will to live. I hate to say this, but I believe he's willing himself to die."

That conversation happened in the doctor's office. I think it was close to midnight. The entire staff had been staying late. None of them wanted to lose the General. I left the office without another word. What could I say? None of us understood the situation.

I went to Jaxon.

He was awake. His head was tilted towards the window. He seemed to be watching the moon, but who could say. His face was illuminated. I could see him clearly, even in the dark room. I hated seeing all the grey in his hair. The long beard was also infused with grey. It didn't look right on him.

"Jax?" I said.

No response.

"You're dying," I said.

No response.

"Is that what you want?" I asked.

No response.

I was crying at that point. I was also angry and frustrated. Hell, I think I was running through pretty much every emotion imaginable.

"I can't believe this," I said. "After all you've done. After all you've survived. Why? What is so terrible? This is the coward's way out. Do you think the rest of us aren't suffering?"

No response.

"What can I say to bring you back?" I asked. "What is it that you want? I don't want to lose you. Everyone's so worried, and you're just giving up."

No response.

The tears were really flowing now. I angrily wiped them away with the back of my hand. I searched frantically for something to say. I needed something that would reach him.

"What do we tell Skie?" I asked. "What do we tell her when she wakes up?"

Jaxon turned his head and looked me in the eyes.

There wasn't much emotion, just the barest hint, but I knew. I figured it out immediately. Everything came together in a great big explosion inside my head. I approached his bed.

"Jaxon," I said. "Listen to me very carefully. Skie is alive. She survived, and she needs you."

I left after that.

"Anything?" Nick asked as I closed the door behind me.

"Maybe," I answered.

That night I went to sleep on a couch in the waiting room. It was the first bit of rest I'd had in a long, long time.

Georgie woke me up in the morning. He was frantic. For a brief moment I thought the worst had happened. It took a second for me to realize Georgie was smiling.

"Dudley!" Georgie shrieked. "You gotta come now. He's asking for you."

"Who's asking for me?" I asked.

"Jaxon!" Georgie said. "He's awake!"

I ran to his room. I shoved my way past the crowd of people at the door. The only person in the room with Jaxon was the doctor, and he was pleading with my uncle to be still.

"What's going on?" I asked.

"He shouldn't be moving," the doctor said. "His body is in a fragile state. This could be a shock to his system."

Jaxon was trying to sit up. He'd already removed all the medical tubes from his body.

"I got this," I said. "Give me some space."

The doctor backed up a bit. I placed my hands on Jaxon's chest. I tried to calm him down but there was something in his eyes that wouldn't be denied.

"Where's my wife?" Jaxon asked.

I laughed out loud.

"She's a couple floors up," I said. "She's waiting for you. All you have to do is walk in the room, and she'll wake up."

"Help me up and get me some clippers," Jaxon said.

I motioned my hand for the doctor to be quiet. Jaxon had made up his mind. Nothing was going to stop him. We could either help him, or he'd do things all on his own. The man was going to see his wife if he had to crawl out of the bed, and search every room in the hospital.

"Get us some hair clippers," I told the doctor as I pulled him up to a sitting position. "He's not going to go and see his wife looking like a hobo."

The doctor didn't move. He argued some more, but it was under his breath and I was able to ignore him. A nurse from outside the room evidently heard us talking. She brought in some hair clippers. Jaxon tried to take them from me but his hands weren't exactly cooperating.

"Let me help," I said.

I ran the clippers through his hair. Fortunately, Jax doesn't have a very difficult haircut. He just likes it short. I slapped on a number three guard and went to work. When I was finished, he asked me to get rid of his beard as well. I left him with his usual stubble.

"What room is she in?" Jaxon asked when I finished.

"I'll take you there," I said.

"All right," the doctor interrupted. "That's enough. I'm putting my foot down. This man can't take a shock to his system."

The doctor tried to get between us, and I shoved him back.

"DO YOU KNOW WHO THIS MAN IS?" I demanded. "THIS MAN IS THE GENERAL! HE HAS FOUGHT LEGIONS OF ZOMBIES! HE HAS BATTLED VAMPIRES! HE HAS SAVED COUNTLESS LIVES! HE WILL NOT BE DENIED!"

Jaxon got off the bed.

I went to help him, and he waved me off. He wanted to do it on his own. Despite my bravado, I was worried sick. Jaxon did indeed look fragile. I'm sure the feeding tubes put some weight on him, but I wasn't seeing it.

He took his first steps. One leg limped badly and the other shook from the added effort. Halfway to the door, he stumbled on his damaged leg but somehow caught himself and didn't fall. The crowd outside parted. Jaxon began again. Step after shaky step he limped forward.

He stumbled again at the door.

He used the doorframe to catch himself. He wasn't going to be able to make it. He was too weak. His body was too broken.

I ran to his side.

"I'm here for you," I said as I threw his arm over my shoulder. "I won't let you down."

He nodded in understanding, and we left the room. The crowd outside the door had grown. There were people all around us. Nick was waiting in the crowd.

"Is this what you want?" he asked Jaxon.

Jaxon nodded.

"Let me help," said Nick, as he took over for me.

The three of us made our way through the crowd. Through the corners of my eyes I saw the astonished faces of those around us. Something was happening. They weren't sure exactly what but they knew they had to watch.

Another thing I should point out is that someone had talked. The news that the General was brought into the hospital had spread far and wide. Reporters were everywhere. Security kept them from entering the building, but they weren't able to stop the hundreds of random fans that had checked themselves in with made-up illnesses in order to try and get a look at him.

More and more people were filling up the hallway.

We walked on. We weren't stopping. I could see the strain on my uncle's face. I could see how weak he'd become, and just before his body gave out, Georgie appeared.

"I believe in you!" he shouted with tears in his eyes. "We will not fail. You will not fail. We won't let you fail. We can do this!"

Georgie took over for Nick.

And then there were four.

"Make way for the General!" Georgie called out.

Jaxon pushed on. I started crying. I'm not a crier, but his will and determination was astounding. Nick was wiping his eyes. Nick is a crier. The crowd began to pat us on our backs as we moved by them.

We made it to the elevator. As soon as the door closed, Nick picked Jaxon up in order to give him a rest. I put my hand on Jaxon's shoulder. Georgie put his hand on his other shoulder.

"We began this together," Georgie said. "We'll finish it together."

Before the doors slid open on Skie's floor, Nick had set my uncle back down on his feet. I took over helping him walk once again. I was blown away by what I saw when I stepped out of the elevator.

The crowd below paled in comparison to the amount of people waiting for us on Skie's floor. The entire hallway was filled with people, and every damn one of them was giving him our salute of the right fist crossed over the heart.

A kind nurse came forward with a wheelchair.

"The General doesn't need a wheelchair, ma'am!" Javie shouted out as he stepped forth from the crowd. "He has us to help him."

I let Javie take over for me, and the five of us made our way past a silent crowd.

"Just a little bit more," Javie whispered in Jaxon's ear. "You're almost there. You can do it."

He pushed himself. He's always pushing himself. His face was strained. He looked sick. His limbs were shaking but he never gave up. He never even thought about quitting. He paused at the doorway. Miriam and Ivana had taken a few steps back to give him room.

Jaxon looked at his wife for the first time in a long, long time.

Tears began to fall from his eyes. He tapped Javie on the shoulder and Javie let him go. Jaxon limped to her bedside. It wasn't easy for him. He stumbled a bit. He even paused a bit to catch his breath, but he did it. I brought over a chair for him to sit in, but he didn't take it. He only saw Skie.

I watched the man—the warrior and invincible force of nature that broke bones and cleaved skulls—turn soft and gentle. I watched as he tenderly placed a kiss on the top of his wife's head. I watched as he stroked her face and held her hand.

The General had been reunited with his wife. No one said a word. We were all too afraid to break the spell. He spoke soft words to her. He touched her hair. He cried softly.

After a while, Ivana couldn't take it anymore. She gently approached Jaxon and placed her hand on his arm.

"Sweetheart," she said. "You need to sit down."

Jaxon looked at her. He nodded once and allowed her to help him into the chair. He never let go of his wife's hand.

Thirty minutes later, Jaxon had a seizure.

It was a bad one. His heart actually stopped beating for over a minute. The hospital staff ran in and went to work. They managed to bring him back, and the doctor was polite enough not to say, "I told you so."

They pulled another bed into the room for my uncle. They hooked him back up to a bunch of machines to monitor his heart, and whatever else those machines do.

"He's stable," the doctor said. "But no more excitement and I mean that. As of now, he's done playing games. I will not allow anyone of you to risk my patient's health once again."

Nick was about to reply and I cut him off.

"We'll go down and grab something to eat," I said. "My grandparents should be arriving with the kids soon. I need to give them the news."

Everyone was in good spirits after my grandparents arrived. We were worried about Skie, of course. Miriam alone seemed unconcerned about her. We bought our lunch and told everybody about what had just occurred.

"I can't believe he just got out of bed and went to visit Skie," Ivana said. "After so many days of nothing, he simply gets up for a stroll."

"Well, he's not out of the woods yet," I said. "In retrospect, it was a bad move to let him do that, but I don't think anyone would've been able to stop him."

"Let's hope he stays put now," Nick added. "What's he going to do if Skie doesn't wake up?"

It was a stupid thing to ask with her kids sitting at the same table. Everyone got quiet. Miriam smiled.

"I don't think we need to talk about that right now," I said.

"Nonsense," Miriam said.

Everyone turned to her.

"Your mother will be waking up very soon," Miriam told the kids. "Never doubt the power of love. Human beings can do amazing things when they're in love."

"Did you put a spell on my mom?" Otis asked.

"I did," Miriam said. "I wanted to keep her safe and sound until your stepfather found his way back to her."

"So, she's like Sleeping Beauty?" Otis asked.

"I believe that's somewhat accurate," Miriam said.

"Doesn't that make you the evil witch?" I asked.

Everyone laughed. Even Miriam gave a chuckle. Lunch was over soon after that. My grandparents wanted to see Jax, the kids wanted to see their mother, and the team wanted to protect everyone.

The elevator doors opened up on a ruckus. The earlier crowd had long since dispersed, but nurses were running in and out of Skie's room. I went to the door and was immediately approached by the rather exasperated looking Doctor.

"Everything is fine," he said. "Your uncle is still stable but he's the most frustrating patient I've ever encountered."

I looked over the doctor's shoulder. Jaxon had moved from his bed to Skie's. He had also unplugged himself from all the tubes and wires in the process.

"Did he hurt himself?" I asked.

"Fortunately, he did not," the doctor answered. "But he could have. He simply cannot be moving around. The staff is getting together now to put him back in the other bed."

I looked to my uncle. He was curled up next to his wife. His head was resting on her shoulder. He wasn't conscious. I wondered if he fell asleep normally, or if he passed out after moving himself.

"Doctor," I said. "Let him stay with her."

"I can't do that," he said. "It's against policy."

"I need you to listen to me," I said. "You don't understand. My uncle will keep moving back to his wife. No matter what you do, he'll keep trying. It's who he is. He'll never quit. If you're worried about him moving around, let him stay with her."

The doctor grumbled and complained but, in the end, he took my advice. All of us piled into the room. My grandma rubbed Jaxon's arm and kissed his cheek. My grandpa laughed at all the chaos Jax was causing.

"I'm shocked he even took the time to get a haircut," Georgie mused.

"I think he was summoning up what little energy he possessed while I cut his hair," I said. "You didn't see his expression. He looked like he was getting ready for a battle."

Eventually, everything calmed down. My grandparents left with the kids. The team rested. I alone stood watch over the sleeping couple. Shortly before dawn, I fell asleep in a soft chair on the far side of the room.

I was awakened by a small voice quietly singing.

It was a relatively pleasant way to wake up. I yawned and stretched. I let my tired eyes gaze out the window upon the forest. Then, I freaked the fuck out. I was the only person in the room with Jaxon and Skie, and it certainly wasn't Jaxon's voice I was hearing.

Sometime during my rest, Skie had woken up.

Chapter 11

JAXON

The next time I met with Jaxon, I looked at him with different eyes. I'm not sure why that was; the man has proven time and time again that he can be put through the grinder and still push forward... but all the suffering he went through—the very country he fought to protect turning against him— and the belief that his wife had died, broke my heart.

He walked into the room wearing jeans, t-shirt, and cowboy boots. He took one look at my face, and let out a groan.

Stop it.

"Stop what?"

Stop feeling sorry for me. I lived through it, didn't I?

"You did. Now tell me how. Tell me what happened after Skie woke up."

It was beautiful, just beautiful. Even the dreams I had while I was sleeping next to her were beautiful. That's why I didn't want to wake up; but there was this soft voice singing in my ear. I've never been woken up by a soft voice singing in my ear, so I figured I might as well crack an eye and see what was going on.

It wasn't easy. My eyes were heavy. I was very tired. My body had been through the ringer, but that voice kept calling to me. Then I felt the softest touch upon my skin as a hand traced my cheekbones.

I opened my eyes.

Sunlight was streaming through the room. The figure next to me was bathed in light. I couldn't make out her details, but I was positive the song came from her. I let her finish. I really didn't have the energy to stop her anyway.

When she was finished, she moved her dark head just a fraction of an inch, and blocked out the sun. I could see my wife smiling down at me. The tubes and wires were no longer connected to her body.

"I've missed you, baby," Skie said. "Where've you been?"

I started crying.

"I tried," I said. "I couldn't find my way home."

"You did find your way home," Skie said. "You woke me up, Jaxon. You woke me up."

I took her in my arms. I probably squeezed her a bit too hard, but she didn't complain. She just laughed that laugh I hadn't heard in way too long. I could feel her smile against my neck, and I started laughing as well.

"We have company," Skie said.

I looked at the foot of the bed. I saw Dudley. He was standing before us bawling his eyes out.

"Thanks, Dudley," I told him.

He left the room. When he returned, he had everyone with him. Twenty minutes after that, my parents arrived with Skie's kids. Against the doctor's wishes, there was a small celebration in our room. I, of course, was strictly forbidden to join in on the festivities but that didn't matter. I kept dozing off anyway, and I wasn't feeling my best.

"What song was Skie singing to you?"

"Down to the River to Pray."

"I'm not familiar with it. I'll have to look it up."

Skie told me she learned it from the pretty young girl that kept watch over her. She said her name was Sally, but no one in the hospital knew anybody named Sally.

Skie didn't let it bother her. She was too happy to be awake. She was also energetic. Unlike me, she was able to get out of bed without any problems. The doctor couldn't explain it. He also couldn't explain how she got unplugged from all the medical contraptions that kept her alive. In essence, it was like Skie had taken a big long nap, and now she was ready to put her dancing shoes on.

The only thing that kept her in bed was my appearance, something she was very unhappy about.

"Jaxon," she said. "I'm okay. You should go heal yourself up in the shower. Your broken nose is starting to freak me out."

I didn't answer her. I didn't know what to say.

"Jax," Skie said with an undertone of worry. "Why do you have an IV in your arm?"

Then she moved the covers off the rest of my body and saw for the first time how skinny I had become through my hospital gown. Her eyes immediately welled up.

"Don't cry," I said. "I'm here. I'm alive, and so are you. That's all that matters."

"I didn't even notice before," Skie cried. "I was so happy to see you. I was so happy to be awake. "

"It's fine," I said. "I'll catch you up on everything. Just relax a bit."

She made a move to take my hand. I pulled it away from her. I had kept my hands hidden from her since she woke up in an effort to not freak her out. She tried to take my hand again, and when I still moved away from her, she grew angry.

"Let me see," she said.

Everyone in the room was quiet. Ivana went to her side and touched her shoulder.

"Maybe this is all a bit much for you right now," Ivana said. "Maybe you should take your time a bit more."

"Have you seen my husband?" Skie demanded. "Who the hell did this to him, and why the hell can't he heal?"

Everyone sort of looked at their feet.

Skie got out of bed, and marched over to Miriam.

"Miriam," Skie said. "I want answers, and I want them now."

"He can't heal because he's lost his powers," Miriam answered. "Your husband is a normal human being, and so is everyone else. His hair is grey because the age he avoided while he was the Guardian has finally caught up with him, now that he is powerless. The scars and the overall damage to his body are the result of his imprisonment, and subsequent torture."

Hardin walked into the room before Skie could gather her thoughts. Everyone looked at him. In turn, he looked over his shoulder. Then he looked back at my wife who was standing before him.

"Did I pick a bad time to visit?" He asked.

Skie began screaming at him. I mean, she really let him have it. She probably called him every name in the book, and when Miriam tried to defend the man, Skie turned on her as well. The bitch-out session lasted damn near thirty minutes, and when it was over, my wife banned both of them from our room.

The festivities were over at that point. Skie asked a nurse for our doctor. Then she got tired of waiting, and marched off in search of him. She wanted to know how bad I was. She wasn't happy to find out.

The only ones allowed to visit after that were the Regulators, family, and the medical staff. Hardin and Miriam didn't even try. I think they were too afraid of angering my wife.

As the days went on, I became stronger and stronger. Eventually, I was strong enough to get out of bed, and walk around with a leg brace and a cane. After that, I had some minor surgeries on my hands. They were still pretty useless after the surgery, but at least all my fingers were pointing in roughly the same direction. I was supposed to have additional surgeries, but I refused them. I told everyone it was due to the pain but in reality, I just wanted to go home.

"Did you get to go home?"

I did. I went home to my family. My days of playing hero were done. I was beat up, busted up, worked over, and pretty much good for nothing at that point. At least that's how I saw myself.

"I'm a bit confused. The public at large thought you went back to El Paso to continue the fight. There are even pictures of you and the team boarding a helicopter at the hospital."

Those were body doubles. The powers that be asked us very politely to keep the country in the dark about our status. They also paid us quite a bit for our discretion.

"Can you explain to me the reason for the deception?"

They felt the country would panic if I wasn't holding down the fort. They wanted people to believe their hero was still out there, keeping them safe. Also, other countries needed to believe that as well. If the truth came out, the panic might even spread throughout the world. They were worried about foreign borders closing on Americans.

"I see. So now that Mr. Hardin was back in the captain's chair, how exactly was he keeping the zombies from breaking out of El Paso?"

Well, that was tricky. Continued operations in the city had been terminated once the Monster turned on Major Crass, because the Monster started killing all the operatives. Nobody was killing the zombies anymore.

Instead, they were feeding them. Since they couldn't enter the city, they had helicopters dropping out fresh corpses onto the streets in order to keep the zombies from searching out new food.

This was a necessity, but it didn't make Hardin very happy at all. Of course, I had no knowledge of this at the time. I was a civilian. The Regulators were civilians. We were all busy living out what was left of our lives. It wasn't much of a life, believe me.

Everyone but Javie was suffering from PTSD. I had nightmares every single time I tried to sleep. They were horrible. Thousands of people reaching out to me for help as the dead closed in upon them. I stood on top of a great hill watching them panic. I turned my back when the dead reached out for them. Their screams would wake me up. I learned to hate sleeping.

Worst of all was when I got home and saw Merrick. Age had caught up to her as well. She was getting pretty long in the tooth when I became the Guardian. The power sort of reversed her age and kept her young.

She wasn't young anymore. She had arthritis in her joints. She had surgery scars where tumors were removed. Still, she wiggled when I came through the doors. I remember sitting down on the floor with her, and wrapping her up in my arms while she licked at my face.

"Why didn't anyone tell me?" I asked.

"We didn't want you to worry," my mom answered. "After all you'd been through, we didn't want to add any more stress."

It couldn't have been easy for Merrick, but she cuddled in even closer to me when she saw I was becoming agitated.

"You should spend time with her," my dad said. "I don't think she has too many more days left in her."

That was some tough news to hear, let me tell you. In the end, I think she held on as long as she did because she was waiting for me. She wanted to see me one last time. My heart was breaking as I scratched her ears.

Months went by.

Merrick held on, but she was just a bit weaker every day. I spend a lot of time with her. It was my turn to be loyal. I gave her treats. I helped her onto the couch when she couldn't get up herself.

"*How long were you in Ruidoso?*"

About six months.

"*So you hadn't been in El Paso for around two years?*"

That's correct.

"*How did you enjoy civilian life?*"

It sucked. I was in pain all the time and my dog was dying. I had anxiety attacks at least twice a week. I could barely get around on my own, and I was developing a large gut due to inactivity. I also lost all of my muscle mass due to the starvation, and with my messed up body, I'd never be able to do the running and exercising necessary to gain it back.

I saw a psychologist that specialized in PTSD four times a week. Fortunately, I was a wealthy man. Fighting zombies pays really well, by the way. I give the man credit. He tried his best with the entire team, but we were damaged goods.

I tried to put on my happy face for my wife, but it wasn't easy. She saw right through me most times. In the end, I went through the motions of living a normal life, but my heart wasn't in it. I missed the action. I missed the challenge. I hated what my life had become. I was tired of the nightmares, and anxiety attacks. The power had somehow protected all of us from the worst of that shit.

I was also worried about Dudley. He rarely got out of bed. He never showered. He seemed to be falling deeper and deeper into madness. Georgie and Nick were also having problems, but at least Georgie stopped having suicidal thoughts. Javie would visit me daily. It was a short drive for him. The military purchased a small resort in the woods for the team, but Javie was the only one that visited me at my parents.

We couldn't work. We weren't supposed to be seen by anyone. The days were long. I couldn't even go to the veterinarian with Merrick. Time sort of dragged along in our meaningless lives.

Hardin visited one day. I was shocked that Skie didn't try and shoot him when he got out of his car.

"How are you feeling Jaxon?" He asked.

"How do I look like I'm feeling?" I answered. The truth was I was in a hell of a mood. At that point, Merrick was unable to get out of her doggie bed. Her time was nearing. Everyone but me thought she should be put down, humanely. They were probably right, but every time I went over to her, her tail would wag. I couldn't let her go.

"Well, I'm sorry about that," Hardin said. "I'm sorry about the way everything went down."

"It wasn't your fault," I said. "You got screwed like the rest of us."

"I guess I did," Hardin said. "Can we talk for a bit? Or would you rather shoot me with the .38 in the waistband of your jeans?"

"Doubt I could pull the trigger," I said as I grabbed a seat on the steps of the front porch. I had problems standing up straight, and I disliked people seeing me all hunched over.

"It's like this," Hardin said after sitting next to me. "I'm doing the best I can with what I've got but it's not enough. I'm only treading water, and Max is going to make his move soon."

"Why do you say that?" I asked

"He called me," Hardin said. "He told me to watch the news tonight. He's going public with something. When that happens, the shit's gonna hit the fan."

"So why are you telling me?" I asked.

"I'd like you to come back," Hardin answered.

"Are you going mental?" I asked. "Have you seen me? I can barely walk."

"It would only be in an advisory capacity," Hardin said. "We need someone that thinks like a Guardian. All we have are military-minded individuals. Guardians think differently than we do. They come up with plans we could never even conceive of."

"No," I said. I wanted my old life back, but that didn't mean I was going to take what was offered to me. Not after all that had happened.

"Well," Hardin said. "Perhaps you could explain that to the man I brought with me."

Hardin motioned his hand towards a man in his car. I turned my head to see who else was with him behind the tinted windows and was shocked to see the President of the United States himself walking towards my porch.

I didn't get up.

The President offered his hand. I didn't accept it.

"That's fair," the President said. "I certainly deserve that. Perhaps you didn't hear how well Major Cross framed the group of you. The video evidence alone was pretty damning. Then you began shooting the Men in Black agents. How was I to know?"

"You should've known," I said.

The President looked at me. He really looked at me.

"I'm sorry," he said. "You're right. I should have known. What happened to you and your team was unforgivable. I wanted to talk to you myself, I really did. My protection detail, however, thought that would be too dangerous. I have failed you, Mr. McQuaid. I will never make that mistake again."

"The man came here to personally apologize, Jax," Hardin said. "That has to count for something."

"Maybe," I said.

"It's not for me," the President said. "The world needs you. If Major Cross is correct, the former Guardian wants to unleash this plague upon the entire world."

"If things go bad, I'll help you boys out," I said. "Now leave me be. My dog's dying."

I left them on the front porch, and I went inside to go sit with Merrick. Her tail wagged once again. I got comfortable next to her doggie bed, and she lifted her head up and rested it on my lap. I stroked her ears, and whispered that I loved her.

I forgot entirely about the President and Mr. Hardin.

Max made his move at around 9:00 p.m. I'm not sure how he managed to get the video to the news station, but inside of ten minutes every station we turned to was covering the story. My family gathered around the television as the anchorwoman set up the clip.

The video showed Max sitting before a desk. I was happy to see that his nose was still pretty messed up. He also hadn't recovered from the burns Dudley had given him. His hair was gone. The flesh on his scalp was an angry red, and in some places, it peeled away from his skull. I could see that, in addition to his metal cheek, he also had a partially metal skull. I then remembered bending my Ti-Lite as I stabbed him, and I figured he was probably thoroughly armored beneath his skin.

"Hear me now, citizens," Max purred in his weird voice. "I am the man who shall bring about the apocalypse. I am the man who shall create a new world; a world forged in my image. Abandon your weak. Forget about your former lives. There will be no law I do not create. Cities will fall. Governments will crumble. The dead will walk the earth. In the ashes of civilization I will rise, and you will follow me. I am the Monster. My legions will march in three days."

Somebody cursed. I think it was Skie.

The phone rang. My mom answered it.

"Jax," my mom said. "It's Mr. Hardin."

I took the phone.

"Did you see that?" Hardin asked.

"I saw it," I answered.

"The son of a bitch is going to attack the borders with an army of zombies," Hardin said. "He's going to break them out and let the plague spread."

"We kinda expected that, didn't we?" I asked.

"I didn't truly believe it," Hardin said. "The possibility was there, but I didn't really believe it. Who would want such a thing?"

"A madman with an ego," I said. "Do you know where he's going to attack?"

"Yes," Hardin answered. "The same place you used to escape the city. He called me just a bit ago to invite me to stop him."

"What happens if his army of zombies crosses into New Mexico?" I asked.

"They're gonna go nuclear if that happens," Hardin said. "They have a new warhead they want to try out with a large fallout range. If they don't kill them in the initial blast, they're hoping the fallout finishes the job. Basically, it's everything we were afraid of. I have one chance to stop him. If I fail... let's just hope I don't fail. Hold on a second."

I heard Hardin talking to someone in the background but I couldn't make out what they were saying.

"This is getting pretty bad." Hardin said when he got back on the phone. "A number of foreign nations have already begun closing their borders to the United States. They're hoping that, by cutting us off, the outbreak won't spread to their countries."

"I can't say I blame them," I said. "I doubt it'll work, but they probably feel the need to do something to protect themselves."

"Hold on another second, Jax," Hardin said.

I waited once again while he discussed things with someone in the background.

"All right," Hardin said. "I need to go. Tomorrow begins the evacuation of all the neighboring areas inside the fallout zone. I need to make sure nothing in the evacuation proceedings will interfere with what I have going on."

"Good luck," I said.

"Thanks," Hardin said. "Let me meet and discuss some strategies with the higher-ups. Then I'll swing by and see what you think about everything. I'll also have your family removed from the area to a location of your choosing."

"Yeah," I said. "Sounds good."

Truth is. I was barely paying attention at that point. Seeing Max again had an effect on me. My thoughts were chaotic. I went over to check on Merrick. She gave her tail a slight wag but she didn't lift her head off her pillow.

I scratched her ears, grabbed my cane and limped my way to the front door. After opening it, Skie called out to me.

"Do they still want your help?" She asked.

"Yeah," I said.

"Shouldn't there be a new Guardian by now?" She asked.

"I guess so," I answered, "but there isn't. Miriam's not sure what happened."

"Close the door," my dad grumbled.

"I'll be back soon," I said and closed the door behind me.

This is where things get weird and unexplainable. Outside a storm was brewing in the distance. The wind had picked up, lightning was flashing in the sky. By morning, the weather was going to be nasty but at that moment the storm was a ways off. There was only a slight drizzle.

I made my way down a nearby path and into the woods. I didn't bring a flashlight. I didn't need one. The moon and stars were bright enough to light my way. At some point I went off the path and ventured down a valley in an effort to get out of the wind. It wasn't really smart of me. I was going to have a bitch of a time climbing back up the hill.

The ground was littered with pine needles. My feet were crunching as I made my way through them. I could hear the wind whistling in the trees above me. I had no destination in mind. I only wanted to wander until my head was clear.

Seeing Max again royally screwed me up. This was the man that had my wife shot. This was the man that wounded my teammates and nearly beat me to death. I wanted to kill him. I really, truly wanted to kill him. I may have missed being the Guardian before, but that was nothing compared to what I was feeling as I walked through the forest.

The rage I felt as I left my dying wife in the hospital was back. It began in my heart and crawled through my veins. I began thinking about the nightmares I'd been having. I had failed everyone, and more people were going to die because I wasn't strong enough to hold onto my power.

I hated myself.

I did. I hated the weakness in my body. I hated the lurching shuffle I was forced to walk. I hated not being able to stand up straight. I hated the ugly, damaged nose I saw in the mirror every morning.

Most of all, I hated Max.

I entered a clearing of green grass. It was an almost perfect circle. I walked to the very center of it and stared up at the moon. I could hear thunder booming in the distance. The sounds rumbled and spread throughout the forest.

I looked in that direction. I watched the lightning flash; sharp etching across the sky. The anger, the hate, and the self-loathing washed over me. I felt their menace as my useless fingers twisted against the grip of my cane.

I imagined what I'd do to Max if I weren't a broken man. Different scenarios flashed across my mind. Each of them grew more violent. Each of them ended with his death. I gnashed my teeth as a soft drizzle turned into a downpour that soaked me to the bone.

I remembered holding my dying wife in my arms. I remembered the beating he gave me. I slammed my cane to the ground. I was trembling. My back was hurting me. My leg was threatening to give out. Even my skeleton ached. The pain only fueled my rage.

A final image of holding my bleeding wife in my arms and I could take no more.

"FUCK YOU!" I screamed out to the nighttime sky. "I gave you everything! I risked my life! I saved people, and this is how you leave me?"

The rain came down even harder. Lightning began to flash above me.

"I fought my heart out for you!" I screamed. "Where are you when I need you the most? Where are you? You coward! You took everything from me!"

Lightning arced down, and lit up the forest. Thunder began to grumble out a menacing warning, but I would not be denied. Not even when the lightning touched the ground only ten feet away, creating a small fire that burned despite the rain.

"I am the Guardian!" I screamed. "I'm not finished! I want it back! I want my revenge!"

Again the lightning touched the ground, and again after that. The hair on my arms was electrified and standing straight up. The clearing was almost glowing and my rage was spent.

"I was a fool for doing your work," I grumbled, and limped away.

Now, I'm not sure how I got my powers. Maybe it was some mysterious entity. Maybe it was a Sasquatch. Maybe it was an alien. Maybe it was God. Maybe it was Mother Nature. I don't know. Miriam doesn't know. Nobody knows, but I'll tell you this, whatever being was responsible finally started paying attention. They also seemed to be a bit pissed off.

More lightning strikes hit the ground in front of me, one after another. I was a bit worried at how close they seemed to be getting. I even backed up a tad but it did me no good. The fourth strike hit me square in the chest.

It wrapped me up in its electrified grip and squeezed the hell out of me. I was shaking and screaming. I levitated eight feet from the ground. All I saw was the bluish-white light. I wondered why the strike was lasting so long. It should have hit me and vanished. Instead, the damn thing was sticking around to torture me.

Blackness.

I woke up in my bed with no memory of walking home. I felt hung-over. Maybe I had a few drinks, I couldn't remember. Skie wasn't in the bed.

I couldn't find my leg brace or my cane. I grabbed a decorative walking stick and used that instead. I made my way out into the kitchen. Everyone had gathered there. All of them were looking sullen.

"Is it Merrick?" I asked.

"She's suffering now, Jax," Skie said. "It would be cruel to keep her any longer."

I left the room and went to my dog. There was no tail wag to greet me. Her eyes were open but she couldn't focus. Tears filled my eyes. I sat down beside her.

"After all the things we've been through," I said. "Who would have thought?"

I started petting her. She didn't even look at me. I talked to her. She didn't respond. Her breathing was labored. Her mouth was hanging open. Skie was correct; keeping her any longer would be cruel.

"What do you think?" My dad asked.

It took me a bit before I could answer him without blubbering.

"Let me take a quick shower, and we'll go."

I don't know why I wanted a shower. Perhaps it was because I smelled like burnt hair. More likely it was just my way of delaying the inevitable.

"You're not supposed to go out in public," my dad said.

"I don't much care about that right now," I said.

Reluctantly, I left Merrick's side and limped my way to the shower. My heart was breaking. I've lost dogs before; it sucks tremendously. Skie tried to hug me. I brushed her off gently. I wanted to be alone with my grief.

In the bathroom, I looked at myself in the mirror. My cheek scruff had gotten a bit charred. I took the clipper, and ran it over the stubble, cutting off the burnt tips. After that I wet my hand and washed away any loose clippings still clinging to my face. My hand ached like a son-of-a-bitch.

As I turned on the water to the shower, my face began to itch terribly. I assumed my skin was sensitive around the burns, so I pushed my face under the warm water of the shower. The itching intensified. I also felt a tremendous pressure in my sinuses.

My hands came away full of grey whiskers after rubbing my cheeks. My nose began to bleed, and the pressure in my nose grew stronger.

SNAP

POP

I could hear the cartilage inside my nose rearranging itself. I cursed out loud. It hurt like a motherfucker. Large drops of blood fell to the floor of the shower. I found myself getting light-headed. I grabbed out at the tiled wall in order to steady myself but the sudden stabbing pain in each of my hands made that impossible.

In the back of my mind, I knew what was happening but that didn't make it feel any better. The crunching bones in my hands laughed at the pain in my nose. The screams came at that point. I couldn't help myself. The pressure on my bones would build and build only to release in a break as they refitted themselves into their correct positions.

My knees gave out.

Consciousness was lost for the briefest of moments, and the water fell directly on my wounded knee. The pain was almost indescribable. Seriously, how do you explain to someone what it feels like to grow back the damaged cartilage in your knee? I'm not sure I can. I swam on the edge of awareness. My brain wanted me to go to sleep, but the pain was having none of that.

Skie was banging on the bathroom door.

She was asking me if I was all right.

"Give Merrick a bath," I shouted through gritted teeth.

"What?" Skie asked.

"Just do it!" I shouted. "Put her in the tub and pour water on her."

The pain spread out from my hands and knee. It circled around my hip and danced along my spine. I heard every bit of it. I felt every bit of it. The pressure was too much. I wasn't as strong as I used to be. When my spine began to crack, I finally passed out, and I wasn't complaining.

I woke up to screaming.

I also woke up feeling like a brand new man. I laughed out loud and found my feet. A loud ruckus was going on at the opposite end of the house. My family was running from something. I went to the mirror and wiped away the condensation.

The face that looked back at me seemed ten years younger than the last time I saw it. The grey stubble and hair had been replaced by light brown. My nose was no longer misshapen.

I flexed my hands. They were a little stiff, but they worked just fine. The scars and burns all over my body had vanished. In their place was healthy pink skin. I was still pretty skinny, but the slight impression of muscle was now evident. Unfortunately, the paunch that hung over my waistband was still there, but even that had begun to shrink away.

I heard my dad laughing. I heard the sound of a table being turned over, and then I heard the giggles of multiple people.

I stepped out of the bathroom.

I went to my closet and dressed in running shorts and a t-shirt. I then threw on some shoes, and stretched.

I was smiling from ear to ear as I stepped out of my bedroom. The smile turned to laughter as soon as I entered the living room. A soaking wet Merrick was chasing my family around the living room. Skie was rubbing her butt where she'd evidently been nipped.

Gone were the signs of age hell-bent on claiming her life. The dog once again had the energy of a puppy. Her paws scrambled against the hardwood floors of the cabin as she tore around the room.

"Merrick," I called out.

The dog stopped in her tracks.

"Come see Daddy," I said.

Merrick ran towards me at full speed. She jumped from five feet away, and I caught her out of the air as if she were weightless. I laughed, and wrestled around with her on the floor. From the corners of my eyes I could see everyone watching us in disbelief. They wanted answers. I was too hyper to give them.

"I'm feeling much better," I said to their astonished faces. "I think I'll go for a run."

I didn't wait for them to say anything. Instead, I scooped up Merrick and bolted out the front door, a soft rain greeting us as we jumped off the front porch. The rain was a friend. The living, beating heart of the forest was our ally, and we tore off through the mud.

I wasn't nearly what I used to be. That became evident almost immediately. My speed was off. My reflexes were slower and I got tired. But I was running! I was running and jumping my way down the trail. I wasn't one hundred percent but I was on my way. It takes time for the power to settle in. Waiting a few months wouldn't be a problem. I was running again.

We ran to the clearing.

There was no evidence of lightning strikes anywhere. Not even the smallest bit of burnt grass could be found. Perhaps I dreamt the entire thing. Perhaps the Guardian power recoiled inside my mind after I was told Skie had died, because I truly gave up at that moment. I lost my will to live, and perhaps the rage I felt upon seeing the Monster on television brought forth the power once again.

I had no idea. I also didn't care. For good or bad, the power was once again mine. I had work to do in the near future. My mind was already churning. However, the moment was mine. I gave myself one day in which to play, and I wasn't about to waste it.

I had gotten my breath back with the brief rest. I wanted to lose it again. Calling out for Merrick, I tore into the woods. I didn't need a trail. Trails were for pussies. Around trees we went, jumping, sliding, crouching. We ran fast. Merrick did a lot better than me. I'm not sure how she managed to stay in respectable shape despite her advanced years, but she was embarrassing me.

I had to stop frequently. When I did, I would lie back in the nearest patch of grass and watch as the living tendrils slowly climbed up my body. A few hours before dark, I took a nap. My heart wanted to keep on running, but my body had reached its limit.

I fell asleep in the forest with Merrick resting beside me.

The sun was slipping past the horizon when I woke up. The grass released me from its grip as I stood. The rain was pouring, and a soaking wet Merrick looked at me rather grumpily for resting so long.

We ran.

We ran all the way back home. I didn't stop: not even when the burning in my chest became almost unbearable. I wanted to push myself. The freedom was what I sought. The thrill of moving fast through the wet forest: I loved it.

I hit the path at a dead run. From there, it wasn't far to my parents' cabin. As I stepped from the forest, I saw the team all standing there in the rain on the muddy driveway. Each of them looked at me as the rain drenched their clothes. None of them said a word.

I joined them.

We stood in a loose circle. Thunder boomed above us. Lightning flashed over our heads.

CRACK

BOOM

Georgie smiled. He then raised his fist over his head.

"REGULATORS!" He shouted.

"REGULATORS!" The rest of us echoed.

We were back. We didn't need to discuss things. We were ready to go. The horrors and regrets inside our minds had quieted down. We were back with a vengeance.

I looked towards the cabin. I saw my wife looking out at me from the window. I told the boys to wait as I went to her.

She was washing the dishes as I entered the kitchen. The rest of my family was nowhere to be found. She heard me walk in but she didn't turn around, a bad sign.

"Skie," I said. "Don't you want to talk to me?"

"Nothing I say matters," she said.

"It does matter," I replied.

"Is this why you stopped your physical therapy?" Skie asked. "Is this why you refused all the surgeries even though they would help you with the pain?"

"I think so," I said. "At least, I hoped my powers would return."

"So now you're back," Skie said. "I love that. I really do. I'm happy for you. Of course I am. All you did since I woke up was mope around. I did my best, but a normal life isn't enough for you anymore. You're only truly alive when you're out there risking your life fighting monsters."

"I'm the only one that can," I said.

"So what?" Skie said.

"I need to go," I said.

"Why?" Skie asked. "Why does it have to be you? Why not just take your life and run? Let someone else deal with the nasty things out there. I saw what they did to you, Jax. I saw your body. I saw the hurt. How do you expect me to let you go?"

"Because everything I do," I said. "I do it for you. I do it for my family. I do it so you can sleep safely at night."

"I don't care about that," Skie screamed as she threw a glass across the room. "He beat you. He hurt you. I don't want you fighting him again. I don't want you to get hurt. Why do you rush off so eagerly to face him again after what happened?"

"How could I not?" I asked. "How can I let him live after what he did to you? I can't stop thinking about it. Every time I close my eyes I see you lying there covered in blood. I couldn't wake you up. I kept trying but you wouldn't answer me. I see that, and I can't go on. I see a man that hurt my wife and I can't go on."

"He'll kill you," Skie said and walked out of the room.

I stood there for a bit and collected my thoughts. I cleaned up the broken glass. My dad walked into the room.

"She needs time," he said. "She was getting used to the idea of having you around all safe and sound."

"I guess so," I said.

"Tell Dudley and the rest of that bunch to take their shoes off before they come in," my dad said. "Your mom will be pissed if they get mud all over her floor."

The team brought booze, lots and lots of booze. Before I knew it, the shots were flowing, and the jokes were rolling out. We were laughing. We were pounding drinks. Georgie was so happy he was literally jumping up and down. Eventually, he made the mistake of humping Nick's leg. Nick, in turn, smacked him on top of his head, which led to Dudley smacking Nick in the balls. All of that led to a free for all.

My mom came running into the kitchen. She didn't want us rough-housing inside. Things ended up getting broken that way. Dudley tried to give her a shot. She refused, but my dad came into the room behind her with no thoughts of turning it down. The kids eventually ventured into the party. Merrick was happy to see them and began running in circles.

The doorbell rang.

Ivana walked into the cabin. All of us cheered out for her and raised our glasses. The poor girl was crying. She made a beeline straight for me, and held my face in her hands.

"My favorite boy," she said. "I didn't want to believe it. I didn't dare to hope."

I heard later that as soon as Georgie hit the shower and got his powers back, he ran up and down the hallways screaming about how the Regulators were back. Word had spread pretty fast after that, though the boys didn't stick around. Instead, they made a beeline straight to my parents' cabin to see what was going on.

"You need a shot?" I asked.

"I need a million shots," Ivana said as I threw her over my shoulder, and made my way over to the liquor.

Two hours later, the doorbell rang again.

Miriam walked in. She smiled when she saw us.

"I knew this day would come," Miriam smiled. "I knew it in my heart. I can't tell you how happy I am."

"Somebody pour her a shot," Dudley said.

The party continued. We were loud. We were rowdy. We told jokes. We told stories. We made up for lost time and we had a great time doing so. It got late. My parents and the kids went to sleep. The rest of us continued.

At one point Dudley tried to convince Miriam to let him color her hair. In turn, Miriam threatened to turn him into a rat. Javie broke out the music and began ripping his shirt off. Nick started crushing beer cans on his forehead, and Georgie began moaning about wanting a fine glass of wine.

"Whiskey is for bad asses," Nick growled. "Bring up wine one more time, and I'll shove a wine bottle up your ass."

"Beer is for high school kids," Georgie laughed. "I'm a classy motherfucker, you beer chugging pantywaist."

Georgie farted loudly.

Nick threw a beer bottle cap and hit Georgie in the forehead. I jumped on Nick's back, and started riding him like a bull as everyone counted out eight seconds.

Skie entered the room.

Her eyes were puffy. She was wearing a t-shirt with my emblem on it. Everyone quieted down immediately as she grabbed a beer and proceeded to chug. When she finished half the bottle, she wiped her mouth with the back of her hand and raised her bottle into the air.

"REGULATORS," she screamed out.

Everyone cheered as she ran over and jumped at me. I caught her easily and spun her around. She was smiling that big smile of hers. My heart was singing.

"Still mad?" I asked.

"I know the man I married," Skie said. "He's not a quitter, and I love him for that. It just took me a few hours to figure things out. Now make me a promise. I won't ask you to not do anything stupid. I know you better than that. Instead, I'm asking you to return to me. I want you to survive this battle. I want you to come home."

"Silly girl," I said. "Haven't you learned anything yet? I always find my way home to you."

Skie tilted her head back and laughed heartily. I spun her around the room. I kept kissing her cheeks as she giggled merrily. This was my wife. This was my life. I had it back. The future would be tough but the present was upon us, and we were going to celebrate.

The party raged on for another two more hours until a soft knock was heard upon the front door. Dudley let Hardin into the room. He was smiling broadly and carrying a wooden box.

"Wow," Hardin said. "I don't even have the words. I won't stay long. I know I'm unwelcome. I only had to see for myself."

"Balls," Skie giggled drunkenly. "You're as much a part of this family as everyone else. Grab a drink and get after it."

Hardin did as asked. He partied with us. I couldn't remember seeing the man unwind before. As far as I knew, all he ever did was work. It was strange seeing him clap the boys on the shoulder and join in on their jokes.

"Awe," Javie said in his best Brad Pitt impression. "What's in the box?"

Everyone looked at the box.

"Yeah," Dudley said. "I was wondering about that myself. Then I drank some more and forgot all about it."

"Best to leave the man and his box alone," Georgie added. "I'm personally uninterested in his vibrator collection, and have no desire to hear all about it."

Hardin laughed.

"This here is a gift for Jaxon," Hardin said. "I found it on the wall of Major Crass's office."

I went to the box. Something about it kept drawing my eyes from the moment Hardin walked into the cabin. It was a plain box, stained a light color. The gloss on the wood was of the highest quality, and it even reflected the light a bit. The two hinges popped open with a slight creak. I lifted the lid.

My fingers twitched. I couldn't believe what I was looking at. The metal had been refinished. I couldn't see a scratch. The handle had been replaced. The new wood was pale and waxed.

My tomahawk.

The weapon called out to me from a bed of velvet cushioning. My hands were shaking as I reached for it. The handle felt warm. The metal felt alive.

"I sent it down to our weapons team," Hardin said. "They were more than happy to fix it up for you. Even went so far as to polish it up and everything. Made them a little nervous to handle it though, I'm not sure why. Where'd you get that thing anyway?"

"To tell the truth," I said. "I can't really remember. I'm sure I ordered it somewhere. I just can't remember ever doing the ordering."

"Well," Hardin said. "There you go. I thought you might want it back."

"Oh fuck yeah," Georgie said. "Now we're talking. Let's see the Monster deal with that shit."

"I've got the dirt on the Monster as well if you want to hear it," Hardin said. "Major Crass held out for a while on that score, but eventually he cracked."

I heard Hardin. I was interested in what he was saying. Yet I had been reunited with an old friend. I needed a moment. I took a practice swing. I tested the weight. I tested the balance. The tomahawk sang with each swing. I smiled.

"Let's go somewhere and talk," I said.

That somewhere ended up being my underground bunker. The girls and Merrick stayed behind. The team, Hardin, and I went to talk.

We each pulled out a seat at the table while Georgie made coffee. Playtime was over. I was in the mood to work.

"Tell me about Max," I said.

"Every read any Mary Shelley?" Hardin asked.

That had to sit a bit. Of course I had read Mary Shelley. I knew immediately what Max had become. But I didn't know the how of it.

"Who's Mary Shelley?" Nick asked.

"She's an author," Dudley said.

"What does that have to do with anything?" Nick asked.

"She wrote *Frankenstein*," Javie said. "Are you trying to tell us that the Monster is the Monster from the book?"

"Not really," Hardin said. "He's had many upgrades that the original creation never had, but he was created in the same way."

"How did Major Crass do this?" I asked.

"The original Monster was created using two different items," Hardin said. "Black energy and ichor: mix them both together, and there you go. You see, ichor is a fluid that stops decomposition and infection completely. Black energy is an energy source that behaves very much like traditional electricity, but it can only be used to power a body."

"Where did you send Crass after I beat him up?" I asked.

"We sent him to the Arctic circle," Hardin answered. "It was a punishment: a horrible job investigating some tunnels that had been discovered. Evidently he found something in those tunnels. He shared what he found with a scientist at his station, and together they created the Monster."

"I don't get it," Georgie said. "How did they get a hold of Max's body?"

"I'm not sure about that one yet," Hardin answered, "But somehow they managed."

"Wait a second," I said. "Let's go back to black energy and ichor. How does all of that work?"

"Sometime in the late 1700s," Hardin said. "A depressed scientist began experimenting with fresh corpses. The first thing he did was pervert electricity into something that would power a corpse. Now, don't ask me to explain how. I'm not a scientist, but he created what we now call black energy. However, this wasn't enough. The bodies were still decaying because they weren't truly alive. For that, he needed ichor. Momo believes ichor was created from that black fluid the vampires like to drool."

"So that glowing disk over Max's heart was his power source?" I asked.

"Yes," Hardin said. "That disk created the black energy that powered his body."

"I destroyed that disk," I said.

"The body can survive up to twenty four hours on the leftover charge," Hardin said.

"Max wasn't the same," I said. "He seemed comprised of a bunch of different pieces."

"All made possible by the ichor in his veins," Hardin said. "With ichor, you could mix and match all sorts of body parts together and make them work. You can also add metal body armor under the skin without fear of killing the host."

"That's why fire got to him," Nick said. "Frankenstein doesn't like fire."

"The Monster isn't called Frankenstein," Javie said. "Try and read a book every now and then."

"Whatever, asshole," Nick said.

"Geez," Dudley interrupted. "How awesome would that be? You could basically upgrade yourself whenever you wanted to."

"It wouldn't be awesome at all," Hardin said. "The creature isn't alive. He doesn't feel things like a human being. He functions, but he feels very little. Pain means almost nothing to him. Only fire can create a strong enough sensation for him to feel."

"So how do I fight him?" I asked.

"You don't," Hardin said. "We'll get a big enough gun and tear him to pieces with the bullets. Not even a Guardian can fight a creature that feels no pain, has no weaknesses, and won't get tired."

"He'll get tired twenty four hours after you pull his battery out," Georgie added.

"Yes," Dudley said, "but who can fight him for that long? Mr. Hardin is right. We need to either light him up or blow him to pieces with the guns."

"How strong is he?" I asked.

"The original creature was incredibly strong," Hardin answered. "Max seems to be an upgrade from the original, so I won't even hazard a guess."

"He gets his strength from the ichor in his veins, doesn't he?" I asked.

"That sounds pretty accurate," Hardin answered. "You can't bleed him out either. ichor is thick. It doesn't flow like blood."

"Jaxon," Dudley said. "You're not going to fight him. You don't need to. We'll take him out at a distance, okay?"

"Yeah," I said only because I didn't have a solution to the problem…yet.

Chapter 12

DUDLEY

Dudley was in an odd mood when he walked into the room. Evidently he was still worried about what questions I might be asking him. He made some jokes, he drank some weird shake, and screamed out "Rock n Roll" every time I tried talking to him.

It wasn't until I promised not to ask him about his feelings during what the team refers to as their "dark days" that he finally calmed down.

"Jaxon took me all the way to the meeting in the underground bunker. I now know how the Monster was resurrected."

What does that tell you about our lives that nobody questioned whether it was true or not? Geez, the world we live in. Still, I guess that's why we get paid the big bucks. Fighting monsters isn't easy.

"Is that what you were thinking when you learned about Max?"

Well, you've seen the video he released to the news stations. It sort of made sense just by looking at him. Fighting him was a nightmare. The son of a bitch was tough. What really made me nervous was my uncle. Jaxon had unfinished business with the Monster. I didn't like the way the gears started turning in his head after we told him not to go out and fight the bastard again.

I was going to beat a dead horse and continue pressing my uncle to control himself, but Georgie interrupted.

"So what are the plans so far?" Georgie asked. "What are we doing to keep the zombies from crossing into New Mexico?"

"I have choppers carrying boulders on the way," Mr. Hardin said. "The plan is to drop these boulders up and down the Rio Grande to make a wall. When the dead climb over the wall, we'll shoot them down."

Jaxon told him how stupid that idea was. Because that's how Jaxon tends to talk to people, and Mr. Hardin then asked my uncle if he had a better plan. Jax smiled. After that, Jaxon began talking, and the rest of us tried to keep up with him.

He had crazy ideas and we ate them up. Crazy wins the day, especially when it's coming from Jaxon. Mr. Hardin was on the phone immediately. He was following Jaxon's plan to the letter, until he asked for swords and shields.

"Why do we want swords and shields?" Mr. Hardin asked. "We have guns."

"This fight will be up close and personal whether you like it or not," Jaxon said. "The zombies will swarm into the biggest horde we've ever seen. Explosions might work, but they won't stop all of them. The dust will get kicked up, and visibility will be tough. Also, Max will be expecting guns."

"Not counting five Special Forces teams, I only have two hundred and forty-three soldiers," Mr. Hardin said. "Those were the volunteers that stayed behind. The military won't give me any more: not with our chance of failure being so high."

"You ever hear about the battle of Thermopylae? Jaxon asked.

Mr. Hardin smiled, and then he made calls. He wanted a surplus of short swords and big shields, and he wanted them by the thousands.

Things were set into motion. Jaxon still wasn't satisfied. He wanted something else. He wanted an ace in the hole. He began to pace the room. The tomahawk twirled in his hand.

"What ever happened to that vampire Ivana found?" He asked abruptly.

More calls were made. Ivana left for New York within the hour.

Eventually, after we had planned and planned, after we had gone over every scenario we could possibly think of, the meeting was over. Mr. Hardin took his leave. The man looked worried. I couldn't blame him. Somehow we had missed the sunrise and were greeted by the sunset when we exited the bunker. All that time planning and it still didn't seem like we were ready.

We said our goodbyes to the family soon after Mr. Hardin left. They were going to be spending some time in Alaska, far away from the troubles in El Paso. Tears were shed. Skie and Jaxon embraced. He whispered something in her ear. She smiled despite herself, and then she hugged him again before getting in the waiting car.

Only the Regulators were left after that. We sat around. We ate. We didn't joke much. We went to sleep. We woke up. We were having coffee on the porch as a car pulled into the driveway. Each of us was given a suitcase.

We hauled the suitcases into the living room and opened them up. Our gear had arrived. All of us began to suit up. It was a surreal moment. It was a moment we had dreamed about but thought would never again happen. I pulled on the pants and shirt of the bite suit. I shoved my feet into the boots. I strapped on the knee and elbow pads. I clicked on the utility belt and zipped up the utility vest.

The need for silenced weapons had passed. All of us were using assault-type shotguns, except for Georgie, and Jaxon. Georgie decided to use an AK47, and my uncle chose his old youth model Winchester twenty gauge that he swore was the best shotgun he'd ever used. Of course, he pulled out the plug, and loaded it up with slugs. He also attached a sling.

"He used a youth gun?"

My grandpa got it for Jaxon when he was a kid. It's a great gun, and Jaxon has always appreciated its smaller size.

We cheered when Jax shoved a Harley Davidson cap backwards on his head. We laughed when Georgie put on a helmet. We were still laughing when a helicopter landed in the driveway to pick us up.

The view of the mountains from the air was breathtaking. I enjoyed the ride. It was peaceful. That is, until we left the mountains. Once we reached the town, things looked differently. A mass exodus of cars filled the roads.

"I thought they'd be finished with the evacuations by now," Nick said.

Nobody replied. We simply watched all the cars driving away to safety. When we flew over the freeways, we saw even more cars. Everyone was leaving. We were headed to war. The Regulators had never gone to war before. We had our little missions, but never was the fate of the world so violently shoved into our hands.

I was scared. It sucks to admit that, but I'm not going to lie. I was going to kill, and I was going to see others get killed. Violence was in my future. There would be no running. I would stand beside my teammates and fight until I was dead, or my enemies had all been destroyed.

I rested my hands on top of my shotgun in order to keep them from shaking, and I watched the evacuation far below us.

Everyone stayed quiet until we crossed over Las Cruces, New Mexico, and Nick opened his mouth.

"Too bad you aren't going to fight the Monster," Nick said. "You could have had your Batman moment."

"My what?" Jaxon asked with a confused look on his face.

"You know," Nick said. "Batman was all badass, and then Bane comes around and beats him up. So, Batman goes to prison until he gets even tougher. Then they have a rematch and Batman saves the day."

"Batman didn't go to prison," Georgie said. "His back was broken."

"Nick is talking about the movie not the comic book," Javie added.

"Regardless," Nick said. "The Monster is Jaxon's Bane."

"Shut up, Nick," I growled. "Don't give my uncle any bad ideas."

"I'm not," Nick said. "We'll take the fucker out like we planned. I'm just saying, is all."

I didn't like the look on Jaxon's face. I didn't like it one bit. He was looking at Nick, but his mind was far away. The gears were turning once again.

We flew over El Paso. The pilot wouldn't show us the gathering horde, but he assured us it was there. For the past couple days Max had been driving around the city blaring out that weird foghorn sound of his in an effort to gather his army.

The chopper flew down Country Club Road, and I saw Jaxon's plan laid out before me. Let me set this up for you, if you don't mind.

"That would be great."

If you remember, Country Club Road goes right over the Rio Grande on a small bridge and ends up in New Mexico. Now, we blew this bridge when we escaped from El Paso way back when. The military had since replaced it with a drawbridge, and they had also cleared all the abandoned vehicles off the street at some point.

Rocks, giant boulders really, were piled up on both sides of the two-lane street leading up to the bridge. They ran down Country Club, away from the bridge for about the length of a football field. The zombies wouldn't be able to climb over them. Hell, they wouldn't even try, because our small army of soldiers would be between those walls of rock with their shields and swords.

"You were going to squeeze the horde into a small area in order to control their massive numbers. Now I see why the General asked Mr. Hardin if he'd ever heard about the battle of Thermopylae."

Then you get it, right? The zombies would head right for the people, and in order to do so, they would have to squeeze their numbers between the walls of rock. By doing that, we wouldn't get surrounded, and we could also control how many attacked at one time.

Since the conception of the plan, Mr. Hardin had the soldiers training to fight with swords and shields. Those poor guys probably never expected to need skills like that.

The helicopter landed.

Mr. Hardin, Snake Charmer, and his new team, approached us immediately. Merrick sniffed each of their hands before allowing them to get too close.

"Our weapons have been sabotaged," Mr. Hardin said. "Most of the explosives have been stolen. The majority of the rifles have been destroyed. How'd you know Max would attack our weapons?"

"Because I would've done the same thing in his shoes," Jaxon said. "How long ago did this happen?"

"My men are trying to piece that together now," Mr. Hardin answered. "We're guessing just a little over an hour ago. Four guards are dead. We had no idea we'd even been struck until the ordinance went off. By then, whoever hit us was long gone."

"He probably sent his men to do that," Jaxon said. "Snake Charmer, are you and your men ready to go?"

"All Special Forces teams have been deployed," Snake Charmer said. "Except for mine."

"Good hunting then," Jaxon said. "Don't let us get shot."

Snake Charmer laughed and set out. His job, and the job of the four other Special Forces teams, was to take out the Albanian Mafia members that worked for Max. They stationed themselves throughout the area and ambushed our ambushers. I have to say, those teams are incredible. We were never once shot at during the entire battle.

"Do you have any other explosives?" Jaxon asked.

"I'm sure I can scrounge up something if you have an idea," Mr. Hardin answered.

"I do," Jaxon said. "I'll also need a remote detonator."

Another helicopter approached from the distance. Ivana ran out of it carrying a large cooler. She immediately ran to Jaxon.

"I've got everything you need," Ivana said. "She was more than happy to help out. Momo has her set up quite nicely, in exchange for her good behavior. They also keep her well fed."

"What do I need to do?" Jaxon asked.

"It's easy," Ivana said. "You draw a symbol with the blood and light it on fire. Just make sure the blood never gets put in the sunlight. It'll dissolve before you need it, and they won't come until nightfall anyway."

"Got it," Jaxon said. "How do I light it up?"

"Momo included a small fire starter gizmo," Ivana said. "After you draw the symbol, place the gizmo in the blood. When you're ready, hit the button on the remote. All of them will burn at the same time."

"Gotcha," Jaxon said. "Now give me a hug and get out of here. I want you safe."

"I'm worried about you," Ivana cried as she hugged my uncle. "Please don't do anything too crazy."

Jaxon laughed at that. Ivana hugged me, and then she was back in the chopper flying far away from El Paso. Jaxon sighed a contentedly as he watched her leave. Our loved ones were safe.

"You wanna go for a walk?" He asked.

"Nothing better to do," I answered.

With that, we had the drawbridge lowered, and Merrick, Jaxon, and I stepped into El Paso. The day was warm, but it wasn't too hot. It was a nice day. The smell of rot was not yet in the air. It would come, though. It would definitely come.

We went from house to house. Jaxon would kick in a door and we'd clear a room. He would then open up the cooler, grab a paintbrush, and paint a weird circle symbol somewhere in a dark corner. After that, he set a tiny box with wires in the blood.

"Is that vampire blood?" I asked.

"Yeah," Jaxon answered.

"How many of these are we going to set up?" I asked.

"How many fire starter gizmos are there?" Jaxon asked in return.

"Looks to be about a hundred," I said.

"Sounds good to me," Jaxon said. "If it works, it'll be worth the work."

It ended up taking most of the day. Every now and then we'd encounter zombies in the houses. Jaxon would take care of them immediately. The tomahawk would flash through the air and bodies would drop. Merrick and I did our best to help him, but he didn't need much in the way of assistance. All in all, there weren't a lot of them in the area.

"AAAAWWWWOOOOAAAA!"

That's the sound we heard about our third house in. It was distant, but Jaxon still stopped his symbol painting.

"That explains why this area is so vacant," Jaxon said. "Any shambler that can, has already set out after Max. He's going to have one hell of an army with him."

I must have looked worried.

"Listen," Jax said. "Just fight. That's all you have to do. Don't worry about anything else. Keep yourself safe. Stay by the team and fight."

I nodded that I understood.

An hour before sunset we made our way across the bridge. Mr. Hardin met us with the last of the explosives.

"Is this big enough to take out the bridge?" Jaxon asked.

"Just set them on the corners," Mr. Hardin said. "It won't be a big explosion, but it'll do what you're asking."

With that, Jaxon and Merrick vanished under the bridge. I didn't know what he was planning. I figured it was a failsafe in case the zombies attempted to cross the border. I should have paid a bit more attention; the bridge was a drawbridge. It didn't need a failsafe.

I watched as some soldiers set up a large camera on a long pole before the drawbridge. The video from that camera was being monitored by the military. If the zombies crossed over the border, they would see it happen. I could only imagine a bunch of old duffers sitting around a big monitor with their fingers on a button.

I didn't want to blow up. The stupid camera was giving me the creeps. I walked away from it and went to sit next to the rest of the team on the banks of the river. Together we watched the Rio Grande flow on by.

A soldier came and dropped off our shields. Nick and I didn't need swords. I was going to use my machete, and Nick was comfortable with his fireman's axe. The round shields were immense. They covered us from shin to jaw. It looked as if they were made from some sort of black-colored, high tech plastic, so they were much lighter than they appeared.

"I wonder where Mr. Hardin got all these swords and shields in such a short amount of time?" Javie asked, as he twirled his sword.

"Mr. Hardin has a lot of contacts," I answered.

"You assholes ready for this shit?" Nick asked. "We're going out in the first row. That's some scary shit."

I chuckled at his honesty. I also agreed with him. Going out in the first row was some scary shit. How else could we gather the support of all the troops? They needed to see us in action. They needed to see the plan work.

"AAAAWWWWOOOOAAAA!"

I had been hearing the Monster's call all throughout the day. It kept getting closer and closer. We had two shooters, armed with .50 cal machine guns, on opposite sides of the boulders. Mr. Hardin had even erected them a flimsy looking stand that raised them up fifteen feet in the air. If the Monster were in the horde, they would get him. They were told to look out for him.

I looked towards the bridge. Jaxon stood on it by himself. He was glaring towards the city, as if he could see the former Guardian. I was worried about my uncle. He wanted his revenge. I knew he did. Unfortunately, he wasn't in top shape, and even if he was, the Monster was too much for one man.

Jaxon simply could not fight him. I wouldn't allow it. The Monster would come. I doubted he'd be stupid enough to walk in front of the machine guns, but he'd come for Jax. Of that, I had no doubt. Unfortunately, I didn't have a plan for it. I was only hoping to prevent my uncle from chasing after him. It would be better to go at him as a team with some really big guns, after we took out the zombies.

I had visions of us chasing down the former Guardian through an empty El Paso. He wasn't so fierce anymore. He wasn't so tough. We would finally corner him in a deserted home, or a filthy alley. There, the team would blow him to pieces with guns big enough to tear through his armor.

"AAAAWWWWOOOOAAAA!"

This time, the call was closer. I looked towards Jaxon once again. He was smiling. He lived for these moments. Pitting himself against impossible odds had become a game for him. He had changed so much since the outbreak. He had become a leader. He had become a symbol that people could follow. Watching him on that bridge, with Merrick sniffing around his shoes, he looked every bit the hero people thought him to be.

The soldiers gathered up behind him. One after another they came. Armed with their shields and swords, they looked a bit like an ancient army preparing to defend their homeland. The sky had turned red around us. I saw Mr. Hardin in the distance watching the scene unfold.

When the soldiers had all come forth, Jaxon turned and faced them. He walked back and forth, and sized them up. His green eyes were on fire. The lust for battle was evident in his powerful stride.

"AAAAWWWWOOOOAAAA!"

The dead were getting closer. The battle was almost upon us. The team joined the soldiers, and Jaxon began to speak.

"I won't lie to you," Jaxon said. "Very soon we will all descend into Hell. The worst visions from your worst nightmares will be thrust upon you. You have a right to be afraid. You should be afraid, because our enemy knows no fear and they will never stop. Many of us will die here tonight. But we will not run. We will not break rank. We will stand strong against the Hell that pounds against our shields, for this is the last stand. If we fail, the entire world will fall. Your wives; your children; your friends; and your loved ones, all of them are depending on you. This is your moment. This is where you make a difference."

Everyone cheered.

"LET'S RAISE SOME HELL!" Jaxon shouted, and after grabbing a shield, he led the way across the bridge. I shoved my way to his right, and Georgie took my right side. Nick was on Jaxon's left, and Javie was on Nick's left. Merrick was out in front sniffing the air. Soldiers were all around us.

We marched slowly to the middle point of the rock barriers. The street lights came on above us as the sun slipped below the horizon. One of the soldiers passed Georgie a flask of whiskey.

"To better days," he said as he drank.

"To a brighter future," I said when he passed the flask to me.

Nick reached out for it and took a big gulp.

"I'm gonna get laid after this," Nick said, and handed the flask to Javie.

"Here's hoping Nick isn't referring to me," Javie said, and passed the flask back down the line to Jax.

"Here's to payback," Jaxon snarled.

A lone figure entered the opposite end of the street. It sort of shambled out of nowhere. It spotted us immediately and screamed in our direction. Our entire army screamed back at it. The figure ran at us. It moved fast.

Jaxon pulled his tomahawk out of his belt sheath.

The figure entered the canyon of rocks. More figures appeared behind it. They began screaming out as well as they entered the canyon and charged towards us.

Our shields came up and overlapped one another. The shields of the men behind us pressed against our backs. I looked to my right. Georgie's eyes were wide, but he was hanging in. On my left, Jaxon's green eyes were shining in the dim light.

The first figure never made his way to us. Merrick brought him down five feet from our shields. We watched as she tore into the back of the corpse's neck, and then we looked past the both of them to the small horde not far beyond.

There must have been forty or fifty of them. They ignored Merrick and her zombie. They rammed straight into our shields, and we stopped them flat. From there it was a massacre. They couldn't get around us, and we hacked them to pieces.

It was over in a matter of seconds.

Everyone was cheering.

"AAAAWWWWOOOOAAAA!" called the former Guardian from somewhere near the mouth of the canyon.

"Brace yourselves!" Jaxon shouted as a massive horde took shape under the dim streetlamps farther down the road.

Brace ourselves we did. First, we steadied our bodies. Then, we steadied our nerves. The horde was too numerous to count. The smell they gave off was nauseating. The sound they created was deafening.

They poured into the mouth of the canyon. There they shoved and trampled on one another in an effort to be the first to reach us. Their numbers were counting against them. The vast size of the horde counted for very little inside the narrow canyon walls.

The dead slammed against our shields. They shoved against us but we lost very little ground as we hacked and pushed back against them. Nick was laughing as he handled his fireman's axe with only one hand to deadly effect.

Jaxon was using the blade tip of his tomahawk as a stabbing weapon. Each thrust punctured a skull. Bodies were mounting up at our feet.

After thirty minutes of battle, my arms began to grow tired. My machete was no longer slicing the air with evil intent. My strikes were getting clumsy. I looked towards Jaxon. He looked tired as well. Of course, he still hadn't nearly recovered from all he'd been through.

"Time!" Jaxon shouted.

Shields opened up behind us. We were pulled backwards down the rows as the men behind us took our place.

"Merrick," Jaxon called, and the black dog followed her master.

In a matter of seconds, the front line was at the back of the formation. We were able to rest. I grabbed a canteen full of water from my utility belt and took a swig.

"Holy shit," I said. "That was crazy. I can't believe it's working."

"Two minutes," Jaxon said. "Then let's get back at it."

More and more zombies piled into the rock canyon. It didn't matter. They couldn't gain an inch on us. The narrow confines of the canyon, combined with our blades and shields, stopped them cold until they were just one big putrid, screaming, mob, waiting to have their skulls cleaved in.

Three or four rows had taken their turn when something bad happened. The dead bodies for the most part aided in our defenses, but the leaking fluids made the ground slippery. A soldier went down. He was torn into immediately, and then the gap closed as another shield took his place. His body was hauled backwards past me. He was just a kid. Younger than me, probably around twenty or so, and screaming that he wanted to go home. Somehow, the dead managed to rip off the pants of his bite suit. His legs were shredded.

Jaxon left his place and followed the soldier to the back of the formation. He put the kid out of his misery. As always, a bite was fatal. The army helping us out wasn't gifted with our abilities to heal. The soldiers were lucky enough to all have bite suits.

We lost people. The ground was becoming too slippery. We couldn't advance forward; there was an army of corpses pushing against us. Not to mention all the fallen bodies blocking our way. Reluctantly, we went backwards until our soldiers once again found traction.

The canyon was filled with the dead and even more were trying to shove their way inside. Our army was getting tired. It wasn't going to be long before we had to give up more ground. The seeds of doubt began to enter my mind. We could only give up so much ground. Our soldiers were getting tired. Would we be able to bring them all down before we ran out of room, and grew too weak to prevent them from overwhelming us, and crossing over?

I never considered the Monster. I should have known he wouldn't be content to sit back and watch the battle unfold.

The explosion wasn't too big, but it was loud. Four people on the front line were killed instantly. Two people in the line behind them later died from their wounds. The dead had broken through our defenses.

"What the fuck?" Jaxon demanded as he left his place and forced his way to the hole in the frontline.

I followed behind him. I watched as he slammed the shamblers with his shield and cut them down with his tomahawk. He shouted out orders. The front line was sealed. Jaxon and I dealt with the zombies inside our formation.

Another explosion took place right as our line made its way to the front once again. I saw it that time. One of the zombies was wearing an explosive vest. Max set it off just as the corpse slammed against our shields.

More people were killed. The first eight lines of our formation were in complete disarray as the zombies swarmed into the gaps. Jaxon didn't miss a beat. He fought, and the Regulators joined him. He ordered the disarrayed soldiers to fall back behind the remaining formation, and we held off the advancing zombies that crowded around us.

Back to back we stood. To see the different styles we each employed made for a heck of a sight. Nick used brute strength. Javie attacked wildly. Georgie reacted defensively. I picked my moments, and Jaxon did what Jaxon does. He mixes everything together, and he seems to be everywhere at once.

Merrick joined up with Georgie. That was good. He needed the help, and I'm sure he appreciated the way Merrick would bring down a zombie so he could easily strike it on the head.

Another explosion blasted out behind us, towards the formation of soldiers still holding their ground. I prayed they would be able to close the gap without us.

"The son of a bitch figured out how to bring us down," I said to Jaxon.

"Yeah," Jaxon agreed.

"What are we going to do?" I asked.

"He's using a remote detonator," Jaxon said. "He has to be. They only blow up when they reach the front line. Max is watching us from somewhere. We need to take his hand off the button."

Not long after that we were able to make our way back to the formation. Thankfully, they had been able to plug the holes. Unfortunately, they had lost more ground in the process. The soldiers allowed us past their shields and we made our way to the back of the line.

The battle was raging, and there was no indication that it was nearing an end. We were slowly losing but not one single person deserted their position.

Another explosion rocked against the frontline. The wave of the undead broke through once again. We were tired. We were injured. The zombies were able to kill many of us before we managed to cut them down and plug the hole.

Still, we pushed on. Well, we tried at least. Our numbers were low. We were being shoved backwards. The force of the great horde was so powerful; those in the front lines were no longer able to strike them down. They had to concentrate all their energy on keeping their shields up.

"This is bad!" Nick shouted.

"We're being overwhelmed," Georgie agreed.

"To the last man!" Jaxon shouted as he pushed with all his considerable might.

"To the last man!" I screamed out, and joined him.

A moment of great despair came from a final explosion. Our formation was ripped apart. The dead were upon us. We fought bravely. We fought like heroes, and we died like heroes. Jaxon tossed away his shield and pulled out his long Bowie knife. He became a whirlwind of destruction but it wasn't enough. We could not reform our wall of shields.

And then when all seemed lost, a bright light came from behind us and I heard a roaring louder than the screams of the zombies. I spared a look, and my eyes grew wide. Help was rushing towards us; a great force over five thousand strong, led by a short man with a roaring chainsaw.

"THIS IS OUR LAND!" Father Monarez shouted as his force thundered over the drawbridge and joined the fight.

As they rushed in around me, I could see that they were young and old, men and women. Some of them had weapons; others had kitchen knives and gardening tools. They came from New Mexico, Mexico, and many other places. They were people that would not be evacuated. They were people that wanted to help, and the entire world should be thankful they came.

I was next to Jaxon and Merrick. I saw the look on Jaxon's face through the tears in my eyes. I don't know exactly how to describe his expression. He was covered in blood. He was battered and tired but he was also alive with hope.

"Not over yet," he grinned, and then I watched as his grin turn to acid.

Immediately, I looked behind me. I saw the large man holding a double-bladed battle axe standing atop the rock wall. He was silhouetted beneath a street lamp, but his proportions were unmistakable. He dropped into the canyon with mighty arrogance and strode forward to meet my uncle.

A blur of movement rushed by me, I tried to grab on to him but he was too fast. I tried to chase after him, but undead hands grabbed me by the shoulders, and I was once again fighting for my life.

Chapter 13

JAXON

Jaxon walked into the meeting room with a bottle of Jack, a pitcher of soda, and two glasses filled with ice. He was smiling as he poured.

If you wanna hear the end of this story, you're gonna need to drink with me.

"That sounds fair enough. Dudley told me all about the battle. It was a good thing Father Monarez and all those people showed up when they did."

You're not kidding. Imagine how we felt.

"What I'd like to know is how you felt when the former Guardian jumped into the canyon?"

I knew he'd make an appearance eventually. I needed him to. The exploding zombies were fucking us up. I needed to see him so I could stop him.

"After what happened before, were you at all worried about fighting him?"

Jaxon scratched his chin and considered my question a bit before answering.

I think I was. I think I was very worried, but I also wanted that fight. I didn't want help. I didn't want to burn him down or shoot him with really big guns. I wanted to beat him myself, and despite what anyone said, that was my plan from the moment my powers returned. I guess I just needed my Batman moment.

Merrick was helping Georgie. The rest of the team was distracted. Dudley was the only obstacle in my way, aside from the machine gunners, and they couldn't fire anyway, for fear of hitting all the humans scattered around the area. I made my move before Dudley could stop me. He tried, I'll give him credit for that, but he wasn't nearly quick enough.

The Monster and I passed each other at full speed. He swung his battle axe. I swung my tomahawk. I opened him up, and he missed me completely.

He growled out his fury, and homed in on me. We ran at one another again. Despite his strength, his battle axe was a slow-moving weapon. It was too heavy to be of much use against somebody as fast as me. I went into a roll at the last possible second. His weapon nicked off a piece of rubber from the sole of my shoe. I sliced his leg open.

A normal human would have been covered in blood and on their way to the morgue after the wounds Max received. However, his pink-tinged, gelatinous, blood refused to pour. My attacks didn't even weaken him, but I expected that.

"I knew you would be here," Max said. "Your pride made you come, but you should have run. Let the outbreak spread. What do you care? You could survive it. You could keep your loved ones safe, at least until I come for you, and I'll always come for you."

We sized each other up from a safe distance.

Max wore only combat boots, and camouflage pants. His body was burned even worse than his face. He had never healed from his wounds. He had merely continued on. From his pale blue-hued skin, to the metal showing beneath his wounds, the man had become a true monster to behold. He had replaced the glowing disk over his heart, and I made a mental note not to strike him in that area. I needed his power source functioning.

He made his move.

I dodged out of the way, but his sudden charge clipped me on the shoulder and knocked me off my feet. Before I knew it, he was standing over me and raining down punches on my face.

I raised an arm to defend myself and sliced away at his stomach. The cuts didn't hurt him or slow him down. Still, he eventually stepped away, as if he was worried about the cosmetic damage I was causing him.

I rose to my feet. I took my time. The effort it took was obvious, and Max started smiling.

"You aren't as tough as you were the last time we fought," Max said. "Back then, you were able to absorb a lot of punishment before your body finally gave out. I'm a bit disappointed."

I ran at him.

He expected me to swing my tomahawk. Instead, I jumped in the air and struck his knee square with the heel of my boot and all my weight behind it. His knee cracked. Max grabbed a hold of my neck and lifted me into the air.

I sliced off his nose.

I dropped and rolled when he tried to kick me. I found my feet, and swung my tomahawk into his other knee. Max wasn't moving very quickly after that. Metal armor under his skin or not, take out the knees and the body will soon follow.

He scooped up the battle axe he had discarded when he was pummeling my face, and hurled it at me. I dodged, but lost my balance. Max was on top of me in an instant. His feet were stomping down at me and I curled in upon myself. His hands began another assault on my face and the arm I raised to defend it with.

In turn, I slashed at his waxy arms and rolled away as quick as I could. I got my feet under me, but as soon as I stood up, Max had me wrapped in a bear hug.

He began squeezing and I began suffocating.

I spun in his grasp. We were facing each other and I leveraged my legs against his pelvis while pushing against him with all my might. After a brief struggle, I escaped his grasp. He was punching; I was slicing.

I went for quick cuts. I wasn't worried about deep cuts. I just wanted to open him up. I had no dreams about bleeding him out and weakening him. That simply wasn't going to happen. The Monster was a living weapon. He would never weaken.

He threw a right cross. I ducked under the swing, and came around behind him. I placed the handle of my tomahawk over his head and under his chin. I squeezed it against his throat as hard as I could.

Max wasn't stupid. The moment he felt pressure against his throat, he ran backwards as fast as his damaged knees would allow. It wasn't extremely fast, but when my back collided onto the wall of rocks behind me, a few of my ribs broke and my spine made a nasty crack.

Max stepped away as my body dropped to the street.

"Judging by the sounds of breaking bones," Max said. "This fight has officially ended. You lost once again."

I crawled to my feet. My legs barely held me upright. My steps were clumsy as I backed away from him towards the bridge.

He came at me moving impossibly fast for someone with messed up knees.

I took a chunk of flesh from his shoulder with my tomahawk, and he in turn lashed out a front kick that connected with my sternum, sending me flying closer to the bridge.

My eyes were beginning to swell shut but I saw him advancing towards me anyway. I couldn't get to my feet. I was trying as he swung a meaty fist into my face, shattering my cheekbone.

I paid him back by chopping down on his foot with my tomahawk. Surprisingly, his feet weren't armored. I split his foot in half. The Monster roared in anger, and possibly a small amount of pain.

He kicked out at me and my body went limp as I slid right in front of the drawbridge. I made a show of trying to rise, only to fall back down. Max limped towards me.

I sliced deeply into his hand as he grabbed a hold of my utility vest and hoisted me into the air. He ignored the cut, so I chopped off his ear with my tomahawk.

"I am done with you disfiguring me!" Max shouted. "DO YOU HEAR ME? I AM DONE WITH YOU!"

He slammed me down hard against the ground, raised me back up and threw my body all the way to the center of the drawbridge.

I didn't rise back up from where I landed on my back. Instead, I started talking.

"I'm not done with you," I said in a garbled voice. "I'll kill you. I won't stop until I kill you."

Max stepped onto the bridge and walked towards me. When he was about five feet away, I stopped talking funny and started laughing.

Max stopped dead in his tracks when I slowly rose to my feet. You see, I was suckering him. I wasn't nearly as injured as I had led him to believe. Don't get me wrong, I was absorbing a lot of punishment and I hurt all over, but I did my very best to make sure he never connected with anything vital.

I wasn't looking very pretty either, but the worst blow I received was cracking my back against the rock. I had learned a thing or two from the last time we faced each other. I knew the areas Max liked to target. Therefore, I protected my head as best I could. His punches that got by my protective arm landed mainly on my face and his kicks to my body landed mainly on my legs as I curled up in defense. I took some pretty decent damage—hell, I even saw double for a bit—but a Guardian is built to absorb damage and keep functioning.

I had more than a bit of fight left in me. Unfortunately for Max, our fight was over.

Max looked at me as I laughed at him. I could see the confusion all over his ugly face. He knew he'd lost. He just didn't know the details.

"How?" Max asked.

I pulled the detonator out of my utility belt.

"This time, I won't leave anything left of you to bring back," I said, and pushed the button.

The corners of the bridge blew immediately, and the bridge dropped into the water of the Rio Grande. I went underwater, and covered myself against the raining debris. When all had settled, I stood up in waist-deep water and searched for Max.

He was twenty feet away from me. His body was jerking around crazily and sparks were shooting out of the many slashes I had cut into him, while he slowly electrocuted.

"*Black energy.*"

Yeah, Hardin said black energy behaves very much like traditional electricity. I decided to put that to the test and see how the current running inside of his body would react to water after I opened him up a bit.

Despite the jerking seizures, Max was still trying to climb out of the river. I stopped him when he reached the banks. He didn't even turn around to look at me when I grabbed his ankle and pulled him back in the water.

That was unfortunate. I really wanted to see the expression on his face as I buried my tomahawk into his head, right on the seam of bone and metal. I have Dudley to thank for that one, by the way. He lit the Monster up. If the flesh hadn't burned away from his skull, I never would have known where to strike.

Max died for the second time.

I left his body smoldering on the bank of the river and ran to where I had stashed my shotgun and the second remote detonator in the rocks. I pushed the button, and imagined a hundred or so small house fires breaking out inside the many homes just beyond the rock walls of the canyon.

I didn't know if Ivana's idea would work, but under the circumstances, it was worth a try. We only had to hold out until our reinforcements arrived and that wasn't going to be easy. Despite the new army led by Father Monarez, we were still grossly outnumbered.

Up ahead, I saw Georgie, and Merrick.

Merrick was fine, since zombies still had zero interest in dogs, but Georgie was underneath a pile of shamblers. I ran up and kicked three of them away. Then I blew their brains out. The kick of the weapon was nice. The pumping action was manly.

"I'm bit," Georgie cried. "Fuckers got me. I'm a goner. I need a hospital."

"If you're a goner," I said, "you won't be needing a hospital."

I looked at the tiny bite mark on his wrist, and I couldn't help but laugh.

"Fuck you, Jaxon," Georgie growled. "You don't know."

"I'm not even sure that's a bite mark," I said. "Go stick your arm in the water until it heals."

I yanked him off the ground, shoved him towards the river, called Merrick, and I was back in the fight. I blasted everything that came my way until I was in the thick of things. After that, I could no longer shoot for fear of hitting a living human by mistake.

I didn't use a shield. I pulled my tomahawk and Bowie knife.

I went to work. Just another day in the office; it was that easy. The water had washed away the tiredness. I was still hurting, but not enough to sit out. I wasn't moving very fast either, but it was fast enough.

My favorite plan of attack was to come up from behind. The zombies all had their intended targets picked out. They never even noticed me until I nailed them, or Merrick dropped them to the pavement.

Working this way, I could help out anyone I saw that needed support. That doesn't mean we didn't have any casualties. We lost many brave souls in that battle, and then we fought against their reanimated remains.

It was a long fight. Dudley eventually made his way to my side.

"I guess you won," Dudley said.

"Are you in awe of my awesomeness?" I asked.

"That was pretty stupid," Dudley said as he hacked down the shambler grabbing onto his shield.

"Actually," I said. "It was pretty brilliant. Besides, those suicide zombies were kicking our ass. I had to do something."

"Well, what are we going to do now?" Dudley asked. "We can't keep up this pace forever. We're losing too many, and we're getting tired."

"Look above you," I said.

Dudley did as I asked. All along the tops of the boulder canyon walls were ghouls. Ivana came up with the idea. The vampire eventually told her how to summon them by drawing a certain symbol in vampire blood, and then setting the blood ablaze.

El Paso was filled with ghouls. They lived under the streets in tunnels, fed upon fallen zombies and the remains of their victims. They were highly aggressive when attacked, and it was about time they earned their keep.

The ghouls were hungry. We hadn't been killing zombies in a long while. I think that's why they crept silently down the boulders and entered the field of battle. At first it was only a few of them. The others were shy. Ghouls don't like to be seen. They normally wait until the battle is finished before they feast.

The braver ones went after the fallen zombies closest to them. They weren't interested in the living dead at all, but that didn't mean the living dead weren't interested in them. The minute a zombie spotted a crouching ghoul, it rushed to attack.

Dudley and I began calling everyone back towards the Rio Grande. I wanted the humans far away from what was about to happen. It took time; one couldn't just up and run from a group of zombies. The zombies would chase after them.

The next time I looked, the zombie that rushed the ghoul was crushed on the street and the ghoul was standing over its remains. More zombies came after that. The ghoul destroyed them as well, but the scuffle attracted attention.

A large group of shamblers bore down on the ghoul. There were enough of them to knock it off its feet. Once they had it down, they really went at it. A great wail screeched out when the many hands and teeth began to tear at the ghoul's flesh.

The call of distress was answered by two more brave ghouls that had climbed down. They tore into the group of zombies. Their battle attracted more zombies. More wails screeched out. The ghouls on top of the canyon wall began to bounce around like agitated monkeys. Then they went to aid their companions.

I couldn't tell you how many ghouls entered the canyon. They just kept coming and coming. Some of them were fighting. Some of them were eating. It was disgusting, but the battle was pretty much over. The zombies were no match for the immense strength and tough skin, of the ghouls.

We gathered our forces before the Rio Grande. Each of the Regulators had survived. We were battered and bruised, but we proudly stood before our army and we shot down any stray zombie that chose to come our way. It was an easy win, despite the vast number of zombies. Or maybe it was an easy win because of all the zombies. You see, never before had an army of corpses come together like this one had. Without meaning to, Max helped us finish the zombie outbreak. He put all the fish in a barrel; we just had to start shooting.

The battle of monster vs. monster raged on until sunrise. The ghouls didn't like the sun, but they had left very little for us to do when they left. A new bridge was brought out. Everyone but the team crossed over into New Mexico.

We stayed behind to mop up the leftovers. We spent the day making sure all the zombies were down for good, chopping up the ones that still had a little life in them. It was nasty work, but we didn't mind. We were looking to the future.

At sunset, we left the dead where they had fallen. The ghouls came back for seconds, and they came back the day after as well. In less than a week, the boulder canyon had been picked clean, and I managed to burn the remains of Max's body. I wasn't taking any more chances with that prick.

The next few months were spent inside the city clearing the stragglers that didn't follow Max. Again, it was easy work. My team never encountered more than ten of them at a time. I believe Snake Charmer fared pretty much the same, as did the other Special Forces teams. None of them had lost a single man, by the way. The Albanian Mafia were outclassed from the beginning of their behind the scenes gunfight.

When we were finished, having gone through every house and every building, the rest of the military came in. They went over everything as well, and when they were finished, the gates were opened and people were finally able to return to their homes. Of course, the military patrolled the streets along with the police on a regular basis, just in case.

This base we're in now was set up for us outside Fort Bliss. We wanted to be close to the city we fought so hard for.

One day, the President even came to the site of our final battle, and dedicated a plaque to all the brave people that died protecting our planet. The boulders on both sides of the street stand to this day and probably always will. People come from miles around to walk that stretch of road where the battle took place. Someone even spray painted "The Regulators were here" in big black letters on one of the boulders.

The Safe Zone still stands as well. Nothing there has been touched, not even the fences we erected. Georgie wasn't too happy about that. He wanted to get his house back. The last I heard, the entire area was being considered for National Monument status. They even conduct tours, just to show people how we lived back then. My favorite part is the souvenir shop they put up by the gate that sells t-shirts and little key chains of my skull and musket pistols emblem.

When the dust finally cleared, I went home to my family. I gave everyone a six-month vacation. I spent the time eating and being lazy. When it was over, I went back to work. The team gets called upon on occasion, but we've never come across anything as big as what went down in El Paso. That's not to say it will never again happen. I'm just hoping that it doesn't.

"What if it does?"

Then I'll be there to fight it. Because I'm the Guardian. I'm the leader of the Regulators. We fight evil shit, and we don't like to lose.

Epilogue

GEORGIE

Jaxon was called away during my wrap up meeting. So, Georgie decided to step in and take his place. It worked out well enough because Georgie happened to be the only witness to the question I was about to ask.

"*What happened to Major Crass?*"

He was sent to Felltrop Prison in Louisiana. He occupied the very same cell he created for Jaxon.

"*Did Jaxon know about this?*"

I was with him when he found out. It was a few days after the final battle. The team was clearing houses. Jaxon was bored out of his mind since most of the zombies were dead, so the two of us, plus Merrick, drove down to a temporary base camp that had been set up outside an old gas station.

We were supposed to be getting food for the rest of the team, but Jaxon wasn't in a hurry to return. He was too busy joking around with all the soldiers asking him for his autograph. Mr. Hardin came out and pulled Jaxon aside.

"With everything slowing down," Mr. Hardin said, "I thought you would want to know that Major Crass is now occupying your former cell at Felltrop."

A sudden change fell over Jaxon. A squint in his eyes, a clenching of his jaw: I'm not sure what it was, but he suddenly became very menacing, and I realized that he hated Major Crass damn near as much as he hated the Monster. How could he not? Major Crass was just as guilty of hurting Skie as the Monster was. My mistake was assuming Jax was satisfied with his imprisonment. I should have known better. He wasn't satisfied with imprisonment at all. He simply had more important things to take care of before he completed his revenge.

In less than ten minutes we were in the air. Jaxon didn't say much during the trip. His mind was elsewhere. I also didn't want to bother him. I didn't like the expression on his face.

We landed in the same place we had landed when we came on our rescue mission. The section we had destroyed had already been rebuilt. Jaxon stared long and hard at the prison and then he marched right up to the front doors and flashed his badge.

Nobody said a word against him as he made his way to a private elevator. If they weren't afraid of him, they were certainly afraid of Merrick, who snarled at anyone in our way. We descended to the lowest point of the prison, went past an open metal door, and entered a brick-lined hallway. Major

Crass was in a small cell at the end of the hallway.

His hands were around the bars as Jaxon approached.

There was a coldness emanating from my friend and leader that forced Merrick and me to keep a few steps away from him. The two men glared at each other for a long time. Major Crass was the first to speak.

"Don't bother gloating," Major Crass said. "You're only where you are, and I'm only where I am, because I couldn't control the Monster."

"You told me that my wife was dead," Jaxon said in a low whisper.

"I lied," Major Crass said. "What are you going to do about it? Face the facts, you idiot! I'm only here on a temporary basis. I'm a very talented man. Eventually, somebody will need my services, and when that day comes, you'd better pray I don't come after you again. Because despite what you see here, I beat you. I crushed you. I took you down, and you know in your heart I could do it again."

"You're right," Jaxon said in that same scary whisper. "You beat me. You came up with a plan that put my wife in a hospital, and caused my team to go into hiding."

"I bet it gives you chills at night," Major Crass gloated.

"It does," Jaxon said. "That's why I'm here."

"What?" Major Crass asked with a laugh. "Do you want to call a truce? Do you want to beg me to leave you and your family alone?"

Jaxon's hand snaked through the bars and wrapped around the back of Major Crass's head. He pressed the man's face between two bars and bent to his ear.

"No," Jaxon whispered. "I'm here because I'm a sore loser."

He continued pressing Major Crass's face between the bars, and he continued to increase the pressure. Eventually the skin on the forehead began to split, and Major Crass let out a scream. He tried to fight. He tried to push his legs against the bars and free himself from Jaxon's grip but Jaxon was too strong.

He begged for mercy. He swore up and down that he'd leave Jaxon alone. He apologized over and over, but the General wasn't listening. One final, vicious yank and I heard the crunch of bone, after watching an eye pop from its socket before I turned away.

The next thing I knew, the screams had stopped and Jaxon was walking by me towards the elevator. Merrick followed him immediately. I hesitated briefly, and then joined them.

It was an hour after we left the prison and were high in the air, rapidly returning to El Paso, when Jaxon finally turned and spoke to me.

"You wanna go eat?"

I laughed out loud! I'm serious! I was really having a fit, and after a fashion, Jaxon laughed right along with me.

THE END?

About the Author

Michael Clary was raised in El Paso, Texas. He is the author of The Guardian Interviews (The Guardian, The Regulators, and Broken).

He is an occasional practitioner of Mixed Martial Arts, and collects bladed weapons of various types. Before he wrote novels, he wrote and directed Independent films.

Currently, Michael is living in Temescal Valley, California with his wife, family, and three Pit Bulls. He is also continuing his writing career with a brand new series of novels.

www.michaelclaryauthor.com